Analyses of Nineteenth- and Twentieth- Century Music: 1940–1985

Compiled By
Arthur Wenk

MLA Index and Bibliography Series
Number 25

Boston
Music Library Association, Inc.

Library of Congress Cataloging in Publication Data

Wenk, Arthur B.
  Analyses of nineteenth- and twentieth-century
music, 1940-1985.

  (MLA Index and bibliography series, ISSN 0094-6478 ;
no.25)
  "Cumulates and updates the indexes originally
published as numbers 13, 14, and 15 in this series"--
Ser. t.p.
  Includes index.
  1. Music--19th century--History and criticism--
Bibliography. 2. Music--20th century--History and
criticism--Bibliography. 3. Musical analysis--
Bibliography. I. Title. II. Series: MLA index and
bibliography series ; 25.
ML113.W45 1987   016.78'0903'4   87-5675
ISBN 0-914954-36-9

MLA Index and Bibliography Series Number 25

ISBN: 0-914954-36-9
ISSN: 0094-6478

Analyses of Nineteenth- and Twentieth-Century Music

MLA Index and Bibliography Series, Number 25
Robert Michael Fling, Editor

This volume cumulates and updates the indexes originally published as Numbers 13, 14, and 15 in this series.

Persons interested in submitting manuscripts for possible publication in this series should correspond with the editor: R. Michael Fling, Indiana University Music Library, Bloomington, Indiana 47405.

For William Austin

CONTENTS

INTRODUCTION

The purpose of this index is to provide rapid access to technical materials of an analytical nature contained in periodicals, monographs, Festschriften and dissertations. Defining "analysis" has become nearly as difficult as defining "music." Edward T. Cone, grappling with this question in "Analysis Today" (MQ 46(1960): 172-186), separates analysis both from description, both from description, which details what happens in a score without explaining why, and from prescription, which explains a explaining why, and from prescription, which explains a composition in terms of an "externally imposed scheme rather than . . . the actual course of the music." Analysis, for Cone, uncovers the logic comprising the relationship of "each event to its predecessors and to its successors, as well as to the whole." Ian Bent's admirable treatment of "Analysis" in the *New Grove Dictionary of Music and Musicians* offers as a working definition, "the resolution of a musical structure into relatively simpler constituent elements, and the investigation of the functions of those elements within that structure." As examples of analytical methods, Bent cites reductive techniques (Schenker), comparative techniques (Reti, Keller), segmentation (Tovey, Riemann), category measurement and feature counting (Jeppesen, LaRue), syntax formulation (Ruwet, Nattiez), probability measurement, and set-theoretic approaches (Forte). The analyses cited in this index represent all of these techniques as well as those which consider a composition in its broader musical context: the relationship between music and text in song, cantata, oratorio, operetta; the relationship of a given work to the norms of its genre, be it sonata form or nineteenth-century Italian opera; the relationship between a composer's intentions as manifested in sketches and the structure of the finished realization; the presence of a program, be it announced, as in Berlioz, or concealed, as in Berg.

The criterion for inclusion in this index may be informally summarized as technical writing on any of the above topics as applied to specific compositions. Dissertations of the "life and works" variety are included only if the title or abstract indicates the presence of analysis rather than simply a *catalogue raisonné*. Discussions of orchestration are included insofar as they bear on analysis as opposed to instrumental technique. (For a more extended treatment of this question, see my "Varieties of analysis: Through the analytical sieve and beyond" [forthcoming].)

Many of the monographs cited in this index form part of ongoing series, including the following:

Au delà des notes
Beihefte zum Archiv für Musikwissenschaft
Beiträge zur Westfalischen Musikgeschichte
Berliner musikwissenschaftlicher Arbeiten
Cambridge opera handbooks
Canadian composers

English national opera guides
Forschungsbeiträge zur Musikwissenschaft
Freiburger Schriften zur Musikwissenschaft
Gesellschaft für Musikforschung
Les Grands opéras
Hamburger Beiträge zur Musikwissenschaft
Kontrapunkte
Mainzer Studien zur Musikwissenschaft
Meisterwerke der Musik
Münchener Veröffentlichungen zur Musikgeschichte
Musikwissenschaftliche Schriften
Neue Heidelberger Studien zur Musikwissenschaft
Neue musikgeschichtliche Forschungen
Princeton studies in music
Regensburger Beiträge zur Musikwissenschaft
Schriften zur Musik
Schriftenreihe zur Musik
Studien zur Musik
Studien zur Musikgeschichte des 19. Jahrhunderts
Veröffentlichungen zur Musikforschung
Veröffentlichungen des Instituts für Neue Musik und Musikerziehung,
    Darmstadt
Wiener Veröffentlichungen zur Musikwissenschaft
Wiener musikwissenschaftliche Beiträge
Wollenweber Beiträge zur Musikwissenschaft
Würzburger musikhistorische Beiträge

Entries are arranged as follows:

1. Alphabetically by composer. (Strict alphabetical order has been followed, thus "Mahler" follows "Machover" and precedes "McPhee.)
2. Alphabetically by genre or by work for composers having more than ten entries.
3. Alphabetically by author. (An index of authors may be found at the back of this volume.)
4. Alphabetically by title, for multiple entries by a single author, disregarding initial articles such as "An," "The," "Die," "Le".

Each entry contains the name of the composer of the work, the title, author and source of the analysis, and the name of the work analyzed if it is not clear from the title of the article. The composers' dates, when not provided within the article, have been taken from one of the following sources:

Altmann, Willhelm and Paul Frank. *Kurzgefasstes Tonkünstler-*
    Lexikon. 15th ed. 3 vols. Wilhelmshaven: Heinrichshofen,
    1964-1974.
Bull, Storm, ed. *Index to biographies of contemporary composers.*
    2 vols. Metuchen, NJ: Scarecrow Press, 1964-1974
Jaques Cattell Press, ed. *Who's who in American music: Classical.*
    2nd ed. New York: R. R. Bowker, 1985.

Kay, Ernest, ed. *International who's who in music and musicians' directory.* 10th ed. Cambridge, Eng.: Melrose Press, 1984.

Sadie, Stanley, ed. *The New Grove dictionary of music and musicians.* 20 vols. London: Macmillan, 1980.

Slonimsky, Nicolas, ed. *Baker's biographical dictionary of musicians.* 7th ed. New York: Schirmer Books, 1984.

Dates remain unavailable for around a dozen composers who have not yet entered any of the standard reference works.

Items dealing with more than three composers have been assigned abbreviations, a list of which may be found below. The complete cumulation of this index has provided an occasion for regularizing the abbreviations assigned to periodicals, which differ in certain details from the sigla employed in previous editions. The date of the last issue examined is indicated in parentheses after the publication dates. Periodicals which have suspended publication are indicated by an asterisk; in this case, the last issue examined is indicated by the closing date.

It may be appropriate to add a retrospective note. The first version of this index, *Analyses of 20th Century Music, 1940-1970,* contained 1225 entries by some 600 authors drawn from 46 periodicals and 7 Festschriften, covering 225 composers. The present cumulation, including both 19th- and 20th-century composers in a single volume, contains 5664 entries by some 2400 authors drawn from 132 periodicals and 93 Festschriften, covering 779 composers. The burgeoning output of analytical material has, in some cases, turned a literature review into a prodigious feat: Consider the 213 items for Bartók, 287 for Beethoven, 289 for Schoenberg, 221 for Stravinsky, or 202 for Webern, to name only the most frequently analyzed composers. One begins to wonder whether the 40 entries on Webern's Opp.21 and 27, for example, represent isolated utterances rather than contributions to an ongoing conversation. The compiler hopes that this volume may promote a greater degree of coherence in analytical colloquy.

I should like to thank Celine Mercier of Université Laval for her assistance in compiling the 1980-1985 update; Karen Bryan, Steven Norquist, Suzanne LaPlante and Julie Schnepel of Indiana University for their assistance in preparing the 1975-1980 update; and the staffs of the music libraries at University of Washington, University of California at Berkeley, and McGill University for their cooperation. Thanks to my wife Peggy for her encouragement and understanding.

This index, though by its nature doomed to incompleteness, enjoys the advantage of regular republication. Readers are fervently urged to point out errors of omission and commission in order that they be may corrected in the next edition.

ABBREVIATIONS

Periodicals

ACA*	-American Composers Alliance. *Bulletin.* 1938-1965.
ACR	*-American choral review.* 1959- (1985).
ACTA	*-Acta musicologica.* 1928- (1985).
AM	*-Archiv für Musikwissenschaft.* 1918- (1985).
AMF*	*-Archiv für Musikforschung.* 1936-1945.
ASO	*-L'Avant-scène opéra.* 1976- (1985).
ASUC*	-American Society of University Composers. *Proceedings.* 1966-1977.
BJ	*-Beethoven Jahrbuch.* 1953- (1981).
BM	*-Beiträge zur Musikwissenschaft.* 1959- (1985).
BOGM	*-Beiträge: Österreichische Gesellschaft für Musik.* 1967- (1981).
BRJ	*-Bruckner Jahrbuch.* 1980- (1983).
BRS	*-Bruckner symposium.* 1980- (1982).
BS	*-Brahms-Studien.* 1974- (1983).
CAD	*-Cahiers Debussy.* 1974- (1984).
CAUSM*	-Canadian Association of University Schools of Music. *Journal.* 1971-1979.
CC	*-Contrechamps: Musique du XXe siècle.* 1983-(1985).
CCM*	*-Cahiers canadiens de musique.* 1970-1976.
CD*	*-Chord and discord.* 1940-1969.
CHI	*-Chigiana.* Nuova ser. 1964- (1984).
CI	*-Critical inquiry.* 1974- (1983).
CM	*-Current musicology.* 1965- (1983).
CMJ*	*-Canadian music journal.* 1956-1962.
CMR	*-Contemporary music review.* 1984- (1985)
CMS	*-College music symposium.* 1961- (1984)
CPS*	*-Contrepoints.* 1946-1953.
CT	*-Contact.* 1971- (1985).
D*	*-Dissonance.* 1969-1975.
DAM	*-Dansk Årbog for Musikforskning.* 1961-(1983)
DBNM	*-Darmstädter Beiträge zur neuen Musik.* 1958-(1984)
DI	*-Dissonanz/Dissonance.* 1984- (1985).
DJM*	*-Deutsches Jahrbuch der Musikwissenschaft.* 1956-1978. [Title changes to *Jahrbuch Peters* with the 1978 volume]
EMM	*-Essays on modern music.* 1984- (1984).
FAM	*-Fontes artis musicae.* 1966- (1985).
HJ	*-Hindemith Jahrbuch.* 1971- (1983)
HJM	*-Hamburger Jahrbuch für Musikwissenschaft.* 1974-(1985).
HS	*-Haydn-Studien.* 1965- (1983)
HY	*-Haydn yearbook.* 1962- (1984)
I	*-Interface.* 1972- (1984).
IABS	-International Alban Berg Society. *Newsletter.* 1968-(1985).

ABBREVIATIONS

IAMB*	-*Inter-American music bulletin.* 1957-1973.
IAMR	-*Inter-American music review.* 1978- (1982).
IKSB	-International Kodály Society. *Bulletin.* 1976-(1985).
IRASM	-*International review of the aesthetics and sociology of music.* 1970- (1985).
ISM	-*Israel studies in musicology.* 1978- (1983).
ITO	-*In theory only.* 1972- (1985).
ITR	-*Indiana theory review.* 1977- (1983).
JALS	-*Journal of the American Liszt Society.* 1977-(1985).
JAMS	-*Journal of the American Musicological Society.* 1948- (1985).
JASI	-*Journal of the Arnold Schoenberg Institute.* 1976-(1984).
JBR	-*Journal of band research.* 1964- (1985)
JM	-*Journal of musicology.* 1982- (1985)
JMP*	-*Jahrbuch der Musikbibliothek Peters.* 1894-1940.
JMR	-*Journal of musicological research.* [Formerly *Music and man*] 1972- (1985).
JMT	-*Journal of music theory.* 1957- (1985).
JP	-*Jahrbuch Peters.* 1978- (1980).
JR*	-*Juilliard review.* 1954-1964.
JSIM	-*Jahrbuch des Staatlichen Instituts für Musikforschung, Preussischer Kulturbesitz.* 1968-(1982).
KJ	-*Kirchenmusikalisches Jahrbuch (Köln).* 1917-(1983).
KN	-*Key notes.* 1975- (1985).
LAMR	-*Latin American music review.* 1980-(1983).
M	-*Musica.* 1947- (1982).
MA	-*Music analysis.* 1982- (1985).
MAN*	-*Musical analysis.* 1972-1974.
MAU	-*Musicologica Austriaca.* 1977- (1985).
MB	-*Musik und Bildung.* 1970- (1983).
ME	-*Musik-Erziehung.* 1947- (1985).
MELOS*	-*Melos: Zeitschrift für neue Musik.* 1920-1933, 1934-1936, 1946-1974. [Merged with NZM in 1975]
Melos/NZM	-1975-1979. [Continues after 1979 as NZM]
MF	-*Die Musikforschung.* 1948- (1985)
MFO	-*Music forum.* 1967- (1980)
MG	-*Musik und Gesellschaft.* 1951- (1984).
MHPG	-*Mitteilungen der Hans Pfitzner-Gesellschaft.* 1954-(1984).
MJ*	-*Musique en jeu.* 1970-1979.
MK	-*Musik und Kirche.* 1929- (1985).
ML	-*Music and letters.* 1920- (1985).
MM*	-*Modern music.* 1924-1947.
MMA	-*Miscellanea musicologica: Adelaide studies in musicology.* 1966- (1985).
MMR*	-*Monthly music record.* 1871-1960.
MN*	-*Musical newsletter.* 1971-1977.
MO	-*Musik des Ostens.* 1962- (1982).
MP	-*Music perception.* 1983- (1985).
MQ	-*Musical quarterly.* 1915- (1985).
MR	-*Music review.* 1940- (1984).
MS	-*Musicology* (Sydney). 1964- (1982).
MSU*	-*Music survey.* 1947-1952.

MTS	*-Music theory spectrum.* 1979- (1985).
MTX	*-Musik Texte: Zeitschrift für neue Musik.* 1983-(1985).
MU*	*-Musicology.* 1945-1949.
MZ*	*-Musik der Zeit.* 1952-1955.
N	*-Neuland: Ansätze zur Musik der Gegenwart.* 1980-(1985).
NCM	*-Nineteenth century music.* 1977- (1985).
NMD*	*-Neue Musik in der Bundesrepublic Deutschland.* 1957-1958.
NOTES	-Music Library Association. *Notes.* 1943-(1985).
NW*	*-Numus West.* 1972-1975.
NZM	*-Neue Zeitschrift für Musik.* 1834- (1985).
OM	*-Orbis musicae.* 1971- (1983).
OMZ	*-Österreichische Musikzeitschrift.* 1946- (1985).
OQ	*-Opera quarterly.* 1983- (1985).
PM	*-Polish music.* 1967- (1981).
PNM	*-Perspectives of new music.* 1962- (1985).
POL*	*-Polyphonie.* 1947-1949.
PQ	*-Piano quarterly.* 1952- (1985).
PRMA	*-Proceedings of the Royal Musical Association.* 1874- (1984).
R*	*-Die Reihe* (English edition). 1957-1964.
RBM	*-Revue Belge de musicologie.* 1946- (1984).
RDM	*-Revue de musicologie.* 1917-1921, 1922-1939, 1945- (1984).
RILM	*-International repertory of music literature.* 1967-(1980).
RIM	*-Rivista Italiana di musicologia* (Firenze). 1966-(1985).
RM	*-La Revue musicale.* 1920-1940, 1946-1972, 1973-(special number 387).
RS	*-Recorded sound.* 1961- (1984).
S*	*-Source.* 1967-1972.
SBM	*-Schweizer Beiträge zur Musikwissenschaft.* 1972-(1980).
SCORE*	*-The Score and I.M.A. magazine.* 1949-1961.
SJM*	*-Schweizerisches Jahrbuch für Musikwissenschaft.* 1924-1938.
SM	*-Studia musicologica.* 1961- (1983).
SMM	*-Student musicologists at Minnesota.* 1966-(1976).
SMU	*-Studies in music* (Australia). 1967- (1984).
SMUWO	*-Studies in music from the University of Western Ontario.* 1976- (1984).
SMZ*	*-Schweizerische Musikzeitung.* 1861-1983. [Continues as DI]
SN	*-Soundings* (Cardiff). 1970- (1985).
SONUS	*-Sonus.* 1980- (1984).
SS*	*-Sonorum speculum.* 1958-1974. [Superseded by KN in 1975]
STM	*-Svensk Tidskrift för Musikforskning.* 1919-(1983).
STU	*-Studi musicali.* 1972- (1985).
SV	*-Studi Verdiana.* 1982- (1982).
SZM	*-Studien zur Musikwissenschaft.* Beihefte der *Denkmäler der Tonkunst in Österreich.* New series. 1955- (1984).
T	*-Tibia: Magazin für Freunde älter und neuer Bläsermusik.* 1976- (1983).
TEMPO	*-Tempo: A review of modern music.* 1939-1946, 1946- (1985).
TP	*-Theory and practice.* Journal of the Music Theory Society of New York State. 1975-(1984).
V	*-Verdi.* Bollettino dell' Instituto di Studi Verdiani (Parma). 1960- (1982).

Y*   -Yearbook for Inter-American musical research. 1965-1975.
ZM*   -Zeitschrift für Musiktheorie. 1970-1978.

Festschriften

Fs. Abert   -Opernstudie: Anna Amalie Abert zum 65. Geburtstag.
                     Klaus Hortschansky, ed. Tutzing: H. Schneider, 1975.
Fs. Abert/H   -Gedenkschrift für Hermann Abert: Von seinen Schülern.
                     Friedrich Blume, ed. Tutzing: H. Schneider, 1974.
                     [Reprint of 1928 edition]
Fs. Abs   -Divertimento für Hermann J. Abs: Beethoven-Studien
                     dargebracht zu seinem 80. Geburtstag. Vom Verein
                     Beethoven-Haus Beethoven-Haus und vom Beethoven-
                     Archiv Bonn. Martin Staehelin, ed. Bonn: Beethoven-
                     Haus, 1981.
Fs. Adorno/60   -Zeugnisse: Theodor W. Adorno zum 60. Geburtstag. Im
                     Auftrag des Instituts für Sozialforschung. Max Hork-
                     heimer, ed. Frankfurt am Main: Europaische Verlagsan-
                     stalt, 1963.
Fs. Albrecht   -Hans Albrecht in Memoriam. Kassel: Bärenreiter, 1962.
Fs. Albrecht/70   -Festschrift Georg von Albrecht zum 70. Geburtstag.
                     Stuttgart: Ichthys, 1962.
Fs. Albrecht/S   -Studies in musicology in honor of Otto E. Albrecht: A
                     collection of essays by his colleagues and former students
                     at the University of Pennsylvania. John Walter Hill, ed.
                     Kassel: Bärenreiter, 1980.
Fs. Alderman   -Festival essays for Pauline Alderman: A musicological
                     tribute. Burton L. Karson, ed. Provo: Brigham Young
                     University Press, 1976.
Fs. Anglés   -Miscelánea en homenaje a Monseñor Higinio Anglés.
                     Barcelona: Consejo Superior de Investigaciones
                     Cient¡ficas, 1958-1961.
Fs. Apel   -Essays in musicology: A birthday offering for Willi Apel.
                     Hans Tischler, ed. Bloomington: Indiana University
                     School of Music, 1968.
Fs. Bartók/S   -Studia memoriae Belae Bartók sacra. Budapest: Aedes
                     Academiae Scientiarum Hungaricae, 1956 (2nd ed., 1957;
                     3rd ed., 1959).
Fs. Bartók/T   -Béla Bartók: A memorial review. New York: Boosey &
                     Hawkes, 1950.
Fs. Becking   -Gustav Becking zum Gedächtnis: Eine Auswahl seiner
                     Schriften und Beiträge seine Schüler. Tutzing: H.
                     Schneider, 1975.
Fs. Benz   -Gegenwart in Geiste: Festschrift für Richard Benz.
                     Hamburg: C. Wegner, 1954.
Fs. Bernstein   -A musical offering: Essays in honor of Martin Bernstein.
                     Edward H. Clinkscale and Claire Brook, eds. New York:
                     Pendragon, 1977.

Fs. Besseler —*Festschrift Heinrich Besseler zum sechzigsten Geburtstag.* Leipzig: VEB Deutshcer Verlag für Musik, 1961.

Fs. Bishop —*Miscellanea musicologica.* Adelaide Studies in Musicology 1. Adelaide: Libraries Board of South Australia in association with the University of Adelaide, 1966.

Fs. Blankburg —*Bach-Interpretationen: Walter Blankenburg zum 65. Geburtstag.* Martin Geck, ed. Gottingen: Vandenhoeck & Ruprecht, 1969.

Fs. Blaukopf —*Festschrift Kurt Blaukopf.* Irmagard Bontinck and Otto Brusatti, eds. Wien: Universal, 1975.

Fs. Blume —*Festschrift Friedrich Blume zum 70. Geburtstag.* Kassel: Bärenreiter, 1963.

Fs. Boetticher —*Convivium musicorum: Festschrift Wolfgang Boetticher zum sechzigsten Geburtstag am 19. August 1974.* Heinrich Huschen and Dietz-Rudiger Moser, eds. Berlin: Merseburger, 1974.

Fs. Brook —*Music in the Classic period: Essays in honor of Barry S. Brook.* Allan W. Atlas, ed. New York: Pendragon, 1985.

Fs. Cage —*A John Cage reader in celebration of his 70th birthday.* Peter Gena and Jonathan Brent, eds. New York: C. F. Peters, 1982.

Fs. Cuyler —*Notations and editions: A book in honor of Louise Cuyler.* Edith Borroff, ed. Dubuque, IA: Wm. C. Brown, 1974.

Fs. Dadelson —*Festschrift Georg von Dadelson zum 60. Geburtstag.* Thomas Kohlhase and Volker Scherliess, eds. Neuhausen-Stuttgart: Hänssler, 1978,

Fs. David —*Ex deo nascimur: Festschrift zum 75. Geburtstag von Johann Nepomuk David.* Gerd Sievers, ed. Wiesbaden: Breitkopf & Härtel, 1970.

Fs. Davison —*Essays in honor of Archibald Thompson Davison by his associates.* Cambridge: Harvard University Department of Music, 1957.

Fs. Deutsch —*Festschrift Otto Erich Deutsch zum 80. Geburtstag am 5. September 1963.* Walter Gersternberg, Jan LaRue and Wolfgang Rihm, eds. Kassel: Bärenreiter, 1963.

Fs. Doflein —*Erich Doflein: Festschrift zum 70. Geburtstag.* Lars Ulrich Abraham, ed. Mainz: Schott, 1972.

Fs. Emmanuel —*Maurice Emmanuel. La Revue Musicale,* numéro special 206. (1947): 1-128.

Fs. Engel —*A birthday offering to Carl Engel.* New York: G. Schirmer, 1943.

Fs. Engel/H —*Festschrift Hans Engel zum seibzigsten Geburtstag.* Kassel: Bärenreiter, 1964.

Fs. Erdmann —*Begegnungen mit Eduard Erdmann.* Christof Bitter and Manfred Schloser, eds. Darmstadt: Erato, 1968.

Fs. Federhofer —*Symbolae historiae musicae: Hellmut Federhofer zum 60. Geburtstag.* Friedrich Wilhelm Riedel and Hubert Unverricht, eds. Mainz: Schott, 1971.

Fs. Federov/65 *-Mélanges offerts à Vladimir Féderov à l'occasion de son soixante-cinquième anniversaire 5 août 1966.* Harold Heckmann and Wolfgang Rehm, eds. *Fontis artis musicae* 13(1966): 1-152.

Fs. Feicht *-Studia Hieronymo Feicht seuptuagenario dedicata.* Zofia Lissa, ed. Kracow: Polskie Wydawnictwo Muzyczne, 1967.

Fs. Fellerer *-Festschrift Karl Gustav Fellerer zum sechzigsten Geburtstag.* Heinrich Hüschen, ed. Regensburg: G. Bosse, 1962.

Fs. Fellerer/60 *-Karl Gustav Fellerer zum 60. Geburtstag überreicht von den Mitgliedern der Arbeitsgemeinschafts für Rheinische Musikgeschichte.* Herbert Druk, ed. Beiträge zur Rheinischen Musikgeschichte 52. Köln: A. Volk, 1962.

Fs. Fellerer/70 *-Musicae scientiae collectanea: Festschrift Karl Gustav Fellerer zum siebzigsten Geburtstag am 7. Juli 1972.* Heinrich Hüschen, ed. Köln: A. Volk, 1973.

Fs. Fox *-Essays on music for Charles Warren Fox.* Jerald C. Grave, ed. Rochester: Eastman School of Music Press, 1979.

Fs. Ghisi *-Memorie e contributi alla musica dal medioevo all'età moderna: Offerti a F. Ghisi nel settantesimo compleanno (1901-1971).* 2 vols. Bologna: Antiquae Musicae Italicae Studiosi, 1971.

Fs. Gudewill *-Beiträge zur Musikgeschichte Nordeuropas: Kurt Gudewill zum 65. Geburtstag.* Uwe Haensel, ed. Wolfenbüttel: Möseler, 1978.

Fs. Haberl *-Festschrift Ferdinand Haberl zum 70. Geburtstag: Sacerdos et cantus gregoriani magister.* Franz A. Stein, ed. Regensburg: G. Bosse, 1977.

Fs. Herz *-Essays in the music of J.S. Bach and other divers subjects: A tribute to Gerhard Herz.* Robert L. Weaver, ed. Louisville: University of Louisville, 1981.

Fs. Hoboken *-Anthony van Hoboken: Festschrift zum 75. Geburtstag.* Joseph Schmid-Görg, ed. Mainz: Schott, 1962.

Fs. Hüschen *-Ars musica, musica scientia: Festschrift Heinrich Hüschen zum fünfundsechzigsten Geburtstag am 2. Marz 1980.* Detlef Altenburg, ed. Köln: Gittare und Laute Verlagsgesellschaft, 1980.

Fs. Husmann *-Speculum musicae artis: Festgabe für Heinrich Husmann zum 60. Geburtstag am 16. Dezember 1968.* Heinz Becker and Reinhard Gerlach, eds. München: Fink, 1970.

Fs. Jeppesen *-Natalicia musicologica Knud Jeppesen suptuagenario collegis oblata.* Bjorn Hjelmburg and Soren Sorensen, eds. Oslo: W. Hansen, 1962.

Fs. Kaufmann/W *-Music East and West: Essays in honor of Walter Kaufmann.* Thomas Noblitt, ed. New York: Pendragon, 1981.

Fs. Kodály/80 *-Zoltano Kodály octogenario sacrum.* Budapest: Akadémia Kiadó, 1962. [Also appeared as *Studia musicologica* 3].

Fs. Kretzschmar *-Festschrift Hermann Kretzschmar zum siebzigsten Geburtstage überreicht von Kollegen, Schülern und Freunden.* Leipzig: C. F. Peters, 1918. [Reprinted, Hildesheim: G. Olms, 1973].

Fs. Lang   -*Music and civilization: Essays in honor of Paul Henry Lang*. Edmond Strainchamps and Maria Rika Maniates, eds. New York: W.W. Norton, 1984.

Fs. Larsen   -*Festskrift Jens Peter Larsen*. Kobenhavn: W. Hansen, 1972.

Fs. Lissa   -*Studia musicologica aesthetica, theoretica, historica*. Krakow: Polskie Wydawnictwo Muzyczne, 1979.

Fs. Marx   -*Festschrift Karl Marx zum 70. Geburtstag*. Erhard Karkoschka, ed. Stuttgart: Ichthys, 1967.

Fs. Mauersberger   -*Credo musicale: Komponistenporträts aus der Arbeit des Dresdener Kreuzchores: Festgabe zum 80. Geburtstag des Nationalpreisträgers Kreuzkantor Professor D. Dr. h. c. Rudolf Mauersberger*. Kassel: Bärenreiter, 1969.

Fs. Merritt   -*Words and music: The scholar's view: A medley of problems and solutions compiled in honor of A. Tillman Merritt by sundry hands*. Laurence Berman, ed. Cambridge: Harvard University Department of Music, 1972.

Fs. Moser   -*Musik in Zeit und Raum*. Berlin: Mersburger, 1960.

Fs. Müller-   -*Festgabe für Joseph Müller-Blattau zum 65. Geburtstag*.
   Blattau/65   Annales Universitatis Saraviensis, Philosophie 9, fasc.1 (1960). Saarbrucken: Universität des Sarrlandes, 1960.

Fs. Orel   -*Festschrift Alfred Orel zum 70. Geburtstag*. Hellmut Federhofer, ed. Wien/Wiesbaden: R.M. Rohrer, 1960.

Fs. Osthoff/70   -*Hellmuth Osthoff zu seinen siebzigsten Geburtstag*. Ursula Aarburg and Peter Cahn, eds. Tutzing: H. Schneider, 1969.

Fs. Osthoff/80   -*Renaissance-Studien: Helmut Ostoff zum 80. Geburtstag*. Ludwig Finscher, ed. Tutzing: H. Schneider, 1979.

Fs. Pepping   -*Festschrift Ernst Pepping zu seinem 70. Geburtstag am 12. September 1971*. Heinrich Poos, ed. Berlin: Merseberger, 1971.

Fs. Pfitzner   -*Festschrift Hans Pfitzner*. Walter Abendroth and Karl-Robert Danler, eds. München: P. Winkler, 1969.

Fs. Philipp   -*Franz Philipp 70 Jahre: Das Bild eines deutschen Musikers in Zeugnissen und Zeitgenossen: Gedruckt als Gabe seiner Freunde zum 70. Geburtstag, 24 August 1960*. [Freiburg im Breisgau?, 1960]

Fs. Pisk   -*Paul A. Pisk: Essays in his honor*. Austin: University of Texas Press, 1965.

Fs. Plamenac   -*Essays in honor of Dragan Plamenac on his 70th birthday*. Gustav Reese and Robert J. Snow, eds. Pittsburgh: University of Pittsburgh, 1967.

Fs. Reger   -*Max Reger 1873-1973: Ein Symposium*. In Verbindung mit dem Max-Reger-Institut (Elsa-Reger-Stiftung). Bonn-Bad Godesberg und der Internationalen Orgelwache Nürnberg. Klaus Röhring, ed. Wiesbaden: Breifkopf & Härtel, 1974.

Fs. Rohlfs   -*Romania cantat: Lieder in alten une neue: Chorsätzen mit sprachlichen, literarischen und musikwissenschaftlichen Interpretationen*. Francisco J. Oroz Anscuren, ed. Tübingen: G. Narr, 1980.

Fs. Ronga	-*Scritti in onore di Luigi Ronga.* Milano: R. Ricciardi, 1973.
Fs. Sachs/C	-*The commonwealth of music: In honor of Curt Sachs.* Gustav Reese and Rose Brandel, eds. Glencoe, NY: Free Press, 1964.
Fs. Savoff	-*Aspekte der musikalischen Interpretation: Sava Savoff zum 70. Geburtstag.* Hermann Danuser and Christoph Keller, eds. Hamburg: K. D. Wagner, 1980
Fs. Schenk	-*De ratione in musica: Festschrift Erich Schenk zum 5. Mai 1972.* Theophil Antonicek, Rudolf Flotzinger, and Othmar Wessely, eds. Kassel: Bärenreiter, 1975.
Fs. Scheurleer	-*Gedenboek aangeboden aan Dr. D. F. Scheurleer op zijn 70sten verjaardag: Bijdragen van urienden en vereerders ophetgebied der muziek.* 's-Gravenhage: M. Nijhoff, 1925.
Fs. Schmidt-Görg	-*Festschrift Joseph Schmidt-Görg zum 60. Geburtstag.* Dagmar Weise, ed. Bonn: Beethoven-Haus, 1957.
Fs. Schmidt-Görg/70	-*Colloquium amicorum: Joseph Schmidt-Görg zum 70. Geburtstag.* Siegfried Kross and Hans Schmidt, eds. Bonn: Beethoven-Haus, 1967.
Fs. Schneider	-*Festschrift für Michael Schneider zum 65. Geburtstag.* Berlin: Merseburger, 1974.
Fs. Schneider/80	-*Festschrift Max Schneider zum achtzigsten Geburtstage.* In Verbindung mit Franz von Wasenapp, Ursula Schneider und Walther Siegmund-Schultze. Walter Vetter, ed. Leipzig: Deutscher Verlag für Musik, 1955.
Fs. Schreiber	-*Festschrift für Ottmar Schreiber zum 70. Geburtstag am 16. Februar 1976. Reger-Studien 1.* Gunther Massenkeil and Susanne Popp, eds. Wiesbaden: Breitkopf & Härtel, 1978.
Fs. Schuh	-*Art Nouveau, Jugendstil und Musik.* Jürg Stenzl, ed. Zürich: Atlantis, 1980.
Fs. Schwarz	-*Russian and Soviet music: Essays for Boris Schwarz.* Malcolm Hamrick Brown, ed. Ann Arbor: UMI Research Press, 1984.
Fs. Seay	-*A Festschrift for Albert Seay: Essays by his friends and colleagues.* Michael D. Grace, ed. Colorado Springs: The Colorado College, 1982.
Fs. Sievers	-*Heinrich Sievers zum 70. Geburtstag.* Richard Jakoby and Gunter Katzenberger, eds. Tutzing: H. Schneider, 1978.
Fs. Strecker	-*Festschrift für einen Verlager: Ludwig Strecker zum 90. Geburtstag.* Carl Dahlhaus, ed. Mainz: Schott, 1973.
Fs. Strunk	-*Studies in music history: Essays for Oliver Strunk.* Harold Powers, ed. Princeton: Princeton University Press, 1968.
Fs. Schuh	-*Art nouveau, Jugenstil und Musik.* Jürg Stenzl. ed. Zürich: Atlantis, 1980.
Fs. Szabolcsi	-*Bence Szabolcsi: Septuagenario.* Denes Bartha, ed. Kassel: Bärenreiter, 1969.
Fs. Tippett	-*Michael Tippett: A symposium on his 60th birthday.* Ian Kemp, ed. London: Faber & Faber, 1965.
Fs. Valentin	-*Festschrift Erich Valentin zum 70. Geburtstag.* Günther Weiss, ed. Regensburg: G. Bosse, 1976.

Fs. Vetter   -*Musa--Mens--Musici: Im Gedenken an Walther Vetter.*
                Heinz Wegener, ed. Leipzig: VEB Deutscher Verlag für
                Musik, 1969.

Fs. Votterle   -*Musik und Verlag: Karl Vötterle zum 65. Geburtstag am
                12. April 1968.* Richard Baum and Wolfgang Rehm, eds.
                Kassel: Bärenreiter, 1968.

Fs. Walcha   -*Bachstunden: Festschrift für Helmut Walcha zum 70.
                Geburtstag, überreicht von seinen Schülern.* Walter
                Dehnhard and Gottlob Ritter, eds. Frankfurt am Main:
                Evangelischer Presseverband in Hessen und Nassau, 1978.

Fs. Wessely   -*Festschrift Othmar Wessely zum 60. Geburtstag.* Manfred
                Angerer, et al., eds. Tutzing: H. Schneider, 1982.

Fs. Wiener   -*Festschrift 1817-1967 Akademie für Musik und Darstel-
                lende Kunst in Wien.* Wien: Lafite, 1967.

Fs. Wiora   -*Festschrift für Walter Wiora zum 30. Dezember 1966.*
                Kassel: Bärenreiter, 1967.

Monographs

In citing dissertations below, the following abbreviations are used: "LC
Mic" indicates are used: "LC Mic" indicates the Library of Congress call
number for microfilm; "DA" refers to Dissertation Abstracts volume, fascicle,
and page; and "UM" refers to University Microfilm order number.

Abraham   -Gerald Abraham. *Essays on Russian and East European
                music.* Oxford: Clarendon Press, 1985.

Abraham/L   -Lars Ulrich Abraham, et al. *Neue Wege der musikali-
                schen Analyse.* Veröffentlichungen des Instituts für neue
                Musik und Musikerziehung, Darmstadt 6. Berlin: Merse-
                burger, 1967.

Anhalt   -Istvan Anhalt. *Alternative voices: Essays on contempo-
                rary vocal and choral composition.* Toronto: University
                of Toronto Press, 1984.

Bachfest   -*Bachfest (55.) der Neuen Bachgesellschaft in Mainz, 22 bis
                27 Oktober 1980: "Johann Sebastian Bach und seine
                Ausstrahlung auf die Nachfolgende Jahrhunderte."* Mainz:
                Neue Bachgesellschaft, 1980.

Badura-Skoda   -*Schubert studies: Problems of style and chronology.* Eva
                Badura-Skoda and Peter Branscombe, eds. Cambridge:
                Cambridge University Press, 1982.

Battcock   -Gregory Battcock. *Breaking the sound barrier: A critical
                anthology of the new music.* New York: E.P. Dutton,
                1981.

Beck   -*Studien zur Musikgeschichte der Stadt Regensburg.*
                Hermann Beck, ed. Regensburg: G. Bosse, 1979.

Benary   -Peter Benary, et al. *Versuch musikalischer Analysen.*
                Veröffentlichungen des Instuts für neue Musik und
                Musikerziehung, Darmstadt 8. Berlin: Merseburger, 1967.

Bersano   -James Richard Bersano. "Formalized aspect analysis of sound texture." PhD dissertation (Theory): Indiana University, 1979. UM 80-16,401. DA XL.1, p.11-A.

Boulez   -Pierre Boulez. *Points de repère*. Jean-Jacques Nattiez, ed. 2nd ed. Paris: Editions du Seuil, 1985.

Brinkmann   -*Die neue Musk und die Tradition: Sieben Kongress-Beiträge und eine analytische Studie*. Reinhold Brinkmann, ed. Mainz: Schott, 1978.

Broekema   -Andrew J. Broekema. "A stylistic comparison of the solo vocal works of Arnold Schoenberg, Alban Berg, and Anton Webern." PhD dissertation (Musicology): University of Texas, 1962. UM 62-4822. DA XXIII.5, p. 1730.

Brusatti   -*Schubert-Kongress Wien 1978: Bericht*. Otto Brusatti, ed. Graz: Akademische Druck- und Verlagsanstalt, 1979.

Buccheri   -John Stephen Buccheri. "An approach to twelve-tone music: Articulation of serial pitch units in piano works of Schoenberg, Webern, Krenek, Dallapiccola, and Rochberg." PhD dissertation (Theory): University of Rochester, 1975. UM 76-12,555. DA XXXVII.2, p.679-A.

Budde   -*Franz-Schrecker-Symposium*. Elmar Budde and Rudolph Stephan, eds. Berlin: Colloquium, 1980.

Carner   -Mosco Carner. *Major and minor*. New York: Holmes & Meier, 1980.

Chailley   -Jacques Chailley. *Florilège d'analyses*. Volume 2: *Classiques et romantiques*. Paris: A. Leduc, 1984.

Chihara   -Paul Seiko Chihara. "Studies in melody in four twentieth-century composers." DMA dissertation: Cornell University, 1965. No DA listing.

Cope   -David H. Cope. *New directions in music*. 4th ed. Dubuque, IA: Wm.C. Brown, 1984.

Curtis   -Brandt B. Curtis. "A comparison of early musical settings of four poems by A.E. Housman." DMA dissertation (Voice): Indiana University, 1979. No DA listing.

Dahlhaus   -*Das Drama Richard Wagners als musikalisches Kunstwerk*. Carl Dahlhaus, ed. Regensburg: G. Bosse, 1970. Dahlhaus/S   -*Studien zur Musikgeschichte Berlins im fruhen 19. Jahrhundert*. Carl Dahlhaus, ed. Regensburg: G. Bosse, 1980.

De la Motte -Diether De la Motte. *Musikalische Analyse*. Kassel: Bärenreiter, 1968.

Dommel-Diény -Amy Dommel-Diény. *L'analyse harmonique en exemples de J.S. Bach à Debussy*. [Imprint varies]

Dorroh   -William James Dorroh. "A study of plainsong in the organ compositions of six twentieth-century French composers." PhD dissertation: George Peabody College for Teachers, 1978. 132 p. UM 79-09,940. DA XXXIX.11, p.6387-A.

Enix   -Margery Ann Enix. "The dissolution of the functional harmonic tonal system: 1850-1910." PhD dissertation (Theory): Indiana University, 1977. 446 p. UM 77-22,646. DA XXXVIII.4, p.1725-A.

Epstein	-David Epstein. *Beyond Orpheus: Studies in musical structure.* Cambridge: MIT Press, 1979.
Forte	-Allen Forte. *Contemporary tone structures.* New York: Columbia University Teachers' College, 1955.
Goldschmidt	-*Bericht über den Internationalen Beethoven-Kongress 20. bis 23. Marz 1977 in Berlin.* Harry Goldschmidt, Karl-Heinz Kohler, and Konrad Niemann, eds. Leipzig: VEB Deutscher Verlag für Musik, 1978.
Grasberger	-*Schubert Studien: Festgabe der Österreichischen Akademie der Wissenschaften zum Schubert-Jahr 1978, Wien 1978.* Franz Grasberger and Othmar Wessely, eds. Wien: Österreichische Akademie der Wissenschaften, 1978.
Hall	-Anne Carothers Hall. "Texture in violin concertos of Stravinsky, Berg, Schoenberg, and Bartók." PhD dissertation (Musicology): University of Michigan, 1971. 356 p. UM 72-14,884. DA XXXII.11, p.6476-A.
Hansler	-George E. Hansler. "Stylistic characteristics and trends in contemporary British choral music." PhD dissertation (Music Edution): New York University, 1957. LC Mic 58-651. DA XVIII.4, p.1454.
Hart	-Ralph E. Hart. "Compositional techniques in choral works of Stravinsky, Hindemith, Honegger, and Britten." PhD dissertation: Northwestern University, 1952. 316 p. No DA listing.
Hines	-*Essays on twentieth-century music by those who wrote it: The orchestral composer's point of view.* Robert Stephan Hines, ed. Norman: University of Oklahoma Press, 1970.
Jeter	-Eulalie Wilson Jeter. "The study, analysis and performance of selected original two-piano music of contemporary American composers." EdD dissertation: Columbia University, 1978. 166 p. No DA listing.
Johnson	-June Durkin Johnson. "Analyses of selected works for the soprano voice written in serial technique by living composers." DMA dissertation: University of Illinois, 1967. No DA listing.
Kirchmeyer	-Helmut Kirchmeyer and Hugo Wolfram Schmidt. *Aufbruch der jungen Musik: Von Webern bis Stockhausen.* Köln: H. Gerig, 1970.
Kniesner	-Virginia Elizabeth Kniesner. "Tonality and form in selected French piano sonatas: 1900-1950." PhD dissertation: Ohio State University, 1977. 437 p. UM 77-31,907. DA XXXVIII.8, p.4439-A.
KNM	-*Kommentare zur neuen Musik.* Köln: Du Mont Schaubert, 1961.
Kolleritsch	-*Gustav Mahler: Sinfonie und Wirklichkeit.* Otto Kolleritsch, ed. Graz: Universal, 1977.
Kolleritsch/S	-*Alexander Skrjabin.* Otto Kolleritsch, ed. Graz: Universal, 1980.
Kresky	-Jeffry Kresky. *Tonal music: Twelve analytic studies.* Bloomington: Indiana University Press, 1977.

Kühn — *Bericht über den Internationalen Musikwissenschaftlichen Kongress, Berlin 1974.* Hellmut Kühn and Peter Nitsche, eds. Kassel: Bärenreiter, 1980.

Lampsatis — Raminta Lampsatis. "Dodekaphonische Werke von Balsys, Juzeliunas und der jüngeren Komponisten-generation Litauens: Dodekaphonie als integrierende Technik." PhD dissertation (Musicology): Technische Universität Berlin, 1977.

Lang — Paul Henry Lang. *Stravinsky: A new appraisal of his work.* New York: W.W. Norton, 1963. [Reprinted from MQ 48(1962): 287-384]

Larsen — *Haydn Studies: Proceedings of the International Haydn Conference, Washington, D.C., 1975.* Jens Peter Larsen, Howard Senwer, James Webster, eds. New York: W.W. Norton, 1981.

Larson — Robert Merl Larson. "Stylistic characteristics in A cappella composition in the U.S., 1940-1953, as indicated by the works of Jean Berger, David Diamond, Darius Milhaud, and Miklós Rozsa." PhD dissertation: Northwestern University, 1953. UM 7047. DA XIV.2, p.371.

Leibowitz — René Leibowitz. *Schoenberg and his school.* New York: Philosophical Library, 1949.

Leibowitz/F — René Leibowitz. *Les fantômes de l'opéra: Essais sur le théâtre lyrique.* Paris: Gallimard, 1972.

Lewis — Beverly Williams Lewis. "A study of the musical and literary significance of the lyric portions of Goethe's Wilhelm Meisters Lehrjahre." DMA dissertation: Memphis State University, 1979. No DA listing.

Ligeti — György Ligeti, Witold Lutoslawski, and Ingvar Lidholm. *Three aspects of new music.* Stockholm: Nordiska Musikförlagt, 1968.

Little — Jean Little. "Architectonic levels of rhythmic organization in selected twentieth-century music." PhD dissertation: Indiana University, 1971. 405 p. No DA listing.

Macy — Carleton Macy. "Musical characteristics in selected Faust works: A study in nineteenth-century music rhetoric." DMA dissertation: University of Washington, 1978. 344 p. No DA listing.

Mertens — Wim Mertens. *American minimal music: An analysis of the music of La Monte Young, Terry Riley, Steve Reich, Philip Glass.* New York: Alexander Broude, 1983.

Mize — Lou Slem Mize. "A study of selected choral settings of Walt Whitman poems." PhD dissertation: Florida State University, 1976. No DA listing.

Morrison — Donald N. Morrison. "Influences of Impressionist tonality on selected works of Delius, Griffes, Falla, and Respighi: Based on the concept developed by Robert Mueller." PhD dissertation (Theory): Indiana University, 1960. LC Mic 60-2829. DA XXI.3, p.641.

Müller	-*Schumann-Tage (1.) des Bezirkes Karl-Marx-Stadt 1976: 1. Wissenschaftliche Arbeitstagung zu Fragen der Schumann-Forschung.* Gunther Müller and Williams Geissler, eds. Zwickau: Robert-Schumann-Gesellschaft der DDR, 1977.
Ogdon	-Wilbur Lee Ogdon. "Series and structure: An investigation into the purpose of the twelve-note row in selected works of Schoenberg, Webern, Krenek and Leibowitz." PhD dissertation (Theory): Indiana University, 1966. UM 14,663. DA XVI.2, p.351.
Pascall	-*Brahms biographical, documentary, and analytical studies.* Robert Pascall, ed. Cambridge: Cambridge University Press, 1983.
Pečman	-*Colloquium musica cameralis, Brno 1971.* Rudolf Pecman, ed. Brno: Mezinárodní hudební festival, 1977.
Pečman/J	-*Colloquium Leos Janacek et musica Europaea: Colloquia on the history and theory of music at the International Musical Festival in Brno.* Rudolf Pecman, ed. International Musical Festival, 1970.
Perle	-George Perle. *Serial composition and atonality.* 3rd ed. Berkeley: University of California Press, 1972.
Pütz	-Werner Pütz. *Studien zum Streichquartettschaffen bei Hindemith, Bartók, Schönberg und Webern.* Regensburg: G. Bosse, 1968.
Rahn	-John Rahn. *Basic atonal theory.* New York: Longman, 1980.
Reichert	-*Bericht über den Internationalen musikwissenschaftlichen Kongress, Kassel 1962.* Georg Reichert and Martin Just, eds. Kassel: Bärenreiter, 1963.
Rexroth	-*Erprobungen und Erfahrungen: Zu Paul Hindemiths Schaffen in den zwanziger Jahren.* Dieter Rexroth, ed. Mainz: Schott, 1978.
Rhoades	-Larry Lynn Rhoades. "Theme and variations in twentieth-century organ literature: Analyses of variations by Alain, Barber, Distler, Dupré, Duruflé, and Sowerby." PhD dissertation (Theory): Ohio State University, 1973. 282 p. UM 73-26,894. DA XXXIV.5, p.2686-A.
Roberts	-Gwyneth Margaret Roberts. "Procedures for analysis of sound masses." PhD dissertation (Theory): Indiana Univesity, 1978. No DA listing.
Rognoni	-Luigi Rognoni. *Espressionismo e dodecafonia: In appendice scritti di Arnold Schoenberg, Alban Berg, Wassily Kandinsky.* Torino: E. Einaudi, 1954.
Schnitzler	-*Musik und Zahl: Interdisziplinäre Beiträge zum Grenzbereich zwischen Musik und Mathematik.* Günter Schnitzler, ed. Bonn-Bad Godesberg: Verlag für systematische Musikwissenschaft, 1976.
Schnitzler/D	-*Dichtung und Musik: Kaleidoscop ihrer Beziehungen.* Günter Schnitzler, ed. Stuttgart: Klett-Cotta, 1979.
Schreker	-Franz Schreker. *Am Beginn der neuen Musik.* Graz: Universal, 1978.

Schultz	-Wolfgang-Andreas Schultz. *Die freien Formen in der Musik des Expressionismus und Impressionismus.* Hamburg: Wagner, 1974. 143 p.
Schultz/D	-Donna Gartman Schultz. "Set theory and its application to compositions by five twentieth-century composers." PhD dissertation (Theory): Michigan State University, 1979. UM 79-21,198. DA XL.3, p.1146-A.
Schweitzer	-Eugene William Schweitzer. "Generation in string quartets of Carter, Sessions, Kirchner, and Schuller: A concept of forward thrust and its relationship to structure in aurally complex styles." PhD dissertation (Theory): University of Rochester, 1965. UM 66-2363. DA XXVII.6, p.1856-A.
Stahmer	-*Form und Idee in Gustav Mahlers Instrumentalmusik.* Klaus Hinrich Stahmer, ed. Wilhelmshaven: Heinrichshofen, 1980.
Stephan	-*Die Musik der sechziger Jahre.* Rudolph Stephan, ed. Mainz: Schott, 1972.
Sterling	-Eugene A. Sterling. "A study of chromatic elements in selected piano works of Beethoven, Schubert, Schumann, Chopin, and Brahms." PhD dissertation (Theory): Indiana University, 1966. UM 66-14,895. DA XXVIII.2, p.714-A.
Stockhausen	-Karlheinz Stockhausen. *Texte zu eigenen Werken zur Kunst anderer Aktuelles.* His *Texte,* vol. 2. Köln: M.D. Schauberg, 1964.
Taruskin	-Richard Taruskin. "Chernomor to Kashchei: Harmonic sorcery; or, Stravinsky's 'Angle'." JAMS 38(1985): 72-142.
Van Solkema	-*The new worlds of Edgard Varèse: A symposium.* Sherman van Solkema, ed. New York: Institute for Studies in American Music, 1979. [Papers by Elliott Carter, Chou Wen-Chung, and Robert P. Morgan]
Vogt	-Hans Vogt. *Neue Musik seit 1945.* 3rd ed. Stuttgart: P. Reclam, 1982.
Webern	-*Webern-Kongress, Vienna 1972: Beiträge.* Österreichische Gesellschaft für Musik, ed. Kassel: Bärenreiter, 1973.
Wennerstrom	-Wennerstrom, Mary Hannah. "Parametric analysis of contemporary music form." PhD dissertation (Theory): Indiana University, 1967.
Winter	-*Beethoven, performers, and critics: The International Beethoven Congress, Detroit 1977.* Robert Winter and Bruce Carr, eds. Detroit: Wayne State University Press, 1980.
Wise	-Ronald Eugene Wise. "Scoring in the Neoclassic woodwind quintets of Hindemith, Fine, Etler, and Wilder." PhD dissertation: University of Wisconsin, 1967. 274 p. No DA listing.
Wozzeck	-*50 Jahre Wozzeck von Alban Berg.* Studien zu Wertungsforschung 10. Graz: Universal, 1978.
Yeston	-*Readings in Schenker analysis and other approaches.* Maury Yeston, ed. New Haven: Yale University Press, 1977.

Zimmerschied   *-Perspectiven neuer Musik: Material und didaktische Information.* Dieter Zimmerschied, ed. Mainz: Schott, 1974.

ANALYSES OF NINETEENTH- AND TWENTIETH-CENTURY MUSIC
1940-1985

ADLER, SAMUEL (born 1928)

1. Lucas, Joan Dawson. "The operas of Samuel Adler: an analytical study." PhD dissertation (Musicology): Louisiana State University, 1978. No DA listing.

ADORNO, THEODOR W. (1903-1969)

2. Leibowitz, René. "Der Komponist Theodor W. Adorno." Fs. Adorno/60:335-359. [Sechs Bagatellen für Singstimme und Klavier, Op. 6]
3. Spahlinger, Mathias. "Der Widersinn von Gesang: Zu Theodor W. Adornos Liedkomposition." MTX 1(1983): 37-39.

AHRENS, JOSEPH (born 1904)

4. Ahrens, Joseph. *Die Formprinzipien des gregorianischen Chorals und mein Orgelstil.* Heidelberg: Müller Süddeutscher Musikverlag, 1977.

ALAIN, JEHAN (1911-1940)

5. Bouchett, Richard Travis. "The organ music of Jehan Alain (1911-1940)." DSM dissertation (Musicology): Union Theological Seminary, 1971. UM 71-23,416. DA XXXII.4, p.2114-A.
6. Dorroh.
7. Dunham, Ervin Jerrol. "A stylistic analysis of the organ music of Jehan Alain." DMA dissertation (Performance): University of Arizona, 1965. UM 65-9578. DA XXVI.6, p.3389.
8. Rhoades.
9. Schauerte, Helga. *Jehan Alain (1911-1940): Das Orgelwerke.* Regensburg: G. Bosse, 1983.

ALBÉNIZ, ISAAC (1860-1909)

10. Mast, Paul Buck. "Style and structure in *Iberia* by Isaac Albéniz." PhD dissertation (Theory): University of Rochester, 1974. 409 p. UM 74-21,529. DA XXXV.4, pp.2322-3-A.

ALBRECHT, GEORG VON (1891-1976)

11. *Festschrift Georg von Albrecht.* [Articles on "Klavier-und Orchesterwerke" (Gerhard Frommel): 11-24; "Kammermusik" (Michael von Albrecht): 25-34; "Vokalwerke" (Johannes Schwermer): 35-44; "Die Rolle der Volksmusik" (Karl Michael Komma): 45-52] Fs. Albrecht/70.

ALIABEV, ALEXANDER ALEXANDROVICH (1787-1851)

12. Green, Carol. "The string quartets of Alexander Alexandrovich Alexandrovich Aliabev." MR 33(1972): 323-329.

ALNAES, EYVIND (1872-1932)

13. Olson, Robert Wallace. "A comparative study of selected Norwegian romances by Halfdan Kjerulf, Edvard Grieg, and Eyvind Alnaes." PhD dissertation (Performance): University of Illinois, 1973. 328 p. UM 73-17,611. DA XXXIV.2, p.812-A.

AMES, CHARLES

14. Hiller, Lejaren and Charles Ames; graphics by Robert Franki. "Automated composition: An installation at the 1985 International Exhibition in Tsukuba, Japan." PNM 23/2 (1984-1985): 196-215. [*Transitions; Mix or Match* (in collaboration with L. Hiller)]

ANDERGASSEN, FERDINAND

15. Gabriel, Ferdinand. "Die Instrumentalwerke von Ferdinand Andergassen." PhD dissertation (Musicology): Universität Innsbruck, 1977.

ANDERSON, T. J. (Thomas Jefferson) (born 1928)

16. Thompson, Bruce Alfred. "Musical style and compositional technique in selected works of T. J. Anderson." PhD dissertation (Theory): Indiana University, 1978. UM 79-09,721. DA XXXIX.11, p.6392-A.

ANDRIESSEN, HENDRIK (1892-1981)

17. Dox, Thurston J. "Hendrik Andriessen: The path to *Il Pensiero.*" KN 13/1(1981): 16-24.
18. ----. "The works of Hendrik Andriessen." PhD dissertation (Theory): University of Rochester, 1970. 244 p. UM 70-12,462. DA XXXI.2, p.782-A.
19. Klerk, Jos de. "Hendrik Andriessen: *Sonata de Chiesa*, 2 studi per organo." SS 17(1963): 14-16.
20. Paap, Wouter. "The *Symphonische Etude* by Hendrik Andriessen." SS 4(1960): 135-136.
21. Schuyt, Nico. "*Philomela*: Opera by Hendrik Andriessen." SS 11(1962): 10-21.

ANDRIESSEN, JURRIAAN (born 1925)

22. Flothuis, Marius. "Jurriaan Andriessen, *Sonata de camera* per flauto, viola e chitarra." SS 15(1963): 19-22.
23. Paap, Wouter. "Jurriaan Andriessen and incidental music." SS 40(1969): 1-19.

ANDRIESSEN, LOUIS (born 1939)

24. Geraedts, Jaap. "Louis Andriessen: *Nocturnen* for Soprano and Orchestra." SS 25(1965): 14-16.
25. Huber, Nicolaus A. "Erlebniswanderung auf schmalem Grat: Das Hörbarmachen von Zeit und Geschwindigkeit bei Louis Andriessen." MTX 9(1985): 24-29.
26. Potter, Keith. "The music of Louis Andriessen: Dialectical double-dutch?" CT 23(1981): 16-22.
27. Sabbe, Hermann. "Pulsierende gegen geronnene Zeit: Stenogramm einer Analyse von Andriessens *Hoketus*." MTX 9(1985): 22-24.
28. Schönberger, Elmer. "Louis Andriessen: On the conceiving of time." KN 13/1(1981): 5-11.

ANHALT, ISTVAN (born 1919)

29. Anhalt, Istvan. "The making of *Cento*." CCM 1(1970): 81-89.

ANTHEIL, GEORGE (1900-1959)

30. Albee, David Lyman. "George Antheil's *La Femme 100 têtes*: A study of the piano preludes." DMA dissertation: University of Texas, 1977. No DA listing.
31. Whitesitt, Linda. *The life and music of George Antheil, 1900-1959*. Ann Arbor: UMI Research Press, 1983.

APOSTEL, HANS ERICH (1901-1972)

32. Bischof, Rainer. "Hans Erich Apostel oder die Schönheit der Ordnung." OMZ 35(1980): 15-27.

ARCHER, VIOLET (born 1913)

33. Huiner, Harvey Don. "The choral music of Violet Archer." PhD dissertation: University of Iowa, 1980. No DA listing.

ARGENTO, DOMINICK (born 1927)

34. Gebuhr, Ann K. "Structure and coherence in *The Diary* from Dominck Argento's cycle, *From the Diary of Virginia Woolf*." ITR 1/3 (1977-1978): 12-21.
35. Sabatino, Trucilla Marie. "A performer's commentary on *To Be Sung Upon the Water* by Dominick Argento." DMA dissertation: Ohio State University, 1980. No DA listing.

AUBER, DANIEL-FRANÇOISE-ESPRIT (1782-1871)

36. Longyear, Rey M. "D.F.E. Auber (1782-1871): A chapter in the history of the *opéra comique*, 1800-1870." PhD dissertation (Musicology): Cornell University, 1957. UM 22,202. DA XVII.9, p.2027.

AUBIN, TONY (1927-1981)

37. Kniesner. [*Sonate en si mineur* (piano)]

AULIN, TOR (1866-1914)

38. Wallner, Bo. "Tor Aulin och det svenska musiklivet." DAM 11 (1980): 31-43.

AUSTIN, LARRY (born 1930)

39. Clark, Thomas. "Duality of process and drama in Larry Austin's *Sonata concertante*." PNM 23/1(1984-1985): 112-125.

BAAREN, KEES VAN (1906-1970)

40. Hill, S. Jackson. "The music of Kees van Baaren: A study of transition in the music of the Netherlands in the second third of the twentieth century." PhD dissertation (Musicology): University of North Carolina, 1970. UM 71-3564. DA XXXI.8, p.4201-A.

41. Straesser, Joep. "Kees van Baaren: *Quintetto a fiati (Sovraposizioni 2).*" SS 22(1965): 12-19.

42. Wouters, Jos. "Kees van Baaren." SS 16(1963): 1-14.

BABBITT, MILTON (born 1916)

Chamber works

43. Arnold, Stephen and Graham Hair. "An introduction and a study: String Quartet No.3." PNM 14/2-15/1(1976): 155-186.

44. Borders, Barbara. "Formal aspects in selected instrumental works of Milton Babbitt." PhD dissertation (Music Theory): University of Kansas, 1979. UM 80-02,810. DA XL.8, p.4290-A. [*Composition for Twelve Instruments*; Sextets for Piano and Viola; String Quartet No.3]

45. Capalbo, Marc. "Charts." PNM 19/2(1980-1981): 309-331. [Sextets]

46. Cone, Richard. "The 12x12 Latin square as found in Babbitt's String Quartet No.2." SONUS 3/1(1982): 57-65.

47. Hush, David. "Asynordinate twelve-tone structures: Milton Babbitt's *Composition for Twelve Instruments*." PNM 21(1982-1883): 152-208, 22(1983-1984): 103-116.

48. Westergaard, Peter. "Some problems raised by the rhythmic procedures in Milton Babbitt's *Composition for Twelve Instruments*." PNM 4/1(1965): 109-118.

49. Zuckerman, Mark. "On Milton Babbitt's String Quartet No.2." PNM 14/2-15/1(1976): 85-110.

Piano works
    50. Perle: 128-134. [Three Compositions for Piano]

Songs
    51. Johnson. [*Du; The Widow's Lament in Springtime*]
    52. Rahn, John. "How do you *Du* (by Milton Babbitt)." PNM 14/2-15/1(1976): 61-80.

Other works
    53. Babbitt, Milton. "On *Relata I.*" PNM 9/1(1970): 1-22.
    54. Hines: 11-38.
    55. Mead, Andrew W. "Detail and the array in Milton Babbitt's *My Complements to Roger.*" MTS 5(1983): 89-109.
    56. ----. "Recent developments in the music of Milton Babbitt." MQ 70(1984): 310-331. [*Paraphrases; Relata I; My Complements to Roger; Arie da Capo*; Quartets No.2 and No.4]
    57. Sward, Rosalie La Grow. "An examination of the mathematical systems used in selected compositions of Milton Babbitt and Iannis Xenakis." PhD dissertation: Northwestern University, 1981. No DA listing.
    58. Wintle, Christopher. "Milton Babbitt's *Semi-Simple Variations.*" PNM 14/2-15/1(1976): 111-154.

BADINGS, HENK (born 1907)

    59. Ameringen, Sylvia van. "Henk Badings: Profil eines holländischen Komponisten von heute." OMZ 7(1952): 297-300.
    60. Badings, Henk. "Henk Badings: Sonata for 'Cello Solo." SS 7 (1961): 23-24.
    61. Clardy, Mary Karen King. "Compositional devices of Willem Pijper (1894-1947) and Henk Badings (b. 1907) in two selected works: Pijper's *Sonata per flauto e pianforte* (1925) and Badings' Concerto for Flute and Wind Symphony Orchestra (1963). DMA dissertation: North Texas State University 1980. No DA listing.
    62. Ditto, John Allen. "The Four Preludes and Fugues, the *Ricercar* and the *Passacaglia* for Timpani and Organ by Henk Badings." DMA dissertation: University of Rochester, 1979. UM 79-21,120. DA XL.3, p.1141-A.
    63. Geraedts, Jaap. "Badings: Symphony for String Orchestra." SS 6 (1961): 9-13.
    64. Kox, Hans. "Henk Badings: Eighth Symphony." SS 16(1963): 15-19.
    65. Wouters, Jos. "Henk Badings: Largo and Allegro." SS 6(1961): 18-20.
    66. ----. "Henk Badings." SS 32(1967): 1-23.

BAIRD, TADEUSZ (1928-1981)

    67. Baird, Tadeusz. "*Sinfonia brevis* of Tadeusz Baird." PM 4/1 (1969): 13-15.

68. Carper, Jeremy Lee. "The interplay of musical and dramatic structures in *Jutro*, an opera by Tadeusz Baird." PhD dissertation (Musicology): Washington University, 1983. No DA listing.

BAJORAS, FELIKSAS (born 1934)

69. Lampsatis.

BALAKAUSKAS, OSWALDAS (born 1937)

70. Lampsatis.

BALAKIREV, MILY ALEXEIEVITCH (1837-1910)

71. Davis, Richard. "Henselt, Balakirev, and the piano." MR 28 (1967): 173-208.
72. Garden, Edward. "Sibelius and Balakirev." Fs. Abraham: 215-218.

BALSYS, EDUARDAS (born 1919)

73. Gerlach, Hannelore. "*Rührt nicht am blauen Globus*: Oratorium des litauischen Komponisten Eduardas Balsys." MG 25(1975): 264-268.
74. Lampsatis.

BARBER, SAMUEL (1910-1981)

Piano works
75. Carter, Susan Blinderman. "The piano music of Samuel Barber." PhD dissertation (Theory): Texas Tech University, 1980. 188 p. UM 80-22,610. DA XLI.4, p.1270-A.
76. Chittum, Donald. "The synthesis of materials and devices in nonserial counterpoint." MR 31(1970): 123-135. [Piano Sonata]
77. Fairleigh, James P. "Serialism in Barber's solo piano works." PQ 72(1970): 13-17.
78. Haberkorn, Michael. "A study and performance of the piano sonatas of Samuel Barber, Elliott Carter, and Aaron Copland." EdD dissertation: Columbia University, 1979. No DA listing.
79. Tischler, Hans. "Barber's Piano Sonata, Op.26." ML 33(1952): 352-354.

Other works
80. Broder, Nathan. "The music of Samuel Barber." MQ 34(1948): 325-335.
81. ----. *Samuel Barber*. Westport, CT: Greenwood Press, 1985.
82. Friedewald, Russell Edward. "A formal and stylistic analysis of the published music of Samuel Barber." PhD dissertation (Theory): University of Iowa, 1957. UM 23,735. DA XVII.2, p.3037.
83. Horan, Robert. "Samuel Barber." MM 20(1943): 161-169.

84. Larsen, Robert L. "A study and comparison of Samuel Barber's *Vanessa*, Robert Ward's *The Crucible*, and Gunther Schuller's *The Visitation.*" DMA dissertation (Conducting): Indiana University, 1971. No DA listing.
85. Rhoades.
86. Wathen, Lawrence Samuel. "Dissonance treatment in the instrumental music of Samuel Barber." PhD dissertation (Theory): Northwestern University, 1960. LC Mic 60-6586. DA XXI.10, p.3118.

BARKAUSKAS, VYTAUTAS (born 1931)

87. Lampsatis.

BARKIN, ELAINE (born 1932)

88. Cory, Eleanor. "Elaine Barkin: String Quartet (1969)." MQ 62 (1976): 618-620. [Record review]

BARLOW, KLARENZ (born 1945)

89. Frisius, Rudolf. "Eine gewisse mechanische Starrheit: Zu *Çoğluotobüsişletmesi* von Klarenz Barlow." TXT 5(1984): 45-47.

BARRIÈRE, JEAN-BAPTISTE

90. Barrière, Jean-Baptiste. "*Chréode*: The pathway to new music with the computer." CMR 1/1(1984-1985): 181-201.

BARTEL, HANS-CHRISTIAN (born 1932)

91. Wolf, Werner. "Neue Werke unserer Komponisten: Max Buttings X. Sinfonien; Bratschenkonzert von Hans-Christian Bartel." MG 14(1964): 80-83.

BARTÓK, BÉLA (1881-1945)

Bluebeard's Castle
92. Kroó, György. "*Duke Bluebeard's Castle.*" SM 1(1959): 251-340.
93. Veress, Sándor. "*Bluebeard's Castle.*" Fs. Bartók/T: 36-53.

Concerto for Orchestra
94. Austin, William. "Bartók's Concerto for Orchestra." MR 18(1957): 21-47.
95. French, Gilbert G. "Continuity and discontinuity in Bartók's Concerto for Orchestra." MR 28(1967): 122-134.
96. Kneif, Tibor. "Zur Entstehung und Kompositionstechnik von Bartóks Konzert für Orchester." MF 26(1973): 36-51.

97. Volek, J. "Über einige interessante Beziehungen zwischen thematischer Arbeit und Instrumentation in Bartóks Werk: Concerto für Orchester." SM 5(1963): 557-586. [Also *Liszt-Bartók: Bericht über die zweite internationale musikwissenschaftliche Konferenz, Budapest 25-30 September, 1961.* Z. Gárdonyi and B. Szabolcsi, eds. Budapest: Akadémiai Kiadó, 1963: 557-586.

98. Weber, Horst. "Material und Komposition in Bartóks Concerto for Orchestra." NZM 134(1973): 767-773.

Concertos

99. Bartók, Béla. "The Second Piano Concerto." TEMPO 65(1963): 5-7.

100. Eimert, Herbert. "Das Violinkonzert von Bartók." MELOS 14 (1947): 335-337.

101. Guerry, Jack E. "Bartók's concertos for solo piano: A stylistic and formal analysis." PhD dissertation: Michigan State University, 1964. UM 65-684. DA XXV.9, p.5319-20.

102. Hall. [Violin Concerto]

103. Kovács, Sándor. "Formprobleme beim Violakonzert von Bartók/ Serly." SM 24(1982): 381-391.

104. Little. [Violin Concerto No.2]

105. Mason, Colin. "Bartók's early Violin Concerto." TEMPO 49 (1958): 11-16.

106. Meyer, John A. "Beethoven and Bartók: A structural parallel." MR 31(1970): 315-321.

107. Michael, Frank. "Analytische Anmerkungen zu Bartóks 2. Klavierkonzert." SM 24(1982): 425-437.

108. ----. *Béla Bartóks Variationstechnik: Dargestellt im Rahmen einer Analyse seines 2. Violinskonzert.* Regensburg: G. Bosse, 1976.

109. Nüll, Edwin von der. "Béla Bartók, Geist und Stil: Aus Anlass der 2. Klavierkonzerts." MELOS 21(1945): 135-138.

110. Serly, Tibor. "A belated account of the reconstruction of a 20th century masterpiece." CMS 15(1975): 7-25. [Posthumous Viola Concerto]

111. Somfai, László. "Strategies of variation in the second movement of Bartók's Violin Concerto of 1937-1938." SM 19(1977): 161-202.

112. Zimmerschied: 110-127. [Violin Concerto 1937-1938]

Contrasts

113. Kárpáti, János. "Alternative structures in Bartók's *Contrasts*." SM 23(1981): 201-207.

114. Oramo, Ilkka. "Marcia und Burletta: Zur Tradition der Rhapsodie in zwei Quartettsatzen Bartóks." MF 30(1977): 14-25.

Forty-four Duos for Two Violins

115. Röbke, Peter. "Analyse im Instrumentalspiel: Ein Unterichtsentwurf: Bartóks Scherzo aus Op.44." MB 15/10(1983): 14-17.

116. Veress, Sándor. "Béla Bartóks 44 Duos für 2 Violinen." Fs. Doflein: 31-57.

Four Pieces
    117. Waldbauer, Ivan. "Bartók's Four Pieces for Two Pianos." TEMPO 53/54(1960): 17-22.

Fourteen Bagatelles, Op.6
    118. Antokoletz, Elliott. "The musical language of Bartók's 14 Bagatelles for piano." TEMPO 137(1981): 8-16.
    119. Forte: 74-90.
    120. Woodward, James. "Understanding Bartók's Bagatelle Op.6/9." ITR 4/2(1980-1981): 11-32.

Improvisations for Piano, Op.20
    121. Agawu, V. Kofi. "Analytical issues raised by Bartók's Improvisations for Piano, Op.20." JMR 5(1984-1985): 131-163.
    122. Wilson, Paul. "Concepts of prolongation and Bartók's Opus 20." MTS 6(1984): 79-89.

Mikrokosmos
    123. Ameringen, Sylvia van. "Teaching with Bartók's *Mikrocosmos*." TEMPO 21(1951): 31-35.
    124. Benary, Peter. "Der zweistimmige Kontrapunkt in Bartóks *Mikrokosmos*." AM 15(1958): 198-206.
    125. Dustin, William. "Two-voiced texture in the *Mikrokosmos* of Béla Bartók." PhD dissertation (Musicology): Cornell University, 1959. LC Mic 60-609. DA XX.9, p.3768.
    126. Engelmann, Hans Ulrich. *Béla Bartóks "Mikrokosmos": Versuch einer Typologie "neuer Musik"*. Würzburg: K. Triltsch, 1953.
    127. ----. "Chromatisches Ausstufung in Béla Bartóks *Mikrokosmos*." MELOS 18(1951): 138-141.
    128. Kapst, Erich. "Bartóks Anmerkungen zum *Mikrokosmos*." MG 20 (1970): 585-595.
    129. Lewin, Harold F. "A graphic analysis of Béla Bartók's *Major Seconds Broken and Together, Mikrokosmos*, Vol. V, No.132." TP 6/2 (1981): 40-46.
    130. Loeb van Zuilenburg, Paul E.O.F. "A study of Béla Bartók's *Mikrokosmos* with respect to formal analysis, compositional techniques, piano-technical and piano-pedagogical aspects." PhD dissertation (Musicology): University of Witwatersrand, Johannesburg, 1969.
    131. Lowman, Edward A. "Some striking propositions in the music of Béla Bartók." *Fibonacci Quarterly* 915(1971): 527-528, 536-537.
    132. Parks, Richard S. "Harmonic resources in Bartók's *Fourths*." JMT 25(1981): 245-274.
    133. Schultz/D. [*Bulgarian Rhythm* from *Mikrokosmos*, Vol. 4]
    134. Simon, Albert. "Béla Bartók: *Secondes mineures--septièmes majeures (Mikrokosmos* VI/144)." SMZ 123(1983): 82-86.
    135. Starr, Lawrence. "*Mikrokosmos*: The tonal universe of Béla Bartók." PhD dissertation (Musicology): University of California, Berkeley, 1973.
    136. Suchoff, Benjamin. "Béla Bartók, and a guide to the *Mikrokosmos*." EdD dissertation: New York University, 1956. UM 17,678. DA XVII.4, p.876.

137. ----. *Guide to the "Mikrokosmos" of Béla Bartók.* New York: Da Capo Press, 1982. (1956)

138. Uhde, Jurgen. *Bartók "Mikrokosmos": Spielanweisungen und Erläuterungen: Die Einführung in das Werk und seine pädagogischen Absichten.* Regensburg: G. Bosse, 1954.

139. Veress, Sándor. "Le *Mikrokosmos* dans l'univers musical de Bartók." SMZ 122(1982): 260-263.

140. Waldbauer, Iván F. "Intellectual construct and tonal direction in Bartók's *Divided Arpeggios.*" SM 24(1982): 527-536.

141. Wolff, Hellmuth Christian. "Der *Mikrokosmos* von Béla Bartók." M 5(1951): 134-140.

Miraculous Mandarin

142. Chailley, Jacques. "Essai d'analyse du *Mandarin merveilleux.*" SM 8(1966): 11-39.

143. Lendvai, Ernö. "*Der wunderbare Mandarin.*" SM 1(1959): 363-431.

144. Lossau, Gunter. "Bartóks Pantomime *Der wunderbare Mandarin.*" MELOS 33(1966): 173-177.

145. Persichetti, Vincent. "Current Chronicle." MQ 35(1949): 122-126.

146. Szabolcsi, Bence. "Bartók's *Miraculous Mandarin.*" *Bartók Studies.* Todd Crow, ed. Detroit: Information Coordinators, 1976: 22-38.

147. ----. "*Le Mandarin miraculeux.*" SM 1(1959): 341-361.

148. Vinton, John. "The case of *The Miraculous Mandarin.*" MQ 50 (1964): 1-17.

Music for Strings, Percussion, and Celesta

149. Bailey, Kathryn. "Bartók's tonal ellipsis in the *Music for String, Percussion and Celeste.*" SMUWO 8(1983): 37-46.

150. Brinkmann, Reinhold. "Einige Aspekte der Bartók-Analyse." SM 24(1983) Supplement: 57-66.

151. Chittum, Donald. "The synthesis of materials and devices in non-serial counterpoint." MR 31(1970): 123-135.

152. Frobenius, Wolf. "Bartók und Bach." AM 41(1984): 54-67.

153. Helm, Everett. "Bartóks *Musik für Saiteninstrumente.*" MELOS 20(1953): 245-249.

154. Howat, Roy. "Debussy, Ravel and Bartók: Towards some new concepts of form." ML 58(1977): 285-293.

155. Hunkemöller, Jurgen. "Bartók analysiert seine *Musik für Saiteninstrumente, Schlagzeug und Celesta.*" AM 40(1983): 147-163.

156. ----. *Béla Bartók: Musik für Saiteninstrumente.* München: W. Fink, 1982.

157. Persichetti, Vincent. "Current Chronicle." MQ 35(1949): 297-301.

158. Smith, Robert. "Béla Bartók's *Music for Strings, Percussion and Celesta.*" MR 20(1959): 264-276.

159. Weiss-Aigner, Günther. "Béla Bartók: *Musik für Saiteninstrumente, Schlagzeug und Celesta.*" MB 7(1975): 440-448.

Piano works [see also individual titles]

160. Fenyo, Thomas. "The piano music of Béla Bartók." PhD dissertation: University of California, Los Angeles, 1956. 293 p. No DA listing.

161. Horn, Herbert A. "Idiomatic writing in the piano music of Béla Bartók." DMA dissertation (Performance): University of Southern California, 1968. UM 64-3811. DA XXIV.12, p.5451-2.

162. Hundt, Theodor. *Bartóks Satztechnik in den Klavierwerken.* Regensburg: G. Bosse, 1971.

163. Lammers, Joseph E. "Patterns of change and identity in shorter piano works by Béla Bartók." PhD dissertation: Florida State University, 1971.

164. Weissmann, John. "Bartók's piano music." Fs. Bartok/T: 60-71.

165. ----. "La Musique de piano de Bartók: L'Évolution d'une écriture." RM 224(1955): 171-222.

Rhapsody No. 2 for Violin and Piano
166. Eastman, Yasuko Tanaka. "Béla Bartók's Second Rhapsody for Violin and its folk melody sources: A study." MM dissertation: University of Alberta, 1977.

Scherzo for Piano and Orchestra
167. Mason, Colin. "Bartók Scherzo for Piano and Orchestra." TEMPO 65(1963): 10-13.

Sonata for Solo Violin
168. Lenoir, Yves. "Contributions à l'étude de la Sonate pour violin solo de Béla Bartók (1944)." SM 23(1981): 209-260.

Sonata for Two Pianos and Percussion
169. Nordwall, Ore. "Béla Bartók and modern music." SM 9(1967): 265-280.

170. Stockhausen: 136-139.

171. ----. "Bartók's Sonata for Two Pianos and Percussion." *The new Hungarian quarterly* 40(1970): 49-53.

Sonata for Violin, No. 2
172. Pleasants, Henry and Tibor Serly. "Bartók's historic contribution." MM 17(1940): 131-140.

173. Szentkirályi, András. "Bartók's Second Sonata for öiolin and Piano (1922)." PhD dissertation: Princeton University, 1976.

174. ----. "Some aspects of Béla Bartók's compositional techniques." SM 20(1978): 157-182.

Songs
175. Gerbers, Hilda. "Béla Bartók's *Öt dal* (Five Songs) Op.15." MR 30(1969): 291-299.

176. Hough, Philip. "The tonal structure of Bartók's *Autumn Tears*, Opus 16, No.1." TP 3/2(1978): 15-20.

177. Leichtentritt, Hugo. "Bartók and the Hungarian folksong." MM 10(1933): 130-139. [Twenty Hungarian Folk Songs]

178. McKinney, Bruce. "Further reflections on 'Autumn Tears'." TP 4/1(1979): 25-27. [Opus 16, No.1]

179. Weissmann, John S. "Notes concerning Bartók's solo vocal music." TEMPO 36(1955): 16-26; 38(1956): 14-20; 40(1956): 18-33.

String Quartets [see also individual quartets]
 180. Abraham, Gerald. "The Bartók of the quartets." ML 26(1945): 185-194.
 181. Babbitt, Milton. "The string quartets of Bartók." MQ 35(1949): 377-385.
 182. Boaz, Mildred Meyer. "T.S. Eliot and music: A study of the development of musical structure in selected poems by T.S. Eliot and music by Erik Satie, Igor Stravinsky, and Béla Bartók." PhD dissertation (Literature): University of Illinois, 1977. No DA listing.
 183. Carner, Mosco. "The string quartets of Bartók." Carner 92-121.
 184. Donahue, Robert Laurence. "A comparative analysis of phrase structure in selected movements of the string quartets of Béla Bartók and Walter Piston." DMA dissertation: Cornell University, 1964. No DA listing.
 185. Fladt, Harmut. *Zur Problematik traditionnel Formtypen in der Musik des frühen zwanzigsten Jahrhunderts: Dargestellt an Sonatensatzen in den Streichquartetten Béla Bartóks.* München: E. Katzbichler, 1974. 182 p.
 186. Kárpáti, János. *Bartók's string quartets.* Budapest: Corvina Press, 1975.
 187. Kreter, Leo Edward. "Motivic and structural delineation of the formal design in the first three Bartók quartets." DMA dissertation: Cornell University, 1960. No DA listing.
 188. Monelle, Raymond. "Bartók's imagination in the later quartets." MR 31(1970): 70-81.
 189. Perle, George. "The string quartets of Béla Bartók." Fs. Bernstein: 193-210.
 190. ----. "Symmetrical formations in the string quartets of Béla Bartók." MR 16(1955): 300-312.
 191. Putz.
 192. Rands, Bernard. "The use of canon in Bartók's quartets." MR 18 (1957): 183-188.
 193. Schwinger, Wolfram. "Béla Bartóks Streichquartette." M 27 (1973): 13-18, 133-137, 245-250, 252, 350-355, 445-451, 569-574.
 194. Seiber, Mátyás. *Béla Bartók: The String Quartets.* New York: Boosey & Hawkes, 1957.
 195. ----. "Béla Bartók's chamber music." Fs. Bartók/T: 23-35.
 196. Siegmund-Schultze, Walther. "Tradition und Neuerertum in Bartóks Streichquartetten." Fs. Kodály/80: 317-328.
 197. Thomason, Leta Nelle. "Structural significance of the motive in the string quartets of Béla Bartók." PhD dissertation (Theory): Michigan State University, 1965. UM 66-6876. DA XXVII.3, p.793-94-A.
 198. Traimer, Roswitha. *Béla Bartóks Kompositionstechnik: Dargestellt an seinen sechs Streichquartetten.* Regensburg: G. Bosse, 1956.
 199. Walker, Mark Fesler. "Thematic, formal, and tonal structure of Bartók string quartets." PhD dissertation (Theory): Indiana University, 1955. UM 14,672. DA XV.12, p.2543.

String Quartet No.1
 200. Gow, David. "Tonality and structure in Bartók's first two string quartets." MR 34(1973): 259-271.

201. Lendvai, Ernö. "Bartók und die Zahl." MELOS 27(1960): 327-331.

String Quartet No.2
202. Gow, David. "Tonality and structure in Bartók's first two string quartets." MR 34(1973): 259-271.
203. Whittall, Arnold. "Bartók's Second String Quartet." MR 32 (1971): 265-270.

String Quartet No.3
204. Berry, Wallace. "Symmetrical interval sets and derivative pitch materials in Bartók's String Quartet No.3." PNM 18/1-2(1979-1980): 289-379.

String Quartet No.4
205. Antokoletz, Elliott Maxim. "Principles of pitch organization in Bartók's Fourth String Quartet." PhD dissertation: City University of New York, 1975. 152 p. UM 75-21,334. No DA listing.
206. ----. "Principles of pitch organization in Bartók's Fourth String Quartet." ITO 3/6(1977): 3-22.
207. Forte: 139-143. [First movement]
208. ----. "Bartók's 'serial' composition." MQ 46(1960): 233-245.
209. Mason, Colin. "An essay in analysis: Tonality, symmetry, and latent serialism in Bartók's Fourth Quartet." MR 18(1957): 189-201.
210. Monelle, Raymond. "Notes on Bartók's Fourth Quartet." MR 29 (1968): 123-129.
211. Perle: 52-54.
212. Travis, Roy. "Tonal coherence in the first movement of Bartók's Fourth String Quartet." MFO 2(1970): 298-371.
213. Treitler, Leo. "Harmonic procedure in the Fourth Quartet of Béla Bartók." JMT 3(1959): 292-298.
214. Vogt: 191-209.

String Quartet No.5
215. Chapman, Roger E. "The Fifth Quartet of Béla Bartók." MR 12(1951): 296-303.
216. Winrow, Barbara. "*Allegretto con indifferenza*: A study of the 'Barrel Organ' episode in Bartók's Fifth Quartet." MR 32(1971): 102-106.

String Quartet No.6
217. Kramolisch, Walter. "Das Leitthema des VI. Streichquartetts von Béla Bartók." Fs. Becking: 437-482.
218. Oramo, Ilkka. "Marcia und Burletta: Zur Tradition der Rhapsodie in zwei Quartettsätzen Bartóks." MF 30(1977): 14-25.
219. Suchoff, Benjamin. "Structure and concept in Bartók's Sixth Quartet." TEMPO 83(1967-1968): 2-11.
220. Vinton, John. "New light on Bartók's Sixth Quartet." MR 25 (1964): 224-238.

Symphony (Kossuth)
221. Clegg, David. "Bartók's *Kossuth* symphony." MR 23(1962): 215-220.

Wooden Prince
222. Wolff, Hellmuth Christian. "Béla Bartóks *Holzgeschnitzter Prinz* und seine Beziehungen zu Igor Strawinsky." MZ 2(1952): 53-56.

Other works
223. Antokoletz, Elliott. *The music of Béla Bartók: A study of tonality and progression in twentieth-century music.* Berkeley: University of California Press, 1984.
224. ----. "Pitch-set derivations from the folk modes in Bartók's music." SM 24(1982): 265-274.
225. Bachmann, Tibor. *Bartók's harmonic language.* R.D. Getz, ed. n.p.: Bachmann, 1976.
226. Bachmann, Tibor and Mario Bachmann. *Studies in Bartók's music.* Russell P. Getz, ed. n.p.: T.& M. Bachmann, 1981.
227. Bachmann, Tibor and Peter J. Bachmann. "An analysis of Béla Bartók's music through Fibonaccian numbers and the golden mean." MQ 65(1979): 72-82.
228. Bartók, Béla. "Gypsy music or Hungarian music?" MQ 33 (1947): 240-257.
229. ----. "Hungarian peasant music." MQ 19(1933): 267-287.
230. ----. "Das Problem der neuen Musik." MELOS 25(1958): 232-235.
231. Berger, Gregor. *Béla Bartók.* Wolfenbüttel: Möseler, 1963.
232. Bratuz, Damiana. "Béla Bartók: A centenary homage." SMUWO 6(1981): 77-111.
233. Brelet, Gisele. "Musique savante et musique populaire." CPS 3 (1946): 38-58.
234. Breuer, János. "Kolinda rhythm in the music of Bartók." SM 17 (1975): 39-58.
235. Browne, Arthur G. "Béla Bartók." ML 12(1931): 35-45.
236. Chihara.
237. Citron, Pierre. *Bartók.* Paris: Éditions du Seuil, 1963.
238. Dobszay, Lásztò. "The absorption of folksong in Bartók's composition." SM 24(1982): 303-313.
239. Downey, John W. *La Musique populaire dans l'oeuvre de Béla Bartók.* Paris: Centre de Documentation Universitaire, 1966.
240. Forner, Johannes. "Die Sonatenform im Schaffen Béla Bartóks." PhD dissertation (Musicology): Wilhelm-Pieck Universität, Rostock, 1975. 158 p. [Works up to 1917]
241. Gergely, Jean Guillaume. "Béla Bartók, compositeur hongrois." PhD dissertation (Musicology): Strasbourg, 1975.
242. ----. "Béla Bartók, compositeur hongrois." RM 328-329(1980): 53-88; 330-332(1980): 137-167; 333-335(1980): 5-114.
243. Gillies, Malcolm. "Bartók's notation: Tonality and modality." TEMPO 145(1983): 4-9.
244. ----. "A theory of tonality and modality: Bartók's last works." MS 7(1982): 120-130.

245. Griffiths, Paul. *Bartók*. London: J.M. Dent, 1984.

246. Händel, Gunter. "Bartók und die Wiener Klassik." MELOS 22 (1955): 103-106.

247. Hartzell, Lawrence W. "Contrapuntal-harmonic factors in selected works of Béla Bartók." PhD dissertation: University of Kansas, 1970.

248. Hawthorne, Robin. "The fugal technique of Béla Bartók." MR 10(1949): 277-285.

249. Hundt, Theodore. "Barocke Formelemente im Kompositionsstil Béla Bartóks." SM 24(1982): 361-372.

250. Kapst, Erich. "Die 'polymodale Chromatik' Béla Bartóks: Ein Beitrag zur stilkritischen Analyse." PhD dissertation (Musicology): Karl-Marx Universität, 1969.

251. ----. "Stilkriterien der polymodal-chromatischen Gestaltungweise im Werk Béla Bartóks." BM 12(1970): 1-28.

252. Kárpáti, János. "Les gammes populaires et le système chromatique dans l'oeuvre de Béla Bartók." SM 11(1969): 227-240.

253. ----. "Tonal divergences of melody and harmony: A characteristic device in Bartók's musical language." SM 24(1982): 373-380.

254. Kramer, Jonathan. "The Fibonacci series in twentieth-century music." JMT 17(1973): 110-148.

255. Kroó György. *A guide to Bartók*. Trans. by Ruth Pataki and Maria Steiner. n.p.: Corvina Press, 1974.

256. ----. "Monothematik und dramaturgie in Bartóks Bühnenwerken." SM 5(1963): 449-467. [Also *Liszt-Bartók: Bericht über die zweite internationale musikwissenschaftliche Konferenz, Budapest 25-30 September, 1961*. Z. Gárdonyi and B. Szabolcsi, eds. Budapest: Akadémiai Kiadó, 1963: 449-467.

257. Kuckertz, Josef. *Gestaltvariation in den von Bartók gesammelten rümanischen Colinden*. Regensburg: G. Bosse, 1963.

258. Lampert, Vera. "Bartók's choice of theme for folksong arrangement: Some lessons of the folk-music sources of Bartók's works." SM 24 (1982): 401-409.

259. Lendvai, Ernö. "Bartók und der goldene Schnitt." OMZ, Sonderheft November 1966: 23-30. [Also OMZ 21(1966): 607-615]

260. ----. *Béla Bartók: An analysis of his music*. London: Kahn & Averill, 1971.

261. ----. "Duality and synthesis in the music of Béla Bartók." *Bartók Studies*. Todd Crow, ed. Detroit: Information Coordinators, 1976: 39-62.

262. ----. "Remarks on Roy Howat's 'Principles of proportional analysis'." MA 3/3(1984): 255-264.

263. ----. Über die Formkonzeption Bartóks." Fs. Szabolcsi: 271-280. [Also SM 11(1969): 271-280]

264. Lesznai, Lajos. *Bartók*. Trans. by Percy M. Young. London: Dent, 1973.

265. ----. "Realistische Ausdrucksmittel in der Musik Béla Bartóks." SM 5(1963): 469-479. [Also MG 11(1961): 722-726.

266. Mason, Colin. "Bartók and folksong." MR 11(1950): 292-302.

267. ----. "Bartók's rhapsodies." ML 30(1949): 26-36.

268. Maxwell, Judith Elaine Shepherd. "An investigation of axis-based structures in two compositions of Béla Bartók." PhD dissertation: University of Oklahoma, 1975. UM 76-03,115. DA XXXVI.8, p.4842-A.

269. Michael, Frank. "Anmerkungen zu Bartóks Variationstechnik." OMZ 36(1981): 303-310.

270. Mila, Massimo. "La natura e il mistero nell'arte di Béla Bartók." CHI 2(2965): 147-168.

271. Olsvai, I. "West-Hungarian (Trans-Danubian) characteristic features in Bartók's works." SM 11(1969): 333-347.

272. Oramo, Ilkka. "Modale Symmetrie bei Bartók." MF 33(1980): 450-464.

273. ----. "Die notierte, die wahrgenommene und die gedachte Strukur bei Bartók: Bermerkungen zu einem Problem der musikalischen Analyse." SM 24(1982): 439-449.

274. Pernecky, John Martin. "A musico-ethnological approach to the instrumental music of Béla Bartók." PhD dissertation (Music Education): Northwestern *University, 1956. UM 19,585. DA XVI.12, p.2476.

275. Petersen, Peter. *Die Tonalität im Instrumentalschaffen von Béla Bartók.* Hamburg: Verlag der Musikalienhandlung, 1971.

276. Petrov, Stojan. "Béla Bartók und die bulgarische musikalische Kultur." Fs. Lissa: 367-377.

277. Pleasants, Henry and Tibor Serly. "Bartók's historic contribution." MM 17(1940): 131-140.

278. Radice, Mark A. "Bartók's parodies of Beethoven." MR 42(1981): 252-260. [Third Piano Concerto; Sixth String Quartet]

279. Reaves, Florence Ann. "Bartók's approach to consonance and dissonance in selected late instrumental works." PhD dissertation (Theory): University of Kentucky, 1983. 481 p. UM 83-25,786. No DA listing.

280. Rosenbloom, Paul David. "A study of phrase rhythm in late Bartók." DMA dissertation: Cornell University, 1979. No DA listing. [String Quartets Nos.5 and 6; Sonata for Two Pianos and Percussion; Sonata for Solo Violin]

281. Rostand, Claude. "Chemins et contrastes de la musique." CPS 3 (1946): 31-37.

282. Schlötterer-Traimer, Roswitha. "Béla Bartók und die Tondichtungen von Richard Strauss." OMZ 36(1981): 311-318.

283. Schoffman, Nachum. "Expanded unisons in Bartók." JMR 4 (1982-1983): 21-38.

284. Seiber, Mátyás. "Béla Bartók's chamber music." TEMPO 13 (1949): 19-31.

285. Somfai, László. "*Per finire*: Some aspects of the finale in Bartók's cyclic form." Fs. Szabolcsi: 391-408.

286. Stenzl, Jürg. "'Wer sich der Einsamkeit ergibt . . .': Zu Béla Bartóks Bühnenwerken." AM 39(1982): 100-112.

287. Stevens, Halsey. *The life and music of Béla Bartók.* Rev. ed. New York: Oxford University Press, 1964.

288. ----. "Some 'unknown' works of Bartók." MQ 52(1966): 37-55.

289. Szabolcsi, Bence. *Bartók: Sa Vie et son oeuvre.* Budapest: Corvina, 1956.

290. ----, ed. *Béla Bartók: Weg und Werk: Schriften und Briefe.* Kassel: Bärenreiter, 1972.

291. Szentkirályi, András. "Some aspects of Béla Bartók's compositional techniques." SM 20(1978): 157-182.

292. Taylor, Vernon H. "Contrapuntal techniques in the music of Béla Bartók." PhD dissertation: Northwestern University, 1950. No DA listing.

293. Thayer, Fred Martin, Jr. "The choral music of Béla Bartók." DMA dissertation (Performance): Cornell University, 1976. UM 77-8414. DA XXXVII.10, p.6136-A.

294. Thyne, Stuart. "Bartók's 'Improvisations'." ML 31(1950): 30-45.

295. Tóth, Anna. "Die Dudelsack-Effekt in Bartóks Werk." SM 24(1982): 505-517.

296. Vauclair, Constant. "Bartók: Beyond bi-modality." MR 42(1981): 243-251. [String Quartets Nos.3 and 6; *Music for Strings, Percussion and Celesta*]

297. Vinton, John. "Hints to the printers from Bartók." ML 49 (1968): 224-230.

298. Weiss, Günter. *Die frühe Schaffensentwicklung Béla Bartóks im Lichte westlicher und östlicher Traditionen*. Erlangen, 1971.

299. Weiss-Aigner, Günther. "Der Spätstil Bartóks in seiner Violinmusik: Stilistische Erscheinungsbild und spieltechnisches Perspectiven." SM 23(1981): 261-293.

300. ----. "Tonale Perspektiven des jungen Bartók." SM 24(1982): 537-548.

301. Weissmann, John S. "Béla Bartók: An estimate." MR 7(1946): 221-241.

302. Wolff, Hellmuth Christian. "Béla Bartók und die Musik der Gegenwart." MELOS 19(1952): 209-217.

303. ----. "Zum Kompositionsstil Béla Bartóks." BM 7(1965): 218-224.

304. Special Issue: MZ 3(1953).

BASTIANELLI, GIONNOTTO (1883-1927)

305. Donadoni, Miriam Omodeo. "Il Concerto per due pianoforti di Giannotto Bastianelli." CHI 15(1983): 97-108.

BATISTE, EDOUARD (1820-1876)

306. Smialek, William. "Edouard Batiste's *Symphonie Militaire*: Some thoughts on its conception." JBR 14/2(1978-79): 20-25.

BAUCKHOLT, CAROLA (born 1959)

307. Bauckholt, Carola. "Anmerkungen zu *Eure Zeichen*." N 4 (1983-1984): 188-196.

BAX, SIR ARNOLD (1883-1953)

308. Foreman, R.L.E. "The musical development of Arnold Bax." ML 52(1971): 59-68.

309. Scott-Sutherland, Colin. "The symphonies of Arnold Bax." MR 23(1962): 20-24.

BEACH, AMY MARCY CHENEY (Mrs. H.H.A.) (1867-1944)

310. Chisholm Flatt, Rose Marie. "Analytical approaches to chromaticism in Amy Beach's Piano Quintet in F-Sharp Minor." ITR 4/3(1980-1981): 41-58.
311. Merrill, Lindsey E. "Mrs. H.H.A. Beach: Her life and music." PhD dissertation (Theory): University of Rochester, 1963. UM 64-6374. DA XXVI.4, p.2257.
312. Miles, Marmaduke Sidney. "The solo piano works of Mrs. H.H.A. Beach." DMA dissertation (Performance): Peabody Conservatory, 1985. 160 p. No DA listing.

BECK, CONRAD (born 1901)

313. Mohr, Ernst. "Zum Kompositionsstil von Conrad Beck." SMZ 101 (1961): 150-156.

BECKWITH, JOHN (born 1927)

314. Anhalt: 244-247. [*Gas!*]

BEDFORD, DAVID (born 1937)

315. Barry, Malcolm and Richard Witts. "David Bedford." CT 15 (1976-1977): 3-7.
316. Whittall, Arnold. "Post-twelve-tone analysis." PRMA 94 (1967-68): 1-17. [*Music for Albion Moonlight*]

BEETHOVEN, LUDWIG VAN (1770-1827)

An die ferne Geliebte, Op.98
317. Hatch, Christopher. "Ideas in common: The *Liederkreis* and other works by Beethoven." Fs. Lang: 56-77.
318. Peake, Luise Eitel. "The antecedents of Beethoven's *Liederkreis*." ML 63(1982): 242-260.

Bagatelles
319. Ratz, Erwin. "Die Bagatellen Op.126 von Beethoven." OMZ 6 (1951): 52-56.

Cello Sonatas
320. Dahlhaus, Carl. "'Von zwei Kulturen der Musik': Die Schlussfuge aus Beethovens Cellosonate Opus 102.2" MF 31(1978): 397-404.

Choral Fantasy, Op.80
321. Hess, Willy. "Zu Beethoven's *Chorfantasie*." SMZ 106(1966): 19-23.
322. Schmidt, Hans. "Die gegenwartige Quellenlage zu Beethovens *Chorfantasie*." Fs. Schmidt-Görg/70: 355-371.

Diabelli Variations, Op.120

323. Abraham, Lars Ulrich. "Trivialität und Persiflage in Beethovens *Diabellivariationen*." Abraham/L: 7-17.

324. Dahlhaus, Carl. "Zur Rhythmik in Beethovens *Diabelli Variationen*." *Veröffentlichungen des Institut für neue Musik und Musikerziehung, Darmstadt* 6(1967): 18-22.

325. Geiringer, Karl. "The structure of Beethoven's *Diabelli Variations*." MQ 50(1964): 496-503.

326. Huber, Anna Gertrud. *Beethoven-Studien*. Zürich: Hug, 1961.

327. Kinderman, William Andrew. "Beethoven's *Variations on a Waltz by Diabelli*: Genesis and structure." PhD dissertation: University of California, Berkeley, 1980. No DA listing.

328. ----. "The evolution and structure of Beethoven's *Diabelli Variations*." JAMS 35(1982): 306-328.

329. Munster, Arnold. *Studien zu Beethovens "Diabelli-Variationen"*. München: Henle, 1982.

330. Porter, David H. "The structure of Beethoven's *Diabelli Variations, Op.120*." MR 31(1970): 295-301.

331. Schaeffer, Erwin. "Die *Diabelli-Variationen* von Beethoven." SMZ 107(1967): 202-210.

332. Uhde, Jurgen. "Reflexionen zu Beethovens Op.120 (*33 Veränderungen über einen Walzer von A. Diabelli*)." ZM 7/1(1976): 30-53.

333. Zenck, Martin. "Rezeption von Geschichte im Beethovens *Diabelli-Variation*: Zur Vermittlung analytischer, ästhetischer und historischer Kategorien." AM 37(1980): 61-75.

Eroica Variations, Op.35

334. Derr, Ellwood. "Beethoven's long-term memory of C.P.E. Bach's Rondo in E Flat, W.61/1 (1787), manifest in the Variations in E Flat for Piano, Opus 35 (1802)." MQ 70(1984): 45-76.

335. Fischer, Kurt von. "*Eroica-Variationen* Op.35 und Eroica-Finale." SMZ 89(1949): 282-286.

336. Hering, Hans. "Beethovens Klaviervariationen Opus 35 und das Eroica-Finale." M 29(1975): 304-306.

337. Huber, Anna Gertrud. *Beethoven-Studien*. Zürich: Hug, 1961.

338. Kunze, Stefan. "Die 'wirklich gantz neue Manier' in Beethovens *Eroica-Variationen* Op.35." AM 29(1972): 124-129.

Fidelio, Op.72

339. ASO 10(1977).

340. Brunswick, Mark. "Beethoven's tribute to Mozart in *Fidelio*." MQ 31(1945): 29-32.

341. Carner: 186-252.

342. Dahlhaus, Carl. "Idylle und Utopie: Zu Beethovens *Fidelio*." NZM 146/11(1985): 4-8.

343. Gossett, Philip. "The arias of Marzelline: Beethoven as a composer of opera." BJ 10(1978-1981): 141-183.

344. Hess, Willy. *Beethovens Oper "Fidelio" und ihre drei Fassungen*. Zürich: Atlantis, 1953.

345. John, Nicholas, ed. *Beethoven: Fidelio*. London: J. Calder, 1980.

346. Leibowitz, René. "Un rêve solitaire: *Fidelio*." Leibowitz/F: 61-106.

347. Nowak, Leopold. "Beethoven's *Fidelio* und die österreichischen Militarsignale." OMZ 10(1955): 373-375.

Missa Solemnis, Op.123

348. Dikenmann-Balmer, Lucie. *Beethovens "Missa Solemnis" und ihre geisten Grundlagen.* Zürich: Atlantis, 1952.

349. Fiske, Roger. *Beethoven's "Missa Solemnis."* London: Elek, 1979.

350. Kirkendale, Warren. "New roads to old ideas in Beethoven's *Missa Solemnis*." MQ 56(1970): 665-701.

351. Klein, Rudolf. "Die Struktur von Beethovens *Missa Solemnis*." Fs. Valentin: 89-108.

352. Langer, Rudolf. *Missa Solemnis: Über das theologische Problem in Beethovens Musik.* Stuttgart: Calwer, 1962.

353. Schmidt-Görg, Joseph. "Zur melodischen Einheit im Beethovens *Missa Solemnis*." Fs. Hoboken: 146-152.

354. Schmitz, Arnold. "Zum Verständnis des *Gloria* in Beethoven's *Missa Solemnis*." Fs. Blume: 320-326.

355. Zickenheimer, Otto. "Untersuchungen zur Credo-Fugue im Beethovens *Missa Solemnis*." PhD dissertation (Musicology): Bonn, 1981.

Overtures

356. Göllner, Theodor. "Beethovens Ouvertüre *Die Weihe des Hauses* und Händels Trauermarsch aus *Saul*." Fs. Hüschen: 181-189.

357. Mies, Paul. "Zur *Coriolan-Ouvertüre* Op.62." BJ 6(1965-1968): 260-268.

358. Oster, Ernst. "The dramatic character of the *Egmont Overture*." MU 2(1948-1949): 269-285.

359. Wieninger, Herbert. "Beethovens *Leonoren-Ouvertüren*." ME 25 (1971-1972): 113-118.

Piano Concertos

360. Collier, Michael. "The rondo movements of Beethoven's Concerto No.3 in C Minor, Op.37, and Brahms's Concerto No.1 in D Minor: A comparative analysis." TP 31(1978): 5-15.

361. Goldschmidt, Harry. "Motivvariation und Gestaltmetamorphose." Fs. Besseler: 389-409.

362. Körner, Klaus. "Formen musikalisicher Aussage im zweiten Satz des G-dur Klavierkonzertes von Beethoven." BJ 9(1973-1977): 202-216. [Op.58]

363. Osthoff, Wolfgang. *Ludwig van Beethoven: Klavierkonzert Nr.3 C-Moll, Op.37.* München: W. Fink, 1965.

364. Rust, Ezra G. "The first movements of Beethoven's piano concertos." PhD dissertation (Musicology): University of California at Berkeley, 1970. UM 71-09,908. DA XXXI.10, p.5452.

Piano Sonatas [see also individual sonatas]

365. Adams, Frank John. "An analysis of seven Adagio and Largo movements from the early piano sonatas of Beethoven." MA dissertation: Harvard University, 1968.

366. Bilson, Malcolm. "The emergence of the fantasy-style in the Beethoven piano sonatas of the early and middle periods." DMA dissertation (Performance): University of Illinois, 1968. UM 68-12,082. DA XXIX.2, p.623.

367. Chase, Howard R. "Tonality and tonal factors in the piano sonatas of Beethoven." PhD dissertation (Musicology): University of Michigan, 1953. UM 5021. DA XII.3, p.408.

368. Dahlhaus, Carl. "Cantabile und thematischer Prozess. Der Übergang zum Spätwerk in Beethovens Klaviersonaten." AM 37(1980): 81-98.

369. Dreyfus, Kay. "Beethoven's last five piano sonatas: A study in analytical method." BJ 9(1973-1977): 37-45.

370. Hauschild, Peter. "Bemerkungen zu Beethovens Klaviernotation." BJ 9(1973-1977): 147-165.

371. Kamien, Roger. "Aspects of the recapitulation in Beethoven piano sonatas." MFO 4(1976): 195-236.

372. Lorince, Frank Edell. "A study of musical texture in relation to sonata-form as evidenced in selected keyboard sonatas from C.P.E. Bach through Beethoven." PhD dissertation (Theory): University of Rochester, 1966. UM 66-5424. DA XXVII.1, p.223-A.

373. Reti, Rudolf. *Thematic patterns in sonatas of Beethoven.* London: Faber & Faber, 1967.

374. Rosenberg, Richard. *Die Klaviersonaten Ludwig van Beethovens: Studien über Form und Vortrag.* Olten: Urs Graf, 1957.

375. ----. "Mozart-Spuren in Beethovens Klaviersonaten." BJ 3 (1957-1958): 51-62.

376. Schmalzriedt, Siegfried. "Charakter und Drama: Zur historischen Analyse von Haydnschen und Beethovenschen Sonatensätzen." AM 42 (1985): 37-66.

377. Shamgar, Beth Friedman. "Dramatic devices in the retransitions of Beethoven's piano sonatas." ISM 2(1979): 63-75.

378. ----. "The retransition in the piano sonatas of Haydn, Mozart and Beethoven." PhD dissertation (Musicology): New York University, 1978. 246 p. UM 79-12,324. DA XL.2, p.534-A.

379. Stainkamph, Eileen. *Form and analysis of the complete Beethoven pianoforte sonatas.* Melbourne: Allans Music, 1968.

380. Szelényi, Istvan. "Monothematische Beziehungen in der Klaviersonaten von Beethoven." SM 12(1970): 205-232.

381. Thompson, Harold Adams. "An evolutionary view of Neapolitan formations in Beethoven's pianoforte sonatas." CMS 20(1980): 144-162.

382. Weber, Friedrich. *Harmonischer Aufbau und Stimmführung in den Sonatensätzen der Klaviersonaten Beethovens.* Würzburg: Triltsch, 1940.

Piano Sonata, Op.2, No.1
383. Broyles, Michael. "The two instrumental styles of classicism." JAMS 36(1983): 210-242.

Piano Sonata, Op.7
384. Kamien, Roger. "Chromatic details in Beethoven's Piano Sonata in E-Flat Major, Op.7." MR 35(1974): 149-156.

Piano Sonata, Op.10, No.3
385. De la Motte, Diether. "Ludwig van Beethoven: Klaviersonate Op.10, Nr.3, zweiter Satz in D-Moll, *Largo e mesto*." Benary: 13-20. [Also found in De la Motte: Vol.I, p.49-60]
386. Federhofer, Hellmut. "Zur Analyse des zweiten Satzes von L. van Beethovens Klaviersonate Op.10, No.3." Fs. Larsen: 339-350.
387. Finscher, Ludwig. "Beethovens Klaviersonate Opus 31, 3: Versuch einer Interpretation." Fs. Wiora: 385-396.
388. Huber, Ernst Friedrich. "Rhythmische Gestalten im *Largo e mesto* der Klaviersonate Op.10, No.3 von L. v. Beethoven." Dissertation: Erlangen, 1954.

Piano Sonata, Op.13
389. Kresky: 92-107. [2nd movement]

Piano Sonata, Op.14, No.1
390. Schachter, Carl. "Beethoven's sketches for the first movement of Op.14, No.1: A study in design." JMT 26(1982): 1-21.

Piano Sonata, Op.27, No.2
391. Krohn, Ilmari. "Die Form des ersten Satzes der *Mondscheinsonate*." *Beethovenzentenarfeier: Internationaler musikhistorischer Kongress, Vienna, 26-31 March 1927.* Wien: Universal, 1927: 58-65.

Piano Sonata, Op.31, No.2
392. Cooper, Barry. "The origins of Beethoven's D Minor Sonata Op.31 No.2." ML 62(1981): 261-280.
393. Dahlhaus, Carl. "Musikalische Forme als Transformation: Bemerkungen zur Beethoven-Interpretation." BJ 9(1973-1977): 27-36. [First movement]
394. ----. "Zur Formidee von Beethovens D-Moll-Sonate Opus 31,2." MF 33(1980): 310-312.

Piano Sonata, Op.31, No.3
395. Finscher, Ludwig. "Beethovens Klaviersonate Opus 31,3: Versuch einer Interpretation." Fs. Wiora: 385-396.

Piano Sonata, Op.53
396. Beach, David, Donald Mintz, and Robert Palmer. "Analysis Symposium." JMT 13(1969): 186-217. [Also in Yeston: 202-226]
397. Chávez, Carlos. "Anatomic analysis: Beethoven's *Waldstein* Op.53." PQ 82(1973): 17-23.

Piano Sonata, Op.57
398. Dommel-Diény, Amy. *Beethoven: Appassionata Sonata.* Dommel-Diény 6. Paris: Dommel-Diény, 1972.

Piano Sonata, Op.90

399. Danuser, Hermann. "Zum Problem musikalischer Ambiguität: Einige Aspekte von Beethovens Klaviersonate in E-Moll Opus 90." ZM 8/2(1977): 22-28.

400. Kalisch, Volker. "Beethovens Klaviersonate Op.90: Ein analytischer Versuch." SZM 35(1984): 89-124.

Piano Sonata, Op.101

401. Schenker, Heinrich. *Beethoven: Die letzten Sonaten: Sonate A Dur Op.101.* Wien: Universal, 1972.

Piano Sonata, Op.106

402. Badura-Skoda, Paul. "Textprobleme in Beethovens *Hammerklaviersonate* Op.106." Melos/NZM 3(1977): 11-15.

403. Friedmann, Michael L. "Hexachordal sources of structure in Beethoven's *Hammerklavier* Sonata, Opus 106." ITO 4/6(1978): 3-17.

404. Hauser, Richard. "Das *AIS* in der Sonate Op.106." BJ 6 (1965-1968): 243-259.

405. Klein, Rudolf. "Beethovens gebundener Stil in Opus 106." BJ 9(1973-1977): 185-199.

Piano Sonata, Op.109

406. Forte, Allen. *The compositional matrix.* Baldwin, NY: Music Teachers National Association, 1961.

407. Mulder, Michael. "An unpublished letter treating the Piano Sonata, Op.109, by Ludwig van Beethoven." ITO 5/4(1979-1981): 16-20. [This is clearly not genuine, but rather Mr. Mulder's idiosyncratic manner of presenting his analysis.]

408. Schenker, Heinrich. *Beethoven: Die letzten Sonaten: Sonata E Dur Op.109.* Wien: Universal, 1971.

Piano Sonata, Op.110

409. Ashforth, Alden. "The relationship of the sixth in Beethoven's Piano Sonata, Opus 110." MR 32(1971): 93-101.

410. Uhde, Jurgen and Renate Wieland. "Von der Analyse zur Darstellung: Zur Artikulation der Zeitgestalt in Beethovens Sonate As-Dur Op.110." M 36(1982): 13-18.

411. Voss, Egon. "Zu Beethovens Klaviersonate As-Dur Op.110." MF 23(1970): 256-268.

Piano Sonata, Op.111

412. Drabkin, William. "The sketches for Beethoven's Piano Sonata in C Minor, Opus 111." PhD dissertation (Musicology): Princeton University, 1977. 378 p. UM 77-14,236. DA XXXVIII.1, p.16-A.

413. ----. "Some relationships between the autographs of Beethoven's Sonata in C Minor, Opus 111." CM 13(1972): 38-47.

414. Hackman, Willis H. "Rhythmic analysis as a clue to articulation in the Arietta of Beethoven's Op.111." PQ 93(1976): 26-37.

415. Schenker, Heinrich. *Beethoven: Die letzten Sonaten: Sonate C Moll Op.111.* Wien: Universal, 1971.

Piano Trios
416. Hiebert, Elfrieda F. "Beethoven's trios for pianoforte, violin and violoncello: Problems in history and style." PhD dissertation (Musicology): University of Wisconsin, 1970. UM 70-22,652. DA XXXI.10, p.5447.

Piano works [see also individual titles]
417. Batta, András and Sándor Kovács. "Typbildung und Grossform in Beethovens frühen Klaviervariationen." SM 20(1978): 125-156.
418. Cockshoot, John V. *The fugue in Beethoven's piano music.* London: Routledge, 1959.
419. Dunsby, Jonathan. "A bagatelle on Beethoven's WoO 60." MA 3/1(1984): 57-68.
420. Goldschmidt, Harry. "Chopiniana bei Beethoven." Fs. Lissa: 209-222.
421. Hertzmann, Erich. "The newly discovered autograph of Beethoven's *Rondo à capriccio*, Op.129." MQ 32(1946): 171-195.
422. Sterling.

Songs [see also individual titles]
423. Broeckx, Jan L. and Walter Landrieu. "Comparative computer study of style, based on five Liedermelodies." I 1(1972): 29-92. [*Kennst du das Land*]
424. Forbes, Elliot. "*Nur wer die Sehnsucht kennt*: An example of a Goethe lyric set to music." Fs. Merritt: 59-82.
425. Lewis. [*Mignon Lieder*]
426. Richter, Lukas. "Zur Kompositionstechnik von Beethovens *Britischen Liedern*." BM 17(1975): 257-279.
427. Schollum, Robert. "Zur Wiedergabe der *Gellert-Lieder* Op.48 von Beethoven." M 33(1979-1980): 99-104, 153-157.
428. Stuber, Robert. *Die Klavierbegleitung im Liede von Haydn, Mozart, und Beethoven: Eine Stilstudie.* Biel: Graphische Anstalt Schüler, 1958.

String Quartets [see also individual titles]
429. Brusatti, Otto. "Klangexperimente in Beethovens Streichquartetten." SZM 29(1978): 69-88.
430. Cooke, Deryck. "The unity of Beethoven's late quartets." MR 24 (1963): 30-49.
431. Drabkin, William. "Beethoven and the open string." MA 4/1-2 (1985): 15-28.
432. Dullo, W. A. "The mysterious four-note motive in Beethoven's late string quartets." MS 1(1964): 10-15.
433. Firca, Gheorge. "Werkanalyse und Möglichkeiten einer neuen Lesert von Beethovens Schaffen." Goldschmidt: 323-327. [Opp.131, 132, 133]
434. Forchert, Arno. "Zur Satztechnik von Beethovens Streichquartetten." Fs. Hüschen: 151-158.
436. Galo, Ellen Gillespie. "Analysis of the *Rasumovsky Quartets* Op.59, No.1, 2, and 3 of Beethoven." MA dissertation (Theory): State University College, Potsdam, New York, 1977.

436. Hubsch, Lini. *Ludwig van Beethoven: Die Rasumowsky Quartette Op.59, Nr.1, F-Dur, Nr.2 E-Moll, Nr.3, C-Dur.* München: W. Fink, 1983.

437. Kerman, Joseph. *The Beethoven quartets.* New York: Knopf, 1967.

438. Kreft, Ekkehard. *Die späten Quartette Beethovens: Substanz und Substanzverarbeitung.* Bonn: Bouvier, 1959.

439. Krummacher, Friedhelm. "Synthesis des Disparaten: Zu Beethovens späten Quartetten und ihrer frühen Rezeption." AM 37(1980): 99-134.

440. Levy, Janet M. "Texture as a sign in classic and early romantic music." JAMS 35(1982): 482-531. [Opp.18, 132, 135]

441. Radliffe, Philip. *Beethoven's string quartets.* London: Hutchinson, 1965.

442. Ratner, Leonard G. "Texture: A rhetorical element in Beethoven's quartets." ISM 2(1979): 51-62.

443. Stephan, Rudolf. "Zu Beethoven's letzten Quartetten." MF 23 (1970): 245-256.

444. Wildberger, Jacques. "Versuch über Beethovens späte Streichquartette." SMZ 110(1970): 1-8.

String Quartet, Op.18, No.1

445. Levy, Janet M. *Beethoven's compositional choices: The two versions of Op.18, No.1, first movement.* Philadelphia: University of Pennsylvania Press, 1982.

String Quartet, Op.18, No.6

446. Mitchell, William J. "Beethoven's *La Malinconia* from the String Quartet, Op.16, No.6: Techniques and structure." MFO 3(1973): 269-280.

String Quartet, Op.59, No.1

447. Chailley, Jacques. "Sur la signification du quatuor de Mozart K.465, dit 'Les Dissonances,' et du 7ème quatuor de Beethoven." Fs. Jeppesen: 283-292.

448. Chailley.

449. Eiseman, David. "Half-notes demystified in the first movement of Beethoven's String Quartet, Op.59, No.1." CMS 24(1984): 21-27.

450. Headlam, Dave. "A rhythmic study of the exposition in the second movement of Beethoven's Quartet Op.59, No.1." MTS 7(1985): 114-138.

String Quartet, Op.59, No.3

451. Hatten, Robert S. "An approach to ambiguity in the opening of Beethoven's String Quartet, Op.59, No.3, I." ITR 3/3(1979-1980): 28-35.

String Quartet, Op.95

452. Carpenter, Patricia. "Musical form and musical idea: Reflections on a theme of Schoenberg, Hanslick and Kant." Fs. Lang: 394-427.

453. Fischer, Kurt von. "*Never to be performed in public*: Zu Beethovens Streichquartett, Op.95." BJ 9(1973-1977): 87-96.

454. Livingstone, Ernest F. "Die Coda in Beethovens Streichquartett F-Moll Op.95." Kühn: 358-369.

455. ----. "The final coda in Beethoven's String Quartet in F Minor, Op.95." Fs. Fox: 132-144.

String Quartet, Op.130
456. MacArdle, Donald. "Beethoven's Quartet in B Flat, Op.130." MR 8(1947): 11-24.

String Quartet, Op.131
457. Glauert, Amanda. "The double perspective in Beethoven's Opus 131." NCM 4(1980-1981): 113-120.
458. Platen, Emil. "Eine Frühfassung zum ersten Satz des Streichquartetts Op.131 von Beethoven." BJ 10(1978-1981): 277-304.
459. Winter, Robert S., III. "Compositional origins of Beethoven's String Quartet in C-Sharp Minor, Op.131." PhD dissertation (Musicology): University of Chicago, 1978. DA XXXIX.4, p.1923-A. [Also Ann Arbor: UMI Research Press, 1982]

String Quartet, Op.132
460. Kirkendale, Warren. "Gregorianischer Stil in Beethovens Streichquartett Op.132." Kühn: 373-376.

String Quartet, Op.133
461. Kirkendale, Warren. "The *Great Fugue* Op.133: Beethoven's *Art of Fugue*." ACTA 35(1963): 14-24.
462. Mila, Massimo. "Lettura della *Grande fuga* Op.133." Fs. Ronga: 345-366.

String Quartet, Op.135
463. Fischer, Kurt von. "*Der schwer gefasste Entschluss*: Eine Interpretationsstudie zu Beethovens Streichquartett Op.135." BM 18(1976): 117-121.
464. Kluge, Reiner. "*Der schwer gefasste Entschluss*: Über eine Verbindung biogener, logogener und musikogener Elemente in Beethovens Op.135." BM 26(1984): 225-236.
465. Kramer, Jonathan D. "Multiple and non-linear time in Beethoven's Opus 135." PNM 11/2(1973): 122-145.

String Quintet, Op.29
466. Hatch, Christopher. "Thematic interdependence in two finales by Beethoven." MR 45(1984): 194-207.
467. Levy, Janet M. "Texture as a sign in classic and early romantic music." JAMS 35(1982): 482-531.

String Trios
468. Kerman, Joseph. "*Tändelne Lazzi*: On Beethoven's Trio in D Major, Opus 70, No.1." Fs. Abraham: 109-122.
469. Platen, Emil. "Beethovens Streichtrio D-Dur, Opus 9, Nr. 2: Zum Problem der thematischen Einheit mehrsätziger Formen." Fs. Schmidt-Görg/70: 260-282.

Symphonies [see also individual titles]

470. Cooper, Barry. "Newly identified sketches for Beethoven's Tenth Symphony." ML 66(1985): 9-18.

471. Gülke, Peter. "Zur Bestimmung des Sinfonsichen bei Beethoven." DJM 15(1970): 67-95.

472. La Rue, Jan. "Harmonic rhythm in the Beethoven symphonies." MR 18(1957): 8-20.

473. Schulze, Werner. *Temporelationen in symphonischen Werk von Beethoven, Schubert und Brahms.* Bern: Kreis und Freude um Hans Kayser, 1981.

474. Steunenberg, Thomas B. "Rhythmic continuity in slow movements from Beethoven's symphonies." PhD dissertation (Theory): University of Rochester, 1954. UR 5456. No DA listing.

Symphony No.1, Op.21

475. Hantz, Edwin. "A pitch for rhythm: Rhythmic patterns in Beethoven's First Symphony: III (Minuetto)." ITO 1/4(1975-1976): 17-21.

476. Misch, Ludwig. "Der persönliche Stil in Beethovens erster Symphonie: Organismus und Idee des ersten Satzes." BJ 2(1955-1956): 55-101.

477. Seidel, Wilhelm. *Ludwig van Beethoven: I. Symphonie C-Dur.* München: W. Fink, 1979.

Symphony No.2, Op.36

478. Hill, Cecil. "Early versions of Beethoven's Second Symphony." MS 6(1980): 90-110.

479. Pazur, Robert. "The development of the fourth movement of Beethoven's Second Symphony considered as a variation of the development of the first movement." ITO 2/1-2(1976): 3-4.

480. Westphal, Kurt. *Vom Einfall zur Symphonie: Einblick in Beethovens Schaffenweise.* Berlin: W.de Gruyter, 1965.

Symphony No.3, Op.55

481. Antonicek, Theophil. "Humanitätssymbolik im *Eroica*-Finale." Fs. Schenk: 144-155.

482. Degen, Helmut. "Der erste Satz der *Eroica*." NZM 118(1957): 156-159.

483. Downs, Philip G. "Beethoven's 'New Way' and the *Eroica*." MQ 56(1970): 585-604.

484. Engelsmann, Walther. "Beethovens Werkthematik: Dargestelle an der *Eroica*." AM 5(1940): 104-113.

485. Epstein, David. "Unity in Beethoven's *Eroica Symphony* (First Movement)." *Beyond Orpheus: Studies in musical structure.* Cambridge: MIT Press, 1979.

486. Floros, Constantin. *Beethovens "Eroica" und "Prometheus" Musik: Subjekt-Studien.* Wilhelmshaven: Heinrichshofen, 1978. 152 p.

487. Hauschild, Peter. "Melodische Tendenzen in Beethovens *Eroica*." DJM 14(1969): 41-75.

488. Hollander, Hans. "Zur Psychologie des Helden in Beethovens *Eroica*." NZM 128(1967): 205-207.

489. Huber, Anna Gertrud. *Der Held der "Eroica": Beethovens Es Dur Symphonie in ihrem Aufbau.* Strassbourg: P.H. Heitz, 1947.

490. Lochhead, Judy. "Musical reference: A source of meaning in the first movement of the *Eroica.*" TP 5/2(1980): 32-39.

491. Lockwood, Lewis. "Beethoven's earliest sketches for the *Eroica Symphony.*" MQ 67(1981): 457-478.

492. Meikle, Robert B. "Thematic transformation in the first movement of Beethoven's *Eroica Symphony.*" MR 32(1971): 205-218.

493. Ringer, Alexander L. "Clementi and the *Eroica.*" MQ 47(1961): 454-468.

Symphony No.4, Op.60

494. Dahlhaus, Carl. *Ludwig van Beethoven: IV. Symphonie B-Dur.* München: W. Fink, 1979.

495. Feil, Arnold. "Zur Satztechnik in Beethovens vierter Sinfonie." AM 16(1959): 391-399.

496. Hatch, Christopher. "Internal and external references in Beethoven's Fourth Symphony." CMS 24(1984): 107-117.

Symphony No.5, Op.67

497. Canisius, Claus Heinrich. "Quellenstudien und satztechnische Untersuchungen zum dritten Satz aus Beethovens C-Moll-Sinfonie." PhD dissertation: Ruprecht-Karl-Universität, Heidelberg, 1966.

498. Forbes, Elliot, ed. *Beethoven: Symphony No.5 in C Minor.* Norton Critical Scores. New York: W.W. Norton, 1971.

499. Gülke, Peter. "Motive aus französischer Revolutionsmusik in Beethovens fünfter Sinfonie." MG 21(1971): 636-641.

500. Lockwood, Lewis. "On the coda of the finale of Beethoven's Fifth Symphony." Fs. Abs: 41-48.

Symphony No.6, Op.68

501. Bockholdt, Rudolf. *Ludwig van Beethoven: VI. Symphonie F-Dur, Op.68, "Pastorale".* Meisterwerke der Musik 23. München: W. Fink, 1981.

502. Gossett, Philip. "Beethoven's Sixth Symphony: Sketches for the first movement." JAMS 27(1974): 248-284.

503. Kirby, F.E. "Beethoven's *Pastoral Symphony* as a *Sinfonia caracteristica.*" MQ 56(1970): 605-623.

504. Taruskin.

505. Ujfalussy, Joszef. "Dramatischer Bau und Philosophie in Beethovens VI. Symphonie." SM 11(1969): 439-447. [Also in Fs. Szabolcsi: 439-447]

Symphony No.7, Op.92

506. Bässler, Hans and Andreas Jung. "Beethoven: Scherzo aus der VII. Sinfonie: Theorie und Praxis." MB 14/1(1982): 27-30.

507. Below, Robert. "Some aspects of tonal relationships in Beethoven's Seventh Symphony." MR 37(1976): 1-4.

508. Carner, Mosco. "A Beethoven movement and its successors." Carner: 9-20.

509. Gerstenberg, Walter. "Das Allegretto in Beethovens VII. Symphonie." Fs. Hüschen: 171-174.

510. Levarie, Siegmund. "A pitch cell in Beethoven's Seventh Symphony." Fs. Brook: 181-194.

511. Osthoff, Wolfgang. "Zum Vorstellungsgehalt des Allegretto in Beethovens 7. Symphonie." AM 34(1977): 159-179.

512. Richter, Christoph. "Beethovens Scherzo aus der VII. Sinfonie: Ein musikalisches Puzzle." MB 12(1980): 595-602.

513. Silliman, A. Cutler. "Familiar music and the a priori: Beethoven's Seventh Symphony." JMT 20(1976): 215-226.

514. Temperley, Nicholas. "Schubert and Beethoven's eight-six chord." NCM 5(1981-1982): 142-154.

515. Winking, Hans. "Ludwig van Beethoven: Sinfonie Nr.7 A-Dur Op.92." NZM 144/7-8(1983): 39-43.

Symphony No.8, Op.93

516. Dahlhaus, Carl. "Bermerkungen zu Beethovens 8. Symphonie." SZM 110(1970): 205-209.

517. De la Motte, Diether. "Scherzando--für wen? Analyse des zweiten Satzes der 8. Sinfonie von Beethoven." Goldschmidt: 130-137.

518. Gauldin, Robert. "A labyrinth of fifths: The last movement of Beethoven's Eighth Symphony." ITR 1/3(1977-1978): 4-11.

519. Gülke, Peter. "Zum Allegretto der 8. Sinfonie." Goldschmidt: 106-112.

520. Holopov, Jurij. "Modulation und Formbildung: Zur Analyse des Allegretto scherzando aus der Sinfonie Nr. 8 F-Dur von Beethoven." Goldschmidt: 97-106.

521. Kaden, Christian. "Ludwig van Beethoven, Sinfonie Nr.8 Op.93, zweiter Satz Allegretto scherzando: Ansätze zu einer statistischen Strukturanalyse." Goldschmidt: 113-130.

522. Laaff, Ernst. "Der musikalische Humor in Beethovens achter Symphonie." AM 19-20(1962-1963): 213-229.

523. Schneider, Frank. "Das Allegretto scherzando aus der 8. Sinfonie von Beethoven." Goldschmidt: 137-146.

524. ----. "Überlegungen zur VIII. Sinfonie." MG 27(1977): 158-164.

Symphony No.9, Op.125

525. Sanders, Ernest. "Form and content in the finale of Beethoven's Ninth Symphony." MQ 50(1964): 59-76.

526. Steglich, Rudolf. "Motivischer Dualismus und thematische Einheit in Beethovens neunter Sinfonie." Fs. Besseler: 411-424.

527. Winter, Robert. "The sketches for the *Ode to Joy*." Winter: 176-214.

Violin Concerto, Op. 61

528. Jander, Owen. "Romantic form and content in the slow movement of Beethoven's Violin Concerto." MQ 69(1983): 159-179.

529. Kojima, Shin Augustinus. "Die Solovioline-Fassungen und -Varianten von Beethovens Violinkonzert Op.61." BJ 8(1971-1972): 97-145.

530. Mohr, Wilhelm. "Die Klavierfassung von Beethovens Violonkonzert." OMZ 27(1972): 71-75.

531. Moser, Hans Joachim. "Die Form von Beethovens Violonkonzert." Fs. Moser: 198-205.

532. Scholz, Werner. "Zur Interpretation des Violinkonzertes von Beethoven." MG 12(1962): 732-736.

Violin Sonatas

533. Hatch, Christopher. "Thematic interdependence in two finales by Beethoven." MR 45(1984): 194-207. [Op.23]

534. Hollander, Hans. "Tektonische Probleme in Beethovens *Kreutzersonate.*" SMZ 115(1975): 237-243. [Op.47]

535. Karmer, Richard A. "The sketches for Beethoven's Violin Sonatas, Opus 30: History, transcription, analysis." PhD dissertation: Princeton University, 1974. UM 74-17,468. No DA listing.

Other works

536. Arnold, Denis and Nigel Fortune, eds. *The Beethoven companion.* London: Faber & Faber, 1971.

537. Badura-Skoda, Paul. "Fehlende und Überzählige Takte bei Schubert und Beethoven." OMZ 33(1978): 284-294.

538. Bartha, Dénes. "Drei Finale-Themen von Beethoven." Fs. Federhofer: 210-216.

539. Becker, Heinz. "Das modulierende Zwischenglied in der engeren Sonatenform: Beobachtungen an Beethovens Frühwerk." Fs. Dadelson: 20-32.

540. Becking, Gustav. "Studien zu Beethovens Personalstil: Das Scherzothema." Fs. Becking: 1-68.

541. Beling, Renate. "Der Marsch bei Beethoven." PhD dissertation (Musicology): Bonn, 1960.

542. Berry, Wallace. "Rhythmic accelerations in Beethoven." JMT 22/2 (1978): 177-240.

543. Blumröder, Christoph von. "Von Wandel musikalischer Aktualität: Anmerkungen zum Spätstil Beethovens." AM 40(1983): 24-37.

544. Broyles, Michael E. "Rhythm, metre and Beethoven." MR 33 (1972): 300-322.

545. Bruce, I.M. "Calculated unpredictability in Beethoven's sonata-designs." SN 1(1970): 36-53.

546. Brusatti, Otto. "Die thematisch-melodische Einheit im Spätwerk Beethovens." MAU 2(1979): 117-140.

547. Cahn, Peter. "Aspekte der Schlussgestaltung in Beethovens Instrumentalwerken." AM 39(1982): 19-31.

548. Chailley.

549. Cole, Malcolm S. "Techniques of surprise in the sonata-rondos of Beethoven." SM 12(1970): 232-262.

550. Cooper, Martin. *Beethoven: The last decade.* Oxford: Oxford University Press, 1985.

551. Dürr, Walther. "Wer vermag nach Beethoven noch etwas zu machen? Gedanken über die Beziehungen Schuberts zu Beethoven." BJ 9(1973-1977): 47-67.

552. Eibner, Franz. "Einige Kriterien für die Apperzeption und Interpretation von Beethovens Werk." BOGM (1976-1978): 20-36.

553. Epstein, David. "Middle-period Beethoven." *Beyond Orpheus: Studies in musical structures.* Cambridge, MA: MIT Press, 1979.

554. Eversole, James Atlee. "A study of orchestrational style through the analysis of representative works of Mozart and Beethoven." EdD dissertation: Columbia University, 1966. UM 67-02,795. DA XXVII.9, p.3072.

555. Fischer, Kurt von. *Die Beziehungen von Form und Motiv in Beethovens Instrumentalwerke.* 2nd augmented ed. Baden-Baden: Korner, 1972.

556. Garner, Chet H. "Principles of periodic structure in the instrumental works of Haydn, Mozart, and Beethoven." PhD dissertation (Theory): University of Iowa, 1977. 279 p. UM 77-28,456. DA XXXVIII.7, p.3791-A.

557. Goldschmidt, Harry. *Beethoven-Studien.* Leipzig: Deutscher Verlag für Musik, 1974.

558. ----. "Zitat oder Parodie?" BM 12(1970): 171-198.

559. Greene, David B. *Temporal processes in Beethoven's music.* New York: Gordon & Breach, 1981.

560. Gülke, Peter. "Kantabilität und thematische Abhandlung." BM 12(1970): 252-273.

561. Hess, Willy. *Beethoven-Studien.* Bonn: Beethoven-Haus, 1972.

562. Kolisch, Rudolf. "Tempo and character in Beethoven's music." MQ 29(1943): 169-187, 291-312.

563. Kopferman, Michael. *Beiträge zur musikalischen Analyse später Werke Ludwig van Beethovens.* München: E. Katzbichler, 1975.

564. Kropfinger, Klaus. "Zur thematischen Funktion der langsamen Einleitung bei Beethoven." Fs. Schmidt-Görg/70: 197-216.

565. Lang, Paul Henry, ed. *The creative world of Beethoven.* New York: W.W. Norton, 1971. [Articles originally published in MQ 56(1970).]

566. Liebermann, Ira. "Some representative works from Beethoven's early period analyzed in light of the theories of Ernst Kurt and Kurt von Fischer." PhD dissertation (Musicology): Columbia University, 1968. 301 p. UM 69-15,692. DA XXX.4, p.1588-A.

567. Linde, Bernard S. van der. "Die Versunkenheitsepisode bei Beethoven." BJ 9(1973-1977): 319-337.

568. Lippman, Edward A. "The formation of Beethoven's early style." Fs. Lang: 102-116.

569. Lubin, Steven. "Techniques for the analysis of development in middle period Beethoven." PhD dissertation (Musicology): New York University, 1974. UM 74-18,187. DA XXXV.2, p.1145-A.

570. Luxner, Michael David. "The evolution of the minuet/scherzo in the music of Beethoven." PhD dissertation (Musicology): University of Rochester, 1978. UM 78-17,561. DA XXXIX.4, p.1918-A.

571. Mahaim, Ivan. *Beethoven.* Paris: Desclée de Brouwer, 1964.

572. Mainka, Jürgen. "Das Weltbild des jungen Beethoven." BM 12 (1970): 199-251.

573. Mies, Paul. "Die Bedeutung der Pauke in den Werken Ludwig van Beethovens." BJ 8(1971-1972): 49-71.

574. ----. "Friedrich Silchers Liederarbeitungen Beethovenscher Melodien." BJ 3(1957-1958): 111-126.

575. ----. "Ludwig van Beethovens Werke über seinen Kontretanz in Es-Dur." BJ 1(1953-1954): 80-102.

576. ----. "Sehnsucht von Goethe und Beethoven." BJ 2 (1955-1956): 112-119.

577. Miller, Hugh. "Beethoven's rhythm: Some observations and problems." Fs. Apel: 165-174.

578. Misch, Ludwig. *Beethoven Studies*. Trans. by G.I.C. De Courey. Norman: University of Oklahoma Press, 1953.

579. ----. "Beethovens *Variierte Themen* Op.105 und Op.107." BJ 4 (1959-1960): 102-142.

580. ----. *Neue Beethoven-Studien und andere Themen*. München: G. Henle, 1967.

581. ----. "Wiedergeburt aus dem Geist der Sonate: Fuge und Fugato in Beethovens Variationsform." NZM 119(1958): 75-81.

582. Newman, William S. "Tempo in Beethoven's instrumental music: Its choice and its flexibility." PQ 116(1981-1982): 22-29, 117(1981-1982): 22-31.

583. Preston, Sandra Elaine. "An investigation of Beethoven's use of tonality." PhD dissertation (Musicology): Sheffield, 1975.

584. Ratner, Leonard G. "Key definition: A structural idea in Beethoven's music." JAMS 23(1970): 472-483.

585. Ratz, Erwin. "Analyse und Hermeneutik in ihrer Bedeutung für die Interpretation Beethovens." OMZ 25(1970): 756-766.

586. ----. "Analysis and hermeneutics, and their significance for the interpretation of Beethoven." Trans. by Mary Whittall. MA 3/3(1984): 243-254.

587. ----. *Einführung in der musikalische Formenlehre: Über Formprinzipien in den Inventionen J.S. Bachs und ihre Bedeutung für die Kompositionstechnik Beethovens*. Wien: Österreichischer Bundesverlag für Unterricht, Wissenschaft und Kunst, 1951.

588. Rienäcker, Gerd. "Zum Problem des attacca in Instrumentalwerken Ludwig van Beethovens." BM 18(1976): 39-68.

589. Rosen, Charles. *The classical style: Haydn, Mozart, Beethoven*. London: Faber & Faber, 1971.

590. Schenkman, Walter. "The tyranny of the formula in Beethoven." CMS 18(1978): 158-174.

591. Schneider, Norbert J. "Mediantische Harmonik bei Ludwig van Beethoven." AM 35(1978): 210-230.

592. Schwager, Myron. "A fresh look at Beethoven's arrangements." ML 54(1973): 142-160.

593. ----. "Some observations on Beethoven as an arranger." MQ 60 (1974): 89-93.

594. Souchay, Marc-André. "Zur Sonate Beethovens." Fs. Abert/H: 133-153.

595. Steglich, Rudolf. "Über Beethovens Märsche." Fs. Orel: 187-195.

596. Steinbeck, Wolfram. "Ein wahres Spiel mit musikalischen Formen: Zum Scherzo Ludwig Beethovens." AM 38(1981): 194-226.

597. Thym, Jurgen. "The instrumental recitative in Beethoven's compositions." Fs. Fox: 230-240.

598. Tyson, Alan. *Beethoven Studies*. New York: W.W. Norton, 1973.

599. Wagner, Günther. "Motivgruppierung in der Expositionsgestaltung bei C.Ph.E. Bach und Beethoven: Zur Kompositionsgeschichtlichen Kontinuität im 18. Jahrhundert." JSIM (1978): 43-71.

600. Warch, Willard F. "A study of the modulation technique of Beethoven." PhD dissertation (Theory): University of Rochester, 1955. No DA listing.

601. Wiesel, Henry Meir. "Thematic unity in Beethoven's sonata works of the period 1796-1802." PhD dissertation (Musicology): City University of New York, 1976. 196 p. UM 76-21,100. DA XXXVII.3, p.1292-A.

602. Zickenheiner, Otto. "Zur kontrapunktischen Satztechnik in späten Werken Beethovens." BJ 9(1973-1977): 553-569.

603. Special Issue: BM 12(1970).

BELCHER, SUPPLY (1751-1836)

604. Owen, Earl M., Jr. "The life and music of Supply Belcher (1751-1836), 'Handel of Maine.'" DMA dissertation (Musicology): Southern Baptist Theological Seminary, 1969. UM 69-4446. DA XXIX.9, p.3172-3-A.

BELLINI, VINCENZO (1801-1835)

605. ASO 29(1980). [*Norma*]

606. Lippmann, Friedrich. "Donizetti und Bellini: Ein Beitrag zur Interpretation von Donizettis Stil." STU 4(1975): 193-243.

607. ----. *Vincenzo Bellini und die italienische Opera seria seiner Zeit: Studien über Libretto, Arienform und Melodik.* Köln: Böhlau, 1969.

608. Weinstock, Herbert. *Vincenzo Bellini: His life and operas.* New York: Knopf, 1971.

BENDER, JAN (born 1909)

609. Herman, H. David. "Jan Bender and his organ music." DMA dissertation (Performance): University of Kansas, 1974. No DA listing.

BENJAMIN, ARTHUR (1893-1960)

610. Keller, Hans. "Arthur Benjamin and the problem of popularity." TEMPO 15(1950): 4-15.

611. Seiber, Mátyás. "Arthur Benjamin: Symphony: An analysis." TEMPO 32(1954): 9-12.

BENNETT, RICHARD (born 1936)

612. Marston, Marlene G. "The serial keyboard music of Richard Rodney Bennett." PhD dissertation (Theory): University of Wisconsin, 1968. UM 68-17,916. DA XXX.3, p.1195-A.

BENOLIEL, BERNARD (born 1943)

    613. MacDonald, Calum. "An American in Albion: The music of Bernard Benoliel." TEMPO 142(1982): 20-30.

BENSON, WARREN (born 1924)

    614. Ferguson, Thomas. "A theoretical analysis of Symphony for Drums and Wind Orchestra by Warren Benson." JBR 10/1(1974): 9-22.

BERG, ALBAN (1885-1935)

Op.2, Four Songs
    615. Ayrey, Craig. "Berg's *Scheideweg*: Analytical issues in Op.2/ii." MA 1(1982): 189-202.
    616. Wennerstrom, Mary H. "Pitch relationships in Berg's Songs, Op.2." ITR 1/1(1977-1978): 12-22.

Op.4, Altenberg Lieder
    617. Chadwick, Nicholas. "Thematic integration in Berg's *Altenberg Songs*." MR 29(1968): 300-304.
    618. De Voto, Mark. "Alban Berg's picture postcard songs." PhD dissertation: Princeton University, 1966. 139 p. No DA listing.
    619. ----. "Alban Berg's picture postcard songs." EMM 1/2(1984): 11-19.
    620. Leibowitz, René. "Alban Berg's Five Orchestral Songs." MQ 34 (1948): 487-511.
    621. Mayer-Rosa, Eugen. "Alban Bergs *Altenberg-Lieder* im Unterricht." MB 4(1972): 123-128.
    622. Redlich, Hans. "Alban Berg's *Altenberg Songs*, Op.4." MR 31 (1970): 43-53.
    623. Ringger, Rolf Urs. "Zur formbildener Kraft des vertonten Wortes: Analytische Untersuchungen an Liedern von Hugo Wolf und Alban Berg." SMZ 99(1959): 225-229.
    624. Stenzl, Jurg. "Franz Schreker und Alban Berg: Bemerkungen zu den *Altenberg-Liedern* Op.4." Schreker: 44-58.
    625. Stroh, Wolfgang Martin. "Alban Bergs *Orchesterlieder*." NZM 130(1969): 89-94.

Op.5, Four Pieces for Clarinet and Piano
    626. Borris, Siegfried. "Vergleichende Stilanalyse: Alban Berg--Paul Hindemith." Benary: 35-47. [No.1]
    627. ----. "Vergleichende Werkanalyse: Alban Berg: Op.5 Nr.1; Paul Hindemith: Aus der Violinsonate 1939." MB 5(1973): 138-141.
    628. De Fotis, William. "Berg's Op.5: Rehearsal instructions." PNM 17/1(1978-1979): 131-137.
    629. De la Motte: 131-145. [No.1]
    630. Leibowitz: 150-152.
    631. Lewis, Christopher. "Tonal focus in atonal music: Berg's Op.5/3." MTS 3(1981): 84-97.

Op.6, Three Orchestral Pieces
632. Archibald, Bruce. "The harmony of Berg's *Reigen*." PNM 6/2 (1968): 73-91.
633. De Voto, Mark. "Alban Berg's 'Marche Macabre'." PNM 22 (1983-1984): 386-447.
634. Jameux, Dominque. "Interminable analyse: Études atonales III: La première pièce de l'Opus 6 de Berg: Präludium." MJ 19(1975): 49-70, 20(1975): 33-41.
635. Rost, Cornelia. "Alban Berg: Drei Orchesterstücke Op.6." NZM 143/12(1982): 37-40.

Op.7, Wozzeck
636. ASO 35(1981).
637. Berg, Alban. "Conférence sur *Wozzeck* (1929)." MJ 14(1974): 77-94.
638. Chittum, Donald. "The triple fugue in Berg's *Wozzeck*." MR 28 (1967): 52-62.
639. Forneberg, Erich. *"Wozzeck" von Alban Berg*. Berlin: R. Lienau, 1963.
640. Hyde, Martha MacLean. [review] "George Perle: *The operas of Alban Berg*, vol.I. *Wozzeck*." JAMS 34(1981): 573-587.
641. Jouve, Pierre and Michel Fano. *"Wozzeck" d'Alban Berg*. Paris: Union Générale d'Éditions, 1964.
642. ----. *"Wozzeck* d'Alban Berg (Acte III, scène IV)." RM 212 (1952): 87-98.
643. Klein, Rudolf. "Zur Frage der Tonalität in Alban Bergs Oper *Wozzeck*." Wozzeck: 32-45.
644. König, Werner. *Tonalitätstruckturen in Alban Bergs Oper "Wozzeck."* Tutzing: H. Schneider, 1974.
645. Lederer, Josef Horst. "Zu Alban Berg's Invention über den Ton H." Wozzeck: 57-67.
646. Leibowitz: 171-177.
647. Mahler, Fritz. *Concerning Alban Berg's opera "Wozzeck": Scenic and musical analysis*. Wien: Universal, 1965.
648. ----. *Zu Alban Bergs Oper "Wozzeck": Szenische und musikalische Übersicht*. Wien: Universal, 1957.
649. Mauser, Siegfried. *Das expressionistische Musiktheater der Wiener Schule: Stilistische und entwicklungsgeschichtliche Untersuchungenen zu Arnold Schönbergs "Erwartung" und "Die glückliche Hand," und Alban Bergs "Wozzeck."* Regensburg: G. Bosse, 1982.
650. McCredie, Andrew D. "A half centennial new look at Alban Berg's *Wozzeck*: Its antecedents and influence on German Expressionist music theatre." MMA 9(1977): 156-205.
651. Perle, George. "The musical language of *Wozzeck*." MFO 1(1967): 204-259.
652. ----. *The operas of Alban Berg*. Vol. I. *Wozzeck*. Berkeley: University of California Press, 1980. 231 p.
653. ----. "Representation and symbol in the music of *Wozzeck*." MR 32(1971): 281-308.
654. ----. *"Woyzeck* and *Wozzeck*." MQ 53(1967): 206-219.

35

655. Petersen, Peter. "Wozzecks persönliche Leitmotive: Ein Beitrag zur Deutung des Sinngehalts der Musik in Alban Bergs *Wozzeck*." HJM 4 (1980): 33-84.

656. Ploebsch, Gerd. *Alban Berg's "Wozzeck."* Strasbourg: P.H. Heitz, 1968. [Includes bibliography of 1172 items]

657. Radice, Mark A. "The anatomy of a libretto: The music inherent in Büchner's *Woyzeck*." MR 41(1980): 223-233.

658. Redlich, Hans. "*Wozzeck*: Dramaturgie und musikalische Form." M 10(1956): 120-125.

659. Reich, Willi. "Alban Berg: *Wozzeck*." MZ 6(1954): 27-34.

660. ----. "A guide to *Wozzeck*." MM Special Supplement: Monograph No.2. [Also MQ 38(1952): 1-21. Also *Alban Berg's "Wozzeck": A guide to the text and music of the opera.* New York: G. Schirmer, 1952]

661. Richter, Christoph. "Die Wirthausszene aus Alban Bergs *Wozzeck*: Unterrichtsmodell: Verhältnis von Musik und Sprache in der Oper." MB 14/9(1982): 553-563.

662. Sabin, Robert. "Alban Berg's *Wozzeck*." *Musical America* (April 1951): 6. [Includes a chart of the form, by Fritz Mahler, more convenient than the well-known brochure of Reich]

663. Schmalfeldt, Janet. *Berg's "Wozzeck": Harmonic language and dramatic design.* New Haven: Yale University Press, 1983.

664. ----. "Berg's *Wozzeck*: Pitch-class set structures and the dramatic design." PhD dissertation: Yale University, 1979. UM 81-21,410. DA XVII.4, p.1370-A.

654. Stephan, Rudolf. "Aspekte der *Wozzeck*-Musik." Wozzeck: 9-21.

666. Treitler, Leo. "*Wozzeck* and the apocalypse: An essay in historical criticism." CI 3/2(1976-1977): 251-270.

667. ----. "*Wozzeck* et l'apocalypse." SMZ 116(1976): 249-262.

Chamber Concerto

668. Hilmar, Rosemary. "Metrische Proportionen und serielle Rhythmik im *Kammerkonzert* von Alban Berg." SMZ 120(1980): 355-360.

Lulu

669. Bitter, Christof. "Notizen zu Mozarts *Don Giovanni* und Bergs *Lulu*." Fs. Strecker: 123-124.

670. Boulez, Pierre. "*Lulu*: Le second opéra." Boulez: 307-325.

671. Ertelt, Thomas F. "'Hereinspaziert . . .': Ein früher Entwurf des Prologs zu Alban Bergs *Lulu*." OMZ 41(1986): 15-25.

672. Foldi, Andrew. "The enigma of Schigolch: A character analysis." IABS 9(1980): 4-7.

673. Jarman, Douglas. "Berg's surrealist opera." MR 31(1970): 232-240.

674. ----. "Dr. Schön's five-strophe aria: Some notes on tonality and pitch association in Berg's *Lulu*." PNM 8/2(1970): 23-48.

675. ----. "*Lulu*: The sketches." IABS 6(1978): 4-8.

676. ----. "Some rhythmic and metric techniques in Alban Berg's *Lulu*." MQ 56(1970): 349-366.

677. Leibowitz: 177-185.

678. Neumann, Karl. "Wedekind's and Berg's *Lulu*." MR 35(1974): 47-57.

679. Perle, George. "The film interlude of *Lulu*." IABS 11(1982): 3-8.
680. ----. "Das Film-Zwischenspiel in Bergs Opera *Lulu*." OMZ 36 (1981): 631-638.
681. ----. "Inhaltliche und formale Strukturen in Alban Bergs Oper *Lulu*." OMZ 32(1977): 427-441.
682. Perle, George. "An introduction to *Lulu*." OQ 3(1985): 87-111.
683. ----. "*Lulu*: The formal design." JAMS 17(1964): 179-192.
684. ----. "*Lulu*: Thematic materials and pitch organization." MR 26(1965): 269-302.
685. ----. "The music of *Lulu*: A new analysis." JAMS 12(1959): 185-200. [Corrections in JAMS 14(1961): 96]
686. ----. *The operas of Alban Berg*. Vol. 2. *Lulu*. Berkeley: University of California Press, 1985.
687. ----. "Die Personen in Berg's *Lulu*." AM 24(1967): 283-290.
688. ----. "Der Tod der Beschwitz." OMZ 36(1982): 19-28.
689. ----. "The tone-row as symbol in Berg's *Lulu*." Fs. Herz: 309-318.
690. Pople, Anthony. "Serial and tonal aspects of pitch structure in Act III of Berg's *Lulu*." SN 10(1983): 36-57.
691. Reich, Willi. "Alban Berg's *Lulu*." MQ 22(1936): 383-401.
692. ----. "*Lulu*: The text and music." MM 12(1935): 103-111.
693. Reiter, Manfred. *Die Zwölftontechnik in Alban Bergs Oper "Lulu*." Regensburg: G. Bosse, 1973.
694. Rognoni: 165-187.
695. Scherliess, Volker. "Alban Bergs analytische Tafeln zur *Lulu*-Reihe." MF 30(1977): 452-464.
696. Stephan, Rudolf. "Zur Sprachmelodie in Alban Bergs *Lulu*-Musik." Schnitzler/D: 246-264.

Lyric Suite
697. Berg, Alban. "Berg's notes for the *Lyric Suite*." IABS 2(1971): 5-7.
698. Blankenship, Shirley Meyer. "Berg. Lines: Opus 3: *Lyrische Suite*." DMA dissertation (Composition): University of Illinois 1977. No DA listing.
699. Bouquet, Fritz. "Alban Berg's *Lyrische Suite*: Eine Studie über Gestalt, Klang und Ausdruck." MELOS 15(1948): 227-231.
700. Brindle, Reginald Smith. "The symbolism in Berg's *Lyric Suite*." SCORE 21(1957): 60-63.
701. Budday, Wolfgang. *Alban Bergs "Lyrische Suite"*. Neuhausen-Stuttgart: Hänssler, 1979.
702. Floros, Constantin. "Das esoterische Programm der *Lyrischen Suite* von Alban Berg: Eine semantische Analyse." HJM 1(1974): 101-145.
703. Green, Douglass. "The Allegro Misterioso of Berg's *Lyric Suite*: Iso- and retrorhythms." JAMS 30(1977): 507-516.
704. ----. "Berg's *De Profundis*: The finale of the *Lyric Suite*." IABS 5(1977): 13-23.
705. ----. "Das Largo Desolato der *Lyrischen Suite* von Alban Berg." OMZ 33(1978): 79-85.

706. Parish, George D. "Motive and cellular structure in Alban Berg's *Lyric Suite*." PhD dissertation (Musicology): University of Michigan, 1970. UM 71-15,262. DA XXXI.12, p.6650-A.

707. Perle: 72-77. 708. ----. "Das geheime Programm der *Lyrischen Suite*." OMZ 33(1978): 64-79, 113-119.

709. ----. "The secret program of the *Lyric Suite*." IABS 5(1977): 4-12.

710. Straus, Joseph N. "Tristan and Berg's *Lyric Suite*." ITO 8/3 (1983-1984): 33-41.

Schliesse mir die Augen beide (Storm)

711. Smith, Joan Allen. "Some sources for Berg's *Schliesse mir bei die Augen beide* II." IABS 6(1978): 9-13.

Songs [see also individual titles]

712. Adorno, Theodor W. "Die Instrumentation von Bergs frühen Lieder." *Klangfiguren-Musikalischen Schriften.* Berlin: Suhrkamp, 1959. I: 138-156.

713. Broekema.

714. Chadwick, Nicholas. "Berg's unpublished songs in the Österreichische Nationalbibliothek." ML 52(1971): 123-130.

715. Eberle, Gottfried. "Alban Berg: Sieben frühe Lieder." NZM 146/2(1985): 23-26.

716. Pittman, Elmer Everett. "Harmony in the songs of Alban Berg." PhD dissertation (Theory): Florida State University, 1966. UM 67-306. DA XXVII.10, p.2554-A.

717. Venus, Dankmar. *Vergleichende Untersuchung zur melodischen Struktur der Singstimmen in den Liedern von Arnold Schönberg, Alban Berg, Anton Webern, und Paul Hindemith.* Göttingen, 1965.

718. Wilkey, Jay W. "Certain aspects of form in the vocal music of Alban Berg." PhD dissertation (Music Education): Indiana University, 1965. UM 65-10,911. DA XXVI.8, p.4720-1.

Violin Concerto

719. Barcaba, Peter. "Zur Tonalität in Alban Bergs Violinkonzert." M 32(1978-1979): 158-164.

720. Floros, Constantin. "Alban Berg 'Requiem': Das verschwiegene Programm des Violinkonzerts." NZM 146/4(1985): 4-8.

721. Forneberg, Erich. "Der Bach-Choral in Alban Bergs Violinkonzert." MELOS 23(1956): 247-249.

722. Fuhrmann, Roderich. "Alban Berg (1885-1935): Violinkonzert (1935)." Zimmerschied: 73-109.

723. Hall.

724. Jarman, Douglas. "Alban Berg, Wilhelm Fliess and the secret programme of the Violin Concerto." IABS 12(1982): 5-11.

725. ----. "Alban Berg, Wilhelm Fliess und das geheime Programm des Violinkonzerts." OMZ 40(1985): 12-21.

726. Knaus, Herwig. "Die Kärntner Volksweise aus Alban Bergs Violinkonzert." ME 23(1970): 117-118.

727. ----. "Die Reihenskizzen zu Alban Bergs Violinkonzert." OMZ 37 (1982): 105-108.

728. ----. "Studien zu Alban Bergs Violinkonzert." Fs. Schenk: 255-274.

729. Leibowitz: 162-167.

730. Little.

731. Redlich, Hans. "Alban Bergs Violinkonzert." MELOS 24(1957): 316-321, 352-357.

732. Schneider, Frank. "Alban Bergs Violinkonzert: Metaphern zu einer transzendierenden Musik." BM 18(1976): 219-233.

733. Schreffler, Theodore Wilson, III. "An analysis of the Violin Concerto (1935) by Alban Berg." PhD dissertation: University of California, Los Angeles, 1979. No DA listing.

Der Wein

734. Jarman, Douglas. "Some row techniques in Alban Berg's *Der Wein*." SN 2(1971-1972): 46-56.

735. Knaus, Herwig. "Alban Bergs Skizzen und Vorarbeiten zur Konzartarie *Der Wein*." Fs. Wessely: 355-380. [Also M 38(1984-1985): 194-204]

Wozzeck see *Op.7, Wozzeck*

Other works

736. Archibald, Robert Bruce. "Harmony in the early works of Alban Berg." PhD dissertation: Harvard University, 1965. No DA listing.

737. Buchanan, Herbert Herman. "An investigation of mutual influences among Schoenberg, Webern, and Berg (with an emphasis on Schoenberg and Webern, ca. 1904-1908)." PhD dissertation (Musicology): Rutgers University, 1974. UM 74-27,592. DA XXXV.6, p.3789-A.

738. Carner, Mosco. *Alban Berg: The man and the work*. London: Duckworth, 1975. 255 p.

739. Chadwick, Nicholas. "Franz Schreker's orchestral style and its influence on Alban Berg." MR 35(1974): 29-46.

740. De Voto, Mark and Joan Allen Smith. "Berg's seventeen four-part canons: The mystery solved." IABS 3(1975): 4-7.

741. Godwin, Paul Milton. "A study of concepts of melody, with particular reference to some music of the twentieth century and examples from the compositions of Schoenberg, Webern, and Berg." PhD dissertation (Theory): Ohio State University, 1972. UM 73-02,003. DA XXXIII.8, p.4453-A.

742. Hier, Ethel Glenn. "To Alban Berg: A tribute." MU 1 (1946-1947): 275-287.

743. Hollander, Hans. "Alban Berg." MQ 22(1936): 375-382.

744. Jarman, Douglas. *The music of Alban Berg*. Berkeley: University of California Press, 1979.

745. Maegard, Jan. "Ein Beispiel atonalen Kontrapunkts im Frühstadium." ZM 3/1(29-34). [17 canons]

746. Murray, Robert P. "The string quartets of Alban Berg." PhD dissertation (Performance): Indiana University, 1975. No DA listing.

747. Nelson, Robert U. "Form and fancy in the variations of Berg." MR 31(1970): 54-69.

748. Perle, George. "Berg's master array of interval cycles." MQ 63 (1977): 1-30.

749. Pernye, A. "Alban Berg und die Zahlen." SM 9(1967): 141-161.

750. Redlich, Hans Ferdinand. *Alban Berg: The man and his music.* New York: Abelard Schumann, 1957.

751. Reich, Willi. *The life and work of Alban Berg.* London: Thames and Hudson, 1965.

752. Rognoni.

753. Schollum, Robert. *Die Wiener Schule: Schönberg-Berg-Webern: Entwicklung und Ergebnis.* Wien: E. Lafite, 1969.

754. Schweitzer, Klaus. *Die Sonatensatzform im Schaffen Alban Bergs.* Stuttgart: Musikwissenschaftliche Verlagsgesellschaft, 1970.

755. Spring, Glenn Ernest, Jr. "Determinants of phrase structure in selected works of Schoenberg, Berg, and Webern." DMA dissertation (Composition): University of Washington, 1972. 61 p. UM 72-28,670. DA XXXIII.5, p.2417-A.

756. Stroh, Wolfgang Martin. "Alban Berg's 'constructive rhythm'." PNM 7/1(1968): 18-31.

BERGER, ARTHUR (born 1912)

757. Barkin, Elaine. "Arthur Berger's Trio for violin, guitar and piano (1972)." Battcock: 215-220. [Also PNM 17/1(1978-1797): 23-37]

758. Silver, Sheila. "Pitch and registral distribution in Arthur Berger's music for piano." PNM 17/1(1978-1979): 68-76.

BERGER, JEAN (born 1909)

759. Johnson, Axie Allen. "Choral settings of the Magnificat by selected twentieth-century composers." DMA dissertation: University of Southern California, 1968. 172 p. RILM 68/3607dd28. No DA listing.

760. Larson.

761. Pritchard, W. Douglas. "The choral style of Jean Berger." ACR 8/1(1965): 4-5, 15.

762. Roller, Dale Alvin. "The secular choral music of Jean Berger." EdD dissertation: University of Illinois, 1974. UM 75-00,416. DA XXXV.7, p.4602-A.

763. Smith, Kenyard Earl. "The choral music of Jean Berger." PhD dissertation (Choral Music): University of Iowa, 1972. 242 p. UM 72-26,742. DA XXXIII.4, p.1774-A.

BERGSMA, WILLIAM (born 1921)

764. Skulsky, Abraham. "The music of William Bergsma." JR 3/2 (1956): 12-26.

BERIO, LUCIANO (born 1925)

Allelujah
765. Berio, Luciano. "Aspects d'un artisanat formel." CC 1(1983): 10-23.

Chemins I, II, III
    766. Osmond-Smith, David. "Joyce, Berio et l'art de l'exposition." CC 1(1983): 83-89.

Circles
    767. Demierre, Jacques. "*Circles*: e.e. cummings lu par Luciano Berio." CC 1(1983): 123-180.
    768. Hermann, Richard. "Luciano Berio's *Circles*, first movement." SONUS 4/2(1984): 26-45.
    769. Schnaus, Peter. "Anmerkungen zu Luciano Berios *Circles*." MB 10(1978): 489-497.

Coro
    770. Anhalt: 252-266.

O King
    771. Stoianowa, Iwanka. "Verbe et son: 'Centre et absence': Sur *Cummings ist der Dichter* de Boulez, *O King* de Berio, et *Für Stimmen ... Missa est* de Schnebel." MJ 16(1974): 79-102.

Omaggio a Joyce see *Thema (Omaggio a Joyce)*

Sequenza I-IX [see also individual titles]
    772. Albèra, Philippe. "Introduction aux neuf séquences." CC 1(1983): 90-122.

Sequenza III
    773. Anhalt, Istvan. "Luciano Berio's *Sequenza III*." CCM 7(1973): 23-60. [Also Anhalt: 25-40]
    774. Gruhn, Wilfried. "Luciano Berio (1925): *Sequenza III* (1965)." Zimmerschied: 234-249.
    775. Lyotard, Jean-François and Dominique Avron. "*A Few Words to Sing* (sur *Sequenza III* de Berio)." MJ 2(1971): 30-44.

Sequenza V
    776. Pellman, Samuel Frank. "An examination of the role of timbre in a musical composition as exemplified by an analysis of *Sequenza V* by Luciano Berio." DMA dissertation: Cornell University, 1979. 160 p. No DA listing.

Sequenza VI
    777. Uscher, Nancy. "Luciano Berio: *Sequenza VI* for Solo Viola: Performance practices." PNM 21(1982-1983): 286-293.

Sequenza VII
    778. Förtig, Peter. "Zu Luciano Berios *Sequenza per Oboe solo.*" T 1/2(1976-1977): 72-76.

Serenata I
    779. Wennerstrom.

Sinfonia
    780. Altmann, Peter. *"Sinfonia" von Luciano Berio: Eine analytische Studie.* Wien: Universal, 1977.
    781. Budde, Elmar. "Zum dritten Satz der *Sinfonia* von Luciano Berio." Stephan: 128-144.
    782. Cope: 345-351.
    783. Hicks, Michael. "Text, music, and meaning in Berio's *Sinfonia*, 3rd movement." PNM 20(1981-1982): 199-224.
    784. Krieger, Georg and Wolfgang Martin Stroh. "Probleme der Collage in der Musik: Aufgezeigt am 3. Satz der *Sinfonia* von Luciano Berio." MB 3(1971): 229-235.
    785. Osmond-Smith, David. "From myth to music: Lévi-Strauss's *Mythologiques* and Berio's *Sinfonia*." MQ 67(1981): 230-260.
    786. ----. *Playing on words: A guide to Luciano Berio's "Sinfonia."* London: Royal Musical Association, 1985.
    787. Ravizza, Victor. "*Sinfonia* für acht Singstimmen und Orchester von Luciano Berio." MELOS 41(1974): 291-297.
    788. Zeichner, Sam. "Sound in Luciano Berio's *Sinfonia*: A La Rue style analysis." D 5/2(1973): 2-12.

Tempi concertati
    789. Jarvlepp, Jan. "Compositional aspects of *Tempi concertati* by Luciano Berio." I 11(1982): 179-193.

Thema (Omaggio a Joyce)
    790. Berio, Luciano. "Poésie et musique: Une Expérience." CC 1 (1983): 24-35.
    791. Delalande, François. "*L'Omaggio a Joyce* de Luciano Berio." MJ 15(1974): 45-54.

Other works
    792. Dressen, Norbert. "Luciano Berios Vokalkompositionen: Sprachliche Vorlagen und kompositorische Beispiele." *Sprache im technischen Zeitalter* 74(1980): 109-122.
    793. ----. *Sprache und Musik bei Luciano Berio.* Regensburg: G. Bosse, 1982.
    794. Flynn, George W. "Listening to Berio's music." MQ 61(1975): 388-421. [*Visage, Laborintus II, Sinfonia*]
    795. Holmes, Reed Kelley. "Relational systems and process in recent works of Luciano Berio." PhD dissertation (Theory): University of Texas, 1981. UM 81-28,638. DA XLII.7, p.2924-A.
    796. Jahnke, Sabine. "Materialien zu einer Unterrichtssequenz: Des Antonius von Padua Fischpredigt bei Orff-Mahler-Berio." MB 5(1973): 615-622.
    797. Miller, Robert W. "A style analysis of the published solo piano works of Luciano Berio, 1950-1975." DMA dissertation (Piano): Peabody Conservatory, 1979. UM 79-21,361. DA XL.4, p.1742-A.
    798. Sams, Carol Lee. "Solo vocal writing in selected works of Berio, Crumb and Rochberg." DMA dissertation (Performance): University of Washington, 1975. UM 76-17,610. DA XXXVII.2, p.685-A.

799. Stoianova, Ivanka. "Luciano Berio: Chemins en musique." RM 375-377(1985): 5-512.

BERKELEY, LENNOX

800. Hull, Robin. "Two symphonies: Eugene Goossens and Lennox Berkeley." MR 4(1943): 229-242.

BERLIOZ, HECTOR (1803-1869)

Damnation de Faust
    801. ASO 22(1979).
    802. Ferchault, Guy. *Faust: Une Légende et ses musiciens.* Paris: Larousse, 1948.
    803. Macy.
    804. Rushton, Julian. "The genesis of Berlioz's *La Damnation de Faust.*" ML 56(1975): 129-146.

Harold en Italie
    805. Dahlhaus, Carl. "Allegro frenetico: Zum Problem des Rhythmus bei Berlioz." Melos/NZM 3(1977): 212-214.
    806. Danuser, Hermann. "Symphonisches Subjekt und Form in Berlioz' *Harold en Italie.*" Meloz/NZM 3(1977): 203-212.
    807. Schenkman, Walter. "Fixed ideas and recurring patterns in Berlioz's melody." MR 40(1979): 24-48.

Lelio, ou Le Retour à la vie
    808. Bloom, Peter. "Orpheus' lyre resurrected: A *Tableau musical* by Berlioz." MQ 61(1975): 189-211.

Messe des morts
    809. Cone, Edward T. "Berlioz's Divine Comedy: The *Grande Messe des Morts.*" NCM 4(1980-1981): 3-16.
    810. George, Graham. "The ambiguities of Berlioz." CAUSM 6(1976): 1-10.

Overtures
    811. Adelson, Deborah M. "Interpreting Berlioz's *Overture to King Lear*, Opus 4: Problems and solutions." CM 35(1983): 46-56.
    812. Sandford, Gordon T. "The overtures of Hector Berlioz: A study in musical style." PhD dissertation (Musicology): University of Southern California, 1964. UM 64-6245. DA XXIV.12, p.5455-6.

Roméo et Juliette
    813. Chailley. [*Scène d'amour*]
    814. Friedheim, Philip. "Berlioz' *Roméo* symphony and the romantic temperament." CM 36(1983): 101-111.

Songs
    815. Bullard, Truman Campbell. "Hector Berlioz and the solo song in France." MA dissertation: Harvard University, 1963.

816.   Dickinson, A.E.F.   "Berlioz's songs."   MQ 55(1969): 329-343.

Symphonie fantastique
817.   Banks, Paul.   "Coherence and diversity in the *Symphonie
fantastique*."   NCM 8(1984-1985): 37-43.
818.   Berger, Christian.   *Phantastik als Konstruktion: Hector Berlioz'
"Symphonie fantastique."*   Kassel: Bärenreiter, 1983.
819.   Bockholdt, Rudolf.   "Die idée fixe der *Phantastischen Symphonie*."
AM 30(1973): 190-207.
820.   Cone, Edward T., ed.   *Berlioz: Fantastic Symphony.* Norton
Critical Scores.   New York: W.W. Norton, 1971.
821.   Schenkman, Walter.   "Fixed ideas and recurring patterns in
Berlioz's melody."   MR 40(1979): 24-48.
822.   Temperley, Nicholas.   "The *Symphonie fantastique* and its
program."   MQ 57(1971): 593-608.

Symphonies [see also individual titles]
823.   Bass, Edward.   "Thematic procedures in the symphonies of
Berlioz."   PhD dissertation: University of North Carolina, 1964.
UM 65-3988.   DA XXV.11, p.6673.
824.   Nowalis, Sister Susan Marie.   "Timbre as a structural device in
Berlioz's symphonies."   PhD dissertation (Theory): Case-Western Reserve
University, 1975.   UM 75-27,945.   DA XXXVI.7, p.4098-A.

Les Troyens
825.   Kühn, Hellmut.   "Antike Massen: Zu einigen Motiven in *Les
Troyens* von Hector Berlioz."   Fs. Abert: 141-152.
826.   Rushton, Julian.   "The overture to *Les Troyens*."   MA 4/1-2
(1985): 119-144.

Other works
827.   Alexander, Metche Franke.   "The choral-orchestral works of
Hector Berlioz."   PhD dissertation (Musicology): North Texas State
University, 1978.   UM 78-16,709.   DA XXXIX.3, p.1177-A.
828.   Bass, Edward.   "Musical time and space in Berlioz."   MR 30
(1969): 211-224.
829.   ----.   "Thematic unification of scenes in multi-movement works
of Berlioz."   MR 28(1967): 45-51.
830.   Bockholdt, Rudolf.   *Berlioz-Studien.*   Tutzing: H. Schneider,
1979.   225 p.
831.   ----.   "Musikalischer Satz und Orchesterklang im Werk von
Hector Berlioz."   MF 32(1979): 122-135.
832.   Chailley, Jacques.   "Berlioz harmoniste."   RM 223(1956): 15-30.
833.   Dickinson, A.E.F.   "Berlioz's Rome Prize works."   MR 25(1964):
163-185.
834.   ----.   "Berlioz' stage works."   MR 31(1970): 136-157.
835.   ----.   *The music of Berlioz.*   London: Faber & Faber, 1972.
836.   Dömling, Wolfgang.   "'En songeant au temps . . . à l'espace . . .'
Über einzige Aspekte der Musik Hector Berlioz."   AM 33(1976): 241-260.
837.   ----.   *Hector Berlioz: Die symphonisch-dramatischen Werke.*
Stuttgart: Reclam, 1979.

838. Friedheim, Philip. "Berlioz and rhythm." MR 37(1976): 5-44.

839. ----. "Radical harmonic procedures in Berlioz." MR 21(1960): 282-295.

840. Guiomar, Michel. *Le Masque et le fantasme: L'Imagination de la matière sonore dans la pensée musicale de Berlioz.* Paris: J. Corti, 1970.

841. Hirshberg, Jehoash. "Berlioz and the fugue." JMT 18(1974): 152-188.

842. Langford, Jeffrey. "The 'dramatic symphonies' of Berlioz as an outgrowth of the French operatic tradition." MQ 69(1983): 85-103.

843. ----. "The operas of Hector Berlioz: Their relationship to the French operatic tradition of the early nineteenth century." PhD dissertation: University of Pennsylvania, 1978. 431 p. UM 78-24,739. DA XXXIX.7, p.3908-A.

844. Primmer, Brian. *The Berlioz style.* New York: Da Capo Press, 1984. (1973)

845. Rushton, Julian. *The musical language of Berlioz.* New York: Cambridge University Press, 1983.

846. Silverman, Richard S. "Synthesis in the music of Hector Berlioz." MR 34(1973): 346-352.

847. Tanner, Peter H. "Timpani and percussion writing in the works of Hector Berlioz." PhD dissertation (Musicology): Catholic University, 1967. UM 67-17,122. DA XXVIII.7, p.2722-A.

BERNSTEIN, LEONARD (born 1918)

848. Boelzner, David E. "The symphonies of Leonard Bernstein: An analysis of motivic character and form." MA dissertation: University of North Carolina, 1976.

849. Gottlieb, Jack. "The choral music of Leonard Bernstein." ACR 10(1958): 156-174.

850. ----. "The music of Leonard Bernstein: A study of melodic manipulations." DMA dissertation (Performance): University of Illinois, 1964. UM 65-3589. DA XXVI.12, p.7355.

851. ----. "Symbols of faith in the music of Leonard Bernstein." MQ 66(1980): 287-295.

852. Gradenwitz, Peter. "Leonard Bernstein." MR 10(1949): 191-202.

853. Lehrman, Leonard Jordan. "Leonard Bernstein's *Serenade* after Plato's *Symposium*: An analysis." DMA dissertation (Performance): Cornell University, 1977. UM 78-06,305. DA XXXVIII.11, p.6390-A.

854. Pearlmutter, Alan Jay. "Leonard Bernstein's *Dybbuk*: An analysis including historical, religious, and literary perspectives of Hasidic life and lore." DMA dissertation (Conducting): Peabody Conservatory, 1985. 345 p. No DA listing.

BERWALD, FRANZ (1796-1868)

855. Brüll, Erich. "*Sinfonie singulière*: Information über Berwald." MG 18(1968): 246-252.

856. Stahmer, Klaus. "Ein Beitrag Berwalds zur romantischen Sonatenform: Das Duo für Violoncello und Klavier (1858)." STM 59/2(1977): 23-33.

857. ----. "Zur zyklischen Sonatenform: Franz Berwalds Duo für Violoncello und Klavier (1858)." Fs. Gudewill: 79-90.

BEVERSDORF, THOMAS (1924-1981)

858. Ferguson, Thomas. "An analysis of Symphony for Winds and Percussion by Thomas Beversdorf." JBR 9/1(1972-1973): 17-31.

BEYERS, FRANK MICHAEL (born 1928)

859. Dorfmüller, Joachim. "Musik der Sensibilität und Transparenz: Zum Orgelschaffen Frank Michael Meyers." MK 48(1948) 273-277.

BIALAS, GÜNTER (born 1907)

860. Huber, Nicolaus. "Der Komponist Günter Bialas." M 26(1972): 333-337.

BIERMANN, WOLF (born 1936)

861. Reinhardt, Klaus. "Eine Ballade von Wolf Biermann." MB 4 (1972): 200-201.

BIJSTER, JACOB (1902-1958)

862. Beechey, Gwilym. "The organ music of Jacob Bijster (1902-1958)." SS 36(1968): 1-7.

BINKERD, GORDON (born 1916)

863. Griffith, Patricia Barnes. "The solo piano music of Gordon Binkerd." DMA dissertation (Performance): Peabody Conservatory, 1985. 134 p. No DA listing.
864. Hawthorne, Loyd Furman. "The choral music of Gordon Binkerd." DMA dissertation (Performance): University of Texas, 1973. UM 74-05,181. DA XXXIV.9, p.6022-A.

BIRTWISTLE, HARRISON (born 1934)

865. Smalley, Roger. "Birtwistle's *Nomos*." TEMPO 86(1968): 7-10.

BITTNER, JULIUS (1874-1939)

866. Zauner, Waltraud. "Studien zu den musikalischen Bühnenwerken von Julius Bittner: Mit Beiträgen zur Lebensgeschichte des Komponisten." PhD dissertation (Musicology): Wien, 1984.

BIZET, GEORGES (1838-1875)

867. ASO 26(1980). [*Carmen*]

868. Bleiler, Ellen H., ed. *Georges Bizet: Carmen.* Dover Opera Guide and Libretto Series. New York: Dover Publications, 1970.

869. Cooper, Martin. *Bizet: Carmen.* London: Boosey & Hawkes, 1947.

870. Dean, Winton. *"Carmen:* An attempt at a true evaluation." MR 7(1946): 209-220.

871. ----. *Georges Bizet: His life and work.* London: J.M. Dent, 1965.

872. John, Nicholas, ed. *Bizet: Carmen.* London: J. Calder, 1982.

873. Luck, Ray. "An analysis of three variation sets for piano by Bizet, d'Indy and Pierné." DMA dissertation: Indiana University, 1978. No DA listing. [*Variations chromatiques*, Op.3]

874. Malherbe, Henry. *Carmen.* Paris: Michel, 1951.

875. Muller, Monique. "L'Oeuvre pianistique originale de Georges Bizet." PhD dissertation (Musicology): Université de Neuchâtel, 1976.

876. Shanet, Howard. "Bizet's suppressed symphony." MQ 44(1958): 461-476.

877. Stefan, Paul. *Georges Bizet.* Zürich: Atlantis, 1952.

BLACHER, BORIS (1903-1975)

878. Gray, John H. "Variable meter and parametric progression in the music of Boris Blacher." DMA dissertation: Cornell University, 1979. No DA listing.

879. Jahnke, Sabine. "Boris Blacher: *Ornamente* für Klavier, Op.37." MB 1(1969): 508-510.

880. Vogt: 253-260. [*Abstrakte Oper Nr.1* (1953)]

BLITZSTEIN, MARC (1905-1964)

881. Dietz, Robert James. "The operatic style of Marc Blitzstein in the American 'Agit-Prop' Era." PhD dissertation (Music Education): University of Iowa, 1970. UM 70-15,591. DA XXXI.3, p.1307-A.

BLOCH, AUGUSTYN (born 1929)

882. Erhardt, Ludwig. *"Wordsworth Songs* by Augustyn Bloch." PM 12/1(1977): 30-35.

883. Kominek, Mieczyslaw. "Augustyn Bloch *Anenaiki, Carmen biblicum."* PM 15/4(1980): 11-14.

BLOCH, ERNEST (1880-1959)

Chamber works

884. Guibbory, Yenoin Ephraim. "Thematic treatment in the string quartets of Ernest Bloch." PhD dissertation (Musicology): University of West Virginia, 1970. UM 71-04,849. DA XXXI.8, p.4199-A.

885. Jones, William M. "Ernest Bloch's five string quartets." MR 28 (1967): 112-121.

886. Raditz, Edward. "An analytical study of the violin and piano works of Ernest Bloch." PhD dissertation (Performance): New York University, 1975. No DA listing.

887. Rimmer, Frederick. "Ernest Bloch's Second String Quartet." TEMPO 52(1959): 11-16.

Orchestral works

888. Kushner, David. "Ernest Bloch and his symphonic works." PhD dissertation: University of Michigan, 1966. UM 67-15,649. DA XXVIII.7, p.2714-A.

889. Sharp, Geoffrey. "Ernest Bloch's Violin Concerto." MR 1(1940): 72-78.

Piano works

890. Wheeler, Charles Lynn. "The solo piano music of Ernest Bloch." DMA dissertation (Performance): University of Oregon, 1976. UM 77-13,217. DA XXXVII.12, p.7400-A.

Other works

891. Knapp, Alexander. "The Jewishness of Bloch: Subconscious or conscious." PRMA 97(1970-1971): 99-112.

892. Jones, William M. "The music of Ernest Bloch." PhD dissertation (Theory): Indiana University, 1963. UM-2292. DA XXIV.12, p.5452-53.

893. Minsky, Henri S. "Ernest Bloch and his music." PhD dissertation: George Peabody College for Teachers, 1945. 227 p. No DA listing.

894. Newlin, Dika. "The later works of Ernest Bloch." MQ 33(1947): 443-459.

BLOMDAHL, KARL BIRGER (1916-1968)

895. Ostrander, Arthur Eugene. "Style in the orchestral works of Karl-Birger Blomdahl." PhD dissertation (Theory): Indiana University, 1973. 317 p. UM 74-404. DA XXXIV.9, p.6025-A.

BON, WILLEM FREDERIK (born 1940)

896. Vermeulen, Ernst. "Willem Frederik Bon: *Usher-Symphony*." SS 48(1971): 1-8.

BORODIN, ALEXANDER (1833-1887)

897. Abraham, Gerald. "Borodin as a symphonist." ML 11(1930): 352-359.

898. ----. *Borodin: The composer and his music: A descriptive and critical analysis of his works and a study of his value as an art-force.* New York: AMS Press, 1975 (1927).

899. Bobeth, M. *Borodin und seine oper "Furst Igor": Geschichte, Analyse, Konsequenzen.* München: E. Katzbichler, 1982.

900. Dianin, Serge Aleksandrovich. *Borodin.* London: Oxford University Press, 1963.

BORTNYANSKY, DMITRI S. (1751-1825)

901. Seaman, Gerald. "D.S. Bortnyansky (1751-1825)." MR 21(1960): 106-113.

BOSSEUR, JEAN-YVES

902. Witts, Richard. "Jean-Yves Bosseur." CT 15(1976-1977): 8-11.

BOUCOURECHLIEV, ANDRÉ (born 1925)

903. Boucourechliev, André. "Le Nom d'Oedipe: Protocole musical." ASO 18(1978): 90-101.

BOULANGER, LILI (1893-1918)

904. Chailley, Jacques. "L'Oeuvre de Lili Boulanger." RM 353-354 (1982): 15-44.
905. Rosenstiel, Leonie. *The life and works of Lili Boulanger*. Rutherford, NJ: Fairleigh Dickinson University Press, 1978.

BOULEZ, PIERRE (born 1925)

Cummings ist der Dichter
906. Stoianowa, Iwanka. "Verbe et son: 'Centre et absence': sur *Cummings ist der Dichter* de Boulez, *O King* de Berio, et *Für Stimmen ... Missa est* de Schnebel." MJ 16(1974): 97-102.

Don
907. Cross, Anthony. "Form and expression in Boulez' *Don*." MR 36 (1975): 215-230.

Improvisations sur Mallarmé
908. Boulez, Pierre. "Construire une improvisation (*Deuxième improvisation sur Mallarmé*)." Bolez: 143-162.
909. ----. "Wie arbeitet die Avantgarde." MELOS 28(1961): 301-308. [Nos.1-2]

Le Marteau sans maître
910. Bard, Maja and Hans Vogt. "Pierre Boulez: *Le Marteau sans maître* (1954)." Vogt: 274-287.
911. Koblyakov, Lev. "P. Boulez *Le Marteau sans maître*: Analysis of pitch structure." ZM 8/1(1977): 24-39.
912. Levin, Gregory. "An analysis of movements III and IX from *Le Marteau sans maître* by Pierre Boulez." PhD dissertation (Theory and Composition): Brandeis University, 1975. 82 p. RILM 75/1533dd28. No DA listing.
913. Piencikowski, Robert T. "René Char et Pierre Boulez: Esquisse analytique du *Marteau sans maître*." SBM 4(1980): 193-264.
914. Stockhausen, Karlheinz. "Music and speech." R 6(1964): 40-64.

Piano Sonata No.2

915. Dechario, Joseph L. "A phrase structure analysis of the third movement of Boulez's Second Piano Sonata: An essay together with a comprehensive project in piano performance." DMA dissertation (Performance): University of Iowa, 1977. UM 77-28,527. DA XXXVIII.7, p.3791-A.

Piano Sonata No.3

916. Black, Robert. "Boulez's Third Piano Sonata: Surface and sensibility." PNM 20(1981-1982): 182-198.

917. Boulez, Pierre. "Sonate, que me veux-tu?" PNM 1/2(1962): 32-44. [Also in Boulez: 163-175]

918. ----. "Zu meiner III. Sonate." DBNM 3(1960): 27-40.

919. Ligeti, György. "À propos de la troisième Sonate de Boulez (1959)." MJ 16(1974): 6-8. [Translated and reprinted from *Die Reihe*]

920. Stahnke, Manfred. *Struktur und Aesthetik bei Boulez: Untersuchung zum Formanten "Trope" der dritten Klaviersonate.* Hamburg: Wagner, 1979. 236 p.

921. Stoianowa, Iwanka. "La Troisième Sonate de Boulez et le projet mallarméen du Livre." MJ 16(1974): 9-28.

922. Trenkamp, Wilma Anne. "The concept of Aléa in Boulez's *Constellation-Miroir*." ML 57(1976): 1-10.

923. Wait, Mark. "Aspects of literary and musical structure as reflected by the Third Piano Sonata of Pierre Boulez." DMA dissertation (Performance): Peabody Conservatory, 1976. No DA listing.

924. ----. "Liszt, Scriabin, and Boulez: Considerations of form." JALS 1(1977): 9-16.

Pli selon pli

925. Krastewa, Iwanka. "*Pli selon pli*: Portrait de Mallarmé." SMZ 113(1973): 16-24, 76-82, 143-150.

926. Miller, Roger L. "*Pli selon pli*: Pierre Boulez and the 'new lyricism.'" PhD dissertation: Case-Western Reserve University, 1978. No DA listing. *Polyphonie X*

927. Boulez, Pierre. "Le système mis à nu: *Polyphonie X* et *Structures* pour deux pianos." Boulez: 129-142.

Répons

928. Gerzso, Andrew. "Reflections on *Répons*." CMR 1/1(1984-1985): 23-34.

929. Oehlschlägel, Reinhard. "Koordination von Akustik und Musik: *Répons 3* von Pierre Boulez." MTX 9(1985): 51-54.

Rituel

930. Beiche, Michael. "Serielles Denken in *Rituel* von Pierre Boulez." AM 38(1981): 24-56.

931. Stoianova, Ivanka. "Narrativisme, téléologie et invariance dans l'oeuvre musicale: à propos de *Rituel* de Pierre Boulez." MJ 25(1976): 15-31.

Sonatine for Flute and Piano
932. Baron, Carol K. "An analysis of the pitch organization in Boulez's Sonatine for Flute and Piano." CM 20(1975): 87-95.

Structures for Two Pianos
933. Boulez, Pierre. "Le système mis à nu (*Polyphonie X* et *Structures* pour deux pianos)." Boulez: 129-142.
934. De Young, Lynden. "Pitch order and duration order in Boulez' *Structure Ia.*" PNM 16/2(1977-1978): 26-34.
935. Febel, Reinhard. *Musik für zwei Klaviere seit 1950 als Spiegel der Kompositionstechnik.* Herrenberg: Döring, 1978.
936. Fuhrmann, Roderich. "Boulez, Pierre (1925): *Structures I* (1952)." Zimmerschied: 170-187.
937. Kirchmeyer: 179-186.
938. Ligeti, György. "Pierre Boulez." R 4(1960): 36-62.
939. Wennerstrom.

Other works
940. Griffiths, Paul. *Boulez.* London: Oxford University Press, 1978.
941. Häusler, Josef and Pierre Stoll. "Musikalische Technik." DBNM 5(1963): 29-123.
942. McCalla, James Wesley. "'Between its human accessories': The art of Stéphane Mallarmé and Pierre Boulez." PhD dissertation: University of California, Berkeley, 1976. UM 77-04,520. DA XXXVII.9, p.5433-A.
943. Trenkamp, Wilma Anne. "A throw of the dice: An analysis of selected works by Pierre Boulez." PhD dissertation (Theory): Case-Western Reserve University, 1973. 247 p. UM 74-02,571. DA XXXIV.8, p.5237-A.

BOYKAN, MARTIN (born 1931)

944. Harbison, John and Eleanor Cory. "Martin Boykan: String Quartet (1967): Two views." PNM 11/2(1973): 204-248. [Includes entire score]

BOZZA, EUGENE (born 1905)

945. Rowan, Denise Cecile Rogers. "The contributions for bassoon with piano accompaniment and orchestral accompaniment of Eugene Bozza with analyses of representative solo compositions." DMA dissertation: University of Southern Mississippi, 1978. No DA listing.

BRAHMS, JOHANNES (1833-1897)

Alto Rhapsody
946. Berry, Wallace. "Text and music in the *Alto Rhapsody.*" JMT 27(1983): 239-253.
947. Forte, Allen. "Motive and rhythmic contour in the *Alto Rhapsody.*" JMT 27(1973): 255-271.

BRAHMS

Chamber works [see also individual titles]
948. Czesla, Werner. "Studien zum Finale in der Kammermusik von Johannes Brahms." PhD dissertation (Musicology): Rheinische Friedrich-Wilhelms-Universität, Bonn, 1968.
949. Fenske, David. "Texture in the chamber music of Johannes Brahms." PhD dissertation (Musicology): University of Wisconsin, 1973. 540 p. UM 73-28,915. DA XXXIV.10, p.6684-5-A.
950. Kohlhase, Hans. "Brahms und Mendelssohn: Strukturelle Parallelen in der Kammermusik für Streicher." HJM 7(1984): 59-86.

Choral works
951. Bellamy, Sister Katherine Elizabeth. "Motivic development in the larger choral works of Johannes Brahms." PhD dissertation (Musicology): University of Wisconsin, 1973. 370 p. UM 73-30,307. DA XXXIV.10, p.6680-A.
952. Blume, Jürgen. "Johannes Brahms: *Schaffe in mir, Gott, ein reine Herz* (Op.29, Nr.2)." NZM 146/5(1985): 34-36.
953. Kross, Siegfried. *Die Chorwerke von Johannes Brahms.* Berlin: Hesse, 1958.
954. ----. "The choral music of Johannes Brahms." ACR 25/4(1983): 5-30.
955. Roeder, Michael T. "The choral music of Brahms: Historical models." CAUSM 5/2(1975): 26-46.
956. Rose, Michael Paul. "Structural integration in selected mixed a capella choral works of Brahms." PhD dissertation (Musicology): University of Michigan, 1971. 269 p. UM 72-4964. DA XXXII.7, p.4051-A.

Clarinet Quintet
957. Häfner, Roland. *Johannes Brahms: Klarinettenquintett.* München: W. Fink, 1978.

Clarinet Sonata
958. Schmidt, Christian Martin. *Verfähren der motivischthematischen Vermittlung in der Musik von Johannes Brahms, dargestellt an der Klarinettensonate F-Moll, Op.120, 1.* München: E. Katzbichler, 1971.

Piano Concertos
959. Collier, Michael. "The rondo movements of Beethoven's Concerto No.3 in C Minor, Op.37, and Brahms's Concerto No.1 in D Minor: A comparative analysis." TP 31(1978): 5-15.
960. Dahlhaus, Carl. *Johannes Brahms: Klavierkonzert Nr.1 D-Moll, Op.15.* München: W. Fink, 1965.
961. Rosen, Charles. "Influence: Plagiarism and inspiration." NCM 4(1980-1981): 87-100. [Piano Concerto No.1 in D Minor]
962. Vallis, Richard. "A study of late Baroque instrumental style in the piano concertos of Brahms." PhD dissertation (Musicology): New York University, 1978. No DA listing.

Piano Fantasias, Op.116
963. Dunsby, Jonathan. "The multi-piece in Brahms: *Fantasien* Op.116." Pascall: 167-190.

964. Mastroianni, Thomas Owen. "Elements of unity in *Fantasies*, Opus 116, by Brahms." DMA thesis: Indiana University, 1970. No DA listing.

965. Smith, Charles Justice, III. "Patterns and strategies: Four perspectives of musical characterization." PhD dissertation (Theory): University of Michigan, 1980. 130 p. UM 81-06,229. DA XLI.9, p.3776-7-A. [Intermezzo in E, Op.116, No.4]

966. Torkewitz, Dieter. "*Die entwickelte Zeit*: Zum Intermezzo Op.116, IV von Johannes Brahms." MF 32(1979): 135-140.

Piano Intermezzi, Op.117

967. Cadwallader, Allen. "Schenker's unpublished graphic analysis of Brahms's Intermezzo Op.117, No.2: Tonal structure and concealed motivic repetition." MTS 6(1984): 1-13.

968. Gamer, Carlton. "Busnois, Brahms, and the syntax of temporal proportions." Fs. Seay: 201-215. [Op.117, No.3]

969. Grippe, Kerry. "An analysis of the Three Intermezzi, Op.117, by Johannes Brahms." DMA dissertation (Piano Performance): Indiana University, 1980. No DA listing.

970. Velten, Klaus. "Entwicklungsdenken und Zeiterfahrung in der Musik von Johannes Brahms: Das Intermezzo Op.117, Nr.2." MF 34(1981): 56-59.

971. Zabrack, Harold. "Musical timing: A view of implicit musical reality." JALS 16(1984): 89-97. [Intermezzo Op.117, No.1]

Piano Pieces, Op.76

972. Kresky: 120-134. [Intermezzo, Op.76, No.7]

973. Lewin, David. "On harmony and meter in Brahms's Op.76, No.8." NCM 4(1980-1981): 261-265.

Piano Pieces, Op.118

974. Cone, Edward T. "Three ways of reading a detective story: Or, a Brahms Intermezzo." *Georgia Review* 31(1977): 554-574. [Op.118, No.1]

975. Lamb, James Boyd. "A graphic analysis of Brahms' Opus 118 with an introduction to Shenkerian theory and the reduction process." PhD dissertation (Fine Arts): Texas Tech University, 1979. 159 p. UM 80-13,258. DA XLI.2, p.454-A.

976. Miller, Lynus Patrick. "From analysis to performance: The musical landscape of Johannes Brahms's Opus 118, No.6." PhD dissertation: University of Michigan, 1979. 2 vols. UM 79-16,777. DA XL.2, p.530-A.

Piano Pieces, Op.119

977. Cadwallader, Allen. "Motivic unity and integration of structural levels in Brahms's B Minor Intermezzo, Op.119, No.1." TP 8/2(1983): 5-24.

978. Clements, Peter J. "Johannes Brahms: Intermezzo, Opus 119, No.1." CAUSM 7(1977): 31-51.

979. Newbould, Brian. "A new analysis of Brahms's Intermezzo in B Minor, Op.119, No.1." MR 38(1977): 33-43.

BRAHMS

Piano Rhapsodies, Op.79
980. Greenberg, Beth. "Brahms' Rhapsody in G Minor, Op.79, No.2."
ITO 1/9(1975): 21-32.

Piano Scherzo in Eb, Op.4
981. Joseph, Charles M. "Origins of Brahms's structural control."
CMS 21(1981): 8-24. [Scherzo in E-Flat Minor, Op.4 and others]

Piano Waltzes, Op.39
982. Kirsch, Winfried. "Die Klavier-Walzer Op.39 von Johannes
Brahms und ihre Tradition." JSIM 1969: 38-67.

Piano works [see also individual titles]
983. Auh, Mijai Youn. "Piano variations by Brahms, Liszt, and
Friedman on a theme by Paganini." DM dissertation (Piano): Indiana
University, 1980. No DA listing.
984. Baud, Jean-Marc. "Con molta espressione." SMZ 123(1983):
141-147. [Opp.116, 117, 118, 119]
985. Floros, Constantin. "Studien zu Brahms' Klaviermusik." BS
5(1983): 25-64.
986. Mason, Colin. "Brahms's piano sonatas." MR 5(1944): 112-118.
987. Mies, Paul. "Zu Werdegang und Strukturen der *Paginini-
Variationen* Op.35 für Klavier von Johannes Brahms." SM 11(1969):
323-332. [Also in Fs. Szabolcsi: 323-332]
988. Neighbour, Oliver. "Brahms and Schumann: Two Opus Nines
and beyond." NCM 7(1983-1984): 266-270. [*Variations on a theme of
Schumann*, Op.9]
989. Schläder, Jürgen. "Zur Funktion der Variantentechnik in den
Klaviersonaten F-Moll von Johannes Brahms und H-Moll von Franz Liszt."
HJM 7(1984): 171-199.
990. Sterling.

Requiem
991. Hollander, Hans. "Gedanken zum strukturellen Aufbau des
Brahmsschen *Requiem*." SMZ 105(1965): 326-333.
992. Musgrave, Michael. "Historical influences in the growth of
Brahms's *Requiem*." ML 53(1972): 3-17.
993. Newman, William S. "A 'basic motive' in Brahms' *German
Requiem*." MR 24(1963): 190-194.
994. Reinhardt, Klaus. "Motivisch-thematisches im *Deutschen Requiem*
von Brahms: Zum 100. Jahrestag der ersten völlstandigen Aufführung im
Leipzig am 28. Februar 1869." MK 39(1969): 13-17.
995. Westafer, Walter. "Over-all unity and contrast in Brahms's *German
Requiem*." PhD dissertation: University of North Carolina, 1973. 330 p.
UM 74-15,404. DA XXXV.1, p.507-A.

Songs
996. Boyer, Margaret Gene. "A study of Brahms' setting of the poems
from Tieck's *Liebesgeschichte der schönen Magelone und des Grafen Peter
von Provence*." PhD dissertation: Washington University, 1980. No DA
listing.

997. Bozart, George Severs, Jr. "Brahms's duets for soprano and alto, Op.61: A study in chronology and compositional process." SM 25(1983): 191-210.

998. ----. "The Lieder of Johannes Brahms, 1868-1871: Studies in chronology and compositional process." PhD dissertation (Musicology): Princeton University, 1978. 153 p. UM 79-05,620. DA XXXIX.9, p.5196-A.

999. ----. "Synthesizing word and tone: Brahms' setting of Hebbel's *Vorüber.*" Pascall: 77-98.

1000. Clarkson, Austin and Edward Laufer. "Analysis Symposium: Brahms Op.105/1." JMT 15/1-2(1971): 2-57. [*Wie Melodien zieht es*] [Also in Yeston: 227-274]

1001. Gerber, Rudolf. "Formprobleme im Brahmsschen Lied." JMP 39(1932): 23-42.

1002. Giebeler, Konrad. *Die Lieder von Johannes Brahms.* Münster/Westfalen: Max Kramer, 1959.

1003. Harrison, Max. *The Lieder of Brahms.* London: Cassell, 1972.

1004. Helms, Siegmund. "Die Melodiebildung in den Liedern von Johannes Brahms und ihr Verhältnis zu Volksliedern und volkstümlichen Weisen." Dissertation: Freie Universität, Berlin, 1968.

1005. Jacobsen, Christiane. *Das Verhältnis von Sprache und Musik in ausgewählten Liedern von Johannes Brahms, dargestellt an Parallelvertonungen.* Hamburg: Wagner, 1975. 2 vol. 724 p.

1006. Kielien, Marianne, Marion A. Guck and Charles J. Smith. "Analysis Symposium: Brahms's *Der Tod, das ist die kühle Nacht.*" ITO 2/6(1976): 16-43.

1007. Kinsey, Barbara. "Mörike poems set by Brahms, Schumann, and Wolf." MR 29(1968): 257-267.

1008. Misch, Ludwig. "Kontrapunkt und Imitation im Brahmsschen Lied." MF 11(1958): 155-160.

1009. Pisk, Paul A. "Dreams of death and life: A study of two songs by Johannes Brahms." Fs. Alderman: 227-234. [*Der Tod, das ist die kühle Nacht; Immer leiser wird mein Schlummer*]

1010. Rieger, Erwin. "Die Tonartencharacteristik im einstimmigen Klavierlied von Johannes Brahms." SZM 22(1955): 142-216.

1011. Stohrer, Sister M. Baptist. "The selection and setting of poetry in the solo songs of Johannes Brahms." PhD dissertation (Musicology): University of Wisconsin, 1974. 247 p. UM 74-18,958. DA XXXV.5, p.3042-A.

1012. Whittall, Arnold. "The *Vier ernste Gesänge* Op.121: Enrichment and uniformity." Pascall: 191-207.

String Quartets

1013. Fenske, David. "Contrapuntal textures in the String Quartets, Op.51, No.2 and Op.67 of Johannes Brahms." Fs. Kaufmann/W: 351-369.

1014. Forte, Allen. "Motivic design and structural levels in the first movement of Brahms's String Quartet in C Minor." MQ 69(1983): 471-502.

1015. Hill, William G. "Brahms' Opus 51: A diptych." MR 13(1952): 110-124.

1016. Wilke, Rainer. *Brahms, Reger, Schönberg, Streichquartette: Motivisch-thematische Prozesse und formale Gestalt.* Hamburg: Wagner, 1980.

String Quintet, Op.88
1017. Ravizza, Victor. "Möglichkeiten des Komischen in der Musik: Der letzte Satz des Streichquintetts in F Dur, Op.88 von Johannes Brahms." AM 31(1974): 137-150.
1018. Redlich, Hans F. "Bruckner and Brahms Quintets in F." ML 36(1955): 253-258.

Symphonies [see also individual titles]
1019. ASO 53(1983).
1020. Cuyler, Louise E. "Progressive concepts of pitch relationships as observed in the symphonies of Brahms." Fs. Fox: 164-180.
1021. Hendrickson, Hugh. "Rhythmic activity in the symphonies of Brahms." ITO 2/6(1976): 5-15.
1022. Klein, Rudolf. "Die konstructiven Grundlagen der Brahms-Symphonien." OMZ 23(1968): 258-263.
1023. Rittenhouse, Robert J. "Rhythmic elements in the symphonies of Johannes Brahms." PhD dissertation (Theory): University of Iowa, 1967. UM 68-971. DA XXVIII.8, p.3212-3-A.
1024. Schulze, Werner. *Temporelationen in symphonischen Werk von Beethoven, Schubert und Brahms.* Bern: Kreis und Freude um Hans Kayser, 1981.
1025. Stellfeld, Bent. "Kontrapunktik og den funktion i Brahms's orkestervoeker." DAM 14(1983): 115-132.

Symphony No.1
1026. Moser, Hans Joachim. "Zur Sinndeutung der Brahms'schen C-Moll Symphonie." OMZ 8(1953): 21-24.
1027. Musgrave, Michael. "Brahms's First symphony: Thematic coherence and its secret origin." MA 2(1983): 117-134.
1028. Ravizza, Victor. "Konflikte in Brahms'scher Musik: Zum ersten Satz der C-Moll-Sinfonie Op.68." SBM 2(1974): 75-90.
1029. Seedorf, Thomas. "Brahms' 1. Symphonie: Komponieren als Auseinandersetzung mit der Geschichte." MB 15/5(1983): 10-14.

Symphony No.2
1030. Epstein.
1031. Komma, Karl Michael. "Das Scherzo der 2. Symphonie von Johannes Brahms." Fs. Wiora: 448-457.
1032. Schachter, Carl. "The first movement of Brahms's Second Symphony: The first theme and its consequences." MA 2(1983): 55-68.

Symphony No.3
1033. Brown, A. Peter. "Brahms' Third Symphony and the New German School." JM 2(1983): 434-452.
1034. Musgrave, Michael. *"Frei aber Froh*: A reconsideration." NCM 3(1979-1980): 251-258.

Symphony No.4

1035. Klein, Rudolf. "Die Doppelgerüsttechnik in der Passacaglia der IV. Symphonie von Brahms." OMZ 27(1972): 641-648.

1036. Osmond-Smith, David. "The retreat from dynamism: A study of Brahms's Fourth Symphony." Pascall: 147-166.

1037. Siegmund-Schultze, Walter. "Brahms' vierte Sinfonie." Fs. Schneider/80: 241-254.

Variations on a Theme of Haydn

1038. Forte, Allen. "The structural origin of exact tempi in the *Brahms-Haydn Variations*." MR 18(1957): 138-149.

1039. McCorkle, Donald M., ed. *Johannes Brahms: Variations on a Theme by Haydn for Orchestra, Op.56a and for Two Pianos, Op.56b.* Norton Critical Scores. New York: W.W. Norton, 1976.

Violin Concerto

1040. Weiss-Aigner, Günter. *Johannes Brahms: Violinkonzert D-Dur.* München: W. Fink, 1979.

1041. ----. "Komponist und Geiger: Joseph Joachims Mitarbeit am Violinkonzert von Johannes Brahms." NZM 135(1974): 232-236.

Violin Sonatas

1042. Fischer, Richard S. "Brahms' technique of motive development in his Sonata in D Minor, Opus 108, for Piano and Violin." DMA dissertation (Performance): University of Arizona, 1964. UM 64-8763. DA XXV.3, p.1956.

1043. Hollander, Hans. "Der melodische Aufbau in Brahms' *Regenlied* Sonate." NZM 125(1964): 5-7. (Op.78)

Other works

1044. Borchardt, Georg. "Ein Viertonmotiv als melodische Komponente in Werken von Brahms." HJM 7(1984): 101-112.

1045. Braun, Hartmut. "Ein Zitat: Beziehungen zwischen Chopin und Brahms." MF 25(1972): 317-321.

1046. Brusatti, Otto. "Zur thematischen Arbeit bei Johannes Brahms." SZM 31(1980): 191-206.

1047. Czesla, Werner. "Motivische Mutationen in Schaffen von Johannes Brahms." Fs. Schmidt-Görg/70: 64-72.

1048. Dunsby, Jonathan Mark. "Analytical studies of Brahms." PhD dissertation: University of Leeds, 1976. 173 p. [Opp.24, 60, 98, 119, No.1]

1049. ----. Structural ambiguity in Brahms: Analytical approaches to four works. Ann Arbor: UMI Research Press, 1981. [Opp.24, 60, 98, 119, No.1]

1050. Federhofer, Hellmut. "Johannes Brahms--Arnold Schönberg und der Fortschritt." SZM 34(1983): 111-130.

1051. Frisch, Walter Miller. *Brahms and the principle of developing variation.* Berkeley: University of California Press, 1984.

1052. ----. "Brahms's sonata structures and the principle of developing variation." PhD dissertation (Musicology): University of California, Berkeley, 1981. UM 82-00,106. DA XLII.7, p.2922-A.

1053. Hiebert, Elfrieda. "The Janus figure of Brahms: A future built upon the past." JALS 16(1984): 72-88.

1054. Hirsch, Hans. *Rhythmisch-metrische Untersuchungen zur Variationstechnik bei Johannes Brahms.* Hamburg, 1963.

1055. Hollander, Hans. "Die Terzformel als musikalisches Bauelement bei Brahms." NZM 133(1972): 439-441.

1056. Jordahl, Robert. "A study of the use of the chorale in the works of Mendelssohn, Brahms, and Reger." PhD dissertation (Theory): University of Rochester, 1965. UM 66-2360. DA XXVII.6, p.1861-2-A.

1057. Klenz, William. "Brahms, Op.38: Piracy, pillage, plagiarism, parody." MR 34(1973): 39-50.

1058. Kross, Siegfried. "Brahms und der Kanon." Fs. Schmidt-Görg: 175-187.

1059. Lesznai, Lajos. "Auf den Spuren einer ungarischen Intonation in den Werken von Johannes Brahms." MG 21(1971): 455-458.

1060. Mitschka, Arno. "Der Sonatensatz in den Werken von Johannes Brahms." PhD dissertation (Musicology): Johannes-Gutenberg-Universität, Mainz, 1961.

1061. Morik, Werner. *Johannes Brahms und sein Verhältnis zum deutschen Volkslied.* Tutzing: H. Schneider, 1965.

1062. Truscott, Harold. "Brahms and sonata style." MR 25 (1964): 186-201.

1063. Velten, Klaus. "Das Princip der entwickelnden Variation bei Johannes Brahms und Arnold Schönberg." MB 6(1974): 547-555.

1064. Webster, James. "Brahms's *Tragic Overture*: The form of tragedy." Pascall: 99-124.

1065. ----. "Schubert's sonata form and Brahms's first maturity." NCM 2/1(1978): 1835, 3(1979-1980): 52-71.

1066. Wetschky, Jürgen. *Der Kanontechnik in der Instrumentalmusik von Johannes Brahms.* Kölner Beiträge zur Musikforschung 35. Regensburg: G. Bosse, 1967.

1067. Zingerle, Hans. "Chromatische Harmonik bei Brahms und Reger: Ein Vergleich." SZM 27(1966): 151-185.

BRANT, HENRY (born 1913)

1068. Drennen, Dorothy Carter. "Henry Brant's use of ensemble dispersion." MR 38(1977): 65-68.

1069. ----. "Relationship of ensemble dispersion to structure in the music of Henry Brant." PhD dissertation (Theory): University of Miami, 1975. UM 76-04,683. DA XXXVI.9, p.5624-A.

1070. Sankey, Stuart. "Henry Brant's *Grand universal circus*." JR 3/3(1956): 21-37.

BREDEMEYER, REINER (born 1929)

1071. Kneipel, Eberhard. "Die Analyse: Konzert für Oboe und Orchester von Reiner Bredemeyer." MG 29(1979): 286-289.

1072. Thiel, Wolfgang. "Reiner Bredermeyers Film- und Fernsehmusiken." MG 23(1973): 648-653.

BRÉGENT, MICHEL-GEORGES (born 1948)

1073. Petrowska-Brégent, Christina. "The concept of *Geste*." CCM 9(1974): 65-79.

BRETTINGHAM SMITH, JOLYON (born 1949)

1074. Schmidt, Christian Martin. "Jolyon Brettingham Smith." NZM 144/6(1983): 22-26.

BRÉVILLE, PIERRE ONFROY DE (1861-1949)

1075. Daitz, Mimi Segal. "The songs of Pierre de Bréville (1861-1949)." PhD dissertation (Music Education): New York University, 1974. 365 p. UM 74-17,137. RILM 74/482dd27. No DA listing.
1076. Kniesner. [*Sonate en ré majeur*, Piano]

BRIAN, HAVERGAL (1876-1972)

1077. Pike, Lionel. "The tonal structure of Brian's *Gothic Symphony*." TEMPO 138(1981): 33-40.
1078. Truscott, Harold and Paul Rapoport. *Havergal Brian's "Gothic" Symphony: Two studies*. Potters Bar: Havergal Brian Society, 1978.

BRICHT, WALTER (1904-1970)

1079. Martin, Paul David. "The seven solo piano sonatas of Walter Bricht." DMA dissertation (Piano Pedagogy): Indiana University, 1977. No DA listing.
1080. Wylie, Ted David. "A survey of the solo vocal compositions of Walter Bricht with analyses of selected songs." DMA dissertation: Indiana University, 1979. No DA listing.

BRIDGE, FRANK (1879-1941)

1081. Howells, Herbert. "Frank Bridge." ML 22(1941): 208-215.
1082. Keating, Roderic Maurice. "The songs of Frank Bridge." DMA dissertation: University of Texas, 1970. No DA listing.
1083. Payne, Anthony. "The music of Frank Bridge." TEMPO 106 (1973): 18-25, 107(1973): 11-18.

BRISTOW, GEORGE F. (1825-1898)

1084. Kauffman, Byron F. "The choral works of George F. Bristow (1825-1898) and William H. Fry (1815-1864)." DMA (Choral Music): University of Illinois, 1975. 107 p. UM 76-06,815. DA XXXVI.9, p.5627-A.

BRITTEN, BENJAMIN (1913-1976)

Albert Herring
    1085. Keller, Hans. *Benjamin Britten: Albert Herring: Analytical notes.* New York: Boosey & Hawkes, 1949.

Beggar's Opera
    1086. Keller, Hans. "Britten's *Beggar's Opera*." TEMPO 10 (1948-1949): 7-13.
    1087. Wolff, Hellmuth Christian. "Britten und die *Beggar's Opera*." MZ 11(1955): 62-65.

Billy Budd
    1088. Porter, Andrew. "Britten's *Billy Budd*." ML 33(1952): 111-118.
    1089. Schuh, Willi. "*Billy Budd*: Zur musikalischen Struktur." MZ 11(1955): 14-17.

Cantata academica
    1090. Bradshaw, Susan. "Britten's *Cantata academica*." TEMPO 53-54(1960): 22-34.

Canticles
    1091. Gordon, Samuel S. "Benjamin Britten's *Canticles I, II* and *III*: A structural and stylistic analysis." DM dissertation (Voice): Indiana University, 1974. 147 p. No DA listing.

Curlew River
    1092. Flynn, William T. "Britten the progressive." MR 44(1983): 44-52.
    1093. Laade, Wolfgang. "Benjamin Brittens Mysterienspiel *Curlew River* und die japanischen Vorbilder." MB 1(1969): 562-565.
    1094. Rhoads, Mary Ruth Schneyer. "Influences of Japanese *hogaku* manifest in selected compositions by Peter Mennin and Benjamin Britten." PhD dissertation (Theory): Michigan State University, 1969. 397 p. No DA listing.

Death in Venice
    1095. Dickinson, A.E.F. "Current Chronicle: Britten's new opera." MQ 60(1974): 470-478.
    1096. Evans, John. "Britten's Venice workshop: 1. The sketch book." SN 12(1984-1985): 7-24.
    1097. Milliman, Joan Ann. "Benjamin Britten's symbolic treatment of sleep, dream and death as manifest in his opera *Death in Venice*." PhD dissertation: University of Southern California, 1977. No DA listing.

Gloriana
    1098. Mitchell, Donald. "Some observations on *Gloriana*." MMR 83(1953): 255-260.

A Midsummer-Night's Dream
    1099. Bach, Jan Morris. "An analysis of Britten's *A Midsummer Night's Dream*." DMA dissertation (Composition): University of Illinois, 1971. 424 p. RILM 71/2916dd28. No DA listing.
    1100. Evans, Peter. "Britten's new opera: A preview." TEMPO 53-54(1960): 34-48.

Missa Brevis
    1101. Roseberry, Eric. "A note on Britten's *Missa Brevis*." TEMPO 53-54(1960): 11-16.

Noye's Fludde
    1102. Roseberry, Eric. "The music of *Noye's Fludde*." TEMPO 49(1958): 2-11.

Peter Grimes
    1103. ASO 31(1981)
    1104. Brett, Philip. *Benjamin Britten: Peter Grimes*. Cambridge: Cambridge University Press, 1983.
    1105. Deavel, R. Gary. "A study of two operas by Benjamin Britten: *Peter Grimes* and *The Turn of the Screw*." PhD dissertation (Theory): University of Rochester, 1970. 268 p. UM 70-17,398. DA XXXI.4, p.1831-A.
    1106. Foerster, Lilian. "Peter Grimes in score and performance." MU 1(1946-1947): 221-241.
    1107. Garbutt, J. W. "Music and motive in *Peter Grimes*." ML 44 (1963): 334-342.
    1108. McGiffert, Genevieve. "The musico-dramatic techniques of Benjamin Britten: A detailed study of *Peter Grimes*." PhD dissertation: University of Denver, 1970.
    1109. Payne, Anthony. "Dramatic use of tonality in *Peter Grimes*." TEMPO 66/67(1963): 22-26.
    1110. Stein, Erwin. "Benjamin Britten: *Peter Grimes*." MZ 6(1954): 51-55.
    1111. ----. "*Peter Grimes*: Form und Geist." MZ 11(1955): 10-14.

Prince of the Pagodas
    1112. Mitchell, Donald. "An afterword on Britten's *Pagodas*: The Balinese sources." TEMPO 152(1985): 7-11.
    1113. ----. "Catching on to the technique in Pagoda-land." TEMPO 146(1983): 13-24.

Rape of Lucretia
    1114. Squire, W. H. Haddon. "The aesthetic hypothesis and *The Rape of Lucretia*." TEMPO 1/(1946): 1-9.

Rejoice in the Lamb
    1115. LePage, Peter V. "Benjamin Britten's *Rejoice in the Lamb*." MR 33(1972): 122-137.

BRITTEN

Saint Nicholas
1116. Holst, Imogen. *"Saint Nicholas."* MZ 7(1954): 33-34.

Sonata for Cello
1117. Evans, Peter. "Britten's Cello Sonata." TEMPO 58(1961): 8-19.

Songs from the Chinese
1118. Noble, Jeremy. "Britten's *Songs from the Chinese*." TEMPO 52(1959): 25-29.

Spring Symphony
1119. Stein, Erwin. "Britten's *Spring Symphony*." TEMPO 15(1950): 19-24.

String Quartet, No.2
1120. Keller, Hans. "Benjamin Britten's Second Quartet." TEMPO 3(1947): 6-8.

Symphony for Cello
1121. Evans, Peter. "Britten's Cello Symphony." TEMPO 66/67(1963): 2-15.

Three Canticles
1122. Brown, David. "Britten's *Three Canticles*." MR 21(1960): 55-65.

The Turn of the Screw
1123. Deavel, R. Gary. "A study of two operas by Britten: *Peter Grimes* and *The Turn of the Screw*." PhD dissertation (Theory): University of Rochester, 1970. 268 p. UM 70-17,398. DA XXXI.4, p.1831-A.
1124. Howard, Patricia. *Benjamin Britten: The Turn of the Screw*. Cambridge: Cambridge University Press, 1985.
1125. Mitchell, Donald. *"Turn of the Screw*: A note on its thematic organization." MMR 85(1955): 95-100.
1126. Stein, Erwin. *"Turn of the Screw* and its musical idiom." TEMPO 34(1955): 6-14.
1127. ----. *"The Turn of the Screw*: Das musikalische Idiom." MZ 11(1955): 53-61.

War Requiem
1128. Bagley, Peter B.E. "Benjamin Britten's *War Requiem*: A structural analysis." DM dissertation (Choral Conducting): Indiana University, 1972. 170 p. No DA listing.
1129. Boyd, Malcolm. "Britten, Verdi, and the Requiem." TEMPO 86(1968): 2-6.
1130. Evans, Peter. "Britten's *War Requiem*." TEMPO 61-62(1961-1962): 20-39.
1131. Whittall, Arnold M. "Tonal instability in Britten's *War Requiem*." MR 24(1963): 201-204.

Wedding Anthem
1132. Mitchell, Donald. *"Wedding Anthem."* MZ 7(1954): 31-32.

Other works
1133. Brewster, Robert G. "The relationship between poetry and music in the original solo-vocal music of Benjamin Britten through 1965." PhD dissertation (Musicology): Washington University, 1967. UM 68-5122. DA XXVIII.10, p.4198-A.

1134. Damp, Alice Bancroft. "The fusion of sacred and secular elements in Benjamin Britten's vocal and choral literature." DMA dissertation (Performance): University of Rochester, 1973. No DA listing.

1135. Dundore, Mary Margaret. "The choral music of Benjamin Britten." DMA dissertation (Choral Music): University of Washington, 1964. UM 65-3257. DA XXV.11, p.6675-6.

1136. Evans, Peter. "Britten's fourth creative decade." TEMPO 106 (1973): 8-17.

1137. ----. *The music of Benjamin Britten.* London: Dent; Minneapolis: University of Minnesota Press, 1979.

1138. Garvie, Peter. "'Darkly Bright': Britten's moral imagination." CCM 1(1970): 59-66.

1139. Handel, Darrell. "Britten's use of the passacaglia." TEMPO 94 (1970): 2-6.

1140. Hansler

1141. Hart.

1142. Holst, Imogen. "Let's make an opera!" MZ 11(1955): 46-50.

1143. Howard, Patricia. *The operas of Benjamin Britten: An introduction.* London: Barrie & Rockcliff, 1969.

1144. Jennings, John Wells. "The influence of W.H. Auden on Benjamin Britten." DMA dissertation (Choral Music): University of Illinois, 1979. UM 79-15,370. DA XL.1, p.19-A. [*Our hunting fathers*, Op.8; *On this island*, Op.11; *Hymn to St. Cecilia*, Op.27]

1145. Mark, Christopher. "Britten's *Quatre chansons françaises.*" SN 10(1983): 22-35.

1146. ----. "Britten's revisionary practice: Practical and creative." TEMPO 66/67(1963): 15-22.

1147. ----. "Contextually transformed tonality in Britten." MA 4/3 (1985): 265-287. [String Quartet No.1, Op.22; *Rats Away!* from *Our hunting fathers*, Op.8; *Villes* from *Les Illuminations*, Op.18.]

1148. ----. Simplicity in early Britten." TEMPO 147(1983): 8-14. [*Seven Sonnets of Michelangelo*, Op.22, and other vocal and chamber music]

1149. Mitchell, Donald and Hans Keller, eds. *Benjamin Britten: A commentary on his works from a group of specialists.* London: C. Tinling, 1952.

1150. Simons, Harriett Rose. "The use of the chorus in the operas of Benjamin Britten." DMA dissertation (Conducting): Indiana University, 1970. No DA listing.

1151. Stein, Erwin. "Benjamin Britten und die englische Tradition." MZ 7(1954): 11-20.

1152. ----. "Brittens Sinfonien." MZ 7(1954): 46-53.

1153. Stimpson, Mansel. "Britten's last work." TEMPO 155(1985): 34-36. [*Praise We Great Men*]
1154. Whittall, Arnold. *The music of Britten and Tippett: Studies in themes and techniques*. Cambridge: Cambridge University Press, 1982.
1155. ----. "The study of Britten: Triadic harmony and tonal structure." PRMA 106(1979-1980): 27-41.
1156. ----. "Tonality in Britten's song cycles with piano." TEMPO 96(1971): 2-11.
1157. Special Issue: MZ 7(1954) *Britten*.
1158. Special Issue: MZ 22(1955) *Britten: Das Opernwerk*.

BRONS, CAREL (1931-1983)

1159. Visser, Piet. "The Schnitger Organ and the Schnitger Prize of the City of Zwolle awarded to Carel Brons for his composition *Prisms*." SS 36(1968): 9-20.

BROWN, EARLE (born 1926)

1160. Quist, Pamela Layman. "Indeterminate form in the work of Earle Brown." DMA dissertation (Composition): Peabody Conservatory, 1984. 139 p. No DA listing.
1161. Vogt: 314-321. [*Available Forms II* (1962)]

BRUCH, MAX (1838-1920)

1162. Vick, Bingham Lafayette, Jr. "The five oratorios of Max Bruch (1838-1920)." PhD dissertation (Musicology): Northwestern University, 1977. UM 77-32,363. DA XXXVIII.8, p.4443-A.

BRUCKNER, ANTON (1824-1896)

Masses
1163. Diether, Jack. "An introduction to Bruckner's Mass in E Minor." CD 2/6(1950): 60-65.
1164. Mathews, Theodore Kenneth. "The masses of Anton Bruckner: A comparative analysis." PhD dissertation (Musicology): University of Michigan, 1974. 382 p. UM 75-00,754. DA XXXV.8, p.5449-A.
1165. Newlin, Dika. "Bruckner's three great masses." CD 2/8(1958): 3-16.
1166. Scholz, Horst-Günther. *Die Form der reifen Messen Anton Bruckners*. Berlin: Merseburger, 1961.
1167. Simpson, Robert. "Thoughts on Bruckner's E Minor Mass." CD 2/4(1946): 30-35.
1168. Wellesz, Egon. "Anton Bruckner and the process of musical creation." MQ 24(1938): 265-290.
1169. Wessely, Othmar. "Vergangenheit und Zukunft in Bruckners Messe in D-Moll." OMZ 29(1974): 412-418.

Os Justi

1170. David, Johann Nepomuk. "Die "Jupiter Symphonie": Eine Studie über die thematische-melodischen Zusammenhänge. Göttingen: Vandenhoeck und Reuprecht, 1960: 35-39.

Quartets

1171. Nowak, Leopold. "Form und Rhythmus in ersten Satz des Streichquartetts von Anton Bruckner." Fs. Engle/H: 260-273.

Symphonies [see also individual titles]

1172. Bauer, Moritz. "Zur Form in den sinfonischen Werken Anton Bruckners." Fs. Kretzschmar: 12-14.

1173. Buschler, David Martin. "Development in the first movements of Bruckner's symphonies." PhD dissertation: City University of New York, 1975. 249 p. UM 75-16,960. DA XXXVI.2, p.589-A.

1174. Dahlhaus, Carl. "Ist Bruckners Symphonik formbildend?" BRJ (1982-1983): 19-26.

1175. Doernberg, Erwin. *The life and symphonies of Anton Bruckner.* London: Barrie & Rockcliff, 1960.

1176. Dokalik, Alfred. "Anton Bruckners Symphonien: Auswahl und Darbietung an der A.HS." ME 28(1974-1975): 8-14, 109-113, 206-212.

1177. Engel, Gabriel. *The symphonies of Anton Bruckner.* New York: Bruckner Society of America, 1955.

1178. Floros, Constantin. "Die Zitate in Bruckners Symphonik." BRJ (1982-1983): 7-18.

1179. Grunsky, Karl. *Bruckners Symphonien.* Berlin: Schlesinger, 1907.

1180. Halm, August. *Die Symphonie Anton Bruckners.* München: G. Müller, 1923.

1181. Krohn, Ilmari Henrik Reinhold. *Anton Bruckners Symphonien: Untersuchung Bber Formenbau und Stimmungsgehalt.* 3 vols. Ser. B, 86, 99, 109. Helsinki: Suomalainen Tiedeakat; Wiesbaden: Harrassowitz, 1955-1957.

1182. Moravesik, Michael J. "The coda in the symphonies of Anton Bruckner." MR 34(1973): 241-258.

1183. Notter, Werner. *Schematismus und Evolution in der Sinfonik Anton Bruckners.* München: E. Katzbichler, 1983.

1184. Oeser, Fritz. *Die Klangstruktur der Bruckner-Symphonie: Eine Studie zur Frage der Originalfassungen.* Leipzig: Musikwissenschaftlicher Verlag, 1939.

1185. Schön, Werner. "Studien zur Symphonik Bruckners: Motivisch-thematische Substanz und musikalischer Prozess." PhD dissertation (Musicology): Marburg, n.d.

1186. Werner, Eric. "Nature and function of the sequence in Bruckner's symphonies." Fs. Plamenac: 365-384.

1187. Wilcox, James H. "Bruckner and symphonic form." CD 2/9(1960): 89-99.

1188. ----. "The symphonies of Anton Bruckner." PhD dissertation (Theory): Florida State University, 1956. UM 18,675. DA XVI.11, p.2180.

1189. Wohlfahrt, Frank. *Anton Bruckners sinfonisches Werk: Stil- und Formerläuterung.* Leipzig: Musikwissenschaftlicher Verlag, 1943.

BRUCKNER

1190. Wünschmann, Theodor. *Anton Bruckners Weg als Symphoniker.* Beiträge zur Musikreflexion 4. Steinfeld: Salvator, 1976.

Symphony No.3
1191. Schnebel, Dieter. "Der erhörte Klang: Höranalyse am Beispiel von Bruckners Dritter." MB 11(1979): 159-164.
1192. Stephan, Rudolf. "Zu Anton Bruckners dritter Symphonie." BRS (1980): 65-73.
1193. Tröller, Josef. *Anton Bruckner: III. Symphonie D-moll.* München: W. Fink, 1976.

Symphony No.4
1194. Nowak, Leopold. "Die Drei Final-Sätze zur IV. Symphonie von Anton Bruckner." OMZ 36(1981): 2-11.
1195. Röder, Thomas. "Motto und symphonischer Zyklus: Zu den Fassungen von Anton Bruckners vierter Symphonie." AM 42(1985): 166-177.

Symphony No.5
1196. Nowak, Leopold. "Anton Bruckners Formwille, dargestellt am Finale seiner V. Symphonie." Fs. Anglés: 609-613.
1197. Wieninger, Herbert. "Das Finale von Bruckners V. Sinfonie." ME 24(1970-1971): 9-13.

Symphony No.6
1198. Halbreich, Harry. "Bruckners Sechste: Kein Stiefkind mehr." BRS (1982): 85-92.

Symphony No.7
1199. Simpson, Robert. "The Seventh Symphony of Bruckner." MR 8(1947): 178-187.
1200. ----. "The Seventh Symphony of Bruckner: An analysis." CD 2/10(1961): 57-67.

Symphony No.8
1201. Dowson-Bowling, Paul. "Thematic and tonal unity in Bruckner's Eighth Symphony." MR 30(1969): 225-236.
1202. Floros, Constantin. "Die Fassungen der Achten Symphonie von Anton Bruckner." BRS 1980: 53-63.
1203. Marschner, Bo. "Den cykliske formproces i Anton Bruckners Symfoni Nr.8 og dens arketypiske grundlag." DAM 12(1981): 19-68.

Symphony No.9
1204. Adensamer, Michael. "Bruckners Einfluss auf die Modern (mit Beispielen aus dem Adagio der 9. Symphonie)." BRJ 1(1980): 27-31.
1205. Floros, Constantin. "Zur Deutung der Symphonik Bruckners: Das Adagio der neunten Symphonie." BRJ (1981): 89-96.

Te Deum
1206. Griesbacher, Peter. *Bruckners "Te Deum": Studie.* Regensburg: F. Pustet, 1919.

Other works

1207. Floros, Constantin. "Parallelen zwischen Schubert und Bruckner." Fs. Wessely: 133-146.

1208. Grant, Parks. "Bruckner and Mahler: The fundamental dissimilarity of their styles." MR 32(1971): 36-55.

1209. Grunsky, Hans. "Rang und Wesen der Musik Anton Bruckners." M 18(1964): 190-197.

1210. Howie, A.C. "Traditional and novel elements in Bruckner's sacred music." MQ 67(1981): 544-567.

1211. Kirsch, Winfried. *Studien zum Vokalstil der mittleren und späten Schaffensperiode Anton Bruckners.* Frankfurt/Main, 1958.

1212. Kurth, Ernst. *Bruckner.* Berlin: Max Hesses Verlag, 1925.

1213. Neumann, Friedrich. "Zum Verhaltnis von Akkordik und Melodik bei Anton Bruckner." BRJ (1981): 167-170.

1214. Newlin, Dika. *Bruckner, Mahler, Schoenberg.* New York: King's Crown Press, 1947.

1215. Redlich, Hans F. *Bruckner and Mahler.* Rev. ed. London: J.M. Dent, 1963.

1216. Schurtz, H. Paul. "The small sacred choral works of Anton Bruckner." MA dissertation (Musicology): Brigham Young University, 1976.

1217. Smith, Warren Storey. "The cyclic principle in musical design and the use of it by Bruckner and Mahler." CD 2/9(1960): 3-32.

1218. Unger, Klaus. "Studien zur Harmonik Bruckners: Einwirkung und Umwandlung älterer Klangstruckturen." PhD dissertation (Musicology): University of Heidelberg, 1969. 193 p.

1219. Vogel, Martin. "Bruckner in reiner Stimmung: Eine Analyse des Orgelpräludiums in C-Dur." BRJ (1981): 159-166.

1220. Wagner, Karl. "Bruckners Themenbildung als Kriterium seiner Stilentwicklung." OMZ 25(1970): 159-165.

1221. Wagner, Manfred. "Der Quint-Octavschrift als 'Maiestas'-Symbol bei Anton Bruckner." KJ 56(1972): 97-103.

1222. Wellesz, Egon. "Anton Bruckner and the process of musical creation." MQ 24(1938): 265-290.

1223. Wessely, Othmar, ed. *Bruckner Studien.* Wien: Verlag der Öesterreichischen Akademie der Wissenschafter, 1975. [Analyses of E Minor Mass by Leopold Nowak and Symphony No.2 by Franz Grasberger]

1224. Special Issue: OMZ 29/9(1974).

BRUNELLI, LOUIS JEAN (born 1925)

1225. Neilson, James. "*Essay for Cyrano*: Concert Overture for Band by Louis Jean Brunelli: Analysis by Dr. James Neilson from notes provided by the composer." JBR 15/1(1979-1980): 58-65.

BRUNSWICK, MARK (1902-1971)

1226. Gideon, Miriam. "The music of Mark Brunswick." ACA 13/1(1965): 1-10.

BRUYNÈL, TON (born 1934)

1227. Paagiviströmm, John. "Ton Bruynèl: Trying to set the ear free." KN 15(1982): 24-29. [*Translucent II, Phases, Soft Song, Serene, Toccare*]
1228. Vermeulen, Ernst. "*Signs* by Ton Bruynèl." SS 42(1970): 17-30.

BRYAR, GAVIN (born 1943)

1229. Potter, Keith. "Just the tip of the iceberg: Some aspects of Gavin Bryar's music." CT 22(1981): 4-15.

BUCK, DUDLEY (1839-1909)

1230. Gallo, William K. "The life and church music of Dudley Buck (1839-1909)." PhD dissertation (Musicology): Catholic University, 1968. UM 69-8886. DA XXIX.11, p.4038-A.

BURKHARD, WILLY (1900-1955)

1231. Burkhard, Simon. "Die Klavierlieder von Willy Burkhard." SMZ 100(1960): 154-158.
1232. Burkhard, Willy. "Mein Oratorium *Das Gesicht Jesajas* und die Musik unserer Zeit." SMZ 100(1960): 136-146.
1233. Eckhardt, Paul. "Musikalische Einführung in Burkhards Oratorium *Das Gesicht Jesajas*." MK 22(1952): 148-154.
1234. Indermühle, Fritz. "Die erzählende Musik im Schaff Willy Burkhards." SMZ 100(1960): 147-154.
1235. ----. "*Die Musikalische Übung*, Op.39, von Willy Burkhard." MK 41(1971): 79-88.
1236. Mohr, Ernst. "Betrachtungen zum Stil Willy Burkhards." SMZ 87(1947): 1-8.
1237. ----. "Die Messe von Willy Burkhard." M 12(1950): 67-72.
1238. Schmidt, Erich. "'Ahnung einer neuen Weltordnung': Willy Burkhard (1900-1955)." Fs. Mauersberger: 111-125.
1239. Sievers, Gerd. "Das Ezzolied in der Vertonung von Willy Burkhard und Johann Nepomuk David: Ein Vergleich." Fs. Engel/H: 335-363.

BUSH, ALAN (born 1900)

1240. Stevenson, Ronald. "Alan Bush: Committed composer." MR 25(1964): 232-242.

BUSONI, FERRUCCIO BENVENUTO (1866-1924)

1241. Leshowitz, Myron Howard. "A study of the life and work of Ferruccio Busoni and analyses of his *Waffentanz, All' Italia!*, and *Toccata* for use in performance and interpretation." PhD dissertation: New York University, 1979. No DA listing.

1242. Meloncelli, Raoul. "La *Turandot* di Busoni." CHI 31(1974): 167-186.

1243. Meyer, Heinz. *Die Klaviermusik Ferruccio Bussonis: Eine stilkritische Untersuchung.* Wolfenbüttel: Möseler, 1969.

1244. Previtali, Fernando. "La *Turandot* di Busoni." CHI 31(1974): 249-258.

1245. Raessler, Daniel M. "The '113' scales of Ferruccio Busoni." MR 43(1982): 51-56.

1246. Sitsky, Larry. "The six sonatinas for piano of Ferruccio Busoni." STU 2(1973): 155-173. [Also SMU 2(1968): 66-85]

1247. Winfield, George. "Ferruccio Busoni's compositional art: A study of selected works for piano solo composed between 1907 and 1923." PhD dissertation (Theory): Indiana University, 1981. No DA listing.

BUTTERWORTH, GEORGE (1885-1916)

1248. Curtis.

BUTTING, MAX (1888-1976)

1249. Vetter, Walther. "Max Butting als schaffender Musiker der Gegenwart: Eine Improvisation zur seinem 75. Geburtstag." MG 13(1963): 604-611.

1250. Wolf, Werner. "Neue Werke unserer Komponisten: Max Buttings X. Sinfonien; Bratschenkonzert von Hans-Christian Bartel." MG 14(1964): 80-83.

CAGE, JOHN (born 1912)

Cartridge Music
1251. Cope: 289-296.

Cheap Imitation
1252. Huber, Nicolaus A. "John Cage: *Cheap Imitation*." N 1(1980): 135-141.

HPSCHD
1253. Cage, John and Lejaren Hiller. "*HPSCHD*." S 2/2(1968): 10-19.

Mushrooms et Variationes
1254. Gronemeyer, Gisela. "'Paul Zukovsky does not agree': *Mushrooms et Variationes*: Eine neue Textkomposition von John Cage." MTX 10(1985): 26-31.

Roaratorio
1255. Reichert, Klaus. "*Finnegans Wake* auf der Spur bei John Cage: James Joyce und *Roaratorio*." MTX 10(1985): 23-26.

Sonata for Prepared Piano
1256. Goebels, Franzpeter. "Cage: Sonata for Prepared Piano 1948." SMZ 113(1973): 331-336.

Themes and Variations
    1257. Radano, Ronald M. "Themes and Variations by John Cage."
PNM 21(1982-1983): 417-424.

Variations I
    1258. Zimmerschied: 188-200.

Variations II
    1259. DeLio, Thomas. "John Cage's *Variations II*: The morphology of
a global structure." PNM 19/2(1980-1981): 351-371.
    1260. ----. "Sound, gesture and symbol: The relation between
notation and structure in American experimental music." I 10(1981):
199-219.

Other works
    1261. Beeler, Charles Alan. *"Winter Music/ Cartridge Music/ Atlas
Eclipticalis*: A study of three seminal works by John Cage." PhD
dissertation (Theory-Composition): Washington University, 1973. 33 p.
UM 74-7030.
    1262. Blum, Eberhard. "John Cage und seine Kompositionen für und
mit Flöten." T 5/6(1980-1981): 407-411.
    1263. Brooks, William. "Choice and change in Cage's recent music."
Fs. Cage: 82-100.
    1264. Duckworth, William Ervin. "Expanding notational parameters in
the music of John Cage." EdD dissertation: University of Illinois, 1972.
    1265. Francis, John Richard. "Structure in the solo piano music of
John Cage." PhD dissertation: Florida State University, 1976.
    1266. Fürst-Heidtmann, Monika. *Das präparierte Klavier des John
Cage.* Regensburg: G. Bosse, 1978.
    1267. Gillmor, Alan. "Satie, Cage, and the new asceticism." CT 25
(1982): 15-20.
    1268. Goebels, Franzpeter. "Bemerkungen und Materialen zum Stu-
dium neuer Klaviermusik." SMZ 113(1973): 265-268.
    1269. Griffiths, Paul. *Cage.* London: Oxford University Press, 1981.
    1270. Hinz, Klaus-Michael. "Ein Museum ohne Taschen: Zum
Hörspiel *James Joyce, Marcel Duchamp, Erik Satie: Ein Alphabet* von
John Cage." MTX 10(1985): 35-38.
    1271. Mahrt, Jürgen. "Die Temperatur der Sprache: Zu Texten von
John Cage." MTX 10(1985): 38-40.
    1272. Metzger, Heinz-Klaus and Rainer Riehn, eds. *John Cage.*
München: Edition Text und Kritik, 1978.
    1273. Shimoda, Kimiko. "Cage and Zen." CT 25(1982): 28-29.
    1274. Zukovsky, Paul. "John Cage's recent violin music." Fs. Cage:
101-106.

CARDEW, CORNELIUS (1936-1981)

    1275. Tilbury, John. "Cornelius Cardew." CT 26(1983): 4-12.

CARPENTER, JOHN ALDEN (1876-1951)

1276. Pierson, Thomas C. "The life and music of John Alden Carpenter." PhD dissertation (Theory): University of Rochester, 1952. No DA listing.

CARRILLO, JULIÁN (1875-1965)

1277. Benjamin, Gerald R. "Julián Carrillo and *Sonido Trece*." Y 3(1967): 33-68.

CARTER, ELLIOTT (born 1908)

Brass Quintet
1278. Lochhead, Judy. "Temporal structure in recent music." JMR 6(1986): 49-93.

Double Concerto
1279. Whittall, Arnold. "Post-twelve-note analysis." PRMA 94 (1967-1968): 1-17.

Duo for Violin and Piano
1280. Derby, Richard. "Carter's Duo for Violin and Piano." PNM 20 (1981-1982): 149-168.

Piano Concerto
1281. Grau, Irene Rosenberg. "Compositional techniques employed in the first movement of Elliott Carter's Piano Concerto." PhD dissertation (Theory): Michigan State University, 1973. UM 73-29,703. DA XXXIV.10, p.6685-A.
1282. Stone, Kurt. "Current Chronicle." MQ 55(1969): 559-572.

Piano Sonata
1283. Below, Robert. "Elliott Carter's Piano Sonata." MR 34(1973): 283-293.
1284. Haberkorn, Michael. "A study and performance of the piano sonatas of Samuel Barber, Elliott Carter and Aaron Copland." EdD dissertation: Columbia University, 1979. No DA listing.

Sonata for Flute, Oboe, Cello and Harpsichord
1285. Shinn, Randall. "An analysis of Elliott Carter's Sonata for flute, oboe, cello, and harpsichord (1952)." DMA dissertation (Composition): University of Illinois, 1975. UM 76-06,957. DA XXXVI.9, p.5631-A.

String Quartets [see also individual titles]
1286. Morgan, Robert P. "Elliott Carter's string quartets." MN 4/3(1974): 3-11.

String Quartet No.1
1287. McElroy, William Wiley. "Elliott Carter's String Quartet No.1: A study of heterogeneous rhythmic elements." MM dissertation: Florida State University, Tallahassee, 1973.
1288. Tingley, George Peter. "Metric modulation and Elliott Carter's First String Quartet." ITR 4/3(1980-1981): 3-11.

String Quartet No.2
1289. Gass, Glenn. "Elliott Carter's Second String Quartet: Aspects of time and rhythm." ITR 4/3(1980-1981): 12-23.
1290. Schweitzer.
1291. Steinberg, Michael. "Elliott Carter's Second String Quartet." SCORE 27(1960): 22-26.
1292. ----. "Elliott Carters 2. Streichquartett." MELOS 28(1961): 35-37.
1293. Wennerstrom.

String Quartet No.3
1294. Mead, Andrew W. "Pitch structure in Elliott Carter's String Quartet No.3." PNM 22(1983-1984): 31-60.

Variations for Orchestra
1295. Stewart, Robert. "Serial aspects of Elliott Carter's Variations for Orchestra." MR 34(1973): 62-65.

Other works
1296. Bernard, Jonathan W. "Spatial sets in recent music of Elliott Carter." MA 2(1983): 5-34.
1297. Breedon, Daniel Franklin. "An investigation of the influence of the metaphysics of Alfred North Whitehead upon the formal-dramatic compositional procedures of Elliott Carter." DMA dissertation (Composition): University of Washington, 1975. UM 76-17,414. DA XXXVII.2, p.678-9-A.
1298. DeLio, Thomas. "Spatial design in Elliott Carter's *Canon for 3*." ITR 4/1(1980-1981): 1-12.
1299. Geissler, Fredrick Dietzmann. "Considerations of tempo as a structural basis in selected orchestral works of Elliott Carter." DMA dissertation (Composition): Cornell University, 1974. UM 74-24,233. DA XXXV.5, p.3036-A.
1300. Glock, William. "A note on Elliott Carter." SCORE 12(1955): 47-52.
1301. Goldman, Richard Franko. "The music of Elliott Carter." MQ 43(1957): 151-170.
1302. Hines: 36-91.
1303. Northcott, Bayan. "Carter the progressive." *Elliott Carter: A 70th-birthday tribute.* London: G. Schirmer, 1978: 4-7, 10-11. 1304. Rosen, Charles. *The music languages of Elliott Carter.* Washington, D.C.: Music Division, Research Services, Library of Congress, 1984.
1305. Schiff, David. "'In Sleep, in Thunder': Elliott Carter's portrait of Robert Lowell." TEMPO 142(1982): 2-9.

1306. ----. *The music of Elliott Carter.* London: Eulenberg Books; New York: Da Capo Press, 1983.
1307. Skulsky, Abraham. "Elliott Carter." ACA 3/2(1953): 2-16.

CASTALDO, JOSEPH (born 1927)

1308. Chittum, Donald. "Current Chronicle." MQ 53(1967): 254-256. [*Dichotomy* for Woodwind Quartet]
1309. ----. "Current Chronicle." MQ 55(1969): 95-99. [*Flight*]
1310. ----. "Current Chronicle." MQ 57(1971): 138-141. [*Cycle*]

CASTELNUOVO-TEDESCO, MARIO (1895-1968)

1311. Higham, Peter Anthony. "Castelnuovo-Tedesco's works for guitar." MM dissertation: University of Alberta, 1977. [Opp.143, 152]
1312. Holmberg, Mark Leonard. "Thematic contours and harmonic idioms of Mario Castelnuovo-Tedesco, as exemplified in the solo concertos." PhD dissertation (Music Theory): Northwestern University, 1974. UM 75-7925. DA XXXV.10, p.6753-A.
1313. Scalin, Burton Howard. "Operas by Mario Castelnuovo-Tedesca." PhD dissertation (Music History): Northwestern University, 1980. UM 80-26,919. DA XLI.8, p.3316-A.

CASTÉRÈDE, JACQUES (born 1926)

1314. Delente, Gail Buchanan. "Selected piano music in France since 1945." PhD dissertation (Performance Practice): Washington University, 1966. UM 66-11,869. DA XXVII.6, p.1849-A. [*Diagrammes*, Four Etudes, Passacaglia and Fugue]

CAZDEN, NORMAN (1914-1980)

1315. Haufrecht, Herbert. "The writings of Norman Cazden: Composer and musicologist." ACA 8/2(1958): 2-9.

CHADWICK, GEORGE WHITEFIELD (1854-1931)

1316. Campbell, Douglas G. "George W. Chadwick: His life and works." PhD dissertation (Theory): University of Rochester, 1957. 363 p. UR 1242.
1317. Yellin, Victor. "The life and operatic works of George Whitefield Chadwick." PhD dissertation: Harvard University, 1957. 421 p. No DA listing.

CHAMPAGNE, CLAUDE ADONAI (1891-1965)

1318. Walsh, Anne. "The life and works of Claude Adonai Champagne." PhD dissertation (Musicology): Catholic University, 1972. 183 p. UM 72-24,581. DA XXXIII.3, p.1191-A.

CHANCE, JOHN BARNES (born 1932)

    1319. Chance, Barnes. "Variations on a Korean folk song." JBR 3/1 (1966-1967): 13-16.

CHANLER, THEODORE WARD (1902-1961)

    1320. Cox, Donald Ray. "Theodore Ward Chanler: A biographical and analytical study of the man and three song cycles." DMA dissertation (Performance): University of Southern Mississippi, 1976. UM 76-23,002. DA XXXVII.4, p.1863-A.
    1321. Kolb, Bruce Lanier. "The published songs of Theodore Chanler." DMA dissertation (Performance): Louisiana State University, 1976. No DA listing.
    1322. Nordgren, Elliott Alfred. "An analytical study of the songs of Theodore Chanler (1902-1961)." PhD dissertation (Music Education): New York University, 1980. UM 81-10,675. DA XLI.12, p.4882-A.

CHAUSSON, ERNEST (1855-1899)

    1323. Barricelli, Jean-Pierre and Leo Weinstein. *Ernest Chausson: The composer's life and works.* Norman: Oklahoma University Press, 1955.
    1324. Chailley. [*Poème*]
    1325. Grover, Ralph S. "The influence of Franck, Wagner, and Debussy on representative works of Ernest Chausson." PhD dissertation: University of North Carolina, 1966. UM 67-992. DA XXVII.9, p.3072-3-A.
    1326. Hirsbrunner, Theo. "Debussy--Maeterlicnk--Chauson: Literary and musical connections." MMA 13(1984): 57-85. [*Serres chaudes*]
    1327. ----. "Debussy-Maeterlinck-Chausson: Musikalische und literarische Querverbindungen." Fs. Schuh: 47-66. [*Serres chaudes*]

CHÁVEZ, CARLOS (1899-1978)

    1328. Nordyke, Diane. "The piano works of Carlos Chávez." PhD dissertation (Fine Arts): Texas Tech University, 1982. 197 p. UM 82-21,981. DA XLIII.7, p.2151-A.
    1329. Parker, Robert L. *Carlos Chávez: Mexico's modern-day Orpheus.* Boston: G.K. Hall, 1983.

CHERUBINI, MARIA LUIGI (1760-1842)

    1330. Saak, Siegfried. *Studien zur Instrumentalmusik Luigi Cherubinis.* Kassel: Bärenreiter-Antiquariat, 1979. [Overtures, D-Major Symphony, String Quartets and Quintets]
    1331. Selden, Margery J. S. "The French operas of Luigi Cherubini." PhD dissertation (Music History): Yale University, 1951. UM 65-1701. DA XXVI.12, p.7360.
    1332. White, Maurice L. "The motets of Luigi Chrubini." PhD dissertation (Musicology): University of Michigan, 1968. UM 69-2406. DA XXIX.8, p.2746-7-A.

CHESLOCK, LOUIS (1898-1981)

1333. Sprenkle, Elam Ray. "The life and works of Louis Cheslock." DMA dissertation (Performance): Peabody Conservatory, 1979. 197 p. UM 79-27,206. DA XL.6, p.2977-A.

CHESNOKOV, PAVEL GREGORYEVICH (1877-1944)

1334. Elzinga, Harry. "The sacred choral compositions of Paval Gregoryevich Chesnokov (1877-1944)." PhD dissertation (Musicology): Indiana University, 1970. UM 71-13,544. DA XXXI.12, p.6645-A.

CHOPIN, FRÉDÉRIC (1810-1849)

Ballades
1335. Griffel, L. Michael. "The sonata design in Chopin's Ballades." CM 36(1983): 125-136.
1336. Witten, Neil David. "The Chopin Ballades: An analytical study." MusED dissertation: Boston University, 1979. No DA listing.

Berceuse, Op.57
1337. Lissa, Zofia. "Max Regers Metamorphosen der Berceuse Op.57 von Frederic Chopin." Fs. Wiener: 35-40.

Études
1338. Ganz, Peter. "The development of the etude for pianoforte." PhD dissertation (Music History and Literature): Northwestern University, 1960. LC Mic 60-6546. DA XXI.10, p.3114.
1339. Phipps, Graham H. "A response to Schenker's analysis of Chopin's Étude, Opus 10, No.12, using Schoenberg's *Grundgestalt* concept." MQ 69(1983): 543-569.
1340. Salzer, Felix. "Chopin's Étude in F Major, Opus 25, No.3: The scope of tonality." MFO 3(1973): 281-290.
1341. Smith, Charles Justice, III. "Patterns and stratagies: Four perspectives of musical characterization." PhD dissertation (Theory): University of Michigan, 1980. 130 p. UM 81-06,229. DA XLI.7, p.3776-A. [Op.10, No.1]
1342. ----. "Registering distinctions: Octave non-equivalence in Chopin's 'Butterfly' Etude." ITO 3/5(1977-1978): 32-40.
1343. ----. "(Supra-) durational patterns in Chopin's 'Revolutionary' Etude." ITO 2/5(1976): 3-12.
1344. ----. "Toward the construction of intersecting divergent models for Chopin's 'Three Against Two' Etude." ITO 1/3(1975-1976): 19-25.

Fantaisie in F Minor
1345. Gojowy, Detlej. "Frédéric Chopin: Fantaisie F-Moll, Op.49." NZM 146/6(1985): 29-31.

Fantaisie-Impromptu
1346. Oster, Ernst. "The Fantaisie-Imprompu: A tribute to Beethoven." MU 1(1946-1947): 407-429.

CHOPIN

Impromptus
1347. Ekier, Jan. "Das Impromptu Cis-Moll von Frédéric Chopin." Melos/NZM 4(1978): 201-204.

Mazurkas
1348. Beach, David. "Chopin's Mazurka, Op.17, No.4: Analysis." TP 2/3(1977): 12-16.

1349. Belotti, Gastone. "Una nuova mazurca di Chopin." STU 6(1977): 161-206.

1350. Bronarski, Louis. "La dernière Mazurka de Chopin." SMZ 95 (1955): 380-387. [Op.68, No.4 in F Minor]

1351. Kallberg, Jeffrey. "Chopin's last style." JAMS 38(1985): 264-315. [Op.68, No.4]

1352. Kresky: 80-91. [Op.68, No.3, post.]

1353. Nowik, Wojciech. "Chopins Mazurka F Moll, Op.68, Nr.4: Die letzte Inspiration des Meisters." AM 30(1973): 109-127.

1354. Swartz, Anne. "Folk dance elements in Chopin's Mazurkas." JMR 4(1982-1983): 417-426.

1355. ----. "The Mazurkas of Chopin: Certain aspects of phrasing." PhD dissertation (Musicology): University of Pittsburgh, 1973. UM 74-08,709. DA XXXIV.10, p.6693.

1356. Viljoen, Nicol. "The drone bass and its implications for the tonal voice-leading structure in two selected mazurkas by Chopin." ITR 6/1-2(1982-1983): 17-35. [Op.6, No.2; Op.56, No.2]

Nocturnes
1357. Levy, Janet M. "Texture as a sign in classic and early romantic music." JAMS 35(1982): 482-531. [Op.27, No.1]

1358. Mainka, Jürgen. "Zu Chopins H-Dur-Nocturno Opus 32 Nr.1: Ein Aspekt der Tonsprache Chopins in ihrem Verstältnis zur deutschen Romantik." BM 22(1980): 309-316.

1359. Rothgeb, John. "Chopin's C-Minor Nocturne, Op.48, No.1, first part: Voice leading and motivic content." TP 5/2(1980): 26-31.

1360. Salzer, Felix. "Chopin's Nocturne in C-Sharp Minor, Op.27, No.1." MFO 2(1970): 283-297.

Polonaise-Fantasy, Op.61
1361. Kallberg, Jeffrey. "Chopin's last style." JAMS 38(1985): 264-315.

1362. Tarasti, Fero. "Pour une narratologie de Chopin." IRASM 15/1(1984): 53-75.

Preludes
1363. Cole, Ronald Eugene. "Analysis of the Chopin Preludes, Opus 28." MM dissertation: Florida State University, Tallahassee, 1968.

1364. Higgins, Thomas. Chopin: Preludes, Op.28. Norton Critical Scores. New York: W.W. Norton, 1975.

1365. Hoyt, Reed J. "Chopin's Prelude in A Minor revisited: The issue of tonality." ITO 8/6(1984-1985): 7-16.

1366. ----. "Harmonic process, melodic process, and interpretive aspects of Chopin's Prelude in G Minor." ITR 5/3(1981-1982): 22-42.

1367. Kresky: 41-55. [Op.28, No.4]

1368. Pierce, Alexandra. "Climax in music: Structure and phrase (Part III)." ITO 7/1(1983-1984): 3-30. [Prelude, Op.28, No.4]

1369. Rogers, Michael R. "Chopin, Prelude in A Minor, Op.28, No.2." NCM 4(1980-1981): 245-250.

1370. Smith, Charles J. "On hearing the Chopin Preludes as a coherent set: A survey of some possible structural models for Op.28." ITO 1/4(1975-1976): 5-16.

Scherzos

1371. Fang, Julia Lam. "Chopin's approach to form in his four piano scherzos." PhD dissertation (Performance): Michigan State University, 1979. 121 p. UM 80-01,552. DA XL.7, p.3617-A.

Sonatas

1372. Bollinger, John Simon. "An integrative and Schenkerian analysis of the B-Flat Minor Sonata by Frederic Chopin." PhD dissertation (Performance): Washington University, 1981. UM 82-01,728. DA XLII.10, p.4346-A.

1373. Wessely, Othmar. "Chopins B-Moll Sonate." OMZ 4(1949): 283-286.

Waltzes

1374. Sittner, Hans. "Der Walzer bei Chopin und Johann Strauss." OMZ 4(1949): 287-293.

Other works

1375. *Annales Chopin.* Warsaw, 1956- [Articles on Chopin's style, published by the Société Frédéric Chopin]

1376. Barbag-Drexler, Irena. "Zur Harmonik Chopins." ME 27 (1973-1974): 202-206.

1377. Belotti, Gastone. *Les origini italiane del "rubato" chopiniano.* Wroclaw: Zakld Narodowy Im. Ossolińskich, 1968.

1378. ----. "Le *Polacche* dell' Op.26 nel testo autentico di Chopin." STU 2(1973): 267-313.

1379. ----. "Le prime composizione di Chopin: Problemi e osservazioni." RIM 7(1972): 230-291.

1380. Braun, Harmut. "Ein Zitat: Beziehungen zwischen Chopin und Brahms." MF 25(1972): 317-321.

1381. Bronarski, Louis. "Le plus 'chopinesque' des accords de Chopin." SMZ 85(1945): 382-385.

1382. Burdick, Michael Francis. "A structural analysis of melodic scale-degree tendencies in selected themes of Haydn, Mozart, Schubert and Chopin." PhD dissertation (Music Theory): Indiana University, 1977. UM 77-22,643. DA XXXVIII.4, p.1724-A.

1383. Chomiński, Józef Michat. "Das Entwicklungsprobleme des chopinschen Stils." Fs. Besseler: 437-446.

1384. Dammeier-Kirpal, Ursula. *Der Sonatensatz bei Frédéric Chopin.* Wiesbaden: Breitkopf und Härtel, 1973.

1385. Dommel-Diény, Amy. *Chopin.* Dommel-Diény 7. Paris: Éditions Transatlantiques, 1970. [Preludes Nos.2, 4, 9, 15; Sonata Op.58, No.3; Fantaisie-Impromptu, Op.66; Nocturne Op.48, No.1]

1386. Eigeldinger, Jean-Jacques. "Un autographe musical inédit de Chopin." SMZ 115(1975): 18-23.

1387. ----. "Chopin et l'heritage baroque." SBM 2(1974): 51-74.

1388. Goepfert, Robert Harold. "Ambiguity in Chopin's rhythmic notation." DMA dissertation (Performance): Boston University, 1981. UM 81-26,665. DA XLII.6, p.2352-A.

1389. Goldschmidt, Harry. "Chopiniana bei Beethoven." Fs. Lissa: 209-222.

1390. Hutchinson, William R. "Implication, closure and interpolated change as exemplified in the works of Frédéric Chopin." PhD dissertation: University of Chicago, 1960. No DA listing.

1391. Kallberg, Jeffrey. "Compatibility in Chopin's multipartite publications." JM 2(1983): 391-417.

1392. Kinzler, Harmuth. *Frédéric Chopin: Über den Zusammenhang von Satztechnik und Klavierspiel.* Freiburger Schriften zur Musikwissenschaft 9. München: E. Katzbichler, 1977.

1393. Klein, Rudolf. "Chopins Sonatentechnik." OMZ 22(1967): 389-399.

1394. Koszewskik, Andrzej. "Das Walzerelement im Schaffen Chopins." DJM 5(1960): 48-66.

1395. Lissa, Zofia, ed. *The book of the first International Musicological Congress devoted to the works of Frédérick Chopin.* Warsaw: Panstwowe Wydawnictwo Naukowe, 1963.

1396. Lissa, Zofia. "Chopin und die polnische Volksmusik." MG 10(1960): 65-74.

1397. ----. "Die chopinische Harmonik aus der Perspective der Klangtechnik des 20. Jahrhunderts." DJM 2(1957): 68-84; 3(1958): 74-91.

1398. ----. "Über den Einfluss Chopins aus Ljadow." DJM 13(1968): 5-42.

1399. Matter, Jean. "De l'harmonie complémentaire et de l'expression du dépaysement dans la musique de Chopin." SMZ 101(1961): 93-97.

1400. McGinnis, Francis. "Chopin: Aspects of melodic style." PhD dissertation (Theory): Indiana University, 1969. UM 69-7108. DA XXIX.11, p.4043-A.

1401. Meloncelli, Raoul. "Coerenza et continuità del linguaggio chopiniano." Fs. Haberl: 187-195.

1402. Moore, Kevin Morris. "Linearity of voice structure in selected works of Frédéric Chopin and its implications in performance." PhD dissertation: New York University, 1979. No DA listing.

1403. Noden-Skinner, Cheryl. "Tonal ambiguity in the opening measures of selected works by Chopin." CMS 24(1984): 28-34. [Mazurka, Op.17, No.4; Prelude, Op.28, No.2; Scherzo, Op.39; Ballade, Op.52]

1404. Parks, Richard S. "Voice leading and chromatic harmony in the music of Chopin." JMT 20(1976): 189-214.

1405. Sterling.

1406. Thomas, Betty J. "Harmonic materials and treatment of dissonance in the pianoforte music of Frédéric Chopin." PhD disssertation (Theory): University of Rochester, 1963. UM 66-6899. DA XXVII.4, p.1076-7-A.

1407. Wagner, Günther. "Die Melodik Chopins unter dem Einfluss italienischer Opernmusik." JSIM (1975): 80-95.

1408. Walker, Alan, ed. *Frédéric Chopin: Profiles of the man and the musician.* London: Barrie & Rockcliff, 1966.

1409. YaDeau, William Ronald. "Tonal and formal structure in selected larger works of Chopin." PhD dissertation: University of Illinois, 1980. No DA listing.

CILENŠEK, JOHANN (born 1913)

1410. Felix, Werner. "Die V. Sinfonie von Johann Cilenšek." MG 10(1960): 541-548.

1411. Junghanns, Bernd. "Johannes Cilenšek: Sein sinfonisches Werk." PhD dissertation (Musicology): Halle-Salle, 1978.

1412. Markowski, Liesel. "Johann Cilenšek: II. Sinfonie." MG 12 (1962): 489-490.

1413. Schmidt, Gerhard. "Johann Cilenšek: Konzertstück für Klavier und Orchester." MG 2(1952): 86-89.

CLARKE, HENRY LELAND (born 1907)

1414. Verrall, John. "Henry Leland Clarke." ACA 9/3(1959): 2-8.

CLARKE, REBECCA (1886-1979)

1415. Richards, Deborah. "*And you should have seen their faces when they saw it was by a woman!*: Gedanken zu Rebecca Clarkes Klaviertrio." N 4(1983-1984): 201-208.

CLEMENTI, ALDO (born 1925)

1416. Bortolotto, Mario. "Aldo Clementi." MELOS 30(1963): 364-369.

1417. Osmond-Smith, David. "*Au creux néant musicien*: Recent work by Aldo Clementi." CT 23(1981): 5-9.

CLEMENTI, MUZIO (1752-1832)

1418. Allorto, Riccardo. *Le Sonate per pianoforte di Muzio Clementi: Studio critico e catalogo tematico.* Firenze: Olschki, 1959.

1419. Grave, Jerald C. "Clementi's self-borrowings: The refinement of a manner." Fs. Fox: 57-71.

1420. Hill, John Walter. "The symphonies of Muzio Clementi." MA dissertation: Harvard University, 1965.

1421. Tighe, Alice Eugene. "Muzio Clementi and his sonatas surviving as solo piano works." PhD dissertation: University of Michigan, 1964. UM 64-12,693. DA XXV.6, p.2612-13.

COE, TONY

1422. Barry, Malcolm. "Tony Coe's *Zeitgeist*." CT 19(1978): 12-14.

COLE, BRUCE (born 1947)

1423. Potter, Keith. "Bruce Cole and *Fenestrae sanctae*." TEMPO 107(1973): 19-22.

COLERIDGE-TAYLOR, SAMUEL (1875-1912)

1424. Batchman, John Clifford. "Samuel Coleridge-Taylor: An analysis of selected piano works and an examination of his influence on Black American musicians." PhD dissertation (Music Education): Washington University, 1977. No DA liasting.

COLTRANE, JOHN (1926-1967)

1425. Cole, William Shadrack. "The style of John Coltrane, 1955-1967." PhD dissertation: Wesleyan University, 1975. UM 74-23,031. DA XXXV.4, p.2316-7-A.

CONVERSE, FREDERICK SHEPHERD (1871-1940)

1426. Garofalo, Robert J. "The life and works of Frederick Shepherd Converse (1871-1940)." PhD dissertation (Musicology): Catholic University, 1969. UM 69-19,710. DA XXX.6, p.2558-9-A.

COOKE, ARNOLD (born 1906)

1427. Clapham, John. "Arnold Cooke's Symphony." MR 11(1950): 118-121.
1428. Gaulke, Stanley Jack. "The published solo and chamber works for clarinet of Arnold Cooke." DMA dissertation (Performance): University of Rochester, 1978. UM 78-16,653. DA XXXIX.6, p.3209-A.

COPLAND, AARON (born 1900)

Connotations
1429. Evans, Peter. "Copland on the serial road." PNM 2/2(1964): 141-149.

Danzon cubano
1430. Jeter.

Nonet
1431. Plaistow, Stephen. "Some notes on Copland's Nonet." TEMPO 64(1962): 6-11.
1432. Salzman, Eric and Paul Des Marais. "Aaron Copland's Nonet: Two views." PNM 1/1(1962): 172-179.

Passacaglia
    1433. Coolidge, Richard. "Aaron Copland's Passacaglia: An analysis." MAN 2(1974): 33-36.

Piano Blues
    1434. Forte: 63-73. [No.3]

Piano Fantasy
    1435. Berger, Arthur. "Aaron Copland's Piano Fantasy." JR 5/1(1957-1958): 13-27.

Piano Sonata
    1436. Haberkorn, Michael. "A study and performance of the piano sonatas of Samuel Barber, Elliott Carter, and Aaron Copland." EdD dissertation: Columbia University, 1979. No DA listing.
    1437. Kirkpatrick, John. "Aaron Copland's Piano Sonata." MM 19 (1942): 246-250.

Symphony No.3
    1438. Berger, Arthur. "The Third Symphony of Aaron Copland." TEMPO 9(1948): 20-27.

Twelve Poems of Emily Dickinson
    1439. Daugherty, Robert Michael. "An analysis of Aaron Copland's *Twelve Poems of Emily Dickinson*." DMA dissertation: Ohio State University, 1980. No DA listing.
    1440. Mabry, Sharon Cody. *"Twelve Poems of Emily Dickinson* by Aaron Copland: A stylistic analysis." DMA dissertation: George Peabody College for Teachers, 1977. No DA listing.
    1441. Young, Douglas. "Copland's *Dickinson Songs*." TEMPO 103(1972): 25-37.

Other Works
    1442. Berger, Arthur. "The music of Aaron Copland." MQ 31(1945): 420-447.
    1443. Brookhart, Charles E. "The choral works of Aaron Copland, Roy Harris, and Randall Thompson." PhD dissertation: George Peabody College for Teachers, 1960. LC Mic 60-5861. DA XXI.9, p.2737.
    1444. Cole, Hugo. "Aaron Copland." TEMPO 76(1966): 2-6, 77(1966): 9-15.
    1445. Evans, Peter. "The thematic technique of Copland's recent works." TEMPO 51(1959): 2-13.
    1446. Smith, Julia Frances. "Aaron Copland: His work and contribution to American music." PhD dissertation (Higher Education): New York University, 1952. UM 4543. DA XIII.1, p.103.
    1447. Starr, Lawrence. "Copland's style." PNM 19/1(1980-1981): 68-89.

CORDERO, ROQUE (born 1917)

1448. Ennett, Dorothy Maxine. "An analysis and comparison of selected piano sonatas by three contemporary Black composers: George Walker, Howard Swanson, and Roque Cordero." PhD dissertation (Performance): New York University, 1973. UM 73-30,062. DA XXXIV.6, p.3450-A.

1449. Sider, Ronald R. "Roque Cordero: The composer and his style seen through three representative works." IAMB 61(1967): 1-17.

CORIGLIANO, JOHN (born 1938)

1450. Dickson, John Howard, Jr. "The union of poetry and music in John Corigliano's *A Dylan Thomas Trilogy*." DMA dissertation (Choral Conducting): University of Texas, 1985. 171 p. No DA listing.

1451. Jeter. [*Kaleidoscope*]

CORNELIUS, PETER (1824-1874)

1452. Federhofer, Hellmut and Kurt Oehl, eds. *Peter Cornelius als Komponist, Dichter, Kritiker und Essayist.* Regensburg: G. Bosse, 1977.

1453. Porter, Ernest Graham. "The songs of Peter Cornelius." MR 27(1966): 202-206.

COSME, LUIZ (1908-1965)

1454. Béhague, Gerard. "Luiz Cosme (1908-1965): Impulso creador versus conciencia formal." Y 5(1969): 67-89.

COULTHARD, JEAN (born 1908)

1455. Rowley, Vivienne Wilda. "The solo piano music of the Canadian composer Jean Coulthard." PhD dissertation: Boston University, 1973. 174 p. UM 73-23,642. DA XXXIV.5, p.2686-A.

COWELL, HENRY (1897-1965)

1456. Cowell, Henry. "Mein Weg zu den Clusters." MELOS 40(1973): 288-296.

1457. Gerschefski, Edwin. "Henry Cowell." MM 23(1946): 255-260.

1458. Godwin, Joscelyn R.J.C. "The music of Henry Cowell." PhD dissertation (Musicology): Cornell University, 1969. No DA listing.

1459. Hitchcock, H. Wiley. "Henry Cowell's *Ostinato pianissimo*." MQ 70(1984): 23-44.

1460. Smith, Leland. "Henry Cowell's *Rhythmicana*." Y 9(1973): 134-147.

1461. Weisgall, Hugo. "The music of Henry Cowell." MQ 45(1959): 484-507.

CRAWFORD, RUTH (1901-1953)

1462. Spragg, Deborah. "Time and intervallic language in Crawford's *Diaphonic Suite No.3*." SONUS 3/1(1982): 39-56.

CROSSE, GORDON (born 1937)

1463. Blacker, Terry. "Gordon Crosse: Towards a style." TEMPO 155(1985): 22-27.

CRUMB, GEORGE (born 1929)

Echoes of Time and the River
1464. Bersano. [Last movement]

Eleven Echoes of Autumn
1465. Thomas, Jennifer. "The use of color in three chamber works of the twentieth-century." ITR 4/3(1980-1981): 24-40.

Madrigals
1466. Chatman, Stephen. "George Crumb's *Madrigals Book III*: A linear analysis." ITO 1/9(1975): 55-79.

Makrokosmos
1467. Moevs, Robert. "George Crumb: *Music for a Summer Evening (Makrokosmos III)*." MQ 62(1976): 293-302. [Record review]
1468. Schultz/D. [*Makrokosmos II*, third movement]

Night Music I
1469. Lewis, Robert Hall. "George Crumb: *Night Music I*." PNM 3/2(1965): 143-151.

Night of the Four Moons
1470. Chatman, Stephen. "George Crumb: *Night of the Four Moons*." JMR 1(1973-1975): 215-224.
1471. White, John D. "Systematic analysis for musical sound." JMR 5(1984-1985): 165-190.

Vox balaenae
1472. Timm, Kenneth N. "A stylistic analysis of George Crumb's *Vox balaenae*." DMA dissertation (Composition): Indiana University, 1977. No DA listing.

Other works
1473. De Dobay, Thomas R. "The evolution of harmonic style in the Lorca works of Crumb." JMT 28/1(1984): 89-112.
1474. Rouse, Christopher Chapman III. "The music of George Crumb: A stylistic metamorphosis as reflected in the Lorca cycle." DMA dissertation: Cornell University, 1977. UM 78-00,063. DA XXXVIII.8, p.4442-A.

1475. Sams, Carol Lee. "Solo vocal writing in selected works of Berio, Crumb and Rochberg." DMA dissertation (Performance): University of Washington, 1975. UM 76-17,610. DA XXXVII.2, p.685-A.

1476. Schuffett, Robert V. "The music, 1971-1975, of George Crumb: A style analysis." DMA dissertation (Compostion): Peabody Conservatory, 1979. UM 79-21,362. DA XL.4, p.1744-A. [*Vox balaenae; Lux aeterna; Makrokosmos*, vols. 1-3]

1477. Steinitz, Richard. "George Crumb." CT 15(1976-1977): 11-13.

1478. ----. "The music of George Crumb." CT 11(1975): 14-22.

CUI, CÉSAR (1835-1918)

1479. Abraham, Gerald. "Heine, Cui, and William Ratcliff." Abraham: 56-67.

CZERNY, KARL (1791-1857)

1480. Sweets, Randall. "Carl Czerny reconsidered: Romantic elements in his Sonata Op.7." JALS 16(1984): 54-71.

DALAYRAC, NICHOLAS (1753-1809)

1481. Charlton, David. "Motif and recollection in four operas of Dalayrac." SN 7(1978): 38-61.

1482. Moss, Llewellyn. "The one-act *opéra comiques* by Nicolas Dalayrac (1753-1809)." PhD dissertation (Music Education): New York University, 1969. UM 70-739. DA XXX.8, p.3494-5-A.

DALLAPICCOLA, LUIGI (1904-1975)

Canti di liberazione
1483. Engelmann, Hans Ulrich. "Dallapiccolas *Canti di liberazione*." MELOS 23(1956): 73-76.

Cinque canti
1484. Wildberger, Jacques. "Dallapiccolas *Cinque canti*." MELOS 26(1959): 7-10.

Commiato
1485. Kamper, Dietrich. "*Commiato*: Bemerkungen zu Dallapiccolas letztem Werk." SMZ 111(1975): 194-200.

Goethe-Lieder
1486. DeLio, Thomas. "A proliferation of canons: Luigi Dallapiccolas's *Goethe Lieder* No.2." PNM 23/2(1984-1985): 186-195.

1487. Eckert, Michael. "Text and form in Dallapiccola's *Goethe-Lieder*." PNM 17/2(1978-1979): 98-111.

1488. Neumann, Peter Horst and Jürg Stenzl. "Luigi Dallapiccolas *Goethe-Lieder*." SBM 4(1980): 171-192.

Piano works
    1489. Buccheri.

Il Prigioniero
    1490. Rufer, Josef. "Luigi Dallapiccola: *Il Prigioniero*." MZ 6(1954):
46-64.

Quaderno musicale di Annalibera
    1491. Shackelford, Rudy. "Dallapiccola and the organ." TEMPO 111
(1974): 15-22.

Ricerca ritmica e metrica
    1492. Kämper, Dietrich. "*Ricerca ritmica e metrica*: Beobachtungen
am Spätwerk Dallapiccolas." NZM 135(1974): 94-99.

Three Questions with Two Answers
    1493. Petrobelli, Pierluigi. "Dallapiccolas's last orchestral piece."
TEMPO 123(1977): 2-6.

Other works
    1494. Brown, Rosemary. "Continuity and recurrence in the creative
development of Luigi Dallapiccola." PhD dissertation (Musicology): Bangor,
1977.
    1495. ----. "Dallapiccola's use of symbolic self-quotation." STU
4(1975): 277-304.
    1496. ----. "La Sperimentazione ritmica in Dellapiccola tra libertà e
determinazione." RIM 13(1978): 142-173.
    1497. Gould, Glen Hibbard. "A stylistic analysis of selected
twelve-tone works of Luigi Dallapiccola." PhD dissertation (Theory):
Indiana University, 1964. UM 65-3480. DA XXV.11, p.6676.
    1498. Johnson. [*Goethe Lieder; Quattro liriche di Antonio Machado*]
    1499. Mereni, Anthony Ekemezie. "Die Chorwerke Luigi Dallapiccolas." PhD dissertation (Musicology): Salzburg Universität, 1979.
    1500. Nathan, Hans. "On Dallapiccola's working methods." PNM 15/2
(1977): 34-57.
    1501. ----. "The twelve-tone compositions of Luigi Dallapiccola." MQ
44(1958): 289-310.
    1502. Perkins, John MacIvor. "Dallapiccola's art of canon." PNM 1/2
(1963): 95-106.
    1503. Vlad, Roman. "Dallapiccola 1948-1966." SCORE 15(1956):
39-62.

DAMASE, JEAN-MICHEL (born 1928)

    1504. Kniesner [Piano Sonata, Op.24]

DANZI, FRANZ (1763-1826)

    1505. Abert, Anna Amalie. "*Oberon* in Nord und Süd." Fs. Gudewill:
51-68. [*Der Triumph der Treue*]

DAVID, JOHANN NEPOMUK (1895-1977)

Choralwerk
1506. Johns, Donald Charles. "Johann Nepomuk David's *Choralwerk*: A study in the evolution of a contemporary liturgical organ style." PhD dissertation (Theory): Northwestern University, 1960. LC Mic 60-6554. DA XXI.9, p.2738.
1507. ----. "Technik und Problematik der Cantus firmus-Bearbeitung in Johann Nepomuk Davids *Choralwerk*." MK 35(1965): 242-252.

Josquin-Variationen
1508. Sievers, Gerd. "Johann Nepomuk Davids *Josquin-Variationen* (1966): Entstehung--Analyse--Deutung." HJM 4(1980): 115-144.

Partita über B-A-C-H
1509. Bertram, Hans George. "Johann Nepomuk David: *Partita über B-A-C-H* für Orgel." MK 40(1970): 411-424.
1510. Klein, Rudolf. "Die jüngsten Werke von Johann Nepomuk David." OMZ 20(1965): 566-571.

Spiegelkabinett
1511. Sievers, Gerd. "Johann Nepomuk Davids *Spiegelkabinett*: Analytische Studie." Fs. David: 160-187.

Symphony No.8, op.59
1502. Klein, Rudolf. "Die jüngsten Werke von Johann Nepomuk David." OMZ 20(1965): 566-571.

Violin Concerto
1513. Kaufmann, Harold. "J.N. David und das Ganzheitsstreben seiner Musik." ME 9(1955): 158-160. [First movement]

Other works
1514. Bertram, Hans Georg. "Flöte und Horn: Instrument und Instrumentatation bei Johann Nepomuk David." Fs. David: 126-149.
1515. ----. *Material, Struktur, Form: Studien zur musikalischen Ordnung bei Johann Nepomuk David.* Wiesbaden: Breitkopf und Härtel, 1965.
1516. ----. "Von der Einheit in der Vielfalt der Stilepochen bei J.N. David." NZM 127(1966): 424-428.
1517. Dallmann, Wolfgang. "Johann Nepomuk Davids späte Orgelwerke." MK 52(1982): 15-23.
1518. Klein, Rudolf. *Johann Nepomuk David: Eine Studie.* Wien: Österreichischer Bundesverlag, 1964.
1519. ----. "Neue Orgelmusik von Johann Nepomuk David." OMZ 26(1971): 691-697.
1520. Kolneder, Walter. "Unbekannte Werke von Johann Nepomuk David." OMZ 20(1965): 572-577.
1521. Marsh, Lawrence Bernhard. "The choral music of Johann Nepomuk David (1895-   )." DMA dissertation (Performance): University of Washington, 1974. UM 74-29,459. DA XXXVII.2, p.1101-A.

1522. Sievers, Gerd. "Das Ezzolied in der Vertonung von Willy Burkhard und Johann Nepomuk David: Ein Vergleich." Fs. Engel/H: 335-363.

DAVIDOWSKY, MARIO (born 1934)

1523. Soule, Richard Lawrence. "*Synchronisms* Nos.1, 2, 3, 5, and 6 of Mario Davidowsky: A style analysis." DMA dissertation (Performance): Peabody Conservatory, 1978. No DA listing.

1524. True, Wesley. "Men, music and machines: Some thoughts generated by the practice and performance of Mario Davidowsky's *Synchronisms* No. 6 for Piano and Electronic Sounds." JALS 9(1981): 50-54.

1525. Wuorinen, Charles. "*Contrasts No.1*." PNM 4/2(1966): 144-149.

DAVIES, PETER MAXWELL (born 1934)

Ave Maris Stella
1526. Pruslin, Stephen. "The triangular space: Peter Maxwell Davies's *Ave Maris Stella*." TEMPO 120(1977): 16-22.

Eight Songs for a Mad King
1527. Cope: 128-133.
1528. Harvey, Jonathan. "Maxwell Davies's *Songs for a Mad King*." TEMPO 89(1969): 2-6.
1529. Skoog, James. "Pitch material in Peter Maxwell Davies's *Eight Songs for a Mad King*." MA dissertation (Theory): University of Rochester, 1976.

Five Klee Pictures
1530. Knussen, Oliver. "Peter Maxwell Davies's *Five Klee Pictures*." TEMPO 124(1978): 17-21.

Five Motets
1531. Payne, Anthony. "Peter Maxwell Davies's *Five Motets*." TEMPO 72(1965): 7-11.

Piano Sonata
1532. Griffiths, Paul. "Maxwell Davies's Piano Sonata." TEMPO 140(1982): 5-9.

Second Taverner Fantasia
1533. Pruslin, Stephen. "Maxwell Davies's *Second Taverner Fantasia*." TEMPO 73(1965): 2-11.
1534. Whittall, Arnold. "Post-twelve-note analysis." PRMA 94 (1967-1968): 1-17.

The Shepherds Calendar
1535. Andrewes, John. "Maxwell Davies's *The Shepherds Calendar*." TEMPO 87(1968): 6-9.
1536. Peart, Donald. "Peter Maxwell Davies: *The Shepherds' Calendar*." MMA 1(1966): 249-255. [Also in Fs. Bishop: 249-255]

Stone Litany

1537. Silsbee, Ann Loomis. "Peter Maxwell Davies's *Stone Litany*: Integration and dynamic process." DMA dissertation: Cornell University, 1979. No DA listing.

Taverner

1538. Harbison, John. "Peter Maxwell Davies's *Taverner*." PNM 11/1(1972): 233-240.

1539. Special Issue: TEMPO 101(1972)

Vesalii Icones

1540. Jacob, Jeffrey Lynn. "Peter Maxwell Davies' *Vesalii Icones*: Origins and analysis." DMA dissertation (Piano): Peabody Conservatory, 1980. No DA listing.

1541. Potter, Keith. "The music of Peter Maxwell Davies." CT 4 (1972): 3-9.

1542. Pruslin, Stephen. "'One if by land, two if by sea': Maxwell Davies the symphonist." TEMPO 153(1985): 2-6.

1543. ----, ed. *Peter Maxwell Davies: Studies from two decades.* London: Boosey & Hawkes, 1979. [Collection of articles which originally appeared in TEMPO]

1544. Taylor, Michael. "Maxwell Davies's *Vesalii Icones*." TEMPO 92(1970): 22-27.

Westerlings

1545. Warnaby, John. "*Westerlings*: A study in symphonic form." TEMPO 147(1983): 15-22.

Other works

1546. Griffiths, Paul. *Peter Maxwell Davies.* London: Robson, 1982.

1547. Pruslin, Stephen. "Returns and departures: Recent Maxwell Davies." TEMPO 113(1975): 22-28. [*Worldes Blis* and *Stone Litany*]

DAVIS, LESLIE N.

1548. Davis, Leslie N. "Chemical composition: Chiral rows (*Lactic No.1*)." PNM 23/1(1984-1985): 108-111.

DEBUSSY, CLAUDE (1862-1918)

Cello Sonata

1549. Moevs, Robert. "Intervallic procedures in Debussy: Serenade from the Sonata for Cello and Piano, 1915." PNM 8/1(1969): 82-101.

Chamber music [see also individual titles]

1550. Derr, Ellwood. "Sein erstes überliefertes Instrumentalwerk: Zur Erstveröffentlichung von Claude Debussys frühem Klaviertrio." NZM 146/12(1985): 10-16.

1551. Seraphin, Hellmut. *Debussys Kammermusik der mittleren Schaffenzeit.* Kassel: Bärenreiter, 1964.

1552. Wilson, Eugene N. "Form and texture in the chamber music of Debussy and Ravel." PhD dissertation (Theory): University of Washington, 1968. UM 68-12,723. DA XXIX.3, p.927-A.

Children's Corner
1553. Koptschewski, Nikolai. "*Children's Corner* von Claude Debussy: Stilistische Parallelen und Probleme der Interpretation." DJM (1978): 173-209. [JP 1(1978): 173-209]

Etudes
1554. Gauldin, Robert, William E. Benjamin, and Elaine Barkin. "Analysis symposium: Debussy, Etude *Pour les sixtes*." JMT 22(1978): 241-312.
1555. Kaufmann, Harold. "Zur Wertung des Epigonentums in der Musik." NZM 129(1968): 397-404. [No.10]
1556. Parks, Richard Samuel. "Organizational procedures in Debussy's *Douze études*." PhD dissertation (Musicology): Catholic University of America, 1973. 597 p. UM 74-07,663. DA XXVIV.9, p.6025-A.
1557. Peterson, William John. "Debussy's *Douze études*: A critical analysis." PhD dissertation (Musicology): University of California, Berkeley, 1981. UM 82-00,236. DA XLII.7, p.2927-A.
1558. Schneider, John. "The Debussy Etudes: A challenge to mind and fingers." JALS 14(1983): 59-63.

Images for Orchestra
1559. Bein, Joseph H. "Debussy's orchestral *Images*: Other features of the style." PhD dissertation: University of Rochester, 1970. UM 70-4456. DA XXX.9, p.3965-6-A.
1560. Schultz: 49-52. [*Rondes de printemps*]

Images for Piano
1561. Howat, Roy. "Debussy, Ravel and Bartók: Towards some new concepts of form." ML 58(1977): 285-293. [*Reflets dans l'eau*]
1562. Reiche, Jens Peter. "Die theoretischen Grundlagen javanischer Gamelan-Musik und ihre Bedeutung für Claude Debussy." ZM 3/1(1972): 5-15. [*Cloches à travers le feuilles*]

Jeux
1563. Berman, Laurence D. "*Prelude to the Afternoon of a Faun* and *Jeux*: Debussy's summer rites." NCM 3(1979-1980): 225-238.
1564. Eimert, Herbert. "Debussy's *Jeux*." R 5(1961): 3-20.
1565. Gut, Serge. "Konstante und bewegliche Elemente in *Jeux* von Claude Debussy." Kühn: 395-398.
1566. Schultz: 53-57.
1567. Zenck-Maurer, Claudia. ""Form- und Farbenspiele: Debussys *Jeux*." AM 33(1976): 28-47.

La Mer
1568. Dömling, Wolfgang. *Claude Debussy: La Mer*. München: W. Fink, 1976. 36 p.

1569. Howat, Roy. "Dramatic shape and form in *Jeux de vagues*, and its relationship to *Pelléas, Jeux* and other scores." CAD 7(1983): 7-23.

1570. Monnard, Jean-François. "Claude Debussy: *La Mer*." SMZ 121 (1981): 11-16.

1571. Rolf, Marie. "Debussy's *La Mer*: A critical analysis in the light of early sketches and editions." PhD dissertation (Theory): University of Rochester, 1976. 357 p. UM 77-08,315. DA XXXVII.11, p.6833-A.

Pelléas et Mélisande

1572. Abbate, Carolyn. "*Tristan* in the composition of *Pelléas*." NCM 5(1981-1982): 117-141.

1573. Appledorn, Mary Jeanne van. "A stylistic study of Claude Debussy's opera *Pelléas et Mélisande*." PhD dissertation (Theory): University of Rochester, 1966. UM 67-1312. DA XXVIII.2, p.716-A.

1574. ASO 9(1977).

1575. Bugeanu, Constantin. "La forme musicale dans le *Pelléas* de Debussy." *Revue roumaine d'histoire de l'art* 6(1969): 243-260.

1576. Emmanuel, Maurice. *"Pelléas et Mélisande" de Claude Debussy: Étude historique et critique, analyse musicale.* Paris: Mellottée, 1925.

1577. Enix.

1578. Gilman, Lawrence. *Debussy's "Pelléas et Mélisande": A guide to the opera with musical examples from the score.* New York: G. Schirmer, 1907.

1579. Grayson, David. "The libretto of Debussy's *Pelléas et Mélisande*." ML 66(1985): 34-50.

1580. John, Nicholas, ed. *Debussy: Pelléas et Mélisande.* London: J. Calder, 1982.

1581. Leibowitz, René. "*Pelléas et Mélisande*, ou les fantômes de la réalité." Leibowitz/F: 291-326.

1582. Neuwirth, Gösta. "Musik um 1900." Fs. Schuh: 89-134.

1583. Philips, Mary Kathryn. "Recitativo-Arioso: A survey with emphasis on contemporary opera." PhD dissertation: University of California, Los Angeles, 1965. UM 65-8797. DA XXVI.3, p.1688-9.

1584. Setaccioli, Giacomo. *Debussy: Eine kritische-aesthetische Studie.* Leipzig: Breitkopf und Härtel, 1911.

1585. Spieth-Weissenbacher, Christine Elisabeth. "Le Recitatif mélodique dans *Pelléas et Mélisande* de Claude Debussy." PhD dissertation (Musicology): Strasbourg, 1979.

1586. Staempfli, Edward. "*Pelléas und Mélisande*: Eine Gegen-überstellung der Werke von Claude Debussy und Arnold Schönberg." SMZ 112(1972): 65-72.

1587. Stirnemann, Knut. "Zur Frage des Leitmotivs in Debussys *Pelléas et Mélisande*." SBM 4(1980): 151-170.

1588. Terrasson, René. *Pelléas et Mélisande*, ou l'initiation. Paris: EDIMAF, 1982.

1589. Van Ackère, Jules. *Pelléas et Mélisande.* Bruxelles: Les Éditions de Librairie Encyclopédique, 1952.

1590. Wenk, Arthur. "Claude Debussy and the Art Nouveau image of woman." MMA 13(1984): 67-74.

Piano works [see also individual titles]
1591. Chun, Edna Breinig. "Debussy's piano music, 1903-1907." DM dissertation (Piano Pedagogy): Indiana University, 1980. No DA listing. [*Estampes; Masques; L'Ile joyeuse; Images* I and II]
1592. Dommel-Diény, Amy. *Debussy.* Dommel-Diény 16. Neuchâtel Editions Delachaux et Niestlé, 1967. [*Jardins sous la pluie; Les Collines d'Anacapri; La Cathédrale engloutie; Bruyères; Canope*]
1593. Holden, Calvin. "The organization of texture in selected piano compositions of Claude Debussy." PhD dissertation: University of Pittsburgh, 1973. UM 74-6793. No DA listing.
1594. Jakobik, Albert. *Die assoziative Harmonik in den Klavierwerkern Claude Debussys.* Würzburg: K. Triltsch, 1940.
1595. Martins, José Eduardo. "Quelques aspects comparatifs dans les langages pianistiques de Debussy et Scriabin." CAD 7(1983): 24-37.
1596. Mies, Paul. "Widmungsstück mit Buchstaben: Motto bei Debussy und Ravel." SZM 25(1962): 363-368. [*Hommage à Haydn*]
1597. Porten, Maria. *Zum Problem der "Form" bei Debussy: Untersuchungen am Beispiel der Klavierwerke.* München: E. Katzbichler, 1974. 121 p.
1598. Schmitz, Elie Robert. *The piano works of Claude Debussy.* New York: Duell, Sloan, & Pearce, 1950.
1599. Storb, Ilse. "Untersuchungen zur Auflösung der funktionalen Harmonik in den Klavierwerken von Claude Debussy." PhD dissertation: University of Cologne, 1967.
1600. Zulueta, Jorge and Jacobo Romano. *Claude Debussy: La Obra completo para piano: Analisis y manuscritos.* Buenos Aires: Universidad Nacional de Tucumona, 1964.

Prélude à l'après-midi d'un faune
1601. Austin, William W., ed. *Claude Debussy: Prelude to the Afternoon of a Faun.* Norton Critical Scores. New York: W.W. Norton, 1970.
1602. Berman, Laurence D. "*Prelude to the Afternoon of a Faun* and *Jeux*: Debussy's summer rites." NCM 3(1979-1980): 225-238.
1603. Crotty, John E. "Symbolist influence in Debussy's *Prelude to the Afternoon of a Faun.*" ITO 6/2(1981-1983): 17-30.
1604. Gülke, Peter. "Musik aus dem Bannkreis einer literarischen Aesthetik: Debussy's *Prélude à l'après-midi d'un faune.*" DJM (1978): 103-146. [JP 1(1978): 103-146]
1605. Haug, Wiltrud. *Claude Debussy: Historische Einordnung: Analyse "L'après-midi d'un faune."* Ravensburg: Holzschuh, 1977.

Preludes
1606. Benedetto, Renato di. "Congetture su *Voiles.*" RIM 13(1978): 312-344.
1607. Böckl, Rudolf. "Claude Debussys *Prélude* II (....*Voiles*): Über Material und Form: Ein Versuch." MF 25(1972): 321-323.
1608. Buck, Charles Henry, III. "Structural coherence in the Preludes for Piano by Claude Debussy." PhD dissertation (Musicology): University of California, Berkeley, 1975. No DA listing.

1609. Freundlich, Irwin. "Random thoughts on the Preludes of Claude Debussy." CM 13(1972): 48-57. [Also PQ 87(1974): 17-24]

1610. Friedmann, Michael L. "Approaching Debussy's *Ondine*." CAD 6(1982): 22-35.

1611. Guck, Marion A. "One path through Debussy's *...Des par sur la neige*." ITO 1/5(1975-1976): 4-8.

1612. ----. "Tracing Debussy's *Des pas sur la neige*." ITO 1/8 (1975-1976): 4-12.

1613. Guertin, Marcelle. "Lecture-audition du texte musical: Une Étude de la mélodie dans le Livre I des Préludes pour piano de Debussy." PhD dissertation (Musicology): Université Laval, 1985.

1614. ----. "A stylistic approach to Debussy's Preludes for Piano." *Three musical analyses*. Toronto Semiotic Circle 4. Toronto: Victoria University, 1981. p.36-58.

1615. Hepokoski, James A. "Formulaic openings in Debussy." NCM 8(1984-1985): 44-59. [Also mentions *Printemps* and *La Damoiselle élue*]

1616. Hirbour-Paquette, Louise. "Analyse sémiologique des Préludes pour piano de Claude Debussy: Vers une characterisation stylistique de la 'mélodie'." PhD dissertation: Université de Montréal, 1975.

1617. Imberty, Michel. *Signification and meaning in music: On Debussy's Préludes pour le piano*. Montréal: Groupe de recherches en sémiologie musicale, Université de Montréal, 1976.

1618. Keil, Werner. *Untersuchungen zur Entwicklung des frühen Klavierstils von Debussy und Ravel*. Wiesbaden: Breitkopf und Härtel, 1982.

1619. Kresky: 151-163. [*La Fille aux cheveux de lin*]

1620. Nadeau, Roland. "*Brouillards*: A tonal music." CAD 4-5 (1980-1981): 38-50.

1621. Parks, Richard Samuel. "Pitch organization in Debussy: Unordered sets in *Brouillards*." MTS 2(1980): 119-134.

1622. Ráfols, Alberto. "Debussy and the symbolist movement: The Preludes." DMA dissertation (Performance): University of Washington, 1975. 195 p. UM 76-17,594. DA XXXVII.2, p.683-A.

1623. Schnebel, Dieter. "*Brouillards*: Tendenzen bei Debussy." R 6 (1964): 33-39.

1624. Schoffman, Nachum. "Pedal points, old and new." JMR 4(1982-1983): 369-398.

1625. Seldin, H.D. "An analytical study of the Debussy Preludes for Piano." Master's thesis: Columbia University, 1965.

1626. Watson, Lorne. "Cadences in Debussy's Preludes, Books I and II." DMA dissertation (Piano): Indiana University, 1976. 80 p. No DA listing.

1627. Wenk, Arthur B. "An analysis of Debussy's Piano Preludes, Book I." MA thesis (Theory): Cornell University, 1967.

Six épigraphes antiques
1628. Hirsbrunner, Theo. "Claude Debussy und Pierre Louÿs. Zu den *Six épigraphes antiques* von Debussy." MF 31(1978): 426-442.

Sonata for flute, viola and harp
   1629. Allen, Judith Shatin. "Tonal allusion and illusion: Debussy's Sonata for flute, viola and harp." CAD 7(1983): 38-48.

Songs
   1630. Briscoe, James R. "Debussy *d'après* Debussy: The further resonance of two early *Mélodies*." NCM 5(1981-1982): 110-116.
   1631. ----. "Debussy's earliest songs." CMS 24/2(1984): 81-94.
   1632. Fischer, Kurt von. "Bemerkungen zu der zwei Ausgaben von Debussys *Ariettes oubliées*." Fs. Federhofer: 283-289.
   1633. Hirsbrunner, Theo. "Debussy--Maeterlinck--Chausson: Literary and musical connections." MMA 13(1984): 57-65. [*Proses lyriques*]
   1634. ----. "Debussy--Maeterlinck--Chausson: Musikalische und literarische Querverbindungen." Fs. Schuh: 47-66.
   1635. ----. "Musik und Dichtung im französischen *Fin de siècle* am Beispiel der *Proses lyriques* von Claude Debussy." Schnitzler/D: 152-174.
   1636. ----. "Zu Debussys und Ravels Mallarmé-Vertonungen." AM 35(1978): 81-103.
   1637. Hsu, Samuel. "Imagery and diction in the songs of Claude Debussy." PhD dissertation (Musicology): University of California, Santa Barbara, 1972. UM 72-26,832. DA XXXIII.5, p.2413-A.
   1638. Koechlin, Charles. "Quelques anciennes mélodies inédites de Claude Debussy." RM Special Number (1926): 115(211)-140(236).
   1639. Nichols, Roger. "Debussy's two settings of *Clair de lune*." ML 48(1967): 229-235.
   1640. Ruschenburg, Peter. "Stilkritische Untersuchungen zu den Liedern Claude Debussys." PhD dissertation: University of Hamburg, 1966.
   1641. Wenk, Arthur B. "Claude Debussy and the poets." PhD dissertation (Musicology): Cornell University, 1970. UM 70-23,094. DA XXXI.6. [Includes several appendices not contained in following entry]
   1642. ----. *Claude Debussy and the poets*. Berkeley: University of California Press, 1976. 345 p. [Includes several chapters not contained in the preceding entry]
   1643. Youens, Susan Lee. "Debussy's setting of Verlaine's *Colloque sentimental*: From the past to the present." SMU 15(1981): 93-105.
   1644. ----. "From the fifteenth century to the twentieth: Considerations of musical prosody in Debussy's *Trois ballades de François Villon*." JM 2(1983): 418-433.

String Quartet
   1645. Dietschy, Marcel. "Wagner et le Quatuor de Debussy." SMZ 121(1981): 243-247.

Syrinx
   1646. Bopp, Joseph. "*Syrinx* von Claude Debussy." T 7/8(1982-1983): 265-267.
   1647. Borris, Siegfried. "Claude Debussy: *Syrinx* für Soloflöte." MB 4(1969): 173-175.

Trois chansons de Charles d'Orléans
1648. Böhmer, Helga. "Claude Debussy (1862-1918): *Yver, vous n'estes qu'un vilain* für vierstimmigen Chor a cappella aus den *Trois chansons de Charles d'Orléans.*" Fs. Rohlfs: 453-454.

Trois nocturnes
1649. Fischer, Kurt von. "Debussy and the climate of Art Nouveau: Some remarks on Debussy's aesthetics." MMA 13(1984): 49-56.
1650. Lang-Becker, Elke. *Debussy: Nocturnes.* München: W. Fink, 1982.

Other works
1651. Alfred, Everett Maurice. "A study of selected choral works of Claude Debussy." PhD dissertation: Texas Tech University, 1980. UM 81-11,943. DA XLI.12, p.4878-A. [*La damoiselle élue; Trois chansons; Ode à la France*]
1652. Berman, Laurence D. "The evolution of tonal thinking in the works of Claude Debussy." PhD dissertation: Harvard University, 1965. No DA listing.
1653. Brăiloiu, Constantin. "Pentatony in Debussy's music." Fs. Bartók/S: 377-417.
1654. Briscoe, James Robert. "The compositions of Claude Debussy's formative years (1879-1887)." PhD dissertation: University of North Carolina, 1979. 448 p. UM 79-25,888. DA XL.8, p.4290-A.
1655. Brynside, Ronald Lee. "Debussy's second style." PhD dissertation (Musicology): University of Illinois, 1971. UM 72-06,878. DA XXXII.8, p.4647-A.
1656. Carner, Mosco. "Debussy and Puccini." Carner: 139-147.
1657. Cnattingius, Claes M. "Notes sur les oeuvres de jeunesse de Claude Debussy." STM 44(1962): 31-53.
1658. Crapps, Lyra Nabors. "Compensatory change as a formal element in selected compositions of Debussy." MM dissertation: Florida State University, Tallahassee, 1970.
1659. DeLone, Peter. "Claude Debussy, *contrapuntiste malgré lui.*" CMS 17/2(1977): 48-63.
1660. Denissow, Edison. "Über einige Besonderheiten der Kompositionstechnik Claude Debussys." DJM (1978): 147-172. [JP 1(1978): 147-172]
1661. Dionisi, Renato. "Aspetti tecnici e sviluppo storica del sistema 'esacordale' da Debussy in poi." RIM 1(1966): 49-67.
1662. Gervais, Françoise. "Étude comparée des langages harmoniques de Fauré et de Debussy." PhD dissertation (Letters): Paris, 1954.
1663. ----. "Structures Debussystes." RM 258(1962): 77-88.
1664. Gitter, Felix. "Die Programmatik in klavieristischen und orchestralen Schaffen von Claude Debussy." PhD dissertation (Musicology): Halle-Salle, 1973.
1665. Gruber, Gernot. "Zur Funktion der 'primären Klangformen' in der Musik Debussys." Fs. Federhofer: 272-282.
1666. Hilse, Walter Bruno. "Hindemith and Debussy." HJ 2(1972): 48-90.
1667. Holloway, Robin. *Debussy and Wagner.* London: Eulenberg Books, 1979. 235 p.

1668. Howat, Roy. *Debussy in proportion: A musical analysis.* Cambridge: Cambridge University Press, 1983. 239 p.

1669. ----. "Proportional structure in the music of Claude Debussy." PhD dissertation (Musicology): King's College, Cambridge, 1979.

1670. Jakobik, Albert. *Claude Debussy oder die lautlose Revolution in der Musik.* Würzburg: K. Triltsch, 1977. 164 p. [*Prélude à l'après-midi d'un faune; Nocturnes; Pelléas et Mélisande* (first scene); *La Mer; Jeux*]

1671. Koechlin, Charles. "Sur l'evolution de la musique française avant et après Debussy." RM 16(1935): 264-280.

1672. Leibowitz, René. "L'Interpretation de Debussy." *Le Compositeur et son double: Essais sur l'interpretation musicale.* Paris: Gallimard, 1971: 201-209. [*Prélude à l'après-midi d'un faune; Jeux*]

1673. Liess, Andreas. "Claude Debussy und der *Art nouveau*: Ein Entwurf." STU 4(1975): 245-276; 5(1976): 143-234.

1674. Lockspeiser, Edward. "Musorgsky and Debussy." MQ 23(1937): 421-427.

1675. Mueller, Robert Earl. "The concept of tonality in Impressionist music: Based on the works of Debussy and Ravel." PhD dissertation (Theory): Indiana University, 1954. UM 54-10,153. DA XIV.11, p.2088.

1676. Orledge, Robert. *Debussy and the theatre.* Cambridge: Cambridge University Press, 1982.

1677. ----. "Debussy's second English ballet: *Le Palais du silence* or *No-Ja-Li*." CM 22(1976): 73-87.

1678. Park, Raymond. "The later style of Claude Debussy." PhD dissertation: University of Michigan, 1966. UM 67-15,699. DA XXVIII.7, p.2718-A.

1679. Ringgold, John Robert. "The linearity of Debussy's music and its correspondances with the symbolist esthetic: Developments before 1908." PhD dissertation (Musicology): University of Southern California, 1972. UM 73-00,762. DA XXXIII.7, p.3700-A.

1680. Schmidt-Garre, Helmut. "Die Klangstruktur Debussy: In ihrem Beziehung zur Mehrstimmigkeit des Mittelalters." MELOS 17(1950): 104-106.

1681. Starr, Lawrence. "The modern composer, the conservative audience . . . and Debussy." CAD 8(1984): 13-17.

1682. Stuckenschmidt, H.H. "Debussy or Berg? The mystery of a chord progression." MQ 51(1965): 453-459.

1683. Warburton, Thomas. "Bitonal miniatures by Debussy from 1913." CAD 6(1982): 5-15.

1684. Watson, Linda Lee. "Debussy: A programmatic approach to form." PhD dissertation: University of Texas, Austin, 1978. No DA listing. [*En blanc et noir; Le martyre de Saint Sebastien; Six épigraphes antiques*]

1685. Weber, Edith, ed. *Debussy et l'évolution de la musique au XXe siècle.* Paris: Editions du Centre National de la Recherche Scientifique, 1965.

1686. Wenk, Arthur B. *Claude Debussy and twentieth-century music.* Boston: G.K. Hall, 1983.

1687. Whitman, Ernestine. "Analysis and performance critique of Debussy's flute works." DMA dissertation: University of Wisconsin, 1977. No DA listing. [*Syrinx*; Sonata for flute, viola and harp]

1688. Winzer, Dieter. *Claude Debussy und die französische musikalische Tradition.* Wiesbaden: Breitkopf und Härtel, 1981.
1689. Whittall, Arnold. "Tonality and the whole-tone scale in the music of Debussy." MR 36(1975): 261-271.
1690. Woollen, Russell. "Episodic compositional techniques in late Debussy." JAMS 11(1958): 79-80.
1691. Zenck-Maurer, Claudia. *Versuch über die wahre Art, Debussy zu analysieren.* München: E. Katzbichler, 1974.

DECAUX, ABEL (1869-1943)

1692. Schenewerk, Joyce L. "Abel Decaux's *Clairs de lune.*" MA dissertation (Theory): University of Rochester, 1977.

DEL BORGO, ELLIOT (born 1938)

1693. Toering, Ronald J. "An analysis of Elliot Del Borgo's *Do Not Go Gentle into that Good Night.*" JBR 21/1(1985): 1-21.

DELDEN, LEX VAN (born 1919)

1694. Delden, Lex van. "Lex van Delden: Impromptu for Solo Harp, Op.48." SS 7(1961): 25-27.

DELIUS, FREDERICK (1862-1934)

Chamber works
1695. Bacon-Shone, Frederic. "Form in the chamber music of Frederick Delius." PhD dissertation (Musicology): University of Southern California, 1976, No DA listing.

Koanga
1696. Randel, William. "*Koanga* and its libretto." ML 52(1971): 141-156.

The Magic Fountain
1697. Threlfall, Robert. "Delius's unknown opera: *The Magic Fountain.*" SMU 11(1977): 60-73.

A Mass of Life
1698. Boyle, Andrew J. "*A Mass of Life* and its 'Bell-Motif'." MR 42 (1982): 44-50.

Requiem
1699. Payne, Anthony. "Delius's Requiem." TEMPO 76(1966): 12-17.

Songs
1700. Holland, Arthur Keith. *The songs of Delius.* London: Oxford University Press, 1951.

1701. Hutchings, Edward Gillmore, III. "The published solo songs of Frederick Delius." DMA dissertation: University of Miami, 1980. No DA listing.

Other works

1702. Cooke, Deryck. "Delius the unknown." PRMA 89(1962-1963): 17-29.

1703. Grimes, Doreen. "Form in the orchestral music of Frederick Delius." PhD dissertation (Theory): North Texas State University, 1966. UM 66-6411. DA XXVII.1, p.221-A.

1704. Jones, Philip B.R. "The American sources of Delius's style." PhD dissertation (Musicology): Birmingham, 1982.

1705. Morrison.

1706. Palmer, Christopher. "Delius and Percy Grainger." ML 52 (1971): 418-415.

1707. Payne, Anthony. "Delius's stylistic development." TEMPO 60(1961): 6-16.

1708. Special Issue: TEMPO 26(1952-1953).

DELLO JOIO, NORMAN (born 1913)

1709. Boston, Nancy J. "The piano sonatas and suites of Norman Dello Joio (1940-1948)." DMA dissertation (Performance): Peabody Conservatory, 1984. 177 p. No DA listing.

1710. Bumgardner, Thomas Arthur. "The solo vocal works of Norman Dello Joio." DMA dissertation: University of Texas, Austin, 1973. 232 p. UM 74-5180. DA XXXIV.9, p.6019-A.

1711. Downes, Edward. "The music of Norman Dello Joio." MQ 48 (1962): 149-172.

1712. Jeter. [*Aria and toccata*]

1713. Mize.

1714. Whalen, J. Robert. "A comparative study of the Sonata Number Three for Piano and the *Variations, Chaconne, and Finale* for Orchestra by Norman Dello Joio." DM dissertation (Piano): Indiana University, 1968. No DA listing.

DEL TREDICI, DAVID (born 1937)

1715. Earls, Paul. "David Del Tredici: *Syzygy.*" PNM 9/2-10/1(1971): 304-313.

1716. Knussen, Oliver. "David Del Tredici and *Syzygy.*" TEMPO 118(1976): 8-15.

DEMESSIEUX, JEANNE (1921-1968)

1717. Dorroh.

DENNIS, BRIAN (born 1941)

1718. Hill, Peter. "The Chinese song-cycles of Brian Dennis." TEMPO 137(1981): 23-29.

DESSAU, PAUL (1894-1979)

1719. Hennenberg, Fritz. "Kosmosforschung als sinfonisches Subjekt: Kommentar zur Orchestermusik Nr.2 *Meer der Stürme* von Paul Dessau." MG 18(1968): 177-183.

1720. ----. "Mozart-Modern: Bermerkungen zu Paul Dessaus 'Sinfonischer Adaptation' des Streichquintetts in Es Dur von W.A. Mozart (KV 614)." MG 16(1966): 375-379.

1721. ----. "Paul Dessaus Theatermusik: Kommentar, Deutung, Werkübersicht: Zum 65. Geburtstag des Komponisten." MG 9/12(1959): 3-10.

1722. Müller, Gerhard. "Paul Dessaus Konzeption einer politischen Musik." JP 3(1980): 9-26.

1723. Rienäcker, Gerd. "Analytische Bemerkungen zu Dessaus Oper *Einstein*." MG 24(1974): 711-717.

1724. ----. "Zur Dialektik musikdramaturgischer Gestaltung: Analytische Notate zum zwölften Bild der Oper *Lanzelot* von Paul Dessau." DJM 64(1972): 79-97.

1725. Spieler, Heinrich. "Tradition und Zeitgenössisches Denken: Paul Dessaus Bach-Variationen." MG 14(1964): 714-724.

DETT, ROBERT NATHANIEL (1881-1943)

1726. McBrier, Vivian F. "The life and works of Robert Nathaniel Dett." PhD dissertation (Musicology): Catholic University, 1967. UM 67-17,142. DA XXVIII.8, p.3212-A.

DE VRIES, KLAAS   see   VRIES, KLAAS DE

DIEPENBROCK, ALPHONS (1862-1921)

1727. Reeser, Eduard. "Alphons Diepenbrock: Music for *Elektra*." SS 12(1962): 12-14.

1728. ----. "Alphons Diepenbrock: The commemoration of the centenary of his birth." SS 12(1962): 1-11.

1729. ----. "Some melodic patterns in the music of Alphons Diepenbrock." KN 3(1976): 16-25.

DIEREN, BERNARD VAN (1884-1936)

1730. Grouse, Gordon. "Bernard van Dieren: Three early songs in relation to his subsequent development." MR 29(1968): 116-122.

1731. Williams, Robert. "The life and work of Bernard van Dieren." PhD dissertation (Musicology): Aberystwyth, 1980.

DIETRICH, KARL (born 1927)

1732. Kober, Kleinhardt. "Karl Dietrichs sinfonisches Schaffen als Ausdruck sozialistischen Lebensgefühls." PhD dissertation (Musicology): Halle-Salle, 1981.

1733. Kneipel, Eberhard. "Die Analyse: Dramatische Szenen für drei Flöteninstrumente und grosses Orchester (1974) von Karl Dietrich." MG 25(19750: 525-529.

DINESCU, VIOLETA (born 1953)

1734. Dinescu, Violeta. "Allgemeine Gedanken zum Komponieren." N 4(1983-1984): 46-52.

DISTLER, HUGO (1908-1942)

1735. Bergaas, Mark Jerome. "Compositional style in the keyboard works of Hugo Distler (1908-1942)." PhD dissertation (Music History): Yale University, 1978. UM 79-15,802. DA XLI.1, p.16-A.
1736. Neumann, Friedrich. "Anmerkungen zum Kompositionsstil Hugo Distlers." M 33(1979-1980): 16-21.
1737. Rhoades.
1738. Schmolzi, Herbert. "Das Wort-Ton-Verhältnis in Distlers Choralpassion." M 7(1953): 556-561.

DITTRICH, PAUL-HEINZ (born 1930)

1739. Hansen, Mathias. "Die Analyse: Violoncellokonzerte von Paul-Heinz Dittrich, Siegfried Matthus und Christfried Schmidt." MG 29(1979): 591-599.

DOHNANYI, ERNST VON (1877-1960)

1740. Hallman, Milton. "Ernö Dohnanyi's solo piano works." JALS 17(1985): 48-54.
1741. Mabry, George Louis. "The vocal and choral works of Ernst von Dohnanyi." PhD dissertation (Musicology): George Peabody College, 1973. 207 p. UM 73-32,643. DA XXXIV.7, p.4316-A.
1742. Mintz, George Jacob. "Textural patterns in the solo piano music of Ernst von Dohnanyi." PhD dissertation (Theory): Florida State University, 1976. UM 76-29,463. DA XXXVII.7, p.3979-A.

DONATONI, FRANCO (born 1927)

1743. Stoianova, Ivanka. "Franco Donatoni: *Souvenir*." MR 20(1975): 4-14.

DONIZETTI, GAETANO (1797-1848)

1744. Ashbrook, William. "*L'Ange de Nisida* di Donizetti." RIM 16(1981): 96-114.
1745. ----. *Donizetti*. London: Cassell, 1965.
1746. ----. *Donizetti and his operas*. Cambridge: Cambridge University Press, 1982.
1747. ASO 55(1983) [*Lucia di Lammermoor*]

1748. Dean, Winton. "Donizetti's serious operas." PRMA 100 (1973-1974): 123-141.
1749. Gossett, Philip. *Anna Bolena and the artistic maturity of Gaetano Donizetti.* Oxford: Clarendon Press, 1985.
1750. Levy, Janet M. "Texture as a sign in classic and early romantic music." JAMS 35(1982): 482-531. [*Anna Bolena*]
1751. Lippmann, Friedrich. "Donizetti und Bellini: Ein Beitrag zur Interpretation von Donizettis Stil." STU 4(1975): 193-243.

DORÁTI, ANTAL (born 1906)

1752. MacDonald, Calum. "Antal Doráti, composer: A catalog of his works." TEMPO 143(1982): 16-24.

DRAESEKE, FELIX (1835-1913)

1753. Follert, Udo-R. "Felix Draeseke (1835-1913): Eine Bekanntmachung am Beispiel seines Requiem H-moll, Op.22." MK 52(1982): 226-235.

DREYFUS, GEORGE (born 1928)

1754. Lucas, Kay. "George Dreyfus's *Garni Sands*: A forward step for Australian opera." SMU 7(1973): 78-87.

DRIESSLER, JOHANNES (born 1921)

1755. Platen, Emil. "Johannes Driesslers Oratorium *Dein Reich komme.*" MK 21(1951): 113-122.

DRUCKMAN, JACOB (born 1928)

1756. Uscher, Nancy. "Two contemporary viola concerti: A comparative study." TEMPO 147(1983): 23-29.

DRUMMOND, JOHN (born 1949)

1757. Drummond, John. "*Narcissus* and tonality." CT 2(1971): 18-19.

DUKAS, PAUL (1865-1935)

1758. Boyd, Everett Vernon, Jr. "Paul Dukas and the impressionist milieu: Stylistic assimilation in three orchestral works." PhD dissertation (Theory): University of Rochester, 1980. UM 80-04,011. DA XLI.3, p.841-A. [*L'Apprenti sorcier; Ariane et Barbe-Bleue; La Péri*]
1759. Favre, Georges. *L'Oeuvre de Paul Dukas.* Paris: Durand, 1969.
1760. Kniesner. [Piano Sonata in E-Flat Minor]
1761. Minger, Frederick. "The piano works of Paul Dukas." DMA dissertation (Peformance): Peabody Conservatory, 1982. No DA listing.
1762. Reinfandt, Karl-Heintz. "Unterrichtsplanung im Fachmusik am Beispiel *Der Zauberlehrling* von Paul Dukas." MB 6(1973): 389-396.

DUNCAN, JOHN

1763. Spence, Martha Ellen Blanding. "Selected song cycles of three contemporary Black American composers: William Grant Still, *Songs of Separation*, Hale Smith, *Beyond the Rim of Day*, John Duncan, *Blue Set*." DMA dissertation (Performance): University of Southern Mississippi, 1977. No DA listing.

DUNHAM, HENRY MORTON (1853-1929)

1764. Gamble, Jane Council. "The organ sonatas of Henry Morton Dunham." DMA dissertation: Memphis State University, 1980. No DA listing.

DUPARC, HENRI (1848-1933)

1765. Elst, Nancy van der. *Henri Duparc: L'Homme et son oeuvre.* Lille Service de Reproduction des Thèses, Université de Lille, 1972.

DUPRÉ, MARCEL (1886-1971)

1766. Delestre, R. *L'Oeuvre de Marcel Dupré.* Paris: Éditions "Musique Sacrée," 1952.

1767. Dorroh.

1768. Pagett, John Mason. "The music of Marcel Dupré." SMD dissertation (Sacred Music): Union Theological Seminary, 1975. UM 75-1923. DA XXXVI.3, p.1159-A.

1769. Rhoades.

1770. Van Wye, Benjamin. "Marcel Dupré's Marian Vespers and the French *alternatim* tradition." MR 43(1982): 192-224.

DURUFLÉ, MAURICE (born 1902)

1771. Beechey, Gwilym. "The music of Maurice Duruflé." MR 32(1971): 146-155.

1772. Dorroh.

1773. McIntosh, John Stuart. "The organ music of Maurice Duruflé." DMA dissertation (Performance): University of Rochester, 1973. 180 p. RILM 76/11056dd28. No DA listing.

1774. Rhoades.

DUSSEK, JOHANN LADISLAUS (1760-1812)

1775. Grossman, Orin Louis. "The solo piano sonatas of Jan Ladislav Dussek." PhD dissertation (Musicology): Yale University, 1975. 258 p. UM 75-24,541. DA XXXVI.5, p.2479-A.

1776. Schwarting, Heino. "The piano sonatas of Johann Ladislaus Dussek." PQ 91(1975): 41-45.

DUTILLEUX, HENRI (born 1915)

    1777. Delente, Gail Buchanan. "Selected piano music in France since 1945." PhD dissertation (Performance Practice): Washington University, 1966. UM 66-11,869. DA XXVII.6, p.1849-A. [Piano Sonata]
    1778. Kniesner.

DVOŘÁK, ANTONÍN (1841-1904)

Cello Concerto
    1779. Clapham, John. "Dvořák's Cello Concerto in B Minor: A masterpiece in the making." MR 40(1979): 123-140.
    1780. ----. "Dvorák's First Cello Concerto." ML 37(1956): 350-355.

Chamber works [see also individual categories]
    1781. Beveridge, David. "Sophisticated primitivism: The significance of pentatonicism in Dvořák's *American Quartet*." CM 24(1977): 25-36.
    1782. Kull, Hans. *Dvořáks Kammermusik*. Bern: Haupt, 1948.
    1783. Šourek, Otakar. *The chamber music of Antonįn Dvořák*. Prague: Artia, 1956.

Operas
    1784. Clapham, John. "The operas of Antonįn Dvořák." PRMA 84(1957-1958): 55-69.
    1785. Schläder, Jurgen. "Märchenoper oder symbolistisches Musikdrama? Zum Interpretationsrahmen der Titelrolle in Dvořáks *Rusalka*." MF 34(1981): 25-39.

Piano Quintet
    1786. Hollander, Hans. "Schubertsches bei Dvořák." M 28(1974): 40-43.

Piano Trios
    1787. Case, Barbara Betty Bacik. "The relation between structure and the treatment of instruments in the first movements of Dvořák's piano trios Opus 21, 26, and 65." DMA dissertation: University of Texas, Austin, 1977. No DA listing.

Symphonies
    1788. Clapham, John. "Dvořák's Symphony in D Minor: The creative process." ML 42(1961): 103-116.
    1789. ----. "The evolution of Dvořák's Symphony *From the New World*." MQ 44(1958): 167-183.

Other works
    1790. Abraham, Gerald. "Verbal inspiration in Dvořák's instrumental music." SM 11(1969): 27-34.
    1791. Beveridge, David. "Romantic ideas in a classical frame: The sonata forms of Dvořák." PhD dissertation (Musicology): University of California, Berkeley, 1980. 409 p. UM 81-12,963. DA XLII.1, p.11-A.

1792. Boese, Helmut. *Zwei Urmusikanten: Smetana, Dvořák.* Zürich: Almathea, 1955.

1793. Clapham, John. *Antonįn Dvořák: Musician and craftsman.* London: Faber & Faber, 1966.

1794. ----. "Dvořák's relations with Brahms and Hanslick." MQ 57 (1971): 241-254.

1795. ----. "The national origins of Dvořák's art." PRMA 89 (1962-1963): 75-88.

1796. Hollander, Hans. "Die tschechisch-amerikanische Synthese in Dvořáks Musik aus der Neuen Welt." M 29(1975): 122-124.

1797. Komma, Karl Michael. "Die Pentatonik in Antonįn Dvořáks Werk." MO 1(1962): 63-75.

1798. Šourek, Otakar. *Antonįn Dvořák: Werkanalysen.* Prague: Artia, 1956.

1799. ----. *The orchestral works of Antonįn Dvořák.* Prague: Artia, 1957.

EBEN, PETR (born 1929)

1800. Landale, Susan. "Die Orgelmusik von Petr Eben." MK 50(1980): 248-259.

EBERL, ANTON (1765-1807)

1801. White, A. Duane. "The piano works of Anton Eberl (1765-1807)." PhD dissertation (Musicology): University of Wisconsin, 1971. UM 71-20,699. DA XXXII.4, p.2125-A.

EGK, WERNER (1901-1983)

1802. Häusler, Josef. "'Choucoun': Reflexion und Verwandlung (*Variations über ein karibisches Thema*)." MELOS 26(1959): 373-376.

EIMERT, HERBERT (1897-1972)

1803. Oesch, Hans. "Herbert Eimert: Pionier der Zwölftontechnik." MELOS 41(1974): 211-214.

EINEM, GOTTFRIED VON (born 1918)

1804. Klein, Rudolf. "Gottfried von Einems Oper *Jesu Hochzeit*." OMZ 35(1980): 189-199.

1805. ----. "Gottfried von Einems Oper *Kabale und Liebe*." OMZ 31(1976): 633-639.

1806. Saathen, Friedrich. "Committed opera: Gottfried von Einem's *The Visit of the Old Lady*." TEMPO 104(1973): 22-29.

1807. Schollum, Robert. "Die Klavierlieder Gottfried von Einems." OMZ 28(1973): 80-86.

EISLER, HANNS (1898-1962)

Cantatas
    1808. Grabs, Manfred. "Über Hanns Eislers Kammerkantaten." MG 18 (1968): 445-454.

Chamber works
    1809. Mainka, Jürgen. "Zum Finale von Eislers Septett Nr.1." MG 28 (1978): 412-413.

Songs
    1810. Elsner, Jürgen. "Zum 70. Geburtstag Hanns Eislers: Die Majakowski-Vertonungen." MG 18(1968): 435-444.
    1811. Grabs, Manfred. *"Wir, so gut es gelang, haben das Unsre getan*: Zur Aussage der Hölderlin-Vertonungen Hanns Eislers." BM 15(1973): 49-60.
    1812. Rösler, Walter. "Zu einigen Tucholsky-Liedern Hanns Eislers." BM 15(1973): 81-92.
    1813. Stephan, Rudolf. *"Zeitungsausschnitte* und *Kinderreime*: Zu einigen Liedern von Hanns Eisler und Theodor W. Adorno." OMZ 39(1984): 18-22.

Symphonies
    1814. Szeskus, Richard. "Bemerkungen zur Eislers *Deutscher Sinfonie*." MG 23(1973): 390-396.

Other works
    1815. Allihn, Ingeborg. "Die Musik Hanns Eislers zu Stücken von Bertolt Brecht." PhD dissertation (Musicology): Humboldt-Universität, Berlin, 1979.
    1816. Csipák, Károly. *Probleme der Volkstümlichkeit bei Hanns Eisler*. München: E. Katzbichler, 1975.
    1817. Hauska, Hans. "Hanns Eisler: Ouvertüre zu einem Lustpiel." MG 13(1963): 148-149.
    1818. ----. "Hanns Eisler: *Winterschlact-Suite*." MG 12(1962): 416-417.
    1819. Knepler, Georg. *"Was des Eislers ist . . ."* BM 15(1973): 29-48.
    1820. Stern, Dietrich. "Hanns Eislers Balladen für Gesang und kleines Orchester." SM 18(1976): 169-182.
    1821. Special Issues: BM 15(1973).

ELGAR, EDWARD (1857-1934)

    1822. Dann, Mary G. "Elgar's use of the sequence." ML 19(1938): 255-264.
    1823. Porte, John F. *Sir Edward Elgar*. London: K. Paul, Trench, Truber, 1921.
    1824. Ridout, Godfrey. "Elgar, the angular Saxon." CMJ 1/4(1957): 33-40.
    1825. Westrup, Jack A. "Elgar's Enigma." PRMA 86(1959-1960): 79-97.

EMMANUEL, MAURICE (1862-1938)

1826. Carlson, Eleanor Anne. "Maurice Emmanuel and the six sonatinas for piano." DMA dissertation (Performance): Boston University, 1974. No DA listing.
1827. Fs. Emmanuel. [Several articles on Emmanuel's music]

ENESCO, GEORGES (1881-1955)

1828. Lejtes, Ruf. "*Oedipe* by Georges Enesco." PhD dissertation (Musicology): Leningrad, 1970.
1829. Newman, Elaine W. "Enesco's *Oedipe*: A little-known masterpiece." CM 26(1978): 99-105.

ERB, DONALD (born 1927)

1830. Cope: 232-235. [*Souvenir* (1970)]

ERDMANN, EDUARD (1896-1958)

1831. Baumgartner, Paul. "Das Konzertstück Op.18." Fs. Erdmann: 152-155.
1832. Scherliess, Volker. "Zum Streichquartett Op.17." Fs. Erdmann: 156-162.

ESCHER, RUDOLF (1912-1980)

1833. Escher, Rudolf. "Rudolf Escher: Musique pour l'esprit en deuil." SS 20(1964): 15-33.
1834. ----. "Rudolf Escher: Quintette a fiati." SS 34(1968): 24-34.
1835. Paap, Wouter. "*Le Tombeau de Ravel* by Rudolf Escher." SS 4 (1960): 136-137.

ESSER, HEINRICH (1818-1872)

1836. Müller, Karl-Josef. *Heinrich Esser als Komponist*. Kassel: Bärenreiter-Antiquariat, 1969.

ETLER, ALVIN (1913-1973)

1837. Nichols, William Roy. "The wind music of Alvin Etler." DMA dissertation (Performance): University of Iowa, 1976. UM 77-13,154. DA XXXVII.12, p.7396-A.
1838. Shelden, Paul Melvin. "Alvin Etler (1913-1973): His career and the two sonatas for clarinet." DMA dissertation: University of Maryland, 1978. UM 79-20,730. DA XL.3, p.1146-A.
1839. Wise.

EYBLER, JOSEPH (1765-1846)

1840. Ricks, Robert W. "The published masses of Joseph Eybler, 1765-1846." PhD dissertation (Musicology): Catholic University, 1967. UM 67-15,445. DA XXVIII.6, p.2282-A.

FALLA, MANUEL DE (1876-1946)

1841. Brownscombe, Peter. "Spanish nationalism and impressionism as represented in Manuel de Falla's *Homenaje: Pour le tombeau de Debussy*." D 5/1(1973): 1-10.

1842. Budwig, Andrew. "Manuel de Falla's *Atlantida*: An historical and analytical study." PhD dissertation (Musicology): University of Chicago, 1984. 385 p. No DA listing.

1843. Concepción, Elman Augusto. "An analysis of twelve published works of Manuel de Falla y Matheu for voice and piano." DMA dissertation (Performance): University of Miami, 1981. No DA listing.

1844. Mayer-Serra, Otto. "Falla's musical nationalism." MQ 29(1943): 1-17.

1845. Morrison.

FANO, MICHEL (born 1929)

1846. Toop, Richard. "Messiaen/Goeyvaerts, Fano/Stockhausen, Boulez." PNM 13/1(1974-1975): 141-169. [Sonata (1951)]

FARWELL, ARTHUR (1872-1952)

1847. Kirk, Edgar L. "Toward American music: A study of the life and music of Arthur Farwell." PhD dissertation (Theory): University of Rochester, 1959. 2 vols. No DA listing.

FAUCHET, PAUL ROBERT MARCEL (1881-1937)

1848. Mitchell, Jon C. "Paul Robert Marcel Fauchet: *Symphonie pour musique d'harmonie* (Symphony in B Flat)." JBR 20/2(1983-1984): 8-26.

FAURÉ, GABRIEL (1845-1924)

Chamber works
1849. Favre, Max. *Gabriel Faurés Kammermusik*. Zürich: Niehans, 1947.

1850. Knox, Roger Martin. "Counterpoint in Gabriel Fauré's String Quartet, Op.121." MA dissertation (Theory): Indiana University, 1978.

1851. Rorick, William C. "The A Major Violin Sonatas of Fauré and Franck: A stylistic comparison." MR 42(1981): 46-55.

Piano works
1852. Austin, William W. "Tonalität und Form in den Preludes Op.103 von Gabriel Fauré." Kühn: 399-401.

1853. Crouch, Richard Henry. "The nocturnes and barcarolles for solo piano of Gabriel Fauré." PhD dissertation (Musicology): Catholic University, 1980. 220 p. UM 80-19,200. DA XLI.3, p.841-A.

1854. Dommel-Diény, Amy. *Gabriel Fauré*. Dommel-Diény 12. Paris: Dommel-Diény, 1974. [Theme and Variations, Op.33; Three Nocturnes: Op.73, No.1; Op.63, No.6; Op.119, No.13]

1855. Sanger, G. Norman. "Chromaticism in the keyboard works of Franck and Fauré." PhD dissertation (Musicology): University of Pittsburgh, 1976. 263 p. UM 77-03,035. DA XXXVII.8, p.4688-A.

1856. Valicenti, Joseph Anthony. "The thirteen nocturnes of Gabriel Faure." DMA dissertation: University of Miami, 1980. No DA listing.

Songs

1857. Bland, Stephen F. "The songs of Gabriel Fauré." PhD dissertation (Theory): Florida State University, 1976.

1858. Dommel-Diény, Amy. *Fauré*. Dommel-Diény 13. Neuchâtel: Delachaux et Niestlé, 1967. [*Prison; Les Roses d'Isapahan; Le Secret; Au cimetière; L'Horizon chimérique*]

1859. Fortassier, Pierre. "Le Rythme dans les mélodies de Gabriel Fauré." RDM 62(1976): 257-274.

1860. Jankélévitch, Vladimir. *Gabriel Fauré et ses mélodies*. Paris: Librarie Plon, 1938.

1861. Kurtz, James Lawrence. "Problems of tonal structure in songs of Gabriel Fauré." PhD dissertation (Theory): Brandeis University, 1970. 80 p. UM 70-24,645. DA XXXI.7, p.3583-A.

1862. Orledge, Robert. "The two endings of Fauré's *Soir*." ML 60 (1979): 316-322.

1863. Sommers, Paul Bartholin. "Fauré and his songs: The relationship of text, melody and accompaniment." DMA dissertation (Performance): University of Illinois, 1969. 175 p. RILM 69/4261dd28. No DA listing.

Other works

1864. Gervais, Françoise. *Étude comparée des langages harmoniques de Fauré et de Debussy*. Paris: La Revue musicale, 1971.

1865. Nectoux, Jean-Michel. "Le *Pelléas* de Fauré." RDM 67(1981): 169-190.

1866. ----. "Works renounced, themes rediscovered: *Elements pour une thématique fauréenne*." NCM 2(1978-1979): 231-244.

FEBEL, REINHARD (born 1952)

1867. Febel, Reinhard. "Anmerkungen zu *Komitas* und Variationen für Orchester." N 2(1981-1982): 35-40.

1868. Heiland, Tilman. "Reinhard Febel: Variationen für Orchester." N 2(1981-1982): 41-44.

FELCIANO, RICHARD (born 1930)

1869. Christiansen, Sigurd Olaf. "The sacred music of Richard Felciano: An analytical study." DMA dissertation (Performance): University of Illinois, 1977. UM 77-14,937. DA XXXVIII.1, p.16-A.

FELDMAN, MORTON (born 1926)

1870. Gronemeyer, Gisela. "Momente von grosser Schönheit: Zu Morton Feldmans neuem Stück *Crippled Symmetry*." MTX 4(1984): 5-9.
1871. Gruhn, Wilfried. "Klang und Stille: Gedanken zur kompositorischen Arbeit Morton Feldmans." MB 14/3(1982): 147-152.

FERGUSON, HOWARD (born 1908)

1872. McBurney, Gerard. "Howard Ferguson in 1983." TEMPO 147(1983): 2-6.
1873. Russell, John. "Howard Fergusons's Concerto for Piano and String Orchestra." TEMPO 24(1952): 24-25.

FERNEYHOUGH, BRIAN (born 1943)

1874. Potter, Keith, Kathryn Lukas, Kevin Corner and Malcolm Barry. "Brian Ferneyhough." CT 20(1979): 4-15.

FERRERO, LORENZO (born 1951)

1875. Ferrero, Lorenzo. "*Marilyn*: Anmerkungen zur Oper." N 3(1982-1983): 142-146.

FIELD, JOHN (1782-1837)

1876. Branson, David. *John Field and Chopin*. London: Barrie & Jenkins, 1972.
1877. Hibbard, Trevor Davies. "John Field's *Rondeaux* on 'Speed the Plough'." MR 24(1963): 139-146.
1878. Piggott, Patrick. *The life and music of John Field, 1782-1837, creator of the nocturne*. Berkeley: University of California Press, 1973.
1879. Southall, Geneva Handy. "John Field's piano concertos: An analytical and historical study." PhD dissertation: University of Iowa, 1966. UM 67-02,680. DA XXVIII.4, p.1461.

FINE, IRVING (1914-1962)

1880. Epstein, David. "Symphony (1962)." PNM 3/2(1965): 160-164.
1881. Wise.

FINNEY, ROSS LEE (born 1906)

1882. Amman, Douglas D. "The choral music of Ross Lee Finney." PhD dissertation (Musicology): University of Cincinnati, 1972. 266 p. RILM 76/10853dd28. No DA listing.

1883. Cooper, Paul. "The music of Ross Lee Finney." MQ 53(1967): 1-21.

1884. Finney, Ross Lee. "Concerning my *Fantasy in Two Movements* (1958)." Fs. Cuyler: 182-190.

1885. Haines, Don Robert. "The eight string quartets of Ross Lee Finney." DMA dissertation (Performance): University of Rochester, 1973. No DA listing.

1886. Hines: 62-75.

1887. Onderdonk, Henry. "Aspects of tonality in the music of Ross Lee Finney." PNM 6/2(1968): 125-145.

FISCHER, IRWIN (born 1903)

1888. Borroff, Edith. "Spelling and intention: A setting of William Alexander Percy's lyric *A Sea-Bird* (1933) by Irwin Fischer." Fs. Cuyler: 172-181.

FIŠER, LUBOŠ (born 1935)

1889. Locke, John R. "An analysis of *Report* by Luboš Fišr." JBR 20/1(1984-1985): 9-19.

FLEURY, ANDRÉ (born 1903)

1890. Dorroh.

FLOTHUIS, MARIUS (born 1914)

1891. Geraedts, Jaap. "Marius Flothuis: *Canti e Giuochi*." SS 25 (1965): 16-19.

FOOTE, ARTHUR WILLIAM (1853-1937)

1892. Alviani, Doric. "The choral church music of Arthur William Foote." SMD dissertation (Sacred Music): Union Theological Seminary, 1962. 2 vols. No DA listing.

FÖRSTER, EMANUEL ALOYS (1748-1823)

1893. Longyear, Rey M. "Klassik und Romantik in Emanuel Aloys Försters Nachlass." MAU 2(1979): 108-116.

FORTNER, WOLFGANG (born 1907)

1894. Dangel, Arthur. "Wolfgang Fortner: Impromptus." MELOS 27(1960): 79-84, 107-112.

1895. Döhl, Friedhelm. "Fortners Lorca-Vertonung: *In seinem Garten liebt Don Perlimplin Belisa.*" NZM 125(1964): 183-187.

1896. Engelmann, Hans Ulrich. "Fortners *Phantasie über B-A-C-H.*" MELOS 21(1954): 131-135.

1897. Günther, Siegfried. "Wolfgang Fortner: *The Creation.*" MELOS 29(1961): 109-112.

1898. Kroeker, Dieter. "Fortners Fantasia aus der Pfingstgeschichte." Fs. Schneider: 50-61.

1899. Lindlar, Heinrich, ed. *Wolfgang Fortner: Eine Monographie, Werkanalysen, Aufsätze, Reden, Offene Briefe 1950-1959.* Rodenkirches/Rhein: P.J. Tonger, 1960.

1900. Lohrmann, Uwe. "Zum geistlichen Werk Wolfgang Fortners: Dem Komponisten zum 75. Geburtstag." MK 52(1982): 215-225.

1901. Schuhmacher, Gerhard. "Aktualität und Geschichtsbewusstsein als Vernügen: Zu Wolfgang Fortners kompositorischen Prinzipien." NZM 143/11(1982): 20-28.

FOSS, LUKAS (born 1922)

1902. Bailey, Donald Lee. "A study of stylistic and compositional elements of *Anthem* (Stravinsky), *Fragments of Archilochos* (Foss), and *Creation Prologue* (Ussachevsky)." DMA dissertation (Performance): University of Northern Colorado, 1976. 218 p. UM 76-23,159. DA XXXVII.4, p.1859-A.

1903. Browne, Bruce Sparrow. "The choral music of Lukas Foss." DMA dissertation (Performance): University of Washington, 1976. UM 76-20,709. DA XXXVIII.7, p.3789-90-A.

1904. Foss, Lukas. "Work-notes for *Echoi.*" PNM 3/1(1964): 54-61.

1905. Gruhn, Wilfried. "Bearbeitung als kompositorische Reflexion in neuer Musik." M 28(1974): 522-528. [*Baroque Variations*]

1906. ----. "Lukas Foss *Phorion*: Die Obsession einer Melodie von Johann Sebastian Bach in den *Baroque Variations.*" MB 13(1981): 140-153.

1907. Wennerstrom. [*Echoi*]

FOSTER, STEPHEN (1826-1864)

1908. Gombosi, Otto. "Stephen Foster and 'Gregory Walker'." MQ 30(1944): 133-146.

FOULDS, JOHN (1880-1939)

1909. MacDonald, Calum. "John Foulds and the string quartet." TEMPO 132(1980): 16-25.

FRANCHETTI, ARNOLD (born 1906)

1910. Morrison, Watson Wilbur. "The piano sonatas of Arnold Franchetti." DMA dissertation (Performance): Boston University, 1972. 239 p. UM 72-25,124. DA XXXIII.4, p.1770-A.

FRANCK, CÉSAR (1822-1890)

Chamber works

1911. Mompellio, Federico. "Valori cromatici nell Quintetto di César Franck." Fs. Ghisi (vol.2): 311-330.

1912. Rorick, William C. "The A Major Violin Sonatas of Fauré and Franck: A stylistic comparison." MR 42(1981): 46-55.

Organ works

1913. Dommel-Diény, Amy. *Franck.* Dommel-Diény 11. Paris: Dommel-Diény, 1973. [*Prelude, choral et fugue; Trois chorals*]

1914. Dufourcq, Norbert. *César Franck et la genèse des premières oeuvres d'orgue.* Paris: Éditions de la Schola Cantorum, 1973.

1915. Haag, Herbert. *César Franck als Orgelkomponist.* Kassel: Bärenreiter, 1936.

Orchestral works

1916. Gülke, Peter. "Wider die Übermacht des Thematischen: Zum Verständnis César Franks anhand seinen D-Moll-Sinfonie." BM 13(1971): 261-272.

1917. Hollander, Hans. "Die tonpoetische Idee in der Sinfonie César Francks." SMZ 99(1959): 425-427.

1918. Kreutzer, Peter. *Die sinfonische Form César Francks.* Düsseldorf: Dissertations-Verlag Nolte, 1938.

1919. Seipt, Angelus. *César Francks symphonische Dichtungen.* Regensburg: G. Bosse, 1981.

Other works

1920. Matter, Jean. "De quelques sources beethoveniennes de César Franck." SMZ 99(1959): 231-234.

1921. Monnikendam, Marius. *César Franck.* Regensburg: G. Bosse, 1976.

1922. Sanger, G. Norman. "Chromaticism in the keyboard works of Franck and Fauré." PhD dissertation (Musicology): University of Pittsburgh, 1976. 263 p. UM 77-03,035. DA XXXVII.8, p.4688-A.

1923. Wegener, Bernd. *César Francks Harmonik.* Regensburg: G. Bosse, 1976.

FRANCK, EDUARD (1817-1893)

1924. Bittner, Johannes. "Die Klaviersonaten Eduard Francks (1817-1893) und anderer Kleinmeister seiner Zeit." PhD dissertation: Hamburg, 1968.

FRAZZI, VITO (1888-1975)

1925. Prosperi, Carlo. "Vito Frazzi e il *Re Lear*." CHI 14(1981): 333-360.

FREEDMAN, HARRY (born 1922)

 1926. Dixon, Gail. "Cellular metamorphosis and structural compartmentalization in Harry Freedman's *Chalumeau.*" SMUWO 6(1981): 48-76.
 1927. ----. "Harry Freedman: A survey." SMUWO 5(1980): 122-144.

FRENCH, JACOB (1754-1817)

 1928. Genuchi, Marvin C. "The life and music of Jacob French (1754-1817), colonial American composer." PhD dissertation: University of Iowa, 1963. UM 64-7918. DA XXV.2, p.1247-8.

FRICKER, PETER RACINE (born 1920)

 1929. Hines: 76-88.
 1930. Kimbell, Michael Alexander. "Peter Racine Fricker's Second String Quartet: An analysis." DMA dissertation (Composition): Cornell University, 1973. No DA listing.

FRID, GÉZA (born 1904)

 1931. Wijdeveld, Wolfgang. "Géza Frid." SS 18(1964): 1-9.

FRIEDMAN, IGNAZ (1882-1948)

 1932. Auh, Mijai Youn. "Piano variations by Brahms, Liszt and Friedman on a theme by Paganini." DM dissertation (Piano): Indiana University, 1980. No DA listing.

FRY, WILLIAM HENRY (1813-1864)

 1933. Kauffman, Byron F. "The choral works of George F. Bristow (1825-1898) and William Henry Fry (1813-1864)." DMA dissertation (Choral Music): University of Illinois, 1975. 107 p. UM 76-06,815. DA XXXVI.9, p.5627-A.

GABURO, KENNETH (born 1926)

 1934. Logan, Jackie Dale. "*Mouthpiece* by Kenneth Gaburo: A performer's analysis of the composition." PhD dissertation (Performance): University of California, San Diego, 1977. UM 77-13,685. DA XXXVIII.2, p.539-A.

GÁL, HANS (born 1890)

 1935. Oliver, Roger. "Hans Gál at 95." TEMPO 155(1985): 2-7.

GALINDO, BLAS (born 1910)

 1936. Conant, Richard Paul. "The vocal music of Blas Galindo: A study of the choral and solo vocal works of a twentieth-century Mexican composer." DMA dissertation: University of Texas, 1977. UM 77-28,987. DA XXXVIII.7, p.3790-A.

GAMER, CARLTON

1937. Gamer, Carlton. "Notes on the structure of *Piano Raga Music*." PNM 12/1-2(1973-1974): 217-230. [Includes complete score: 191-216]

GÄNSBACHER, JOHANN BAPTIST (1778-1844)

1938. Schneider, Manfred. "Studien zu den Messenkompositionen Johann Baptist Gänsbachers (1778-1884)." PhD dissertation (Musicology): University of Innsbruck, 1976.

GASSER, ULRICH (born 1950)

1939. Gasser, Ulrich. "Bilderbuch für zwei Klaviere: *Vier Paprikafrüchte*." N 2(1981-1982): 110-119.
1940. ----. "*Passion II/Stationen* (75)1976(77)." SMZ 119(1979): 274-279.

GAUDIBERT, ERIC (born 1936)

1941. Gaudibert, Eric. "*Variations lyriques* pour violoncello solo (1966-1976)." SZM 117(1977): 150-153.

GEHLHAAR, ROLF (born 1943)

1942. Gehlhaar, Rolf. "*Fünf deutsche Tänze*." DBNM 16(1977): 56-64.

GEISSLER, FRITZ (1921-1984)

Orchestral works
1943. Heinecke-Oertel, Walther. "*Sinfonische Suite* von Fritz Geissler." MG 16(1966): 242-243.
1944. Hennenberg, Fritz. "Das Sinfonische und das Dramatische: Kommentar zu Fritz Geisslers III. Sinfonie." MG 18(1968): 610-615.
1945. Kapst, Erich. "Fritz Geisslers *Sinfonische Sätze*." MG 10(1960): 146-149.
1946. Klement, Udo. "Analysen: Sinfonie Nr.9 von Fritz Geissler." MG 30(1980): 325-329.
1947. Schneider, Frank. "Gedenken zur V. Sinfonie von Fritz Geissler." MG 20(1970): 595-599.
1948. ----. "Gedenken zur VIII. Sinfonie von Fritz Geissler." MG 25 (1975): 204-207.
1949. Schönfelder, Gerd. "VII. Sinfonie von Fritz Geissler." MG 24(1974): 199-202.
1950. Wolf, Werner. "Fritz Geisslers II. Sinfonie." MG 16(1966): 91-98.

Other works
>   1951. Kapst, Erich. "Fritz Geisslers *Handzettel an einige Nachbarn.*" MG 9/1(1959): 10-14.
>   1952. Schneider, Frank. "*Der zerbrochene Krug*: Oper von Fritz Geissler." MG 24(1974): 11-18.
>   1953. Schönfelder, Gerd. "Fritz Geisslers Oratorium *Schöpfer Mensch.*" MG 23(1973): 408-412.

GENZMER, HARALD (born 1909)

>   1954. Müllisch, Hermann. *Die A-Capella-Chorwerke Harald Genzmers: Stilkritische Untersuchungen zur Textausdeutung.* Berlin: Ries und Erler, 1982.

GERHARD, ROBERTO (1896-1970)

Symphonies
>   1955. Ballantine, Christopher. "The symphony in the twentieth century: Some aspects of its tradition and innovation." MR 32(1971): 219-232. [First Symphony]
>   1956. Bradshaw, Susan. "Symphony No.2/Metamorphosis: The compositional background." TEMPO 39(1981): 28-32.
>   1057. Cunningham, Michael Gerald. "An analysis of the First Symphony of Roberto Gerhard." PhD dissertation (Composition): Indiana University, 1973. 27 p. No DA listing.
>   1958. MacDonald, Calum. "Sense and sound: Gerhard's Fourth Symphony." TEMPO 100(1972): 25-29.

Other works
>   1959. Davies, Hugh. "The electronic music." TEMPO 139(1981): 36-38.
>   1960. Donat, Misha. "Thoughts on the late works." TEMPO 139(1981): 39-43.
>   1961. Glock, William, ed. "A tribute to Roberto Gerhard on his sixtieth birthday." SCORE 17(1956): 5-72. [Special issue]
>   1962. MacDonald, Calum. "*Soirées de Barcelone*: A preliminary report." TEMPO 139(1981): 19-26.
>   1963. Nash, Peter Paul. "The Wind Quintet." TEMPO 139(1981): 5-11.
>   1964. Walker, Geoffrey J. and David Drew. "Gerhard's Cantata." TEMPO 139(1981): 12-18.

GERSCHEFSKI, EDWIN (born 1909)

>   1965. Vaglio, Anthony Joseph, Jr. "The compositional significance of Joseph Schillinger's *System of Musical Composition* as reflected in the works of Edwin Gerschefski." PhD dissertation (Theory): University of Rochester, 1977. UM 78-01,785. DA XXXVIII.9, p.5119-A.
>   1966. Yerlow, Stanley Clinton. "Edwin Gerschefski's Preludes, Op.6, Nos.1-6 and Three Dances, Op.11, Nos.1-3." DMA dissertation: University of Rochester, 1980. No DA listing.

GERSHWIN, GEORGE (1898-1937)

1967. Gilbert, Steven E. "Gershwin's art of counterpoint." MQ 70 (1984): 423-456.
1968. Schwartz, Charles M. "The life and orchestral works of George Gershwin." PhD dissertation (Musicology): New York University, 1969. UM 70-3105. DA XXX.9, p.3977-A.

GERTILUCCI, ARMANDO (born 1939)

1969. Heister, Hanns-Werner. "Kantabilität und Klangkonstruktion: Ein Werkporträt des italienischen Komponisten Armando Gentilucci." MTX 12(1985): 6-10.

GIANNINI, VITTORIO (1903-1966)

1970. Mullins, Joe Barry. "A comparative analysis of three symphonies for band." JBR 6/1(1969-1970): 17-28. [Symphony No.3]
1971. Parris, Robert. "Vittorio Giannini and the romantic tradition." JR 4/2(1957): 32-46.
1972. Wynn, James Leroy. "An analysis of the first movement of the Symphony No.3 for Band by Vittorio Giannini." JBR 1/2(1964-1965): 19-26.

GIBBS, CECIL ARMSTRONG (1889-1960)

1973. Curtis.

GIDEON, MIRIAM (born 1906)

1974. Fertig, Judith Pinnolis. "An analysis of selected works of the American composer Miriam Gideon (1906-   ) in light of contemporary Jewish musical trends." MA dissertation: University of Cincinnati, 1978.
1975. Perle, George. "The music of Miriam Gideon." ACA 7/4(1957): 2-8.

GILBERT, HENRY FRANKLIN BELKNAP (1868-1928)

1976. Longyear, Katherine E. "Henry F. Gilbert: His life and works." PhD dissertation (Theory): University of Rochester, 1968. UM 68-12,647. DA XXIX.4, p.1244-A.
1977. ---- and Rey M. Longyear. "Henry F. Gilbert's unfinished *Uncle Remus* opera." Y 10(1974): 50-67.

GINASTERA, ALBERTO (1916-1983)

1978. Chase, Gilbert. "Alberto Ginastera: Argentine composer." MQ 43(1957): 439-460.
1979. Hanley, Mary Ann. "The solo piano compositions of Alberto Ginastera (1916-   )." DMA dissertation (Performance): University of Cincinnati, 1969. No DA listing.

1980. Kuss, Malena. "Type, derivation, and use of folk idioms in Ginastera's *Don Rodrigo* (1964)." LAMR 1(1980): 176-195.

1981. Paik, Eui. "An analysis of the First Piano Concerto (1961) by Alberto Ginastera." DMA dissertation (Composition): Indiana University, 1979. 76 p. No DA listing.

1982. Suarez Urtubey, Pola. "Alberto Ginastera's *Don Rodrigo*." TEMPO 74(1965): 11-18.

1983. ----. "Ginastera's *Bomarzo*." TEMPO 84(1968): 14-21.

1984. Wallace, David Edward. "Alberto Ginastera: An analysis of his style and technique of composition." PhD dissertation (Theory): Northwestern University, 1964. UM 65-3320. DA XXV.11, p.6680.

GIULIANI, MAURO (1781-1829)

1985. Heck, Thomas F. "The birth of the classic guitar and its cultivation in Vienna, reflected in the career and compositions of Mauro Giuliani (d.1829)." PhD dissertation (Music History): Yale University, 1970. UM 71-16,249. DA XXXI.12, p.6648.

GLASS, PHILIP (born 1937)

1986. Mertens: 67-86.

1987. Smith, Dave. "The music of Phil Glass." CT 11(1975): 27-33.

1988. York, Wesley. "Form and process in *Two Pages* by Philip Glass." SONUS 1/2(1980): 28-50.

GLAZUNOV, ALEXANDER (1865-1936)

1989. Abraham, Gerald. "Glazunov and the string quartet." TEMPO 73(1964): 16-21.

1990. Cherbuliez, Antoine-Elisée. "Alexander Glasunows Kammermusik." MO 4(1967): 45-64.

1991. Taruskin. [Symphony No.3; *The Seasons*]

GLINKA, MIKHAIL IVANOVICH (1804-1857)

1992. Rowen, Ruth Halle. "Glinka's tour of folk modes on the wheel of harmony." Fs. Schwarz: 35-54. [*Ruslan and Ludmila*]

GLOBOKAR, VINKO (born 1934)

1993. Bachmann, Claus-Henning. "Der Weg nach draussen." NZM 144/1(1983): 15-18. [*Miserere*]

1994. Klüppelholz, Werner. "Von Nächtlichen Schrecken: Zu Vinko Globokars *Discours VI* für Streichquartett." N 5(1984-1985): 252-255.

1995. König, Wolfgang. *Vinko Globokar: Komposition und Improvisation*. Wiesbaden: Breitkopf und Härtel, 1977.

GOEHR, ALEXANDER (born 1932)

1996. Ballantine, Christopher. "The symphony in the twentieth century: Some aspects of its tradition and innovation." MR 32(1971): 219-232. [*Little Symphony*]

1997. Northcott, Bayan. "Alexander Goehr: The recent music." TEMPO 124(1978): 10-15, 125(1978): 12-18.

1998. Wood, Hugh. "The choral work of Alexander Goehr." ACR 8/2(1965): 6-8.

GOETHALS, LUCIEN (born 1931)

1999. Sabbe, Hermann. "Lucien Goethals: Le Constructivisme bifonctionnel." *Jaarboek IPEM* (1967): 33-59.

GOEYVAERTS, KAREL (born 1923)

2000. Sabbe, Hermann. "Vom Serialismus zum Minimalismus: Der Werdegang eines Manierismus: Der Fall Goeyvaerts, 'Minimalist avant la lettre'." N 3(1982-1983): 203-208.

2001. Toop, Richard. "Messiaen/Goeyvaerts, Fano/Stockhausen, Boulez." PNM 13/1(1974-1975): 141-169. [Sonata for Two Pianos, 1950-1967]

GOLDMAN, RICHARD FRANKO (1910-1980)

2002. Lester, Noel K. "Richard Franko Goldman: His life and works." DMA dissertation (Performance): Peabody Conservatory, 1984. 338 p. No DA listing.

GOLDMANN, FRIEDRICH (born 1941)

2003. Schneider, Frank. "Die Analyse: Friedrich Goldmann: *Sing', Lessing*, Komposition für Bariton und 6 Spieler." MG 29(1979): 137-143.

2004. ----. "Die Analyse: Sinfonie 2 von Friedrich Goldmann." MG 28(1978): 30-35.

2005. ----. "Sinfonie für Orchester von Friedrich Goldmann." MG 24 (1974): 143-149.

2006. ----. "Analysen: *Fünf Gesichtspunkte zum Konzert für Oboe und Orchester* von Friedrich Goldman." MG 30(1980): 329-333.

GOLDSCHMIDT, BERTHOLD (born 1903)

2007. Matthews, David. "Berthold Goldschmidt: The chamber and instrumental music." TEMPO 145(1983): 20-25.

GOOSSENS, SIR EUGENE (1893-1962)

2008. Hull, Robin. "Two symphonies: Eugene Goossens and Lennox Berkeley." MR 4(1943): 229-242.

GÓRECKI, HENRYK MIKOTAJ (born 1933)

2009. Thomas, Adrian. "The music of Henryk Mikotaj Górecki: The first decade." CT 27(1983): 10-20.
2010. ----. "A pole apart: The music of Górecki since 1965." CT 28(1984): 20-31.

GÖRNER, HANS GEORG (born 1908)

2011. Vetter, Walther. "Görners Cello-Konzert Opus 41: Uraufführung in Gotha." MG 14(1964): 533-534.

GOTTSCHALK, LOUIS MOREAU (1829-1869)

2012. Doyle, John G. "The piano music of Louis Moreau Gottschalk (1829-1869)." PhD dissertation (Music Education): New York University, 1960. LC Mic 61-107. DA XXI.10, p.3113.
2013. Korf, William E. "Gottschalk's one-act opera scene, *Escenas campestres*." CM 26(1978): 62-73.
2014. ----. *The orchestral music of Louis Moreau Gottschalk.* Henryville, Pa.: Institute of Mediaeval Music, 1983.
2015. Marrocco, W. Thomas. "America's first nationalist composer Louis Moreau Gottschalk (1829-1869)." Fs. Ronga: 293-313.

GOULD, MORTON (born 1913)

2016. Mullins, Joe Barry. "A comparative analysis of three symphonies for band." JBR 6/1(1969-1970): 17-28. [Symphony for Band]
2017. ----. "Morton Gould: Symphony for Band." JBR 4/2(1967-1968): 24-35; 5/1(1968-1969): 29-47.

GOUNOD, CHARLES FRANÇOIS (1818-1893)

2018. ASO 2(1976) [*Faust*]
2019. ASO 41(1982) [*Roméo et Juliette*]
2020. Ferchault, Guy. *Faust: Une Legende et ses musiciens.* Paris: Larousse, 1948.
2021. Langevin, Kenneth W. "*Au silence des belles nuits*: The earlier songs of Charles Gounod." PhD dissertation (Musicology): Cornell University, 1978. 207 p. UM 78-09,495. DA XXXVIII.12, p.7014-A.
2022. Macy. [*Faust*]

GRAETTINGER, ROBERT (1923-1957)

2023. Morgan, Robert Badgett. "The music and life of Robert Graettinger." DMA dissertation (Composition): University of Illinois, 1974. 124 p. UM 75-375. DA XXXV.7, p.4596-A.

GRAINGER, PERCY (1882-1961)

2024. Anderson, Peter James. "The innovative music of Percy Grainger: An examination of the origins and development of free music." MM dissertation (Arts): University of Melbourne, 1979.

2025. Fred, Herbert W. "Percy Grainger's Music for Wind Band." JBR 1/1(1964-1965): 10-16.

2026. Slattery, Thomas C. "The Hill Songs of Percy Aldridge Grainger." JBR 8/1(1971-1972): 6-10.

2027. ----. "The wind music of Percy Aldridge Grainger." PhD dissertation: University of Iowa, 1967. UM 67-9104. DA XXVIII.2, p.713-A.

GRANGE, PHILIP (born 1956)

2028. Williamson, Clive. "Philip Grange." TEMPO 146(1983): 25-30.

GRETCHANINOV, ALEXANDER (1864-1956)

2029. Yasser, Joseph. "Gretchaninoff's 'Heterdox' compositions." MQ 28(1942): 309-317.

GRIEG, EDVARD (1843-1907)

2030. Abraham, Gerald. *Grieg: A symposium.* London: L. Drummond, 1948.

2031. Bauer, Werner. "Edvard Grieg." SMZ 97(1957): 349-352.

2032. Fischer, Kurt von. *Griegs Harmonik und die nordländische Folklore.* Bern: P. Haupt, 1938.

2033. Kortsen, Bjarne. *Zur Genesis von Edvard Griegs G-Moll Streichquartett, Op.27.* Haugesund, 1967.

2034. Olson, Robert Wallace. "A comparative study of selected Norwegian romances by Halfdam-Kjerulf, Edvard Grieg, and Eyvind Alnaes." PhD dissertation (Performance): University of Illinois, 1973. 328 p. UM 73-17,611. DA XXXIV.2, p.812-A.

2035. Sandvik, O. M. "Edward Grief und die norwegische Volksmusik." Fs. Scheurleer: 271-275.

2036. Schjelderup-Ebbe, Dag. *A study of Grieg's harmony, with special references to his contributions to musical impressionism.* Oslo: J.G. Tanum, 1953.

GRIESBACH, KARL-RUDI (born 1916)

2037. Felix, Werner. "*Afrikanische Sinfonie* von Karl-Rudi Griesbach." MG 17(1967): 460-466.

2038. Marfordt, Torsten. "Noch einmal *Kolumbus*." MG 10(1960): 203-208, 278-283.

2039. Pollack, Hans. "Das *Planetarische Manifest* von Karl-Rudi Griesbach." MG 14(1964): 530-532.

2040. Winter, Ilse. "*Marike Weiden*: Karl-Rudi Griesbachs neue Oper." MG 10(1960): 707-712.

GRIFFES, CHARLES (1884-1920)

2041. Boda, Daniel. "The music of Charles T. Griffes." PhD dissertation (Theory): Florida State University, 1962. UM 63-1802. DA XXIII.10, p.3919.

2042. Johnson, Richard Oscar. "The songs of Charles Tomlinson Griffes." DMA dissertation (Performance): University of Iowa, 1977. UM 77-21,184. DA XXXVIII.4, p.1727-8-A.

2043. Morrison.

2044. Nash, Nancy Lee. "Syllogistic form as a heuristic principle in musical analysis: Based on the music of Charles Griffes." MM dissertation: Florida State University, 1972. No DA listing.

2045. Pratt, Hoon Mo Kim. "The complete piano works of Charles Griffes." DMA dissertation (Performance): Boston University, 1975. UM 75-20,938. DA XXXVI.3, p.1159-A.

GROLL, EVERMOD (1755-1810)

2046. Lederer, Franz. *Evermod Groll (1755-1810): Leben und Werke eines süddeutschen Klosterkomponisten.* Regensburger Beiträge zur Musikwissenschaft 5. Regensburg: G. Bosse, 1978. 577 p.

GRÜNEWALD, JEAN-JACQUES (1911-1982)

2047. Dorroh.

GUILMANT, FÉLIX ALEXANDRE (1837-1911)

2048. Johnson, Calvert. "The organ sonatas of Félix-Alexandre Guilmant." DMA dissertation (Organ): Northwestern University, 1973. 138 p. No DA listing.

GÜMBEL, MARTIN (born 1923)

2049. Gümbel, Martin. "Zu meinem Divertimento für Streicher (1960)." Fs. Marx: 98-101.

HÁBA, ALOIS (1893-1973)

2050. Vyslouzil, Jirį. "Alois Hába und die Dodekaphonie." SMZ 118 (1978): 95-102.

HADLEY, HENRY (1871-1937)

2051. Canfield, John Clair, Jr. "Henry Kimball Hadley: His life and work (1871-1937)." EdD dissertation: Florida State University, 1960. LC Mic 60-3306. DA XXII.1, p.280-281.

HAHN, REYNALDO (1875-1947)

2052. Schuh, Willi. "Zum Liedwerk Reynaldo Hahns." SBM 2(1974): 103-126.

HALFFTER, CHRISTÓBAL (born 1930)

2053. Andraschke, Peter. "Traditionsmomente in Kompositionen von Christóbal Halffter, Klaus Huber und Wolfgang Rihm." Brinkmann: 130-152.

HALLER, HERMANN (born 1914)

2054. Haller, Hermann. "Komponisten präsentieren neue Arbeiten: 2. Streichquartett." SMZ 113(1973): 348-352.

HAMBRAEUS, BENGT (born 1928)

2055. Schmiedeke, Ulrich. *Der Beginn der neuen Orgelmusik: Die Orgelkompositionen von Hambraeus, Kagel und Ligeti.* München: E. Katzbichler, 1981.

HAMEL, PETER MICHAEL (born 1947)

2056. Vill, Suzanne. "Gral-Bilder: Zu Peter Michael Hamels *Merlin*-Musik." NZM 143/11(1982): 8-13.

HAMILTON, IAIN (born 1922)

2057. Ballantine, Christopher. "The symphony in the twentieth century: Some aspects of its tradition and innovation." MR 32(1971): 219-232. [Sinfonia for Two Orchestras]
2058. Thompson, Randall Scott. "The solo clarinet works of Iain Hamilton." DMA dissertation (Performance): University of Maryland, 1976. UM 76-29,017. DA XXXVII.6, p.3262-A.

HANISCH, JOSEPH (1812-1892)

2059. Kraus, Eberhard. "Der gregorianische Choral im Orgelschaffen der Regensburger Domorganisten Joseph Hanisch (1812-1892) und Joseph Renner (1868-1934)." Fs. F. Haberl: 151-167.

HANKE, KARL (1750-1803)

2060. Abert, Anna Amalie. "*Oberon* in Nord und Süd." Fs. Gudewill: 51-68. [*Huon und Amande*]

HANSON, HOWARD (1896-1981)

2061. Carnine, Albert, Jr. "The choral music of Howard Hanson." DMA dissertation (Performance): University of Texas, 1977. UM 77-28,986. DA XXXVIII.7, p.3789-90-A.
2062. Mize.
2063. Tuthill, Burnet C. "Howard Hanson." MQ 22(1936): 140-153.

HARRIS, ROY (1898-1979)

2064. Brookhart, Charles E. "The choral works of Aaron Copland, Roy Harris, and Randall Thompson." PhD dissertation: George Peabody College for Teachers, 1960. LC Mic 60-5861. DA XXI.9, p.2737.
2065. Cox, Sidney Thurber. "The autogenic principle in the melodic writing of Roy Harris." DMA dissertation: Cornell University, 1948. No DA listing.
2066. Evett, Robert. "The harmonic idiom of Roy Harris." MM 23 (1946): 100-107.
2067. Farwell, Arthur. "Roy Harris." MQ 18(1932): 18-32.
2068. Mendel, Arthur. "The Quintet of Roy Harris." MM 17(1939): 25-28.
2069. Mize.
2070. Piston, Walter. "Roy Harris." MM 11(1934): 73-83.
2071. Slonimsky, Nicolas. "Roy Harris." MQ 33(1947): 17-37.
2072. Stehman, Dan. "The symphonies of Roy Harris: An analytical study of linear materials." PhD dissertation (Musicology): University of Southern California, 1973. UM 74-11,709. DA XXXIV.11, p.7272-A.

HARRISON, LOU (born 1917)

2073. Rutman, Neil Clark. "The solo piano works of Lou Harrison." DMA dissertation (Performance): Peabody Conservatory, 1983. No DA listing.

HARTMANN, KARL AMADEUS (1905-1963)

2074. Distefano, Joseph P. "The symphonies of Karl Amadeus Hartmann." PhD dissertation (Theory): Florida State University, 1972. UM 73-04,199. DA XXXIII.8, p.4452-A.
2075. Günther, Siegfried. "Hartmanns achte Sinfonie." MELOS 30 (1963): 190-193.
2076. ----. "6. Sinfonie von Karl Amadeus Hartmann." MELOS 29 (1962): 74-77.
2077. Heister, Hanns-Werner. "Karl Amadeus Hartmann: 2. Klaviersonate '27. April 1945'." NZM 146/10(1985): 29-31.
2078. ----. "Voller Angst vor dem Nazi-Terror: Wort und Sinn in Karl Amadeus Hartmanns Instrumentalmusik: Die Klaviersonate '27. April 1945'." MTX 11(1985): 9-15.
2079. ----. "Zur Semantik musikalischer Strukturen: Der Schluss-Satz aus K.A. Hartmanns 1. Symphonie." BM 18(1976): 137-147.

2080. McCredie, Andrew D. "Karl Amadeus Hartmann (1905-1963): New documents and sources in a decennial perspective." MMA 7(1975): 142-187.
2081. ----, ed. *Karl Amadeus Hartmann: Symphonische Hymnen für grosser Orchester.* Mainz: Schott, 1976.
2082. ----. "The role of sources and antecedents in the compositional process of Karl Amadeus Hartmann." MMA 10(1979): 166-212.
2083. Vogt: 260- [Konzert für Klavier, Bläser und Schlagzeug (1953)]

HARVEY, JONATHEN DAVID (born 1939)

2084. Griffiths, Paul. "Three works by Jonathan Harvey: The electronic mirror." CMR 1/1(1984-1985): 87-109. [*Bhakti; Mortuos plango, vivos vovo; Inner Light*]
2085. Harvey, Jonathan, Denis Lorrain, Jean-Baptiste Barrière and Stanley Haynes. "Notes on the realization of *Bhakti*." CMR 1/1(1984-1985): 111-129.

HASELBACH, JOSEF (born 1936)

2086. Haselbach, Josef. "Komponisten präsentieren neue Arbeiten: *Moving-Theatre I*." SMZ 114(1974): 149-154.

HAUER, JOSEF MATTHAIS (1883-1959)

2087. Leuchtmann, Horst. "'Möglichkeiten logischer Formgebung bei der Benützung von 12 Tönen.' J.M. Hauers Op.22,1." Fs. Sievers: 103-114.
2088. Sengstschmid, Johann. "Anatomie eines Zwolftonspiels: ein Block in der Werkstatt Josef Matthais Hauers." ZM 2/1(1971): 14-34.
2089. ----. *Zwischen Trope und Zwölftonspiel: J.M. Hauers Zwölftontechnik in ausgewählten Beispielen.* Regensburg: G. Bosse, 1980. 144 p.
2090. Szmolyan, Walter. "Hauer als Opernkomponist." OMZ 21(1966): 226-232.
2091. Special Issue: OMZ 21(1966): 98-144.

HAUFRECHT, HERBERT

2092. Cazden, Norman. "Herbert Haufrecht: The composer and the man." ACA 8/4(1958): 2-11.

HAWKINS, JOHN (born 1944)

2093. Mather, Bruce. "Le collage musical: *Remembrances* de John Hawkins." CCM 3(1971): 99-102.
2094. Plawutsky, Eugene. "The music of John Hawkins." CAUSM 8/1(1978):112-134.

HAYDN, JOSEPH (1732-1809)

Chamber works

2095. Barrett-Ayres, Reginald. *Joseph Haydn and the string quartet.* London: Barrie & Jenkins, 1974.

2096. Bartha, Dénes. "Thematic profile and character in the quartet-finales of Joseph Haydn." SM 11(1969): 35-62.

2097. Brook, Barry. "Haydn's string trios: A misunderstood genre." CM 36(1983): 61-77.

2098. Chapman, Roger E. "Modulation in Haydn's piano trios in the light of Schoenberg's theories." Larsen: 471-475.

2099. Demaree, Robert W., Jr. "The structural proportions of the Haydn quartets." PhD dissertation (Theory): Indiana University, 1973. UM 74-09,419. DA XXXIV.10, p.6682.

2100. Germann, Jörg. *Die Entwicklung der Exposition in Joseph Haydn Streichquartetten.* Teufen AR: Kunz-Druck, 1964.

2101. Kaschmitter, Walter. "Streichquartett Op.33 Nr.2 oder Humor bei Joseph Haydn." M 36(1982-1983): 168-171.

2102. Löber, Burckhard. *Strukturwissenschaftliche Darstellung der ersten und letzten Satze der sechs Streichquartette Op.76 von Joseph Haydn.* Münster: Forschungsstelle für theoretische Musikwissenschaft, 1983.

2103. Moe, Orin, Jr. "The significance of Haydn's Op.33." Larsen: 445-450.

2104. ----. "Texture in Haydn's early quartets." MR 35(1974): 4-22.

2105. ----. "Texture in the string quartets of Haydn to 1787." PhD dissertation (Musicology): University of California, Santa Barbara, 1970. UM 71-11,482. DA XXXI.11, p.6100.

2106. Pankaskie, Lewis V. "Tonal organization in the sonata-form movements of Haydn's string quartets." PhD dissertation: University of Michigan, 1957. UM 21,344. DA XVII.6, p.1352.

2107. Randall, J. K. "Haydn: String Quartet in D, Op.76, No.5." MR 21(1960): 94-105.

2108. Reed, Carl H. "Motivic unity in selected keyboard sonatas and string quartets of Joseph Haydn." PhD dissertation: University of Washington, 1966. UM 66-7893. DA XXVII.2, p.501-A.

2109. Salzer, Felix. "Haydn's Fantasia from the String Quartet, Opus 76, No.6." MFO 4(1976): 161-194.

2110. Silbert, Doris. "Ambiguity in the string quartets of Joseph Haydn." MQ 36(1950): 562-573.

2111. Steinbeck, Wolfram. "Mozarts 'Scherzi': Zur Beziehung zwischen Haydns Streichquartetten Op.33 und Mozarts Haydn-Quartetten." AM 41(1984): 208-231.

2112. Steinberg, Lester. "A numerical approach to activity and movement in the sonata-form movements of Haydn's piano trios." Larsen: 515-522.

2113. ----. "The piano trios of Joseph Haydn: Analysis of style in sonata-form movements." PhD dissertation (Musicology): New York University, 1976. 377 p. UM 77-16,528. DA XXXVIII.2, p.541-A.

2114. Webster, James. "Freedom of form in Haydn's early string quartets." Larsen: 522-530.

2115. Wiesel, Siegfried. "Klangfarbendramaturgie in den Streichquartetten von Joseph Haydn." HS 5(1982-1983): 16-22.

The Creation

2116. Ravizza, Victor. *Joseph Haydn: Die Schöpfung.* München: W. Fink, 1981.

Masses

2117. Brand, Carl Maria. *Die Messen von Joseph Haydn.* Würzburg: Triltsch, 1941. Reprint: Walluf bei Wiesbaden: Sandig, 1973.

2118. Gibbs, Thomas Jordan, Jr. "A study of form in the late masses of Joseph Haydn." PhD dissertation (Musicology): University of Texas, 1972. UM 73-18,430. DA XXXIV.2, p.807.

2119. Kalisch, Volker. "Haydn und die Kirchenmusik: Ein analytischer Versuch am Beispiel des Benedictus aus der *Schöpfungsmesse.*" MK 54(1984): 159-170.

2120. Nafziger, Kenneth J. "The masses of Haydn and Schubert: A study in the rise of romanticism." DMA dissertation (Music History): University of Oregon, 1970. UM 71-10,765. DA XXXII.10, p.5451-A.

2121. Otto, Craig A. "The use of the sonata-allegro form in the Kyrie movements of Joseph Hadyn's late masses." D 4/2(1972): 3-12.

2122. Runestad, Cornell J. "The masses of Joseph Haydn: A stylistic study." DMA dissertation (Choral Music): University of Illinois, 1970. UM 71-14,932. DA XXXI.12, p.6652.

Piano works

2123. Andrews, Harold L. "Tonality and structure in the first movements of Haydn's solo keyboard sonatas." PhD dissertation: University of North Carolina, 1967. UM 68-6714. DA XXXVIII.11, p.4656-A.

2124. Brown, Alfred P. "The solo and ensemble keyboard sonatas of Joseph Haydn: A study of structure and style." PhD dissertation (Music History and Literature): Northwestern University, 1970. UM 71-1805. DA XXXI.8, p.4195.

2125. Fillion, Michelle. "Sonata-exposition procedures in Haydn's keyboard sonatas." Larsen: 475-481.

2125. Moss, Lawrence K. "Haydn's Sonata Hob.XVI:52 (ChL.62) in E-Flat Major: An analysis of the first movement." Larsen: 496-501.

2127. Reed, Carl H. "Motivic unity in selected keyboard sonatas and string quartets of Joseph Haydn." PhD dissertation: University of Washington, 1966. UM 66-7893. DA XXVII.2, p.501-A.

2128. Shamgar, Beth Friedman. "The retransition in the piano sonatas of Haydn, Mozart and Beethoven." PhD dissertation (Musicology): New York University, 1978. 246 p. UM 79-12,324. DA XL.2, p.534-A.

2129. Vignal, Marc. "L'Oeuvre pour piano seul de Joseph Haydn." RM 249(1961): 7-19.

2130. Wackernagel, Bettina. *Joseph Haydns frühe Klaviersonaten: Ihre Beziehungen zur Klaviermusik um d. Mitte d. 18. Jahrhunderts.* Tutzing: H. Schneider, 1975.

Operas

2131. Lawner, George. "Form and drama in the operas of Joseph Haydn." PhD dissertation: University of Chicago, 1959. 241 p. No DA listing.

2132. Lippmann, Friedrich. "Haydns *La Fedelta premiatà* und Cimarosas *L'Infedeltà fedele.*" HS 5(1982-1983): 1-15.

2133. ----. "Haydns opere serie: Tendenzen und Affinitäten." STU 12(1983): 301-332.

2134. Rice, John A. "Sarti's *Giulio Sabino*, Haydn's *Armida*, and the arrival of opera seria at Eszterháaza." HY 15(1984): 181-198.

The Seasons

2135. Moe, Orin, Jr. "Structure in Hadyn's *The Seasons.*" HY 9(1975): 340-348.

2136. Schmidt, Karl. "Die Sprache der Tonarten in Hadyns *Jahreszeiten.*" M 36(1982-1983): 211-214.

Symphonies

2137. Alston, Charlotte LeNora. "Recapitulation procedures in the mature symphonies of Haydn and Mozart." PhD dissertation (Theory): University of Iowa, 1972. UM 73-00,590. DA XXXIII.7, p.3690-A.

2138. Bard, Raimund. "Untersuchungen zur motivischen Arbeit in Haydns sinfonischem Spätwerken." PhD dissertation (Musicology): Saarbrücken, 1980. Kassel: Bärenreiter, 1982.

2139. Bawel, Frederick Henry. "A study of developmental techniques in selected Hadyn symphonies." PhD dissertation (Theory): Ohio State University, 1972. UM 73-01,934. DA XXXIII.8, p.4450.

2140. Butcher, Norma Perkins. "A comparative-analytical study of sonata-allegro form in the first movements of the London symphonies of Franz Joseph Haydn." PhD dissertation (Theory): University of Southern California, 1971. 179 p. UM 72-06,042. DA XXXII.8, p.4647-A.

2141. Cole, Malcolm S. "Haydn's symphonic rondo finales: Their structural and stylistic evolution." - HY 13(1982): 113-142.

2142. ----. "Momigny's analysis of Hadyn's Symphony No.103." MR 30(1969): 261-284.

2143. Eberle, Gottfried. "Joseph Haydn: Sinfonia G-Dur Hob.1:100 ('Militär-Sinfonie')." NZM 143/2(1982): 31-33.

2144. Fisher, Stephen C. "Sonata procedures in Hadyn's symphonic rondo finales of the 1770s." Larsen: 481-487.

2145. Geiringer, Karl, ed. *Franz Joseph Haydn: Symphony No.103 in E-Flat Major ("Drum-Roll").* Norton Critical Scores. New York: W.W. Norton, 1974.

2146. Gresham, Carolyn D. "Stylistic features of Hadyn's symphonies from 1768 to 1772." Larsen: 431-434.

2147. Gwilt, Richard. "Sonata-allegro revisited." ITO 7/5-6 (1983-1984): 3-33. [Symphonies 93, 94, 95, 96, 97, 100, 103]

2148. Klein, Rudolf. "Wo kann die Analyse von Haydns Symphonik ansetzen?" OMZ 37(1982): 234-241.

2149. Kresky: 12-26. [Symphony No.104, 1st movement]

2150. Lazar, Joel. "Thematic unity in the first movements of Haydn's London symphonies." MA dissertation: Harvard University, 1963.

2151. Livingston, Ernest F. "Unifying elements in Hadyn's Symphony No.104." Larsen: 493-496.

2152. Marillier, C. G. "Computer assisted analysis of tonal structure in the classical symphony." HY 14(1983): 187-199.

2153. Martinez-Gollner, Marie Louise. *Joseph Haydn: Symphonie Nr.94 (Paukenschlag)*. München: W. Fink, 1979.

2154. Marx, Karl. "Über thematische Beziehungen in Haydns Londoner Symphonien." HS 4(1976-1980): 1-20.

2155. Menk, Gail E. "The symphonic introductions of Joseph Haydn." PhD dissertation (Theory): University of Iowa, 1960 LC Mic 60-6851. DA XXI.7, p.1963.

2156. Riehm, Diethard. *Die ersten Sätze von Joseph Haydns Londoner Sinfonien*. n.p.: 1971, cover 1975.

2157. ----. "Zur Anlage der Exposition in Joseph Haydns letzten Sinfonien." OMZ 21(1966): 255-260.

2158. Schlager, Karl-Heinz. *Joseph Haydn: Sinfonie Nr.104 D-Dur*. München: W. Fink, 1983.

2159. Schroeder, David Peter. "Audience reception and Haydn's London symphonies." IRASM 16/1(1985): 57-72.

2160. ----. "Joseph Haydn's symphonic language: A critical approach." PhD dissertation (Musicology): King's College, Cambridge, 1982.

2161. Schwartz, Judith L. "Thematic asymmetry in first movements of Haydn's early symphonies." Larsen: 501-509.

2162. Wolf, Eugene K. "The recapitulations in Hadyn's London symphonies." MQ 52(1966): 71-89.

2163. Worbs, Hans Christoph. *Die Sinfonik Haydns*. Heidenau/Sa.: Mitteldeutsche Kunstanstalt, 1956.

Other works

2164. Andrews, Harold L. "The submediant in Hadyn's development sections." Larsen: 465-471.

2165. Arnold, Denis. "Haydn's counterpoint and Fux's *Gradus*." MMR 87(1957): 52-58.

2166. Bartha, Dénes. "Volkstanz-Stilisierung in Joseph Haydns Finale-Themen." Fs. Wiora: 375-384.

2167. Brown, A. Peter. "Critical years for Haydn's instrumental music: 1787-1790." MQ 62(1976): 374-394.

2168. ----. "Tommaso Traetta and the genesis of a Haydn aria (Hob.XXIVb:10)." CHI 16(1984): 101-142.

2169. Broyles, Michael. "The two instrumental styles of classicism." JAMS 36(1983): 210-242. [Symphony No.76, Piano Sonatas Hob.XVI/20, XVI/52/, XVI/50]

2170. Burdick, Michael Francis. "A structural analysis of melodic scale-degree tendencies in selected themes of Haydn, Mozart, Schubert and Chopin." PhD dissertation (Theory): Indiana University, 1977. UM 77-22,643. DA XXXVIII.4, p.1724-A.

2171. Cushman, David Stephen. "Joseph Haydn's melodic materials: An exploratory introduction to the primary and secondary sources together with an analytical catalogue and tables of proposed melodic correspondence and/or variance." PhD dissertation (Musicology): Boston University, 1973. UM 73-14,135. DA XXXIII.12, p.6947.

2172. Danckwardt, Marianne. *Die langsame Einleitung: Ihre Herkunft und ihr Bau bei Haydn und Mozart.* Tutzing: H. Schneider, 1977. 2 vols. 435 p.

2173. Edwall, Harry R. "Ferdinand IV and Haydn's Concertos for the *Lira organizzata.*" MQ 48(1962): 190-203.

2174. Feder, Georg. "Haydn und Bach: Versuch eines musikhistorischen Vergleichs." Fs. Durr: 75-87.

2175. ----. "Typisches bei Haydn: Eine Methode der Stiluntersuchung." OMZ 24(1969): 11-17.

2176. Finscher, Ludwig. "Joseph Haydn: Ein unbekannten Komponist?" NZM 143/10(1982): 12-18.

2177. Garner, Chet H. "Principles of periodic structure in the instrumental works of Haydn, Mozart, and Beethoven." PhD dissertation (Theory): University of Iowa, 1977. 279 p. UM 77-28,456. DA XXXVIII.7, p.3791-A.

2178. Goebels, Franzpeter. "'Meine Sprache versteht man durch die ganze Welt': Bemerkungen zu den Variationen F-Moll (Hob.XVII.6) von Joseph Haydn." MB 14(1982): 338-340, 349-350.

2179. Hailparn, Lydia. "Haydn: The *Seven Last Words*: A new look at an old masterpiece." MR 34(1973): 1-21.

2180. Harutunian, John Martin. "Haydn and Mozart: A study of their mature sonata-style procedures." PhD dissertation (Musicology): University of California, Los Angeles, 1981. No DA listing.

2181. Lang, Paul Henry, ed. *Haydn commemorative issue of The Musical Quarterly.* Introduction by Karl Geiringer. New York: Da Capo Press, 1982.

2182. Levy, Janet M. "Texture as a sign in classic and early romantic music." JAMS 35(1982): 482-531. [String Quartets Op.74, Nos.1,3; Op.76, No.1; Symphony No.92]

2183. Möllers, Christian. "De Einfluss des Konzertsatzes auf die Formentwicklung im 18. Jahrhundert." ZM 9/2(1978): 34-46.

2184. Neubacher, Jürgen. "'Idee' und 'Ausführung': Zum Kompositionsprozess bei Joseph Haydn." AM 41(1984): 187-207.

2185. Prey, Stefan. "Originalität in Haydns Harmonik." M 36(1982): 136-139.

2186. Reindl, Johannes. "Zur Entstehung des Refrains der Kaiserhymne Joseph Haydns." SZM 25(1966): 417-433.

2187. Riedel-Martiny, Anke. "Das Verhältnis von Text und Musik in Haydns Oratorien." HS 1(1965-1967): 205-240.

2188. Rosen, Charles. *The classical style: Haydn, Mozart, Beethoven.* London: Faber & Faber, 1971.

2189. Scholz, Gottfried. "Der dialektische Prozess in Hadyns Doppelvariationen." MAU 2(1979): 97-107.

2190. Schroeder, David. "Melodic source material and Haydn's creative process." MQ 68(1982): 496-515.

2191. Schwarting, Heino. "Ungewöhnliche Repriseneintritte in Haydns späterer Instrumentalmusik." AM 17(1960): 168-182.

2192. Sisman, Elaine Rochelle. "Haydn's variations." PhD dissertation (Musicology): Princeton University, 1978. 357 p. UM 78-18,353. DA XXXIX.4, p.1921-A.

2193. Sponheuer, Bernd. "Haydns Arbeit am Finalproblem" ZM 34 (1977): 199-224.

2194. Steinbeck, Wolfram. *Das Menuett in der Instrumentalmusik Joseph Haydns.* München: E. Katzblichler, 1973.

2195. Stuber, Robert. *Die Klavierbegleitung im Liede von Haydn, Mozart, und Beethoven: Eine Stilstudie.* Biel: Graphische Anstalt Schuler, 1958.

2196. Wollenberg, Susan. "Haydn's Baryton trios and the *Gradus.*" ML 54(1973): 107-178.

HAYDN, MICHAEL (1737-1806)

2197. Pauly, Reinhard G. "Michael Haydn's Latin *Proprium Missae* compositions." PhD dissertation (Music History): Yale University, 1956. UM 67-04,125. DA XXXVII.11, p.3896.

HAYER, RALF

2198. Hansen, Mathies. "Die Analyse: Streichquartett Nr.1 von Ralf Hayer." MG 30(1980): 528-532.

HEIDEN, BERNHARD (born 1910)

2199. Langosch, Marlene Joan. "The instrumental chamber music of Bernhard Heiden." PhD dissertation (Musicology): Indiana University, 1974. UM 74-9431. DA XXXIV.10, p.6688-A.

HEIDER, WERNER (born 1930)

2200. Kelber, Sebastian. "Werner Heiders *Katalog für einen Blockflötenspieler:* Eine Analyse." T 1/2(1976-1977): 145-148.

HEILLER, ANTON (1923-1979)

2201. Gant, Robert Edward. "The organ works of Anton Heiller." DMA dissertation (Performance): University of Rochester, 1975. UM 76-15,589. DA XXXVII.2, p.680-A.

2202. Wieninger, Herbert. "Anton Heiller: Choralmotette *Ach, wie nichtig, ach, wie flüchtig.*" ME 21(1968): 122-127.

HEINRICH, ANTHONY PHILIPP (1781-1861)

2203. Maust, Wilbur. "The symphonies of Anthony Philip Heinrich based on American themes." PhD dissertation (Musicology): Indiana University, 1973. UM 73-19,743. DA XXXIV.3, p.1315.

HEISS, HERMANN (1897-1966)

2203. Special Issue: DBNM 15(1975).

HELLER, STEPHEN (1813-1888)

2205. Booth, Ronald E., Jr. "The life and music of Stephen Heller."
PhD dissertation (Performance): University of Iowa, 1969. UM 70-4334.
DA XXX.9, p.3966-7-A.

HEMEL, OSCAR VAN (1892-1982)

2206. Paap, Wouter. "The Second Violin Concerto by Oscar van
Hemel." SS 45(1970): 1-5.
2207. Wouters, Jos. "Oscar van Hemel." SS 13(1962): 1-7.

HENKEMANS, HANS (born 1913)

2208. Flothuis, Marius. "Hans Henkemans" SS 14(1963): 1-9.
2209. ----. "Hans Henkemans: Quintet No.2 for flute, oboe, clarinet,
bassoon, and horn." SS 22(1965): 19-24.
2210. Geraedts, Jaap. "Henkemans: *Partita per orchestra*." SS 6(1961):
13-15.
2211. ----. "*Winter Cruise*: An opera by Hans Henkemans." KN 9
(1979): 13-16.
2212. Henkemans, Hans. "Hans Henkemans: Piano Sonata." SS 7
(1961): 20-22.

HENSELT, ADOLPH VON (1814-1889)

2213. Graham, Daniel M. "An analytical study of twenty-four etudes
by Adolph von Henselt." DMA dissertation (Piano performance): Peabody
Conservatory, 1979. 127 p. UM 80-08,046. DA XL.10, p.5240-A.
2214. Ho, Allan. "A stylistic analysis of the piano music of Adolph
von Henselt (1814-1889)." MA dissertation (Musicology): University of
Hawaii, Manoa, 1980.

HENZE, HANS WERNER (born 1926)

Operas
2215. De la Motte, Diether. *Hans Werner Henze: Der Prinz von
Hamburg: Ein Versuch über die Komposition und den Komponisten.*
Mainz: Schott, 1960.
2216. Flammer, Ernst Helmuth. "Form und Gehalt III: Eine Analyse
von Hans Werner Henzes *Der langwierige Weg in die Wohnung der Nata-
scha Ungeheuer*." Melos/NZM 4(1978): 486-495.
2217. Klüppelholz, Werner. "Henzes *El Cimarrón*: Eine didaktische
Analyse für die Sekundarstufe II." MB 10(1978): 95-104.

Piano Concertos
2218. Berger, Gregor. "Henzes zweites Klavierkonzert." MELOS
40(1973): 33-40.
2219. Fuhrmann, Roderich. "Hans Werner Henze (1926): 2.
Konzert für Klavier und Orchester (1967)." Zimmerschied:
267-285.

Symphonies

2220. Hamilton, Phillips Howard. "Serialism in the Third, Fourth and Fifth Symphonies of Hans Werner Henze." PhD dissertation (Theory): University of Rochester, 1981. UM 81-24,648. DA XLII.7, p.2923-A.

2221. Ketas, Sheila. "Current Chronicle." MQ 57(1971): 141-148. [Sixth Symphony]

2222. Schmidt, Christian Martin. "Über die Unwichtigkeit der Konstruktion: Anmerkungen zu Hans Werner Henzes 6. Symphonie." Melos/NZM 2(1976): 275-280.

Other works

2223. Flammer, Ernst Helmuth. "Hans Werner Henze: *Six Absences*: Strukturanalyse und Gegenüberstellung zur Jazzfassung von George Gruntz." MB 10(1978): 88-95.

2224. Hines: 89-104.

2225. Pauli, Hansjürg. "Hans Werner Henze's Italian music." SCORE 25(1959): 26-37.

2226. Symons, David. "Hans Werner Henze: The emergence of a style." SMU 3(1969): 35-52.

2227. Vogt, Hans. "*Being Beauteous* von Hans Werner Henze." MELOS 40(1973): 359-365. [Also in Vogt: 322-333]

2228. Wennerstrom. [Piano Sonata]

HEPPENER, ROBERT (born 1925)

2229. Paap, Wouter. "The composer Robert Heppener." SS 39(1969): 1-11.

HERSCHEL, WILLIAM F. (1738-1822)

2230. Duckles, Vincent. "William F. Herschel's concertos for oboe, viola and violin." Fs. Deutsch: 66-74.

HESELTINE, PHILIP *see* WARLOCK, PETER

HESPOS, HANS-JOACHIM (born 1938)

2231. Brauen, Gerhard. "'--schattenhaft ruhig--grob gekaut--': Anmerkungen zu den Flötenkompositionen von H.-J. Hespos." T 7/8 (1982-1983): 418-421.

2232. Oehlschlägel, Reinhard. "Zwischen Handlungsoper und absurdem Theater: Zu Itzo-Hux von Hans-Joachim Hespos und Peter Wagenbreth." MTX 8(1985): 46-48.

HESSENBERG, KURT (born 1908)

2233. Albrecht, Christoph. "'. . . weil ich die Möglichkeiten der Tonalität noch nicht für erschöpt halte': Kurt Hessenberg (geboren 17-8-1908)." Fs. Mauersberger: 165-175.

2234. Riemer, Otto. "Unausgeschöpfte Tonalität: Gedanke zum Schaffen von Kurt Hessenberg." M 7(1953): 56-60.

2235. Zimmermann, Heinz Werner. "Kurt Hessenbergs Motette *O Herr, mache mich zum Werkzeug deines Friedens*, Opus 37, Nr.1." MK 48(1978): 211-217.

HILL, WILLIAM H.

2236. Harbinson, William G. "Analysis: William Hill's *Dances Sacred and Profane.*" JBR 19/1(1983-1984): 5-10.

HILLER, LEJAREN ARTHUR (born 1924)

2237. Cage, John and Lejaren Hiller. "*HPSCHD.*" S 2/2(1968): 10-19.
2238. Hiller, Lejaren and Charles Ames; graphics by Robert Franki. "Automated composition: An installation at the 1985 International Exhibition in Tsukusa, Japan." PNM 23/2(1984-1985): 196-215. [*Circus Piece; Mix or Match*]

HINDEMITH, PAUL (1895-1963)

Cardillac
2239. Rexroth, Dieter. "Zum Stellenwert der Oper *Cardillac* im Schaffen Hindemiths." Rexroth: 56-59.
2240. Schilling, Hans Ludwig. *Paul Hindemith's "Cardillac": Beitrage zu einem Vergleich der beiden Opernfassungen: Stilkriterien im Schaffen Hindemiths.* Würzburg: K. Triltsch, 1964.
2241. Willms, Franz. *Führer zur Oper "Cardillac" von Paul Hindemith.* Mainz: Schott, 1926.

Cello Sonata
2242. Zimmerschied: 153-169.

Chamber Concerti, Op.36
2243. Ross, Walter Beghtol. "Principles of melodic construction in Paul Hindemith's Chamber Concerti, Op.36." DMA dissertation: Cornell University, 1966. No DA listing.

Chamber works [see also individual titles]
2244. Borris, Siegfried. "Tonal concepts in the instrumental chamber works of Paul Hindemith." ISM 2(1979): 141-156.
2245. Dorfman, Joseph. "Tonal concepts in the instrumental chamber works of Paul Hindemith." ISM 2(1979): 141-156.
2246. Kohlhase, Hans. "Aussermusikalische Tendenzen im Frühschaffen Paul Hindemiths: Versuch über die Kammermusik No.1 mit Finale 1921." HJM 6(1983): 183-224.
2247. Mason, Colin. "Hindemiths Kammermusik." MELOS 24(1957): 171-177, 255-258.
2248. ----. "Some aspects of Hindemith's chamber music." ML 41(1960): 150-155.

2249. Ohlsson, Jean Mary. "Paul Hindemith's music for flute: Analysis of solo works and stylistic and formal considerations of chamber works." DMA dissertation (Performance): Ohio State University, 1975. UM 76-3361. DA XXXVII.1, p.27-8-A.

2250, Payne, Dorothy Katherine. "Contrapuntal techniques in the accompanied brass and woodwind sonatas of Hindemith." PhD dissertation (Theory): University of Rochester, 1974. 227 p. UM 74-21,530. DA XXXV.4, p.2325-A.

2251. Wise.

Choral works [see also individual titles]

2252. Fehn, Ann Clark. "*Das Unaufhörliche*: Gottfried Benns Text in der Vertonung von Paul Hindemith." HJ 5(1976): 43-101.

2253. Gros, Raymond. "Hindemith et les poèmes français de Rilke." HJ 8(1979): 79-101. [*Six chansons*]

2254. Hart.

2255. Klyce, Stephen W. "Hindemith's Madrigals: Some analytical comments." ACR 14(1972): 3-13.

2256. Neumann, Friedrich. "Kadenzen, Melodieführung und Stimmführung in den *Six chansons* und *Five Songs on Old Texts* von Hindemith." HJ 8(1979): 49-78.

2257. Rubeli, Alfred Ulrich. *Paul Hindemiths a cappella Werke.* Mainz: Schott, 1975.

2258. Thilman, Johannes Paul. "Zu Hindemiths Motetten." M 28 (1974): 15-17.

2259. Walker, Alvah John. "The a cappella choral music of Paul Hindemith." PhD dissertation (Theory): University of Rochester, 1971. 399 p. UM 72-18,223. DA XXXII.12, p.7036-A.

Clarinet Sonata

2260. Kidd, James C. "Aspects of mensuration in Hindemith's Clarinet Sonata." MR 38(1977): 211-222.

Concert Music for Brass and Strings

2261. Schubert, Giselher. "Kontext und Bedeutung der Konzertmusiken Hindemiths." HJM 4(1980): 85-114.

Concerto for Orchestra

2262. Booth, Paul J.H. "Hindemith's analytical method and an alternative: Two views of his Concerto for Orchestra." SN 7(1978): 117-136.

2263. Haack, Helmut. "Der Finalsatz aus Hindemiths Konzert für Orchester Op.38." HJ 1(1971): 63-79.

Concerto for Trumpet, Bassoon and String Orchestra

2264. Schubert, Giselher. "Zu einigen Spätwerken Hindemiths." Melos/NZM 3(1977): 108-114.

Frau Musica

2265. Austin, William W. "Hindemith's *Frau Musica*: The versions of 1928 and 1943 compared." Fs. Davison: 265-271.

Harmonie der Welt
    2266. Briner, Andres. "Eine Bekenntnisoper Paul Hindemiths: Zu seiner Oper *Die Harmonie der Welt.*" SMZ 99(1959): 1-5, 50-56.

Ludus tonalis
    2267. Forte: 91-190. *[Fuga undecima in B]*
    2268. Neumann, Friedrich. "Hindemith: *Ludus tonalis, Fuga nona in B.*" ZM 8/1(1977): 19-33.
    2269. Neumeyer, David. "The genesis and structure of Hindemith's *Ludus tonalis.*" HJ 7(1978): 72-103.
    2270. Saguer, Louis. "*Ludus tonalis* de Paul Hindemith." CPS 4(1946): 20-40.
    2271. Tischler, Hans. "Hindemith's *Ludus tonalis* and Bach's *Well-Tempered Clavier:* A comparison." MR 20(1959): 217-227.

Das Marienleben
    2272. Davis, Donna Loomis. "Hindemith's theory of composition and *Das Marienleben.*" D 5/2(1973): 13-15.
    2273. Schilling, Hans Ludwig. "Hindemith's Passacagliathemen in den beiden *Marienleben.*" MELOS 23(1956): 106-109. [Also in AM 11(1954): 65-70]
    2274. Stephan, Rudolf. "Hindemith's *Marienleben* (1922-1948)." MR 15 (1954): 275-287.

Mass
    2275. French, Richard F. "Hindemith's *Mass* 1963: An introduction." Fs. Merritt: 83-91.
    2276. Gottwald, Clytus. "Hindemiths *Messe.*" MELOS 32(1965): 386-391.
    2277. ----. "Hindemiths *Messe.*" MB 6(1974): 370-373.
    2278. Vogt: 333-348.

Mathis der Maler
    2279. Hitchcock, H. Wiley. "Trinitarian symbollism in the 'Engelkonzert' of Hindemith's *Mathis der Maler.*" Fs. Seay: 217-229.
    2280. Schneider, Norbert J. "Prinzipien der rhythmischen Gestaltung in Hindemiths Oper *Mathis der Maler.*" HJ 8(1979): 7-48.

Octet
    2281. Worner, Karl H. "Hindemiths neues Oktett." MELOS 25(1958): 356-359.

Organ works
    2282. Bolitho, Albert G. "The organ sonatas of Paul Hindemith." PhD dissertation (Performance): Michigan State University, 1969. UM 69-11,073. DA XXX.1, p.353-A.
    2283. Gibson, Emily. "A study of the major organ works of Hindemith: The three sonatas and the two concerti." DMA dissertation (Performance): University of Rochester, 1968. No DA listing.

2284. Rehm, Gottfried. "Ein Beitrag zur tonal-atonikalen Harmonik: Harmonische Analyse von Hindemiths 1. Orgelsonate (letzter Satz) und Strawinskys *Agnus Dei*." MK 55(1985): 172-180.

2285. Schilling, Hans Ludwig. "Hindemiths Orgelsonaten." MK 33 (1963): 202-209.

Piano Sonatas

2286. Billeter, Bernhard. "Die kompositorische Entwicklung Hindemiths am Beispiel seiner Klavierwerke." HJ 6(1977): 104-121. [Piano Sonata No.1]

2287. Kraemer, Uwe. "Hindemiths 2. Klaviersonate (1936), 1. Satz." MB 1(1969): 74-77.

Pittsburgh Symphony

2288. Briner, Andres. "Hindemith's *Pittsburgh Symphony*." MELOS 26(1959): 252-255.

2289. Metz, Günther. "Das Webern-Zitat in Hindemiths *Pittsburgh Symphony*." AM 42(1985): 200-212.

Serenades

2290. Konold, Wulf. "Paul Hindemiths Serenaden." HJ 4(1974): 88-96.

2291. Neumeyer, David Paul. "Letter-name mottoes in Hindemith's *Gute Nacht*." HJ 6(1977): 22-46. [Also in ITO 2/8(1976): 5-19]

Songs

2292. Fischer, Kurt von. "Hindemith's early songs for voice and piano." PRMA 109(1982-1983): 147-159.

2293. Metz, Gunther. "Hindemiths Lied *Stillung Maria mit dem Auferstandenen*." HJ 12(1983): 53-78.

2294. Venus, Dankmar. *Vergleichende Untersuchung zur melodischen Struktur der Singstimmen in den Liedern von Arnold Schönberg, Alban Berg, Anton Webern, und Paul Hindemith*. Göttingen, 1965.

String Quartets

2295. Doflein, Erich. "Die sechs Streichquartette von Paul Hindemith." SMZ 95(1955): 413-421.

2296. Dorfman, Joseph. "Hindemith's Fourth Quartet." HJ 7(1978): 54-71.

2297. ----. "Thematic organization in the string quartets of Paul Hindemith." OM 6(1978): 45-58.

2298. Espey, Sister Jule Adele. "Formal, tonal and thematic structure of the Hindemith string quartets." PhD dissertation (Theory): Indiana University, 1974. UM 74-9422. DA XXXIV.10, p.6683-4-A.

2299. Pütz.

2300. Rexroth, Dieter. "Tradition und Reflexion beim frühen Hindemith: Analytische und interpretatorische Anmerkungen zu Op.16." HJ 2(1972): 91-113. [String Quartet No.2]

Symphonic Metamorphoses

2301. Brennecke, Wilfried. "Die Metamorphosen: Werke von Richard Strauss und Paul Hindemith." SMZ 103(1963): 129-136, 199-208. [Also in Fs. Albrecht: 268-284]

Symphony for Band

2302. Gallagher, Charles. "Hindemith's Symphony for Band." JBR 2/1 (1966): 19-27.

Symphony Serena

2303. Laaft, Ernst. "Hindemiths *Symphony Serena.*" MELOS 15(1948): 328-333.

Variations for Orchestra

2304. Sannemüller, Gerd. "Das 'Philharmonische Konzert' von Paul Hindemith." HJ 6(1977): 76-103.

Viola Sonata

2305. Hilse, Walter Bruno. "Hindemith and Debussy." HJ 2(1972): 48-90. [Op.11, No.4]

Violin Sonatas

2306. Borris, Siegfried. "Vergleichende Werkanalyse: Alban Berg: Op.5 Nr.1; Paul Hindemith: Aus der Violinsonate 1939." MB 5(1973): 138-141. [Also in Benary: 35-47]
2307. Chihara.
2308. Hambourg, Klement Main. "Three sonatas for violin and piano by Paul Hindemith: A stylistic and interpretive study." DMA dissertation (Performance): University of Oregon, 1977. UM 78--02,523. DA XXXVIII.10, p.5786-7-A.
2309. Hilse, Walter Bruno. "Hindemith and Debussy." HJ 2(1972): 48-90. [Op.11, No.1]

Other works

2310. Bobbitt, Richard. "Hindemith's twelve-tone scale." MR 26 (1965): 104-117.
2311. Brennecke, Dietrich. "'. . . ein Ideal edler und möglichst vollkommenen Musik . . .:' Paul Hindemiths Verhältnis zur Tradition." JP 3(1980): 86-115.
2312. Briner, Andres. *Paul Hindemith.* Zürich: Atlantis; Mainz: Schott, 1971.
2313. Browne, Arthur G. "Paul Hindemith and neo-classic music." ML 13(1932): 42-58.
2314. Cahn, Peter. "Hindemiths Cadenzen." HJ 1(1971): 80-134.
2315. Decker, Jay C. "A comparative textural analysis of selected orchestral works of William Walton and Paul Hindemith." DMA dissertation (Performance): University of Missouri, 1971. UM 72-29,458. DA XXXIII.5, p.2409-A.
2316. Hilse, Walter B. "Factors making for coherence in the works of Paul Hindemith, 1919-1926." PhD dissertation (Musicology): Columbia University, 1972. 499 p. RILM 76/1676dd66. No DA listing.

2317. Hindemith, Paul. "Methods of music theory." MQ 30(1944): 20-28.

2318. Hymanson, William. "Hindemith's variations: A comparison of early and recent works." MR 13(1952): 20-33.

2319. Kleemann, Paul. "Die Kompositionsprinzip Paul Hindemiths und sein Verhältnis zur Atonalität." Fs. Albert/H: 80-92.

2320. Koper, Robert Peter. "A stylistic and performance analysis of the bassoon music of Paul Hindemith." EdD dissertation (Education): University of Illinois, 1972. UM 72-19,863. DA XXXIII.1, p.349-A.

2321. Landau, Victor. "The harmonic theories of Paul Hindemith in relation to his practice as a composer of chamber music." PhD dissertation (Music Education): New York University, 1957. LC Mic 58-664. DA XVIII.3, p.1062.

2322. ----. "Hindemith the system builder: A critique of his theory of harmony." MR 22(1961): 137-151.

2323. ----. "Paul Hindemith: A case study in theory and practice." MR 21(1960): 36-54.

2324. Lanza, Andrea. "Libertà e determinazione formale nel giovane Hindemith." RIM 5(1970): 234-291.

2325. Metz, Günther. *Melodische Polyphonie in der Zwölftonordnung: Studien zum Kontapunkt Paul Hindemiths.* Baden-Baden: Koener, 1976.

2326. Neumeyer, David Paul. "Counterpoint and pitch structure in the early music of Hindemith." PhD dissertation (Theory): Yale University, 1976. 292 p. UM 76-30,240. DA XXXVII.7, p.3979-A.

2327. Redlich, Hans. "Paul Hindemith: A re-assessment." MR 25 (1964): 241-253.

2328. Reich, Willi. "Paul Hindemith." MQ 17(1931): 486-496.

2329. Salmen, Walter. "Alte Töne und Volksmusik in Kompositionen Paul Hindemiths." MB 6(1974): 362-369.

2330. Sannemüller, Gerd. *Der "Plöner Musiktag" von Paul Hindemith.* Neumünster: K. Wachholtz, 1976.

2331. Schilling, Hans Ludwig. "Melodischer Sequenzbau im Werke Paul Hindemiths." SMZ 96(1956): 429-433.

2332. Schollum, Robert. "Metamorphosen über Thema Hindemith." M 9(1955): 533-538.

2333. Strobel, Heinrich. *Paul Hindemith.* Mainz: Schott, 1948.

2334. Thomson, William. "Hindemith's contribution to music theory." JMT 9(1965): 52-71.

2335. Tischler, Hans. "Remarks on Hindemith's contrapuntal technique." Fs. Apel: 175-184.

2336. Zwinck, Eberhard. *Paul Hindemiths "Unterweisung im Tonsatz" als Konsequenz der Entwicklung seiner Kompositonstechnik: Graphische und statistische Musikanalyse.* Goppingen: A. Kummerle, 1974.

HOCH, FRANCESCO (born 1943)

2337. Hoch, Francesco. "*Idra* per 11 archi (1973)." SMZ 115(1975): 77-85.

HODDINOTT, ALUN (born 1929)

2338. Clark, Stewart Jay. "The choral music of Alun Hoddinott: An analysis and related conclusions concerning performance." DMA dissertation (Performance): University of Texas, 1977. UM 77-22,905. DA XXXVIII.5, p.2400-1-A.

HOFFMANN, E.T.A. (1776-1822)

2339. Dechant, Hermann. *E.T.A. Hoffmanns Oper "Aurora."* Regensburg: G. Bosse, 1975. 294 p.

2340. Garlington, Aubrey S., Jr. "Notes on dramatic motives in opera: Hoffmann's *Undine.*" MR 32(1971): 136-145.

HOHENSEE, WOLFGANG (born 1927)

2341. Rebling, Eberhard. "Ein gelungenes Experiment: Das Poem für zwei Klaviere und Orchester von Wolfgang Hohensee." MG 16(1966): 659-662.

HÖLLER, YORK (GEORG) (born 1944)

2342. Battier, Marc and Thierry Lancino. "Simulation and extrapolation of instrumental sounds using direct synthesis at IRCAM (a propos of *Resonance*)." CMR 1/1(1984-1985): 77-81.

2343. Haynes, Stanley. "Report on the realization of York Höller's *Arcus.*" CMR 1/1(1984-1985): 41-66.

2344. Höller, York. "*Resonance*: Composition today." CMR 1/1 (1984-1985): 67-76.

2345. Karallus, Manfred. "Schlangenbeschwörung und Pythagoras verbindend . . . der Komponist York Höller." NZM 144/11(1983): 14-18.

HOLLIGER, HEINZ

2346. Häusler, Josef. "Heinz Holliger: Versuch eines Porträts." SMZ 107(1967): 64-73.

HOLLOWAY, ROBIN (born 1943)

2347. Burn, Andrew. "Holloway's Viola Concerto and Ballad." TEMPO 155(1985): 33-34.

2348. Nash, Peter Paul. "*Cantata on the Death of God* and *Clarissa.*" TEMPO 129(1979): 27-34.

HOLST, GUSTAV (1874-1934)

2349. Boyer, D. Royce. "Holst's *The Hymn of Jesus*: An investigation into mysticism in music." MR 36(1975): 272-283.

2350. Cantrick, Robert. "*Hammersmith* and the two worlds of Gustav Holst." JBR 12/1(1975-1977): 3-11.

2351. Gallagher, Charles. "Thematic derivations in the Holst First Suite in E Flat." JBR 1/2(1964-1965): 6-10.

2352. Holst, Imogen. *The music of Gustav Holst.* London: Oxford University Press, 1951.

2353. Krone, Max T. "The choral works of Gustav Holst." PhD dissertation: Northwestern University, 1940. 575 p. No DA listing.

2354. Mitchell, Jon Ceander. "Gustav Holst: The works for military band." EdD dissertation (Music Education): University of Illinois, 1980. 314 p. UM 81-08,607. DA XLI.12, p.5019-A.

2355. ----. "Gustav Holst's Three Folk Tunes: A source for the Second Suite in F." JBR 19/1(1983-1984): 1-4.

HÖLSZKY, ADRIANA (born 1953)

2356. Stegen, Gudrun. "Komponistenporträt Adriana Hölszky." N 4 (1983-1984): 54-67.

HOLT, SIMEON TEN (born 1923)

2357. Holt, Simeon ten. "*Tripticon* by Simeon ten Holt." SS 39(1969): 33-40.

HONEGGER, ARTHUR (1892-1955)

2358. Calmel, Huguette. "La collaboration Valéry-Honegger à travers *Amphion* (1929)." SMZ 120(1980): 5-11.

2359. Hart.

2360. Headley, Harrold Eugene. "The choral works of Arthur Honegger." PhD dissertation (Musicology): North Texas State University, 1959. LC Mic 59-1372. DA XIX.11, p.2968.

2361. Maillard, Jean and Jacques Nahoum. *Les Symphonies d'Arthur Honegger.* Paris: A. Leduc, 1974.

2362. Silver, Hector. "Honegger: Lithurgische Sinfonie." MELOS 14(1947): 383-386.

2363. Spratt, Geoffrey Kenneth. "A critical study of the complete works of Arthur Honegger with particular reference to his dramatic works." PhD dissertation (Musicology): Bristol, 1980.

2364. ----. "Honegger's *Le Roi David*: A reassessment." MR 39 (1978): 54-60.

2365. Tappolet, Willy. *Arthur Honegger.* Zürich: Atlantis, 1954.

2366. Trickey, Samuel Miller. "*Les Six.*" PhD dissertation (Musicology): North Texas State University, 1955. UM 14,373. DA IV.12, p.2542.

2367. Voss, Hans-Dieter. "Die Oratorien von Arthur Honegger." PhD dissertation (Musicology): Heidelberg, 1982.

HORN, CHARLES EDWARD (1786-1849)

2368. Montague, Richard A. "Charles Edward Horn: His life and works (1786-1849)." EdD dissertation (Music Education): Florida State University, 1959. LC Mic 59-6921. DA XX.8, p.3325.

HORST, ANTHON VAN DER (1899-1965)

2369. Geraedts, Jaap. "Anthon van der Horst: *Réflexions* pour orchester." SS 21(1964): 35-41.
2370. Wouters, Jos. "Dr. Anthon van der Horst (1899-1965)." SS 23(1965): 1-17.

HOVHANESS, ALAN (born 1911)

2371. Cox, Dennis Keith. "Aspects of the compositional styles of three selected twentieth-century American composers of choral music: Alan Hovhaness, Ron Nelson, and Daniel Pinkham." DMA dissertation: University of Missouri, 1978. No DA listing.
2372. Gerbrandt, Carl James. "The solo vocal music of Alan Hovhaness." DMA dissertation (Performance): Peabody Conservatory, 1974. No DA listing.
2373. Jeter. [*Vijag*, Op.37]
2374. Johnson, Axie Allen. "Choral settings of the Magnificat by selected twentieth century composers." DMA dissertation: University of Southern California, 1968. 172 p. RILM 68/3607dd28. No DA listing.
2375. Rosner, Arnold. "An analytical survey of the music of Alan Hovhaness." PhD dissertation: State University of New York, Buffalo, 1979. 377 p. RILM 76/1016dd28. No DA listing.
2376. Tircuit, Heuwell. "Alan Hovhaness: An American choral composer." ACR 9/1(1966): 8, 10-11, 17.

HOWELLS, HERBERT NORMAN (1892-1983)

2377. Hodgson, Peter John. "The music of Herbert Howells." PhD dissertation (Musicology): University of Colorado, 1970. 345 p. UM 71-21,593. DA XXXII.3, p.1551-A.

HUBER, KLAUS (born 1924)

2378. Andraschke, Peter. "Traditionsmomente in Kompositionen von Christobal Halffter, Klaus Huber und Wolfgang Rihm." Brinkmann: 130-152.
2379. Flammer, Ernst Helmuth. "Form und Gehalt (II): Eine Analyse von Klaus Hubers *Tenebrae*." Melos/NZM 4(1978): 294-304.
2380. Gasser, Ulrich. "Klaus Hubers *Senfkorn*: Informatives, Analytisches, und Spekulatives." SMZ 118(1978): 142-149.
2381. Keller, Kjell. "*Tempora*: Konzert für Violine und Orchester von Klaus Huber." MELOS 40(1973): 165-172.
2382. Muggler, Fritz. "Das Porträt Klaus Hubers." MELOS 41(1974): 339-344.
2383. Pauli, Hansjurg. "Klaus Huber." M 17(1963): 10-17. [*Litania instrumentalis*]
2384. Schweizer, Klaus. "Geschichte, eingespannt in Gegenwart: Choräle in Partituren von Klaus Huber." NZM 146/7-8(1985): 32-38.

HUBER, NICOLAUS (born 1939)

    2385. Huber, Nicolaus. *"Gespenster*: Vorspruch--Tutti--Lied." N 2 (1981-1982): 51-67.

HUGGLER, JOHN (born 1928)

    2386. Chihara.

HUMMEL, JOHANN NEPOMUK (1778-1837)

    2387. Davis, Richard. "The music of J.N. Hummel: Its derivations and development." MR 26(1965): 169-191.
    2388. Mitchell, Francis H. "The piano concertos of Johann Nepomuk Hummel." PhD dissertation: Northwestern University, 1957. UM 23-529. DA XVII.12, p.3041.
    2389. Zimmerschied, Dieter. "Die Kammermusik Johann Nepomuk Hummels." PhD dissertation (Musicology): Mainz, 1966.

HUMPERDINCK, ENGELBERT (1854-1921)

    2390. Gerstner, Annette. *Drei Klavierlieder Engelbert Humperdincks.* Berlin: Merseburger, 1984.

HURÉ, JEAN (1877-1930)

    2391. Kniesner. [*Première sonate*]

HUSA, KAREL (born 1921)

    2392. Hartzell, Lawrence W. "Karel Husa: The man and the music." MQ 62(1976): 87-104.
    2393. Molineux, Allen. "The elements of unity and their applications on various levels of the first movement of Karel Husa's Concerto for Wind Ensemble." JBR 21/1(1985): 43-49.

IBERT, JACQUES (1890-1962)

    2394. Timlin, Francis Eugene. "An analytic study of the flute works of Jacques Ibert." DMA dissertation: University of Washington, 1980. No DA listing.

IMBRIE, ANDREW (born 1921)

    2395. Boykan, Martin. "Third Quartet." PNM 3/1(1964): 139-146.
    2396. Reynolds, Christopher A. "A new cantata by Andrew Imbrie: *Prometheus Bound*." ACR 23/2(19810: 3-10.

INDY, VINCENT D' (1851-1931)

    2397. Kniesner. [Piano Sonata in E major, Op.63]

2398. Luck, Ray. "An analysis of three variations sets for piano by Bizet, d'Indy and Pierné." DMA dissertation: Indiana University, 1978. No DA listing.

IRELAND, JOHN (1879-1962)

2399. Dickinson, A.E.F. "The progress of John Ireland." MR 1(1940): 343-353.
2400. Rankin, W. Donald. "The solo piano music of John Ireland." DMA dissertation (Performance): Boston University, 1970. 254 p. RILM 70/2130dd28. No DA listing.
2401. Townsend, Nigel. "The achievement of John Ireland." ML 24 (1943): 65-74.
2402. Yenne, Vernon Lee. "Three twentieth-century English song composers: Peter Warlock, E.J. Morran, and John Ireland." DMA dissertation (Performance): University of Illinois, 1969. No DA lisitng.

IVES, CHARLES (1874-1954)

Chamber works [see also individual titles]
2403. Maske, Ulrich. *Charles Ives in seiner Kammermusik für drei bis sechs Instrumente.* Kölner Beiträge zur Musikforschung 64. Regensburg: G. Bosse, 1971.
2404. Milligan, Terry G. "Charles Ives: A survey of the works for chamber ensemble which utilize wind instruments (1898-1908)." JBR 18/1 (1982-1983): 60-68.
2405. Quackenbush, Margret Diane. "Form and texture in the works for mixed chamber ensemble by Charles Ives." MA dissertation (Music History): University of Oregon, 1976. 125 p.

Choral works [see also individual titles]
2406. Kumlien, Wendell C. "The sacred choral music of Charles Ives: A study in style development." DMA dissertation (Choral Music): University of Illinois, 1969. 387 p. UM 69-15,339. DA XXX.5, p.2061-A.

Concord Sonata
2307. Albert, Thomas Russell. "The harmonic language of Charles Ives' *Concord Sonata.*" DMA dissertation (Composition): University of Illinois, 1974. UM 75-254. DA XXXV.7, p.4580-A.
2308. Babcock, Michael J. "Ives's *Thoreau*: A point of order." ASUC 9-10(1974-1975): 89-102.
2309. Clark, Sondra Rae. "The element of choice in Ives's *Concord Sonata.*" MQ 60(1974): 167-186.
2410. ----. "The evolving *Concord Sonata*: A study of choices and variants in the music of Charles Ives." PhD dissertation (Musicology): Stanford University, 1972. 382 p. No DA listing.
2411. Conen, Hermann. "'All the wrong notes are wright': Zu Charles Ives 2. Klaviersonate 'Concord, Mass. 1840-60.'" N 1(1980): 28-42.
2412. Fischer, Fred. "Ives's *Concord Sonata.*" PQ 92(1975-1976): 23-27.

2413. ----. *Ives's Concord Sonata*. Denton, TX: C/G Productions, 1981.
2414. Ghandar, Ann. "Charles Ives: Organization in *Emerson*." MS 6 (1980): 111-127.
2415. Schubert, Giselher. "Die *Concord-Sonata* von Charles Ives: Anmerkungen zur Werkstruktur und Interpretation." Fs. Savoff: 121-138.

The Fourth of July
2416. Maisel, Arthur. "*The Fourth of July* by Charles Ives: Mixed harmonic criteria in a twentieth-century classic." TP 6/1(1981): 3-32.
2417. Nelson, Mark D. "Beyond mimesis: Transcendentalism and processes of analogy in Charles Ives's *The Fourth of July*." PNM 22 (1983-1984): 353-384.

Piano Sonata No.1
2418. Greenfield, John Wolkowsky. "Charles Edward Ives and the stylistic aspects of his First Piano Sonata." DMA dissertation: University of Miami, 1976. 88 p. No DA listing.

Piano Sonata No.2 see *Concord Sonata]*

Psalm 90
2419. Grantham, Donald. "A harmonic *Leitmotif* system in Ives's Psalm 90." ITO 5/2(1979-1981): 3-14.

Robert Browning Overture
2420. Hüsken, Renate. "Charles Ives *Robert Browning Overture*." N 1 (1980): 16-24.
2421. Kolter, Horst. "Zur Kompositionstechnik von Charles Edward Ives." NZM 113(1972): 559-567.

Songs
2422. Argento, Dominick. "A digest analysis of Ives's *On the Antipodes*." SMM 6(1975-1976): 192-200.
2423. Euteneuer-Rohrer, Ursula Henrietta. "Charles Ives *The Cage*: Eine Werkbetrachtung." N 1(1980): 47-53.
2424. Lorenz, Christof. "Das Liedschaffen Charles Ives." PhD dissertation (Musicology): Köln, 1978.
2425. Newman, Philip. "The songs of Charles Ives." PhD dissertation (Theory): University of Iowa, 1967. UM 67-16,823. DA XXVIII.7, p.2716-A.
2426. Schoffman, Nachum. "Charles Ives's song *Vote for Names*." CM 23(1977): 56-68.
2427. ----. "The songs of Charles Ives." PhD dissertation: Hebrew University, Jerusalem, 1977.
2428. Starr, Lawrence. "Style and substance: *Ann Street* by Charles Ives." PNM 15/2(1977): 23-33.
2429. Velten, Klaus. "Ein Komponist zwischen den Zeiten: Traditionelle Geist und fortschrittliche Gestaltungsweise in Klavierliedern von Charles Ives." MB 15/12(1983): 11-15.

2430. ----. "Der Künstler und die Natur: Ein Interpretationsbeitrag zum Liedschaffen von Charles Ives." MB 13(1981): 544-546.

String Quartets

2431. Budde, Elmar. "Anmerkungen zum Streichquartett Nr.2 von Charles E. Ives." *Bericht über den Internationalen Musikwissenschaftlichen Kongress Bonn 1970, Gesellschaft für Musikforschung.* Carl Dahlhaus, ed. Kassel: Bärenreiter, 1971, p.303-307, 317-319.

2432. Walker, Gwyneth. "Tradition and breaking of tradition in the string quartets of Ives and Schoenberg." DMA dissertation: University of Hartford, 1976. No DA listing.

Symphonies [see also individual titles]

2433. Badolato, James Vincent. "The four symphonies of Charles Ives: A critical, analytical study of the musical style of Charles Ives." PhD dissertation (Musicology): Catholic University, 1978. 231 p. No DA listing.

2434. Herrmann, Bernard. "Four symphonies by Charles Ives." MM 22(1945): 215-222.

2435. Magers, Roy Vernon. "Aspects of form in the symphonies of Charles E. Ives." PhD dissertation (Musicology): Indiana University, 1975. UM 75-23,484. DA XXXVI.5, p.2482-A.

Symphony No.2

2436. Charles, Sydney Robinson. "The use of borrowed material in Ives's Second Symphony." MR 28(1967): 102-111.

2437. Sterne, Colin. "The quotations in Charles Ives's Second Symphony." ML 52(1971): 39-45.

Symphony No.4

2438. Brooks, William. "Unity and diversity in Charles Ives's Fourth Symphony." Y 10(1974): 5-49.

2439. Cyr, Gordon. "Intervallic structural elements in Ives's Fourth Symphony." PNM 9/2-10/1(1971): 291-303.

2440. Kolter, Horst. "Zur Kompositionstechnik von Charles Edward Ives." NZM 113(1972): 559-567.

2441. Rathert, Wolfgang. "Charles Ives: Symphony Nr.4, 1911-1916." N 3(1982-1983): 226-241.

2442. Stone, Kurt. "Ives's Fourth Symphony: A review." MQ 52 (1966): 1-16.

Three Places in New England

2443. Josephson, Nors S. "The initial sketches for Ives's *St. Gaudens in Boston Common.*" SN 12(1984-1985): 46-63.

2444. Stein, Alan. "The musical language of Charles Ives's *Three Places in New England.*" DMA dissertation (Theory): University of Illinois, 1975. 173 p. UM 76-06,974. DA XXXVI.10, p.6362-A.

The Unanswered Question

2445. Enke, Heinz. "Charles Ives *The Unanswered Question.*" Benary: 30-34. [Also in Gerhard Schumacher, ed. *Zur musikalischen Analyse.* Darmstadt: Wissenschaftliche Buchgesellschaft, 1974, p.232-240]

2446. Jolas, Betsy. "Sur Ives *The Unanswered Question*." MJ 1(1970): 13-16.

Other works

2447. Bellamann, Henry. "Charles Ives: The man and his music." MQ 19(1933): 45-58.

2448. Blum, Stephen. "Ives's position in social and musical history." MQ 63(1977): 459-482.

2449. Boatwright, Howard. "Ives's quarter-tone impressions." PNM 3/2 (1965): 22-31.

2450. Burkholder, James Peter. *Charles Ives: The ideas behind the music*. New Haven: Yale University Press, 1985.

2451. ----. "The evolution of Charles Ives's music: Aesthetics, quotation, technique." PhD dissertation: University of Chicago, 1983. 724 p. No DA listing.

2452. ----. "'Quotation' and emulation: Charles Ives's uses of his models." MQ 81(1985): 1-26.

2453. Cowell, Henry. *Charles Ives and his music*. New York: Oxford University Press, 1955.

2454. Danner, Gregory. "Ives's harmonic language." JMR 5 (1984-1985): 237-249.

2455. Ellison, Mary. "Ives's use of American 'popular' tunes as thematic material." F.W. O'Reilly, ed. *Charles Edward Ives* South Florida's Historic Festival 1974-1976. Coral Gables, FL: University of Miami, 1976, p.30-34.

2456. Helm, Everett. "Charles Ives: Pionier der modernen Musik." MELOS 25(1958): 119-123.

2457. Henderson, Clayton W. "Quotation as a style element in the music of Charles Ives." PhD dissertation (Musicology): Washington University, 1969. UM 69-22,533. DA XXX.7, p.3041-2-A.

2458. ----. "Structural importance of borrowed music in the works of Charles Ives: A preliminary assessment." *Report of the 11th Congress (International Musicological Society) Copenhagen, 1972*. H. Glahn, et al., eds. København: W. Hansen, 1974, p.437.

2459. Hitchcock, H. Wiley. *Ives*. Oxford: Oxford University Press, 1977.

2460. Hutchinson, Mary Ann. "Unrelated simultaneity as an historical index to the music of Charles Ives." MM dissertation: Florida State Universty, 1970.

2461. Josephson, Nors S. "Charles Ives: Intervallische Permutationen im Spätwerk." ZM 9/2(1978): 27-33.

2462. ----. "Zur formalen Struktur einiger später Orchesterwerke von Charles Ives (1874-1954)." MF 27(1974): 57-64.

2463. Kolosick, J. Timothy. "A computer-assisted, set-theoretic investigation of vertical simultaneities in selected piano compositions by Charles E. Ives." PhD dissertation (Theory): University of Wisconsin, 1981. UM 81-24,615. DA XLII.7, p.2925-A.

2464. Marshall, Dennis. "Charles Ives's quotations: Manner or substance?" PNM 6/2(1968): 45-56.

2465. Montague, Stephen Rowley. "The simple and complex in selected works of Charles Ives." MM dissertation: Florida State University, 1967. No DA listing.

2466. Perison, Harry. "The quarter-tone system of Charles Ives." CM 18(1974): 96-104.

2467. Rinehart, John McLain. "Ives's compositional idioms: An investigation of selected short works as microcosms of his musical language." PhD dissertation (Theory): Ohio State University, 1971. RILM 74/734dd28. No DA listing.

2468. Schoffman, Nachum. "Serialism in the works of Charles Ives." TEMPO 138(1981): 21-32.

2469. Starr, Lawrence. "Charles Ives: The next hundred years: Towards a method of analysing the music." MR 38(1977): 101-111.

2470. ----. "The early styles of Charles Ives." NCM 7(1983-1984): 71-81.

2471. Tick, Judith. "Ragtime and the music of Charles Ives." CM 18 (1974): 105-113.

2472. Ward, Charles W. "Charles Ives: The relationship of his aesthetic theories and compositional processes." PhD dissertation (Theory): University of Texas, 1974. UM 74-24,947. DA XXXV.5, p.3403-A.

JACOB, GORDON (1895-1984)

2473. Hall, Louis Ollman. "A stylistic and performance analysis of selected solo oboe works of Gordon Jacob." EdD dissertation: University of Illinois, 1979. No DA listing.

2474. Lee, Walter F. "Analysis of selected compositions by Gordon Jacob for solo oboe: Sonata for Oboe and Piano, Sonatina for Oboe and Harpsichord, Two pieces for Two Oboes and Cor anglais, and Concerto No.2 for Oboe." DMA dissertation: Peabody Conservatory, 1978. No DA listing.

2475. Pusey, Robert Samuel. "Gordon Jacob: A study of the solo works for oboe and English horn and their ensemble literature." DMA dissertation: Peabody Conservatory, 1980. 369 p. UM 80-21,962. DA XLI.4, p.1275-A.

JANÁČEK, LEOŠ (1854-1928)

Chamber works
2476. Kaderavek, Milan R. "Stylistic aspects of the late chamber music of Leoš Janáček: An analytic study." DMA dissertation (Composition): University of Illinois, 1970. 2 vols. RILM 72/1976dd28. No DA listing.

2477. Wehnert, Martin. "Anmerkungen zu Semantik in der Streichquartetten Leoš Janáčeks." Pecman: 177-197.

Glagolithic Mass
2478. Hollander, Hans. "Janáčeks *Glazolitische Messe*." M 12(1958): 329-333.

Jenufa
2479. Ströbel, Dietmar. *Motiv und Figur in den Kompositionen der Jenufawerkgruppe Leoš Janáčeks.* München: E. Katzbichler, 1975.

Kátya Kabanová
2480. Tyrrell, John. *Leoš Janáček: Kát'a Kabanová.* Cambridge: Cambridge University Press, 1982.
2481. Wörner, Karl H. "Katjas Tod: Die Schlussszene der Oper *Katja Kabanowa* von Leoš Janáček." SMZ 99(1959): 91-96.

Operas [see also individual titles]
2482. Evans, Michael. *Janácek's tragic operas.* London: Faber, 1977.
2483. Kneif, Tibor. *Die Bühnenwerke von Leoš Janáček.* Wien: Universal, 1975.
2484. Schön, Eva-Maria. "Darstellung der Charaktere in Leoš Janáčeks Opern." PhD dissertation (Musicology): Halle-Salle, 1976.
2485. Shawe-Taylor, Desmond. "The operas of Leoš Janáček." PRMA 85(1958-1959): 49-64.
2486. Tyrrell, John R. "Janáček's stylistic development as an operatic composer as evidenced in his revisions of the first five operas." PhD dissertation (Musicology): Oxford University, 1969. 2 vols. RILM 70/2162dd28.

Piano works
2487. Jiránek, Jaroslav. "Janáčeks Klavierkompositionen vom Standpunkt ihres dramatischen Charakters: Versuch einer semantischen Analyse." AM 39(1982): 179-197.
2488. Uhde, Jürgen. "Ein musikalisches Monument: Zu Leoš Janáčeks Klaviersonaten-Fragment '1.10.1905'." ZM 6/2(1975): 89-95.

Sinfonietta
2489. Hollander, Hans. "Der Klassizismus in Janáčeks Sinfonietta." NZM 135(1974): 685-687.

Taras Bulba
2490. Goren, Richard. "Janáček and *Taras Bulba*." MR 22(1961): 302-306.
2491. Wehnert, Martin. "Imagination und thematisches Verständnis bei Janáček: Dargestellt an *Taras Bulba*." BM 22(1980): 292-308.

Other works
2492. Barvik, Miroslav. "Interpretationsprobleme der Musik von Leoš Janáček." JP 2(1979): 170-189.
2493. Beckerman, Michael. "Janáček and the Herbartians." MQ 69(1983): 388-407. [*Glagolithic Mass*; Sinfonietta; String Quartet No.1; *Makropulos; Cunning Little Vixen*]
2494. Geck, Adelheid. *Der Volksliedmaterial Leoš Janáčeks: Analysen der Strukturen unter Einbeziehung von Janáčeks Randbemerkungen und Volksliedstudien.* Forschungsbeiträge zur Musikwissenschaft 26. Regensburg: G. Bosse, 1975.

2495. Gerlach, Reinhard. "Leoš Janáček und die erste und zweite Wiener Schule: Ein Beitrag zur Stilkritik seines instrumentalen Spätwerks." MF 24(1971): 19-34.

2496. Gülke, Peter. "Protokolle des schöpferischen Prozesses zur Musik von Leoš Janáček." NZM 134(1973): 407-412, 498-503.

2497. ----. "Versuch zur Aesthetik der Musik Leoš Janáceks." DJM 12 (1967): 5-39.

2498. Helman, Zofia. "Zur Modalität im Schaffen Szymanowskis und Janáčeks." Pecman/J: 201-211.

2499. Hollander, Hans. "The music of Leoš Janáček: Its origin in folklore." MQ 41(1955): 171-176.

2500. Salocks, Christopher Stephen. "Form and interpretation in Leoš Janáček's *Po zarostlém chodnicku*." DMA dissertation: Stanford University, 1980. No DA listing.

2501. Schönfelder, Gerd. "Einige Gesichtspunkte zu musikalischer Struktur und Bedeutung im Schaffen Leoš Janáčeks." BM 22(1980): 280-292.

2503. Trojan, Jan. "Leoš Janáček: Entdecker und Theoretiker der harmonischen Struktur im mährischen Volkslied." Pecman/J: 243-250.

2503. Vetterl, Karel. "Janáček's creative relationship to folk music." Pecman/J: 235-242.

JELINEK, HANNS (1901-1969)

2504. Redlich, Hans F. "Hans Jelinek." MR 21(1960): 66-72.

JENEY, ZOLTÁN (born 1943)

2505. Lück, Harmut. "Zustand, Kreis und Continuum: Drei Aspekte der Stile: Über den ungarischen Komponisten Zoltán Jeney." MTX 10 (1985): 17-21.

JEPPESEN, KNUD (1892-1974)

2506. Mathiassen, Finn. "Jeppesen's *Passacaglia*." Fs. Jeppesen: 293-308.

JOHNSTON, BENJAMIN (born 1926)

2507. Childs, Barney. "Ben Johnston: Quintet for Groups." PNM 7/1(1968): 110-121.

JOLAS, BETSY (born 1926)

2508. Krastewa, Iwanka. "Betsy Jolas." SMZ 114(1974): 342-349.

JOLIVET, ANDRÉ (born 1905)

2509. Kniesner. [Piano Sonata]

JOPLIN, SCOTT (1868-1917)

2510. Reed, Addison Walker. "The life and works of Scott Joplin."
PhD dissertation (Musicology): University of North Carolina, 1973. 190 p.
UM 74-5961. DA XXXIV.9, p.6028-A.

JUZELIUNAS, JULIUS (born 1916)

2511. Lampsatis.

KABALEVSKY, DMITRY BORISOVICH (born 1904)

2512. Adams, John P. "A study of the Kabalevsky Preludes, Op.38."
PhD dissertation: Indiana University, 1976. 60 p. No DA listing.

KAGEL, MAURICIO (born 1931)

Anagrama
2513. Knockaert, Yves. "An analysis of Kagel's *Anagrama*." I 5(1976):
173-188.

Exotica
2514. Pelinski, Ramon. "Mauricio Kagel's *Exotica*: Aspects of
exoticism in new music." CAUSM 3/2(1974): 1-9.

Kantrimiusik
2515. Condé, Gerard. "La charrue avant les boeufs: Essai sur
Kantrimiusik [sic]." MJ 27(1977): 58-71.

Match
2516. Schmidt, Christian Martin. "Mauricio Kagel: *Match* für drei
Spieler." Stephan: 145-153.
2517. Tibbe, Monika. "Schwierigkeiten und Möglichkeiten der Analyse
zeitgenossischer Musik, dargestellt an *Match* von Mauricio Kagel." ZM
3/2(1972): 18-21.

Repertoire
2518. Karger, Reinhard. "Mauricio Kagels *Repertoire*." Melos/NZM
2(1976): 375-380.

Rezitativarie
2519. Klüppelholz, Werner. "Musik als Theologie: Zu Kagels *Rezitativarie*." Melos/NZM 3(1977): 483-489.

Sankt-Bach-Passion
2510. Oehlschlägel, Reinhard. "Mild traditionalistische Festmusik: Zur
Sankt-Bach-Passion von Maurice Kagel." MTX 11(1985): 53-55.

Staatstheater

2521. Stoianova, Ivanka. "Multiplicité, non-directionnalité et jeu dans les pratiques contemporaines du spectacle musico-theatral (I): Théâtre instrumental et *impromuz*: Mauricio Kagel, *Staatstheater*; Ghedalia Tazartes, *Ghédal et son double*." MJ 27(1977): 38-48.

2522. Zarius, Karl-Heinz. "Composition en tant qu'analyse: Destruction et construction dans *Staatstheater* de Kagel." MJ 27(1977): 25-37.

Unguis incarnatus est

2523. Decarsin, François. "Liszt's *Nuages gris* and Kagel's *Unguis incarnatus est*: A model and its issue." Trans. by Jonathan Dunsby. MA 4/3(1985): 259-263.

Variationen ohne Fuge

2524. Klüppelholz, Werner. "'Ohne das Wesentliche der Ideen unkenntlich zu machen': Zu Kagels *Variationen ohne Fuge* . . ." Brinkmann: 114-129.

Other works

2525. Bernager, Olivier. "Notes sur une pratique du théâtre musical: à partir de *Repertoire* et de *Pas de cinq* de Mauricio Kagel." MJ 27(1977): 13-24.

2526. Frisius, Rudolf. "Kompositions als Kritik an Inventionen: Tendenzen in neueren Stücken von Mauricio Kagel und ihre Betdueung für den Musikunterricht." MB 9(1977): 600-606. [*Rezitativarie; Siegfriedp* [sic]; *Unguis incarnatus est; Generalbass*]

2527. Klüppelholz, Werner. "Mauricio Kagel und die Tradition." Brinkmann: 102-113.

2528. ----. *Mauricio Kagel, 1970-1980*. Köln: Dumont, 1981.

2529. Noller, Joachim. "Fluxus und die Musik der sechziger Jahre: Über vernachlässigte Aspekte am Beispiel Kagels und Stockhausens." NZM 146/9(1985): 14-19.

2530. Perrin, Glyn. "Mauricio Kagel." CT 15(1976-1977): 13-16.

2531. Schmiedeke, Ulrich. *Der Beginn der neuen Orgelmusik: Die Orgelkompositionen von Hambraeus, Kagel und Ligeti*. München: E. Katzbichler, 1981.

KALOMIRIS, MANOLIS (1883-1962)

2532. Zack, George. "The music dramas of Manolis Kalomiris." PhD dissertation (Musicology): Florida State University, 1971. UM 72-21,338. DA XXXIII.2, p.7800-A.

KAMINSKI, HEINRICH (1886-1946)

2533. Reck, Albert von. "Mystik und Form in *Magnificat* von Heinrich Kaminski." SMZ 96(1956): 153-160.

2534. Samson, Ingried. *Das Vokalschaffen von Heinrich Kaminski*. Franfurt am Main, 1956.

KATZER, GEORG (born 1935)

2535. Klement, Udo. "Die Analyse: Orchesterkonzerte von Ernst Hermann Meyer, Siegfried Matthus und Georg Katzer." MG 28(1978): 599-603. [Konzert für Orchester]

2536. Schneider, Frank. "'Und das Schöne blüht nur im Gesang': Zwei Versuche über Georg Katzers Komposition." MTX 7(1984): 25-29.

KAY, ULYSSES SIMPSON (born 1917)

2537. Hadley, Richard Thomas. "The published choral music of Ulysses Simpson Kay, 1943-1968." PhD dissertation (Choral Literature): University of Iowa, 1972.

2538. Hayes, Laurence Melton. "The works of Ulysses Kay: A stylistic study of selected works." PhD dissertation (Musicology): University of Wisconsin, 1971. 342 p. UM 71-23,306. DA XXXII.6, p. 3351-A.

KEE, COR (born 1900)

2539. Heusinkveld, Frances Mary. "The psalm-based organ music of Cor Kee." PhD dissertation (Music Literature and Performance): University of Iowa, 1978. UM 79-02,909. DA XXXIX.8, p.4581-A.

KELEMEN, MILKO (born 1924)

2540. Gligo, Nikša. "Milko Kelemen: *Passionato* für Flöte und gemischten Chor: Voraussetzungen für eine mögliche Analyse." ZM 6/2(1975): 71-75.

KELTERBORN, RUDOLF (born 1931)

2541. Kelterborn, Rudolf. "*Changements* pour grand orchestre (1972/73)." SMZ 117(1977): 24-27.

2542. Mohr, Ernst. "Rudolf Kelterborn: Analytische Hinweise zu seiner *Missa* für Sopran, Tenor, Chor und Orchester." M 16(1962): 232-236.

2543. Weber, Martin. *Die Orchesterwerke Rudolf Kelterborns.* Regensburg: G. Bosse, 1981.

KERN, MATHIAS (born 1928)

2544. Dorfmüller, Joachim. "'Eigene Wege im Umfeld der Zeitströmungen': Zur Orgelmusik von Mathias Kern." MK 50(1980): 68-75.

KERR, HARRISON (1897-1978)

2545. Kohlenberg, Randy Bryan. "Harrison Kerr: Portrait of a twentieth-century composer." PhD dissertation: University of Oklahoma, 1978. No DA listing.

KETTING, OTTO (born 1935)

2546. Hartsuiker, Ton. "Otto Ketting and his time machine." SS 57(1974): 1-13.

2547. Leeuw, Ton de. "Otto Ketting: *Due Canzoni*." SS 18(1964): 10-15.

2548. Samama, Leo. "Otto Ketting's Symphony for Saxophones and Orchestra: Elements of a technique." KN 10(1979): 14-19.

KETTING, PIET (born 1905)

2549. Bakker, M. Geerink. "Piet Ketting: Trio per flauto, clarinette e fagotto." SS 22(1965): 24-29.

KHANDOSHKIN, IVAN (1747-1804)

2550. Schwarz, Boris. "Khandoshkin's earliest printed work rediscovered." Fs. Abraham: 81-86.

KILLMAYER, WILHELM (born 1927)

2551. Mauser, Siegfried. "Musik als Sprache: Anmerkungen zu Wilhelm Killmayers Klavierstück I." NZM 143/12(1982): 23-26.

KILPINEN, YRJÖ (1892-1959)

2552. Pullano, Frank Louis. "A study of the published German songs of Yrjö Kilpinen." DMA dissertation (Performance): University of Illinois, 1970. UM 70-21,039. DA XXXI.5, p.2425-A.

KIM, EARL (born 1920)

2553. Barkin, Elaine. "Earl Kim: *Earthlight*." PNM 19/2(1980-1981): 269-277. [part of *Narratives*]

KIRCHNER, LEON (born 1919)

2554. Ringer, Alexander L. "Leon Kirchner." MQ 43(1957): 1-20.

2555. Schweitzer. [First Quartet]

2556. True, Nelita. "A style analysis of the published piano works of Leon Kirchner." DMA dissertation (Performance): Peabody Conservatory, 1976. No DA listing.

KJERULF, HALFDAN (1815-1868)

2557. Olson, Robert Wallace. "A comparative study of selected Norwegian romances by Halfdan Kjerulf, Edvard Grieg, and Eyvind Alnaes." PhD dissertation (Performance): University of Illinois, 1973. 328 p. UM 73-17,611. DA XXXIV.2, p.812-A.

2558. Schjeldreup-Ebbe, Dag. "Modality in Halfdan Kjerulf's music." ML 38(1957): 238-246.

KLEBE, GISELHER (born 1925)

2559. Lewinski, Wolf-Eberhard von. "Giselher Klebe." R 4(1958): 89-97. [*Elegia appassionata*, Op.22; String Quartet, Op.9]

2560. McCredie, Andrew D. "Giselher Klebe." MR 26(1965): 220-235.

KLEIN, BERNHARD (1793-1832)

2561. Mies, Paul. "Ein Sinfonie-Fragment von Bernard Klein." Fs. Fellers/60: 144-154.

KLERK, ALBERT DE (born 1917)

2562. Visser, Piet. "Albert de Klerk: *Missa Mater Sanctae Laetitiae.*" SS 23(1965): 26-30.

2563. ----. "Ricercare for Organ, *Hommage à Sweelinck.*" SS 23 (1965): 31-35.

KOCHAN, GÜNTER (born 1930)

2564. Gerlach, Hannelore. "Günter Kochan: *Mendelssohn-Variationen* für Klavier und Orchester." MG 24(1974): 86-90.

2565. Klement, Udo. "Die Analyse: Oratorium *Das Friedenfest* von Günter Kochan." MG 31(1981): 213-216.

2566. Müller, Hans Peter. "*Die Asche von Birkenau:* Zu Günter Kochans neuer Solo-Kantate." MG 16(1966): 453-462.

2567. ----. "Revision mit Konsequenz: Bemerkungen zu zwei Fassungen von Günter Kochans Sinfonie mit Chor." MG 16(1966): 263-267.

2568. Schäfer, Hansjürgen. "Konzert für Klavier und Orchester Op.16 von Günter Kochan." MG 9/5(1959): 22-25.

2569. ----. Reichtum der Gedanken und Empfindungen: Bemerkungen zu Günter Kochans Sinfonietta 1960." MG 12(1962): 286-289.

2570. Wolf, Werner. "Sinfonie für grosses Orchester mit Chor: Ein neues bedeutendes Werk von Günter Kochan." MG 14(1964): 143-146.

KODÁLY, ZOLTÁN (1882-1967)

Cello Sonata

2571. Brewer, Linda Rae Judd. "Progressions among non-twelve-tone sets in Kodály's Sonata for Violoncello and Piano, Op.41: An analysis for performance interpretation." DMA dissertation: University of Texas, 1978. No DA listing.

Choral works

2572. Bárdos, Lajos. "On Kodály's children's choruses." IKSB 1979/1: 32-47, 2: 36-43; 1980/2: 44-53; 1981/1: 27-35, 2: 26-35; 1982/1: 20-36.

2573. Lindlar, Heinrich. "Einige Kodály-Chöre." MZ 9(1954): 29-32.

2574. Steen, Philip Lewis. "Zoltán Kodály's choral music for children and youth choirs." PhD dissertation (Music Education): University of Michigan, 1970. UM 71-15,316. DA XXXI.12, p.6653-A.

2575. Stevens, Halsey. "The choral music of Zoltán Kodály." MQ 54(1958): 147-168.
2576. Young, Percy. "Zoltán Kodály and the choral tradition." ACR 8/1(1965): 1-3, 8, 10-11, 17.

Háry János
2577. Blasl, Franz. "Zoltán Kodálys *Háry János*." ME 21(1968): 221-227.

Hungarian Dances
2578. Weissman, John S. "Notes to Kodály's recent setting of *Hungarian Dances*." TEMPO 32(1954): 29-32.

Missa brevis
2579. Seiber, Matyas. "Kodály: *Missa brevis*." TEMPO 4(1947): 3-6.

Piano works
2580. Korody, István Paku. "Influence of French impressionism and the essence of the Hungarian national character in Zoltán Kodály's piano music." DMA dissertation: Ohio State University, 1978. No DA listing.

Songs
2581. Jolly, Cynthia. "The art songs of Kodály." TEMPO 63(1962): 2-12.

Symphony
2582. Breuer, János. "Zoltán Kodálys Symphonie: Ein Schweizer Auftragswerk." Trans. by Michel R. Flechter. SMZ 122(1983): 157-163.
2583. Weissman, John S. "Kodály's Symphony: A morphological study." TEMPO 60(1961): 19-36.

Other works
2584. Bónis, Ferenc. "Zoltán Kodály: Der Meister der ungarischen Neoklassik." OMZ 35(1980): 129-143.
2585. Ittzés, Mihály. "The musical world of Kodály's instrumental pieces for children." IKSB 1980/2: 13-23.
2586. Mellers, Wilfred H. "Kodály and the Christian epic." ML 22 (1941): 155-161.
2587. Sárosi, Bálint. "Instrumental folk music in Kodály's works: The Galánta and Marosszék Dances." SM 25(1983): 23-28.
2588. Szöllösy, Andras. "Kodály's melody." TEMPO 63(1962): 12-16.
2589. Vargyas, Lajos. "Wirkung der Volksmusikforschung auf Kodály's Schöpfungen." SM 25(1983): 39-60.
2580. Weissman, John S. "Kodály's later orchestral music." TEMPO 17(1950): 16-23.
2591. ----. "Kodály's späte Orchesterwerke." MZ 9(1954): 16-28.

KOECHLIN, CHARLES (1867-1950)

2592. Fortassier, Pierre. "La Musique des choeurs de l'*Alceste* d'Euripide." RM 340-341(1981): 73-80.

2593. Guieysse, Jules. "Charles Koechlin: L'Oeuvre d'orchestre." Revised by Paul-Gilbert Langevin." RM 324-325-326 (1979): 147-167.

2594. Kirk, Elise Kuhl. "Art nouveau and the melodic style of Charles Koechlin." MMA 13(1984): 117-129.

2595. ----. "The chamber music of Charles Koechlin (1867-1950)." PhD dissertation (Musicology): Catholic University, 1977. UM 77-21,339. DA XXXVIII.4, p.1728-A.

2596. Koechlin, Charles. "Étude sur Charles Koechlin par lui-même." RM 340-341(1981): 39-72.

2597. Langevin, Paul-Gilbert. "Charles Koechlin: Musicien de l'avenir." RM 324-325-326(1979): 135-145.

2598. McGuire, Thomas Howard. "The piano works of Charles Koechlin (1867-1950)." PhD dissertation (Musicology): University of North Carolina, 1975. 272 p. UM 76-9266. DA XXXVI.10, p.6361-A.

2599. Orledge, Robert F. "A study of the composer Charles Koechlin (1867-1950)." PhD dissertation (Musicology): Cambridge, 1973.

KÖHLER, SIEGFRIED (1927-1984)

2600. Felix, Werner. "*Reich des Menschen*: Poem nach Dichtungen von Johannes R. Beicher/Musik: Siegfried Köhler." MG 18(1968): 5-10.

2601. Schönfelder, Gerd. "Die Analyse: IV. Sinfonie von Siegfried Köhler." MG 29(1979): 398-402.

KÖHLER, WOLFGANG (born 1923)

2602. Hopf, Helmuth. "Zu Kompositionstechniken im Konzert für Orchester von Wolfgang Köhler." Fs. Boetticher: 120-129.

2603. ----. "Zu Wolfgang Köhlers Sinfonie Nr.3, Op.42." Fs. Valentin: 53-60.

KOMITAS, SOGOMON (1869-1935)

2604. Vagramian, Violet. "Representative secular choral works of Gomidas: An analytical study and evaluation of his musical style." PhD dissertation (Theory): University of Miami, 1973. No DA listing.

KOX, HANS (born 1930)

2605. Geraedts, Jaap. "Hans Kox: Concerto for Violin and Orchestra." SS 21(1964): 12-16.

2606. Rossum, Frans van. "*Dorian Gray*: An opera to strike joy into a director's heart." KN 6(1977): 12-18.

2607. Werker, Gerard. "*In Those Days* by Hans Kox: A musical memory of the Battle of Arnhem." SS 43(1970): 24-30.

KRAFT, WILLIAM (born 1923)

2608. Harbinson, William G. "Analysis: William Kraft's *Dialogues and Entertainments*." JBR 19/1(1983-1984): 16-25.

KRÄTZSCHMAR, WILFRIED

2609. Raab, Hans-Heinrich. "Die Analyse: II. Sinfonie von Wilfried Krätzschmar." MG 31(1981): 73-76.

KRAUS, EBERHARD (born 1931)

2610. Stein, Franz A. "Historische Aspekte in den Zwölftonkompositionen von Eberhard Kraus." Beck: 193-212.

KRAUSE-GRAUMNITZ, HEINZ (1911-1979)

2611. Hennenberg, Fritz. *"An die Nachgeborenen."* MG 10(1960): 299-301.

KRENEK, ERNST (born 1900)

Eleven Transparencies for Orchestra
2612. Wennerstrom

Lamentatio Jeremiae Prophetae
2613. Vogt: 239-248.

Operas
2614. Knoch, Hans. *Orpheus und Eurydike: Der antike Sagenstoff in den Opern von Darius Milhaud und Ernst Krenek.* Regensburg: G. Bosse, 1977.
2615. Rogge, Wolfgang. *Ernst Krenek: Opern.* Wolfenbüttel: Möseler; Hamburg: Vera, 1970.

Organ works
2616. Haselböck, Martin. "Die Orgelwerke Ernst Kreneks: Eine Überschau: Zum 80. Geburtstag des Komponisten am 23 August 1980." MK 50(1980): 114-122.

Piano works
2617. Buccheri.
2618. Huetteman, Albert George. "Ernst Krenek's theories on the sonata and the relations to his six piano sonatas." PhD dissertation (Theory): University of Iowa, 1968. UM 69-08,747. DA XXX.2, p.751-A.

Sestina
2619. Krenek, Ernst. *"Sestina."* MELOS 25(1958): 235-238.

Songs
2620. Johnson, June Durkin. "Ernst Krenek: *Fünf Lieder nach Worten von Franz Kafka."* Johnson.
2621. Schollum, Robert. "Anmerkungen zum Liedschaffen Ernst Kreneks." OMZ 35(1980): 446-452.

Other works

2622. Erikson, Robert. "Krenek's later music (1930-1947)." MR 9 (1948): 29-43.

2623. Hines.

2624. Houser, James D. "The evolution of Ernst Krenek's twelve-tone technique." MA dissertation (Theory): University of Rochester, 1977. [*Zwölf Variationen in drei Sätzen* (1937); Eight Piano Pieces (1926); *Sechs Vermessene* (1960)]

2625. Neuwirth, Gösta. "Rotas-Sator: Für Ernst Krenek zum 23. August 1980." OMZ 35(1980): 461-472.

2626. Ogdon. [*Lamentations*; Piano Sonata No.3; *Symphonic Elegy*]

2627. Reich, Willi. "Ernst Kreneks Arbeit in der Zwölftontechnik." SMZ 89(1949): 49-53.

2628. Schuh, Willi. "Zur Zwölftontechnik bei Ernst Krenek." SMZ 74(1934): 217-223.

KREUTZER, CONRADIN (1780-1849)

2629. Peake, Luise Eitel. "Kreutzer's *Wanderlieder*: The other *Winterreise*." MQ 65(1979): 83-102.

KRÖLL, GEORG (born 1934)

2630. Gruhn, Wilfried. "Bearbeitung als kompositorische Reflexion in neuer Musik." M 28(1974): 522-528. [*Parodia ad Perotinum* (1972)]

KRUYF, TON DE (born 1937)

2631. Vermeulen, Ernst. "Pleasure in virtuosity: *Serenata* by Ton de Kruyf." SS 40(1969): 23-28.

2632. ----. "Ton de Kruyf: *Spinoza*." SS 47(1971): 1-14.

KUBIK, GAIL (1914-1984)

2633. Lyall, Max Dail. "The piano music of Gail Kubik." DMA dissertation: Peabody Conservatory, 1980. No DA listing.

KUBIZEK, AUGUSTIN (born 1918)

2634. Suyka, Ulf-Diether. "Augustin Kubizek: *Mater castisissima* Op.22c/2." ME 30(1976-1977): 70-72.

KUNAD, RAINER (born 1936)

2635. Härtwig, Dieter. "Rainer Kunads *Sinfonie 64*." MG 16(1966): 816-822.

2636. Kneipel, Eberhard. "Klavierkonzert von Rainer Kunad." MG 21(1971): 625-629.

KUNZEN, FRIEDRICH LUDWIG AEMILIUS (1761-1817)

2637. Abert, Anna Amalie. *"Oberon* in Nord und Süd." Fs. Gudewill: 51-68. [*Holger Danske*]

KURTÁG, GYÖRGY (born 1926)

2638. Spangemacher, Friedrich. "György Kurtág." NZM 143/9(1982): 28-33.

2639. Walsh, Stephen. "György Kurtág: An outline study." TEMPO 140(1982): 11-21; 142(1982): 10-19.

KURZ, SIEGFRIED (born 1930)

2640. Gülke, Peter. "Bemerkungen zur Musik für Orchestra 1960 von Siegfried Kurz." MG 13(1963): 198-201.

2641. Kneipel, Eberhard. "Klavierkonzert von Rainer Kunad." MG 21(1971): 625-629.

2642. Schönewolf, Karl. "Bemerkungen zur II. Sinfonie von Siegfried Kurz." MG 12(1962): 724-727.

KURZBACH, PAUL (born 1902)

2643. Brock, Hella. "Das Freundliche: Ein Wesenzug unserer Musik zum Violonkonzert Paul Kurzbachs." MG 20(1970): 757-762.

KUTZVIČIUS, BRONISLOVAS (born 1932)

2644. Lampsatis.

KUULA, TOIVO (1883-1918)

2645. Hillila, Ruth Ester. "The songs of Toivo Kuula and Leevi Madetoja and their place in twentieth-century Finnish art song." PhD dissertation (Musicology): Boston University, 1964. UM 64-11,620. DA XXV.5, p.3017-8.

LA CASINIÈRE, YVES DE (1897-1971)

2646. Kniesner. [Piano Sonata in B minor]

LA HACHE, THEODORE VON (1822/3-1869)

2647. Fields, Warren C. "The life and works of Theodore von la Hache." PhD dissertation (Musicology): University of Iowa, 1973. 2 vols. UM 74-16,618 Da XXXV.2, p.1143-A.

LACHENMANN, HELMUT (born 1935)

2648. Baucke, Ludolf. "'Mensch, erkenn dich doch . . .': Anmerkungen zu Helmut Lachenmann: *Harmonica*." MTX 3(1984): 6-9.

2649. Mäckelmann, Michael. "Helmut Lachenmann oder 'Das neu zu rechtfertigende Schöne': Zum 50. Geburtstag des Komponisten." NZM 146/11(1985): 21-25.
2650. Shaked, Yuval. "'Wie ein Käfer, auf dem Rücken zappelnd': Zu *Mouvement (-vor der Erstarrung-)* (1982-1984): Von Helmut Lachenmann." MTX 8(1985): 9-16.

LACHNER, FRANZ PAUL (1803-1890)

2651. Wagner, Günter. *Franz Lachner als Liederkomponist nebst einem biographischen Teil und dem thematischer Verzeichnis sämtlicher Lieder.* München: E. Katzbichler, 1970. 313 p.

LACK, THÉODORE (1846-1921)

2652. Kniesner. [*Sonate pastorale*, Op.253, for Piano]

LAJTHA, LÁSZLÓ (1892-1963)

2653. Weissman, John S. "László Lajtha: The symphonies." MR 36 (1975): 197-214.

LALO, EDOUARD (1823-1892)

2654. ASO 65(1984) [*Le Roi d'Ys*]
2655. Macdonald, Hugh. "A fiasco remembered: *Fiesque* dismembered." Fs. Abraham: 163-185.

LANDRÉ, GUILLAUME (1905-1968)

2656. Flothuis, Marius. "Guillaume Landré: Fourth String Quartet (1965)." SS 40(1969): 20-22.
2657. Wouters, Jos. "Guillaume Landré." SS 15(1963): 1-17.
2658. ----. "Guillaume Landré: Symphony No.3." SS 20(1964): 34-37.
2659. ----. "Guillaume Landré: *Symphonic Permutations*." SS 8(1961): 10-13.

LANGLAIS, JEAN (born 1907)

2660. Krellwitz, Janet. "The relationship of the plainsong and the organ music of Jean Langlais." EdD dissertation (Music Education): New York University, 1981. UM 81-11,521. DA XLI.12, p.5018-A.
2661. Kurr, Doreen Barbara. "The organ works of Jean Langlais." DMA dissertation (Performance): University of Washington, 1971. 235 p. UM 71-28,435. DA XXXII.5, p.2730-A.

LANNER, JOSEPH (1801-1843)

2662. Barford, Philip T. "The early dances of Josef Lanner." MR 21(1960): 114-120.

2663. ----. "Joseph Lanner: A further appraisal." MR 21(1960): 179-185.

LASSEN, EDUARD (1830-1904)

2664. Marx-Weber, Magda. "Die Lieder Eduard Lassens." HJM 2(1974): 147-185.

LAYTON, BILLY JIM (born 1924)

2665. Browne, Richmond. *"Dance Fantasy."* PNM 4/1(1965): 161-170.

LAZAROF, HENRI (born 1932)

2666. Applebaum, Edward. "An analysis of Lazarof's *Textures."* NW 3(1973): 26-29.

LEBOFFE, ENRICO

2667. Webster, Jesser Alfred, Jr. "The discovery of Enrico Leboffe, immigrant American-Italian composer." DMA dissertation: University of Oklahoma, 1978. No DA listing.

LECHTHALER, JOSEF (1891-1948)

2668. Klein, Rudolph. "Ein unbekanntes Werk von Josef Lechthaler." ME 5(1952): 139-144. [*Orgelphantasie*, Op.31]

LEES, BENJAMIN (born 1924)

2669. Cooke, Deryck. "Benjamin Lees' *Visions of Poets."* TEMPO 68(1964): 25-31.
2670. ----. "The music of Benjamin Lees." TEMPO 51(1959): 16-29.
2671. ----. "The recent music of Benjamin Lees." TEMPO 64(1963): 11-21.
2672. Kim, Hyung Bae. "The solo piano works of Benjamin Lees published from 1956 to 1976." DMA dissertation (Performance): Peabody Conservatory, 1981. UM 81-18,944. DA XLII.3, p.908-A.
2673. Slonimsky, Nicolas. "Benjamin Lees *In Excelsis."* TEMPO 113(1975): 14-21.
2674. Westwood, Shirley Ann. "Poetic imagery in the songs of Benjamin Lees." DMA dissertation: University of Missouri, 1980. No DA listing.

LEEUW, REINBERT DE (born 1938)

2675. Markus, Wim. *"Axel* or the rejection of life." KN 6(1977): 19-32.

LEEUW, TON DE (born 1926)

2676. Dominick, Lisa R. "Mode and movement in recent works of Ton de Leeuw." KN 17(1983): 15-23. [*Modal Music for Accordion; Car nos vignes sont en fleur; And They Shall Reign For Ever; The Magic of Music II; The Birth of Music II; Chronos; Clair-Obscur*]

2677. Leeuw, Ton de. "Ton de Leeuw: *Mouvements rétrogrades*." SS 8(1961): 14-15.

2678. Manneke, Daan. "Ton de Leeuw: *Music for Organ and 12 Players*." SS 49(1971-1972): 7-12.

2679. ----. "Ton de Leeuw: *Music for Strings*." SS 48(1971): 17-26.

2680. Paap, Wouter. "A new string quartet by Ton de Leeuw." SS 25 (1965): 24-28. [Second String Quartet]

2681. Vermeulen, Ernst. "*Lamento pacis* by Ton de Leeuw." SS 39 (1969): 23-32.

2682. Wouters, Jos. "Ton de Leeuw." SS 19(1964): 1-29.

LEHAR, FRANZ (1870-1948)

2683. ASO 45(1982). [*The Merry Widow*]

LEIBOWITZ, RENÉ (1913-1972)

2684. Maguire, Jan. "René Leibowitz." PNM 21(1982-1983): 241-256. [Opera *Todos Caeran*]

2685. Ogdon: 252-311. [Third String Quartet]

2686. Saby, Bernard. "Un Aspect des problèmes de la thématique sérielle: A propos de la *Symphonie de chambre*, Op.16, de René Leibowitz." POL 4(1949): 54-63.

LEKBERG, SVEN (born 1899)

2687. Lamb, Gordon Howard. "The choral music of Sven Lekberg." PhD dissertation (Choral Literature): University of Iowa, 1973. 195 p. UM 73-30,942. DA XXXIV.6, p.3453-A.

LEONCAVALLO, RUGGIERO (1857-1919)

2688. ASO 50(1983). [*I Pagliacci*]

LESSER, WOLFGANG (born 1923)

2689. Schaefer, Hansjürgen. "'. . . gesellschaftlich Konkret': Bemerkungen zum Violinkonzert von Wolfgang Lesser." MG 14(1964): 331-335.

LEVY, ERNST (1895-1981)

2690. Levarie, Siegmund. "La Musique d'Ernst Levy." SMZ 108(1968): 178-187.

LEWIN, DAVID (born 1933)

    2691. Levy, Burt J. "David Lewin: *Classical Variations on a Theme by Schoenberg* for Cello and Piano (1960)." PNM 7/2(1969): 167-171.

LIAPUNOV, SERGEI MIKHAILOVICH (1859-1924)

    2692. Kaiserman, David. "The piano works of S.M. Liapunov." JALS 3(1978): 25-26.

LIDHOLM, INGVAR (born 1921)

    2693. Brolsma, Bruce Edward. "The music of Ingvar Lidholm: A survey and analysis." PhD dissertation: Northwestern University, 1979. No DA listing.
    2694. Lidholm, Ingvar. "*Poesis* for Orchestra." Ligeti: 55-80.
    2695. ----. "*Poesis* für Orchester." MELOS 36(1969): 63-76.

LIEBERMANN, ROLF (born 1910)

    2696. Stuckenschmidt, H. H. "Rolf Liebermann: Bildnis eines Komponisten." SMZ 92(1952): 137-143.

LIER, BERTUS VAN (1906-1972)

    2697. Wouters, Jos. "Bertus van Lier: Sonatina No.2." SS 13(1962): 9-11.

LIGETI, GYÖRGY (born 1923)

Artikulation
    2698. Miereanu, Costin. "Une musique électronique et sa 'partition': *Artikulation*." MJ 15(1974): 102-109.

Atmosphères
    2699. Kaufmann, Harold. "Strukturen im Strukturlosen." MELOS 31 (1964): 391-398.
    2700. Roberts.
    2701. Schneider, Sigrun. "Zwischen Statik und Dynamik: Zur formalen Analyse von Ligetis *Atmosphères*." MB 7(1975): 507-510.
    2702. Vogt: 307-314.

Aventures, Nouvelles aventures
    2703. Anhalt, Istvan. "Ligeti's *Nouvelles aventures*: A small group as a model for composition." Anhalt: 41-92.
    2704. Kaufmann, Harald. "Un Cas de musique absurde: *Aventures* et *Nouvelles aventures* de Ligeti." MJ 15(1974): 75-98.
    2705. Klüppelholz, Werner. "Aufhebung der Sprache: Zu Gyorgy Ligetis *Aventures*." Melos/NZM 2(1976): 1976): 11-15.

Cello Concerto
    2706. Bersano.
    2707. Schultz, Wolfgang-Andreas. "Zwei Studien über das Cello-Konzert von Ligeti." ZM 6/2(1975): 97-104.
    2708. Stephan, Rudolf. "György Ligeti: Konzert für Violoncello und Orchester: Anmerkungen zur Cluster-Komposition." Stephan: 117-127.

Chamber Concerto
    2709. Bernager, Olivier. "Autour du *Concerto de chambre* de Ligeti." MJ 15(1974): 99-101.

Continuum
    2710. Urban, Uve. "Serielle Technik und barocker Geist in Ligetis Cembalo-Stück *Continuum*." MB 5(1973): 63-70.

Le Grand macabre
    2711. Fanselau, Rainer. "György Ligeti: *Le Grand macabre*: Gesichtspunkte für eine Behandlung im Musikunterricht." MB 15/5(1983): 17-24.

Lontano
    2712. Dadelsen, Hans-Christian von. "Hat Distanz Relevanz: über Kompositionstechnik und ihre musikdidaktischen Folgen: Dargestelle an György Liegtis Orchesterstück *Lontano* (1967)." MB 7(1975): 502-506.
    2713. ----. "Über die musikalischen Konturen der Entfernung: Entfernung als räumliche, historische und ästhetische Perspektive in Ligetis *Lontano*." Melos/NZM 2(1976): 187-190.
    2714. Müller, Karl-Josef. "György Ligeti (1923): *Lontano* für grosses Orchester (1967)." Zimmerschied: 286-308.
    2715. Reiprich, Bruce. "Transformation of coloration and density in Gyorgy Ligeti's *Lontano*." PNM 16/2(1977-1978): 167-180.
    2716. Rollin, Robert L. "The genesis of the technique of canonic sound mass in Ligeti's *Lontano*." ITR 2/2(1978-1979): 23-33.
    2717. ----. "Ligeti's *Lontano*: Traditional canonic technique in a new guise." MR 41(1980): 289-296.
    2718. ----. "The process of textural change and the organization of pitch in Ligeti's *Lontano*." DMA dissertation (Composition): Cornell University, 1973. UM 74-06,383. DA XXXIV.10, p.6691-A.

Lux aeterna
    2719. Gottwald, Clytus. "*Lux aeterna*: Ein Beitrag zur Kompositionstechnik György Ligetis." M 25(1971): 12-17.
    2720. Ligeti, György. "Auf dem Weg zu *Lux aeterna*." OMZ 24 (1969): 80-88.
    2721. Michel, Pierre. "Les Rapports texte/musique chez György Ligeti de *Lux aeterna* au *Grand macabre*." CC 4(1985): 128-138.
    2722. Rummenhöller, Peter. "Möglichkeiten neuester Chormusik." *Der Einfluss der technischen Mittler auf die Musikerziehung unserer Zeit.* Mainz: Schott, 1968: 311-317.

Organ works

2723. Collins, Glena Whitman. "Avant-garde techniques in the organ works of György Ligeti." DMA dissertation: North Texas State University, 1980. 88 p. No DA listing.

2724. Schmiedeke, Ulrich. *Der Beginn der neuen Orgelmusik: Die Orgelkompositionen von Hambraeus, Kagel und Ligeti.* München: E. Katzbichler, 1981.

String Quartet No.2

2725. Borio, Gianmario. "L'Eredità bartókiana nel Secondo Quartetto di G. Ligeti: Sul concetto de tradizione nella musica contemporanea." STU 13(1984): 289-308.

2726. Kaufmann, Harold. "Ligetis zweites Streichquartett." MELOS 37(1970): 181-186.

Ten Pieces for Wind Quintet

2727. Yannay, Yehuda. "Toward an open-ended method of analysis of contemporary music: A study of selected works by Edgard Varèse and György Ligeti." DMA dissertation (Composition): University of Illinois, 1974. 131 p. RILM 74/3024dd28. No DA listing.

Three Fantasies after Friedrich Hölderlin

2728. Floros, Constantin. "Ligetis *Drei Phantasien nach Friedrich Hölderlin* (1982)." NZM 146/2(1985): 18-20.

Three Pieces for Two Pianos

2729. Febel, Reinhard. "György Ligeti: Monument--Selbstporträt--Bewegung (*3 Stücke für 2 Klaviere*)." ZM 9/1(1978): 35-51; 9/2(1978): 4-14.

2730. ----. *Musik für zwei Klaviere seit 1950 als Spiegel der Kompositionstechnik.* Herrenberg: Doring, 1978.

Other works

2731. Christensen, Louis. "Introduction to the music of György Ligeti." NW 2(1972): 6-15.

2732. Dibelius, Ulrich. "Reflexion und Reaktion über den Komponisten György Ligeti." MELOS 37(1970): 89-96.

2733. Dobson, E. "Illusion in the music of György Ligeti, 1958-1968." MM dissertation: University of Queensland, 1977.

2734. Frisius, Rudolf. "Tonal oder postseriell." MB 7(1975): 490-501.

2735. Griffiths, Paul. *György Ligeti.* London: Robson, 1983.

2736. Gruhn, Wilfried. "Textvertonung und Sprachkomposition bei György Ligeti: Aspekte einer didaktischen Analyse zum Thema *Musik und Sprache.*" MB 7(1975): 511-519.

2737. Häusler, Josef. "György Ligeti oder die Netzstruktur." NZM 144/5(1983): 18-21.

2738. Lichtenfeld, Monika. "György Ligeti oder das Ende der seriellen Musik." MELOS 39(1972): 74-80.

2739. Ligeti, György. *György Ligeti in conversation.* London: Eulenberg Books, 1983.

2740. Nordwall, Ore. *György Ligeti: Eine Monographie*. Mainz: Schott, 1971.

2741. Salmenhaara, Erkki. *Das musikalische Material und seine Behandlung in den Werken "Apparitions," "Atmosphères," "Aventures," und "Requiem" von György Ligeti*. Trans. from the Finnish by Helke Sander. Regensburg: G. Bosse, 1969.

LILBURN, DOUGLAS (born 1915)

2742. Harris, Ross. "Douglas Lilburn's Symphony No.3 (in one movement)." *Canzona* 2/5(1980): 3-7.

LISZT, FRANZ (1811-1886)

Les Années de pèlerinage

2743. Presser, Diether. "Liszts *Années de pèlerinage, Prèmiere année: Suisse* als Dokument der Romantik." *Liszt Studien* 1. Kongress-Bericht, Eisenstadt 1975. Wolfgang Suppan, ed. Graz: Akademische Druck- u. Verlagsanstalt, 1977: 137-158.

2744. Wilson, Karen Sue. "A historical study and stylistic analysis of Franz Liszt's *Années de pèlerinage*." PhD dissertation (Musicology): University of North Carolina, 1977. 313 p. UM 78-10,526. DA XXXIX.1, p.20-A.

Choral works

2745. Cheung, Andrew Y. K. "Thematic and motivic transformation in selected sacred choral works of Franz Liszt." MA dissertation (Music History and Literature): State University College, Potsdam, New York, 1979.

2746. Fudge, James Thompson. "The male chorus music of Franz Liszt." PhD dissertation (Choral Literature): University of Iowa, 1972. UM 73-13,536. DA XXXIII.12, p.6951.

2747. Palotai, Michael. "Liszt's concept of oratorio as reflected in his writings and in *Die Legende von der Heiligen Elisabeth*." PhD dissertation: University of Southern California, 1977. No DA listing.

Christus

2748. Orr, Nathaniel Leon. "Liszt, *Christus*, and the transformation of the oratorio." JALS 9(1981): 4-18.

2749. ----. "Liszt's *Christus* and its significance for nineteenth-century oratorio." PhD dissertation (Musicology): University of North Carolina, 1979. 401 p. UM 79-25,952. DA XL.5, p.2343-A.

Consolations

2750. Diercks, John. "The *Consolations*: 'Delightful things hidden away'." JALS 3(1978): 19-24.

Dante Symphony

2751. Barricelli, Jean-Pierre. "Liszt's journey through Dante's hereafter." JALS 14(1983): 3-15.

2752. Knight, Ellen. "The harmonic foundation of Liszt's *Dante Symphony*." JALS 10(1981): 56-63.

Fantasy and Fugue on "Ad nos ad salutarem undam"
2753. Edler, Arnfried. "'In ganz neuer und freier Form geschrieben': Zu Liszts Phantasie und Fuge über den Choral *Ad nos ad salutarem undam*." MF 25(1972): 249-258.
2754. Todd, R. Larry. "Liszt: Fantasy and Fugue for Organ on *Ad nos, ad salutarem undam*." NCM 4(1980-1981): 250-261.

Faust Symphony
2755. Macy.
2756. Niemöller, Klaus Wolfgang. "Zur nicht-tonalen Thema-Struktur von Liszts *Faust-Symphonie*." MF 22(1969): 69-72.
2757. Ott, Leonard W. "The orchestration of the *Faust Symphony*." JALS 12(1982): 28-37.
2758. Ritzel, Fred. "Materialdenken bei Liszt: Eine Untersuchung der 'Zwölftonthemas' der *Faust-Symphonie*." MF 20(1967): 289-294.
2759. Somfai, László. "Die Metamorphose der *Faust-Symphonie* von Liszt." SM 5(1963): 283-294.
2760. ----. "Die musikalische Gestaltwandlungen der *Faust-Symphonie* von Liszt." SM 2(1962): 87-137.

Malediction
2761. Johns, Keith T. "*Malediction*: The concerto's history, programme and some notes on harmonic organization." JALS 18(1985): 29-35.

Masses
2762. Loos, Helmut. "Franz Liszts Graner Festmesse." KJ 67(1983): 45-60.
2763. White, Charles Willis. "The masses of Franz Liszt." PhD dissertation (Musicology): Bryn Mawr College, 1973. UM 74-08,963. DA XXXIV.10, p.6694.

Mephisto Waltz
2764. Feofanov, Dmitry. "How to transcribe the *Mephisto Waltz* for piano." JALS 11(1982): 18-27.
2765. Hunt, Mary Angela. "Franz Liszt: The Mephisto waltzes." DMA dissertation (Performance): University of Wisconsin, 1979. 176 p. UM 79-22,120. DA XL.6, p.2971-A.

Organ music [see also individual titles]
2766. Schwarz, Peter. *Studien zur Orgelmusik Franz Liszts: Ein Beitrag zur Geschichte der Orgelkomposition im 19. Jahrhundert.* München: E. Katzbichler, 1973.
2767. Zacher, Gerd. "Eine Fuge ist eine Fuge ist eine Fuge. (Liszts B-A-C-H Komposition für Orgel)." MK 47(1977): 15-23.

Piano works [see also individual titles]

2768. Auh, Mijai Youn. "Piano variations by Brahms, Liszt, and Friedman on a theme by Paganini." DM dissertation (Piano): Indiana University, 1980. No DA listing.

2769. Decarsin, François. "Liszt's *Nuages gris* and Kagel's *Unguis incarnatus est*: A model and its issue." Trans. by Jonathan Dunsby. MA 4/3(1985): 259-263.

2770. Fowler, Andrew. "Multilevel motivic projection in selected piano works of Liszt." JALS 16(1984): 20-34. [*Années de pèlerinage, 2e année, Italie; Harmonies poétiques et religieuses*]

2771. Goebel, Albrecht. "Franz Liszt: *Die drei Zigeuner*: Ein Beitrag zum Balladenschaffen im 19. Jahrhundert." M 35(1981): 241-245.

2772. Goode, William M. "The late piano works of Franz Liszt and their influence on some aspects of modern piano composition." PhD dissertation (Music Education): Indiana University, 1965. UM 66-1449. DA XXIV.11, p.6761.

2773. Grabócz, Márta. "Die Wirkung des Programms auf die Entwicklung der instrumentalen Formen in Liszts Klavierwerken." SM 22(1980): 299-325.

2774. Johns, Keith T. "*De profundis, Psaume instrumental*: An abandoned concerto for piano and orchestra by Franz Liszt." JALS 15(1984): 96-104.

2775. Kabisch, Thomas. "Struktur und Form im Spätwerk Franz Liszts: Das Klavierstück *Unstern* (1886)." AM 42(1985): 178-199.

2776. Kokai, Rudolf. *Franz Liszt in seinen frühen Klavierwerken.* Budapest: Akadémiai Kiadó, 1969.

2777. Lee, Robert C. "Some little known late piano works of Liszt (1869-1886): A miscellany." PhD dissertation (Musicology): University of Washington, 1970. UM 71-00,992. DA XXXI.7, p.3584.

2778. Lemoine, Bernard C. "Tonal organization in selected late piano works of Liszt." PhD dissertation (Theory): Catholic University, 1976. UM 76-20,423. DA XXXVII.3, p.1289-A.

2779. Ott, Leonard. "Closing passages and cadences in the late piano music of Liszt." JALS 5(1979): 64-74.

2780. Reich, Nancy B. "Liszt's Variations on the March from Rossini's *Siège de Corinthe*." JALS 7(1980): 35-41.

2781. Schenkman, Walter. "Liszt's Reminiscences of Bellini's *Norma*." JALS 9(1981): 55-64.

2782. ----. "The *Venezia e Napoli* Tarentella: Genesis and metamorphosis." JALS 6(1979): 10-24, 7(1980): 42-58, 8(1980): 44-59.

2783. Sievers, Gerd. "Franz Liszts Legende *Der Heilige Franziskus von Paula auf den Wegen schretend* für Klavier in Max Regers Bearbeitung für die Orgel." HJM 2(1976): 125-146.

2784. Stewart, Arthur Franklin. "*La Notte* and *Les Morts*: Investigations into progressive aspects of Franz Liszt's style." JALS 18(1985): 67-106.

2785. Taruskin. [*Étude de concert* Nr. 3; *Totentanz*]

2786. Thompson, Harold Adams. "The evolution of whole-tone sound in Liszt's original piano works." PhD dissertation: Louisiana State University, 1974. 333 p. UM 75-14,290. DA XXXVI.1, p.22-A.

2787. Torkewitz, Dieter. "Anmerkungen zu Liszts Spätstil: Das Klavierstück *Preludio funèbre* (1885)." AM 35(1978): 231-236.

2788. Wait, Mark. "Liszt, Scriabin, and Boulez: Considerations of form." JALS 1(1977): 9-16. [*Vier kleine Klavierstücke*]

2789. Wolff, Konrad. "Beethovenian dissonances in Liszt's piano works." JALS 1(1977): 4-8.

2790. Wuellner, Guy S. "Franz Liszt's Prelude on *Chopsticks*." JALS 4(1978): 37-44.

Les Préludes

2791. Haraszti, Emile. "Genèse des préludes de Liszt qui n'ont aucun rapport avec Lamertine." RDM 35(1953): 112-113.

2792. Main, Alexander. "Liszt after Lamartine: *Les Préludes*." ML 60(1979): 133-148.

Sonata in B Minor

2793. Becker, Ralf-Walter. "Formprobleme in Liszts H-Moll-Sonate: Untersuchungen zu Liszts Klaviermusik um 1850." PhD dissertation (Musicology): Universität Marburg, 1980.

2794. Dommel-Diény, Amy. *Schubert-Liszt*. Dommel-Diény 9. Paris: Dommel-Diény, 1976.

2795. Kánski, Josef. "The problem of form in Franz Liszt's Sonata in B Minor." JALS 5(1979): 4-15.

2796. Longyear, Rey M. "Liszt's B Minor Sonata: Precedents for a structural analysis." MR 34(1973): 198-209.

2797. Ott, Bertrand. "An interpretation of Liszt's Sonata in B Minor." JALS 10(1981): 30-38, 11(1982): 40-41.

2798. Rea, John Rocco. "Franz Liszt's 'new path of composition': The Sonata in B Minor as paradigm." PhD dissertation: Princeton University, 1978. No DA listing.

2799. Saffle, Michael. "Liszt's Sonata in B Minor: Another look at the 'double function' question." JALS 11(1982): 28-39.

2800. Sandresky, Margaret Vardell. "Tonal design in Liszt Sonata in B Minor." JALS 10(1981): 15-29.

2801. Schläder, Jürgen. "Zur Funktion der Variantentechnik in der Klaviersonaten F-Moll von Johannes Brahms und H-Moll von Franz Liszt." HJM 7(1984): 171-199.

2802. Szász, Tibor. "Liszt's divine and diabolical symbolism: Key to the religious program in the Sonata in B Minor." DMA dissertation (Performance): University of Michigan, 1985. No DA listing.

2803. ----. "Liszt's symbols for the divine and diabolical: their revelation of a program in the B Minor Sonata." JALS 15(1984): 39-95.

Sonetto 104 del Petrarca

2804. Cinnamon, Howard. "Chromaticism and tonal coherence in Liszt's *Sonetto 104 del Petrarca*." ITO 7/3(1983-1984): 3-19.

2805. Neumeyer, David. "Liszt's *Sonetto 104 del Petrarca*: The romantic spirit and voice leading." ITR 11/2(1978-1979): 2-22.

Songs

2806. Broeckx, Jan L. and Walter Landrieu. "Comparative computer study of style, based on five Liedmelodies." I 1(1972): 29-92. [*Kennst du das Land*]

2807. Cinnamon, Howard. "Tonal structure and voice-leading in Liszt's *Blume und Duft.*" ITO 6/3(1981-1983): 12-24.

2808. Dart, William J. "Revisions and reworkings in the Lieder of Franz Liszt." SMU 9(1975): 41-53.

2809. Hantz, Edwin. "Motivic and structural unity in Liszt's *Blume und Duft.*" ITO 6/3(1981-1983): 3-11.

2810. Lewis. [*Mignon Lieder*]

2811. Montu-Berthon, Suzanne. "Un Liszt méconnu: Mélodies et Lieder, vol. I." RM 342-343-344(1981): 17-184. Musical examples, RM 345-346 (1981): 5-56.

2812. Turner, Ronald. "A comparison of two sets of Liszt-Hugo songs." JALS 5(1979): 16-31.

Symphonic Poems [see also individual titles]

2813. Bergfeld, Joachim. *Die formale Struktur der symphonische Dichtungen Franz Liszts.* Eisenach: Kühner, 1931.

2814. Dahlhaus, Carl. "Liszts Bergsymphonie und die Idee der symphonischen Dichtung." JSIM (1975): 96-130.

2815. Schläder, Jürgen. "Der schöne Traum vom Ideal: Die künstlerische Konzeption in Franz Liszts letzter symphonische Dichtung." HJM 6(1983): 47-62. [*Von der Wiege bis zum Grabe*]

2816. Taruskin. [*Ce qu'on entend sur la montagne; Orpheus*]

Transcriptions

2817. Bellak, Richard Charles. "Compositional technique in the transcriptions of Franz Liszt." PhD dissertation (Musicology): University of Pennsylvana, 1976. 156 p. UM 76-22,653. DA XXXVII.4, p.1860-A.

2828. Crockett, Barbara Allen. "Liszt's opera transcriptions for piano." DMA dissertation: University of Ilinois, 1968. UM 69-01,325. DA XXIX.7, p.2292.

2819. Suttoni, Charles. "Liszt's operatic fantasies and transcriptions." JALS 8(1980): 3-14.

Via Crucis

2810. Hill, Cecil. "Liszt's *Via Crucis.*" MR 25(1964): 202-208.

Other works

2821. Anderson, Lyle John. "Motivic and thematic transformation in selected works of Liszt." PhD dissertation: Ohio State University, 1977. UM 77-24,591. DA XXXVIII.5, p.2400-A. [Sonata in B Minor; Piano Concerto No.2; *Les Préludes; Faust Symphony*]

2822. Bárdos, Lajos. "Ferenc Liszt, the innovator." SM 17(1975): 3-38.

2823. Claus, Linda W. "An aspect of Liszt's late style: The composer's revisions for *Historische, ungarische Portäts.*" JALS 3(1978): 3-18.

2824. Dahlhaus, Carl. "Franz Liszt und die Vorgeschichte der neuen Musik." NZM 122(1961): 387-391.

2825. Damschroder, David Allen. "The structural foundations of 'The music of the future': A Schenkerian study of Liszt's Weimar repertoire." PhD dissertation (Theory): Yale University, 1981. UM 81-24,336. DA XLII.5, p.1843-A.

2826. Eckhardt, Maria P. "Ein Spätwerk von Liszt: Der 129. Psalm." SM 18(1976): 296-333.

2827. Esteban, Julio. "On Liszt's technical exercises." JALS 1(1977): 17-19.

2828. Gárdonyi, Z. "Neue Tonleiter- und Sequenztypen in Liszts Frühwerken." SM 11(1969): 169-200. [Also in Fs. Szabolcsi: 169-199]

2829. Gibbs, Dan Paul. "A background and analysis of selected Lieder and opera transcriptions of Franz Liszt." DMA dissertation: North Texas State University, 1980. No DA listing.

2830. Gut, Serge. *Franz Liszt: Les Éléments du langage musical.* Paris: Klincksieck, 1975.

2831. Haraszti, Emile. "Les Origines de l'orchestration de Franz Liszt." RDM 34(1952): 81-100.

2832. Hering, Hans. "Franz Liszt und die Paraphrase." M 28(1974): 231-234.

2833. Jiránek, Jaroslav. "Liszt and Smetana." SM 5(1963): 139-192.

2834. Johnsson, Bengt. "Modernities in Liszt's works." STM 46(1964): 83-117.

2835. Kaplan, Richard. "Sonata form in the orchestral works of Liszt: The revolutionary reconsidered." NCM 8(1984-1985): 142-152. [*Faust Symphony*; Symphonic poems]

2836. Main, Alexander. "Liszt *Lyon*: Music and the social con-science." NCM 4(1980-1981): 228-243.

2837. Mastroianni, Thomas. "The Italian aspects of Franz Liszt." JALS 16(1984): 6-19.

2838. Revitt, Paul J. "Franz Liszt's harmonizations of linear chromaticism." JALS 13(1983): 25-52.

2839. Rummenhöller, Peter. "Die verfremdete Kadenz: Zur Harmonik Franz Liszts." ZM 9/1(1978): 4-16.

2840. Saffle, Michael Benton. "Franz Liszt's compositional develop-ment: A study of his principal published and unpublished instrumental sketches and revisions." PhD dissertation (Musicology): Stanford University, 1977. 203 p. No DA listing.

2841. Searle, Humphrey. *The music of Liszt.* New York: Dover, 1966.

2842. Suppan, Wolfgang, ed. *Liszt Studien* 1. Kongress-Bericht, Eisenstadt 1975. Graz: Akademische Druck- und Verlangsanstalt, 1977.

2843. Szelényi, Istvan. "Der unbekannte Liszt." SM 5(1963): 311-331.

2844. Szelényi, Laszlo. "Franz Liszt: *Wiegenlied--Chant de berceau.*" M 34(1980-1981): 19-24.

2845. Taruskin. [Piano Concerto No.1; *Dante Symphony; Faust Symphony*]

2846. Torkewitz, Dieter. *Harmonisches Denken im Frühwerk Franz Liszts.* München: E. Katzbichler, 1978. 128 p.

2847. ----. "Innovation und Tradition: Zur Genesis eines Quartenak-kords: Über Liszts *Prometheus*-Akkord." MF 33(1980): 291-302.

2848. Walker, Alan, ed. *Franz Liszt: The man and his music.* London: Barrie & Jenkins, 1970.

LITOLFF, HENRY CHARLES (1818-1891)

2849. Blair, Ted M. "Henry Charles Litolff: His life and music." PhD dissertation (Musicology): University of Iowa, 1968. UM 68-10,647. DA XXIX.1, p.624-A.

LLOYD, JONATHAN

2850. Uscher, Nancy. "Two contemporary viola concerti: A compara-tive study." TEMPO 147(1983): 23-29.

LOCKWOOD, NORMAND (born 1906)

2851. MacDowell, John. "A note on some facets of Normand Lock-wood's music." ACA 6/4(1956): 7-11.

LOEFFLER, CHARLES MARTIN (1861-1935)

2852. Colvin, Otis H. "Charles Martin Loeffler: His life and works." PhD dissertation (Theory): University of Rochester, 1959. 230 p. No DA listing.

LOEWE, CARL (1796-1869)

2853. Schleicher, Jane Ernestine. "The ballads of Carl Loewe." DMA dissertation: University of Illinois, 1966. UM 66-07,809. DA XXXVII.3, p.792.

LOGAN, WENDELL

2854. Wilson, Olly. "Wendell Logan: *Proportions.*" PNM 9(1970): 135-142.

LOHSE, FRED (born 1908)

2855. Beythien, Jürgen. "Fred Lohses Divertimento für Streichorches-ter." MG 15(1965): 394-399.

2856. Raschke, Siegfried. "Charakteristik und Wirksamkeit der Prinzipien linearen Gestaltens: Untersucht und dargestellt an Komposi-tionen von Fred Lohse." PhD dissertation (Musicology): Karl-Marx Universität, 1969.

LOMBARDI, LUCA

2857. Heister, Hanns-Werner. "Verzweifeln und Standhalten: Zu Luca Lombardis Kantate *Majakowski*." MG 33(1983): 530-535.

2858. Lombardi, Luca. "Construction of freedom." Trans. by Franco Betti. PNM 22(1983-1984): 253-264. [*Wiederkehr; Tui--Gesänge; Majakowski*]

LUCIER, ALVIN (born 1931)

2859. Mumma, Gordon. "Alvin Luciers *Music for Solo Performer 1965*." S 1/2(1967): 68-69.

LUTOSLAWSKI, WITOLD (born 1913)

Cello Concerto
2860. Huber, Alfred. "Witold Lutoslawski: Cellokonzert." MELOS 40(1973): 229-236.

Concerto for Orchestra
2861. Sannemüller, Gerd. "Das Konzert für Orchester von Witold Lutoslawski." SMZ 107(1967): 258-264.

Double Concerto
2862. Lutoslawki, Witold. "Interview with the composer: *Double Concerto* for oboe, harp and chamber orchestra by Witold Lutoslawski." PM 15/4(1980): 7-10.

Les Espaces du sommeil
2863. Cope: 256-259.

Livre pour orchestre
2864. Lutoslawski, Witold. "*Livre pour orchestre* by Witold Lutoslawski." PM 4/1(1969): 9-12.

Paroles tissées
2865. Sannemüller, Gerd. "*Paroles tissées* von Witold Lutoslawski." Fs. Gudewill: 101-110.

Preludes and Fugue
2866. Petersen, Peter. "Witold Lutoslawski: Prelüdien und Fuge (1972)." HJM 1(1974): 147-180.

String Quartet
2867. Gülke, Peter. "Lutoslawskis Streichquartett als Kammermusik." Pečman: 243-249.
2868. Hansberger, Joachim. "Begrenzte Aleatorik: Das Streichquartett Witold Lutoslawskis." M 25(1971): 248-257.
2869. Schmidt, Christian Martin. "Witold Lutoslawski: Streichquartett." Stephan: 154-162.
2870. Selleck, John. "Pitch and duration as textural elements in Lutoslawski's String Quartet." PNM 13/2(1974-1975): 150-161.
2871. Stucky, Steven. "The String Quartet of Witold Lutoslawski." MFA dissertation: Cornell University, 1973.

Symphony No.1
    2872. Vogt: 348-357.
    2873. Sannemüller, Gerd. "Die 1. Sinfonie von Witold Lutoslawski."
MB 18(1981): 766-772.

Symphony No.2
    2874. Dibelius, Ulrich. "Lutoslawski's Second Symphony." PM 2/4
(1967): 8-12.
    2875. Sannemüller, Gerd. "Witold Lutoslawskis 2. Sinfonie." MB 10
(1978): 588-595.

Trauermusik
    2876. Brennecke, Wilfried. "Die *Trauermusik* von Witold Lutoslawski."
Fs. Blume: 60-73. [Also in Fs. Feicht: 457-471]
    2877. Brumbeloe, Joseph. "Symmetry in Witold Lutoslawski's *Trauer-musik*." ITR 6/3(1982-1983): 3-17.

Trois Poèmes d'Henri Michaux
    2878. Anhalt: 93-147.
    2879. Roberts.
    2880. Thomas, Adrian. "A deep resonance: Lutoslawski's *Trois Poèmes d'Henri Michaux*." SN 1(1970): 58-70.

Venetian Games
    2881. Thomas, Adrian. "*Jeux vénitiens*: Lutoslawski at the
crossroads." CT 24(1982): 4-7.

Other works
    2882. Casken, John. "Transition and transformation in the music of
Witold Lutoslawski." CT 12(1975): 3-12.
    2883. Hines.
    2884. Homma, Martina. "Horizontal-Vertikal: Zur Organisation der
Tonhöhe bei Witold Lutoslawski." N 5(1984-1985): 91-99.
    2885. ----. *Das kompositorische Schaffen von Witold Lutoslawski*.
Köln: I. Staatsarbeit, 1983.
    2886. Kaczyński, Tadeusz. *Conversations with Witold Lutoslawki*.
London: J. & W. Chester, 1984. [*Trois poémes d'Henri Michaux*; String
Quartet; *Paroles tissées*; Second Symphony; *Livre pour orchestre*; Cello
Concerto; *Les Espaces du sommeil; Mi-parti*]
    2887. Stucky, Steven. *Lutoslawski and his music*. Cambridge:
Cambridge University Press, 1981.
    2888. ----. "The music of Witold Lutoslawski: A style-critical
study." DMA dissertation: Cornell University, 1978. No DA listing.
    2889. Thomas, Adrian T. "Rhythmic articulation in the music of
Lutoslawski." MA dissertation: University of Cardiff, 1970.

LYAPUNOV, SERGEI (1859-1924)

    2890. Davis, Richard. "Sergei Lyapunov (1859-1924): The piano
works: A short appreciation." MR 21(1960): 186-206.

MACHOVER, TOD (born 1953)

    2891. Machover, Tod. "Computer music with and without instruments." CMR 1/1(1984-1985): 203-230. [*Fusione Fugace; Electric Etudes; Spectres Parisiens*]

MADERNA, BRUNO (1920-1973)

    2892. Fearn, Raymond. "Bruno Maderna: From the Café Pedrocchi to Darmstadt." TEMPO 155(1985): 8-14.

MAGNARD, ALBÉRIC (1865-1914)

    2893. Halbreich, Harry. "Magnard, le solitaire." RM 324-326 (1979): 77-86.
    2894. Maillard, Jean. "Albéric Magnard: Les Quatre symphonies: Étude analytique." RM 324-325-326(1979): 89-104.

MAGRILL, SAMUEL

    2895. Magrill, Samuel. "*Dao Song*: Instructions." PNM 23/1 (1984-1985): 86-97.
    2896. ----. "*Dao Song*: Report to the National Endowment for the Arts." PNM 23/1(1984-1985): 134-142.

MAHLER, ALMA *see* **WERFEL, ALMA (SCHINDLER) MAHLER**

MAHLER, GUSTAV (1860-1911)

Kindertotenlieder
    2897. Agawu, Kofi. "The musical language of *Kindertotenlieder* No.2." JM 2(1983): 81-93.
    2898. Grant, Parks. "Mahler's *Kindertotenlieder*." CD 2/9(1960): 62-72.
    2899. Kravitt, Edward F. "Mahler's dirges for his death: February 24, 1901." MQ 64(1978): 329-353.

Klagende Lied
    2900. Diether, Jack. "Mahler's *Klagende Lied*: Genesis and evolution." MR 29(1968): 268-287.
    2901. Zenck, Martin. "Mahlers Streichung des *Waldmarchens* aus dem *Klagenden Lied*: Zum Verhältnis von philologischer Erkenntnis und Interpretation." AM 38(1981): 179-193.

Das Lied von der Erde
    2902. Baur, Uwe. "Pentatonische Melodiebildung in Gustav Mahlers *Das Lied von der Erde*." MAU 2(1979): 141-150.
    2903. Carner: 52-55.
    2904. Danuser, Hermann. "Gustav Mahlers Symphonie *Das Lied von der Erde* als Problem der Gattungsgeschichte." AM 40(1983): 276-286.

2905. ----. "Mahlers Lied *Von der Jugend*: Ein musikalisches Bild."
Fs. Schuh: 151-169.

2906. Enix.

2907. Roman, Zoltan. "Aesthetic symbiosis and structural metaphor in Mahler's *Das Lied von der Erde*." Fs. Blaukopf: 110-119.

2908. Tischler, Hans. "Mahler's *Das Lied von der Erde*." MR 10 (1949): 111-114.

2909. Wenk, Arthur. "The composer as poet in *Das Lied von der Erde*." NCM 1(1977-1978): 33-47.

Lieder eines fahrenden Gesellen

2910. Roman, Zoltan. "The pianoforte and orchestral manuscripts of Mahler's *Lieder eines fahrenden Gesellen*: Compositional process as a key to chronology." Kühn: 402-404.

2911. Waeltner, Ernst Ludwig. "Lieder-Zyklus und Volkslied-Metamorphose: Zu den Texten der Mahlerischen Gesellenlieder." JSIM (1977): 61-95.

Songs [see also individual titles]

2912. Agawu, V. Kofi. "Mahler's tonal strategies: A study of the song cycles." JMR 6(1986): 1-47.

2913. Borris, Siegfried. "Mahlers holzschnitthafter Liedstil." MB 5 (1973): 578-587.

2914. Dargie, Elizabeth Mary. "Music and poetry in the songs of Gustav Mahler." PhD dissertation (Musicology): Aberdeen, 1979.

2915. Gerlach, Reinhard. "Mahler, Rückert und das Ende des Liedes: Essay über lyrisch-musikalisches Form." JSIM (1975): 7-45.

2916. Jahnke, Sabine. "Materialien zu einer Unterrichtssequenz: Das Antonius von Padua Fischpredigt bei Orff--Mahler--Berio." MB 5(1973): 615-622.

2917. Kravitt, Edward F. "Bar form in Mahler's songs: Omission and misconception." *Report of the Eleventh Congress, Copenhagen 1972*, vol.2. Henrik Glahn, Søren Sørensen and Peter Ryan, eds. København: W. Hansen, 1974: 617-622.

2918. ----. "The folk element in Mahler's songs." CAUSM 8/2(1978): 67-84.

2919. Roman, Zoltan. "Mahler's songs and their influence on his symphonic thought." PhD dissertation (Musicology): University of Toronto, 1970. 2 vols. RILM 70/2002dd27.

2920. ----. "Structure as a factor in the genesis of Mahler's songs." MR 35(1974): 157-166.

Symphonies [see also individual titles]

2921. Bekker, Paul. *Gustav Mahlers Sinfonien*. Berlin: Schuster & Loeffler, 1921.

2922. Greene, David B. *Mahler, consciousness and temporality*. New York: Gordon & Breach, 1984. [Symphonies No.3, 5, 8, 9]

2923. Kneif, Tibor. "Collage oder Naturalismus? Anmerkungen zu Mahlers *Nachtmusik I*." NZM 134(1973): 623-628.

2924. McGuiness, Rosamund. "Mahler und Brahms: Gedanken zu Reminiszenzen in Mahlers Sinfonien." Melos/NZM 3(1977): 215-224.

2925. Murphy, Edward W. "Sonata-rondo form in the symphonies of Gustav Mahler." MR 36(1975): 54-62.

2926. Roman, Zoltan. "The chorus in Mahler's music." MR 43(1982): 31-43.

2927. ----. "Connotative irony in Mahler's *Todtenmarsch in 'Callots Manier'*." MQ 59(1973): 207-222.

2928. Schmitt, Theodor. *Der langsame Symphoniesatz Gustav Mahlers: Historisch-vergleichende Studien zu Mahlers Kompositionstechnik.* München: W. Fink, 1983.

2929. Sponheuer, Bernd. *Logik des Zerfalls: Untersuchungen zum Finalproblem in den Symphonien Gustav Mahlers.* Tutzing: H. Schneider, 1978.

2930. Tibbe, Monika. *Über die Verwendung von Lieder und Liederelementen in instrumental Symphoniensätzen Gustav Mahlers.* München: E. Katzbichler, 1971.

2931. Vestdijk, Simon. *Gustav Mahler: Over de strucktuur van zijn symfonisch oeuvre.* The Hague: Daamen, 1960.

2932. Vetter, Walther. "Gustav Mahlers sinfonische Stil: Eine Skizze." DJM 6(1961): 7-18.

2933. Wellesz, Egon. "The symphonies of Gustav Mahler." MR 1(1940): 2-23.

Symphony No.1

2934. Dahlhaus, Carl. "Geschichte eines Themas: Zu Mahlers erster Symphonie." (JSIM) 1977: 45-60.

2935. Eberle, Gottfried. "Gustav Mahler: Sinfonie Nr.1 D-Dur." NZM 143/10(1982): 33-36.

2936. Hoyer, Michael. "Die multiperspectivische Tonalität von Mahlers 1. Symphonie." Stahmer: 29-116.

2937. Jones, Robert Frederick. "Thematic development and form in the first and fourth movements of Mahlers's First Symphony." PhD dissertation: Brandeis University, 1980. No DA listing.

2938. Osthoff, Helmuth. "Zu Gustav Mahlers erster Symphonie." AM 29(1971): 217-227.

2939. Sponheuer, Bernd. "Der Durchbruch Gustav Mahlers: Eine Untersuchung zum Finalproblem der 1. Symphonie." Stahmer: 117-164.

Symphony No.2

2940. Reilly, Edward R. "Die Skizzen zu Mahlers zweiter Symphonie." OMZ 34(1979): 266-285.

2941. Stephan, Rudolf. *Gustav Mahler: II. Sinfonie C-Moll.* München: W. Fink, 1979.

2942. Zenck, Claudia Maurer. "Technik und Gehalt im Scherzo von Mahlers zweiter Symphonie." Melos/NZM 2(1976): 179-184.

Symphony No.3

2943. Danuser, Hermann. "Schwierigkeiten der Mahler-Interpretation: Ein Versuch am Beispiel der ersten Satzes der dritten Symphonie." SBM 3(1978): 165-181.

2944. Schnebel, Dieter. "Sinfonie und Wirklichkeit am Beispiel von Mahlers Dritter." Kolleritsch: 103-117.

2945. ----. "Über Mahlers Dritte." NZM 135(1974): 283-288.

2946. Williamson, John. "Mahler's compositional process: Rejections of an early sketch for the Third Symphony's first movement." ML 61(1980): 338-345.

Symphony No.4

2947. Stephan: 23-42.

2948. ----. *Mahler: IV. Symphonie G-dur.* Meisterwerke der Musik 5. München: W. Fink, 1966.

Symphony No.5

2949. Forte, Allen. "Middleground motives in the Adagietto of Mahler's fifth symphony." NCM 8(1984-1985): 153-163.

2950. Grant, Parks. "Mahler's Fifth Symphony." CD 2/10(1963): 125-137.

Symphony No.6

2951. Andraschke, Peter. "Struktur und Gehalt im ersten Satz von Gustav Mahlers sechster Symphonie." AM 35(1978): 275-296.

2952. Del Mar, Norman. *Mahler's Sixth Symphony.* New York: Da Capo, 1982.

2953. Ratz, Erwin. "Musical form in Gustav Mahler: An analysis of the finale of the Sixth Symphony." MR 29(1968): 34-48.

2954. ----. "Zum Formproblem bei Gustav Mahler: Eine Analyse des Finales der VI. Symphonie." MF 9(1956): 156-171.

2955. Redlich, Hans. "Mahler's enigmatic Sixth." Fs. Deutsch: 250-256.

Symphony No.7

2956. De la Motte: 107-114.

2957. Williamson, John. "Deceptive cadences in the last movement of Mahler's Seventh Symphony." SN 9(1982): 87-96.

Symphony No.8

2958. Landmann, Ortun. "Vielfalt und Einheit in der achten Sinfonie Gustav Mahlers: Beobachtungen zu den Themen und zur Formgestalt des Werkes." BM 17(1975): 29-43.

Symphony No.9

2959. Andraschke, Peter. *Gustav Mahlers IX. Symphonie: Kompositionsprozess und Analyse.* Beiheft zum Archiv für Musikwissenshaft 14. Wiesbaden: Franz Steiner, 1976.

2960. Dahlhaus, Carl. "Form und Motiv in Mahlers neunter Symphonie." NZM 135(1974): 296-299.

2961. De la Motte, Diether. "Das komplizierte Einfache: Zum ersten Satz der 9. Sinfonie von Gustav Mahler." MB 10(1978): 145-151. [Also in Kolleritsch: 52-67]

2962. Diether, Jack. "The expressive content of Mahler's Ninth: An interpretation." CD 2/10(1963): 69-107.

2963. Fischer, Kurt von. "Die Doppelschlagfigur in den zwei letzten Sätzen von Gustav Mahlers 9. Symphonie: Versuch einer Interpretation." AM 32(1975): 99-105.

2964. Lewis, Christopher Orlo. *Tonal coherence in Mahler's Ninth Symphony.* Ann Arbor: UMI Research Press, 1984.

2965. Ratz, Erwin. "Zum Formproblem bei Gustav Mahler: Eine Analyse des I. Satzes der IX. Symphonie." MF 8(1955): 169-177.

2966. Revers, Peter. "Liquidation als Formprinzip: Die formprägende Bedeutung des Rhythmus für das Adagio der 9. Symphonie von Gustav Mahler." OMZ 33(1978): 527-533.

2967. Schenk, Rüdiger. "Zur neunten Symphonie Gustav Mahlers." Stahmer: 165-221.

2968. Spinnler, Burkhard. "Zur Angemessenheit traditioneller Formbegriffe in der Analyse mahlerscher Symphonik: Eine Untersuchung des ersten Satzes der neunten Symphonie." Stahmer: 223-276.

Symphony No.10

2969. Bergquist, Peter. "The first movement of Mahler's Tenth Symphony: An analysis and an examination of the sketches." MFO 5(1980): 335-394.

2970. Cooke, Deryck. "The Adagio of Mahler's Tenth Symphony." MT 106(1965): 288.

2971. ----. "The facts concerning Mahler's Tenth Symphony." CD 2/10(1963): 3-27.

2972. Kaplan, Richard A. "The interaction of diatonic collections in the Adagio of Mahler's Tenth Symphony." ITO 6/1(1981-1982): 29-39.

2973. ----. "Interpreting surface harmonic connections in the Adagio of Mahler's Tenth Symphony." ITO 4/2(1978): 32-44.

2974. Klemm, Eberhardt. "Über ein Spätwerk Gustav Mahlers." DJM 6(1961): 19-32.

2975. Ratz, Erwin. "Gustav Mahlers X. Symphonie." NZM 125(1964): 307-308.

2976. Reid, Charles. "Mahler's Tenth." MR 26(1965): 318-325.

2977. Rohland, Tyll. "Zum Adagio aus der X. Symphonie von Gustav Mahler." MB 6(1973): 605-615.

2978. Zenck, Martin. "Ausdruck und Konstrucktion im Adagio der 10. Sinfonie Gustav Mahlers." Carl Dahlhaus, ed. Beitrage zur musikalischen Hermeneutik. Regensburg: G. Bosse, 1975: 205-222.

Other works

2979. Banks, Paul. "An early symphonic prelude by Mahler?" NCM 3 (1979-1980): 141-149.

2980. Barford, Philip T. "Mahler: A thematic archetype." MR 21 (1960): 297-316.

2981. Cardus, Neville. *Gustav Mahler: His mind and his music.* London: V. Gollancz, 1965.

2982. Danuser, Hermann. "Versuch über Mahlers Ton." JSIM (1975): 46-79.

2983. Diether, Jack. "Notes on some Mahler juvenalia." CD 3/1 (1969): 3-100.

2984. Eggebrecht, Hans Heinrich. *Die Musik Gustav Mahlers.* München: R. Piper, 1982.

2985. Filler, Susan M. "Mahler's sketches for a Scherzo in C Minor and a Presto in F Major." CMS 24(1984): 69-80.

2986. Grant, Parks. "Bruckner and Mahler: The fundamental dissimilarity of their styles." MR 32(1971): 35-55.

2987. Hansen, Mathias. "Zur Funktion von Volksmusikelementen in Kompositionstechniken Gustav Mahlers." BM 23(1981): 31-35.

2988. James, Burnett. *The music of Gustav Mahler.* Rutherford, NJ: Fairleigh Dickinson University Press, 1985.

2989. Mitchell, Donald. "Gustav Mahler . . . prospect and retrospect." PRMA 87(1960-1961): 83-97.

2990. ----. *Gustav Mahler: The "Wunderhorn" years: Chronicles and commentaries.* London: Faber, 1975. 461 p.

2991. ----. *Mahler: The early years.* Rev. and ed. by Paul Banks and David Matthews. Berkeley: University of California Pres, 1980. (1958)

2992. Newlin, Dika. *Bruckner, Mahler, Schoenberg.* New York: King's Crown Press, 1947.

2993. Ratz, Erwin. "Zum Formproblem." *Gustav Mahler.* Tübingen: R. Wunderlich, 1966: 90-141.

2994. Redlich, Hans. *Bruckner and Mahler.* Rev. ed. London: J.M. Dent, 1963.

2995. Schnebel, Dieter. "Das Spätmusik als neue Musik." *Gustav Mahler.* Tübingen: R. Wunderlich, 1966: 157-188.

2996. Schoenberg, Arnold. "Gustav Mahler." *Style and Idea.* New York: Philosophical Library, 1950: 7-36.

2997. Smith, Warren Storey. "The cyclic principle in musical design and the use of it by Bruckner and Mahler." CD 2/9(1960): 3-22.

2998. Stahmer, Klaus Hinrich. "Mahlers Frühwerk: Eine Stiluntersuchung." Stahmer: 9-28. [C-Minor Quartet movement (1876)]

2999. Tischler, Hans. "Mahler's impact on the crisis of tonality." MR 12(1951): 113-121.

3000. ----. "Musical form in Gustav Mahler's works." MU 2 (1948-1949): 231-242.

3001. Truscott, Harold. "Some aspects of Mahler's tonality." MMR 87 (1957): 203-208.

3002. Vill, Susanne. *Vermittlungsformen verbalisierte und musikalische Inhalte in der Musik Mahlers.* Tutzing: H. Schneider, 1979.

3003. Whaples, Miriam K. "Mahler and Schubert's A Minor Sonata D.784." ML 65(1984): 255-263. [Symphonies No.3, 4, 6; *Lieder eines fahrenden Gesellen*]

MAIGUASHCA, MESIAS (born 1938)

3004. Maiguashca, Masias. "Zu *FMelodies*." N 5(1984-1985): 288-296.

MALIPIERO, GIAN FRANCESCO (1912-1983)

3005. Bontempelli, Massimo. *Gian Francesco Malipiero.* Milano: Bompiani, 1942.

MANOURY, PHILIPPE

3006. Manoury, Philippe. "The arrow of time." Trans. by Tod Machover and Nigel Osborne. CMR 1/1(1984-1985): 131-144. [*Zeitlauf*]

MARBE, MYRIAM-LUCIA (born 1931)

3007. Dănceanu, Liviu. "Myriam Marbe Porträt." N 4(1983-1984): 68-78.

MARKEVITCH, IGOR (1912-1983)

3008. Bennett, Clive. "*Icare*." TEMPO 133-134(1980): 44-51.
3009. De Graeff, Alex. "Partita for Piano and Small Orchestra." TEMPO 133-134(1980): 39-43.
3010. Mavrodin, Alice. "*Variations, Fugue, and Envoi* on the theme of Handel." TEMPO 133-134(1980): 61-67.

MARSCHNER, HEINRICH AUGUST (1795-1861)

3011. Palmer, Allen Dean. "Heinrich August Marschner (1795-1861) and his stage works." PhD dissertation (Musicology): University of California, Los Angeles, 1978. 698 p. UM 78-11,371. DA XXXIX.1, p.18-A.

MARTIN, FRANK (1890-1974)

3012. Billeter, Bernhard. *Die Harmonik bei Frank Martin: Untersuchungen zur Analyse neuerer Musik.* Bern, Stuttgart: Haupt, 1971.
3013. ----. "Die letzten Vokalwerke von Frank Martin." SMZ 116(1976): 344-351.
3014. Fischer, Kurt von. "Frank Martin: Überblick über Werk und Stil." SMZ 91(1951): 91-96.
3015. Hines: 152-165.
3016. Menasce, Jacques de. "Current Chronicle." MQ 34(1948): 271-278. [*Petite symphonie concertante*]
3017. Regamey, Constantin. "Les Éléments flamenco dans les dernières oeuvres de Frank Martin." SMZ 116(1976): 351-359.
3018. Rochester, Marc Andrew. "Frank Martin at Golgatha: Frank Martin's compositional technque as shown by his Passion oratorio *Golgatha*." MA dissertation: University of Wales, 1976.
3019. Tupper, Janet E. "Stylistic analysis of selected works by Frank Martin." PhD dissertation (Theory): Indiana University, 1964. UM 65-1552. DA XXV.8, p.4746.

MARTINO, DONALD (born 1931)

3020. Rothstein, William. "Linear structure in the twelve-tone system: An analysis of Donald Martino's *Pianississimo*." JMT 24(1980): 129-165.

MARTINŮ, BOHUSLAV (1890-1959)

3021. Cable, Susan Lee. "The piano trios of Bohuslav Martinů (1890-1959)." DA dissertation: University of Northern Colorado, 1984. 191 p. UM 84-29,821. No DA listing.

3022. Clapham, John. "Martinů's instrumental style." MR 24(1963): 158-167.

3023. Evans, Peter. "Martinů the symphonist." TEMPO 55-56(1960): 19-33.

3024. Hirsbrunner, Theo. "Bohuslav Martinů: Die Soloklavierwerke der dreissiger Jahre." AM 39(1982): 64-77.

3025. Perry, Richard Kent. "The violin and piano sonatas of Bohuslav Martinů." DMA dissertation (Performance): University of Illinois, 1973. UM 73-17,621. DA XXXIV.2, p.812-A.

3026. Petrella, Robert Louis. "The solo and chamber compositions for flute by Bohuslav Martinů." DMA dissertation (Performance): University of Southern Mississippi, 1980. UM 81-09,889. DA XLI.11, p.4537-A.

3027. Pettway, B. Keith. "The solo and chamber compositions for flute by Bohuslav Martinů." DMA dissertation: University of Southern Mississippi, 1980. UM 81-09,889. DA XLI.11, p.4537-A.

3028. Šafránek, Miloš. "Bohuslav Martinů." MQ 29(1943): 329-354.

MARTIRANO, SALVATORE (born 1927)

3029. Brock, Gordon Ray. "Salvatore Martirano: A study of his *Mass*." DMA dissertation: University of Illinois, 1978. No DA listing.

MARX, JOSEPH (1882-1964)

3030. Meyers, Joseph Kenneth. "The songs of Joseph Marx." DMA dissertation (Performance): University of Missouri, 1972. UM 72-29,465. DA XXXIII.5, p.2414-5-A.

3031. Paxinos, Socrates. "Late romantic harmony and counterpoint in the music of Joseph Marx (1882-1964)." PhD dissertation (Musicology): University of South Africa, 1976.

MARX, KARL JULIUS (born 1897)

3032. Doppelbauer, Josef Friedrich. "Die *a cappella* Chorwerke von Karl Marx." Fs. Marx: 18-41.

3033. ----. "*Missa psalmodica*." Fs. Marx: 94-97.

3034. Gümbel, Martin. "Marginalien zur Hölderinkantate, Opus 52." Fs. Marx: 42-56.

3035. Karkoschka, Erhard. "Über späte Instrumentalwerke von Karl Marx." M 26(1972): 542-547.

3036. Wöhler, Willi. "Anmerkungen zur Instrumentation Marxcher Orchesterwerke." Fs. Marx: 74-76.

MASCAGNI, PIETRO (1863-1945)

3037. ASO 50(1983). [*Cavalliera rusticana*]

MASON, DANIEL GREGORY (1873-1953)

3038. Lewis, Ralph B. "The life and music of Daniel Gregory Mason." PhD dissertation (Theory): University of Rochester, 1959. 161 p. No DA listing.
3039. McDonald, Gail Faber. "The piano music of Daniel Gregory Mason: A performance-tape and study of his original works for piano solo and two pianos." DMA dissertation: University of Maryland, 1977. No DA listing.

MASSENET, JULES (1842-1912)

3040. ASO 61(1984). [*Werther*]
3041. Dorminy, Wendell Larry. "The song cycles of Jules Massenet." DMA disertation (Vocal Literature): Indiana University, 1977. No DA listing.
3042. John, Nicholas, ed. *Massenet: Manon.* London: J. Calder, 1984.

MATHER, BRUCE (born 1939)

3043. Evangelista, José. "Une analyse de *Madrigal III* de Bruce Mather." CCM 6(1973): 81-109.

MATHIAS, WILLIAM (born 1934)

3044. Forbes, Elliot. "The choral music of William Mathias." ACR 21/4(1979): 1-32.

MATHIEU, RODOLPHE (1890-1962)

3045. Bourassa-Trépanier, Juliette. "La Langue musicale de Rodolphe Mathieu." CCM 5(1972): 19-30.

MATTHUS, SIEGFRIED (born 1934)

3046. Hansen, Mathias. "Die Analyse: Violoncellokonzerte von Paul-Heinz Dittrick, Siegfried Matthus und Christfried Schmidt." MG 29(1979): 591-599.
3047. Klement, Uda. "Die Analyse: Orchesterkonzerte von Ernst Hermann Meyer, Siegfried Matthus und George Katzer." MG 28(1978): 599-603. [*Responso*: Konzert für Orchester]
3048. Schaefer, Hansjürgen. "Anmerkungen zu *Noch einen Löffel Gift, Liebling?*" MG 23(1973) 535-539.
3049. ----. "*Jede Stunde deines Lebens*: Bemerkungen zum Fernsehspiel von Armin Müller und Siegfried Matthus." MG 19(1969): 845-848.
3050. ----. "*Lazarillo vom Tormes*: Bemerkungen zur Oper von Siegfried Matthus und Horst Seeger." MG 15(1965): 579-586.
3051. Vogt: 381-391. [*Der letzte Schuss* (1967)]

MAW, NICHOLAS (born 1935)

3052. Payne, Anthony. "The music of Nicholas Maw." TEMPO 68 (1964): 2-13.

3053. ----. "Nicholas Maw's *One Man Show*." TEMPO 71 (1964-1965): 2-14.

3054. ----. "Nicholas Maw's String Quartet." TEMPO 74(1965): 5-11.

3055. Walsh, Stephen. "Nicholas Maw's new opera." TEMPO 92(1970): 2-15. [*The Rising of the Moon*]

3056. Whittall, Arnold. "The instrumental music of Nicholas Maw: Questions of tonality." TEMPO 106(1973): 26-33.

3057. ----. "Maw's *Personae*: Chromaticism and tonal allusion." TEMPO 125(1978): 2-5.

MAYR, SIMONE (1763-1845)

3058. Carner: 148-171. [*L'Amor coniugale*]

McGUIRE, JOHN (born 1942)

3059. Henck, Herbert. "Skizzen zu John McGuires *Cadence Music*." N 5(1984-1985): 302-313.

3060. McGuire, John. "Über *Pulse Music III*." N 3(1982-1983): 252-267.

McPHEE, COLIN (1901-1964)

3051. Cowell, Henry. "Current Chronicle." MQ 34(1948): 410-415. [*Tabuh Tabuhan*]

MEALE, RICHARD (born 1932)

3062. Ghandar, Ann. "Pitch and time structure in *Clouds Now and Then* of Richard Meale." MMA 10(1979): 82-92.

3063. Laubenthal, Annegrit. "Hörvergnügen als ästhetisches Gesetz: Der australische Komponist Richard Meale." NZM 146/9(1985): 21-24.

MEDETOJA, LEEVI

3064. Hillila, Ruth Ester. "The songs of Toivo Kuula and Leevi Medetoja and their place in twentieth-century Finnish art song." PhD dissertation (Musicology): Boston University, 1964. UM 64-11,620. DA XXV.5, p.3017-8.

MEDTNER, NIKOLAI KARLOVICH (1880-1951)

3065. Elmore, Cenieth Catherine. "Some stylistic considerations in the piano sonatas of Nikolai Medtner." PhD dissertation (Musicology): University of North Carolina, 1972. UM 72-24,783. DA XXXIII.3, p.1186-A.

3066. Keller, Charles William. "The piano sonatas of Nicolas Medtner." PhD dissertation: Ohio State University, 1971. 349 p. UM 72-4534. DA XXXII.7, p.4046-A.

3067. Loftis, Bobby Hughes. "The piano sonatas of Nicolai Medtner." PhD dissertation: University of West Virginia 1970. 232 p. RILM 70/761dd28. No DA listing.

3068. Truscott, Harold. "Medtner's Sonata in G Minor, Op.22." MR 22(1961): 112-123.

MÉHUL, ETIENNE NICHOLAS (1763-1817)

3069. Grace, Michael D. "Méhul's *Ariodant* and the early leitmotif." Fs. Seay: 173-197.

3070. Ringer, Alexander L. "A French symphonist at the time of Beethoven: Etienne Nicholas Méhul." MQ 37(1951): 543-565.

MENDELSSOHN-BARTHOLDY, FELIX (1809-1847)

Chamber works [see also individual entries]

3071. Krummacher, Friedhelm. *Mendelssohn: Der Komponist: Studien zur Kammermusik für Streichen.* München: W. Fink, 1978.

3072. McDonald, John A. "The chamber music of Felix Mendelssohn-Bartholdy." PhD dissertation (Music History and Literature): Northwestern University, 1970. UM 71-01,916. DA XXI.8, p.4205.

3073. Reiningdaus, Frieder. "Zwischen Historismus und Poesie: Über die Notwendigkeit umfassender Musikanalyse und ihre Erprobung an Klavierkammermusik von Felix Mendelssohn Bartholdy und Robert Schumann." ZM 4/2(1973): 22-29, 5/1(1974): 34-44.

Choral works

3074. Chamber, Robert Ben. "The shorter choral works with sacred text of Felix Mendelssohn-Bartholdy." DMA dissertation: Southwestern Baptist Theological Seminary, 1984. 153 p. No DA listing.

3075. Jessop, Craig Don. "An analytical survey of the unaccompanied choral works for mixed voices by Felix Mendelssohn-Bartholdy." DMA dissertation (Performance): Stanford University, 1981. UM 81-09,025. DA XLI.11, p.4536-A.

3076. Jonas, Oswald. "An unknown Mendelssohn work." ACR 9/2 (1967): 16-22. [Chorale-cantata, *Jesu, meine Freude*]

3077. Pritchard, Brian W. "Mendelssohn's chorale cantatas: An appraisal." MQ 62(1976): 1-24.

3078. Todd, R. Larry. "A passion cantata by Mendelssohn." ACR 25/1(1983): 3-17. [*O Haupt voll Blut und Wunden*]

Elijah

3079. Ellison, Ross Wesley. "Unity and contrast in Mendelssohn's *Elijah*." PhD dissertation (Musicology): University of North Carolina, 1978. 381 p. UM 79-14,345. DA XL.1, p.16-A.

3080. Werner, Jack. *Mendelssohn's "Elijah": A historical and analytical guide to the oratorio.* London: Chappell, 1965.

Erster Walpurgisnacht

3081. Dahlhaus, Carl. "Hoch symbolisch intentioniert: Zu Mendelssohns *Erster Walpurgisnacht*." OMZ 36(1981): 290-297.

3082. Szeskus, Reinhard. "*Die erste Walpurgisnacht*, Op.60, von Felix Mendelssohn Bartholdy." BM 17(1975): 171-180.

Hebrides Overture

3083. Kielian, Marianne. "Sketches after an overture: Presented musical spans as structural models in Mendelssohn's *Hebrides Overture*." ITO 1(1975): 6-10.

3084. Todd, R. Larry. "Of sea gulls and counterpoint: The early versions of Mendelssohn's *Hebrides Overture*." *NCM 2(1979): 197-213.*

Melusine

3085. Mintz, Donald. "*Melusine*: A Mendelssohn draft." MQ 43 (1957): 480-499.

Octet

3086. Gerlach, Reinhard. "Mendelssohns schöpferische Erinnerung: Der 'Jugendzeit': Die Beziehungen zwischen den Violinkonzert Op.64 und dem Oktett für Streicher, Op.20." MF 25(1972): 142-152.

Organ works

3087. Bötel, Friedhold. "Felix Mendelssohn Bartholdys Präldien und Fugen für Orgel Op.37: Studien zur Orgelmusik Mendelssohns unter Berücksichtigung ihrer gattungsgeschichtlichten Stellung." PhD (Musicology): Heidelberg, 1982.

3088. Butler, Douglas Lamar. "The organ works of Felix Mendelssohn-Bartholdy." PhD dissertation: University of Oregon, 1973. UM 74-6812. No DA listing.

Piano works

3089. De la Motte: 125-130. [*Venetianisches Gondellied*, Op.30, No.6]

3090. Konold, Wulf. "Felix Mendelssohn Bartholdys *Rondo brillant* Op.29: Ein Beitrag zur Geschichte des einsätzigen Konzertstücks im 19. Jahrhundert." MF 38(1985): 169-183.

3091. Tischler, Louise H. and Hans Tischler. "Mendelssohn's *Songs Without Words*." MQ 33(1947): 1-16.

3092. ----. "Mendelssohn's style: The *Songs Without Words*." MR 8 (1947): 256-273.

3093. Todd, R. Larry. "An unfinished piano concerto by Mendelssohn." MQ 68(1982): 80-101.

Songs

3094. Stoner, Thomas Alan. "Mendelssohn's published songs." PhD dissertation (Musicology): University of Maryland, 1972. UM 73-13,636. DA XXXIII.12, p.6956.

String Quartets

3095. Kohlhase, Hans. "Studien zur Form in den Streichquartetten von Felix Mendelssohn Bartholdy." HJM 2(1976): 75-104.

3096. Schuhmacher, Gerhard. "Zwischen Autograph und Erstveröffentlichung: Zu Mendelssohns Kompositionsweise, dargestellt an den
Streichquartetten Op.44." BM 15(1973): 253-262.

Violin Concerto
3097. Gerlach, Reinhard. "Mendelssohns schöpferische Erinnerung:
Der 'Jugendzeit': Die Beziehungen zwischen den Violinkonzert Op.64 und
dem Oktett für Streicher, Op.20." MF 25(1972): 142-152.

Other works
3098. Dahlhaus, Carl. *Das Problem Mendelssohn*. Regensburg:
G. Bosse, 1974.
3099. Filosa, Albert J. "The early symphonies and chamber music of
Felix Mendelssohn-Bartholdy." PhD dissertation (Music History): Yale
University, 1970. UM 71-16,236. DA XXXI.12, p.6646.
3100. Friedrich, Gerda Bertram. "Die Fugenkomposition in Mendelssohns Instrumentalwerk." PhD dissertation: Rheinische Friedrich-Wilhelms-
Universität, Bonn, 1969.
3101. Godwin, Joscelyn. "Early Mendelssohn and late Beethoven."
ML 55(1974): 272-285.
3102. Jordahl, Robert. "A study of the use of the chorale in the
works of Mendelssohn, Brahms, and Reger." PhD dissertation (Theory):
University of Rochester, 1965. UM 66-2360. DA XXVII.6, p.1851-A.
3103. Schönfelder, Gerd. "Zur Frage des Realismus bei Mendelssohn."
BM 14(1972): 169-184.
3104. Schuhmacher, Gerhard, ed. *Felix Mendelssohn-Bartholdy*.
Darmstadt: Wissenschaftliches Buchgesellschaft, 1982.
3105. Thomas, Mathias. *Das Instrumentalwerk Felix Mendelssohn-
Bartholdys: Ein systematische Untersuchung unter besonderer
Berücksichtigung der zeitgenossischen Musiktheorie*. Göttinger musikwissenschaftliche Arbeiten 4. Kassel: Bärenreiter, 1972.
3106. Todd, Ralph Larry. "The instrumental music of Felix Mendelssohn-Bartholdy: Selected studies based on primary sources." PhD
dissertation (Music History): Yale University, 1979. 544 p. UM 79-27,141.
DA XL.6, p.2978-A.
3107. ----. "An unfinished symphony by Mendelssohn." ML
61(1980): 293-309.
3108. Weiss, Günther. "Eine Mozartspur in Felix Mendelssohn-
Bartholdys Sinfonie A-Dur Op.90 ('Italienische')." *Mozart: Klassik für die
Gegenwart*. Oldenburg: Stalling-Druck, 1978: 87-89.

MENGAL, MARTIN JOSEPH (1784-1851)

3109. Andrews, Ralph E. "The woodwind quartets of Martin Joseph
Mengal." PhD dissertation (Theory): Florida State University, 1970. No
DA listing.

MENGELBERG, MISHA (born 1935)

3110. Vermeulen, Ernst. "Misha Mengelberg: *Anatoloose*." SS 48
(1971): 9-16.

MENNIN, PETER (1923-1983)

3111. Goldman, Richard Franko. "Current Chronicle." MQ 35(1949): 111-115. [Third Symphony]

3112. Rhoads, Mary Ruth Schneyer. "Influences of Japanese *hogaku* manifest in selected compositions by Peter Mennin and Benjamin Britten." PhD dissertation (Theory): Michigan State University, 1969. 397 p. No DA listing.

MERCADANTE, SAVERIO (1795-1870)

3113. Mioli, Pero. "Tradizione melodrammatica e crisi di forme nelle *Due illustri rivali* di Saverio Mercadante." STU 9(1980): 317-328.

MESSIAEN, OLIVIER (born 1908)

Ascension

3114. Ameringen, Sylvia van. "Olivier Messiaens *Ascension*." M 6(1952): 500-503.

Catalogue d'oiseaux

3115. Hold, Trevor. "Messiaen's *Birds*." ML 52(1971): 113-122.

3116. Philips, John Douglass. "The modal language of Olivier Messiaen: Principles of *Technique de mon langage musical* reflected in *Catalogue d'oiseaux*." DMA dissertation (Performance): Peabody Conservatory, 1977. No DA listing.

Chronochromie

3117. Bersano. [*Antistrophe I*]

Couleurs de la cité céleste

3118. Shepard, Brian K. "The symbolic elements of Messiaen's work for wind ensemble, *Couleurs de la cité céleste*." JBR 18/1(1982-1983): 52-59.

Livre d'orgue

3119. Frischknecht, Hans Eugen. "Rhythmen und Dauerwerte im *Livre d'orgue* von Olivier Messiaen." *Musik und Gottesdienst* 1(1968): 1-12.

3120. Heiss, Hellmut. "Analysen aus dem *Livre d'orgue* von Olivier Messiaen, 1951." ZM 1/2(1970): 32-38.

3121. ----. "Struktur und Symbolik in *Les Yeux dans les roues* aus Olivier Messiaens *Livre d'orgue*." ZM 3/2(1972): 22-27.

3122. Kemmelmeyer, Karl-Jürgen. "Olivier Messiaen: *Livre d'orgue I*." MB 7(1975): 448-453.

Méditations sur le mystère de la Sainte Trinité

3123. Gilmer, Carl DuVall, III. "Messiaen's musical language in *Méditations sur le mystère de la Sainte Trinité*." DMA dissertation: Memphis State University, 1978. No DA listing.

3124. Weir, Gillian. "Messiaen's musical language: A review of his *Méditations sur le mystère de la Sainte Trinité* for organ." SMU 13(1979): 66-76.

Messe de la Pentecôte
3125. Hohlfeld-Ufer. *Die musikalische Sprache Olivier Messiaens dargestellt an dem Orgelzyklus "Die Pfingstmesse."* Duisburg: Gilles und Francke, 1978.
3126. Raiss, Hans-Peter. "Olivier Messiaen: *Messe de la Pentecôte* für Orgel (1950)." Vogt: 249-253.

La Nativité du Seigneur
3127. Ernst, Karin. "Olivier Messiaen: *La Nativité du Seigneur* für Orgel (1935)." NZM 146/12(1985): 37-39.
3128. Hochreither, Karl. "Olivier Messiaen: *La Nativité du Seigneur.*" Fs. Schneider: 64-78.

Organ works [see also individual titles]
3129. Adams, Beverly Decker. "The organ compositions of Olivier Messiaen." PhD dissertation (Musicology): University of Utah, 1969. No DA listing.
3130. Ahrens, Sieglind, Hans-Dieter Möller, and Almut Rössler. *Das Orgelwerk Messiaens*. Duisberg: Gilles und Francke, 1976.
3131. Ernst, Karin. *Der Beitrag Olivier Messiaens zur Orgelmusik des 20. Jahrhunderts.* Friburg: Hochschulverlag, 1980.
3132. Gárdonyi, Zsolt. "Zur Harmonik Olivier Messiaens: Versuch einer Handreichung zur Einstudierung seiner Orgelmusik." MK 48(1978): 217-227.
3133. Holloway, Clyde. "The organ works of Olivier Messiaen and their importance in his total oeuvre." SMD dissertation (Musicology): Union Theological Seminary, 1974. UM 74-20,075. DA XXXV.3, p.1686-7-A.
3134. Kemmelmeyer, Karl-Jürgen. *Die gedrückten Orgelwerke Olivier Messiaens bis zum "Verset pour la fête de la dédicace."* Regensburg: G. Bosse, 1974. 2 vols.

Piano works [see also individual titles]
3135. Goebels, Franzpeter. "Bemerkungen und Materialen zum Studium neuer Klaviermusik." SMZ 113(1973): 265-268, 336-340.
3136. Lee, John M. "A look at Olivier Messiaen: The man, his philosophy and his piano preludes." PQ 128(1984-1985): 52-56.
3137. Reverdy, Michele. *L'Oeuvre pour piano d'Olivier Messiaen.* Paris: A. Leduc, 1978.

Quatre études rythmiques
3138. Kirchmeyer: 175-179. [*Mode de valeurs et d'intensités*]
3139. Lee, John Madison. "Harmonic structures in the *Études rythmiques* of Olivier Messiaen." PhD dissertation (Theory): Florida State University, 1972. UM 72-18,619. DA XXXIII.1, p.350-A.
3140. Schweizer, Klaus. "Olivier Messiaens Klavieretude *Mode de valeurs et d'intensités.*" AM 30(1973): 128-146.

3141. Toop, Richard. "Messiaen/Goeyvaerts, Fano/Stockhausen, Boulez." PNM 13/1(1974-1975): 141-149.

Quatuor pour la fin du temps
3142. Bernstein, David Stephen. "Messiaen's *Quatuor pour la fin du temps*: An analysis based upon Messiaen's theory of rhythm and his use of modes of limited transposition." DMA dissertation (Composition): Indiana University, 1974. 133 p. RILM 74/633dd28. No DA listing.
3143. Ross, Mark Alan. "The perception of multitonal levels in Olivier Messiaen's *Quatuor pour la fin du temps* and selected vocal compositions." PhD dissertation (Music Theory): University of Cincinnati, 1977. UM 78-01,680. DA XXXVIII.9, p.5117-A. [*Poèmes pour mi; Chants de terre et de ciel*]

Songs
3144. Messiaen, Olivier. "Gedanken zu meiner *Transfiguration*." BOGM (1974-1975): 23-28.

Trois petites liturgies de la présence divine
3145. Günther, Siegfried. "Olivier Messiaen: *Trois petites liturgies de la présence divine*." MK 28(1959): 153-159.

Turangalîla Symphony
3146. Burkat, Leonard. "Current Chronicle." MQ 36(1950): 259-268.
3147. Schweizer, Klaus. *Olivier Messiaen: Turangalîla-symphonie*. München: W. Fink, 1982.

Vingt regards sur l'enfant-Jésus
3148. Ennis, Paula. "A study of coherence and unity in Messiaen's cycle *Vingt regards sur l'enfant-Jésus*." PhD dissertation (Piano): Indiana University, 1979. No DA listing.
3149. Marie, Jean-Etienne. "Inverse function: Differentiation and integration in Messiaen and Boulez." SONUS 2/1(1981): 26-33.
3150. Michaely, Aloyse. "Verbum caro: Die Darstellung des Mysteriums der Inkarnation in Olivier Messiaens *Vingt Regards sur l'enfant-Jésus*." HJM 6(1983): 225-346.
3151. Morris, Betty Ann Walker. "Symbolism and meaning in *Vingt regards sur l'enfant-Jésus* by Olivier Messiaen." DMA dissertation: North Texas State University, 1978. No DA listing.

Other works
3152. Bell, Carl Huston. *Olivier Messiaen*. Boston: Twayne, 1984.
3153. ----. "A structural and stylistic analysis of representative works by Olivier Messiaen." DMA dissertation: Columbia University, 1976. 358 p. No DA listing.
3154. Drew, David. "Messiaen: A provisional study." SCORE 10 (1954): 33-49, 13(1955): 59-73, 14(1955): 41-61.
3155. Forster, Max. *Technik modaler Komposition bei Olivier Messiaen*. Tübinger Beiträge zur Musikwissenschaft 4. Neuhausen-Stuttgart: Hänssler, 1976.

3156. Fremiot, Marcel. "Le Rythme dans le langage d'Olivier Messiaen." POL 2(1948): 58-64.
3157. Griffiths, Paul. *Olivier Messiaen and the music of time.* Ithaca: Cornell University Press, 1985.
3158. Gunden, Heidi Cecilia von. "Timbre as symbol in selected works of Olivier Messiaen." PhD dissertation: University of California at San Diego, 1977. UM 77-17,199. DA XXXVIII.2, p.542-3-A.
3159. Hold, Trevor. "Messiaen's *Birds*." ML 52(1971): 113-122.
3160. Johnson, Robert Sherlaw. *Messiaen.* Berkeley: University of California Press, 1975.
3161. Krastewa, Iwanka. "Le Langage rythmique d'Olivier Messiaen et la métrique ancienne grecque." SMZ 112(1972): 79-86.
3162. Messiaen, Olivier. *La Technique de mon langage musical.* Paris: A. Leduc, 1956.
3163. Nichols, Roger. *Messiaen.* Oxford: Oxford University Press, 1975.
3164. Peterson, Larry Wayne. "Messiaen and rhythm: Theory and practice." PhD dissertation: University of North Carolina, 1973. 239 p. UM 74-5958. DA XXXIV.9, p.6027-A.
3165. Rostand, Claude. "Messiaen et ses trois styles." SMZ 97(1957): 133-139.
3166. Schlee, Thomas Daniel. "Hommage à Olivier Messiaen." OMZ 34 (1979): 28-40.
3167. Schweizer, Klaus. "Dokumentarische Materialen bei Olivier Messiaen." Melos/NZM 4(1978): 477-485.
3168. Tremblay, Gilles. "Oiseau, nature, Messiaen, musique." CCM 1(1970): 15-40.

MEYER, ERNST HERMANN (born 1905)

3169. Hennenberg, Fritz. "Vielschichtigkeit von Form und Inhalt: Bemerkungen zu Ernst Hermann Neyers Poem für Viola und Orchester." MG 15(1965): 804-808.
3170. Klement, Uda. "Die Analyse: Orchesterkonzerte von Ernst Hermann Meyer, Siegfried Matthus und Georg Katzer." MG 28(1978): 599-603. [Konzert für Orchester mit obligaten Pianoforte]
3171. Markowski, Liesel. "Biennale-Eregnis: Meisterliches Kammermusikspiel: Das Berliner Streichquartett spielt Ernst Hermann Meyer." MG 19(1969): 313-316.
3172. ----. "Ernst Hermann Meyers 3. Streichquartett." MG 19(1969): 451-456.
3173. Rienacker, Gerd. "*Reiter der Nacht*: Analytischen Bemerkungen zur Oper von Ernst Hermann Meyer." MG 24(1974): 525-530.
3174. Schaefer, Hansjürgen. "Bemerkungen zu Ernst Hermann Meyers Streichsinfonie." MG 11(1961): 656-660.
3175. ----. "*. . . dass kein Unheil komme über unser Erden*: Ein neuer Liederzyklus von Ernst Hermann Meyer." MG 15(1965): 809-811.
3176. ----. "Ernst Hermann Meyers Violinkonzert." MG 15(1965): 330-332.
3177. Schönewolf, Karl. "Ardens sed virens: Zwei Streichquartette von Ernst Hermann Meyer." MG 9/10(1959): 3-7, 9/11(1959): 13-15.

MEYERBEER, GIACOMO (1791-1864)

3178. ASO 76(1985). [*Robert le Diable*]

3179. Frese, Christhard. *Dramaturgie der grossen Opern Giacomo Meyerbeers*. Berlin-Lichterfelde: Lienau, 1970.

3180. Gibson, Robert Wayne. "Meyerbeer's *Le Prophète*: A study in operatic style." PhD dissertation (Musicology): Northwestern University, 1972. UM 72-32,439. DA XXXIII.6, p.2968-A. [Listed as "The ensemble technique in the grand operas of Giacomo Meyerbeer (1791-1864)" in Cecil Adkins and Alis Dickinson, eds., *Doctoral dissertations in musicology*, 7th North American edition; 2d international edition (Philadelphia: American Musicological Society; International Musicological Society, 1984)]

MIASKOVSKY, NIKOLAI YAKOVLEVICH (1881-1950)

3181. Foreman, George Calvin. "The symphonies of Nikolai Yakovlevich Miaskovsky." PhD dissertation (Musicology): University of Kansas, 1981. UM 81-28,752. DA XLII.7, p.2922-A.

MICHAEL, DAVID MORITZ (1751-1825)

3182. Roberts, Dale Alexander. "The sacred vocal music of David Moritz Michael: An American Moravian composer." DMA dissertation (Theory): University of Kentucky, 1978. 199 p. No DA listing.

MIDDELSCHULTE, WILHELM (1863-1943)

3183. Belcher, Euel H., Jr. "The organ music of Wilhelm Middelschulte." PhD dissertation (Performance): Indiana University, 1975. No DA listing.

MIGNONE, FRANCISCO (born 1897)

3184. Verhaalen, Sister Marion. "Francisco Mignone: His music for piano." IAMB 79(1970-1971): 1-36.

MIHALOVICH, EDMUND VON (1842-1929)

3185. Szerzo, Katalin. "Eine Oper der ungarischen Wagner-Schule: Edmund von Mihalovich: *Eliane*." SM 19(1977): 109-160.

MILHAUD, DARIUS (1892-1974)

Chamber works [see also individual titles]
3186. Mason, Colin. "The chamber music of Milhaud." MQ 43(1957): 326-341.

Choral works

3187. Hodgson, Kenneth Dorsey. "An examination of the compositions by Darius Milhaud for unaccompanied mixed voices." DMA dissertation (Performance): University of Illinois, 1979. UM 80-09,060. DA XL.10, p.5241-A.

3188. Larson.

Octet

3189. Helm, Everett. "Milhaud: XIV + XV = Oktett." MELOS 22(1955): 71-75.

Operas

3190. Knoch, Hans. *Orpheus und Eurydike: Der antike Sagenstoff in den Opern von Darius Milhaud und Ernst Krenek.* Regensburg: G. Bosse, 1977.

Organ works

3191. Goetze, Wilhelm Albin Arthur. "An analytical study of Milhaud's *Neuf préludes* for organ." EdD dissertation (Music Education): Columbia University, 1976. UM 76-21,018. DA XXXVII.3, p.1289-A.

3192. Schaeffer, Stephen Gleim. "The organ works of Darius Milhaud." DMA dissertation: University of Cincinnati, 1977. No DA listing.

Piano works

3193. Kniesner. [Piano Sonata]

Septet

3194. Purrone, Kevin. "The *Septuor à cordes* of Darius Milhaud." ITR 3/3(1979-1980): 36-61.

Songs

3195. Noble, Natoma Nash. "The neoclassic aesthetic in two early song cycles by Darius Milhaud." DMA dissertation (Performance): University of Texas, 1981. UM 81-28,598. DA XLII.7, p.2927-A.

String Quartets

3196. Cherry, Paul Wyman. "The string quartets of Darius Milhaud." PhD dissertation (Musicology): University of Colorado, 1980. UM 81-03,081. DA XLI.8, p.3312-A.

Symphonies

3197. Swickard, Ralph James. "The symphonies of Darius Milhaud: An historical perspective and critical study of their musical content, style, and form." PhD dissertation (Musicology): University of California, Los Angeles, 1973. UM 73-28,988. DA XXXIV.6, p.3458-A.

Une Journée

3198. Forte: 39-47. [Midi]

Other works

3199. Bauer, Marion. "Darius Milhaud." MQ 29(1942): 139-159.

3200. Daniel, Keith W. "A preliminary investigation of pitch-class set analysis in the atonal and polytonal works of Milhaud and Poulenc." ITO 6/6(1981-1983): 22-48.

3201. Laughton, John Charles. "The woodwind music of Milhaud." DMA dissertation (Performance): University of Iowa, 1980. UM 81-14,323. DA XLII.1, p.14-A.

3202. McCarthy, Peter J. "The sonatas of Darius Milhaud." PhD dissertation (Musicology): Catholic University, 1972. UM 73-04,353. DA XXXIII.8, p.4458-A.

3203. MacKenzie, Nancy Mayland. "Selected clarinet solo and chamber music of Darius Milhaud." PhD dissertation (Performance): University of Wisconsin, 1984. 353 p. No DA listing.

3204. Trickey, Samuel Miller. "*Les Six*." PhD dissertation (Musicology): North Texas State University, 1955. UM 14,373. DA XV.12, p.2542.

MOE, DANIEL (born 1926)

3205. Erickson, Karle Joseph. "The choral music of Daniel Moe (1926-   ) written between 1952 and 1967." EdD dissertation: University of Illinois, 1970. UM 71-14,740. DA XXXI.12, p.6645-A.

MOERAN, ERNEST JOHN (1894-1950)

3206. Curtis.

3207. Statham, Heathcote. "Moeran's Symphony in G Minor." MR 1 (1940): 245-254.

MOLCHANOV, KIRILL (BORN 1922)

3208. Taruskin, Richard. "Current Chronicle." MQ 62(1976): 105-115. [*The Dawns are Quiet Here*]

MONIUSZKO, STANISLAW (1819-1872)

3209. Abraham, Gerald. "The operas of Stanislaw Moniuszko." Abraham: 156-171.

3210. Hunt, R. E. "Moniuszko's musical treatment of poems by Mickiewica." PhD dissertation (Musicology): London, 1980.

MONNIKENDAM, MARIUS (1896-1977)

3211. Schouten, Jan. "Marius Monnikendam: *Via Sacre*." SS 55(1974): 29-36.

MOÓR, EMMANUEL (1863-1931)

3212. Truscott, Harold. "The piano concertos of Emmanuel Moór." MR 21(1960): 121-129.

MOORE, DOUGLAS (1893-1969)

3213. Reagan, Donald Joseph. "Douglas Moore and his orchestral works." PhD dissertation (Theory): Catholic University, 1972. No DA listing.
3214. Weitzel, Harold. "A melodic analysis of selected vocal solos in the operas of Douglas Moore." PhD dissertation (Music Education): New York University, 1971. 344 p. UM 71-28,570. DA XXXII.5, p.2736-A.

MOORE, UNDINE SMITH (born 1904)

3215. Jones, John Robert Douglas. "The choral works of Undine Smith Moore: A study of her life and work." EdD dissertation (Music Education): New York University, 1980. 165 p. UM 81-10,694. DA XLI.12, p.4881-A.

MORRAN, E.J.

3216. Yenne, Vernon Lee. "Three twentieth-century English song composers: Peter Warlock, E.J. Morran, and John Ireland." DMA dissertation (Performance): University of Illinois, 1969. No DA listing.

MOSCHELES, IGNAZ (1794-1870)

3217. Heussner, Ingeborg. "Formale Gestaltungsprinzipe bei Ignaz Moscheles." Fs. Engel/H: 155-165.

MOSOLOV, ALEXANDER (1900-1973)

3218. Barsova, Inna. "Das Frühwerk von Alekandr Mosolov." JP 2 (1979): 117-169.

MOSS, LAWRENCE (born 1927)

3219. Barkin, Elaine. "Lawrence K. Moss: Three Rilke songs from *Das Studenbuch* (1963)." PNM 6/1(1967): 144-152.
3220. Kelley, Danny Roy. "The solo piano works of Lawrence K. Moss." DMA dissertation (Performance): Peabody Conservatory, 1985. 147 p. No DA listing.

MUL, JAN (1911-1971)

3221. Mul, Jan. "Jan Mul: Sinfonietta." SS 12(1962): 14-16.

MURAIL, TRISTAN (born 1947)

3222. Murail, Tristan. "Spectra and pixies." CMR 1/1(1984-1985): 157-170. [*Désintégrations*]

MUSGRAVE, THEA (born 1928)

3223. Freedman, Deborah. "Thea Musgrave's opera *Mary, Queen of Scots.*" DMA dissertation (Conducting): Peabody Conservatory, 1985. 175 p. No DA listing.

3224. McDonald, Kenneth Allan. "Dramatic concerto elements as manifested in Thea Musgrave's Concerto for Orchestra." DMA dissertation: University of Washington, 1979. No DA listing.

3225. McGregor, R. E. "An analysis of Thea Musgrave's compositional style from 1958 to 1967." PhD dissertation (Musicology): Liverpool, 1980.

MUSSORGSKY, MODEST (1839-1881)

Boris Godunov
3226. ASO 27-28(1980).

3227. Carr, Maureen Ann. "Keys and modes, functions and progressions in Mussorgsky's *Boris Godounov.*" PhD dissertation (Theory): University of Wisconsin, 1972. UM 72-33,844. DA XXXIII.10, p.5762-A.

3228. Hoffmann-Erbrecht, Lothar. "Die russischen Volklieder in Mussorgskis *Boris Godunov.*" Fs. Wiora: 458-465.

3229. John, Nicholas, ed. *Mussorgsky: Boris Godunov.* London: J. Calder, 1982.

3230. Le Roux, Maurice. *Moussorgski: Boris Godounov.* Paris: Aubier Montaigne, 1980.

3231. Oldani, Robert W. "New perspectives on Mussorgsky's *Boris Godunov.*" Ann Arbor: UMI Research Press, 1979.

3232. Taruskin. [Prologue]

3233. Taruskin, Richard. "Musorgsky vs. Musorgsky: The versions of *Boris Godunov.*" NCM 8(1984-19850: 91-118.

Khovantchina
3234. ASO 58-57(1983).

The Nursery
3235. Agawu, V. Kofi. "Pitch organizational procedures in Mussorgsky's *Nursery.*" ITR 5/1(1981-1982): 23-59.

Piano works
3236. Angerer, Manfred. "Genrestück und Expressivität: Zu Mussorgskys kleinen Klavierstücken." OMZ 36(1981): 298-303.

Pictures at an Exhibition
3237. Hubsch, Lini Pfleger. *Modest Mussorgski: Bilder einer Ausstellung.* München: W. Fink, 1978.

3238. Lehmann, Dieter. "Charakter und Bedeutung der *Promenaden* in Mussorgskis *Bilder einer Ausstellung.*" SM 4(1963): 235-255.

3239. Mayer-Rosa, Eugen. "*Das Grosse Tor von Kiew* im Bild und in der Musik." ME 24(1971): 117-122.

Songs [see also individual titles]

3240. Fox, Andrew Criddle. "Evolution of style in the songs of Modest Mussorgsky." PhD dissertation: Florida State University, 1974. 142 p. UM 75-00,953. DA XXXV.7, p.4585-A.

3241. Friehl, Heather McMaster. "A study of Mussorgsky's use of declamation in the song cycle *Without Sun*." MA dissertation: Brigham Young University, 1978.

3242. Lehmann, Dieter. "Satire und Parodie in den Liedern Modest Mussorgskis." BM 9(1967): 105-111.

3243. Sydow, Brigitte. "Untersuchungen über die Klavierlieder M P. Mussorgskis." PhD dissertation (Musicology): Göttingen, 1974.

3244. Weber-Bockholdt, Petra. *Die Lieder Mussorgskijs: Herkunft und Erscheinungsform*. München: W. Fink, 1982.

Other works

3245. Leyda, Jay and Sergie Bertensen, eds. *The Mussorgsky Reader*. New York: W.W. Norton, 1947.

3246. Taruskin, Richard. "Serov and Musorgsky." Fs. Abraham: 139-161.

3247. Will, Roy T. "A stylistic analysis of the works of Moussorgsky." PhD dissertation (Theory): University of Rochester, 1949. 189 p. No DA listing.

MYHILL, JOHN

3248. Hiller, Lejaren and Charles Ames; graphics by Robert Franki. "Automated composition: An installation at the 1985 International Exhibition in Tsukuba, Japan." PNM 23/2(1984-1985) 196-215. [*Toy Harmonium*]

NANCARROW, CONLON (born 1912)

3249. Jarvlepp, Jan. "Conlon Nancarrow's *Study Nr. 27 for Player Piano* viewed analytically." PNM 22(1983-1984): 218-222.

NAYLOR, BERNARD (born 1907)

3250. Baerg, William John. "A study of selected choral works of Bernard Naylor." DMA dissertation: Peabody Conservatory, 1979. No DA listing.

NELSON, RON (born 1929)

3251. Cox, Dennis Keith. "Aspects of the compositional styes of three selected twentieth-century American composers of choral music: Alan Hovhaness, Ron Nelson, and Daniel Pinkham." DMA dissertation: University of Missouri, 1978. No DA listing.

NIBLOCK, PHILL (born 1933)

    3252. Groneymer, Gisela. "Ein radikale Minimalist: Ein Porträt des amerikanischen Klang-Technikers Phill Niblock." MTX 12(1985): 14-17.

NIELSEN, CARL (1865-1931)

    3253. Jones, William Isaac. "A study of tonality in the symphonies of Carl Nielsen." PhD dissertation (Theory): Florida State University, 1973. UM 73-25,118. DA XXXIV.4, p.1951-A.
    3254. Konold, Wulf. "Carl Nielsens Violinkonzert Op.33: Ein analytischer Versuch." Fs. Gudewill: 91-100.
    3255. Miller, Mina Florence. "The solo piano music of Carl Nielsen: An analysis for performance." PhD dissertation: New York University, 1978. No DA listing.
    3256. ----. "Some thoughts upon editing the music of Carl Nielsen." CM 34(1982): 64-74.
    3257. Simpson, Robert. *Carl Nielsen, symphonist.* Rev. ed. London: Kahn & Averill, 1979.
    3258. Waterhouse, John C.G. "Nielsen reconsidered." MT 106(1965): 425-427, 514-517, 593-595.
    3259. Wilson, Dean C. "An analytical and statistical study of the harmony in Carl Nielsen's six symphonies." PhD dissertation (Theory): Michigan State University, 1967. UM 68-04,235. DA XXVIII.10, p.4205-A.

NIXON, ROGER (born 1921)

    3260. Nixon, Roger. "Fiesta del pacifico." JBR 3/1(1966-1967): 29-32.
    3261. ----. "Reflections." JBR 4/1(1967-1968): 53-60.

NONO, LUIGI (born 1924)

Al gran sole
    3262. Vogt, Harry. "*Al gran solo* carico d'autocitazione: Oder, zwischen Patchwork und Pasticcio: Zur dramaturgisch-musikalischen Gestaltung der 2. szenischen Aktion *Al gran sole carico d'amore* von Luigi Nono." N 5(1984-1985): 125-139.

Il Canto sospeso
    3263. Raiss, Hans-Peter. "Luigi Nono: *Il canto sospeso* (1956)." Vogt: 287-291.
    3264. Stockhausen: 157-165.
    3265. Stockhausen, Karlheinz. "Music and Speech." R 6(1964): 40-64.

La Fabbrica illuminata
    3266. Flammer, Ernst Helmuth. "Form und Gehalt: Eine Analyse von Luigi Nonos *La fabbrica illuminata*." Melos/NZM 3(1977): 401-411.
    3267. Gruhn, Wilfried. "Didaktische Reflexionen zu Luigi Nonos *La Fabbrica illuminata*." MB 9(1977): 285-291.

Incontri
    3268. Stenzl, Jürg. "Nonos *Incontri*." MELOS 39(1972): 150-153.
    3269. Wennerstrom.

Intolleranza
    3270. Gilbert, Janet Monteith. "Dialectic music: An analysis of Luigi Nono's *Intolleranza*." DMA dissertation (Composition): University of Illinois, 1979. UM 80-09,043. DA XL.10, p.5240-A.

Prometeo
    3271. Oehlschlägel, Reinhard. "Klanginstallation und Wahrnehmungs-komposition: Zur Nuova Versione von Luigi Nonos *Prometeo*." MTX 12(1985): 10-13.

Other works
    3272. Gentilucci, Armando. "La Tecnica corale di Luigi Nono." RIM 2(1967): 111-129.
    3273. Kolisch, Rudolf. "Nonos Varianti." MELOS 24(1957): 292-296.
    3274. Kramer, Jonathan. "The Fibonacci series in twentieth-century music." JMT 17(1973): 110-148.
    3275. Lachenmann, Helmut. "Luigi Nono oder Rückblick auf die serielle Musik." MELOS 38(1971): 225-230.
    3276. Poné, Gundaris. "Webern and Luigi Nono: The genesis of a new compositional morphology and syntax." PNM 10/2(1972): 111-119.
    3277. Spangemacher, Friedrich. *Luigi Nono: Die elektronische Musik: Historische Kontext, Entwicklung, Kompositionstechnik.* Regensburg: G. Bosse, 1983.
    3278. Stenzl, Jürg, ed. *Luigi Nono: Texte: Studien zu seiner Musik.* Zürich: Atlantis, 1975. 478 p.

NØRGAARD, PER (born 1932)

    3279. Nørgaard, Per. "Inside a symphony." NW 8(1975): 4-16. [Third Symphony]

NUFFEL, JULES VAN (1883-1953)

    3280. Chase, Robert Allen. "Jules van Nuffel and his music." PhD dissertation: Columbia University Teachers College, 1978. No DA listing.

NYSTEDT, KNUT (born 1915)

    3281. Spicher, Linda Krakowski. "An analysis of selected choral works by Knut Nystedt." MA dissertation: University of Iowa, 1974.

NYSTROEM, GÖSTA (1890-1966)

    3282. Christenson, Peter Louis. "The orchestral works of Gösta Nystroem: A critical study." PhD dissertation: University of Washington, 1961. LC Mic 61-2095. DA XXI.12, p.3807.

OFFENBACH, JACQUES (1819-1880)

3283. ASO 25(1980). [*Les Contes d'Hoffmann*]
3284. ASO 66(1984). [*La Périchole*]
3285. Lyon, Raymond and Louis Saguer. *Les Contes d'Hoffmann: Étude et analyse*. Paris: Mellottée, 1948

OHANA, MAURICE (born 1914)

3286. Marcel, Odile. "L'"Ibérisme' de Maurice Ohana." RM 351-352(1982): 11-26.

OLIVEROS, PAULINE (born 1932)

3287. Von Gunden, Heidi. *The music of Pauline Oliveros*. Metuchen, NJ: Scarecrow Press, 1983.
3288. ----. "The theory of sonic awareness in *The Greeting* by Pauline Oliveros." PNM 19/2(1980-1981): 409-415.

ORFF, CARL (1895-1982)

Antigone
3289. Ptak, Milos O. "Current Chronicle." MQ 36(1950): 105-109.
3290. Stäblein, Bruno. "Schöpferische Tonalität: Zum Grossaufbau von Orffs *Antingonae*." M 6(1962): 145-148.

De temporum fine comoedia
3291. Thomas, Werner and Rudolf Klein. "Zu Carl Orffs *De temporum fine comoedia*." OMZ 28(1973): 290-300.

Prometheus
3292. Kaufmann, Harold. "Carl Orffs Musik heute: An Beispielen aus *Prometheus* verdeutlich." NZM 134(1973): 421-416.

Other works
3293. Helm, Everett. "Carl Orff." MQ 41(1955): 285-304.
3294. Jahnke, Sabine. "Materialien zu einer Unterrichtssequenz: Des Antonius von Padua Fischpredigt bei Orff-Mahler-Berio." MB 5(1973): 615-622.
3295. Keller, Wilhelm. "Wie komponiert Karl Orff?" OMZ 17(1962): 431-443.
3296. Kiekert, Ingeborg. *Die musikalische Form in den Werken Carl Orffs*. Regensburg: G. Bosse, 1957.
3297. Liess, Andreas. "Die musiké techni Carl Orffs." M 9(1955): 305-309.
3298. Seifert, Wolfgang. "Die humanistische Botschaft eines zeitgemässen Unzeitgemässen: Kleines und grosses Welttheater." NZM 143/5(1982): 4-15.

ORNSTEIN, LEO (born 1892)

    3299. Darter, Thomas Eugene, Jr. "The futurist piano music of Leo Ornstein." DMA dissertation (Composition): Cornell University, 1979. UM 79-10,738. DA XXXIX.11, p.6386-A.

ORR, CHARLES WILFRED (1893-1976)

    3300. Curtis.
    3301. Rawlins, Joseph Thomas. "The songs of Charles Wilfred Orr with special emphasis on his Houseman settings." DMA dissertation (Performance): Louisiana State University, 1972. UM 73-02,979. DA XXXIII.8, p.4461-A.

ORREGO-SALAS, JUAN (born 1919)

    3302. Curtis, Brandt B. "Rafael Alberti and Chilean composers." DMA dissertation (Voice): Indiana University, 1977. No DA listing. [*Et alba del alheli*, Op.29]

ORTHEL, LÉON (born 1905)

    3303. Geraedts, Jaap. "Léon Orthel: Scherzo No.2." SS 25(1965): 20-23.
    3304. Wouters, Jos. "Léon Orthel: *Piccola sinfonia*." SS 6(1961): 20-25.

OTTE, HANS (born 1926)

    3305. Baucke, Ludolf. "In Augenblicken Verweilen: Anmerkungen zu Hans Ottes *Das Buch der Klänge*." N 5(1984-1985): 140-145.

OTTERLOO, WILLEM VAN (1907-1978)

    3306. Flothuis, Marius. "Willem van Otterloo: Sinfonietta for 16 Wind Instruments." SS 16(1963): 20-23.

PAART, ARVO (born 1935)

    3307. Bradshaw, Susan. "Arvo Paart." CT 26(1983): 25-28.

PAGH-PAAN, YOUNGHI (born 1945)

    3308. Pagh-Paan, Younghi. "Unterwegs: Reflexionen über meine Tätigkeit als Komponisten." N 4(1983-1984): 20-37.

PAINE, JOHN KNOWLES (1839-1906)

    3309. Schmidt, John Charles. "The life and works of John Knowles Paine." PhD dissertation (Musicology): New York University, 1979. 857 p. UM 79-25,522. DA XL.5, p.2347-A.

PAISIELLO, GIOVANNI (1740-1816)

3310. Hunt, Jno [sic] Leland. "The life and keyboard works of Giovanni Paisiello (1740-1816)." PhD dissertation (Musicology): University of Michigan, 1973. UM 74-15,761. DA XXXV.1, p.499.

PALMER, ROBERT (born 1915)

3311. Austin, William. "The music of Robert Palmer." MQ 42(1956): 35-50.
3312. Chihara.

PANUFNIK, ANDRZEJ (born 1914)

3313. Hall, Barrie. "Andrzej Panufnik and his *Sinfonia sacra*." TEMPO 71(1964-1965): 14-22.
3314. Panufnik, Andrezj. "About my *Autumnal Music* and *Universal Prayer*." TEMPO 96(1971): 11-15.
3315. Truscott, Harold. "Andrzej Panufnik." TEMPO 55-56(1960): 13-18.
3316. Walsh, Stephen. "The music of Andrjez Panufnik." TEMPO 111 (1974): 7-14.

PAPINEAU-COUTURE, JEAN (born 1916)

3317. Beckwith, John. "Jean Papineau-Couture." CMJ 3/2(1958): 4-20.
3318. Dixon, Gail. "The *Pièces concertantes* Nos. 1, 2, 3 and 4 of Jean Papineau-Couture." SMUWO 9(1984): 93-123.

PARKER, HORATIO (1863-1919)

3319. Kearns, William Kay. "Horatio Parker (1863-1919): A study of his life and music." PhD dissertation (Musicology): Univesity of Illinois, 1965. UM 65-11,805. DA XXVI.5, p.2795.

PARROTT, IAN (born 1916)

3320. Thomas, A.F. Leighton. "A note on Parrott's *Jubilate Deo*." *Welsh Music* 3/3 (Summer 1968): 20-23.

PARTCH, HARRY (1901-1976)

3321. Earls, Paul. "Harry Partch: Verses in preparation for *Delusion of the Fury*." Y 3(1967): 1-32.
3300. Hackbarth, Glenn Allen. "An analysis of Harry Partch's *Daphne of the Dunes*." DMA dissertation: University of Illinois, 1979. No DA listing.
3323. Woodbury, Arthur. "Harry Partch: Corporeality and monophony." S 1/2(1967): 91-93.

PARTOS, OEDOEN (1907-1977)

    3324. Bahat, Avner. "Traditional elements and dodecaphonic technique in the music of Odeoen Partos (1907-1977)." ISM 1(1978): 175-191.

PAYNE, ANTHONY (born 1936)

    3325. Bradshaw, Susan and Richard Rodney Bennett. "Anthony Payne and his *Paean*." TEMPO 100(1972): 40-44.

PAZ, JUAN CARLOS (1901-1972)

    3326. Sargent, David H. "The twelve-tone row technique of Juan Carlos Paz." Y 11(1975) 82-105.

PENDERECKI, KRZYSZTOF (born 1933)

Anaklasis
    3327. Huber, Alfred. "Pendereckis *Anaklasis* für Streicher und Schlagzeuggruppen." MELOS 38(1971): 87-91.
    3328. Müller, Karl-Joseph. "Krzysztof Penderecki (1933): *Anaklasis* (1959-1960) für Streicher und Schlagzeuggruppen." Zimmerschied: 215-233.

Capriccio for Violin and Orchestra
    3329. Cope: 78-81.

De natura sonoris
    3330. Albers, Bradley Gene. "*De natura sonoris* I and II by Krzysztof Penderecki: A comparative analysis." DMA dissertation (Composition): University of Illinois, 1978. UM 78-20,890. DA XXXIX.5, p.2605-A.
    3331. Roberts.

The Devils of Loudun
    3332. Jahnke, Sabine. "Musikdramatischer Exorzismus in Pendereckis Oper *Die Teufel von Loudun*." MB 7(1975): 615-617.
    3333. Kellner, Hans. "Devils and angels: A study of the demonic in three twentieth-century operas." JMR 2(1976-1978): 255-272.

Dimension der Zeit und der Stille
    3334. Müller, Karl-Joseph. "Pendereckis Musik im 'mobilen Netz trigonometrischer Punkte'." MB 7(1975): 622-629.

Fluorescences
    3335. Bersano.

Pittsburgh Overture
    3336. Tyra, Thomas. "An analysis of Penderecki's *Pittsburgh Overture*." JBR 10/1(1973-1974): 37-38, 10/2(1973-1974): 5-12.

Psalms
3337. Müller, Karl-Joseph. "Krzysztof Penderecki (1933): aus den *Psalmen Davids* für gemischten Chor und Instrumental-ensemble (1958)." Zimmerschied: 201-214.

St. Luke Passion
3338. Kaack, Brunhilde. "Pendereckis Zwölftonreihe." M 29(1975): 9-15.
3339. Müller, Karl-Joseph. *Informationen zu Pendereckis Lukas-Passion.* Frankfurt am Main: M. Diesterweg, 1973.
3340. Robinson, Ray and Allen Winold. *A study of the Penderecki St. Luke Passion.* Celle: Moeck; Totowa, NJ: US representative, European American Music Distributors, 1982.
3341. Schuler, Manfred. "Das B-A-C-H Motiv in Pendereckis *Lukaspassion.*" KJ 65(1981): 105-111.
3342. ----. "Tonale Phänomene in Pendereckis *Lukaspassion.*" Melos/NZM 1(1976): 457-460.
3343. Stroh, Wolfgang Martin. "Penderecki und das Hören erfolgreicher Musik." MELOS 37(1970): 452-460.
3344. Vogt: 358-371.

Threnody
3345. Gruhn, Wilfried. "Strukturen und Klangmodelle in Pendereckis *Threnos.*" MELOS 38(1971): 409-411.

Other works
3346. Schwinger, Wolfram. *Penderecki: Begegnung, Lebensdaten, Werkkommentare.* Stuttgart: Deutsche Verlags-Anstalt, 1979.
3347. Zielinski, Tadeusz A. "Der einsame Weg des Krzysztof Penderecki." MELOS 29(1962): 318-323.

PENTLAND, BARBARA (born 1912)

3348. Eastman, Sheila and Timothy McGee. *Barbara Pentland.* Toronto: University of Toronto Press, 1983.
3349. McGee, Timothy J. "Barbara Pentland in the 1950s: String Quartet No.2 and Symphony for Ten Parts." SMUWO 9(1984): 133-152.
3350. Turner, Robert. "Barbara Pentland." CMJ 2/4(1958): 15-26.

PEPPING, ERNST (1901-1981)

A-capella-Messe
3351. Adrio, Adam. "Zu Ernst Peppings *A-capella-Messe.*" M 5(1951): 203-210.

Choral music [see also individual titles]
3352. Grote, Gottfried. "Der Weg zum *Passionsbericht des Matthaus* von Ernst Pepping: Strukturelle Untersuchungen." Fs. Pepping: 57-83.
3353. Poos, Heinrich. "Ernst Peppings Chorlied *Anakreons Grab: In memoriam.*" NZM 142(1981): 252-258.

3354. ----. *Ernst Peppings Liederkreis für Chor nach Gedichten von Goethe "Heut und Ewig": Studien zum Personstil Peppings.* Berlin: Merseburger, 1965.

3355. ----. "Ernst Peppings Liedmotetten nach Weisen der böhmischen Brüder." MK 51(1981): 67-82, 177-189.

3356. ----. "Ernst Peppings Prediger-Motette." MK 38(1968): 176-182.

3357. Witte, Gerd. "Die Weihnachtsgeschichte des Lukas in der Fassung Ernst Peppings: Ein Beitrag zum Verhältnis von Sprache und Musik in Ernst Peppings Vokalmusik." Fs. Pepping: 84-104.

Organ works

3358. Hochreither, Karl. "Ernst Peppings Toccata und Fuge *Mitten wir im Leben sind*." Fs. Pepping: 116-146.

3359. Manicke, Dietrich. "Ernst Peppings Orgelwerke." Fs. Pepping: 105-115.

3360. Weeks, William B. "The use of the chorale in the organ works of Ernst Pepping." DMA dissertation: University of Arizona, 1970. No DA listing.

Piano works

3361. Blume, Friedrich. "Ernst Pepping: Sonatine für Klavier." Fs. Pepping: 46-47.

3362. Hamm, Walter. *Studien über Ernst Peppings drei Klaviersonaten.* Würzburg: K. Triltsch, 1955.

Songs

3363. Blankenburg, Walter. "Ernst Peppings *Liederbuch nach Gedichten von Paul Gerhart* in geschichtlicher Beleuchtung." Fs. Pepping: 147-157.

Other works

3364. Adrio, Adam. "Junge Komponisten: 4. Ernst Pepping." Fs. Pepping: 38-45.

3365. ----. "Die Welsen der bömischen Brüder im Werk Ernst Peppings." Fs. Fellerer/70: 23-34.

3366. Baumgärtel, Lothar. "Lebendige Aussage: Ernst Pepping (geboren 12-9-1901)." Fs. Mauersberg: 127-134.

3367. Dürr, Alfred. "Gedanken zum Kirchen-Musikschaffen Ernst Peppings." MK 31(1961): 145-172.

PERLE, GEORGE (born 1915)

3368. Custer, Arthur. "Current Chronicle." MQ 53(1967): 252-254. [Second Wind Quintet]

3369. Kraft, Leo. "The music of George Perle." MQ 57(1971): 444-465.

3370. Saylor, Bruce. "Current Chronicle: A new work by George Perle." MQ 61(1975): 471-475. [*Songs of Praise and Lamentation*]

3371. Swift, Richard. "A tonal analog: The tone-centered music of George Perle." PNM 21(1982-1983): 257-284.

3372. Weinberg, Henry. "The music of George Perle." ACA 10/3(1962): 6-11.

PERSICHETTI, VINCENT (born 1915)

3373. Ashizawa, Theodore Fumio. "The choral music of Vincent Persichetti (b.1915)." DMA dissertation: University of Washington, 1977. UM 78-00,906. DA XXXVIII.9, p.5111-A.

3354. Barnard, Jack Richard. "The choral music of Vincent Persichetti: A descriptive analysis." PhD dissertation: Florida State University, 1974. UM 75-12,629. DA XXXV.12, p.7940-A.

3375. Evett, Robert. "The music of Vincent Persichetti." JR 2/2 (1955): 15-30.

3376. Farrell, Laurence. "Vincent Persichetti's piano sonatas from 1943 to 1965." PhD dissertation (Theory): University of Rochester, 1976. UM 76-21,656. DA XXXVII.6, p.3254-A.

3377. Hilfiger, John Jay. "A comparison of some aspects of style in the band and orchestra music of Vincent Persichetti." PhD dissertation (Music Literature): University of Iowa, 1985. 105 p. No DA listing.

3378. Hines.

3379. Jeter. [Sonata for Two Pianos, Op.13]

3380. Mullins, Joe Barry. "A comparative analysis of three symphonies for band." JBR 6/1(1969-1970): 17-28. [Symphony No.6]

3381. Persichetti, Vincent. "Symphony No.6 for Band." JBR 1/1(1964-1965): 17-20.

PETERSON-BERGER, WILHELM (1867-1942)

3382. Scriven, Marianne Sjoren. "The art songs of Wilhelm Peterson-Berger." DMA dissertation (Performance): University of Missouri, 1973. 140 p. UM 73-25,944. DA XXXIV.5, p.2687-A.

PETRASSI, GOFFREDO (born 1904)

Concerto for Orchestra
3383. Vlad, Roman. "Goffredo Petrassi Orchesterkonzerte." MELOS 26 (1959): 174-178.

Piano Concerto
3384. Stone, Olga. "Goffredo Petrassi's Concerto for Pianoforte and Orchestra: A study of twentieth-century neo-classic style." MR 39(1978): 240-257.

Piano works
3385. Stone, Olga. "Petrassi's Eight Inventions for Piano." MR 33 (1972): 21-27.

Sonata da camera
3386. Stone, Olga. "Petrassi's *Sonata da camera* for harpsichord and ten instruments: A study of twentieth-century linear style." MR 37(1976): 283-294.

205

PFITZNER

Other works
3387. Bonelli, Anthony Eugene. "Serial techniques in the music of Goffredo Petrassi: A study of his compositions from 1950 to 1959." PhD dissertation (Theory): University of Rochester, 1970. 248 p. UM 71-04,451. DA XXXI.9, p.4813-A.
3388. Bortolotto, Mario. "Petrassi Stil 1960." MELOS 33(1966): 48-50.
3389. ----. "Zwei neue Werke von Goffredo Petrassi." MELOS 30 (1963): 114-117. [*Serenade*; String Quartet]
3390. Marinelli, Carlo. "La Musica strumentate de camera di Goffredo Petrassi." CHI 4(1967): 245-284.
3391. Pinzauti, Leonardo. "Petrassi *Sacro*." CHI 3(1966): 297-303.
3392. Weissman, John S. "Current Chronicle." MQ 61(1975): 588-594. [*Tre per sette; Estri*]
3393. ----. "Goffredo Petrassi and his music." MR 22(1961): 198-211.

PFITZNER, HANS ERICH (1869-1949)

Abbitte
3394. Mohr, Wilhelm. "Von Pfitzners *Abbitte* in einer Sammlung von Hölderlin-Vertongungen." MHPG 24(1969): 8-10.

Armer Heinrich
3395. Hirtler, Franz. *Hans Pfitzners "Armer Heinrich" in seiner Stellung zur Musik des ausgehender 19. Jahrhunderts*. Würzburg: K. Triltsch, 1940.

Cello Concerto
3396. Osthoff, Wolfgang. "Jugendwerk, Früh-, Reife-, und Alterstil: Zum langsamen Satz des Cellokonzerts in A-Moll Op.52 von Hans Pfitzner." AM 33(1976): 89-118.

Lethe
3397. Ringger, Rolf Urs. "*Lethe*: Hans Pfitzners Orchesterlied Op.37." MHPG 43(1981): 91-98.

Palestrina
3398. Fleury, Albert. "Historische und stilgeschichtliche Probleme in Pfitzners *Palestrina*." Fs. Osthoff/70: 229-240.
3399. Henderson, Donald Gene. "Hans Pfitzner's *Palestrina*: A twentieth-century allegory." MR 31(1970): 32-42.
3400. Kleinknecht, Friedrich. "Der Kontrapunkt in Pfitzners *Palestrina*." MHPG 41(1981): 20-27.
3401. Osthoff, Wolfgang. "Eine neue Quelle zu Palestrinazitat und Palestrinasatz in Pfitnzers musikalischer Legende." Fs. Osthoff/80: 185-209.
3402. Rectanus, Hans. "Die musikalische Zitate in Hans Pfitzners *Palestrina*." Fs. Pfitzner: 22-27.
3403. Stein, Herbert von. "Äusserungen Hans Pfitzners über eine thematische Analyse zu *Palestrina*." MHPG 28(1972): 2-11.

Phantasie for Orchestra
   3404. Mohr, Wilhelm. "Hans Pfitzners Phantasie für Orchester Opus 56." MHPG 10(1962): 4-12.

Sextet
   3405. Mohr, Wilhelm. "Hans Pfitzners Sextett Opus 55." MHPG 7 (1960): 2-12.

Songs
   3406. Diez, Werner. *Hans Pfitzners Lieder: Versuch einer Stilbetrachtung.* Regensburg: G. Bosse, 1968. 126 p.
   3407. Habelt, Hans-Jürgen. "Hans Pfitzners Lieder auf Texte von Heinrich Heine." MHPG 46(1984): 3-17.
   3408. Lindlar, Heinrich. *Hans Pfitzner Klavierlied.* Würzburg: K. Triltsch, 1940.

String Quartet
   3409. Mohr, Wilhelm. "Pfitzners Streichquartett in D-Moll (1886): Eine Analyse." M 27(1973): 483-485.

Other works
   3410. Abendroth, Walter. *Deutsche Musik der Zeitwende: Eine Kulturphilosophische Persönlichkeitstudie über Anton Bruckner und Hans Pfitzner.* Hamburg: Haneseatische Verlagsanstalt, 1937.
   3411. Henderson, Donald Gene. "Hans Pfitzner: The composer and his instrumental works." PhD dissertation: University of Michigan, 1963. UM 63-4965. DA XXIV.2, p.766.
   3412. Seebohm, Reinhard. "Pfitzners Verhältnis zu Joseph Haydn." MHPG 34(1975): 34-54.
   3413. Truscott, Harold. "Pfitzner's orchestral music." TEMPO 104 (1973): 2-10.

PHILIPP, FRANZ (1890-1972)

   3414. Rahner, Hugo Ernst. "Zwischen Zeit und Ewigkeit." Fs. Philipp: 124-144.
   3415. Steinert, Bernhard. "Zwischen Zeit und Ewigkeit." Fs. Philipp: 103-109.

PIERNÉ, GABRIEL (1863-1937)

   3416. Luck, Ray. "An analysis of three variation sets for piano by Bizet, d'Indy and Pierné." DMA dissertation: Indiana University, 1978. No DA listing.

PIJPER, WILLEM (1894-1947)

3417. Clardy, Mary Karen King. "Compositional devices of Willem Pijper (1894-1947) and Henk Badings (b.1907) in two selected works: Pijper's *Sonata per flauto e pianoforte* (1925) and Badings' Concerto for Flute and Wind Symphony Orchestra (1963)." DMA dissertation: North Texas State University, 1980. No DA listing.

3418. Dickinson, Peter. "The instrumental music of Willem Pijper (1894-1947)." MR 24(1963): 327-332.

3419. Hoogerwerf, Frank W. "The chamber music of Willem Pijper (1894-1947)." PhD dissertation (Musicology): University of Michigan, 1974. 469 p. No DA listing.

3420. ----. "The string quartets of Willem Pijper." MR 38(1977): 44-64.

3421. Ringer, Alexander L. "Willem Pijper and the Netherlands School of the 20th century." MQ 41(1955): 427-445.

3422. Ritsema, Herbert. "The germ cell principle in the works of Willem Pijper (1894-1947)." PhD dissertation (Theory): University of Iowa, 1974. UM 75-01,247. DA XXXV.7, p.4601-A.

3423. Ryker, Harrison Clinton. "The symphonic music of Willem Pijper (1894-1947)." PhD dissertation (Musicology): University of Washington, 1972. 239 p. UM 71-24,077. DA XXXII.3, p.1556-A.

3424. Wouters, Jos. "Willem Pijper." SS 30(1967): 1-38.

PINKHAM, DANIEL (born 1923)

3425. Corzine, Michael Loyd. "The organ works of Daniel Pinkham." DMA dissertation (Performance): University of Rochester, 1979. 295 p. UM 80-05,139. DA XL.11, p.5641-A.

3426. Cox, Dennis Keith. "Aspects of the compositional styles of three selected twentieth-century American composers of choral music: Alan Hovhaness, Ron Nelson, and Daniel Pinkham." DMA dissertation: University of Missouri, 1978. No DA listing.

3427. Johnson, Marlowe W. "The choral music of Daniel Pinkham." PhD dissertation (Musicology): University of Iowa, 1968. 180 p. UM 68-16,814. DA XXIX.6, p.1917-A.

3428. ----. "The choral writing of Daniel Pinkham." ACR 8/4(1966): 1, 12, 14-16.

PISK, PAUL A. (born 1893)

3429. Collins, Thomas William. "The instrumental music of Paul A. Pisk." DMA dissertation (Performance): University of Missouri, 1972. UM 72-29,457. DA XXXIII.5, p.2408-A.

3430. Kennen, Kent. "Paul A. Pisk." ACA 9/1(1959): 7-16.

PISTON, WALTER (1894-1976)

3431. Archibald, Bruce. "Current Chronicle." MQ 59(1973): 121-125. [Concerto for Flute and Orchestra, 1971]

3432. Austin, William. "Piston's Fourth Symphony: An analysis." MR 16(1955): 120-137.

3433. Carter, Elliott. "Walter Piston." MQ 32(1946): 354-375.

3434. Donahue, Robert Laurence. "Comparative analysis of phrase structure in selected movements of the string quartets of Béla Bartók and Walter Piston." DMA dissertation: Cornell University, 1964. No DA listing.

3435. Pollack, Howard Joel. "Walter Piston and his music." PhD dissertation (Musicology): Cornell University, 1981. No DA listing.

3436. Taylor, Clifford. "Walter Piston: For his seventieth birthday." PNM 3/1(1964): 102-114.

PLATZ, ROBERT HP (born 1951)

3437. Platz, Robert HP. "Über *Schwelle* (1973-1978)." N 1(1980): 87-94.

3438. Van den Hoogen, Eckhardt. "Raumform: Formpolyphonie von Robert HP Platz." M 5(1984-1985): 220-225.

POLDOWSKI, LADY DEAN PAUL (1879-1932) [pen name of Regina Wieniawski]

3439. Brand, Myra Jean. "Poldowski (Lady Dean Paul): Her life and her song settings of French and English poetry." DMA dissertation (Vocal Performance): University of Oregon, 1979. UM 79-27,229. DA XL.6, p.2966-A.

POOLE, GEOFFREY RICHARD (born 1949)

3440. Burn, Andrew. "Geoffrey Poole: An introductory note on his music." TEMPO 145(1983): 12-18.

PONSE, LUCTOR (born 1914)

3441. Wouters, Jos. "Luctor Ponse: *Concerto da camera* with Solo Bassoon." SS 19(1964): 32-34.

PORCELIJN, DAVID (born 1947)

3442. Vermeulen, Ernst. "David Porcelijn: *Cybernetica* for Orchestra." SS 49(1971-1972): 13-22.

PORTER, COLE (1893-1964)

3443. Siebert, Lynn Laitman. "Cole Porter: An analysis of five musical comedies and a thematic catalogue of the complete works." PhD dissertation (Musicology): City University of New York, 1975. UM 75-10,762.

PORTER, QUINCY (1897-1966)

3444. Frank, Robert Eugene. "Quincy Porter: A survey of the mature style and a study of the Second Sonata for Violin and Piano." DMA dissertation (Composition): Cornell University, 1973. 128 p. No DA listing.

PORTER, TIM

3445. Head, Raymond. "Tim Porter's *The Irish Blackbird*." TEMPO 155(1985): 36-38.

FRANCIS POULENC (1899-1963)

Chamber works
3446. Poulin, Pamela. "Three stylistic traits in Poulenc's chamber works for wind instruments." PhD dissertation (Theory): University of Rochester, 1983. No DA listing.

Choral works
3447. Almond, Frank Ward. "Melody and texture in the choral works of Francis Poulenc." PhD dissertation: Florida State University, 1970. UM 71-06,956. DA XXXI.9, p.4811-A.
3448. Daniel, Keith. "The choral music of Francis Poulenc." ACR 24/1(1982): 5-36.
3449. Ebensberger, Gary Lee. "The motets of Francis Poulenc." PhD dissertation: University of Texas, 1970. No DA listing.

Dialogues des Carmelites
3450. ASO 52(1983).

Piano works
3451. Davies, Laurence. "The piano music of Poulenc." MR 33(1972): 194-203.
3452. Nelson, Jon Ray. "The piano music of Francis Poulenc." PhD dissertation: University of Washington, 1978 UM 78-20,754. DA XXXIX.5, p.2611-A.
3453. Romain, Edwin Philip. "A study of Francis Poulenc's *Fifteen Improvisations* for piano solo." DMA dissertation: University of Southern Mississippi, 1978. UM 78-18,981. DA XXXIX.4, p.1920-A.

Songs
3454. Hargrove, Guy Arnold, Jr. "Francis Poulenc's settings of Guillaume Apollinaire and Paul Eluard." PhD dissertation: University of Iowa, 1971. UM 71-22,031. DA XXXII.3, p.1550-A.
3455. Weide, Marion. "Style and imagery in the song cycles of Poulenc." PhD dissertation (Musicology): University of California, Santa Barbara, 1976. No DA listing.
3456. Wood, Vivian Poates. "Francis Poulenc's songs for voice and piano." PhD dissertation (Musicology): Washington University, 1973. UM 74-07,072. DA XXXIV.9, p.6031-A.

Other works
3457. Daniel, Keith W. *Francis Poulenc: A study of his artistic development and his musical style.* Ann Arbor: UMI Research Press, 1982.
3458. ----. "A preliminary investigation of pitch-class set analysis in the atonal and polytonal works of Milhaud and Poulenc." ITO 6/6 (1981-1983): 22-48.
3459. Werner, Warren Kent. "The harmonic style of Francis Poulenc." PhD dissertation (Theory): University of Iowa, 1966. UM 66-7234. DA XXII.3, p.794-A.

POUSSEUR, HENRI (born 1929)

3460. Lee, Marjorie Huffman. "The piano compositions of Henri Pousseur." DMA dissertation: University of Maryland, 1977. No DA listing.
3461. Pousseur, Henri. "Der Jahrmarkt von *Votre Faust.*" BOGM (1968-1969): 25-40.
3462. Witts, Dick. "Pousseur's *L'Effacement du Prince Igor.*" TEMPO 122(1977): 10-17.
3463. ----. "Report on Henri Pousseur." CT 13(19760: 13-22. [*Die Erprobung des Petrus Hebraicus*]

POWELL, MEL (born 1923)

3464. Sollberger, Harvey. "Haiku Settings." PNM 3/1(1964): 147-155.
3465. Thimmig, Leslie. "The music of Mel Powell." MQ 55(1969): 31-44.

PRAEGER, FERDINAND (1815-1891)

3466. Ryberg, James Stanley. "Four string quartets by Ferdinand Praeger: An analytical study." PhD dissertation (Theory): Northwestern University, 1978. No DA listing.

PRÉVOST, ANDRÉ (born 1934)

3467. Loranger, Pierre. "André Prévost: *Evanescence.*" CCM 4(1972): 168-172.
3468. Prévost, André. "Formulation et conséquences d'une hypothèse." CCM 1(1970): 67-79. [*Terre des hommes*]

PROKOFIEV, SERGEI (1891-1953)

The Flaming Angel
3469. Henderson, Lyn. "How *The Flaming Angel* became Prokofiev's Third Symphony." MR 40(1979): 49-52.
3470. Kellner, Hans. "Devils and angels: A study of the demonic in three twentieth-century operas." JMR 2(1976-1978): 255-272.
3471. Swarsenski, Hans. "Sergeii Prokofieff: *The Flaming Angel.*" TEMPO 39(1956): 16-27.

The Gambler
3472. Robinson, Harlow. "Dostoevsky and opera: Prokofiev's *The Gambler*." MQ 70(1984): 96-106.

Operas [see also individual titles]
3473. McAllister, Margaret Notman. "The operas of Sergei Prokofiev." PhD dissertation (Musicology): New Hall, Cambridge, 1970.

Piano works
3474. Ashley, Patricia Ruth. "Prokoviev's piano music: Line, chord and key." PhD dissertation (Theory): University of Rochester, 1963. UM 64-6375. DA XXVI.4, p.2248.
3475. Brown, Malcolm. "Prokofiev's Eighth Piano Sonata." TEMPO 70 (1964): 9-15.
3476. Chaikin, Lawrence. "The Prokofieff sonatas: A psychograph." PQ 86(1974): 8-19.
3477. Forner, Johannes. "Tradition und veränderte Struktur: Gestaltungsprinzipien im Klavierschaffen des jungen Prokofjew (geb. am 23.4.1891)." MG 16(1966): 273-279.
3478. Kinsey, David Leslie. "The piano sonatas of Serge Prokofiev: A critical study of the elements of their style." MA dissertation: Columbia University, 1959.
3479. Vlahcevic, Sonia Klosek. "Thematic-tonal organization in the piano sonatas of Sergei Prokofiev." PhD dissertation (Theory): Catholic University, 1975. UM 75-21,272. DA XXXIV.4, p.1897-A.

Symphonies [see also individual entries]
3480. Brown, Malcolm. "The symphonies of Sergei Prokofiev." PhD dissertation (Theory): Florida State University, 1967. UM 67-11,151. DA XXVIII.7, p.2706-A.
3481. Henderson, Lyn. "How *The Flaming Angel* became Prokofiev's Third Symphony." MR 40(1979): 49-52.
3482. Streller, Friedbert. "Die frühen Sinfonien Sergej Prokofjews: Ein Beitrag zu semantischer Analyse von Musik." PhD dissertation (Musicology): Berlin, 1972.

Symphony No.5
3483. Austin, William W. "Prokofiev's Fifth Symphony." MR 17(1956): 205-220.

Symphony No.7
3484. Lockspeiser, Edward. "Prokofieff's Seventh Symphony." TEMPO 37(1955): 24-27.

Other works
3485. Berka, Zdenka. "Themes of Prokofiev's early period: A melodic analysis." MM dissertation: University of Alberta, 1976.
3486. Cholopov, Juri N. "Der russische Neoklassizismus bei Sergej Prokof'ev und Dimitrij Šostakovič." JP 3(1980): 170-199.
3487. Cholopowa, W. "Zur Rhythmik Prokofjews." MG 20(1970): 372-381.

3488. Jahn, Renate. "Zum 70. Geburtstag Serge Prokofjews: Vom 'Spieler' zur 'Erzählung vom wahren Mensch'." MG 11(1961): 232-238.
3489. Samuel, Claude. *Prokofiev.* Paris: Editions du Seuil, 1960.
3490. Streller, Friedbert. *Serge Prokofiev.* Leipzig: Breitkopf und Härtel, 1960.
3491. Swarsenski, Hans. "Prokofieffs Orchesterwerke." MZ 5(1953): 41-49.
3492. ----. "Prokofieff's orchestral works." TEMPO 11(1949): 10-25.
3493. Special Issue: MZ 5(1953).

PUCCINI, GIACOMO (1858-1924)

La Bohème
3494. ASO 20(1979).
3495. John, Nicholas, ed. *Puccini: La Bohème.* London: J. Calder, 1983.

Gianni Schicchi
3496. ASO 82(1985).

Madama Butterfly
3497. ASO 56(1983).
3498. Berg, Karl Georg Maria. "Das Liebesduett aus *Madame Butterfly*: Überlegungen zur Szenendramaturgie bei Giacomo Puccini." MF 38 (1985): 183-194.
3499. John, Nicholas, ed. *Puccini: Madam Butterfly.* London: J. Calder, 1984.
3500. Krohn, Ilmari. "Puccini: *Butterfly*." Fs. Scheurleer: 181-190.

Tosca
3501. ASO 1(1977).
3502. Courtin, Michèle. *"Tosca" de Giacomo Puccini.* Paris: Aubier, 1983.
3503. John, Nicholas, ed. *Puccini: Tosca.* London: J. Calder, 1982.
3504. Leibowitz/F: 259-274.
3505. Winterhoff, Hans-Jürgen. *Analytische Untersuchungen zu Puccinis "Tosca".* Regensburg: G. Bosse, 1973.

Il Trittico [see also individual titles]
3506. Leukel, Jürgen. *Studien zu Puccinis "Il Trittico: Il Tabarro--Suor Angelica--Gianni Schicchi".* München: E. Katzbichler, 1983.

Turandot
3507. ASO 33(1981).
3508. Girardi, Michele. "*Turandot*: Il futuro interrotto del melodramma italiano." RIM 17(1982): 155-181.
3509. John, Nicholas, ed. *Puccini: Turandot.* London: J. Calder, 1984.
3510. Revers, Peter. "Analytische Betrachtungen zu Puccinis *Turandot*." OMZ 34(1979): 342-351.

Other works

3511. Ashbrook, William. *The operas of Puccini.* Ithaca: Cornell University Press, 1985.

3512. Carner, Mosco. "Debussy and Puccini." Carner: 139-147.

3513. Christen, Norbert. *Giacomo Puccini: Analytische Untersuchungen der Melodik, Harmonik und Instrumentation.* Hamburg: Verlag der Musikalienhandlung Wagner, 1978.

3514. D'Ecclesiis, Rev. Gennaro A. "The aria technique of Giacomo Puccini: A study in musico-dramatic style." PhD dissertation (Music Education): New York University, 1961. LC Mic 61-2548. DA XXII.2, p.592.

3515. Valente, Richard. *The verismo of Giacomo Puccini: From scapigliatura to expressionism.* Ann Arbor: Braun-Blumfield, 1971.

RACHMANINOFF, SERGEI (1873-1943)

Aleko

3516. Norris, Geoffrey. "Rakhmaninov's student opera." MQ 59(1973): 441-448.

Night Vigil

3517. Loftis, Eric Kenneth. "An investigation of the textural contrasts in Sergei Rachmaninov's *Night Vigil*, Opus 37." PhD dissertation: University of Southern Mississippi, 1980. No DA listing.

Piano Concertos

3518. Butzbach, Fritz. *Studien zum Klavierkonzert Nr.1 Fis-Moll Op.1 von Rachmaninov.* Regensburg: G. Bosse, 1979.

3519. Coolidge, Richard. "Architectonic technique and innovation in the Rakhmaninov piano concertos." MR 40(1979): 176-216.

3520. Yasser, Joseph. "The opening theme of Rachmaninoff's Third Piano Concerto and its liturgical prototype." MQ 55(1969): 313-328.

Preludes

3521. Baca, Richard. "A style analysis of the Thirteen Preludes, Opus 32, of Sergei Rachmaninoff." DMA dissertation (Performance): Peabody Conservatory, 1975. No DA listing.

3522. Rummenhöller, Peter. "Zum Warencharakter in der Musik: Analyse von Sergej Rachmaninovs Prelude Op.32, Nr.1." ZM 4/2(1973): 30-36.

Songs

3523. Simpson, Anne. "Dear Re: A glimpse into the six songs of Rachmaninoff's Opus 38." CMS 24/1(1984) 97-106.

Symphonies

3524. Rubin, David. "Transformations of the *Dies Irae* in Rachmaninov's Second Symphony." MR 23(1962): 132-136.

Vespers
3525. Prussing, Stephen Henry. "Compositional techniques in Rachmaninoff's *Vespers*, Op.37." PhD dissertation: Catholic University, 1980. No DA listing.

Other works
3526. Walsh, Stephen. "Sergei Rachmaninoff 1873-1943." TEMPO 195 (1973): 12-21.
3527. Yasser, Joseph. "Progressive tendencies in Rachmaninoff's music." MU 2(1948-1949): 1-22.

RADULESCU, HORATIU (born 1942)

3528. Heaton, Roger. "Horatiu Radulescu: *Sound Plasma.*" CT 26 (1983): 23-24.

RANDALL, JAMES K. (born 1929)

3529. Capalbo, Marc. "Charts." PNM 19/2(1980-1981): 309-333. [*Greek Nickle Pieces; Mead; 8va*; parts of *Sound Scroll*]

RATHAUS, KAROL (1895-1954)

3530. Schwarz, Boris. "Karol Rathaus." MQ 41(1955): 481-495.

RAVEL, MAURICE (1875-1937)

Chamber works
3531. Braun, Jürgen. *Die Thematik in dem Kammermusikwerken von Maurice Ravel*. Regensburg: G. Bosse, 1966.
3532. Fruehwald, Edwin Scott. "Harmonic organization in the large-scale instrumental chamber works of Maurice Ravel's 'style pépouillé'." MA dissertation (Musicology): University of North Carolina, 1979. [Sonata for Violin and Cello; Sonata for Violin and Piano]
3533. Sannemüller, Gerd. "Die Sonate für Violine und Violoncello von Maurice Ravel." MF 28(1975): 408-419.
3534. Wilson, Eugene N. "Form and texture in the chamber music of Debussy and Ravel." PhD dissertation (Theory): University of Washington, 1968. UM 68-12,723. DA XXIX.3, p.927-A.

Daphnis et Chloé
3535. Sannemüller, Gerd. *Maurice Ravel: Daphnis und Chloé, 1. und 2. Suite*. München: W. Fink, 1983.
3536. Schultz: 58-60.

L'Enfant et les sortilèges
3537. Green, Marcia S. "Ravel and Krenek: Cosmic music makers." CMS 24/2(1984): 96-104.

Gaspard de la nuit
    3538. Pohl, Norma Davis. "*Gaspard de la nuit* by Maurice Ravel: A theoretical and performance analysis." PhD dissertation: Washington University, 1978. 283 p.

Jeux d'eau
    3539. Light, Edwin Hamilton. "Ravel's *Jeux d'eau*." DMA dissertation (Performance): Boston University, 1983. No DA listing.

Ma Mère l'oye
    3540. Sannemüller, Gerd. "*Ma Mère l'oye* von Maurice Ravel: Fünf Stücke für Kinder." MB 6(1974): 174-178.

Piano works [see also individual titles]
    3541. Howat, Roy. "Debussy, Ravel and Bartók: Towards some new concepts of form." ML 58(1977): 285-293. [*Oiseaux tristes* from *Miroirs*]
    3542. Keil, Werner. *Untersuchungen zur Entwicklung des frühen Klaveristils von Debussy und Ravel.* Wiesbaden: Breitkopf und Härtel, 1982.
    3543. Mies, Paul. "Widmungsstücke mit Buchstaben-Motto bei Debussy und Ravel." SZM 25(1962): 363-368. [*Menuet sur le nom d'Haydn; Berceuse sur le nom de Fauré*]

Rapsodie espagnole
    3544. Sannemüller, Gerd. "Die *Rapsodie espagnole* von Maurice Ravel." MB 11(1979): 675-682.

Shéhérazade
    3545. Schultz: 45-48. [*Asie*]

Sonatine
    3546. Dommel-Diény, Amy. "L'harmonie de Ravel vue à travers le second mouvement de la Sonatine." SMZ 117(1977): 4-10.

Songs
    3547. Gronquist, Robert. "Ravel's *Trois poèmes de Stéphane Mallarmé*." MQ 64(1978): 507-523.
    3548. Hirsbrunner, Theo. "Zu Debussys und Ravels Malarmé-Vertonungen." AM 35(1978): 81-103.
    3549. Orenstein, Arbie. "The vocal works of Maurice Ravel." PhD dissertation (Musicology): Columbia University, 1968. UM 68-16,924. DA XXIX.6, p.1918-A.

Valses nobles et sentimentales
    3550. McCrae, Elizabeth. "Ravel's *Valses nobles et sentimentales*: Analysis, stylistic considerations, performance problems." DMA dissertation (Performance): Boston University, 1974. 196 p. UM 74-20,474. DA XXXV.3, p.1688-A.
    3551. Pepin, M. Natalie. "Dance and jazz elements in the piano music of Maurice Ravel." DMA dissertation (Performance): Boston University, 1972. 289 p. UM 72-25,126. DA XXXIII.4, p.1772-A.

Other works

3552. Hopkins, James F. "Ravel's orchestral transcription technique." PhD dissertation (Composition): Princeton University, 1969. UM 69-18,167. DA XXX.6, p.2560-A.

3553. Landormy, Paul. "Maurice Ravel (1875-1937)." MQ 25(1939): 430-431.

3554. Mueller, Robert Earl. "The concept of tonality in impressionist music, based on the works of Debussy and Ravel." PhD dissertation (Theory): Indiana University, 1954. UM 10,153. DA XIV.11, p.2088.

3555. Orenstein, Arbie. "Maurice Ravel's creative process." MQ 53 (1967): 467-481.

3556. Weiss-Aigner, Günter. "Eine Sonderform der Skalenbildung in der Musik Ravels." MF 25(1972): 323-326.

RAWSTHORNE, ALAN (1905-1971)

3557. Allison, Rees Stephen. "The piano works of Alan Rawsthorne (until 1968)." PhD dissertation (Performance): Washington University, 1970. UM 70-26,844. DA XXXI.7, p.3578-A.

3558. Cooper, Martin. "Current Chronicle." MQ 35(1949): 305-311.

3559. Dickinson, A.E.F. "The progress of Alan Rawsthorne." MR 12(1951): 87-104.

REBIKOV, VLADIMIR (1866-1920)

3560. Dale, William Henry. "A study of the musico-psychological dramas of Vladimir Ivanovitch Rebikov." PhD dissertation (Musicology): University of Southern California, 1955. 611 p. UM 1761. No DA listing.

REDA, SIEGFIED (1916-1968)

3561. Hattlestad, Roger Merle. "Siegfried Reda's *Vorspiele zu den Psalm-Liedern*." DMA dissertation (Performance): University of Iowa, 1974. UM 75-1285. DA XXXV.7, p.4586-7-A.

REGER, MAX (1873-1916)

Chamber works

3562. Fischer, Kurt von. "Bemerkungen zum ersten Satz des Klaviertrios Op.102 von Max Reger." STU 9(1980): 151-159.

3563. Möller, Martin. *Untersuchungen zur Satztechnik Max Regers: Studien an den Kopfsätzen der Kammermusikwerke*. Wiesbaden: Breitkopf und Härtel, 1980.

3564. Wilke, Rainer. *Brahms, Reger, Schönberg, Streichquartette: Motivisch-thematische Prozesse und formale Gestalt*. Hamburg: Wagner, 1980.

Choral works

3565. Troskie, Albert J.J. "Die Tonsymbolik in Regers Chorwerken." Fs. Schreiber: 119-125.

Clarinet Quintet

3566. Häfner, Roland. *Max Reger: Klarinettenquintett, Op.146.* München: W. Fink, 1982.

3567. Kühn, Hellmut. "Sang und Gegensang: Zu Regers Klarinettenquintett Opus 146." NZM 134(1973): 141-143. [Also MB 5(1973): 670-672]

Orchestral works

3568. Ehrenforth, Karl Heinrich. "Max Reger: *Variationen und Fuge über ein Thema von W. A. Mozart* für grosses Orchester, Op.132 (1914)." MB 5(1973): 673-676.

Organ works

3569. Barker, John Wesley. "The organ works of Max Reger." MMA 1(1966): 56-73. [Also in Fs. Bishop: 56-73]

3570. Haupt, Helmut. "Max Regers letztes Orgelwerk Op.135b." *Mitteilungen des Max-Regers-Instituts* 17(1968): 6-12.

3571. ----. "Max Regers symphonisches Orgelschaffen: *Introduktion, Passacaglia und Fugue* Op.127." MK 47(1977): 225-232.

3572. ----. "*Symphonische Phantasie und Fugue* Op.57: Ein Markstein in Max Regers Orgelschaffen." MK 49(1979): 120-126.

3573. Kalkoff, Artur. *Das Orgelschaffen Max Regers im Lichte der deutschen Orgelneurungsbewegung.* Kassel: Bärenreiter, 1950.

3574. Manz, André. "Max Reger als Orgelkomponist: 'Extremer Fortschrittsmann'?" Fs. Schreiber: 105-117.

3575. Sievers, Gerd. "Franz Liszts Legende *Der Heilige Franziskus von Paul auf den Wogen schreitend* für Klavier in Max Regers Bearbeitung für die Orgel." Fs. Schreiber: 9-27.

3576. Walter, Rudolf. "Max Regers Choralvorspiele." KJ 40(1956): 127-138.

3577. Wuensch, Gerhard. "Max Regers *Symphonische Phantasie und Fuge* Opus 57: Betrachtungen zum musikalischen Hörerlebnis." Fs. Schenk: 237-254.

Piano works

3578. Holliman, Janesetta. "A stylistic study of Max Reger's solo piano variations and fugues on themes by Johann Sebastian Bach and Georg Philipp Telemann." PhD dissertation (Music Education): New York University, 1973. 97 p. UM 76-01,739. DA XXXVI.7, p.4095-A.

3579. Hopkins, William Thomas. "The short piano compositions of Max Reger (1873-1916)." PhD dissertation (Musicology): Indiana University, 1971. 243 p. UM 72-15,914. DA XXXII.11, p.6477-8-A.

3580. Kranz, Maria Hinrichs. "Max Reger's piano variations on themes of Bach, Beethoven and Telemann." DMA dissertation (Performance): American Conservatory of Music, 1985. 75 p. No DA listing.

3581. Lissa, Zofia. "Max Regers Metamorphosen der *Berceuse* Op.57 von Frédéric Chopin." Fs. Wiener: 35-40. [Also Fs. Federov/65: 79-83] [Piano pieces Op.82, No.12 and Op.143, No.9]

Songs

3582. Wehmeyer, Grete. *Max Reger als Liederkomponist: Ein Beitrag zum Problem der Wort-Ton-Beziehung.* Regensburg: G. Bosse, 1955.

Violin Concerto

3583. Weiss-Aigner, Günter. "Max Reger und die Tradition: Zum Violinkonzert A-Dur Op.101." NZM 135(1974): 614-620.

Other works

3584. Gatscher, Emanuel. *Die Fugentechnik Max Regers in ihrer Entwicklung.* Stuttgart: J. Engelhorns Nachfolge, 1925.

3585. Grabner, Hermann. *Regers Harmonik.* 2d ed. Wiesbaden: Breitkopf und Härtel, 1961.

3586. Herbst, Wolfgang. *"Ben marcato*: Max Regers Bemühungen um die Erkennbarkeit musikalischer Strukturen." Fs. Walcha: 107-113.

3587. Kaufmann, Harold. "Ausholung der Tonalität bei Reger." NZM 128(1967): 28-33.

3588. Sievers, Gerd. "Die Harmonik im Werk Max Regers." Fs. Reger: 55-82.

3589. Zingerle, Hans. "Chromatische Harmonik bei Brahms und Reger: Ein Vergleich." SZM 27(1966): 151-185.

REICH, STEVE (born 1936)

3590. McGuire, John. "Steve Reich: *Drumming*: ein Werkkommentar." N 1(1980): 142-148.

3591. ----. "Steve Reich: Octet: ein Werkkommentar." N 1(1980): 149-155.

3592. Mertens: 47-66.

3593. Pardey, Wolfgang. "Repetitive Musik von Steve Reich: Analysen, Interpretation und didaktische Ansätze." MB 14/3(1982): 153-162.

3594. Potter, Keith. "The recent phases of Steve Reich." CT 29 (1985): 28-34.

3595. Reich, Steve. *Écrits et entretiens sur la musique.* Paris: Christian Bourgeois, 1981.

3596. Schwarz, K. Robert. "Steve Reich: Music as a gradual process." PNM 19/2(1980-1981): 373-392; 20(1981-1982): 225-286.

3597. Scott, Stephen. "The music of Steve Reich." NW 6(1974): 21-28.

REICHA, ANTON (1770-1836)

3598. Laing, Millard M. "Anton Reicha's quintets for flute, oboe, clarinet, horn and bassoon." EdD dissertation (Education): University of Michigan, 1952. UM 3697. DA XXI.4, p.432.

3599. Morris, Mellasenah Young. "A style analysis of the Thirty-Six Fugues for Piano, Opus 36, by Anton Reicha." DMA dissertation (Piano): Peabody Conservatory, 1980. 141 p. UM 80-21,959. DA XLI.4, p.1274-A.

RIEMANN, ARIBERT (born 1936)

3600. Vogt: 409- [*Six Poems by Sylvia Plath* (1975)]

RENNER, JOSEPH (1868-1934)

3601. Kraus, Eberhard. "Der gregorianische Choral im Orgelschaffen der Regensburg Domorganisten Joseph Hanisch (1812-1892) und Joseph Renner (1868-1934)." Fs. F.Haberl: 151-167.

REUBKE, FRIEDRICH JULIUS (1834-1858)

3602. Chorzempa, Daniel Walter. "Julius Reubke: Life and works." PhD dissertation (Musicology): University of Minnesota, 1971. UM 71-00,343. DA XXXII.6, p.3347.
3603. Keller, Hermann. "Der Orgelkomponist Julius Reubke." MK 29 (1959): 35-39.
3604. Songayllo, Raymond. "A neglected masterpiece." JALS 18(1985): 122-128. [Piano Sonata in B-Flat Minor]

REUTER, FRITZ (1896-1963)

3605. Wichtmann, Kurt. "Fritz Reuters *Sechs Lieder auf Gedichte von Louis Fürnberg*." MG 13(1963): 169-171.

REUTTER, HERMANN (1900-1985)

3606. Reutter, Hermann. "Meine Lieder-Zyklen auf Gedichte von Lorca." MELOS 30(1963): 283-291.

RHEINBERGER, JOSEPH (1839-1901)

3607. Hunsberger, David Ritchie. "Fugal style in the organ sonatas and fughettas of Josef Rheinberger." PhD dissertation: Washington University, 1979. 170 p. UM 79-18,602. DA XL.2, p.529-A.

RIDOUT, GEODFREY (born 1918)

3608. Gilpin, Wayne George William. "Godfrey Ridout: Choral music with orchestra." MM dissertation: University of Alberta, 1978.

RIEDL, JOSEF ANTON (born 1929)

3609. Frisius, Rudolf. "Variable Lautkonstellationen: Variable Kompositionen: Kompositorische und metakompositorische Tendenzen bei Josef Anton Riedl: Anmerkungen zu seinen Lautgedichten." N 5(1884-1985): 169-185.
3610. Zeller, Hans Rudolf. "Experimentelle Klangerzeugung und Instrument: Versuch über Joseph Anton Riedl." MTX 3(1984): 46-57.
3611. ----. "Soli für Schlagzeug: Unbekannte(re)s von Josef Anton Riedl." N 5(1984-1985): 151-168.

RIEGGER, WALLINGFORD (1885-1961)

3612. Buccheri, Elizabeth C. "The piano chamber music of Wallingford Riegger." DMA dissertation (Performance): University of Rochester, 1978. UM 79-15,037. DA XL.2, p.524-A.

3613. Freeman, Paul D. "The compositional technique of Wallingford Riegger as seen in seven major twelve-tone works." PhD dissertation (Theory): University of Rochester, 1963. 335 p. UM 69-4146. DA XXXI.6, p.2955-A.

3614. Gatewood, Dwight Dean, Jr. "Wallingford Riegger: A biography and analysis of selected works." PhD dissertation: George Peabody College for Teachers, 1970. UM 71-4260. DA XXXI.9, p.4817-A.

3615. Goldman, Richard Franko. "Current Chronicle." MQ 34(1948): 594-599. [Third Symphony]

3616. ----. "The music of Wallingford Riegger." MQ 36(1950): 39-61.

3617. Ott, Leonard William. "An analysis of the later orchestral style of Wallingford Riegger." PhD dissertation: Michigan State University, 1970. UM 71-18,265. DA XXXII.1, p.476-A.

3618. Savage, Newell Gene. "Structure and cadence in the music of Wallingford Riegger." PhD dissertation: Stanford University, 1972. 281 p. UM 72-16,788. DA XXXII.12, p.7032-A.

3619. Schmoll, Joseph Benjamin. "An analytical study of the principal instrumental compositions of Wallingford Riegger." PhD dissertation: Northwestern University, 1954. UM 10,318. DA XV.1, p.130.

RIES, FERDINAND (1784-1838)

3620. Darbellay, Etienne. "Epigonalité ou originalité? Les Sonates pour piano seul de Ferdinand Ries (1784-1838)." SBM 4(1980): 51-101.

RIESCO, CARLOS (born 1925)

3621. Curtis, Brandt B. "Rafael Alberti and Chilean composers." DMA dissertation (Voice): Indiana University, 1977. No DA listing. [*Sobre los angeles*]

RIHM, WOLFGANG (born 1952)

3622. Andraschke, Peter. "Traditionsmomente in Kompositionen von Christobal Halffter, Klaus Huber und Wolfgang Rihm." Brinkmann: 130-152.

3623. Frisius, Rudolf. "Werk und Werkzyklus: Bemerkungen zum *Chiffre*-Zyklus von Wolfgang Rihm." MTX 11(1985): 17-20.

3624. Heister, Hanns-Werner. "Sackgasse oder Ausweg aus dem Elfenbeinturm? Zur musikalischen Sprache in Wolfgang Rihms *Jakob Lenz*." BM 24(1982): 3-16.

3625. Schmierer, Elisabeth. "Wolfgang Rihm: Klavierstück Nr.5 (*Tombeau*)." N 1(1980): 110-113.

RILEY, TERRY (born 1935)

    3626. Mertens: 35-46.

RIMSKY-KORSAKOV, NIKOLAY (1844-1908)

    3627. Abraham, Gerald. "*Pskovityanka*: The original version of Rimsky-Korsakov's first opera." Abraham: 68-82. [Also in MQ 54(1968): 58-73]

    3628. ----. "Rimsky-Korsakov's Gogol operas." ML 21(1931): 242-452.

    3629. Feinberg, Saul. "Rimsky-Korsakov's Suite from *Le Coq d'or*." MR 30(1969): 47-64.

    3630. Griffiths, Steven A. K. "A critical study of the music of Rimsky-Korsakov up to 1890." PhD dissertation (Musicology): Sheffield, 1982.

    3631. Lischké, André. "Les Leitmotive de *Snegourotchka* analysés par Rimsky-Korsakov." RDM 65(1979): 51-75. [*The Snow Maiden*]

    3632. Slonimskij, S. "Die lebendige, moderne Kunst Rimski-Korsakows." *Kunst und Literatur* 17/12(1969): 1307-1316.

    3633. Taruskin.

RISSET, JEAN-CLAUDE (born 1936)

    3634. Cope: 198-202. [*Inharmonic Soundscapes*]

    3635. Koblyakov, Lev. "Jean-Claude Risset: *Songes* (1979)(9')." CMR 1/1(1984-1985): 171-173.

    3636. Lorrain, Denis. *"Inharmoniques": Analyse de la bande magnetique de l'oeuvre de Jean-Claude Risset*. Rapports IRCAM 26/80. Paris: Centre Georges Pompidou, 1980.

RITTER, PETER (1763-1846)

    3637. Elsen, Josephine C. "The instrumental works of Peter Ritter (1763-1846)." PhD dissertation (Music History and Literature): Northwestern University, 1967. UM 67-15,226. DA XXVIII.7, p.2710.

    3638. Jessel, Sister Mary Lisa, O.P. "The vocal works of Peter Ritter (1763-1846)." PhD dissertation (Musicology): Catholic University, 1962. UM 62-3793. DA XXIII.4, p.1381-2.

ROCHBERG, GEORGE (born 1918)

    3639. Buccheri.

    3640. Johnson. [*Blake Songs*]

    3641. Reise, Jay. "Rochberg the progressive." PNM 19/2(1980-1981): 395-407. [Third String Quartet]

    3642. Ringer, Alexander L. "Current Chronicle." MQ 58(1972): 128-132. [Third Symphony; *Sacred Song of Reconciliation; David the Psalmist; Songs in Praise of Krishna*]

    3643. ----. "The music of George Rochberg." MQ 52(1966): 409-430.

3644. Sams, Carol Lee. "Solo vocal writing in selected works of Berio, Crumb and Rochberg." DMA dissertation (Performance): University of Washington, 1975. UM 76-17,610. DA XXXVII.2, p.685-A.

3645. Smith, Joan Templar. "The string quartets of George Rochberg." PhD dissertation (Theory): University of Rochester, 1976. 331 p. UM 76-21,657. DA XXXVII.5, p.2488-A.

RODGERS, RICHARD (1902-1979)

3646. Kaye, Milton. "Richard Rodgers: A comparative melody analysis of his songs with Hart and Hammerstein lyrics." EdD dissertation (Music Education): New York Univerity, 1969. 497 p. UM 70-15,995. DA XXXI.3, p.1310-A.

ROGATIS, PASCUAL DE (1881-1980)

3647. Kuss, Malena. "*Huemac* by Pascual de Rogatis: Native identity in the Argentine lyric theater." Y 10(1974): 68-87.

ROGERS, BERNARD (1893-1968)

3648. Diamond, David. "Bernard Rogers." MQ 33(1947): 207-227.

3649. Fox, Charles Warren. "Current Chronicle." MQ 34(1948): 415-417. [Symphony No.4]

3650. Intili, Dominic Joseph. "Text-music relationships in the large choral works of Bernard Rogers." PhD dissertation (Musicology): Case-Western Reserve University, 1977. UM 77-18,826. DA XXXVIII.4, p.1726-A.

ROPARTZ, JOSEPH-GUY MARIE (1864-1955)

3651. Maillard, Jean. "Guy Ropartz, chantre d'armor." RM 324-326 (1979): 107-113.

3652. ----. "Guy Ropartz: Les Six symphonies: Étude analytique." RM 324-325-326(1979): 118-132.

3653. ----. "Guy Ropartz: Un Drame de l'exil: *Le Pays* (1912)." RM 324-325-326(1979): 114-117.

ROREM, NED (born 1923)

3654. Davis, Deborah Louise Bodwin. "The choral works of Ned Rorem." PhD dissertation: Michigan State University, 1978. No DA listing.

3655. Griffiths, Richard Lyle. "Ned Rorem: Music for chorus and orchestra." DMA dissertation: University of Washington, 1979. No DA listing.

3656. Johnson, Bret. "Still sings the voice: A portrait of Ned Rorem." TEMPO 153(1985): 7-12.

3657. Miller, Philip Lieson. "The songs of Ned Rorem." TEMPO 127(1978): 25-81.

3658. North, William Sills. "Ned Rorem as a twentieth-century song composer." DMA dissertation: University of Illinois, 1965. No DA listing.

3659. Pilar, Lillian Nobleza. "The vocal style of Ned Rorem in the song cycle *Poems of Love and the Rain*." PhD dissertation: Indiana University, 1972. No DA listing.

ROSENFELD, GERHARD (born 1931)

3660. Kneipel, Eberhard. "Cellokonzert von Gerhard Rosenfeld." MG 20(1970): 186-191.

ROSSINI, GIOACCHINO (1792-1868)

3661. ASO 37(1981). [*Le Barbier de Seville*]
3662. ASO 81(1985). [*Le Siège de Corinthe*]
3663. Conati, Marcello. "Between past and future: The dramatic world of Rossini in *Mosè in Egitto* and *Moïse et Pharaon*." NCM 4(1980): 32-48.
3664. Gerhard, Anselm. "L'Eroe titubante e il finale aperto: Un Dilemma insolubile nel *Guillaume Tell* di Rossini." RIM 19(1984): 113-130.
3665. Gossett, Philip. "The 'candeur virginale' of *Tancredi*." MT 172 (1971): 326-329.
3666. ----. "The overtures of Rossini." NCM 3(1979-1980): 3-31.
3667. John, Nicholas, ed. *Rossini: La Cenerentola*. London: J. Calder, 1981.
3668. Tartak, Marvin H. "The Italian comic operas of Rossini." PhD dissertation (Musicology): University of California at Berkeley, 1968. UM 69-708. DA XXIX.9, p.3176-A.

ROUSSEL, ALBERT (1869-1937)

3669. Doskey, Henry. "The piano music of Albert Roussel." DM dissertation (Piano): Indiana University, 1980. No DA listing.
3670. Eddins, John M. "The symphonic music of Albert Roussel." PhD dissertation (Theory): Florida State University, 1967. UM 67-289. DA XXVII.11, p.3890-A.
3671. Stevens, James William. "The complete songs for voice and piano of Albert Roussel." DMA dissertation (Performance): University of Maryland, 1976. UM 77-13,033. DA XXXVII.12, p.7399-A.

ROUTH, FRANCIS (born 1927)

3672. Routh, Francis. "A sacred tetralogy." TEMPO 119(1976): 23-29.

RÓZSA, MIKLÓS (born 1907)

3673. Larson.

RUBBRA, EDMUND (1901-1980)

Chamber works
3674. Rubbra, Edmund. "String Quartet No.2 in E Flat, Op.73." MR 14(1953): 36-44.

Choral works
3675. Lyne, Gregory Kent. "The choral works of Edmund Rubbra." DMA dissertation (Conducting): University of Northern Colorado, 1976. UM 77-11,074. DA XXXVII.11, p.6830-A.

Piano works
3676. Dawney, Michael. "Edmund Rubbra and the piano." MR 31 (1970): 241-248.

Symphonies
3677. Hutchings, Arthur. "Rubbra's Third Symphony: A study of its texture." MR 2(1941): 14-28.
3678. Mason, Colin. "Rubbra's four symphonies." MR 8(1947): 131-139.
3679. Mellers, W. H. "Rubbra and the dominant seventh: Notes on an English symphony." MR 4(1943): 145-156.
3680. Payne, Elsie. "Rubbra's Sixth Symphony." MMR 85(1955): 201-207.
3681. Rubbra, Edmund. "Symphony No.5 in B Flat, Op.63." MR 10(1949): 26-35.

Other works
3682. Payne, Elsie. "Rubbra's contrapuntal textures." MMR 84(1954): 143-150.
3683. ----. "Some aspects of Rubbra's style." MR 16(1955): 198-217.

RUDIN, ANDREW

3684. Chittum, Donald. "Current Chronicle." MQ 55(1969): 99-102. [*Tragoedia*]

RUGGLES, CARL (1876-1971)

Angels
3685. Dombek, Stephen. "A study of harmonic interrelationships and sonority types in Carl Ruggles' *Angels*." ITR 4/1(1980-1981): 29-44.
3686. Ziffrin, Marilyn J. "*Angels*: Two views." MR 29(1968): 184-196.

Evocations for Piano
3687. Chapman, Alan. "A theory of harmonic structures for non-tonal music." PhD disserttion (Musicology): Yale University, 1978. 368 p. UM 78-18,589. DA XXXIX.4, p.1914-A.
3688. Gilbert, Steven E. "The 'twelve-tone' system of Carl Ruggles: A study of the *Evocations* for Piano." JMT 14/1(1970): 68-91.

Sun-Treader
3689. Gilbert, Steven E. "Carl Ruggles and total chromaticism." Y 7 (1971): 43-50.

Other works
3690. Babcock, David. "Carl Ruggles: Two early works and *Sun-Treader.*" TEMPO 135(1980): 3-12.
3691. Gilbert, Steven E. "Carl Ruggles (1876-1971): An appreciation." PNM 11/1(1972): 224-232. [*Evocations; Sun-Treader; Organum for Orchestra*]
3692. Harrison, Lou. "Carl Ruggles." SCORE 12(1955): 15-26.
3693. Kirkpatrick, John. "The evolution of Carl Ruggles." PNM 6/2(1968): 144-166.
3694. Peterson, Thomas E. "The music of Carl Ruggles." PhD dissertation (Musicology): University of Washington, 1967. UM 67-210. DA XXVIII.5, p.1850-1-A.
3695. Tenney, James. "The chronological development of Carl Ruggles' melodic style." PNM 16/1(1977): 36-69.

RUSSELL, ARMAND (born 1932)

3696. Russell, Armand. *"Themes and Fantasia* (Armand Russell): Analysis by the composer, edited by Dr. James Neilson." JBR 14/1(1978-1979): 50-53.

RZEWSKI, FREDERIC (born 1938)

3697. Cope. [*Coming Together* (1972)]
3698. Oehlschlägel, Reinhard. "Ein Anti-Kriegstuck: *Les Perses* von Frederic Rzewski." MTX 11(1985): 28-31.
3699. Sherr, Larry. "Vereinigung der Vielfalt: *The People United Will Never Be Defeated!* von Frederic Rzewski." MTX 1(1985): 38-48.

SAINT-SAËNS, CAMILLE (1835-1921)

3700. ASO 15(1978). [*Samson et Dalila*]
3701. Fallon, Daniel. "The symphonies and symphonic poems of Camille Saint-Saëns." PhD dissertation (Music History): Yale University, 1973. 498 p. UM 74-10,672. DA XXXIV.1, p.7266-A.
3702. Pollei, Paul C. "Lisztian piano virtuoso style in the piano concerti of Camille Saint-Saëns." JALS 7(1980): 59-79.
3703. Scherperel, Loretta Fox. "The solo organ works of Camille Saint-Saëns." DMA dissertation: University of Rochester, 1978. 179 p. No DA listing.
3704. Stegemann, Michael. "Die Solokonzertwerke von Camille Saint-Saëns." PhD dissertation (Musicology): Münster, 1981.

SAMINSKY, LAZARE (1882-1959)

3705. Slonimsky, Nicolas. "Lazare Saminsky." MM 12(1935): 69-72.

SANDI, LUIS (born 1905)

3706. Gomez, Leslie M. "The choral music of Luis Sandi (1905-   )."
DMA dissertation: Southwestern Baptist Theological Seminary, 1984. No
DA listing.

SATIE, ERIK (1866-1925)

Musique d'ameublement
3707. Blickhan, Charles Timothy. "Erik Satie: *Musique
d'ameublement*." DMA dissertation (Composition): University of Illinois,
1976. UM 77-08,940. Da XXXVII.10, p.6127-A.

Sports et divertissements
3708. Porter, David H. "Recurrent motifs in Erik Satie's *Sports et
divertissements*." MR 39(1978): 227-230.

Trois gymnopédies
3709. Boaz, Mildred Meyer. "T.S. Eliot and music: A study of the
development of musical structures in selected poems by T.S. Eliot and
music by Erik Satie, Igor Stravinsky, and Béla Bartók." PhD dissertation
(Literature): University of Illinois, 1977. No DA listing.
3710. Geeraert, Nicole. "Erik Satie: *3 gymnopédies*." NZM 146/4
(1985): 32-35.

Other works
3711. Austin, William W. "The rhythm of Satie and 'Oriental timeless-
ness'." MMA 13(1984): 97-111. [*Gnossienne* No.3; *Uspud; Le Fils des
étoiles; Prélude de la porte héroïque du ciel*]
3712. Dickinson, Peter. "Erik Satie (1866-1925)." MR 28(1967):
139-146.
3713. Gillmor, Alan. "Satie, Cage, and the new asceticism." CAUSM
5/2(1975): 47-66. [Also CT 25(1982): 15-20] [*Le Fils des étoiles;
Vexations*]
3714. Gowers, Patrick. "Satie's Rose Croix music (1891-1895)."
PRMA 92(1965-1966): 1-25.
3715. Koon, Margery A. "Aspects of harmonic structure in piano
works of Erik Satie." DMA dissertation (Performance): University of
Wisconsin, 1974. UM 74-19,340. DA XXXV.5, p.3038-A.
3716. Wehmeyer, Grete. *Erik Satie*. Regensburg: G. Bosse, 1974.
3717. ----. "Saties Instantaneismus." Fs. Fellerer/70: 626-639.

SAUGUET, HENRI (born 1901)

3718. Bril, France-Yvonne. "Henri Sauguet et la musique lyrique."
RM 361-362-363(1983): 139-149.
3719. Hofmann, André. "Les Ballets." RM 361-362-363(1983):
155-169.
3720. Holstein, Jean-Paul. "Les Symphonies." RM 361-362-363(1983):
185-210.
3721. Kniesner. [Piano Sonata in D Major]

3722. Mari, Pierrette. "Aperçu esthétique." RM 361-362-363(1983): 131-137.

3723. Robert, Frederic. "Les Mélodies d'Henri Sauguet." RM 361-363 (1983): 173-183.

SCHACHT, THEODOR VON (1748-1823)

3724. Färber, Sigfrid. "Der fürstlich Thorn und taxissche Hofkomponist Theodor von Schacht und seine Opernwerke." *Studien zur Musikgeschichte der Stadt Regensburg I*, ed. Hermann Beck. Regensburger Beiträge zur Musikwissenschaft 6. Regensburg: G. Bosse, 1979: 11-122.

SCHAEFFER, PIERRE (born 1910)

3725. Wehinger, Rainer. "Belebte Klänge: Analytische Skizze von P. Schaeffers *Étude aux sons animés*." MB 11(1979): 746-751.

SCHAFER, R. MURRAY (born 1933)

3726. Adams, Stephen. *R. Murray Schafer*. Toronto: University of Toronto Press, 1983.

3727. Anhalt: 247-252. [*In Search of Zoroaster*]

3728. Mather, Bruce. "Notes sur *Requiems for the Party-Girl* de Schafer." CCM 1(1970): 91-97.

3729. Schafer, R. Murray. "Notes for the stage work *Loving* (1965)." CCM 8(1974): 9-26.

SCHÄFFER, BOGUSLAW (born 1929)

3730. Fessmann, Klaus. "Bergson zu Klang gebracht: Beobachtungen zur *Bergsoniana* von Boguslaw Schäffer." Melos/NZM 3(1977): 28-32.

3731. Hubisz, Boguslawa. "Boguslaw Schäffer's new composition." PM 12/2(1977): 5-10. [*Missa elettronica*]

SCHAT, PETER (born 1935)

3732. Baaren, Kees van. "Peter Schat: *Entelechy No.1* for 5 Groups of Instruments." SS 9(1961): 8-12.

3733. Samama, Leo. "Symphony No.1: A short analysis." KN 9(1979): 34-42.

3734. Schat, Peter. "*Monkey Subdues the White-Bone Demon*: The development of characters composed." KN 12(1980): 17-30.

3735. ----. "Peter Schat's Symphony No.1." KN 9(1979): 31-34.

3736. Schuyt, Nico. "Peter Schat: *Improvisations and Symphonies* for Wind Quintet." SS 7(1961): 12-19.

SCHENKER, FRIEDRICH (born 1942)

3737. Schneider, Frank. "Analyse: *Epitaph für Neruda* von Friedrich Schenker." MG 25(1975): 269-274.

3738. ----. "Ein Appell zur Wachsamkeit: Friedrich Schenkers *Fanal Spanien 1936*." MTX 12(1985): 4-6.

SCHMIDT, CHRISTFRIED (born 1932)

3739. Hansen, Mathias. "Die Analyse: Violoncellokonzerte von Paul-Heinz Dietrich, Siegfried Matthus und Christfried Schmidt." MG 29 (1979): 591-599.

SCHMIDT, FRANZ (1874-1939)

Das Buch mit sieben Siegeln
3740. Blasl, Franz. "*Das Buch mit sieben Siegeln* von Franz Schmidt." ME 18(1964): 63-67, 107-115, 157-164, 210-215.
3741. Wickes, Lewis. "Franz Schmidt's oratorio *The Book with Seven Seals*." MMA 1(1966): 37-55. [Also in Fs. Bishop: 37-55]

Organ works
3742. Nemeth, Carl. "Studien zur Tokkata und Fuge As-Dur von Franz Schmidt." ME 12(1958): 79-87.
3743. Rapf, Kurt. "Franz Schmidt und die Orgel." ME 28 (1974-1975): 3-8.
3744. Scholz, Rudolf. "Die Orgeltoccata in C-Dur von Franz Schmidt." ME 22(1968): 155-160, 25(1969): 206-210.
3745. ----. *Die Orgelwerke von Franz Schmidt: Strukturelle und kompositions-technische Untersuchungen an seinen Orgelwerken mit Fugen.* Wien: Notring, 1971.

Symphonies
3746. Wildner, Johannes. "Die Symphonien von Franz Schmidt." PhD dissertation (Musicology): Universität Wien, 1979.

Other works
3747. Herrmann, Hellmut. "Franz Schmidts Harmonik." OMZ 29(1974): 534-540.
3748. Neuman, Konrad. "Folkloristischen Einflüsse in den Werken Franz Schmidts." OMZ 24(1969): 26-30. [*Variationen über ein Husarenlied*]
3749. Special Issue: OMZ 29/11(1974).

SCHNEBEL, DIETER (born 1930)

3750. Dibelius, Ulrich. "Vision zum Weltenbrand: Zu Dieter Schnebel: *Jowaegerli*." MTX 1(1983): 6-8.
3751. Karkoschka, Erhard. "Schnebels Musik zum Lesen." MELOS 41 (1974): 350-364. [Mo-No]
3752. Rummenhöller, Peter. "Möglichkeiter neuster Chormusik." *Der Einfluss der technischen Mittler auf die Musikerziehung unserer Zeit.* Mainz: Schott, 1968: 311-317. [*Deuteronomium 31,6*]
3753. Stoianowa, Iwanka. "Verbe et son: 'Centre et absence': Sur *Cummings ist der Dichter* de Boulez, *O King* de Berio, et *Für Stimmen ... Missa est* de Schnebel." MJ 16(1974): 79-102.

3754. Zeller, Hans Rudolf. "Choralbearbeitung als Arbeitsprozess."
MELOS 40(1973): 79-103. [Choralvorspielen]

SCHNITZLER, ARTHUR

3755. Green, Jon Dean. "The impact of musical theme and structure
on the meaning and dramatic unity of selected works by Arthur Schnitzler." PhD dissertation (Humanities): Syracuse University, 1972. UM
72-20,334. DA XXXIII.1, p.312-A.

SCHOECK, OTHMAR (1886-1957)

Festlicher Hymnus
3756. Vogel, Werner. "Othmar Schoecks *Festlicher Hymnus*." SMZ 91
(1951): 237-242.

Penthesilea
3757. Eidenbenz, Richard. "Über Harmonik und tonale Einheit in
Othmar Schoecks *Penthesilea*." SJM 4(1929): 94-130.
3758. Schuh, Willi. "Marginalien zu Othmar Schoecks *Penthesilea-*
Melodik." SMZ 108(1968): 167-173.

Ritornelle und Fughetten
3759. Andreae, Hans. "Othmar Schoecks *Ritornelle und Fughetten*:
Eine pädagogische Parallel zu Bach's *Wohltempierten Klavier*." SMZ 101
(1961): 222-228.

Schloss Dürande
3760. Schuh, Willi. "Idee und Tongestalt in Schoecks *Schloss Dürande*."
SMZ 83(1943): 74-83.

Songs
3761. Mohr, Ernst. "Das Problem der Form in Schoecks Liederzyklen."
SMZ 83(1953): 85-91.
3762. Puffett, Derrick. "The song cycles of Othmar Schoeck: A
critical survey." PhD dissertation (Musicology): Wolfson College, Oxford,
1976.
3763. ----. *The song cycles of Othmar Schoeck*. Bern: P. Haupt,
1982.
3764. Tiltmann-Fuchs, Stefanie. *Othmar Schoecks Liedzyklen für
Singstimme und Orchester: Studien zum Wort-Ton-Verhältnis*. Regensburg: G. Bosse, 1976.
3765. Vogel, Werner. "Wesenzüge Schoeckscher Lyrik (Eine Studie)."
SMZ 86(1946): 314-320.
3766. ----. *Wesenzüge von Othmar Schoecks Liedkunst*. Zürich:
Juris, 1950.

Other works
3767. Arnold, Willy. "Othmar Schoecks Harmonik." PhD dissertation
(Musicology): Zürich, 1971.

3768. Hirsbrunner, Theo. "Othmar Schoeck: Zwischen Romantik und Moderne." M 35(1981): 246-249.

SCHOENBERG, ARNOLD (1874-1951)

Opus 4: Verklärte Nacht
    3769. Heinz, Rudolf. "Das Sujet der *Verklärten Nacht*: Eine Interpretation des Dehmelschen Gedichts." ZM 5/1(1974): 21-28.
    3770. Pfannkuch, Wilhelm. "Zu Thematik und Form in Schönbergs Streichsextett." Fs. Blume: 258-271.
    3771. Schultz: 93-97.
    3772. Swift, Richard. "1/XII/99: Tonal relations in Schoenberg's *Verklärte Nacht*." NCM 1/(1977): 3-14.

Opus 5: Pelleas und Melisande
    3773. Berg, Alban. *Arnold Schönbergs "Pelleas und Melisande": Kurze thematische Analyse.* Wien: Universal, n.d.
    3774. Harvey, Jonathan. "Schoenberg: Man or woman?" ML 56(1975): 371-385.
    3775. Schultz: 98-105.
    3376. Staempfli, Edward. "*Pelleas und Melisande*: Eine Gegenüberstellung der Werke von Claude Debussy und Arnold Schonberg." SMZ 112(1972): 65-72.

Opus 6: Eight Songs
    3777. Jalowetz, Heinrich. "On the spontaneity of Schoenberg's music." MQ 30(1944): 388-390.

Opus 7: String Quartet No.1
    3778. Leibowitz: 61-65.
    3779. Neff, Severine. "Aspects of *Grundgestalt* in Schoenberg's First String Quartet, Op.7." TP 9(1984): 7-56.
    3780. Schmidt, Christian Martin. "Schonbergs analytische Bemerkungen zum Streichquartett Op.7." OMZ 39(1984): 296-300.

Opus 9: Kammersymphonie
    3781. Berg, Alban. *Arnold Schönberg Kammersymphonie Op.9: Thematische Analyse.* Wien: Universal, n.d.
    3782. Leibowitz: 65-66.

Opus 10: String Quartet No.2
    3783. Neff, Severine. "Ways to imagine two successive pieces of Schoenberg: The Second String Quartet, Opus 10, movement one; the song *Ich darf nicht dankend*, Opus 14, No.1." PhD dissertation (Theory): Princeton University, 1979. UM 79-13,994. DA XXXIX.12, p.7048-A.
    3784. Pfisterer, Manfred. "Zur Frage der Satztechnik in den atonalen Werken von Arnold Schonberg." ZM 2/1(1971): 4-13.

Opus 11: Three Piano Pieces

3785. Brinkmann, Reinhold. *Arnold Schönberg: Drei Klavierstuck Op.11: Studien zur frühen Atonalität bei Schönberg.* Wiesbaden: F. Steiner, 1969.

3786. Forte, Allen. "The magical kaleidoscope: Schoenberg's first atonal masterwork, Opus 11, No.1." JASI 5/2(1981): 127-168.

3787. Gostomsky, Dieter. "Tonalität-Atonalität: Zur Harmonik von Schönbergs Klavierstück Op.11, Nr.1." ZM 7/1(1976): 54-71.

3788. Lewin, David. "Some notes on Schoenberg's Op.11." ITO 3/1 (1977-1978): 3-7.

3789. Ogdon, Will. "How tonality functions in Schoenberg's Opus 11, No.1." JASI 5/2(1981): 169-181.

3790. Perle: 10-15.

3791. Reible, John Joseph, III. "Tristan-Romanticism and the expressionism of the Three Piano Pieces, Opus 11 of Arnold Schoenberg." PhD dissertation (Theory): Washington University, 1980. No DA listing.

3792. Schultz: 106-107.

3793. Schultz/D. [No.2]

3794. Wittlich, Gary. "Interval set structure in Schoenberg's Op.11, No.1." PNM 13/1(1974-1975): 41-55.

Opus 12: Two Ballads

3795. Harbinson, William G. "Rhythmic structure in Schoenberg's *Jane Grey*." JASI 7/2(1983): 222-237. [No.2]

3796. Martin, Henry. "A structural model for Schoenberg's *Der verlorene Haufen* Op.12/2." ITO 3/3(1977): 4-22.

Opus 14: Two Songs

3797. Cinnamon, Howard. "Some elements of tonal and motivic structure in *In diesen Wintertagen*, Op.14, No.2, by Arnold Schoenberg: A Schoenbergian-Schenkerian study." ITO 7/7-8(1983-1984): 23-49.

3798. Neff, Severine. "Ways to imagine two successive pieces of Schoenberg: The Second String Quartet, Opus 10, movement one; the song *Ich darf nicht dankend*, Opus 14, No.1." PhD dissertation (Theory): Princeton University, 1979. UM 79-13,994. DA XXXIX.12, p.7048-A.

Opus 15: Das Buch der hängenden Gärten

3799. Brinkmann, Reinhold. "Schönberg und George: Interpretation eines Liedes." AM 26(1969): 1-28.

3800. Dahlhaus, Carl. "Musikalische Prosa." NZM 125(1964): 176-182.

3801. ----. "Schönberg's Lied *Streng ist uns das Glück und Spröde*." Abraham/L: 45-52.

3802. Dean, Jerry Mac. "Evolution and unity in Schoenberg's George Songs, Op.15." PhD dissertation: University of Michigan, 1971. No DA listing.

3803. Dill, Heinz J. "Schoenberg's George-Lieder: The relationship between text and music in light of some expressionist tendencies." CM 17 (1974): 91-95.

3804. Domek, Richard. "Some aspects of organization in Schoenberg's *Book of the Hanging Gardens*, Opus 15." CMS 19(1979): 111-128.

3805. Dümling, Albrecht. *Die fremden Klänge der hängenden Gärten.* München: Kindler, 1981.

3806. ----. "Öffentliche Einsamkeit: Untersuchungen zur Situation von Lied und Lyrik um 1900 am Beispiele des *Buches der hängenden Gärten* von Stephan George und Arnold Schönberg." PhD dissertation (Musicology): Technische Universität, Berlin, 1978.

3807. Ehrenforth, Karl Heinrich. *Ausdruck und Form: Schönbergs Druchbruch zur Atonalität in den George-Liedern, Op.15.* Bonn: H. Bouvior, 1963.

3808. ----. "Schönberg und Webern: Das XIV. Lied aus Schönbergs George-Liedern Op.15." NZM 126(1965): 102-105

3809. Falck, Robert. "Fear and hope: Schoenberg's Opus 15, No.VII." CAUSM 7(1977): 91-105.

3810. Fisher, George. "Text and music in Song VIII of *Das Buch der hängenden Gärten.*" ITO 6/2(1981-1983): 3-16.

3811. Jacobs, Jann B. "*Grundgestalt* analysis." MA dissertation (Theory): Northwestern University, 1979. [Nos.2 and 5]

3812. Kaufmann, Harald. "Struktur in Schönberg's Georgeliedern." Abraham/L: 53-61.

3813. Krebs, Harald. "Three versions of Schoenberg's Op.15, No.14: Obvious differences and hidden similarities." JASI 8/2(1984): 131-140.

3814. Lewin, David. "Toward the analysis of a Schoenberg song (Op.15, No.XI)." PNM 12(1973-1974): 43-86.

3815. ----. "A way into Schoenberg's Opus 15, number 7." ITO 6/1 (1981-1982): 3-24.

3816. Smith, Glenn Edward. "Schoenberg's *Book of the Hanging Gardens*: An analysis." DMA dissertation (Music Theory-Composition): Indiana University, 1973. 34 p. No DA listing.

3817. Stroh, Wolfgang Martin. "Schoenberg's use of text: The text as a musical control in the 14th Georgelied, Op.15." PNM 6/2(1968): 34-44.

Opus 16: Five Pieces for Orchestra

3818. Avshalomov, David. "Arnold Schoenberg's *Five Pieces for Orchestra*, Op.16: The story of the music and its revisions, with a critical study of his 1949 revision." DMA dissertation (Performance): University of Washington, 1976. UM 76-25,385. DA XXXVII.5, p.2475-A.

3819. Burkhart, Charles. "Schoenberg's *Farben*: An analysis of Op.16, No.3." PNM 12(1973-1974): 141-172.

3820. Cogan, Robert. "Reconceiving theory: The analysis of tone color." CMS 15(1975): 52-69.

3821. Doflein, Erich. "Schönbergs Opus 16 Nr.3: Der Mythos der Klangfarbenmelodie." MELOS 36(1969): 203-205.

3822. ----. "Schönbergs Op.16 Nr.4: Geschichte einer Überschrift." MELOS 36(1969): 206-209.

3823. Förtig, Peter. "Analyse des Opus 16, Nr.4 von Arnold Schönberg." MELOS 36(1969): 206-209.

3824. Lansky, Paul. "Pitch-class consciousness." PNM 13/2 (1974-1975): 30-56.

3825. Rahn: 59-73. [No.3, *Farben*]

3826. Rufer, Josef. "Noch einmal Schönbergs Op. 16." MELOS 36(1969): 366-368.

Opus 17: Erwartung

3827. Buchanan, Herbert H. "A key to Schoenberg's *Erwartung* (Op.17)." JAMS 20(1967): 434-449.

3828. Budde, Elmar. "Arnold Schönbergs Monodram *Erwartung*: Versuch einer Analyse des ersten Satzes." AM 36(1979): 1-20.

3829. Just, Martin. "Schönbergs *Erwartung* Op.2, Nr.1." Kühn: 425-427.

3830. Laborda, José Maria Garcia. *Studien zu Schonbergs Monodram "Erwartung," Op.17.* Laaber: Laaber-Verlag, 1981.

3831. Mauser, Siegfried. *Das expressionistische Musiktheater der Wiener Schule: Stilistische und entwicklungsgeschichtliche Untersuchungen zu Arnold Schönbergs "Erwartung" und "Die glückliche Hand" und Alban Bergs "Wozzeck".* Regensburg: G. Bosse, 1982.

3832. Schultz: 108-111.

3833. Suderburg, Robert Charles. "Tonal cohesion in Schoenberg's twelve-tone music." PhD dissertation (Theory): University of Pennsylvania, 1966. UM 66-10,672. DA XXVII.5, p.1397-8-A.

Opus 18: Die glückliche Hand

3834. Albèra, Philippe. "A propos de *Die glückliche Hand*." CC 1 (1984): 156-166.

3835. Beck, Richard Thomas. "The sources and significance of *Die glückliche Hand*." Kühn: 427-429.

3836. Crawford, John C. "*Die glückliche Hand*: Schoenberg's *Gesamtkunstwerk*." MQ 60(1974): 583-601.

3837. Demierre, Jacques. "Repères analytiques." CC 2(1984): 167-177.

3838. Mauser, Siegfried. *Das expressionistische Musiktheater der Wiener Schule: Stilistische und entwicklungsgeschichtliche Untersuchungen zu Arnold Schönbergs "Erwartung" und "Die glückliche Hand" und Alban Bergs "Wozzeck".* Regensburg: G. Bosse, 1982.

3839. Rodean, Richard William. "An analysis of structural elements and performance practice in Arnold Schoenberg's *Die glückliche Hand*, Op.18." PhD dissertation (Fine Arts): Texas Tech University, 1980. UM 80-22,631. DA XLI.4, p.1276-A.

3840. Schultz: 112-122.

3841. Truman, Philip. "Synaesthesia and *Die glückliche Hand*." I 12 (1983): 481-503.

Opus 19: Six Little Piano Pieces

3842. Cooper, Grosvenor and Leonard Meyer. *The rhythmic structure of music.* Chicago: University of Chicago Press, 1960.

3843. Forte, Allen. "Context and continuity in an atonal work: A set-theoretic approach." PNM 1/2(1963): 72-82.

3844. Grandjean, Wolfgang. "Form in Schönbergs Op.19, 2." ZM 8/1 (1977): 15-18.

3845. Lewin, David. "Transformational techniques in atonal and other music theories." PNM 21(1982-1983): 312-371. [No.6]

3846. Lubet, Alex. "Vestiges of tonality in a work of Arnold Schoenberg." ITR 5/3(1981-1982): 11-21. [No.3]

3847. Stein, Deborah. "Schoenberg's Opus 19, No.2: Voice-leading and overall structure." ITO 2/7(1976): 27-43.

3848. Stuckenschmidt, H.H. "Opus 19, Nummer 3: Eine Schönberg-Analyse." OM 1(1971-1972): 88-90.

3849. Travis, Roy. "Directed motion in Schoenberg and Webern." PNM 4/2(1966): 85-89.

3850. Vlad, Roman. "Una pagina di Schoenberg." STU 14(1985): 171-192.

Opus 20: Herzgewächse

3851. Carlson, David. "*Exempli gratia*: Two instances of 'bilingual text-painting' in Schoenberg's *Herzgewächse*, Op.20." ITO 6/1(1981-1982): 25-28.

3852. Clifton, Thomas. "On listening to *Herzgewächse*." PNM 11/2 (1975): 87-103.

3853. Diettrich, Eva. "Schönbergs *Herzgewächse*." Fs. Wessely: 103-112.

3854. Hough, Bonny Ellen. "Schoenberg's *Herzgewächse*, Op.20: An integrated approach to atonality through complementary analyses." PhD dissertation (Performance): Washington University, 1982. 298 p. No DA listing.

3855. Ruf, Wolfgang. "Arnold Schönbergs Lied *Herzgewächse*." AM 41 (1984): 257-273.

3856. Wood, Jeffrey. "Tetrachordal and inversional structuring in Arnold Schoenberg's *Herzgewächse*, Op.20." ITO 7/3(1983-1984): 23-34.

Opus 21: Pierrot Lunaire

3857. Asarnow, Elliot Bruce. "Arnold Schoenberg's *Heimweh* from *Pierrot Lunaire*: Registral partitioning of the harmonic structure." PhD dissertation: Brandeis University, 1979. No DA listing.

3858. Bailey, Kathryn. "Formal organization and structural imagery in Schoenberg's *Pierrot Lunaire*." SMUWO 2(1977): 93-107.

3859. Beiringer, Gene. "Musical metaphors in Schoenberg's *Der kranke Mond* (*Pierrot Lunaire*, No.7)." ITO 8/7(1984-1985): 3-14.

3860. Dreyer, Martin. "Pierrot's voice: New monody or old prosody." CT 10(1974-1975): 15-20.

3861. Gilbert, Jan. "Schoenberg's harmonic visions: A study of text painting in *Die Kreuze*." JASI 8/2(1984): 117-130.

3862. Lessem, Alan. "Text and music in Schoenberg's *Pierrot Lunaire*." CM 19(1975): 103-112.

3863. Lewin, Harold F. "Schoenberg's *Pierrot Lunaire*: The rhythmic relation between *Sprechstimme* and instrumental writing in *Eine blasse Wascherin*." TP 5/1(1980): 25-39.

3864. Perle, George. "*Pierrot Lunaire*." Fs. Sachs/C: 307-312.

3865. Smyth, David H. "The music of *Pierrot Lunaire*: An analytic approach." TP 5/1(1980): 5-24.

3866. Sterne, Colin C. "Pythagoras and Pierrot: An approach to Schoenberg's use of numerology in the construction of *Pierrot Lunaire*." PNM 21(1982-1983): 506-534.

3867. Youens, Susan. "Excavating an allegory: The texts of *Pierrot Lunaire*." JASI 8/2(1984): 95-115.

Opus 22: Four Orchestral Songs
    3868. Dunsby, Jonathan M. "Schoenberg's *Premonition*, Op.22, No.4, in retrospect." JASI 1(1976-1977): 137-149.
    3869. Falck, Robert. "Schoenberg's (and Rilke's) *Alle, welche dich suchen*." PNM 12(1973-1974): 87-98. [No.2]
    3870. Hill, Richard S. "Schoenberg's tone-rows and the tonal system of the future." MQ 22(1936): 14-37.
    3871. Schoenberg, Arnold. "Une analyse des Lieder avec orchestre d'Arnold Schoenberg par le compositeur." MJ 16(1974): 43-53.
    3872. ----. "Analysis of the Four Orchestral Songs, Opus 22." PNM 3/2(1965): 1-21.

Opus 23: Five Piano Pieces
    3873. Bailey, Kathryn. "Transitional aspects of Schoenberg's Opus 23, No.2." CAUSM 2/2(1972): 24-30.
    3874. Barkin, Elaine. "Pitch-time structure in Arnold Schoenberg's Opus 23, No.1: A contribution toward a theory of notational music." PhD dissertation (Theory): Brandeis University, 1971. UM 71-30,114. DA XXXII.7, p.4041-A.
    3875. ----. "Registral procedures in Schoenberg's Op.23/1." MR 34 (1973): 141-145.
    3876. ----. "A view of Schoenberg's Op.23/1." PNM 12(1973-1974): 99-127.
    3877. Graziano, John. "Serial procedures in Schoenberg's Op.23." CM 13(1972): 58-63.
    3878. Hasty, Christopher. "Segmentation and process in post-tonal music." MTS 3(1981): 54-73.
    3879. Oesch, Hans. "Schönberg im Vorfeld der Dodekaphonie: Zur Bedeutung des dritten Satzes aus Opus 23 für die Herausbildung der Zwölfton-Technik." ZM 5/1(1974): 2-10. [Also in MELOS 41(1974): 330-338]
    3880. Perle: 42-52.

Opus 24: Serenade
    3881. Lester, Joel. "Pitch structure articulation in the variations of Schoenberg's Serenade." PNM 6/2(1968): 22-34.
    3882. ----. "A theory of atonal prolongations as used in an analysis of the Serenade, Op.24, by Arnold Schoenberg." PhD dissertation (Theory): Princeton University, 1970. 2 vols. RILM 70/2103dd28. No DA listing.

Opus 26: Wind Quintet
    3883. Corson, Langdon. *Arnold Schoenberg's Woodwind Quintet, Op.26: Background and analysis*. Roy Christensen, ed. Nashville, TN: Gasparo, 1984.
    3884. Maxwell, John. "Symmetrical partitioning of the row in Schoenberg's Wind Quintet, Op.26." ITR 5/2(1981-1982): 1-15.
    3885. Stephan, Rudolf. "Gedanken zu A. Schönbergs Bläserquintett Op.26." Benary: 42-49.

Opus 28: Three Satires
    3886. Konold, Wulf. "Schönbergs Kantate *Der neue Klassizismus.*" M 29(1975): 388-393. [No.3]

Opus 29: Suite
    3887. Hyde, Martha M. *Schoenberg's twelve-tone harmony: The Suite Op.29 and the compositional sketches.* Ann Arbor: UMI Research Press, 1982.

Opus 30: String Quartet No.3
    3888. Dietrich, Norbert. *Arnold Schönbergs drittes Streichquartett Op.30.* München: E. Katzbichler, 1983.
    3889. Möllers, Christian. *Reihentechnik und musikalische Gestalt bei Arnold Schonberg: Eine Untersuchung zum III. Streichquartett Op.30.* Wiesbaden: Steiner, 1977. 168 p.
    3890. Niemöller, Klaus Wolfgang. "Klassische Formsynthese im 1. Satz von Schonbergs 3. Streichquartett." Kühn: 429-432.
    3891. Odegard, Peter Sigurd. "Schoenberg's variations: An addendum." MR 27(1966): 102-121.
    3892. Peles, Stephen V. "Interpretations of sets in multipole dimensions: Notes on the second movement of Arnold Schoenberg's String Quartet No.3." PNM 22(1983-1984): 303-352.
    3893. Stein, Erwin. "Schoenberg's new structural form." MM 7/4 (1929): 3-10.

Opus 31: Variations for Orchestra
    3894. Dahlhaus, Carl. *Schönberg: Variationen für Orchester.* München: W. Fink, 1968.
    3895. Engelmann, Hans Ulrich. "Schönbergs *Variationen für Orches-ter.*" MELOS 33(1966): 396-400.
    3896. Hicken, Kenneth Lambert. "Schoenberg's atonality: Fused bitonality?" TEMPO 109(1974): 27-36.
    3897. ----. "Structure and prolongation: Tonal and serial organization in the Introduction of Schoenberg's *Variations for Orchestra.*" PhD dissertation: Brigham Young University, 1970. 192 p. UM 71-8856. DA XXXI.10, p.5446-A.
    3898. Leibowitz, René. *Introduction à la musique de douze sons: Les "Variations pour orchestre," Op.31 d'Arnold Schoenberg.* Paris: L'Arche, 1949.
    3899. Phipps, Graham Howard. "Schoenberg's *Grundgestalt* principle: A new approach with particular application to the *Variations for Orchestra.*" PhD dissertation: University of Cincinnati, 1976. UM 77-06,195. DA XXXVII.10, p.6133-A.
    3900. Pousseur, Henri. "La Polyphonie en question (à propos de Schoenberg, Opus 31)." *Jaarboek I.P.E.M.* (1969): 47-80. [Also in Henri Pousseur, *Musique, semantique, société.* Tournai: Casterman, 1972: 27-77]
    3901. Schoenberg, Arnold. "La Composition à douze sons." POL 4 (1949): 7-31.
    3902. ----. "The *Orchestral Variations*, Op.31." SCORE 27(1960): 27-40.

Opus 32: Von Heute auf Morgen
  3903. Keller, Hans. "Schoenberg's comic opera." SCORE 23(1958): 27-36.

Opus 33: Two Piano Pieces
  3904. Bailey, Kathryn. "Row anomalies in Opus 33: An insight into Schoenberg's understanding of the serial procedure." CM 22(1976): 42-66.
  3905. Glofcheskie, John. "'Wrong' notes in Schoenberg's Op.33a." SMU 1(1976): 88-104.
  3906. Graebner, Eric. "An analysis of Schoenberg's *Klavierstück*, Op.33a." PNM 12(1973-1974): 128-140.
  3907. Perle: 111-116.
  3908. Schoffman, Nachum. "Schoenberg Opus 33a revisited." TEMPO 146(1983): 31-42.

Opus 34: Accompaniment to a Cinema Scene
  3909. Hush, David. "Modes of continuity in Schoenberg's *Begleitungsmusik*, Op.34." JASI 8/1(1984) supplement: 1-45.

Opus 36: Violin Concerto
  3910. Hall, Anne C. "A comparison of manuscript and printed scores of Schoenberg's Violin Concerto." PNM 14/1(1975): 182-196.
  3911. Hall.
  3912. Leibowitz, René. "Le Concerto pour violon et orchestre d'Arnold Schoenberg." *Le Compositeur et son double: Essais sur l'interpretation musicale*. Paris: Gallimard, 1971: 210-222.
  3913. Perle, George and Milton Babbitt. "Babbitt, Lewin, and Schoenberg: A critique." PNM 2/1(1963): 120-132.
  3914. Suderburg, Robert Charles. "Tonal cohesion in Schoenberg's twelve-tone music." PhD dissertation (Theory): University of Pennsylvania, 1966. UM 66-10,672. DA XXVII.5, p.1397-8-A.

Opus 37: String Quartet No.4
  3915. Cubbage, John Rex. "Directed pitch motion and coherence in the first movement of Arnold Schoenberg's Fourth String Quartet." PhD dissertation: Washington University, 1979. No DA listing.
  3916. Gradenwitz, Peter. "Beethoven Op.131--Schönberg Op.37." Kühn: 369-372.
  3917. Klemm, Eberhardt. "Zur Theorie der Reihenstruktur und Reihendisposition in Schönbergs 4. Streichquartett." BM 8(1966): 27-49.
  3918. Lake, William E. "Structural functions of segmental interval-class 1 dyads in Schoenberg's Fourth Quartet, first movement." ITO 8/2(1984-1985): 21-29.
  3919. Neighbour, Oliver. "A talk on Schoenberg for Composer's Concourse." SCORE 16(1956): 19-28.

Opus 40: Variations on a Recitative
  3920. Radulescu, Michael. "Arnold Schönbergs *Variationen über ein Rezitativ* Op.40: Versuch einer Deutung." MK 52(1982): 175-183.

3921. Traber, Jürgen Habakuk. "Versuch über ein 'Nebenwerk': Zu Arnold Schönbergs *Variations on a Recitative*, Op.40." ZM 5/2(1974): 29-41.

3922. Watkins, Glenn E. "Schoenberg and the organ." PNM 4/1 (1965): 119-135.

Opus 41: Ode to Napoleon
3923. List, Kurt. "*Ode to Napoleon*." MM 21(1944): 139-145.

Opus 42: Piano Concerto
3924. Garst, Marilyn M. "The early twentieth-century piano concerto as formulated by Stravinsky and Schoenberg." PhD dissertation (Musicology): Michigan State University, 1972. UM 73-05,376. DA XXXIII.9, p.5224-A.

3925. Jalowetz, Heinrich. "On the spontaneity of Schoenberg's music." MQ 30(1944): 394-408.

3926. Leibowitz, René. "Schönbergs Klavierkonzert, Op.42." MELOS 16 (1949): 44-48.

3927. Newlin, Dika. "Secret tonality in Schoenberg's Piano Concerto." PNM 13/1(1974-1975): 137-139.

3928. Wall, Byron E. "A comparison of two great piano concertos: Mozart's in C Minor and Schoenberg's." D 1/1(1969): 8-20.

Opus 43a: Theme and Variations for Wind Band
3929. Nail, James Isaac. "The concept of developing variations as a means of producing unity and variety in Schoenberg's Theme and Variations, Op.43a." DMA dissertation: University of Texas, 1978. No DA listing.

3930. Schmidt-Brunner, Wolfgang. "Arnold Schönbergs 'pädagogische' Musik: Suite für Streichorchester (1934) und Thema und Variationen für Bläserorchester Op.43A (1943)." Fs. Valentin: 215-224.

Opus 44: Prelude to a "Genesis" Suite
3931. Leibowitz, René. "Aspects récents de la technique de douze sons." POL 4(1949): 32-53.

Opus 45: String Trio
3932. Hymanson, William. "Schoenberg's String Trio (1946)." MR 11(1950): 184-194.

3933. Jordan, Roland Carroll, Jr. "Schoenberg's String Trio, Op.45: An analytical study." PhD dissertation (Composition): Washington University, 1973. 279 p. RILM 75/1506dd28. No DA listing.

3934. Leibowitz, René. "Aspects récents de la technique de douze sons." POL 4(1949): 32-53.

3935. Peel, John M. "On some celebrated measures of the Schoenberg String Trio." PNM 14/2-15/1(1976): 260-279.

3936. Staempfli, Edward. "Das Streichtrio Op.45 von Arnold Schönberg." MELOS 37(1970): 35-39.

Opus 46: A Survivor from Warsaw
3937. Gruhn, Wilfried. "Arnold Schönberg (1874-1951): *Ein Überlebender aus Warschau*, Op.46." Zimmerschied: 128-152.
3938. ----. "Zitat und Reihe in Schönbergs *Ein Überlebender aus Waschau*." ZM 5/1(1974): 29-33.
3939. Heller, Charles. "Traditional Jewish material in Schoenberg's *A Survivor from Warsaw*, Op.46." JASI 3(1979): 69-74.
3940. Leibowitz, René. "Aspects récents de la technique de douze sons." POL 4(1949): 32-53.
3941. Schmidt, Christian Martin. "Schönbergs Kantate *Ein Überlebender aus Warschau*, Op.46." AM 33(1976): 174-188, 261-277.
3942. Schweizer, Klaus. "*Ein Überlebender aus Warschau* für Sprecher, Männerchor und Orchester von Arnold Schönberg." MELOS 41(1974): 365.

Opus 47: Fantasy for Violin and Piano
3943. Forte: 110-127.
3944. Friedmann, Michael L. "A methodology for the discussion of contour: Its application to Schoenberg's music." JMT 29/2(1985): 223-247.
3945. Lewin, David. "A study of hexachord levels in Schoenberg's Violin Fantasy." PNM 6/1(1967): 18-32.
3946. Raab, Claus. "*Fantasia quasi una sonata*: Zu Schönbergs *Phantasy for Violin with Piano Accompaniment*, Op.47." Melos/NZM 2(1976): 191-196.
3947. Whittall, Arnold. "The Violin Fantasy: Schoenberg's serial scaffolding." CT 6(1973): 3-6.

Opus 50a: Dreimaltausend Jahre
3948. Hufschmidt, Wolfgang. "Sprache und 'Sprachgebrauch' bei Schönberg." ZM 5/1(1974): 11-20.

Concerto for String Quartet and Orchestra in Bb
3949. Floreen, John Eric. "Arnold Schoenberg's Concerto for String Quartet and Orchestra after the Concerto Grosso, Op.6, No.7 by G.F. Handel: Transcription, arrangment and recomposition." DMA dissertation: University of Iowa, 1980. No DA listing.
3950. Hübler, Klaus-K. "Schönberg und Händel: Über systembedingtes Unverständnis." MB 14/12(1982): 791-800.

Gurrelieder
3951. Berg, Alban. *Arnold Schönberg: "Gurrelieder" Führer*. Wien: Universal, n.d.

Die Jakobsleiter
3952. Christensen, Jean Marie. "Arnold Schoenberg's oratorio *Die Jakobsleiter*." PhD dissertation (Musicology): University of California, Los Angeles, 1979. 2 vols. UM 80-02,474. No DA listing.
3953. ----. "Schoenberg's sketches for *Die Jakobsleiter*: A study of a special case." JASI 2(1978): 112-121.
3954. Ringer, Alexander L. "Faith and symbol: On Arnold Schoenberg's last musical utterance." JASI 6/1(1982): 80-95.

3955. Zillig, Winfried. "Arnold Schönbergs *Jakobsleiter*." OMZ 16 (1961): 193-204.

3956. ----. "Bericht über Arnold Schönbergs *Jakobsleiter*." NMD 4 (1960-1961): 29-40.

3957. ----. "Notes on Arnold Schoenberg's unfinished oratorio *Die Jakobsleiter*." SCORE 25(1959): 7-16.

Moses and Aron

3958. Fleischer, Robert Jay. "Schoenberg, dualism, and *Moses und Aron*." DMA dissertation (Performance): University of Illinois, 1980. 151 p. UM 80-08,502. DA XLI.11, p.4534-A.

3959. Goehr, Alexander. "Schoenberg and Karl Kraus: The idea behind the music." MA 4/1-2(1985): 59-71. [Also *Die Jakobsleiter*]

3960. Hair, Graham. "Schoenberg's *Moses and Aron*." PhD dissertation: Sheffield, 1973.

3961. Keller, Hans. "Schoenberg: *Moses and Aron*." SCORE 21(1957): 30-45.

3962. Lewin, David. "*Moses and Aron*: Some general remarks and analytic notes for Act I, Scene I." PNM 6/1(1967): 1-17.

3963. Newlin, Dika. "The role of the chorus in Schoenberg's *Moses and Aaron*." ACR 9/1(1966): 1-4, 18.

3964. Stuckenschmidt, H.H. "An introduction to Schoenberg's opera *Moses and Aron*." Fs. Pisk: 243-256.

3965. Vogt: 229-238.

3966. White, Pamela C. *Schoenberg and the God-Idea: The opera "Moses and Aron."* Ann Arbor: UMI Research Press, 1985.

3967. Wörner, Karl H. *Gotteswort und Magie: Die Oper "Moses und Aron" von Arnold Schönberg*. Heidelberg: Schneider, 1959.

3968. ----. "Polyphonie der Symbole: Die 39 Schlusstakte von Schönberg's *Moses und Aron*." MELOS 24(1957): 350-352.

3969. ----. *Schoenberg's "Moses and Aron."* New York: St. Martin's Press, 1963.

String Quartet in D Major (1897)

3970. Gerlach, Reinhard. "War Schönberg von Dvořák beeinflusst? Zu Arnold Schönbergs Streichqartett D-Dur." NZM 133(1972): 122-127.

3971. Maegaard, Jan. "Arnold Schönbergs Scherzo in F-Dur für Streichquartett." DAM 14(1983): 133-140.

Other works

3972. Adorno, Theodor W. *Klangfiguren: Musikalisiche Schriften* I. Berlin: Verlag, 1959: 94-120.

3973. Ashforth, Alden Banning. "Linear and textural aspects of Schoenberg's cadences." PNM 16/2(1977-1978): 195-224.

3974. ----. "Schoenberg's cadential devices." PhD dissertation (Composition): Princeton University, 1971. 282 p. UM 71-23,341. DA XXXV.5, p.2723-A.

3975. Babbitt, Milton. "Since Schoenberg." PNM 12(1973-1974): 3-28.

3976. Bailey, Walter B. *Programmatic elements in the works of Schoenberg*. Ann Arbor: UMI Research Press, 1984.

3977. Berg, Alban. "Why is Schoenberg's music so hard to understand?" MR 13(1952): 187-196.

3978. Broekema.

3979. Buccheri. [Piano works]

3980. Buchanan, Herbert Herman. "An investigation of mutual influences among Schoenberg, Webern, and Berg (with an emphasis on Schoenberg and Webern, ca.1904-1908)." PhD dissertation (Musicology): Rutgers University, 1974. UM 74-27,592. DA XXXV.6, p.3789-A.

3981. Carpenter, Patricia. "The piano music of Arnold Schoenberg." PQ 41(1962): 26-31, 42(1962-1963): 23-29.

3982. Clifton, Thomas James. "Types of ambiguity in tonal compositions of Arnold Schoenberg." PhD dissertation: Stanford University, 1966. UM 66-14,641. DA XXVII.7, p.2169-A. [Opp. 1-10]

3983. Cone, Edward T. "Sound and syntax: An introduction to Schoenberg's harmony." PNM 13/1(1974-1975): 21-40.

3984. Crawford, John. "The relationship of text and music in the vocal works of Schoenberg, 1908-1924." PhD dissertation: Harvard University, 1963. 364 p. No DA listing.

3985. Dean, Jerry. "Schoenberg's vertical-linear relationships in 1908." PNM 12(1973-1974): 173-179.

3986. Emsley, Richard. "Schoenberg as rhythmic innovator." CT 8(1974): 3-9.

3987. Epstein, David M. "Schoenberg's *Grundgesalt* and total serialism: Their relevance to homophonic analysis." PhD dissertation (Composition): Princeton University, 1968. UM 69-2738. DA XXIX.9, p.3168-A.

3988. Forte, Allen. "Schoenberg's creative evolution: The path to atonality." MQ 64(1978): 133-176.

3989. ----. "Sets and nonsets in Schoenberg's atonal music." PNM 11/1(1972): 43-64.

3990. Friedburg, Ruth. "The solo keyboard works of Arnold Schoenberg." MR 23(1962): 39-43.

3991. Friedheim, Philip Alan. "Rhythmic structure in Schoenberg's atonal compositions." JAMS 19(1966): 60-62.

3992. ----. "Tonality and structure in the early works of Schoenberg." PhD dissertation (Musicology): New York University, 1963. UM 64-06,464. DA XXVI.3, p.1685-6. [Opp.1-15]

3993. Godwin, Paul Milton. "A study of concepts of melody, with particular reference to some music of the twentieth century and examples from the compositions of Schoenberg, Webern and Berg." PhD dissertation (Theory): Ohio State University, 1972. UM 73-02,003. DA XXXIII.8, p.4453-A.

3994. Gradenwitz, Peter. "The idiom and development in Schoenberg's quartets." ML 26(1945): 123-142.

3995. Hansen, Mathias. "Arnold Schönbergs Kompositionsverständnis und seine Auseinandersetzung mit neoklassizistischen Tendenzen in den zwanzigen Jahren." JP 3(1980): 66-85.

3996. Hyde, Martha MacLean. "The roots of form in Schoenberg's sketches." JMT 24(1980): 1-36.

3997. ----. "The telltale sketches: Harmonic structure in Schoenberg's twelve-tone method." MQ 66(1980): 560-580.

3998. ----. "A theory of twelve-tone meter." MTS 6(1984): 14-51. [Opp.25, 27, 29, 30, 37, 45]

3999. Johnson, P. "Studies in atonality: Non-thematic structural processes in the early atonal music of Schoenberg and Webern." PhD dissertation (Musicology): Worchester, Oxford, 1978.

4000. Kassler, Michael. "A trinity of essays: Toward a theory that is the twelve-note class system; toward development of a constructive tonality theory based on writing by Heinrich Schenker; toward a simple programming language for musical information retrieval." PhD dissertation (Theory): Princeton University, 1967. UM 68-2490. DA XXVIII.9, p.3702-A.

4001. Kelly, Claire Bennett. "Declaration, dissolution, and reassembly: A creative principle in the string quartets of Arnold Schoenberg." MM dissertation: Florida State University, 1970.

4002. Kraus, Elsie C. "Schönbergs Klavierwerk steht lebendig vor mir." MELOS 41(1974): 134-139.

4003. Krieger, Georg. *Schönbergs Werke für Klavier.* Göttingen: Vandenhoeck und Ruprecht, 1968.

4004. Leibowitz, René. "Les Oeuvres d'Arnold Schoenberg ou la conscience du drame futur dans la musique contemporaine." POL 1(1947): 84-104.

4005. Lessem, Alan Philip. "Music and text in the works of Arnold Schoenberg: The critical years, 1908-1922." PhD dissertation (Musicology): University of Illinois, 1973. 423 p. UM 74-5623. DA XXXIV.9, p.6024-A.

4006. Lewin, David. "The intervallic content of a collection of notes, intervallic relations between a collection of notes and its complement: An application to Schoenberg's hexachordal pieces." JMT 4(1960): 98-100.

4007. ----. "Inversional balance as an organizing force in Schoenberg's music and thought." PNM 6/2(1968): 1-21.

4008. ----. "Vocal meter in Schoenberg's atonal music, with a note on a serial *Hauptstimme.*" ITO 6/4(1981-1983): 12-26. [Op.15, No.5; Op.20; Op.21, No.2]

4009. Lichtenfeld, Monika. "Schönberg und Hauer." MELOS 32(1965): 118-121.

4010. Lohman, Peter Nathan. "Schoenberg's atonal procedures: A non-serial analytic approach to the instrumental works, 1908-1921." PhD dissertation (Theory): Ohio State University, 1981. UM 81-15,133. DA XLII.2, p.446-A.

4011. Lück, Rudolf. "Arnold Schönberg und das deutsche Volkslied." NZM 124(1963): 86-91.

4012. Maegaard, Jan. "Schönberg's Zwölftonreihen." MF 29(1976): 385-424.

4013. ----. *Studien zur Entwicklung des dodekaphonen Satzes bei Arnold Schönberg.* København: W. Hansen, 1972. 3 vols.

4014. Morgan, Robert P. "Schoenberg and the musical tradition: The four string quartets." MN 1/4(1971): 3-10.

4015. Musgrave, Michael Graham. "Schoenberg and Brahms: A study of Schoenberg's response to Brahms's music as revealed in his didactic writings and selected early compositions." PhD dissertation (Musicology): King's College, London, 1980. [String Quartets in D Major (1897) and D Minor (Opus 7); *Verklärte Nacht*]

4016. Naumann, Peter. "Untersuchungen zum Wort-Ton-Verhältnis in der Einaktern Arnold Schönbergs." PhD dissertation (Musicology): Köln, 1972.

4017. Neighbour, O. W. "In defense of Schoenberg." ML 33(1952): 10-27.

4018. Nelson, Robert U. "Schoenberg's variation seminar." MQ 50 1964): 143-163. [Opp.10, 21, 24, 29, 31, 40, 43]

4019. Newlin, Dika. "The piano music of Arnold Schoenberg." PQ 105 (1979): 38-43.

4020. Odegard, Peter Sigurd. "The variation sets of Arnold Schoenberg." PhD dissertation: University of California, Berkeley, 1964. UM 64-13,068. DA XXV.7, p.4186.

4021. Ogdon.

4021a. Paz, Juan Carlos. *Arnold Schoenberg: O el fin de la era tonal.* Buenos Aires: Nueva Vision, 1958.

4022. Perle, George. "Schoenberg's late style." MR 13(1952): 274-282.

4023. Pfisterer, Manfred. *Studien zur Kompositionstechnik in den fröhen atonalen Werken von Arnold Schönberg.* Neuhausen-Stuttgart: Hänssler, 1978.

4024. Phipps, Graham H. "The tritone as an equivalency: A contextual perspective for approaching Schoenberg's music." JM 4(1985-1986): 51-69. [Opp.19, 25, 30]

4025. Pillin, Boris William. *Some aspects of counterpoint in selected works of Arnold Schoenberg.* Los Angeles: Western International Music, 1971.

4026. Putz. [String quartets]

4027. Rauchhaupt, Ursula van, comp. *Die Streichquartette der Wiener Schule, Schönberg, Berg,Webern: Eine Dokumentation.* München: H. Ellermann, 1971.

4028. Reich, Willi. *Schoenberg: A critical biography.* Trans. by Leo Black. New York: Praeger, 1971. 268 p.

4029. Rexroth, Dieter. "Arnold Schönberg als Theoretiker der tonalen Harmonik." PhD dissertation: Rheinischer Friedrich-Wilhelms-Universität, 1971.

4030. Richter, Lukas. "Schönbergs Harmonielehre und die freie Atonalität." DJM (1968): 43-71. [Also in Pečman/J: 339-354]

4031. Rogge, Wolfgang. *Das Klavierwerk Arnold Schönbergs.* Regensburg: G. Bosse, 1964. 54 p.

4032. Rosen, Charles. *Arnold Schoenberg.* New York: Viking, 1975. 113 p.

4033. Rufer, Josef. *Composition with twelve notes related only to one another.* London: Rockcliff, 1954.

4034. ----. *Das Werk Arnold Schönbergs.* Kassel: Bärenreiter, 1974 (1959).

4035. Samson, Jim. "Schoenberg's 'atonal' music." TEMPO 109(1974): 16-25.

4036. Schmid, Erich. "Studie über Schönbergs Streichquartette." SMZ 74(1934): 1-8, 84-91, 155-163.

4037. Schmidt, Christian Martin. "Ansätze zu einem harmonischen System in späten tonalen Kompositionen Schönbergs." MF 29(1976): 425-430.

4038. Schmidt, Wolfgang. *Gestalt und Funktion rhythmischer Phänomene in der Musik Arnold Schönbergs.* Erlangen, 1973. 195 p.

4039. Schneider, Frank. "Schönberg und die tschechische Musik." BM 23(1981): 26-30.

4040. Schoenberg, Arnold. "My evolution." MQ 38(1952): 517-527.

4041. ----. "Problems of harmony." MM 11(1934): 167-187.

4042. Schollum, Robert. *Die Wiener Schule: Schonberg-Berg-Webern: Entwicklung und Ergebnis.* Wien: E. Lafite, 1969.

4043. Schubert, Giselher. *Schönbergs frühe Instrumentation: Untersuchungen zu den "Gurrelieder", zu Op.5 und Op.8.* Baden-Baden: Koerner, 1975.

4044. Schubli, Sigfried. "Ein Stück praktisch gewordener Ideologie: Zum Problem der Komplexen einsätzigen Form in Frühwerken Arnold Schönbergs." AM 41(1984): 274-294. [Opp. 4, 5, 7, 9]

4045. Specht, Robert John, Jr. "Relationships between text and music in the choral works of Arnold Schoenberg." PhD dissertation (Musicology): Case-Western Reserve University, 1976. UM 77-12,012. DA XXXVII.12, p.7398-A.

4046. Spies, Claudio. "The organ supplanted: A case for differentiations." PNM 11/2(1975): 24-25. [Transcriptions of Bach]

4047. Spring, Glenn Ernest, Jr. "Determinants of phrase structure in selected works of Schoenberg, Berg, and Webern." DMA dissertation (Composition): University of Washington, 1972. 61 p. UM 72-28,670. DA XXXIII.5, p.2417-A.

4048. Stadlen, Peter. "Schoenberg's speech-song." ML 62(1981): 1-11. [*Pierrot Lunaire; Gurrelieder; Die glückliche Hand; Moses und Aron*]

4049. Steiner, Ena. "Suchen um des Suchens Willen: Neuentdeckte Jugendwerke Arnold Schönbergs." OMZ 29(1974): 279-291.

4050. Stephan, Rudolf. "Schönberg als Symphoniker." OMZ 29(1974): 267-278.

4051. Suderberg, Robert Charles. "Tonal cohesion in Schoenberg's twelve-tone music." PhD dissertation (Theory): University of Pennsylvania, 1966. UM 66-10,672. DA XXVII.5, p.1397-8-A.

4052. Thieme, Ulrich. *Studien zum Jugendwerk Arnold Schönbergs.* Regensburg: G. Bosse, 1979.

4053. Tuttle, T. Temple. "Schoenberg's compositions for piano solo." MR 18(1957): 301-304.

4054. Velten, Klaus. "Das Prinzip der entwickelnden Variation bei Johannes Brahms und Arnold Schönberg." MB 6(1974): 547-555.

4055. Venus, Dankmar. *Vergleichende Untersuchung zur melodischen Struktur der Singstimmen in den Liedern von Arnold Schönberg, Alban Berg, Anton Webern, und Paul Hindemith.* Göttingen, 1965.

4056. Walker, Alan. "Back to Schoenberg." MR 21(1960): 140-147.

4057. ----. "Schoenberg's classical background." MR 19(1958): 283-289.

4058. Walker, Gwyneth. "Tradition and breaking of tradition in the string quartets of Ives and Schoenberg." DMA dissertation: University of Hartford, 1976. No DA listing.

4059. Watkins, Glenn. "Schoenberg re-cycled." Fs. Fox: 72-81.

4060. Webern, Anton. "Schonberg's Musik." *Arnold Schonberg*. München: R. Piper, 1912: 22-48.

4061. Wee, A. DeWayne. "The twelve-tone piano compositions of Arnold Schoenberg." DM dissertation (Performance): Indiana University, 1968. No DA listing.

4062. Wellesz, Egon. "Schoenberg and beyond." MQ 2(1916): 76-95.

4063. Whittall, Arnold. *Schoenberg Chamber Music*. BBC music guides 21. Seattle: University of Washington Press, 1972.

4064. Wilke, Rainer. *Brahms, Reger, Schönberg, Streichquartette: Motivisch-thematische Prozesse und formale Gestalt*. Hamburg: Wagner, 1980.

4065. Williams, Roger B. "The early development of Arnold Schoenberg: 1897-1905." PhD dissertation (Musicology): Cambridge University, 1976.

4066. Yasser, Joseph. "A letter from Arnold Schoenberg." JAMS 6(1953): 53-62.

4067. Special Issue: SCORE 6(1952): 3-43.

SCHOLLUM, ROBERT (born 1913)

4068. Schollum, Robert. "Mein Mosaik: Versuch einer Werkeinführung" ME 31(1977-1978): 60-63.

SCHOOF, MANFRED (born 1936)

4069. Krumpf, Hans H. "*Ode* von Manfred Schoof." MB 9(1977): 532-535.

SCHREKER, FRANZ (1878-1934)

Der Ferne Klang
4070. Neuwirth, Gösta. *Die Harmonik in der Oper "Der Ferne Klang" von Franz Schreker*. Regensburg: G. Bosse, 1972.

Die Gezeichneten
4071. Granzow, Peter. "Franz Schrekers Kompositionstil in seiner Oper *Die Gezeichneten*." PhD dissertation (Musicology): Innsbruck, 1972.

4072. Molkow, Wolfgang. "Untergang der Transzendenz Franz Schrekers Oper *Die Gezeichneten*." Melos/NZM 4(1978): 304-311.

4073. Neuwirth, Gösta. "Musik um 1900." Fs. Schuh: 89-134.

4074. Wickes, Lewis. "A *Jugendstil* consideration of the opening and closing sections of the *Vorspiel* to Schreker's opera *Die Gezeichneten*." MMA 13(1984): 203-222.

Kammersinfonie
4075. Brinkmann, Reinhold. "Franz Schreker: In ferner Klang? Bemerkungen zur Forschungslag und Anhand der *Kammersinfonie*." Budde: 27-36.

Songs
4076. Budde, Elmar. "Über Metrik und Deklamation in den *Fünf Gesangen* für tiefe Stimme." Budde: 37-48.
4077. Danuser, Hermann. "Über Franz Schrekers Whitman-Gesänge." Budde: 49-73.

Other works
4078. Chadwick, Nicholas. "Franz Schreker's orchestral style and its influence on Alban Berg." MR 35(1974): 29-46.
4079. Hoogen, Eckhardt van der. "Die Orchesterwerke Franz Schrekers in ihrer Zeit." PhD dissertation (Musicology): Köln, 1980.
4080. ----. *Die Orchesterwerke Franz Schrekers in ihrer Zeit: Werkanalytische Studien.* Regensburg: G. Bosse, 1981.
4081. Stephan, Rudolf. "Zu Franz Schrekers *Vorspiel zu einem Drama*." Schreker: 115-121.

SCHROEDER, HERMANN (born 1904)

4082. Campbell, John Coleman. "Musical style in the three organ sonatas of Hermann Schroeder." DMA dissertation (Performance): University of Rochester, 1975. UM 76-3690. DA XXXVI.8, p.4836-A.
4083. Keusen, Raimund. *Die Orgel- und Vokalwerke von Hermann Schroeder.* Köln: A. Volk, 1974. 203 p.
4084. Schulze, Frederick Bennett. "The organ works of Hermann Schroeder." DMA dissertation (Performance): University of Washington, 1970. 95 p. UM 71-1026. DA XXXI.7, p.3588-A.

SCHUBAUR, JOHANN LUKAS (1749-1815)

4085. Sieber, Wolfgang. "Johann Lukas Schubaur als Sinfonie-Komponist." *Operpfälzer Documente der Musikgeschichte*, ed. Hermann Beck. Regensberger Beiträge zur Musikwissenschaft 1. Regensburg: G. Bosse, 1976: 129-200.

SCHUBERT, FRANZ (1797-1828)

Chamber works [see also individual genres]
4086. Chusid, Martin. "The chamber music of Franz Schubert." PhD dissertation: University of California, Berkeley, 1961. No DA listing.
4087. Depew, Laurienne Joyce. "Franz Schubert's music for violin and piano." MA dissertation (Musicology): University of Kentucky, 1977.

Choral works
4088. Badura-Skoda, Eva. "On Schubert's choral works." ACR 24/2-3(1982): 83-90. [Especially Masses in E Flat and A Flat]

4089. Cox, Richard G. "Choral texture in the music of Franz Schubert." PhD dissertation (Music History and Literature): Northwestern University, 1963. UM 64-2740. DA XXIV.9, p.2779-80.

4090. Dürr, Walther. "*Dona nobis pacem*: Gedanken zu Schuberts spätem Messen." Fs. Durr: 62-74.

4091. Heider, Anne Harrington. "A survey of Schubert's part-songs for mixed voices." ACR 22/3(1980): 3-17.

4092. Nafziger, Kenneth J. "The Masses of Haydn and Schubert: A study in the rise of romanticism." DMA dissertation (Music History): University of Oregon, 1970. UM 71-10,765. DA XXXIV.10, p.5451-A.

4093. Stringham, Ronald S. "The Masses of Franz Schubert." PhD dissertation (Musicology): Cornell University, 1964. UM 64-8760. DA XXV.3, p.1958-9.

4094. Taruskin. [Mass in E-Flat Major, D.950]

Moments musicaux

4095. Cone, Edward T. "Schubert's promissary note: An exercise in musical hermeneutics." NCM 5(1981-1982): 233-241.

4096. Gauldin, Robert. "Schubert's *Moment Musical* No.6." ITO 6/8 (1979-1981): 17-30.

4097. Holland, Mark. "Schubert's *Moment Musical* in F Minor, Op.94, No.3: An analysis." TP 7/2(1982): 5-32.

4098. Hughes, Matt, Lawrence Moss and Carl Schachter. "Analysis Symposium." JMT 12/1(1968): 184-239. [Also in Yeston: 141-201] [Op.94, No.1]

4099. McCreless, Patrick. "Schubert's *Moment Musical* No.2: The interaction of rhythmic and tonal structures." ITO 3/4(1977-1978): 3-11.

4100. Rothgeb, John. "Another view on Schubert's *Moment Musical*, Op.94/1." JMT 13/1(1969): 129-139.

4101. Schachter, Carl. "More about Schubert's Op.94/1." JMT 13/2 (1969): 219-229.

4102. Wittlich, Gary E. "Compositional premises in Schubert's Opus 94, Number 6." ITO 5/8(1979-1981): 31-43.

Octet

4103. Klein, Theodor. "Zu Franz Schuberts Oktett Op.166." Fs. Haberl: 143-149.

Operas

4104. Citron, Marcia Smith. "Schubert's seven complete operas: A musico-dramatic study." PhD dissertation (Musicology): University of North Carolina, 1971. UM 72-10,699. DA XXXII.9, p.5262.

Piano Duets

4105. Weekley, Dallas Alfred. "The one-piano, four-hand compositions of Franz Schubert: An historical and interpretive analysis." EdD dissertation: Indiana University, 1968. UM 69-02,796. DA XXXIX.8, p.2746.

4106. Weekley, Dallas Alfred and Nancy Argenbright Weekley. "Schubert: Master of the piano duet." PQ 104(1978-1979): 41-48.

4107. Zipp, Friedrich. "Bemerkungen zu einem zyklischen Klavierwerk zu vier Händen von Franz Schubert." M 32(1978-1979): 18-22. [*Divertissement, Andantino varié e rondeau brillant*]

Piano Fantasies

4108. Brody, Elaine. "Mirror of his soul: Schubert's Fantasy in C (D.760)." PQ 104(1978-1979): 23-31.

4109. Demus, Jorg. "Two fantasies: Mozart's Fantasy in C Minor (K.475) and Schubert's Fantasy in C Minor (D.993)." PQ 104(1978-1979): 9-11.

4110. Godel, Arthur. "Zum Eigengesetz der Schubertschen Fantasien." Brusatti: 199-206.

Piano Sonatas

4111. Bante-Knight, Mary Martha. "Tonal and thematic coherence in Schubert's Piano Sonata D.960." PhD dissertation (Theory): Washington University, 1983. 122 p. No DA listing.

4112. Chusid, Martin. "Cyclicism in Schubert's Piano Sonata in A Major (D.959)." PQ 104(1978-1979): 38-40.

4113. Dommel-Diény, Amy. *Schubert-Liszt*. Dommel-Diény 9. Paris: Dommel-Diény, 1976. [Op.42]

4114. Geiringer, Karl. "Schubert's *Arpeggione* Sonata and the Super Arpeggio." MQ 65(1979): 513-523.

4115. Godel, Arthur. "Schuberts drei letzte Klaviersonaten (D.958-960)." PhD dissertation (Musicology): Zürich, n.d.

4116. Goldberger, David. "A stylistic analysis and performance of three piano sonatas by Franz Schubert." EdD dissertation: Columbia University Teachers College, 1978. No DA listing.

4117. Hanna, Albert L. "A stylistic analysis of some style elements in the solo piano sonatas of Franz Schubert." PhD dissertation (Theory): Indiana University, 1965. UM 65-10,832. DA XXVI.7, p.3994.

4118. Hill, William G. "The genesis of Schubert's Posthumous Sonata in B-Flat Major." MR 12(1951): 269-278.

4119. Komma, Karl Michael. "Franz Schuberts Klaviersonte A-Moll, Op. posth. 164, D.537: Zur Wandel des klassischen Formbegriffs." Fs. Becking: 413-436. [Also in ZM 3/2(1972): 2-15.

4120. Mainka, Jürgen. "Schuberts B-Dur-Klaviersonate: Ohnmacht und Grösse des 'Trotzdem'." MG 28(1978): 656-662.

4121. Schnebel, Dieter. "Klangraume-Zeitraume: Zweiter Versuch über Schubert." Fs. Savoff: 111-120. [Sonata in E Major, D.457]

4122. Truscott, Harold. "Schubert's unfinished Piano Sonata in C Major (1925)." MR 18(1957): 114-137.

4123. Tusa, Michael C. "When did Schubert revise his Opus 122?" MR 45(1984): 208-219.

4124. Whaples, Miriam K. "Mahler's and Schubert's A Minor Sonata D.784." ML 65(1984): 255-263.

4125. Wolff, Konrad. "Observations on the Scherzo of Schubert's B-Flat Sonata Op.posth. (D.960)." PQ 92(1975-1976): 28-29.

Piano Trios

4126. Fleischhauer, Gunther. "Franz Schubert: Trio für Klavier, Violine und Violoncello Nr.2 Es-Dur D.929 (Op.100)." NZM 144/6(1983): 31-34.

4127. Levenson, Irene Montefiore. "Smooth moves: Schubert and theories of modulation in the nineteenth century." ITO 7/5-6(1983-1984): 35-53. [Op.99/1]

4128. Levy, Janet M. "Texture as a sign in classic and early romantic music." JAMS 35/3(1982): 482-531. [D.898]

4129. Willfort, Manfred. "Das Urbild des Andante aus Schuberts Klaviertrio Es-Dur, D.929." OMZ 33(1978): 277-283.

Piano works [see also individual genres]

4130. Levenson, Irene Montefiore. "Smooth moves: Schubert and theories of modulation in the nineteenth century." ITO 7/5-6(1983-1984): 35-53. [*Impromptu* D.935, No.4; *Moment musical* Op.94, No.2; *Lebensstürme*, Op.144]

4131. Pierce, Alexandra. "Climax in music: Structure and phrase (Part III)." ITO 7/1(1983-1984): 3-30. [*Impromptu*, D.935]

4132. Sterling.

4133. Whaples, Miriam K. "Style in Schubert's piano music from 1817 to 1818." MR 35(1974): 260-280.

Quartettsatz

4134. Danckwardt, Marianne. "Funktionen von Harmonik und tonaler Anlage in Franz Schuberts Quartettsatz C-Moll, D.703." AM 40(1983): 50-60.

Die schöne Müllerin

4135. Feil, Arnold. *Franz Schubert: Die schöne Müllerin, Winterreise.* Stuttgart: Reclam 1975. 197 p.

4136. Neumann, Friedrich. *Musikalische Syntax und Form im Liederzyklus "Die schöne Müllerin" von Franz Schubert: Eine morphologische Studie.* Tutzing: H. Schneider, 1978.

4137. Pazur, Robert. "An interpretation of the pitch-structure of *Die schöne Müllerin*." ITO 1/6(1975-1976): 9-13.

4138. Reed, John. "*Die schöne Müllerin* reconsidered." ML 59(1978): 411-419.

4139. Schmidt, Karl. "Harmonie-Beispiele aus Schuberts Liederzyklus *Die schöne Müllerin*." M 32(1978-1979): 6-12, 55-60.

4140. Thigpen, Raymond Owen. "A study of the piano accompaniments of Franz Schubert's *Die schöne Müllerin*." EdD dissertation: Columbia University, 1964. UM 65-04,751. DA XXV.9, p.5327.

Schwanengesang

4141. Kerman, Joseph. "A romantic detail in Schubert's *Schwanengesang*." MQ 48(1962): 36-49. [*Ihr Bild*]

4142. Thomas, J. H. "Schubert's modified strophic songs with particular reference to *Schwanengesang*." MR 34(1973): 83-99.

Songs [see also individual cycles]

4143. Agawa, V. Kofi. "On Schubert's *Der greise Kopf.*" ITO 8/1 (1984-1985): 3-21.

4144. Baggett, Bruce A. "Analytical guide to the understanding and performance of selected song cycles of Franz Schubert." EdD dissertation: Columbia University, 1964. UM 65-02,263. DA XXXVI.4, p.2248.

4145. Branscombe, Peter. "Schubert and the melodrama." Badura-Skoda: 105-141. [*Die Zauberharfe; Fierrabras*]

4146. Brauner, Charles S. "Irony in the Heine Lieder of Schubert and Schumann." MQ 67(1981): 261-281.

4147. Broeckx, Jan L. and Walter Landrieu. "Comparative computer study of style, based on five Liedmelodies." I 1(1972): 29-92. [*Kennst du das Land*]

4148. De la Motte: 61-72. [*Nacht und Träume, D.827*]

4149. Dommel-Diény, Amy. *Schubert-Liszt.* Dommel-Diény 9. Paris: Dommel-Diény, 1976. [*Der Doppelgénger; Der Wegweiser; Kriegers Ahnung; Der Tod und das Mädchen; Der Lindenbaum*]

4150. Dräger, Hans Heinz. "Zur Frage des Wort-Ton-Verhältnisses im Hinblick zu Schuberts Strophenlied." AM 11(1954): 39-59.

4151. Düring, Werner-Joachim. *Erlkönig-Vertonungen: Eine historische und systematische Untersuchung.* Regensburg: G. Bosse, 1972.

4152. Dürr, Walther. "Schubert's songs and their poetry: Reflections on poetic aspects of song composition." Badura-Skoda: 1-24. [*Der Taucher; Wer sich der Einsamkeit ergibt; Die Stadt*]

4153. Eggebrecht, Hans Heinrich. "Prinzipien des Schubert-Liedes." AM 27(1970): 89-109.

4154. Fischer, Kurt von. "Zur semantischen Bedeutung von Textrepetition in Schuberts Liederzyklen." Brusatti: 335-342.

4155. Forbes, Elliot. "*Nur wer die Sehnsucht kennt*: An example of a Goethe lyric set to music." Fs. Merritt: 59-82.

4156. Gauldin, Robert. "Intramusical symbolism in the last strophe of Schubert's *Der Wegweiser.*" ITO 3/12(1977-1978): 3-6.

4157. Georgiades, Thrasybulos. *Schubert: Musik und Lyrik.* Göttingen: Vandenhoeck und Ruprecht, 1967.

4158. ----. "*Das Wirthaus* von Schubert und das Kyrie aus dem gregorianischen Requiem." Fs. Benz: 126-135.

4159. Goldschmidt, Harry. "Welches war die ursprüngliche Reihenfolge in Schuberts Heine-Liedern?" DJM 64(1972): 52-62.

4160. Gray, Walter. "The classical nature of Schubert's Lieder." MQ 57(1971): 62-72.

4161. Gruber, Gernot. "Romantisch Ironie in den Heine-Liedern?" Brusatti: 321-334.

4162. Haas, Hermann. *Über die Bedeutung der Harmonik in den Liedern Franz Schuberts: Zugleich ein Beitrag zur Methodik der harmonischen Analyse.* Bonn: Bouvier, 1957.

4163. Hallmark, Rufus. "Schubert's *Auf dem Strom.*" Badura-Skoda: 25-46.

4164. Hohlov, Jurij N. "Zur Frage vom Verhältnis der Musik und des poetischen Textes in Schuberts Liedern." Brusatti: 353-361.

4165. Kramarz, Joachim. "Das Rezitativ im Liedschaffen Franz Schuberts." PhD dissertation: Freie Universität, Berlin, 1959.

4166. Kresky: 68-79. [*Heidenröslein*]

4167. Lewis. [*Mignon Lieder*]

4168. McNamee, Ann K. "The Introduction in Schubert's Lieder." MA 4/1-2(1985): 95-106.

4169. Moman, Carl Conway, Jr. "A study of the musical setting by Franz Schubert and Hugo Wolf for Goethe's *Promethus, Ganymed*, and *Grenzen der Menschheit*." PhD dissertation: Washington University, 1980. 164 p. UM 81-03,693. DA XLI.9, p.3776-A.

4170. Porter, Ernest Graham. *Schubert's song technique*. London: D. Dobson, 1961.

4171. Salmen, Walter. "Zur Semantik von Schuberts Harfenspiel-ergesängen." Grasberger: 141-149. [*Gesänge des Harfners*, D.478-480]

4172. Schnebel, Dieter. "Klangraume-Zeitraume: Zweiter Versuch über Schubert." Fs. Savoff: 111-120. [*Ihr Bild*]

4173. Schollum, Robert. "Schubarts und Schuberts *Forelle*-Vertonungen." ME 28(1974-1975): 19-23.

4174. Schwarmath, Erdmute. *Musikalischer Bau und Sprachvertonung in Schuberts Liedern*. Tutzing: H. Schneider, 1969.

4175. Seelig, Harry E. "Schuberts Beitrag zu besseren Verständnis von Goethes Suleika-Gestalt: Eine literarisch-musiklische Studie der *Suleika-Lieder* Op.14 und 31." BM 17(1975): 299-316.

4176. Spirk, Arthur. "Theorie, Beschreibung und Interpretation in der Lied-Analyse." AM 34(1977): 225-235.

4177. Stovall, Francis D. "Schubert's Heine songs: A critical and analytical study." DMA dissertation: University of Texas, 1967. UM 68-04,243. DA XXVIII.10, p.4204.

4178. Thomas, Werner. "*Der Doppelgänger* von Franz Schubert." AM 11(1954): 252-267.

4179. Wildberger, Jacques. "Verschiedene Schichten der musikalischen Wortdeutung in den Liedern Franz Schuberts." SMZ 109(1969): 4-9.

4180. Wolff, Christoph. "Schubert's *Der Tod und das Madchen*: Analytical and explanatory notes on the song D.531 and the quartet D.810." Badura-Skoda: 143-171.

String Quartets

4181. Coolidge, Richard A. "Form in the string quartets of Franz Schubert." MR 32(1971): 309-325.

4182. Dahlhaus, Carl. "Formprobleme in Schuberts frühen Streichquar-tetten." Brusatti: 191-197.

4183. ----. "Die Sonatenform bei Schubert: Der erste Satz des G-Dur-Quartetts, D.887." M 32(1978): 125-130.

4184. Gillet, Judy. "The problem of Schubert's G Major String Quartet (D.887)." MR 35(1974): 281-292.

4185. Hollander, Hans. "Stil und poetische Idee in Schuberts D-Moll-Streichquartett." NZM 131(1970): 239-241.

4186. Levy, Janet M. "Texture as a sign in classic and early romantic music." JAMS 35/3(1982): 482-531. [D.887]

4187. Sachse, Hans Martin. *Franz Schuberts Streichquartette*. Münster; Westf.: M. Kramer, 1958.

4188. Truscott, Harold. "Schubert's D Minor String Quartet." MR 19(1958): 27-36.

4189. ----. "Schubert's String Quartet in G Major." MR 20(1959): 119-145.

4190. Wolff, Christoph. "Schubert's *Der Tod und das Mädchen*: Analytical and explanatory notes on the song D.531 and the quartet D.810." Badura-Skoda: 143-171.

String Quintet

4191. Abert, Anna Amalie. "Rhythmus und Klang in Schuberts Streichquintett." Fs. Fellerer: 1-11.

4192. Allen, Judith Shatin. "Schubert's C Major String Quintet, Opus 163/1: The evolving dominant." ITO 6/5(1981-1983): 3-16.

4193. Gülke, Peter. "Zum Bilde des späten Schubert: Vorwiegend analytische Betrachtungen zum Streichquintett, Op.163." DJM 65(1973-1977): 5-58.

Symphonies [see also individual titles]

4194. Brown, Maurice John Edwin. "Schubert's unfinished Symphony in D." ML 31(1950): 101-109.

4195. Hansen, Mathias. "Marsch und Formidee: Analytische Bemerkungen zu sinfonischen Sätzen Schuberts und Mahlers." BM 22(1980): 3-23.

4196. Horvath, Roland. "Schuberts Symphonieschaffen." ME 26 (1972-1973): 149-153.

4197. Langevin, Paul-Gilbert. "Franz Schubert et la symphonie: Les Nouvelles donnés historiques et musicales." RM 355-356-357(1982): 7-56.

4198. ----. "La Structure cellulaire dans les grandes symphonies." RM 355-357(1982): 110-117.

4199. Levenson, Irene M. "Motivic-harmonic transfer in the late works of Schubert: Chromaticism in large and small spans." PhD dissertation (Theory): Yale University, 1981. UM 81-24,373. DA XLII.5, p.1846-A.

4200. Schulze, Werner. *Tempo relationen im symphonischen Werk von Beethoven, Schubert und Brahms.* Bern: Kreis und Freude um Hans Kayser, 1981.

4201. Weber, Rudolf. *Die Sinfonien Franz Schuberts im Versuch einer strukturwissenschaftlichen Darstellung und Untersuchung.* Münster: Forschungsstelle für theoretische Musikwissenschaft an der Universität, 1971. Kassel: Bärenreiter, n.d.

Symphony in B Minor (Unfinished)

4202. Chusid, Martin. *Schubert: Symphony in B Minor (Unfinished).* Norton Critical Scores. New York: W.W. Norton, 1971.

4203. Dahlhaus, Carl. "Studien zu romantischen Symphonien: Zur musikalischen Syntax in Schuberts 'Unvollendeter'." JSIM (1972): 104-119.

4204. Kunze, Stefan. *Franz Schubert: Sinfonie H-Moll, unvollendete.* München: W. Fink, 1965.

4205. Laaff, Ernst. "Schuberts H-Moll Symphonie: Motivische Analyse zum Nachweis von erkennbaren Grundlagen ihrer Einheitlichkeit." Fs. Abert/H: 93-115.

Symphony in C Major

4206. Hollander, Hans. "Die Beethoven-Reflexe in Schuberts grosser C-Dur-Sinfonie." NZM 126(1965): 183-185.

4207. Laaff, Ernst. "Schuberts grosse C-Dur-Symphonie: Erkennbare Grundlagen ihrer Einheitlichkeit." Fs. Blume: 204-213.

4208. Levenson, Irene Montefiore. "Smooth moves: Schubert and theories of modulation in the nineteenth century." ITO 7/5-6(1983-1984): 35-53.

4209. Taruskin.

4210. Truscott, Harold. "Schubert's C Major Symphony." MMR 87(1957): 95-105.

Symphony No.4

4211. Weber, Horst. "Schuberts IV. Symphonie und ihre satztechnischen Vorbilder bei Mozart." M 32(1978): 147-151.

Symphony No.6

4212. Feil, Arnold. "Zur Satztechnik in Schuberts VI. Sinfonie." Grasberger: 69-83.

Symphony No.7

4213. Newbould, Brian. "La Symphonie No.7 en mi majeur (D.729) et sa réalisation." RM 355-356-357(1982): 57-70.

Symphony No.10

4214. Halbreich, Harry. "La Symphonie No.10 en re majeur (D.936A): Étude musicale." RM 355-356-357(1982): 83-102.

Die Winterreise

4215. Chailley, Jacques. *"Le Voyage d'Hiver" de Schubert.* Paris: A. Leduc, 1975.

4216. ----. "Le *Winterreise* et l'énigme de Schubert." SM 11(1969): 107-112. [Also in Fs. Szabolcsi: 107-112]

4217. Feil, Arnold. *Franz Schubert: Die schöne Müllerin, Winterreise.* Stuttgart: Reclam 1975. 197 p.

4218. Greene, David B. "Schubert's *Winterreise*: A study in the aesthetics of mixed media." *Journal of Aesthetics and Art Criticism* 29/2(1970): 181-193.

4219. Seidel, Elmar. "Ein chromatisches Harmonieiserungsmodell in Schuberts *Winterreise*." AM 26(1969): 285-296.

4220. Youens, Susan. "Poetic rhythm and musical metre in Schubert's *Winterreise*." ML 65(1984): 28-44.

Other works

4221. Abraham, Gerald. *The music of Schubert.* New York: W.W. Norton, 1947.

4222. ----, ed. *Schubert: A symposium.* London: L. Drummond, 1946.

4223. Badura-Skoda, Paul. "Fehlende und überzählige Takte bei Schubert und Beethoven." OMZ 33(1978): 284-294.

4224. Benary, Peter. "Zum Personalstil Franz Schuberts in seinen Instrumentalwerken." JP 2(1979): 190-208.

4225. Boyd, Malcolm. "Schubert's short cuts." MR 29(1968): 12-21.

4226. Brown, Maurice John Edwin. *Essays on Schubert.* London: Macmillan, 1966.

4227. ----. "Schubert's settings of the *Salve Regina*." ML 37(1956): 234-249.

4228. ----. *Schubert's variations.* London: Macmillan, 1954.

4229. Bruce, Robert. "The lyrical element in Schubert's instrumental forms." MR 30(1969): 131-137.

4230. Burdick, Michael Francis. "A structural analysis of melodic scale-degree tendencies in selected themes of Haydn, Mozart, Schubert and Chopin." PhD dissertation (Theory): Indiana University, 1977. UM 77-22,643. DA XXXVIII.4, p.1724-A.

4231. Chusid, Martin. "Schubert's cyclic composition of 1824." ACTA 36(1964): 37-45.

4232. Clarke, F.R.C. "Schubert's use of tonality: Some unique features." CAUSM 1/2(1971): 25-38.

4233. Cone, Edward T. "Schubert's unfinished business." NCM 7(1983-1984): 222-232. [Cello Quintet, Op.163; *Unfinished Symphony*; Piano Sonatas D.840 and D.959]

4234. Coren, Daniel. "Ambiguity in Schubert's recapitulations." MQ 60 (1974): 568-582.

4235. Dale, Kathleen. "Schubert's indebtedness to Hadyn." ML 21 (1940): 23-30.

4236. Downs, Philip. "On an aspect of Schubert's expressive means." SMUWO 2(1977): 41-51.

4237. Edler, Arnfried. "Hinweise auf die Wirkung Bachs im Werk Franz Schuberts." MF 33(1980): 279-291.

4238. Federhofer, Hellmut. "Terzverwandle Akkorde und ihre Funktion in der Harmonik Franz Schuberts." Brusatti: 61-70.

4239. Feil, Arnold. *Studien zu Schuberts Rhythmik.* München: W. Fink, 1966.

4240. Floros, Constantin. "Parallelem zwischen Schubert und Bruckner." Fs. Wessely: 133-146.

4241. Goldschmidt, Harry. "Die Frage der Periodisierung im Schaffen Schuberts." BM 2(1959): 2-28.

4242. Gülke, Peter. "Musikalische Lyrik und instrumentale Grossform." Brusatti: 199-206.

4243. Keller, Hermann. "Schuberts Verhältnis zur Sonatenform." Fs. Vetter: 287-295.

4244. Krebs, Harald. "The background level in some tonally deviating works of Franz Schubert." ITO 8/8(1984-1985): 5-18.

4245. Marggraf, Wolfgang. "Franz Schubert und die slawische Folklore." BM 23(1981): 20-25.

4246. Misch, Ludwig. "Ein Lieblingsmotiv Schuberts." MF 15(1962): 146-152.

4247. Möllers, Christian. "Einfall und Darstellung: Eine Untersuchung zu Schuberts 'Rosamundethema'." M 32(1978): 141-146.

4248. Norman, Elizabeth. "Schubert's incidental music to *Rosamunde*." MR 21(1960): 8-15.

4249. Pfrogner, Hermann. "Der Dominantseptklang und seine enharmonische Stellung in Schuberts Harmonik." OMZ 2(1947): 14-18.

4250. Porter, Ernest Graham. "Schubert's harmonies." MR 19(1958): 20-26.

4251. Pritchard, T.C.L. "Franz Schubert." MR 1(1940): 103-122.

4252. Rhein, Robert. "Franz Schuberts Variationswerke." PhD dissertation: Universität des Saarlandes, 1960.

4253. Riezler, Walter. *Schuberts Instrumentalmusik: Werkanalysen.* Zürich: Atlantis, 1967.

4254. Seidel, Elmar. "Die Enharmonik in den harmonischen Grossformen Schuberts." PhD dissertation: Johann Wolfgang Goethe-Universität, Frankfurt am Main, 1963.

4255. Temperley, Nicholas. "Schubert and Beethoven's eight-eix chord." NCM 5(1981-1982): 142-154.

4256. Webster, James. "Schubert's sonata form and Brahms's first maturity." NCM 2/1(1978): 18-35, 3(1979-1980): 52-71.

4257. Wollenberg, Susan. "Schubert and the dream." STU 9(1980): 135-150.

SCHUBERT, MANFRED (born 1937)

4258. Rienäcker, Gerd. "Die Analyse: *Cantilena e capriccio* per violino et orchestra von Manfred Schubert." MG 29(1979): 6-7.

SCHULLER, GUNTHER (born 1925)

4259. Hines: 183-202.

4260. Larsen, Robert L. "A study and comparison of Samuel Barber's *Vanessa*, Robert Ward's *The Crucible*, and Gunther Schuller's *The Visitation*." DMA dissertation (Conducting): Indiana University, 1971. No DA listing.

4261. Schweitzer.

4262. Wennerstrom. [*Music for Brass Quintet*]

SCHUMAN, WILLIAM (born 1910)

4263. Broder, Nathan. "The music of William Schuman." MQ 31(1945): 17-28.

4264. Griffin, Malcolm Joseph. "Style and dimension in the choral works of William Schuman." DMA dissertation (Choral Conducting): University of Illinois, 1972. UM 72-19,835. DA XXXIII.1, p.348-A.

4265. McKinley, Lily. "Stylistic development in selected symphonies of William Schuman: A comparison of symphonies number three and nine." PhD dissertation: New York University, 1977. UM 77-20,751. DA XXXVIII.4, p.1965-A.

4266. Mize.

SCHUMANN, CLARA WIECK (1819-1896)

4267. Susskind, Pamela Gertrude. "Clara Wieck Schumann as pianist and composer: A study of her life and works." PhD dissertation: University of California, Berkeley, 1977. 2 vols. No DA listing.

SCHUMANN, ROBERT (1810-1856)

Carnaval

4268. Chailley, Jacques. *"Carnaval" de Schumann, Op.9.* Au delà des notes 2. Paris: A. Leduc, 1971.

4269. Neighbour, Oliver. "Brahms and Schumann: Two Opus Nines and beyond." NCM 7(1983-1984): 266-270.

4270. Simonett, Hans Peter. "Taktgruppengliederung und Form in Schumanns *Carnaval*." PhD dissertation: Freie Universität Berlin, 1978.

4271. Summer, Averill Vanderipe. "A discussion and analysis of selected unifying elements in Robert Schumann's *Carnaval*, Opus 9." DMA dissertation (Piano): Indiana University, 1979. No DA listing.

Chamber works

4272. Bunyan, Christine Elizabeth. "Aspects of tradition and originality in the chamber music of Robert Schumann." PhD dissertation (Musicology): Rhodes University, Grahamstown, South Africa, 1978.

4273. Helms, Siegmund. "Der Melodiebau in der Kammermusik Robert Schumanns." NZM 131(1970): 194-196.

4274. Hollander, Hans. "Das Variationsprinzip in Schumanns Klavierquintett." NZM 124(1963): 223-225.

4275. Kohlhase, Hans. *Die Kammermusik Robert Schumanns: Stilistische Untersuchung.* Hamburg: Wagner, 1979. 3 vols.

4276. Reiningdaus, Frieder. "Zwischen Historismus und Poesie: Über die Notwendigkeit umfassender Musikanalyse und ihre Erprobung an Klavierkammermusik von Felix Mendelssohn Bartholdy und Robert Schumann." ZM 4/2(1973): 22-29, 5/1(1974): 34-44.

Choral works

4277. Godwin, Robert C. "Schumann's choral works and the romantic movement." DMA dissertation: University of Illinois, 1967. UM 67-11,854. DA XXVIII.4, p.1457.

4278. Popp, Susanne. *Untersuchungen zu Robert Schumanns Chorkompositionen.* PhD dissertation: Rheinische Friedrich-Wilhelms Universität, Bonn, 1971.

Dichterliebe

4279. Agawu, V. Kofi. "Structural 'highpoints' in Schumann's *Dichterliebe*." MA 3/2(1984): 159-180.

4280. Benary: 21-29. [No.1]

4281. Hallmark, Rufus. "The sketches for *Dichterliebe*." NCM 1/2(1977): 110-136.

4282. Komar, Arthur, ed. *Schumann: Dichterliebe.* Norton Critical Scores. New York: W.W. Norton, 1971.

4283. Neumeyer, David. "Organic structure and the song cycle: Another look at Schumann's *Dichterliebe*." MTS 4(1982): 92-105.

4284. Rothgeb, John. "Comment: On the form of *Ich grolle nicht*." ITO 5/2(1979-1981): 15-17.

Genoveva

4285. ASO 71(1985).

4286. Oliver, Willie-Earl. *Robert Schumanns vergessene Oper "Genoveva."* Freiburg im Breisgau: J. Krause, 1978.

4287. Siegel, Linda. "A second look at Schumann's *Genoveva.*" MR 36 (1975): 17-41.

Kinderszenen

4288. Brendel, Alfred. "Der Interpret muss erwachsen sein: Zu Schumanns *Kinderszenen.*" M 35(1981): 429-433.

4289. Kühn, Clemens. "*Kinderszenen*: Analytische Bausteine zu Schumanns Op.15." M 35(1981): 434-437.

4290. Lesznai, Lajos. "Robert Schumann: *Kinderszenen* Op.15." SM 13(1971): 87-94.

4291. Réti-Forbes, Jean. *"Kinderszenen" of Robert Schumann: An interpretive and thematic commentary.* Tallulah Falls, GA: W. Stanton Forbes, 1979.

4292. Traub, Andreas. "Die *Kinderszenen* als zyklisches Werk." M 35 (1981): 424-428.

Liederkreis

4293. Knaus, Herwig. *Musiksprache und Werkstruktur in Robert Schumanns "Liederkreis": Mit dem Faksimile des Autographs.* München: E. Katzbichler, 1974. 105 p.

4294. Ringger, Rolf Urs. "Zu Eichendorff-Schumanns *Liederkreis.*" SMZ 106(1966): 339-345.

Papillons

4295. Chailley.

Piano works [see also individual titles]

4296. Barela, Margaret Mary. "A comparative study of metric displacement in Schumann's *Intermezzi*, Op.4. and *Waldszenen*, Op.82." PhD dissertation (Piano Performance and Music History and Literature): Indiana University, 1977. No DA listing.

4297. Beaufils, Marcel. *La Musique de piano de Schumann.* Paris: Larousse, 1951.

4298. Becker, Claudia Stevens. "A new look at Schumann's Impromptus." MQ 67(1981): 568-586.

4299. Boetticher, Wolfgang. *Robert Schumanns Klavierwerke* (Vol.1, Opp.1-6). Wilhelmshaven: Heinrichshofen, 1976.

4300. ----. "Zur Zitatpraxis in Robert Schumanns frühen Klavierwerken." Fs. Husmann: 63-73.

4301. Brown, Thomas Alan. *The aesthetics of Robert Schumann.* New York: Philosophical Library, 1968.

4302. Dommel-Diény, Amy. *Schumann.* Dommel-Diény 8. Neuchâtel: Delachaux et Niestlé, 1967. [*Études symphoniques; Cinq variations* (posthumous)]

4303. Dubal, David. "Robert Schumann's piano music: An overview." PQ 131(1984-1985): 59-63.

4304. Fugo, Charles Leonard. "A comparative study of melodic motives in selected piano cycles of Robert Schumann." DM dissertation: Indiana University, 1973. 100 p. RILM 73/1936. No DA listing. [*Intermezzi; Carnaval; Davidsbündlertänze; Noveletten*]

4305. Gruber, Gernot. "Robert Schumann: *Fantasia* Op.17, 1. Satz: Versuch einer Interpretation." MAU 4(1984): 101-130.

4306. Harwood, Gregory W. "Robert Schumann's Sonata in F-Sharp Minor: A study of creative process and romantic inspiration." CM 29 (1980): 17-30.

4307. Hering, Hans. "Das Variation in Schumanns frühem Klavier-werk." Melos/NZM 1(1975): 347-354.

4308. Kollen, John L. "Robert Alexander Schumann (1810-1856): *Tema*, Op.13." Fs. Cuyler: 163-171.

4309. Leipold, Eugen. "Die romantische Polyphonie in der Klaviermu-sik Robert Schumanns." PhD dissertation: Friedrich-Alexander-Universität, Erlangen, 1954.

4310. ----. "Vom Melodieklang in Schumanns Klaviermusik." NZM 117 (1956): 415-418.

4311. Lester, Joel. "Substance and illusion in Schumann's *Erinnerung*, Op.68: A structural analysis and pictorial (*geistliche*) description." ITO 4(1978): 9-17.

4312. McNab, Duncan Robert. "A study of classical and romantic elements in the piano works of Mozart and Schumann." PhD dissertation: University of Southern California, 1961. UM 61-03,203. DA XXII.5, p.1658.

4313. Rathbun, James Ronald. "A textual history and analysis of Schumann's Sonatas Op.11, Op.14, and Op.22." DMA dissertation (Perfor-mance): University of Iowa, 1976. UM 77-03,789. DA XXXVII.8, p.4688-A.

4314. Roesner, Linda Correll. "Schumann's revisions in the first movement of the Piano Sonata in G Minor, Op.22." NCM 1(1977-1978): 97-109.

4315. Sterling.

4316. Stevens, Claudia A. "A study of Robert Schumann's *Impromp-tus*, Op.5: Its sources and a critical analysis of its revisions." DMA dissertation (Performance): Boston University, 1977. UM 77-21,693. DA XXXVIII.4, p.1732-3-A.

Scenes from Goethe's Faust

4317. Ferchault, Guy. *Faust: Une Légende et ses musiciens*. Paris: Larousse, 1948.

4318. Macy.

4319. Mintz, Donald. "Schumann as an interpreter of Goethe's *Faust*." JAMS 14(1961): 235-236.

4320. Seyfarth, Winfried. "Die unvollendeten *Faust*-Szenen: ein bedeutender Beitrag Robert Schumanns zu den Goethe-Gedächtnisferien im Jahre 1849." Muller: 42-51.

Songs [see also individual cycles]
4321. Ashley, Douglas Daniels. "The role of the piano in Schumann's song." PhD dissertation (Music History and Literature): Northwestern University, 1973. UM 73-30,522. DA XXXIV.6, p.3449.
4322. Brauner, Charles S. "Irony in the Heine Lieder of Schubert and Schumann." MQ 67(1981): 261-281.
4323. Broeckx, Jan L. and Walter Landrieu. "Comparative computer study of style, based on five Liedmelodies." I 1(1972): 29-92. [*Kennst du das Land*]
4324. Conrad, Dieter. "Schumanns Liederkomposition: Von Schubert hergesehen." MF 24(1971): 135-153.
4325. Dommel-Diény, Amy. *Schumann*. Dommel-Diény 8. Neuchâtel; Paris: Delachaux et Niestlé, 1967. [*In der Fremde; Das ist ein Flöten und Geigen; Ich hab' im Traum geweinet; Am leuchtenden Sommermorgan; Nun hast du mir; Der Nussbaum*]
4326. Felner, Rudolf. "Schumann's place in German song." MQ 26 (1940): 340-354.
4327. Geissler, William. "Vergleichende Analyse zu Robert Schumanns Vertonungen *Die Lotusblume* nach Worten von Heinrich Heine." Müller: 34-41.
4328. Gerstmeier, August. *Die Lieder Schumanns: Zur Musik des frühen 19. Jahrhunderts*. Tutzing: H. Schneider, 1982.
4329. Hernried, Robert. "Four unpublished compositions by Robert Schumann." MQ 28(1942): 50-62.
4330. Kinsey, Barbara. "Mörike poems set by Brahms, Schumann, and Wolf." MR 29(1968): 257-267.
4331. Körner, Klaus. "Eichendorff/Schumann: *Mondnacht*: Ein exemplarischer Fall." MB 9(1977): 381-384.
4332. Lewis. [*Mignon Lieder*]
4333. Mahlert, Ulrich. "Schumanns späte Lieder." PhD dissertation (Musicology): Freiburg Universität, Breisgau, 1982.
4334. Mayeda, Ako. "Das Reich der Nacht in den Liedern Robert Schumanns." Fs. Schenk: 202-227.
4335. Mertens, Paul-Heinrich. *Die Schumannschen Klangfarbengesetze und ihre Bedeutung für die Übertragung von Sprache und Musik*. Frankfurt am Main: E. Bochinsky, 1975.
4336. Phillips, Edward R. "The Mary Stuart songs of Robert Schumann: Key as an aspect of cycle." CAUSM 9/2(1979): 91-99. [Op.135]
4337. Pierce, Alexandra. "Climax in music: Structure and phrase (Part III)." ITO 7/1(1983-1984): 3-30. [*Mondnacht*]
4338. Sams, Eric. *The songs of Robert Schumann*. London: Methuen, 1969.
4339. Schlager, Karl-Heinz. "Erstarrte Idylle: Schumanns Eichendorff-Verständnis im Lied Op.39/VII (*Auf einer Burg*)." AM 33(1976): 119-132.
4340. Simmons, Margaret Rymer. "The cyclic characteristics of Robert Schumann's Lieder, Op.35." MM dissertation: Florida State University, 1967.
4341. Thym, Jurgen. "The solo song settings of Eichendorff's poems by Schumann and Wolf." PhD dissertation (Musicology): Case-Western Reserve University, 1974. UM 74-25,687. DA XXXV.5, p.3043.

4342. ----. "Text-music relationships in Schumann's *Frühlingsfahrt.*" TP 5/2(1980): 7-25.

4343. Walsh, Stephen. *The Lieder of Schumann.* London: Cassell, 1971.

Symphonies

4344. Abraham, Gerald. "Schumann's *Jugendsinfonie* in G Minor." MQ 37(1951): 45-60.

4345. Boetticher, Wolfgang. "Zur Kompositonstechnik und Originalfassung von Robert Schumanns III. Sinfonie." ACTA 53(1981): 144-156.

4346. Finson, Jon William. "Robert Schumann: The creation of the symphonic works." PhD dissertation (Musicology): University of Chicago, 1980. 342 p. DA XLI.8, p.3313-A.

4347. ----. "The sketches for Robert Schumann's C Minor Symphony." JM 1(1982): 395-418.

4348. Gebhardt, Armin. *Robert Schumann als Symphoniker.* Regensburg: G. Bosse, 1968.

4349. Gülke, Peter. "Zu Robert Schumanns *Rheinischer Sinfonie.*" BM 16(1974): 123-135.

4350. Just, Martin. *Robert Schumann: Symphonie Nr. 4, D-Moll.* München: W. Fink, 1982.

4351. Maniates, Maria Rika. "The D Minor Symphony of Robert Schumann." Fs. Wiora: 441-447.

4352. Newcomb, Anthony. "Once more 'between absolute and program music': Schumann's Second Symphony." NCM 7(1983-1984): 233-248.

4353. Voss, Egon. "Robert Schumanns Sinfonie in G-Moll." NZM 133 (1972): 312-319.

Violin works

4354. Melkus, Eduard. "Schumanns letzte Werke." OMZ 15(1960): 565-571. [Violin Concerto; Thirrd Violin Sonata]

4355. ----. "Eine vollständige 3. Violinsonata Schumanns." NZM 121(1960): 190-195.

Other works

4356. Abraham, Gerald. *Schumann: A symposium.* London: Oxford University Press, 1952.

4357. Ahrens, Christian. "Innovative Elemente in Schumanns Konzertstück für vier Horner und Orchester F-Dur Op.86." SMZ 123(1983): 148-156.

4358. Finson, Jon W. "Schumann, popularity, and the *Ouverture, Scherzo, und Finale*, Opus 52." MQ 69(1983): 1-26.

4359. Honsa, Melitta. "Synkope, Hemiole und Taktwechsel in den Instrumentalwerken Robert Schumanns." PhD dissertation: Leopold Franzens Universität, Innsbruck, 1965.

4360. Johnson, Mary Imogene Evans. "Characteristic metrical anomalies in the insturmental music of Robert Schumann: A study of rhythmic intention." PhD dissertation: University of Oklahoma, 1979. No DA listing.

4361. Keil, Siegmar. *Untersuchungen zur Fugentechnik in Robert Schumanns Instrumentalschaffen.* Hamburg: K.D. Wagner, 1973.

4362. Longyear, Rey M. "Unusual tonal procedures in Schumann's sonata-type cycles." ITO 3/12(1977-1978): 22-30.

4363. Marsoner, Karin. "Sonatenkonzept Robert Schumanns in Theorie und Praxis." Kolleritsch:172-181.

4364. Probst, Gisela. *Robert Schumanns Oratorien.* Wiesbaden: Breitkopf und Härtel, 1975.

4365. Sachs, Klaus-Jürgen. "Robert Schumanns Fugen über den Namen BACH (Op.60): Ihr künstliersches Vorbild und ihr kritischer Mass-stab." Bachfest: 151-175.

4366. Sams, Eric. "Hat Schumann in seinen Werken Chriffen benutzt?" NZM 127(1966): 218-224.

4367. ----. "The tonal analogue in Schumann's music." PRMA 96 (1969-1970): 103-117.

4368. Whitesell, L. A. "E.T.A. Hoffmann and Robert Schumann: The blending of music and literature in German romanticism." JALS 13(1983): 73-101.

4369. Wolff, Hellmuth Christian. "Robert Schumann: Der Klassizist." M 2(1948): 47-54.

SCHWAEN, KURT (born 1909)

4370. Kleinschmidt, Klaus. "*Der neue Kolumbus*: Ein Poem von Heinz Rusch/Musik von Kurt Schwaen." MG 13(1963): 601-603.

4371. Matties, Ludwig. "*Komm wieder zur kunft'gen Nacht*: Ein Zyklus für Chor a cappella nach deutschen Volksdichtungen von Kurt Schwaen." MG 11(1961): 92-95.

4372. ----. "Sturm und Gesang: Über Kurt Schwaens *Wartburg-Kantate*: Zu seinem 50. Geburtstag." MG 9/6(1959): 15-18.

SCHWARTZ, ELLIOTT (born 1936)

4373. Schwartz, Elliott. "Electronic music and live performance." Battcock: 331-338. [*Five Mobiles; Cycles and Gongs; Music for Napoleon and Beethoven; The Harmony of Maine*]

SCHWITTER, KURT

4374. Mizelle, Dary John. "Kurt Schwitter's *Ursonate* and *Quanta* and *Hymn to Matter*." PhD dissertation: University of California, San Diego, 1977. UM 77-32,822. DA XXXVIII.9, p.5155-A.

SCOTT, CYRIL (1879-1970)

4375. Darson, Thomas H. "The solo piano works of Cyril Scott." PhD dissertation (Musicology): City University of New York, 1979. UM 79-23,716. DA XL.5, p.2338-A.

SCRIABIN, ALEXANDER (1872-1915)

Piano works [see also individual titles]
4376. Cook, Marcia. "Scriabin's Etudes: Form and style." MA dissertation (Musicology): University of Southern California, 1977.
4377. Herndon, Claude H. "Skryabin's new harmonic vocabulary in his Sixth Sonata." JMR 4(1982-1983): 353-368.
4378. Hymovitz, Edwin. "Playing the Scriabin Etudes: Problems of keyboard technique and style." JALS 14(1983): 43-58.
4379. Martins, José Eduardo. "Quelques aspects comparatifs dans les langages pianistiques de Debussy et Scriabine." CAD 7(1983): 24-37.
4380. Meeks, John Samuel. "Aspects of stylistic evolution in Scriabin's Piano Preludes." DMA dissertation (Performance): Peabody Conservatory, 1975. UM 76-23,204. DA XXXVII.4, p.1866-A.
4381. Pinnix, David Clemmons. "Evolution of stylistic elements in selected solo piano works by Scriabin." DMA dissertation (Performance): University of Rochester, 1969. 142 p. RILM 76/1556dd66. No DA listing.
4382. Pople, Anthony. "Skryabin's Prelude, Op.67, No.1: Sets and structure." MA 2(1983): 151-174.
4383. Randlett, Samuel. "Elements of Scriabin's keyboard style." PQ 74(1970-1971): 20-24; 75(1971): 18-24; 76(1971): 22-27; 78(1971-1972): 26-30.
4384. ----. "The nature and development of Scriabin's piano vocabulary." DMA dissertation: Northwestern University, 1966. UM 68-2676. DA XXIX.1, p.287-A.
4385. Ruger, Christof. "Ethische Konstanz und stilistische Kontinuität im Schaffen Alexander Nikolaevič Skrjabins unter besonderer Berücksichtigung seiner Klavierkompositionen." PhD dissertation (Musicology): Leipzig, 1971.
4386. Steger, Hanns. "Beiträge zum Klavierwerk von A. Skrjabin." PhD dissertation (Musicology): Regensburg, 1977.
4387. ----. Materialstrukturen in den fünf späten Klaviersonaten Alexander Skrjabins. Regensburg: G. Bosse, 1977. 300 p.
4388. ----. *Der Weg der Klaviersonate bei Alexander Skrjabin.* München: Wollenweber, 1979.
4389. Wait, Mark. "Liszt, Scriabin, and Boulez: Considerations of form." JALS 1(1977): 9-16. [10th Sonata]
4390. Woolsey, Timothy Dwight. "Organizational principles in piano sonatas of Alexander Scriabin." DMA dissertation (Performance): University of Texas, 1977. UM 77-22,907. DA XXXVIII.5, p.2408-A.

Prometheus
4391. Peacock, Kenneth John. "Alexander Scriabin's *Prometheus*: Philosophy and structure." PhD dissertation (Musicology): University of Michigan, 1976. UM 76-19,213. DA XXXVII.3, p.1291-A.
4392. Weber, Horst. "Zur Geschichte der Synästhesie, oder: Von den Schwierigkeiten, die Luce-Stimme in *Prometheus* zu interpretieren." Kolleritsch/S: 50-57.

Symphonic works

4393. Gleich, Clemens Christoph von. *Die sinfonische Werke von Alexander Skrjabin.* Bilthoven: A.B. Creyghton, 1963.

4394. Nussgruber, Walther. "Über des sinfonische Werk von Alexander Skrjabin." ME 26(1972-1973): 59-64, 106-110.

Other works

4395. Angerer, Manfred. *Musikalischer Aesthetizismus: Analytische Studien zu Skrjabins Spätwerk.* Tutzing: H. Schneider, 1984.

4396. Baker, James Marshall. "Alexander Scriabin: The transition from tonality to atonality." PhD dissertation (Theory): Yale University, 1977. No DA listing

4397. ----. "Scriabin's implicit tonality." MTS 2(1980): 1-18.

4398. Brinkmann, Reinhold. "Kette und Kreis: Hinweise zum Formdenken Skrjabins." Kolleritsch/S: 66-74.

4399. Chapman, Alan. "A theory of harmonic structures for non-tonal music." PhD dissertation (Musicology): Yale University, 1978. 368 p. UM 78-18,589. DA XXXIX.4, p.1914-A. [*Caresse dansée*, Op.57, No.2]

4400. Cooper, Martin. "Alexander Skriabin and the Russian renaissance." Fs. Abraham: 219-239.

4401. Dahlhaus, Carl. "Struktur und Expression bei Alexander Skrjabin." MO 6(1971): 179-203.

4402. Dickenmann, P. *Die Entwicklung der Harmonik bei A. Skrjabin.* Bern: P. Haupt, 1935.

4403. Dickinson, Peter. "Skryabin's later music." MR 26(1965): 19-22.

4404. Eberle, Gottfried. *Zwischen Tonalität und Atonalität: Studien zur Harmonik Alexander Skrjabins.* München: E. Katzbichler, 1977. 142 p.

4405. Forchert, Arno. "Bemerkungen zum Schaffen Alexander Skrjabins: Ordnung und Ausdruck in der Grenzen der Tonalität." Fs. Pepping: 298-311.

4406. Guenther, Roy James. "Varvara Dernova's *Garmonia Skriabina*: A translation and critical commentary." PhD dissertation (Musicology): Catholic University, 1979. 455 p. UM 79-18,573. DA XL.3, p.1142-A.

4407. Gut, Serge. "Skrjabin: Vermittler zwischen Debussy und Schöberg." Kolleritsch/S: 85-94.

4408. Kelkel, Manfred. *Aleksandr Skrjabin: Sa vie, l'éotéisme et le langage musical dans son oeuvre.* Paris: Champion, 1978.

4409. ----. "Esoterik und formale Gestaltung in Skrjabins Späwerken." Kolleritsch/S: 22-49.

4410. Lederer, Josef-Horst. "Die Funktion der Luce-Stimme in Skrjabin's Op.60." Kolleritsch/S: 128-141.

4411. Lissa, Zofia. "Zur Genesis des 'Promethesischen Akkords' bei A.N. Skrjabin." MO 2(1963): 170-183.

4412. Macdonald, Hugh. "Skryabin's conquest of time." Kolleritsch/S: 58-65.

4413. Mast, Dietrich. *Struktur und Form bei Alexander N. Skrjabin.* Müchen: W. Wollenweber, 1981.

4414. Peacock, Kenneth. "Synaesthetic perception: Alexander Scriabin's color hearing." MP 2(1984-1985): 483-506. [*Tastiera per luce*]

4415. Perle, George. "Scriabin's self-analyses." MA 3/2(1984): 101-122.

4416. Schibli, Sigfried. "Skrjabin spricht: Sieben Stichworte zu einem Problem." NZM 143/3(1982): 22-26.

4417. Shitomirskij, Daniel Wladimirowitsch. "Die Harmonik Skrjabins." Fs. Boetticher: 344-358.

4418. Strangeland, Robert A. "Some structural elements in Opus 11 of Scriabin." CAUSM 5/1(1975): 32-41.

SCULTHORPE, PETER (born 1929)

4419. Boyd, Anne. "Peter Sculthrope's *Sun Music I*." MMA 3(1968): 3-20.

4420. Hannan, Michael Francis. "The music of Peter Sculthorpe: An analytical study with particular reference to those social and other cultural forces which have shaped the development of an Australian vision." PhD dissertation (Musicology): University of Sidney, 1978.

4421. ----. *Peter Sculthorpe: His music and ideas, 1929-1979.* New York: University of Queensland Press, 1982.

SEARLE, HUMPHREY (1915-1982)

4422. Searle, Humphrey. "A note on *Gold Coast Customs*." MSU 3(1950-1951): 18-23.

SEEGER, RUTH PORTER CRAWFORD (1901-1953)

4423. Gaume, Mary Matilda. "Ruth Crawford Seeger: Her life and works." PhD dissertation (Musicology): Indiana University, 1974. UM 74-4672. DA XXXIV.9, p.6020-1-A.

SEIBER, MÁTYÁS (1905-1960)

4424. Carner, Mosco. "Matyas Seiber and his *Ulysses*." Carner: 172-182.

4425. Seiber, Matyas. "A note on *Ulysses*." MSU 3(1950-1951): 263-270.

4426. Silberman, Julian. "Some thoughts on Mátyás Seiber." TEMPO 132 (1982): 12-14.

4427. Varro, Michael Franklin. "The music of Mátyás Seiber (1905-1960)." DMA dissertation (Performance): University of Washington, 1975. UM 76-17,671. DA XXXVII.2, p.687-A.

4428. Weissman, John S. "Die Streichquartette von Mátyás Seiber." MELOS 22(1955): 344-347, 23(1956): 38-41.

SEROCKI, KAZIMIERZ (1922-1981)

4429. Davies, Lyn. "Serocki's *Spatial Sonoristics*." TEMPO 145(1983): 28-32.

4430. Zielinski, Tadeusz A. "Anmerkungen zu *Arrangements* für 1 bis 4 Blockflöten von Kazimierz Serocki." T 5/6(1980-1981): 23-28.

SEROV, ALEKSANDR NIKOLAEVICH (1820-1871)

4431. Abraham, Gerald. "The operas of Serov." Abraham: 40-55.
4432. Taruskin, Richard. "Opera and drama in Russia: The case of Serov's *Judith*." JAMS 32(1979): 74-117.
4433. ----. "Serov and Musorgsky." Fs. Abraham: 139-161.

SESSIONS, ROGER (1896-1985)

Choral works
4434. Gorelick, Brian. "Movement and shape in the choral music of Roger Sessions." DMA dissertation (Choral Music): University of Illinois, 1985. No DA listing.

Montezuma
4435. Laufer, Edward C. "Roger Sessions: *Montezuma*." PNM 4/1(1965): 95-108.
4436. Olmstead, Andrea. "The plum'd serpent: Antonio Borgese and Roger Sessions' *Montezuma*." TEMPO 152(1985): 13-22.

Organ works
4437. McClain, Charles Sharland. "The organ choral preludes of Roger Sessions." DMA dissertation: Cornell University, 1957. No DA listing.

Piano works
4438. Campbell, Michael Ian. "The piano sonatas of Roger Sessions: Sequel to a tradition." DMA dissertation (Performance): Peabody Conservatory, 1982. No DA listing.

Songs
4439. Cone, Edward T. "In defense of song: The contribution of Roger Sessions." CI 2/1(1975-1976): 93-112.

String Quartet
4440. Cone, Edward T. "Roger Sessions' String Quartet." MM 18 (1941): 159-163.
4441. Schweitzer.

Symphonies
4442. Cowell, Henry. "Current Chronicle." MQ 36(1950): 94-98. [Symphony No.1]
4443. Imbrie, Andrew. "The symphonies of Roger Sessions." TEMPO 103(1972): 24-32.

Violin Concerto
4444. Imbrie, Andrew. "Roger Sessions: In honor of his sixty-fifth birthday." PNM 1/1(1962): 117-147. [Also Quintet]

When Lilacs Last in the Dooryard Bloom'd
4445. Powers, Harold S. "Current Chronicle." MQ 58(1972): 297-307.

Other works
4446. Cone, Edward T. "Sessions' Concertino." TEMPO 115(1975): 2-10.
4447. Forte: 48-62. [*From My Diary*, No.3]
4448. Henderson, Ronald D. "Tonality in the pre-serial instrumental music of Roger Sessions." PhD dissertation (Theory): University of Rochester, 1974. UM 74-21,528. DA XXXV.4, p.2319-20-A.
4449. Olmstead, Andrea. *Roger Sessions and his music.* Ann Arbor: UMI Research Press, 1985.
4450. Schubert, Mark A. "Roger Sessions: Portrait of an American composer." MQ 32(1946): 196-214.

SÉVERAC, DÉODAT DE (1873-1921)

4451. Brody, Elaine. "The piano music of Déodat de Séverac: A stylistic analysis." PhD dissertation (Musicology): New York University, 1964. UM 65-10,003. DA XXVI.4, p.2249.

SHARIFF, NOAM

4452. Chittum, Donald. "Current Chronicle." MQ 57(1971): 135-138. [*Chaconne* for Orchestra]

SHEPHERD, ARTHUR (1880-1958)

4453. Loucks, Richard. *Arthur Shepherd: American composer.* Provo: Brigham Young University Press, 1980.
4454. Newman, William S. "Arthur Shepherd." MQ 36(1950): 159-179.

SHIFRIN, SEYMOUR (1926-1980)

4455. Brody, Martin. "An anatomy of intentions: Observations on Seymour Shifrin's *Responses* for Solo Piano." PNM 19/2(1980-1981): 278-304.

SHOSTAKOVICH, DMITRI (1906-1975)

Cello Concerto
4456. Nestjew, Iwan. "Das Cellokonzert von Schostakowitsch." MG 10(1960): 198-203.

Lady Macbeth of Mtzensk
4457. Shostakovitch, Dmitri. "My opera, *Lady Macbeth of Mtzensk*." MM 12(1935): 23-30.

Piano works
4458. Danuser, Hermann. "Dmitri Schostakowitschs musikalischpolitisches Revolutionsverständnis (1926-27): Zur Ersten Klaviersonate und zur zweiten Symphonie." Melos/NZM 4(1978): 3-11.

4459. Thomas, Robert Jay. "The Preludes and Fugues, Opus 87 of Dmitri Shostakovich." PhD dissertation (Piano Performance and Literature): Indiana University, 1979. No DA listing.

Songs
4460. Braun, Joachim. "Shostakovich's song cycle *From Jewish Folk Poetry*: Aspects of style and meaning." Fs. Schwarz: 259-286.

String Quartets
4461. Dyer, Paul Eugene. "Cyclic techniques in the string quartets of Dmitri Shostakovich." PhD dissertation (Musicology): Florida State University, 1977. No DA listing.

4462. Fay, Laurel Elizabeth. "The last quartets of Dmitrii Shostakovich: A stylistic investigation." PhD dissertation (Musicology): Cornell University, 1978. UM 79-02,266. DA XXXIX.7, p.3905-A.

4463. Keller, Hans. "Shostakovich's Twelfth Quartet." TEMPO 94 (1971): 6-15.

4464. Munneke, Russell Edward. "A comprehensive performance project in viola literature and a stylistic study of string quartets 1-13 of Dmitri Shostakovich." DMA dissertation: University of Iowa, 1977. No DA listing.

4465. Ochs, Ekkehard. "Bemerkungen zum Streichquartettschaffen Dmitri Schostakowitschs." Pečman: 455-470.

4466. O'Loughlin, Niall. "Schostakovitch's string quartets." TEMPO 87 (1968): 9-16.

4467. Siegmund-Schultze, Walther. "Meister des Streichquartetts: Eine stilkritisches Betrachtung." MG 16(1966): 596-601.

4468. Smith, Arthur Duane. "Recurring motives and themes as a means of unity in selected string quartets of Dmitri Shostakovich." DME dissertation (Music Education): University of Oklahoma, 1976. UM 76-24,392. DA XXXVII.5, p.2487-8-A.

String Quintet
4469. Maróthy, Jánas. "Harmonic disharmony: Shostakovich's Quintet." SM 19(1977): 325-348.

Symphonies
4470. Brock, Hella. "Konkretheit der emotionalen Aussage in Schostakowitschs XII. Sinfonie *Das Jahr*." MG 12(1962): 555-559.

4471. Danuser, Hermann. "Dmitri Schostakowitschs musikalischpolitisches Revolutionsverständnis (1926-27): Zur ersten Klaviersonate und zur zweiten Symphonie." Melos/NZM 4(1978): 3-11.

4472. Kay, Norman. "Shostakovich's 15th Symphony." TEMPO 100 (1972): 36-40.

4473. Körner, Klaus. "Schostakowitschs vierte Sinfonie." AM 31(1974): 116-136, 214-236.

4474. Lawson, Peter. "Shostakovitch's Second Symphony." TEMPO 91 (1970): 14-17.

4475. Mattner, Lothar. "Dmitri Schostakowitsch: 4. Sinfonie Op.43." NZM 146/7-8(1985): 43-46.

4476. Müller, Hans-Peter. "*Die Fünfzehnte*: Gedanken zur jungsten Sinfonie von Dmitri Schostakowitsch." MG 22(1972): 714-720.

4477. Ottaway, Hugh. "Beyond Babi Yar." TEMPO 105(1973): 26-30. [Symphony No.13]

4478. ----. "Looking again at Shostakovich 4." TEMPO 115(1975): 14-24.

4479. Sabinina, Marina. "Shostakovitch as symphonist: Dramaturgy, aesthetics, style." PhD dissertation (Music History): Institute Istorii Iskusstv, 1973.

4480. Souster, Tim. "Shostakovitch at the crossroads." TEMPO 78 (1966): 2-9. [Symphonies Nos.4 and 5]

Other works

4481. Brockhaus, Heinz Alfred. *Dmitri Schostakowitsch*. Leipzig: Breitkopf und Härtel, 1962.

4482. Cholopov, Juri N. "Der russische Neoklassizismus bei Sergej Prokof'ev und Dmitrij Sostakovič." JP 3(1980): 170-199.

4483. Masel, Leo A. "Über den Stil Dmitri Schostakowitschs." BM 9 (1967): 208-220.

4484. Ottaway, Hugh. "Shostakovich: Some later works." TEMPO 50 (1959): 2-14.

4485. Rosebery, Eric. "Ideology, style, content and thematic process in the symphonies, cello concertos, and string quartets of Shostakovich." PhD dissertation (Musicology): Bristol, 1982.

4486. Slonimsky, Nicolas. "Dmitri Dmitrievitch Shostakovitch." MQ 28(1942): 425-444.

4487. Zeck, Carlferdinand. "Die Solokonzerte von Dmitri Schostakowitsch: Untersuchungen über Aufbau der Werke und ihre ästhetische Wertung." PhD dissertation (Musicology): Halle, 1972.

SIBELIUS, JEAN (1865-1957)

Symphonic Poems

4488. Jacobs, Robert L. "Sibelius' *Lemminkaïnen and the Maidens of Saari*." MR 24(1963): 147-157.

4489. Tammaro, Ferruccio. "Sibelius e il silenzio di *Tàpiola*." RIM 12(1977): 100-129.

Symphonies

4490. Ballantine, Christopher. "The symphony in the twentieth century: Some aspects of its tradition and innovation." MR 32(1971): 219-232. [Seventh Symphony]

4491. Gerschefski, Peter Edwin. "The thematic, temporal and dynamic processes in the symphonies of Jean Sibelius." PhD dissertation (Theory): Florida State University, 1962. UM 63-1813. DA XXIII.10, p.3920-21.

4492. Goddard, Scott. "Sibelius's Second Symphony." ML 12(1931): 156-163.

4493. Hill, William G. "Some aspects of form in the symphonies of Sibelius." MR 10(1949): 165-182.

4494. Hollander, Hans. "Stilprobleme in den Symphonien von Sibelius." M 19(1965): 1-4.

4495. Krohn, Ilmari. *Der Stimmungsgehalt der Symphonien von Jean Sibelius.* Helsinki: Druckerei A.G. der Finnschen Literaturgesellschaft, 1945.

4496. Matter, Jean. "Quelques aspects de l'être symphonique de Sibelius." SMZ 106(1966): 31-36.

4497. Meyer, Alfred H. "Sibelius: Symphonist." MQ 22(1936): 68-86.

4498. Parmet, Simon. *The symphonies of Sibelius: A study in musical appreciation.* London: Cassell, 1959.

4499. Roiha, Eino Vilho Pretari. *Die Symphonien von Jean Sibelius: Ein form-analytische Studie.* Jyväskylä, 1941.

Other works

4500. Abraham, Gerald, ed. *The music of Sibelius.* New York: Da Capo, 1975. (1947)

4501. Chernizvsky, David. "The use of germ motives by Sibelius." ML 23(1942): 1-9.

4502. Garden, Edward. "Sibelius and Balakirev." Fs. Abraham: 215-218.

4503. Mäckelmann, Michael. "Sibelius und die Programmusik: Eine Studie zu seinen Tondichtungen und Symphonien." HJM 6(1983): 121-168.

4504. Pike, Lionel. "Sibelius's debt to renaissance polyphony." ML 55(1974): 317-326.

4505. Ringbom, Nils Eric. *Sibelius: Symphonien; Symphonische Tondichtungen; Violinkonzert; Voces intimae; Analytische Beschreibung.* Helsinki: Fazer, 1957.

4506. Tanzberg, Ernst. *Jean Sibelius: Eine Monographie.* Wiesbaden: Breitkopf und Härtel, 1962.

SIKORSKI, KAZIMIERZ (born 1895)

4507. Marek, Tadeusz. "Composer's workshop: The Fourth Symphony by Kazimierz Sikorski." PM 9/1(1974): 20-24.

SIMPSON, ROBERT (born 1921)

4508. Pike, Lionel. "Robert Simpson's 'new way'." TEMPO 153(1985): 20-29. [String Quartet No.8]

SKEMPTON, HOWARD WHITE (born 1947)

4509. Parsons, Michael. "The music of Howard Skempton." CT 21 (1980): 12-16.

4510. Zimmermann, Walter. "Stillgehaltene Musik: Zu Howard Skemptons Kompositionen." MTX 3(1984): 35-37.

SKILTON, CHARLES SANFORD (1868-1941)

4511. Smith, James A. "Charles Sanford Skilton (1868-1941): Kansas composer." MA dissertation (Musicology): Unversity of Kansas, 1979.

SMALLEY, ROGER (born 1943)

4512. Walsh, Stephen. "Roger Smalley's *Gloria tibi Trinitas I*." TEMPO 91(1970): 17-20.

SMETANA, BEDŘICH (1824-1884)

4513. Clapham, John. "Smetana's sketches for *Dalibor* and *The Secret*." ML 61(1980): 136-146.

4514. Hirsbrunner, Theo. "Das Erhabene in Bedřich Smetanas *Mein Vaterland*." AM 41(1984): 35-41. [*Ma Vlast*]

4515. Honolka, Kurt. "Smetana's *Dalibor*: Eine monothematische Oper." M 24(1970): 554-556.

4516. Jiránek, Jaroslav. "Liszt and Smetana." SM 5(1963): 139-192.

4517. Large, Brian. *Smetana*. New York: Praeger, 1970. 473 p.

4518. Schuffenhauser, Gerhart. "Die tschechoslowakische Volkmusik und ihr Einfluss auf die Opern Friedrich Smetanas." PhD dissertation: Freie Universität, Berlin, 1957.

SMITH, HALE (born 1925)

4519. Breda, Malcolm Joseph. "Hale Smith: A biographical and analytical study of the man and his music." PhD dissertation (Music Education): University of Southern Mississippi, 1975. UM 76-04,434. DA XXXVI.8, p.4835-A.

4520. Spence, Martha Ellen Blanding. "Selected song cycles of three contemporary Black American composers: William Grant Still, *Songs of Separation*, Hale Smith, *Beyond the Rim of Day*, John Duncan, *Blue Set*." DMA dissertation (Performance): University of Southern Mississipi, 1977. No DA listing.

SMITH, STUART (born 1948)

4521. Fiore, Linda. "Notes on Stuart Smith's *Return and Recall*: A view from within." PNM 22(1983-1984): 290-302.

4522. Welsh, John P. ". . . a flight . . . *FLIGHT*." PNM 23/1(1984-1985): 144-161.

SOMERS, HARRY (born 1925)

4523. Butler, Edward Gregory. "Harry Somers: The culmination of a pianistic style in the Third Piano Sonata." SMUWO 9(1984): 124-132.

4524. ----. "The piano sonatas of Harry Somers." DMA dissertation (Performance): University of Rochester, 1974. UM 75-579. DA XXXV.7, p.4582-3-A.

4525. Cherney, Brian. *Harry Somers*. Toronto: University of Toronto Press, 1975.

4526. Houghton, Diane. "The solo vocal works of Harry Somers." DMA dissertation (Performance): University of Missouri, 1980. UM 80-19,143. DA XLI.3, p.844-A.

4527. Loranger, Pierre. "Harry Somers: The Picasso Suite, *Light Music* for Small Orchestra." CCM 1(1970): 147-152.

SOMERVELL, ARTHUR (1863-1937)

4528. Curtis.

SORABJI, KAIKHOSRU SHAPURJI (born 1892)

4529. Browne, Arthur G. "The music of Kaihosru Sorabji." ML 11 (1930): 6-16.

4530. Garvelmann, Donald. "Kaikhosru Shapurji Sorabji." JALS 4 (1978): 18-22.

4531. Gula, Robert J. "Kaikhosru Shapurji Sorabji (1892-   ): The published piano works." JALS 12(1982): 38-51.

4532. Habermann, Michael R. "A style analysis of the nocturnes for solo piano by Kaikhosru Shapurji Sorabji with special emphasis on *Le Jardin parfumé*." DMA dissertation (Performance): Peabody Conservatory, 1984. 238 p. No DA listing.

4533. Rapoport, Paul. "Sorabji and the computer." TEMPO 117(1976): 23-26. [*Opus clavicemabalistum*]

SOUSTER, TIM (born 1943)

4534. Jeffries, David. "Tim Souster." CT 27(1983): 20-27.

SOWERBY, LEO (1895-1968)

4535. Guiltinan, Michael Patrick. "The absolute music for piano solo by Leo Sowerby." DMA dissertation (Piano Performance and Literature): University of Rochester, 1977. UM 78-01,395. DA XXXVIII.9, p.5113-A.

4536. Rhoades.

4537. Rieke, Edwin Allen. "The organ choral preludes of Leo Sowerby." DMA dissertation (Performance): University of Rochester, 1975. UM 75-29,844. DA XXXVI.7, p.4100-A.

4538. Seeley, Robert James. "A performer's study of the sacred solo songs of Leo Sowerby, with organ accompaniment." DMA dissertation (Voice): Southwestern Baptist Theological Seminary, 1980. No DA listing.

4539. Tuthill, Burnet C. "Leo Sowerby." MQ 24(1938): 249-264.

SPIES, CLAUDIO (born 1925)

4540. Lansky, Paul. "The music of Claudio Spies: An introduction." TEMPO 103(1972): 38-44.

SPIES, LEO (1899-1965)

4541. Brennecke, Dietrich. "Sprache des Lebens: Blick auf das Kammermusikschaffen von Leo Spies: Zum 60. Geburtstag des Komponisten." MG 9/6(1959): 8-12.

SPINNER, LEOPOLD (born 1906)

4542. Graubart, Michael. "Leopold Spinner: The last phase." TEMPO 138(1981): 2-18.

4543. ----. "Leopold Spinner's later music." TEMPO 110(1974): 14-29.

4544. ----. "The music of Leopold Spinner: A preliminary study." TEMPO 109(1974): 2-14.

SPOHR, LOUIS (1784-1859)

4545. Berrett, Joshua. "Characteristic conventions of style in selected instrumental works of Louis Spohr." PhD dissertation (Musicology): University of Michigan, 1974. 244 p. UM 75-00,633. DA XXXV.7, p.4582-A.

4546. Möllers, Christian. "Louis Spohr (1784-1859)." M 34(1980): 452-456. [String Quartet Op.29, No.1]

SPONTINI, GASPARO LUIGI (1774-1851)

4547. Döhring, Sieghart. "Spontinis Berliner Opern." Dahlhaus/S: 469-489. [*Nurmahal; Alcidor; Agnes von Hohenstaufen*]

4548. Libby, Dennis A. "Gasparo Spontini and his French and German operas." PhD dissertation (Musicology): Princeton University, 1969. UM 70-08,376. DA XXX.12, p.5472.

STÄBLER, GERHARD (born 1949)

4549. Stäbler, Gerhard. "*Für Später: Jetzt*: Gedanken über eine Art zu komponieren." N 3(1982-1983): 104-119.

STAEMPFLI, EDWARD (born 1908)

4550. Staempfli, Edward. "*Der Zöllner Matthäus*." SMZ 115(1975): 131-135.

STAHNKE, MANFRED

4551. Stahnke, Manfred. "Mein drittes Streichquartett *Penthesilea*: Anmerkungen zur Entstehung eines Musikstücks mit Programm." HJM 6 (1983): 347-363.

STANFORD, CHARLES VILLIERS (1852-1924)

4552. Wilkinson, Harry. "The vocal and instrumental technique of Charles Villiers Stanford." PhD dissertation (Theory): University of Rochester, 1959. 2 vols. No DA listing.

STARER, ROBERT (born 1924)

4553. Lewis, Dorothy. "The major piano solo works of Robert Starer: A style analysis." DMA dissertation: Peabody Conservatory, 1978. No DA listing.

STEVENS, HALSEY (born 1908)

4554. Berry, Wallace. "The music of Halsey Stevens." MQ 54(1968): 287–308.

4555, Johnson, Axie Allen. "Choral settings of the Magnificat by selected twentieth-century composers." DMA dissertation: University of Southern California, 1968. 172 p. RILM 68/3607dd28. No DA listing.

4556. Murphy, James Lawson. "The choral music of Halsey Stevens." PhD dissertation (Theory): Texas Tech University, 1980. 228 p. UM 80-22,629. DA XLI.4, p.1274-A.

STEVENS, LEITH

4557. Hamilton, James Clifford. "Leith Stevens: A critical analysis of his works." DMA dissertation: University of Missouri, 1976. UM 76-25,145. DA XXXVII.5, p.2481-A.

STEVENSON, RONALD (born 1928)

4558. Scott-Sutherland, Colin. "The music of Ronald Stevenson." MR 26(1965): 118-128.

STILL, WILLIAM GRANT (1895-1978)

4559. Simpson, Ralph R. "William Grant Still: The man and his music." PhD dissertation: Michigan State University, 1964. UM 65-727. DA XXV.12, p.7310.

4560. Spence, Martha Ellen Blanding. "Selected song cycles of three contemporary Black American composers: William Grant Still, *Songs of Separation*, Hale Smith, *Beyond the Rim of Day*, John Duncan, *Blue Set*." DMA dissertation (Performance): University of Southern Mississippi, 1977. No DA listing.

STOCKHAUSEN, KARLHEINZ (born 1928)

Aus den sieben Tagen
4561. Kohl, Jerome. "Serial determinism and 'intuitive music': An analysis of Stockhausen's *Aus den sieben Tagen*." ITO 3/12(1977-1978): 7-19.

Ensemble
4562. Gehlhaar, Rolf. "Zur Komposition *Ensemble*." DBNM 11(1968). 77 p.

Gesang der Jünglinge
    4563. Stockhausen, Karlheinz. "Music and speech." R 6(1964): 40-64.

Klavierstück II
    4564. Schultz/D. [Third movement]

Klavierstück VIII
    4565. Toop, Richard. "Stockhausen's *Klavierstuck VIII* (1954)." MMA
10(1979): 93-130. [Also in CT 28(1984): 4-19]

Klavierstück IX
    4566. Henck, Herbert. "Karlheinz Stockhausens *Klavierstück IX*: Eine
analytische Betrachtung." Schnitzler: 171-200.

Klavierstuck X
    4567. Henck, Herbert. "Karlheinz Stockhausens *Klavierstuck IX*: Eine
analytische Betrachtung." Schnitzler: 171-200.
    4568. ----. *Karlheinz Stockhausen's "Klavierstück X": A contribution
toward understanding serial technique.* Translation of the 2nd rev. ed.
Köln: Neuland, 1980.

Klavierstück XI
    4569. Piencikowski, Robert. "Perspective initiale (KS IX)." DI 2(1984):
11-13.
    4570. Truelove, Stephen. "Karlheinz Stockhausen's *Klavierstuck XI*:
An analysis of its composition via a matrix system of serial polyphony and
the translation of rhythm into pitch." PhD dissertation: University of
Oklahoma, 1984. No DA listing.

Kontakte
    4571. Blumröder, Christoph von. "Serielle Musik um 1960: Stockhau-
sens *Kontakte*": Analysen: Beiträge zu einer Problemgeschichte des
Komponierens." *Festschrift für H.H. Eggebrecht.* Wiesbaden, 1984:
423-435.
    4572. Kirchmeyer, Helmut. "Zur Entstehungs- und Problemgeschichte
der *Kontakte* von Karlheinz Stockhausen." N 3(1982-1983): 152-176.
    4573. Kirchmeyer: 193-210.

Kreuzspiel
    4574. Keller, Max Eugen. "Gehörte und komponierte Struktur in
Stockhausens *Kreuzspiel*." MELOS 39(1972): 10-18.
    4575. Stenzl, Jürg. "Karlheinz Stockhausens *Kreuzspiel* (1951)." ZM
3/1(1972): 35-42.

Licht
    4576. Frisius, Rudolf. "Komposition als Versuch der strukturellen und
semantischen Synthese: Karlheinz Stockhausen und sein Werk-projekt
Licht." N 2(1981-1982): 160-178.
    4577. Kohl, Jerome. "Stockhausen at La Scala: *Semper idem sed non
eodem modo*." PNM 22(1983-1984): 483-501. [*Samstag*]

4578. Oehlschlägel, Reinhard. "Annäherung und Versuch: Zur Uraufführung von *Luzifers Traum* von Karlheinz Stockhausen." N 2 (1981-1982): 179-182.
4579. Stockhausen, Karlheinz. "Electronic music for *Kathinka's Chant as Lucifer's Requiem*." PNM 23/2(1985): 40-60.
4580. ----. "Elektronische Musik zu *Kathinkas Gesang als Luzifers Requiem*." N 5(1984-1985): 31-49.

Mantra
4581. Blumröder, Christoph von. "Karlheinz Stockhausens *Mantra* für 2 Pianisten: Ein Beispiel für eine symbiotische Kompositionsform." Melos/NZM 2(1976): 94-104.
4582. Febel, Reinhard. *Musik für zwei Klaviere seit 1950 als Spiegel der Kompositionstechnik*. Herrenberg: Döring, 1978.

Mikrophonie I
4583. Günther, Ulrich. "*Mikrophonie I* von Karlheinz Stockhausen im Musikunterricht." MB 4(1972): 84-87.
4584. Maconie, Robin. "Stockhausen's *Mikrophonie I*." PNM 10/2 (1972): 92-101.

Momente
4585. McElheran, Brock. "Preparing Stockhausen's *Momente*." PNM 4/1(1965): 33-38.

Musik für ein Haus
4586. Raiss, Hans-Peter. "Karlheinz Stockhausen: *Musik für ein Haus* (1968)." Vogt: 391-399.
4587. Ritzel, Fred. "*Musik für ein Haus*." DBNM 12(1970): 7-88. [Entire issue]

Refrain
4588. Wennerstrom.

Stimmung
4589. Rose, Gregory and Simon Emmerson. "Stockhausen--1: *Stimmung*." CT 20(1979): 20-25.

Studie II
4590. Bozzetti, Elmar. "Analyse der *Studie II* von Karlheinz Stockhausen." ZM 4(1973): 37-47.
4591. ----. "Reihenvariationen über ein Tongemisch: Analyse der *Studie II* von Karlheinz Stockhausen." MB 5(1973): 17-24.
4592. Burow, Winfried. *Stockhausens "Studie II"*. Frankfurt am Main: Diesterweg, 1973.
4593. Silberhorn, Heinz. *Die Reihentechnik in Stockhausens "Studie II."* Herrenberg: Döring, 1978.
4594. Stroh, Wolfgang Martin. "Zur Dialektik kompositorischer Verfügungsgewalt." AM 30(1973): 208-229.

Telemusik
4595. Fuhrmann, Roderich. "Karlheinz Stockhausen (1928): *Telemusik* (1966)." Zimmerschied: 250-266.

Tierkreis
4596. Gruhn, Wilfried. "'Neue Einfachheit?' Zu Karlheinz Stockhausens Melodien des *Tierkreis*." Wilfried Gruhn, ed. *Reflexionen über Musik heute: Texte und Analysen.* Mainz, 1981: 185-202.
4597. Stockhausen, Christel. "Karlheinz Stockhausens *Tierkreis*." T 3/4(1978-1979): 95-99.

Zeitmasse
4598. Marcus, Genevieve. "Stockhausen's *Zeitmasse*." MR 29(1968): 142-156.

Zyklus für einen Schlagzeuger
4599. Kirchmeyer: 189-193.
4600. Silberhorn, Heinz. "Analyse von Stockhausens *Zyklus für einen Schlagzeuger*." ZM 8/2(1977): 29-50.

Other works
4601. Brinkmann, Reinhold. "Stockhausens *Ordnung*: Versuch, ein Modell einer terminologischen Untersuchung zu beschreiben." H.H. Eggebrecht, ed. *Zur Terminologie der Musik des 20. Jahrhunderts.* Stuttgart: Veroff. der Walker-Stiftung H.S., 1974: 205-213.
4602. Cloete, Johan. "Pluralism and inter-relation: Mediation between extremes of materials in Stockhuasen's works." Bachelor of Music, Kapstadt, 1979.
4603. Cott, Jonathan. *Stockhausen: Conversations with the composer.* New York: Simon & Schuster, 1973.
4604. Fass, Ekbert. "Interview with Karlheinz Stockhausen held August 11, 1976." I 6(1977): 187-204.
4605. Frisius, Rudolf. "Karlheinz Stockhausen: Melodie als Gestalt und Form." NZM 144/7-8(1983): 23-29.
4606. Gebura, Alice. "Spectral shape as a reflection of the text in Stockhausen's *In the Sky* from *Indianlieder*." SONUS 1/1(1980): 48-62.
4607. Harvey, Jonathan. *The music of Stockhausen: An introduction.* Berkeley: University of California Press, 1975.
4608. ----. "Stockhausen: Theory and music." MR 29(1968): 130-141.
4609. Heikinheimo, Seppo. *The electronic music of Karlheinz Stockhausen: Studies on the esthetical and formal problems of its first phase.* Helsinki: Suomen Musiikkitieteellienen Seura, 1972.
4610. Karkoschka, Erhard. "Stockhausen Theorien." MELOS 32(1965): 5-13.
4611. Kelsall, John Lawrence. "Compositional processes in the music of Karlheinz Stockhausen." PhD dissertation (Musicology): Glasgow, 1976.
4612. Koenig, Gottfried Michael. "Karlheinz Stockhausen: Musik und Graphik." DBNM 3(1960): 5-25.

4613. Kohl, Jerome. "The evolution of macro- and micro-time relations in Stockhausen's recent music." PNM 22(1983-1984): 147-185. [*Tierkreis; Klavierstuck XIII*]

4614. ----. "Serial and non-serial techniques in the music of Karlheinz Stockhausen from 1962-1968." PhD dissertation (Theory): University of Washington, 1981. 264 p. UM 82-12,566. DA XLII.12, p.4969-A.

4615. Kramer, Jonathan. "The Fibonacci series in twentieth-century music." JMT 17(1973): 110-148.

4616. Kruger, Walther. *Karlheinz Stockhuasen: Allmacht und Ohnmacht in der neuesten Musik.* Regensburg: G. Bosse, 1971.

4617. Maconie, Robin. *The works of Karlheinz Stockhausen.* London: Boyars, 1981 (1976).

4618. Morgan, Robert P. "Stockhausen's writings on music." MQ 61 (1975): 1-16.

4619. Noller, Joachim. "Fluxus und die Musik der sechziger Jahre: Über vernachlässigte Aspekte am Beispiel Kagels und Stockhausens." NZM 146/9(1985): 14-19.

4620. Pflugradt, William Charles. "Continuity and discontinuity in the piano music of Karlheinz Stockhausen." MM dissertation, Indiana University, 1972.

4621. Purce, Jill. "The spiral in the music of Karlheinz Stockhausen." *Main currents in modern thought* 30(1973): 18-27.

4622. ----. "La Spirale dans la musique de Stockhausen." MJ 15 (1974): 7-23.

4623. Sabbe, H. "Das Musikdenken von Karel Goeyvaerts in Bezug auf das Schaffen von Karlheinz Stockhausen: Ein Beitrag zur Geschichte der frühseriellen und elektronischen Musik 1950-1956." I 2(1973): 101-114.

4624. Stockhausen, Karlheinz. *Texte zur Musik: 1970-1977*, vol.4. Köln: Dumont, 1978.

4625. Stockhausen. [*Schlagquartett*: 13-18; *Komposition 1953 No.2*: 23-36; *Studie II*: 37-42; *Gesang der Jünglinge*: 49-68; *Zyklus für einen Schlagzeuger*: 73-100; *Originale*: 107-129]

4626. Toop, Richard. "Karlheinz Stockhausen: From *Kreuzspiel* to *Trans.*" *Atti dal terzo e quarto seminario di studi e ricerche sul linguaggio musicale.* Randolph Shackelford, ed. Padova: G. Zanibon, 1975: 58-86. [*Kreuzspiel; Formel; Elektronische Studie II; Klavierstück VIII; Carre; Adieu; Stimmung; Trans*]

4627. ----. "*O alter Duft*: Stockhausen and the return to melody." SMU 10(1976): 79-97.

4628. ----. "Stockhausen's electronic works: Sketches and work-sheets from 1952-1967." I 10(1981): 149-197.

4629. ----. "Stockhausen's *Konkrete Etude*." MR 37(1976): 295-300.

4630. ----. "Stockhausen--2: On writing about Stockhausen." CT 20(1979): 25-27.

4631. Volans, Kevin. *An introduction to the music of Karlheinz Stockhausen.* Vortragstext Kapstadt, 1976.

4632. ----. "The *Klavierstüke*: Stockhausen's microcosm." Bachelor of Music, Johannesburg, 1971.

4633. Westerman, Richard Martyn. "Stockhausen: The way ahead? A study of Stockhausen's orchestral work." Bachelor of Arts, Liverpool, 1982.

4634. Wörner, Karl Heinrich. *Karlheinz Stockhausen: Werk und Wollen 1950-1962.* Rodenkirchen/Rhein: P.J. Tonger, 1963.
4635. ----. *Stockhausen: Life and work.* Berkeley: University of California Press, 1973.

STOCKIGT, MICHAEL (born 1929)

4636. Kleinschmidt, Klaus. "Die Analyse: *Orchestermusik I* von Michael Stockigt." MG 33(1983): 397-399.

STRAESSER, JOEP (born 1934)

4637. Berkenkamp, Heske. "Joep Straesser: Espressivity and complexity as constants in a development." KN 17(1983): 24-32. [*Ramasasiri; Spring Quartet; Intersections; Splendid Isolation; Longing for the Emperor; Signal and Echoes*]
4638. Manneke, Daan. "About Joep Straesser's *Intersections III* for Piano." SS 53(1973): 24-36.
4639. Vermeulen, Ernst. "*Musique pour l'homme* by Joep Straesser." SS 38(1969): 15-25.
4640. ----. "*22 Pages* by Joep Straesser." SS 31(1967): 15-18.
4641. Vriend, Jan. "*The Autumn of Music* by Joep Straesser." SS 31 (1967): 11-14.

STRAUSS, JOHANN (1825-1899)

4642. ASO 49(1983). [*Die Fledermaus*]
4643. Sittner, Hans. "Der Walzer bei Chopin und Johann Strauss." OMZ 4(1949): 287-293.

STRAUSS, RICHARD (1864-1949)

Alpine Symphony
4644. Palmer, Christopher. "Strauss's *Alpine Symphony*." MR 29(1968): 106-115.

Ariadne auf Naxos
4645. ASO 77(1985).
4646. Daviau, Donald G. and George Buelow. *The "Ariadne auf Naxos" of Hugo von Hofmannsthal and Richard Strauss.* Chapel Hill: University of North Carolina Press, 1975.
4647. Erwin, Charlotte E. "Richard Strauss's presketch planning for *Ariadne auf Naxos*." MQ 67(1981): 348-365.
4648. Forsyth, Karen. *Ariadne auf Naxos: Its genesis and meaning.* Oxford: Oxford University Press, 1982.
4649. Gräwe, Karl Dietrich. "Sprache, Musik, und Szene in *Ariadne auf Naxos* von Hugo von Hofmannsthal und Richard Strauss." PhD dissertation (Dramatic Arts): München, 1969.
4650. Schuh, Willi. "Metamorphosen einer Ariette von Richard Strauss." Fs. Abert: 197-208.

Capriccio
 4651. Tenschert, Roland. "The Sonnet in Richard Strauss's opera
Capriccio: A study in the relation between metre and the musical phrase."
TEMPO 47(1958): 6-11.
 4652. ----. "Das Sonnett in Richard Strauss's Oper *Capriccio*." SMZ
98(1958): 1-6.

Don Juan
 4653. Gerlach, Reinhard. *"Don Juan" und "Rosenkavalier."* Bern:
P. Haupt, 1966.
 4654. Lorenz, Alfred. "Neue Formerkenntnisse, angewandt auf
Richard Strauss's *Don Juan*." AM 1(1936): 452-466.

Elektra
 4655. Dinerstein, Norman Myron. "Polychordality in *Salome* and
Elektra: A study of the application of reinterpretation technique." PhD
dissertation (Theory): Princeton University, 1974. UM 75-23,194. DA
XXXVI.4, p.1888-A.
 4656. Enix, Margery. "A reassessment of *Elektra* by Strauss." ITR
2/3(1978-1979): 31-38.
 4657. Enix.
 4658. McDonald, Lawrence Francis. "Compositional procedures in
Richard Strauss's *Elektra*." PhD dissertation (Musicology): University of
Michigan, 1976. UM 76-19,190. DA XXXVII.3, p.1290-A.
 4659. Noe, Günther von. "Das Leitmotiv bei Richard Strauss dargestellt am Beispiel der *Elektra*." NZM 132(1971): 418-422.
 4660. Overhoff, Kurt. *Die Elektra-Partitur von Richard Strauss: Ein
Lehrbuch für die Technik der dramatischen Komposition.* Salzburg:
Pustet, 1978.
 4661. Wittelsbach, Rudolf. "Betrachtungen zu *Salome* und *Elektra*."
Fs. Wiener: 93-99.

Die Frau ohne Schatten
 4662. Graf, Erich. "Zur Thematik der *Frau ohne Schatten*." OMZ 19
(1964): 228-233.
 4663. Knaus, Jakob. *Hofmannthals Weg zur Oper "Die Frau ohne
Schatten" und Einflüsse auf die Musik.* Berlin; New York: De Gruyter,
1971.
 4665. Overhoff, Kurt. *"Die Frau ohne Schatten" von Richard Strauss.*
München: E. Katzbichler, 1976.
 4665. Pantle, Sherrill Hahn. *"Die Frau ohne Schatten" by Hugo von
Hofmannsthal and Richard Strauss: An analysis of text, music, and their
relationship.* Bern; Las Vegas: Lang, 1978.

Friedenstag
 4666. Potter, Pamela M. "Strauss's *Friedenstag* A pacifist attempt at
political resistance." MQ 69(1983): 408-424.

Ein Heldenleben
 4667. Enix.

Die Liebe der Danae

    4668. Birken, Kenneth W. "The last meeting: *Die Liebe der Danae* reconsidered." TEMPO 153(1985): 13-19.

    4669. Tenschert, Roland. "A 'Gay myth': The story of *Die Liebe der Danae*." TEMPO 24(1952): 5-11.

Metamorphosen

    4670. Brennecke, Wilfried. "Die *Metamorphosen*: Werke von Richard Strauss und Paul Hindemith." SMZ 103(1963): 129-136, 199-208. [Also in Fs. Albrecht: 268-284]

    4671. Kusche, Ludwig and Kurt Wilhelm. "Richard Strauss's *Metamorphosen*." TEMPO 19(1951): 19-22.

Der Rosenkavalier

    4672. ASO 69-70(1984).

    4673. Gerlach, Reinhard. "Die Ästhetische Ton'sprache' als Problem im *Rosenkavalier*: Die Musik der ersten Szene oder die Konst des Buchschmucks." Melos/NZM 1(1975): 278-286.

    4674. ----. *"Don Juan" und "Rosenkavalier."* Bern: P. Haupt, 1966.

    4675. ----. "Der lebendige Inhalt und die tote Form: Marginalien zum *Rosenkavalier*." NZM 135(1974): 411-419.

    4676. John, Nicholas, ed. *Strauss: Der Rosenkavalier*. London: J. Calder, 1981.

    4677. Pörnbacher, Karl. *Der Rosenkavalier*. München: R. Oldenbourg, 1964.

    4678. Pryce-Jones, Alan. *Richard Strauss: Der Rosenkavalier*. London: Boosey & Hawkes, 1947.

Salome

    4679. ASO 47-48(1983).

    4680. Dinerstein, Norman Myron. "Polychordality in *Salome* and *Elektra*: A study of the application of reinterpretation technique." PhD dissertation (Theory): Princeton University, 1974. UM 75-23,194. Da XXXVI.4, p.1888-A.

    4681. Schuh, Willi. "Zur harmonischen Deutung des *Salome*-Schlusses." SMZ 86(1946): 452-458.

    4682. Wittelsbach, Rudolf. "Betrachtungen zu *Salome* und *Elektra*." Fs. Wiener: 93-99.

Die schweigsame Frau

    4683. Partsch, Erich Wolfgang. "Artifizialität und Manipulation: Studien zu Genese und Konstitution der Spieloper bei Richard Strauss unter besonderer Berücksichtigung der *Schweigsamen Frau*." PhD dissertation (Musicology): Wien, 1983.

Songs

    4684. Colson, William Wilder. *"Four Last Songs* by Richard Strauss." DMA dissertation (Composition): University of Illinois, 1975. 137 p. UM 75-14,096. DA XXXVI.1, p.16-17-A.

    4685. Finscher, Ludwig. "Richard Strauss and Jugendstil: The Munich years." MMA 18(1984): 169-178.

4686. Jefferson, Alan. *The Lieder of Richard Strauss.* New York: Praeger, 1972.

4687. Lienenluke, Ursula. *Lieder von Richard Strauss nach zeitgenos-sischer Lyrik.* Regensburg: G. Bosse, 1977.

4688. Petersen, Barbara E. *Ton und Wort: The Lieder of Richard Strauss.* Ann Arbor: UMI Research Press, 1980.

4689. Strickert, Jane Elizabeth. "Richard Strauss's *Vier letzte Lieder:* An analytical study." PhD dissertation (Performance): Washington University, 1975. UM 76-04,781. DA XXXVI.9, p.5632-A.

Tod und Verklärung

4690. Armstrong, Thomas. *Strauss's Tone-Poems.* London: Oxford University Press, 1931.

4691. Longyear, Rey M. "Schiller, Moszkowski and Strauss: *Joan of Arc's Death and Transfiguration.*" MR 28(1967): 209-217.

Other works

4692. Abert, Anna Amalie. *Richard Strauss: Die Opern: Einführung und Analyse.* Hannover: Friedrich, 1972. 133 p.

4693. Adorno, Theodor W. "Richard Strauss." PNM 4/1(1965): 14-32.

4694. Albrecht, Klaus. "Untersuchungen zum Schaffensprozess von Richard Strauss." PhD dissertation (Musicology): Bochum, 1979.

4695. Del Mar, Norman. *Richard Strauss.* London: Barrie & Rockcliff, 1962. 2 vols.

4696. Federhofer, Hellmut. "Die musikalische Gestaltung des Krämerspiegels von Richard Strauss." Fs. Vötterle: 260-267.

4697. Floros, Constantin. "Richard Strauss und die Programmusik." Fs. Hüschen: 143-150.

4698. Forchert, Arno. "Techniken motivisch-thematischer Arbeit in Werken von Strauss und Mahler." HJM 2(1974): 187-200.

4699. Gerlach, Reinhard. "Richard Strauss: Prinzipien seiner Kompositionstechnik (mit einem Brief von Strauss)." AM 23(1966): 277-288.

4700. Krause, Ernst. *Richard Strauss: Gestalt und Werk.* Leipzig: Breitkopf und Härtel, 1955.

4701. Lehman, Lotte. *Five operas and Richard Strauss.* New York: Macmillan, 1964.

4702. Mann, William. *Richard Strauss: A critical study of the operas.* London: Cassell, 1964.

4703. Murphy, Edward W. "Harmony and tonality in the large orchestral works of Richard Strauss." PhD dissertation (Theory): Indiana University, 1963. UM 64-12,064. DA XXVI.1, p.408.

4704. ----. "Tonal organization in five Strauss tone poems." MR 44 (1983): 223-233.

4705. Natan, Alex. *Richard Strauss: Die Opern.* Basel: Basilius, 1963.

4706. Partsch, Erich Wolfgang. "Dimensionen des Erinnerns: Musikal-ische Zitattechnik bei Richard Strauss." MAU 5(1985): 101-120.

4707. Schlötterer-Traimer, Roswitha. "Béla Bartók und die Tondich-tungen von Richard Strauss." OMZ 36(1981): 311-318.

4708. Schuh, Willi. "Zum Melodie und Harmoniestil der Richard Strauss'schen Spätwerke." SMZ 89(1949): 236-243.

4709. Schulken, Samuel Benhardt. "Buffa and seria: Musical features in the operas of Richard Strauss." PhD dissertation: Florida State University, 1970. UM 70-07,100. DA XXXI.9, p.4824-A.

4710. Thurston, Richard Elliott. "Musical representation in the symphonic poems of Richard Strauss." PhD dissertation (Musicology): University of Texas, 1971. 186 p. UM 72-11,427. DA XXXII.10, p. 5832-3-A.

4711. Walden, Herwarth. *Richard Strauss: Symphonien und Tondichtungen erläutert von G. Brecher (et al.).* Berlin: Schlesinger, [1905?]

4712. Wilde, Denis S. "The melodic process in the tone poems of Richard Strauss." PhD dissertation (Theory): Catholic University, 1984. No DA listing.

4713. Winterhager, Wolfgang. "Zur Struktur der Operndialogs: Komparative Analysen des musikdramatischen Werks von Richard Strauss." PhD dissertation (Musicology): Bochum, 1982.

STRAUSS, WOLFGANG (born 1927)

4714. Pommer, Max. "Zur I. Sinfonie von Wolfgang Strauss." MG 20(1970): 454-457.

STRAVINSKY, IGOR (1882-1971)

Abraham and Isaac
4715. Payne, Anthony. "Stravinsky's *Abraham and Isaac* and *Elegy for J.F.K.*" TEMPO 73(1965): 12-15.

4716. Spies, Claudio. "Notes on Stravinsky's *Abraham and Isaac.*" PNM 3/2(1965): 104-126.

4717. Thomas, Jennifer. "The use of color in three chamber works of the twentieth century." ITR 4/3(1980-1981): 24-40.

4718. Whittall, Arnold. "Thematicism in Stravinsky's *Abraham and Isaac.*" TEMPO 89(1969): 12-16.

4619. Young, Douglas. "*Abraham and Isaac.*" TEMPO 97(1971): 27-37.

Agnus Dei
4720. Rehm, Gottfried. "Ein Beitrag zur tonalen-atonikalen Harmonik: Harmonische Analyse von Hindemiths 1. Orgelsonate (letztet Satz) und Strawinskys *Agnus Dei.*" MK 55(1985): 172-180.

Agon
4721. Craft, Robert. "Ein Ballett für zwölf Tänzer." MELOS 24(1957): 284-288.

4722. Jahnke, Sabine. "Igor Strawinskys *Agon.*" MB 3(1971): 594-599.

4723. Janzen, Howard. "A stylistic analysis of Stravinsky's *Agon.*" MM dissertation: University of Alberta, 1975.

4724. Pousseur, Henri. "Stravinsky by way of Webern: The consistency of a syntax." PNM 10/2(1972): 13-51, 11/1(1972): 112-145.

4725. ----. "Stravinsky selon Webern selon Stravinsky." MJ 4(1971): 21-47, 5(1971): 107-126.

4726. Vogt: 293-307.

4727. Wiesel, Meir. "Motivic unity in Stravinsky's *Agon*." OM 7 (1979-1980): 119-124.

Anthem: The Dove Descending

4728. Bailey, Donald Lee. "A study of stylistic and compositional elements of *Anthem* (Stravinsky), *Fragments of Archilochos* (Foss), and *Creation prologue* (Ussachevsky)." DMA dissertation (Performance): University of Northern Colorado, 1976. 218 p. UM 76-23,159. DA XXXVII.4, p.1859-A.

Apollo Musagètes

4729. Gutknecht, Dieter. "Strawinskys zwei Fassungen des *Apollon Musagète*." Fs. Fellerer/70: 199-210.

Le Baiser de la fée

4730. Marschner, Bo. "Stravinsky's *Baiser de la fée* and its meaning." DAM 8(1977): 51-83.

4731. Morton, Lawrence. "Stravinsky and Tschaikovsky." Lang: 47-60.

Cantata

4732. Lindlar, Heinrich. "*Cantata*." MZ 12(1955): 30-34.

4733. ----. "Igor Stravinsky: *Cantata*." TEMPO 27(1953): 27-33.

4734. ----. "Igor Stravinsky's *Cantata*." SMZ 93(1953): 397-401.

4735. Mason, Colin. "Serial procedures in the *Ricercare II* of Stravinsky's *Cantata*." TEMPO 61-62(1962): 6-9.

Canticum sacrum

4736. Craft, Robert. "A concert for St. Mark." SCORE 18(1956): 35-51.

4737. ----. *Le musiche religiose di Igor Stravinsky*. Venezia: Lombroso Editore, 1957.

4738. Reck, Albert von. "Gestaltzusammenhänge im *Canticum sacrum*." SMZ 98(1958): 49-68.

4739. ----. "Möglichkeiten tonaler Audition." MF 15(1962): 105-122.

4740. Swarowsky, Hans. "*Canticum sacrum*." OMZ 11(1956): 399-405.

Concerto for Piano and Wind Instruments

4741. Benjamin, William E. "Tonality without fifths: Remarks on the first movement of Stravinsky's Concerto for Piano and Wind Instruments." ITO 2/11-12(1977): 53-70.

Concerto in D for Violin and Orchestra

4742. Little.

Danse russe

4743. Berger, Arthur. "Problems of pitch organization in Stravinsky." PNM 2/1(1963): 11-42.

Dumbarton Oaks Concerto
    4744. Eimert, Herbert. "Stravinsky's *Dumbarton Oaks*." MELOS 14 (1947): 247-250.

Ebony Concerto
    4745. Hunkemöller, Jurgen. "Igor Strawinskys Jazz-Porträt." AM 29 (1972): 45-63.

Elegy for J.F.K.
    4746. Payne, Anthony. "Stravinsky's *Abraham and Isaac* and *Elegy for J.F.K.*" TEMPO 73(1964): 12-15.

The Firebird
    4747. Pfaff, Herbert. "Igor Strawinsky, *Feuervogel: Danse infernale du roi Kastchei*: Eine didaktische Analyse." MB 15/12(1983): 16-19.

Fireworks
    4748. Just, Martin. "Tonordnung und Thematik in Strawinskys *Feu d'artifice*, Op.4." AM 40(1983): 61-72.

The Flood
    4749. Payne, Anthony. "Stravinsky's *The Flood*." TEMPO 70(1964): 2-8.
    4750. Rostan, Daniel. "Set design and formal symmetry in Stravinsky's *The Flood*." SONUS 2/2(1982): 26-40.

Four Norwegian Moods
    4751. Kraemer, Uwe. "*Four Norwegian Moods* von Igor Strawinsky." MELOS 39(1972): 80-84.

In Memoriam Dylan Thomas
    4752. Clemmons, W. Ronald. "The coordination of motivic and harmonic elements in the 'Dirge-Canons' of Stravinsky's *In Memoriam Dylan Thomas*." ITO 3/1(1977): 8-21.
    4753. Gauldin, Robert and Warren Benson. "Structure and numerology in Stravinsky's *In Memoriam Dylan Thomas*." PNM 23/2(1984-1985): 167-185.
    4754. Keller, Hans. "*In Memoriam Dylan Thomas*: Stravinsky's Schoenbergian technique." TEMPO 35(1955): 13-20.
    4755. ----. "*In Memoriam Dylan Thomas*: Strawinskys schönbergische Technik." MZ 12(1955): 39-42.

Introitus T.S. Eliot in Memoriam
    4756. Spies, Claudio. "Some notes on Stravinsky's Requiem settings." PNM 5/2(1967): 98-123.
    4757. White, Eric Walter. "Two new memorial works by Stravinsky." TEMPO 74(1965): 18-21.

Mass
    4758. Bieske, Werner. "Igor Strawinsky: *Messe* 1948." MK 21(1951): 12-19.

285

Monumentum pro Gesualdo

4759. Mason, Colin. "Stravinsky and Gesualdo." TEMPO 55-56(1960): 39-48.

Movements for Piano and Orchestra

4760. Boykan, Martin. "Neoclassicism and late Stravinsky." PNM 1/2 (1963): 155-169.

4761. Briner, Andres. "Guillaume de Machaut 1958/59 oder Stravinsky *Movements for Piano and Orchestra.*" MELOS 27(1960): 184-186.

4762. Jers, Norbert. "Strawinskys *Movements for Piano and Orchestra* (1958/59) als Schlüsselwerk seiner letzten Schaffenphase." Kühn: 432-434.

4763. Mason, Colin. "Stravinsky's newest works." TEMPO 53-54 (1960): 2-10.

4764. Walden, William G. "Igor Stravinsky's *Movements for Piano and Orchestra*: The relationships of formal structure, serial technique, and orchestration." CAUSM 9/1(1979): 73-95.

4765. Wennerstrom.

Les Noces

4766. Berger, Arthur. "Problems of pitch organization in Stravinsky." PNM 2/1(1963): 11-42.

4767. Lindlar, Heinrich. "Christ-kultische Elementen in Strawinskys Bauenhochzeit." MELOS 25(1958): 63-66.

Octet for Wind Instruments

4768. Waeltner, Ernest Ludwig. "Aspekte zum Neoklassizismus Strawinskys: Schlussrhythmus, Thema und Grundriss im Finale des Bläser-Oktetts 1923." *Bericht über den internationalen musikwissenschaftlichen Kongress, Bonn 1970.* Carl Dahlhaus, Hans Joachim Marx, Magda Mary-Weber and Gunther Massenkeil, eds. Kassel: Bärenreiter, 1971: 265-276.

Oedipus Rex

4769. Hansen, Mathias. "Wort-Ton-Verhältnis in Igor Strawinskys *Oedipus Rex.*" MG 28(1978): 329-334.

4770. Hirsbrunner, Theo. "Ritual und Spiel in Igor Strawinskys *Oedipus Rex.*" SMZ 114(1974): 1-5.

4771. Mellers, Wilfred. "Stravinsky's *Oedipus* as 20th-century hero." Lang: 34-46.

4772. Möller, Dieter. *Jean Cocteau und Igor Strawinsky: Untersuchungen zur Ästhetik und zu "Oedipus Rex."* Hamburg: Wagner, 1981.

4773. Vinay, Gianfranco. "Da ' Οἰδίπους. ' a *Oedipus Rex* e ritorno: Un Itinerario metrico." RIM 17(1982): 333-345.

Orpheus

4774. Shatzkin, Merton. "A pre-*Cantata* serialism in Stravinsky." PNM 16/1(1977-1978): 139-143.

Petrushka

4775. Hallquist, Robert Nels, Jr. "Stravinsky and the transcriptional process: An analytical and historical study of *Petrouchka*." DMA dissertation: North Texas State University, 1979. No DA listing.

4776. Hamm, Charles E. *Stravinsky: Petrushka*. Norton Critical Scores. New York: W.W. Norton, 1967.

4777. Pfaff, Herbert. "Igor Strawinsky: *Petrushka*: Versuch einer Synopsis (Malerei, Grafik, Plastik, Dichtung)." MB 14/11(1982): 700-712.

4778. Sternfeld, Frederick W. "Some Russian folk songs in Stravinsky's *Petrouchka*." NOTES 2(1945): 95-104.

Piano Concerto

4779. Garst, Marilyn M. "The early twentieth-century piano concerto as formulated by Stravinsky and Schoenberg." PhD dissertation (Musicology): Michigan State University, 1972. UM 73-05,376. DA XXXIII.9, p.5224-A.

Piano-Rag-Music

4780. Joseph, Charles M. "Structural coherence in Stravinsky's *Piano-Rag-Music*." MTS 4(1982): 76-91.

Pulcinella

4781. Cone, Edward T. "The uses of convention: Stravinsky and his models." Lang 24-29.

4782. Hucke, Helmut. "Die musikalischen Vorlagen zu Igor Strawinskys *Pulcinella*." Fs. Osthoff/70: 241-250.

Ragtime for Eleven Instruments

4783. Heyman, Barbara B. "Stravinsky and ragtime." MQ 68(1982): 543-562.

The Rake's Progress

4784. Abert, Anna Amalie. "Strawinskys *The Rake's Progress*: Strukturell betrachtet." M 25(1971): 243-247.

4785. Cooke, Deryck. "The *Rake* and the 18th century." MT 103 (1962): 20-23.

4786. Craft, Robert. "Reflections on *The Rake's Progress*." SCORE 9 (1954): 24-30.

4787. Danes, Robert Harold. "Stravinsky's *The Rake's Progress*: Paradigm of neoclassic opera." PhD dissertation (Musicology): Washington University, 1972. 226 p. UM 73-05,031. DA XXXIII.8, p.4452-A.

4788. Griffiths, Paul. *Igor Stravinsky: The Rake's Progress*. Cambridge: Cambridge University Pres, 1982.

4789. Kerman, Joseph. "Opera à la mode." *Hudson Review* 6 (1953-1954): 560-577.

4790. Schneider, Frank. "*The Rake's Progress* oder die Oper der verspielten Konventionen: Eine dramaturgische Studie." JP 3(1980): 135-169.

4791. Schuh, Willi. "Zur Harmonik Igor Strawinskys." SMZ 92(1952): 243-252.

4792. White, Eric Walter. *"The Rake's Progress."* TEMPO 20(1951): 10-18.

Requiem Canticles
4793. Cole, Vincent Lewis. "Analyses of *Symphony of Psalms* (1930, rev. 1948) and *Requiem Canticles* (1966) by Igor Stravinsky." PhD dissertation: University of California, Los Angeles, 1980. No DA listing.
4794. Payne, Anthony. *"Requiem Canticles."* TEMPO 81(1967): 10-19.
4795. Spies, Claudio. "Some notes on Stravinsky's Requiem settings." PNM 5/2(1967): 98-123.

The Rite of Spring
4796. Boaz, Mildred Meyer. "T.S. Eliot and music: A study of the development of musical structures in selected poems by T.S. Eliot and music by Erik Satie, Igor Stravinsky, and Béla Bartók." PhD dissertation (Literature): University of Illinois, 1977. No DA listing.
4797. Boulez, Pierre. "Stravinskys remains." *Notes of an apprenticeship.* New York: Knopf, 1968: 72-145.
4798. Forte, Allen. *The harmonic organization of "The Rite of Spring."* New Haven: Yale University Press, 1978.
4799. Kielian-Gilbert, Marianne. "Relationships of symmetrical pitch-class sets and Stravinsky's metaphor of polarity." PNM 21(1982-1983): 209-240. [Also *Three Pieces for String Quartet*; Octet; *Symphony of Psalms*]
4800. Morton, Lawrence. "Footnotes to Stravinsky studies: *Le Sacre du Printemps.*" TEMPO 128(1979): 9-16.
4801. Petzold, Friedrich. "Formbildende Rhythmik: Zu Strawinskys *Sacre du printemps.*" MELOS 20(1953): 46-47.
4802. Pousseur, Henri. "Stravinsky by way of Webern: The consistency of a syntax." PNM 10/2(1972): 13-51, 11/1(1972): 112-145.
4803. ----. "Stravinsky selon Webern selon Stravinsky." MJ 4(1971): 21-47, 5(1971): 107-126.
4804. Scharschuch, Horst. *Analyse zu Igor Stravinskys "Sacre du printemps."* Regensburg: G. Bosse, 1960.
4805. Scherliess, Volker. *Igor Strawinsky: Le Sacre du printemps.* München: W. Fink, 1982.
4806. Siddons, James. "Rhythmic structures in *Le Sacre du printemps.*" MAN 1(1972): 6-11.
4807. Smalley, Roger. "The sketchbooks of *The Rite of Spring.*" TEMPO 91(1970): 2-13.
4808. Sonntag, Brunhilde. "Die Formen in Strawinskys *Sacre du printemps.*" MELOS 37(1970): 232-235.
4809. Taruskin, Richard. "Russian folk melodies in *The Rite of Spring.*" JAMS 33(1980): 501-543.
4810. Travis, Roy. "Towards a new concept of tonality." JMT 3(1959): 257-284.
4811. Whittall, Arnold. "Music analysis as human science? *Le Sacre du Printemps* in theory and practice." MA 1(1982): 33-54.

Scherzo

4812. Joseph, Charles M. "Stravinsky's Piano Scherzo (1902) in perspective: A new starting point." MQ 67(1981): 82-93.

Septet

4813. Hoogerwerf, Frank. "Tonal and referential aspects of the set in Stravinsky's Septet." JMR 4(1982-1983): 69-84.

4814. Schatz, Hilmar. "Igor Stravinsky: Septet." MELOS 25(1958): 60-63.

4815. Schilling, Hans Ludwig. "Zur Instrumentation in Igor Strawinskys Spätwerk, aufgezeigt an seinem Septett 1953." AM 13(1956): 181-196.

4816. Stein, Erwin. "Strawinsky's Septet (1953)." TEMPO 31(1954): 7-10.

Serenade in A

4817. Cone, Edward T. "Stravinsky: The progress of a method." PNM 1/1(1962): 18-26.

A Sermon, a Narrative and a Prayer

4818. Clifton, Thomas. "Types of symmetrical relations in Stravinsky's *A Sermon, a Narrative, and a Prayer*." PNM 9(1970): 96-112.

4819. Mason, Colin. "Stravinskys's new work." TEMPO 59(1961): 5-14.

4820. Morton, Lawrence. "Igor Strawinskys Kantate *A Sermon, a Narrative, and a Prayer*." MK 36(1966): 126-129.

4821. Regamey, Constantin. "Strawinskys jüngstes Werk: *A Sermon, a Narrative, and a Prayer*." SMZ 102(1962): 134-141.

The Soldier's Tale

4822. Bailey, Kathryn. "Melodic structures in the Overture and Scene-Music of *Histoire du Soldat*." CAUSM 4(1974): 1-7.

4823. Bradshaw, Susan. "Suite from *The Soldier's Tale*." TEMPO 97 (1971): 15-18.

4824. Heyman, Barbara B. "Stravinsky and ragtime." MQ 68(1982): 543-562.

4825. Marti, Christoph. "Zur Kompositionstechnik von Igor Strawinsky: Das *Petit concert* aus der *Histoire du soldat*." AM 38(1981): 93-109.

4826. Reinhardt, Klaus. "Igor Strawinskys Konzertsuite nach der *Geschichte vom Soldaten*." MB 3(1971): 548-554.

4827. Trapp, Michael. *Studien zu Strawinskys "Geschichte vom Soldaten" (1918)*. Regensburg: G. Bosse, 1978.

4828. Traub, Andreas. *Igor Strawinsky: L'Histoire du soldat*. München: W. Fink, 1981.

4829. Zur, Menachem. "Tonal ambiguities as a constructive force in the language of Stravinsky." MQ 68(1982): 516-526.

Sonata for Two Pianos

4830. Burkhart, Charles. "Stravinsky's revolving canon." MR 29(1968): 161-164.

4831. Johns, Donald C. "An early serial idea of Stravinsky." MR 23 (1962): 305-313.

4832. ----. "Eine frühe Reihenarbeit Strawinskys." OMZ 19(1964): 248-253.

4833. Kirchmeyer, Helmut. *Igor Strawinsky, Zeitgeschichte in Persönlichkeitsbild, Grundlagen und Voraussetzung zur modernen Konstruktionstechnik.* Regensburg: G. Bosse, 1958: 537-546.

4834. Tangeman, Robert. "Stravinsky's two-piano works." MM 22 (1945): 93-98.

Symphonies of Wind Instruments

4835. Bowles, Richard W. "Stravinsky's *Symphonies of Wind Instruments* for 23 winds: An analysis." JBR 15/1(1979-1980): 32-37.

4836. Cone, Edward T. "Stravinsky: The progress of a method." PNM 1/1(1962): 18-26.

4837. Kramer, Jonathan. "Moment form in twentieth century music." MQ 64(1978): 177-194.

4838. Somfai, L. "*Symphonies of Wind Instruments* (1920): Observations on Stravinsky's organic construction." SM 14(1972): 355-383.

4839. Tyra, Thomas. "An analysis of Stravinsky's *Symphonies of Wind Instruments.*" JBR 8/2(1971-1972): 6-39.

Symphony in C

4840. Babitz, Sol. "Stravinsky's *Symphony in C* (1940)." MQ 27(1941): 20-25.

4841. Williams, B. M. "Time and structure of Stravinsky's *Symphony in C.*" MQ 59(1973): 355-369.

Symphony in Three Movements

4842. Dahl, Ingolf. "Stravinsky in 1946." MM 23(1946): 159-165.

4843. Strobel, Heinrich. "Strawinskys *Symphony in Three Movements.*" MELOS 15(1948): 271-276.

Symphony of Psalms

4844. Berger, Arthur. "Problems of pitch organization in Stravinsky." PNM 2/1(1963): 11-42.

4845. Chittum, Donald. "Compositional similarities in Beethoven and Stravinsky." MR 30(1969): 285-290.

4846. Cole, Vincent Lewis. "Analyses of *Symphony of Psalms* (1930, rev. 1948) and *Requiem Canticles* (1966) by Igor Stravinsky." PhD dissertation: University of California, Los Angeles, 1980. No DA listing.

4847. Cone, Edward T. "Stravinsky: The progress of a method." PNM 1/1(1962): 18-26.

4848. Mellers, Wilfred. "*Symphony of Psalms.*" TEMPO 97(1971): 19-27.

4849. Zimmerschied: 41-54.

Three Pieces for String Quartet

4850. Kolneder, Walter. "Strawinskys Drei Stücke für Streichquartett." OMZ 26(1971): 631-638.

4851. Turkalo, Alexis. "A new approach to similarity relations in set-theory analysis." PhD dissertation (Theory): Michigan State University, 1980. 256 p UM 81-12,169. DA XLI.12, p.4883-A.

Three Songs from William Shakespeare
    4852. Eimert, Herbert. "Die drei Shakespeare-Lieder (1953)." MZ 12 (1955): 35-38. [Also in Kirchmeyer: 186-188]

Threni
    4853. Hogan, Clare. "*Threni*: Stravinsky's 'debt' to Krenek." TEMPO 142(1982): 22-25, 28-29.
    4854. Pauli, Hansjürg. "On Stravinsky's *Threni*." TEMPO 49(1958): 16-33.
    4855. ----. "Zur seriellen Struktur von Igor Strawinskys *Threni*." SMZ 98(1958): 450-456.
    48856 Schuh, Willi. "Struckturanalyze eines Fragments aus Stravinskys *Threni*." SMZ 98(1958): 456-460.
    4857. Vlad, Roman. "Igor Strawinskys *Threni*." MELOS 26(1959): 36-39.

Variations Aldous Huxley in Memoriam
    4858. Kohl, Jerome. "Exposition in Stravinsky's orchestral *Variations*." PNM 18/1-2(1979-1980): 391-405.
    4859. Phillips, Paul Schuyler. "The enigma of *Variations*: A study of Stravinsky's final work for orchestra." MZ 3/1(1984): 69-89.
    4860. Spies, Claudio. "Notes on Stravinsky's variations." PNM 4/1 (1965): 62-74.
    4861. White, Eric Walter. "Two new memorial works by Stravinsky." TEMPO 74(1965): 18-21.

Violin Concerto
    4862. Hall.

Vom Himmel Hoch Variations
    4863. Craft, Robert. "A concert for St. Mark." SCORE 18(19560: 35-51.
    4864. ----. *Le Musiche religiose di Igor Stravinsky*. Venezia: Lombroso Editore, 1957.
    4865. ----. "Stravinsky komponiert Bach." MELOS 24(1957): 35-39.
    4866. Schilling, Hans Ludwig. "Igor Strawinskys Erweiterung und Instrumentation der canonischen Orgelvariationen, *Vom Himmel hoch, da komm ich her* von J.S. Bach." MK 27(1957): 257-275.

Zvezdoliki
    4867. Gottwald, Clytus. "*Swesdoliki* und die musikalische Archetype." MELOS 38(1971): 360-364.
    4868. Matthews, David. "*Zvezdoliki*." TEMPO 97(1971): 9-14.

Other works
    4869. Babbitt, Milton. "Remarks on the recent Stravinsky." PNM 2/2(1964): 35-55.
    4870. Bass, Claude L. "Phrase structure and cadence treatment in the music of Stravinsky." PhD dissertation (Theory): North Texas State University, 1972. UM 73-02,888. DA XXXIII.8, p.4450-A.

4871. Blitzstein, Marc. "The phenomenon of Stravinsky." MQ 21(1935): 330-337.

4872. Boys, Henry. "Stravinsky: Critical categories needed for a study of his music." SCORE 1(1949): 3-12.

4873. Brantley, John Paul. "The serial choral music of Igor Stravinsky." PhD dissertation (Theory): University of Iowa, 1978. UM 79-02,877. DA XXXIX.8, p.4577-A.

4874. Browne, Arthur G. "Aspects of Stravinsky's work." ML 11 11(1930): 360-366.

4875. Chadabe, Joel. "Stravinsky and his easy duets for piano." PQ 75 (1971): 27-29.

4876. Cholopova, Valentina. "Russische Quellen der Rhythmik Strawinskys." MF 27(1974): 435-446.

4877. Cogan, Robert. "Stravinsky's sound: A phonological view: Stravinsky the progressive." SONUS 2/2(1982): 4-21.

4878. Collaer, Paul. *Stravinsky.* Bruxelles: F. Larcier, 1930.

4879. Craft, Robert. "Reihencompositionen: Vom Septett zum *Agon.*" MZ 12(1955): 43-54.

4880. Davies, Laurence. "Stravinsky as Litterateur." ML 49(1968): 135-144.

4881. Donington, Robert. *Stravinsky ballet music.* London: Cassel, 1952.

4882. Edwards, William Pope, Jr. "The variation process in the music of Stravinsky." PhD dissertation: Indiana University, 1974. 196 p. No DA listing.

4883. Evenson, David. "The piano in the compositions of Igor Stravinsky." PQ 118(1981-1982): 26-31.

4884. Fleischer, Herbert. *Strawinsky.* Berlin: Russischer Musik Verlag, 1931.

4885. Hart.

4886. Hirsbrunner, Theo. "Zu Strawinskys Reihentechnik." MF 35(1982): 356-363.

4887. Hopkins, G. W. "Stravinskys's chords." TEMPO 76(1966): 6-12, 77(1966): 2-9.

4888. Huff, H. A. "Linear structures and their relation to style in selected compositions by Igor Stravinsky." PhD dissertation (Theory): Northwestern University, 1965. UM 65-12,205. DA XXVI.6, p.3393.

4889. Jers, Norbert. *Igor Strawinskys späte Zwölftonwerke (1958-1966).* Regensburg: G. Bosse, 1977.

4890. Joseph, Charles Mensore. *Stravinsky and the piano.* Ann Arbor: UMI Research Press, 1983.

4891. ----. "A study of Igor Stravinskys's piano compositions." PhD dissertation: University of Cincinnati, 1974. 339 p. UM 74-28,471. DA XXXV.6, p.3793-4-A.

4892. Karallus, Manfred. "Igor Strawinsky: Der Übergang zur seriellen Kompositionstechnik." PhD dissertation (Musicology): Frankfurt am Main, 1977.

4893. ----. "Mit Quinten und chromatischen Zirkel harmonische Feldvermessung in Strawinskys Spätwerk." NZM 146/1(1985): 8-12. [*In Memoriam Dylan Thomas; Threni; Mass*]

4894. Kirchmeyer, Helmut. *Igor Strawinsky, Zeitgeschichte im Persönlichkeitsbild, Grundlagen und Voraussetzung zur modernen Konstruktionstechnik.* Regensburg: G. Bosse, 1958.

4895. ----. "Optisches und analytisches zu Strawinskys Klaviersonaten." MZ 12(1955): 57-62.

4896. Klein, Lothar. "Stravinsky and opera: Parable as ethic." CCM 4(1972): 65-71.

4897. Kraemer, Uwe. "Das Zitat bei Igor Strawinsky." NZM 131(1970): 135-141.

4898. Lang.

4899. Lindlar, Heinrich. "Bläserchorale bei Strawinsky." SMZ 96(1956): 394-398.

4900. ----. *Igor Strawinskys sakraler Gesang: Geist und Form der Christ-kultischen Kompositionen.* Regensburg: G. Bosse, 1957.

4901. Maconie, Robin. "Stravinsky's final cadence." TEMPO 103 (1972): 18-23.

4902. Mahar, William John. "Neoclassicism in the twentieth century: A study of the idea and its relationship to selected works of Stravinsky and Picasso." PhD dissertation (Fine Arts): Syracuse University, 1972. No DA listing.

4903. Mason, Colin. "Stravinsky's contributions to chamber music." TEMPO 43(1957): 6-16.

4904. Meylan, Pierre. *Une amitie celebre.* Paris: Librairie Ploix, 1962.

4905. Middleton, Richard. "Stravinsky's development: A Jungian approach." ML 54(1973): 289-301.

4906. Moevs, Robert. "Mannerisms and stylistic consistency in Stravinsky." PNM 9/2(1971): 92-103.

4907. Monnikendam, Marius. *Igor Stravinsky.* Haarlem: S.K. Gottmer, 1966.

4908. Murrill, Herbert. "Aspects of Stravinsky." ML 32(1951): 118-124.

4909. Reade, Eugene Walter. "A study of rhythm in the serial works of Igor Stravinsky." PhD dissertation (Theory): Indiana University, 1979. UM 79-21,327. DA XL.4, p.1743-A.

4910. Schneider, Herbert. "Die Parodieverfahren Igor Strawinskys." ACTA 54(1982): 280-293. [In particular, *Pulcinella; Le Baiser de la fée; Petrushka; Apollon Musagète*]

4911. Schönberger, Elmer and Louis Andriessen. "The Apollonian clockwork: Extracts from a book." Trans. by Jeff Hamburg. TEMPO 142 (1982): 13-21.

4912. Shafer, Sharon Guertin. "A survey of Igor Stravinsky's songs." DMA dissertation: University of Maryland, 1973. UM 74-09,816. DA XXXIV.11, p.7271-A.

4913. Stephan, Rudolf. "Aus Igor Strawinskys Spielzeugschachtel." Fs. Doflein: 27-30.

4914. Straus, Joseph. "A principle of voice leading in the music of Stravinsky." MTS 4(1982): 106-124. [*Symphonies of Wind Instruments; Symphony in C; Les Noces; Agon; Oedipus Rex*]

4915. ----. "Stravinsky's tonal axis." JMT 26(1982): 261-290. [*Symphony of Psalms; Dumbarton Oaks; Symphony in C; Oedipus Rex*]

4916. ----. "A theory of harmony and voice leading in the music of Igor Stravinsky." PhD dissertation (Theory): Yale University, 1981. UM 81-25,509. DA XLII.6, p.2359-A.

4917. Strauss, Virginia Rose Fattaruso. "The stylistic use of the violin in selected works by Stravinsky." DMA dissertation: University of Texas, 1980. No DA listing.

4918. Strube, Roger W. "Folk music and folk idioms in Stravinsky's early works." D 5(1973): 16-27.

4919. Struth, Sigrid. "Klassische Symphonik." MZ 12(1955): 53-68.

4920. Taruskin. [Symphony Op.1; *Favi i pastushka*]

4921. Thal, Marlene. "The piano music of Igor Stravinsky." DMA dissertation: University of Washington. 1978. No DA listing.

4922. Van den Toorn, Pieter C. *The music of Igor Stravinsky*. New Haven: Yale University Press, 1983.

4923. ----. "Some characteristics of Stravinsky's diatonic music." PNM 14/1(1975): 104-138.

4924. Vlad, Roman. *Stravinsky*. London: Oxford University Press, 1967.

4925. Wade, Carroll D. "A selected bibliography of Igor Stravinsky." MQ 48(1962): 372-384.

4926. Ward-Steinman, David. "Serial technique in the recent music of Igor Stravinsky." PhD dissertation: University of Illinois, 1961. No DA listing.

4927. White, Eric Walter. *Stravinsky: The composer and his works*. Berkeley: University of California Press, 1966.

4928. Wildberger, Jacques. "Eine musikalisch-rhetorische Figur bei Strawinsky." SMZ 113(1973): 65-69.

4929. Wolterink, Charles Paul. "Harmonic structure and organization in the early serial works of Igor Stravinsky, 1952-1957." PhD dissertation: Stanford University, 1979. UM 79-12,422. DA XXXIX.12, p.7050-A. [*Cantata*; Septet; *Three Songs from William Shakespeare; In Memoriam Dylan Thomas; Canticum Sacrum; Agon*]

4930. Special Issue: MQ 48(1962): 278-384. [Reprinted as Lang]

4931. Special Issue: MZ 1(1952).

4932. Special Issue: MZ 12(1955).

4933. Special Issue: RM 191(1939).

4934. Special Issue: SCORE 20(1957).

4935. Special Issue: TEMPO 97(1971).

STREICHER, THEODOR (1874-1940)

4936. Wursten, Richard Bruce. "The life and music of Theodor Streicher: Hugo Wolf *redivivus*?" PhD dissertation (Musicology): University of Wisconsin, 1980. 566 p. DA 80-11,408. DA XLI.9, p.3778-A.

STRINGFIELD, LAMAR (1897-1959)

4937. Nelson, Douglas. "The life and works of Lamar Stringfield (1897-1959)." PhD dissertation (Musicology): University of North Carolina, 1971. 263 p. UM 72-18,434. DA XXXII.12, p.7031-A.

STSCHEDRIN, RODION (born 1932)

4938. Gerlach, Hannelore. *"Tschastuschki--Kontraste--Poeme*: zum Schaffen von Rodion Stschedrin." MG 22(1972): 721-728.

SUK, JOSEF (1874-1935)

4939. Doubravová, Jarmila. "Sound and structure in Josef Suk's *Zrání.*" IRASM 6(1977): 73-87.

SULLIVAN, SIR ARTHUR (1842-1900)

4940. Helyar, James. *Gilbert and Sullivan: Papers.* First International Conference on Gilbert and Sullivan. Lawrence: University of Kansas Libraries, 1971.
4941. Hughes, Gervase. *The music of Arthur Sullivan.* New York: St. Martin's Press, 1960.

SWANSON, HOWARD (1907-1978)

4942. Ennett, Dorothy. "An analysis and comparison of selected piano sonatas by three contemporary Black Composers: George Walker, Howard Swanson, and Roque Cordero." PhD dissertation (Performance): New York University, 1973. UM 73-30,062. DA XXXIV.6, p.3450-A.

SZYMANOWSKI, KAROL (1882-1937)

4943. Bristiger, Michael, Roger Scruton and Petra Weber-Bockholdt, eds. *Karol Szymanowski in seiner Zeit.* München: W. Fink, 1984.
4944. Gray, Frances M. "Karol Szymanowski: Three representative works for piano." DMA dissertation (Piano Literature and Pedagogy): Indiana University, 1979. No DA listing. [Opp. 4, 34, 50]
4945. Helman, Zofia. "Zur Modalität im Schaffen Szymanowskis und Janáceks." Pecman/J: 201-211.
4946. Samson, Jim. *The music of Szymanowski.* New York: Taplinger, 1981.
4947. ----. "Szymanowski and tonality." STU 5(1976): 291-312.
4948. Schultz: 61-62 [*Dryades et Pan*]; 63-73 [Violin Concerto No.1, Op.35]; 74-82 [Symphony No.3, Op.27]

TAKEMITSU, TORU (born 1930)

4949. Gibson, James Robert. "Toru Takemitsu: A survey of his music with an analysis of three works." DMA dissertation: Cornell University, 1979. No DA listing. [*Requiem* for String Orchestra; *Landscape I* for String Quartet; *Masque* for Two Flutes]

TALMA, LOUISE (born 1906)

4950. Barkin, Elaine. "Louise Talma: *The Tolling Bell.*" PNM 10/2(1972): 142-152.

TAVERNER, JOHN KENNETH (born 1944)

    4951. Parsons, Larry Russell. "An analysis of six major choral works by John Taverner." DMA dissertation (Choral Music): University of Illinois, 1978. UM 79-13,572. DA XXXIX.12, p.7048-A.
    4952. Phillips, Peter. "The ritual music of John Taverner." CT 26 (1983): 29-30.

TAZARTÈS, GHÉDALIA (born 1947)

    4953. Stoianova, Ivanka. "Des scénarios imaginaires en impromuz: Ghédal et son double." MJ 29(1977): 85-93.
    4954. ----. "Multiplicité, non-directionnalité et jeu dans les pratiques contemporaines du spectacle musico-théâtral I): Théâtre instrumental et impromuz, Mauricio Kagel, *Staatstheatre*, Ghédalia Tazartès, *Ghedal et son double*." MJ 27(1977): 38-48.

TCHAIKOVSKY, PETER ILICH (1840-1893)

Ballets
    4955. Wiley, Roland John. "Dramatic time and music in Tchaikovsky's ballets." Fs. Abraham: 187-195.

Eugene Onegin
    4956. Asafev, Boris Vladimirovich. *Tschaikowsky's "Eugen Onegin": Versuch einer Analyse des Stils und der musikalischen Dramaturgie*. Potsdam: Akademische Verlagsgesellschaft Athenaion, 1949.
    4957. ASO 43(1982).

Francesa di Rimini
    4958. Barricelli, Jean-Pierre. "Liszt's journey through Dante's hereafter." JALS 14(1983): 3-15.

Piano Concertos
    4959. Niebuhr, Ulrich. "Der Einfluss Anton Rubinsteins auf die Klavierkonzerte Peter Tschikowskis." MF 27(1974): 412-434.

The Queen of Spades
    4960. Leibowitz, René. "Une fantasmagorie lyrique: *La Dame de pique*." Leibowitz/F: 227-258.

Symphonies
    4961. Hollander, Hans. "Das Finale-Problem in Tschaikowskys sechster Symphonie." NZM 118(1957): 13-15.
    4962. Wolfurt, Kurt von. *Die sinfonischen Werke von Peter Tschaikowski: Einführungen*. Berlin: Bote und Bock, 1947.
    4963. Zajaczkowski, Henry. "Tchaikovsky's Fourth Symphony." MR 45 (1984): 265-276.

Other works

4964. Abraham, Gerald, ed. *The music of Tchaikovsky*. New York: W.W. Norton, 1974 (1946, 1969).

4965. Abraham, Gerald. *Tchaikovsky: A new study*. London: L. Drummond, 1945.

4966. Hanson, Lawrence and Elizabeth Hanson. *Tchaikovsky: A new study of the man and his music*. London: Cassell, 1965.

4967. Kohlhase, Thomas. "Tschaikowskij als Kirchenmusiker: Die *Vsenoščnaja* und ihre liturgischen Vorlagen." Fs. Dadelson: 189-229.

4968. Zagiba, Frantisek. *Tschaikovskij: Leben und Werk*. Zürich: Amalthea, 1953.

4969. Zajaczkowski, Henry. "The function of obsessive elements in Tchaikovsky's style." MR 43(1982): 24-30.

TCHEREPNIN, ALEXANDER (1899-1977)

4970. Layton, Robert. "Alexander Tcherepnin at 75." TEMPO 108 (1974): 11-14.

4971. Thrash, Lois Leventhal. "A stylistic analysis and discussion of Alexander Tcherepnin's preludes and etudes for piano." DMA dissertation (Performance): Indiana University, 1981. No DA listing.

4972. Wuellner, Guy. "Alexander Tcherepnin, in youth and maturity: Bagatelles, Opus 5 and Expressions, Opus 81." JALS 9(1981): 88-94.

4973. ----. "The complete piano music of Alexander Tcherepnin." DMA dissertation (Performance): University of Iowa, 1973. UM 75-01,290. DA XXXV.7, p.4606-A.

THIELE, SIEGRIED (born 1934)

4974. Gülke, Peter. "Siegfried Thiele Sinfonie in 5 Sätzen." MG 16 (1966): 340-342.

4975. Kneipel, Eberhard. "Polarität und Metamorphose: Anmerkungen zu Siegfried Thieles Sinfonie in fünf Sätzen." MG 19(1969): 322-328.

THILMAN, JOHANNES PAUL (1906-1973)

4976. Hauska, Hans. "Johannes Paul Thilman: *Partita piccola*." MG 12(1962): 679-680.

4977. Rubisch, Egon. "Eine neue Sinfonie von Thilman." MG 10 (1960): 549-599. [Sinfonie Nr.6 in E, Op.92]

4978. Schwinger, Eckart. "Rhapsodie für Orchester von Johannes Paul Thilman." MG 16(1966): 338-340.

THOMPSON, RANDALL (1899-1984)

4979. Brookhart, Charles E. "The choral works of Aaron Copland, Roy Harris, and Randall Thompson." PhD dissertation: George Peabody College for Teachers, 1960. LC Mic 60-5861. DA XXI.9, p.2737.

4980. Forbes, Elliot. "The music of Randall Thompson." MQ 35(1949): 1-25.

4981. McGilvray, Byron Wendol. "The choral music of Randall Thompson, an American eclectic." DMA dissertation (Choral Conducting): University of Missouri, 1979. UM 79-26,591. DA XL.6, p.2973-A.

4982. Urrows, David Francis. "Five Love Songs: Reflections on a recent work." ACR 22/2(1980): 28-38.

THOMSON, VIRGIL (born 1896)

4983. Anagnost, Dean Z. "The choral music of Virgil Thomson." PhD dissertation (Music Education): Columbia University Teachers College, 1977. No DA listing.

4984. Cowell, Henry. "Current Chronicle." MQ 35(1949): 619-622. [*A Solemn Music*]

4985. Glanville-Hicks, Peggy. "Virgil Thomson." MQ 35(1949): 209-235.

4986. Sternfeld, Frederick W. "Current Chronicle." MQ 35(1949): 115-121.

4987. Ward, Kelly Mac. "An analysis of the relationship between text and musical shape and an investigation of the relationship between text and surface rhythmic detail in *Four Saints in Three Acts* by Virgil Thomson." PhD dissertation: University of Texas, 1978. No DA listing.

THURM, JOACHIM (born 1927)

4988. Gülke, Peter. "Joachim Thurms Orchestermusik 1965." MG 17 (1967): 101-102.

TIPPETT, SIR MICHAEL (born 1905)

Choral works
4989. Hansler.

Operas
4990. Jones, R.E. "The operas of Michael Tippett." PhD dissertation: Cardiff, 1976.

4991. Scheppach, Margaret. "The operas of Michael Tippett in the light of 20th-century opera aesthetics." PhD dissertation: University of Rochester, 1974. No DA listing.

Piano Concerto
4992. Mason, Colin. "Tippett's Piano Concerto." SCORE 16(1956): 63-68.

Symphonies
4993. Rodda, Richard Earl. "The symphonies of Sir Michael Tippett." PhD dissertation (Musicology): Case-Western Reserve University, 1979. UM 80-01,479. DA XL.7, p.3621-A.

Other works
4994. Atkinson, Neville. "Michael Tippett's debt to the past." MR 23 (1962): 195-204.

4995. Hines.

4996. Kemp, Ian, ed. *Michael Tippett: A symposium on his 60th birthday.* London: Faber & Faber, 1965.

4997. ----. "Rhythm in Tippett's early music." PRMA 105 (1978-1979): 142-153.

4998. Milner, Anthony. "The music of Michael Tippett." MQ 50(1964): 423-438.

4999. Whittall, Arnold. *The music of Britten and Tippett: Studies in themes and techniques.* Cambridge: Cambridge University Press, 1982.

TOCH, ERNST (1887-1964)

5000. Johnson, Charles Anthony. "The unpublished works of Ernst Toch." PhD dissertation (Musicology): University of California, Los Angeles, 1973. UM 73-28,717. DA XXXIV.6, p.3451-A.

5001. Pisk, Paul. "Ernst Toch." MQ 24(1938): 438-450.

TOEBOSCH, LOUIS (born 1916)

5002. Geraedts, Jaap. "Louis Toebosch: *Philippica moderata*, Op.88." SS 21(1964): 30-35.

5003. Paap, Wouter. "Louis Toebosch." SS 21(1964): 1-10.

5004. Visser, Piet. "Louis Toebosch: Finale from *Tryptique pour orgue*." SS 23(1965): 35-46.

TOURNEMIRE, CHARLES (1870-1939)

5005. Dorroh.

TREDICI, DAVID DEL *see* DEL TREDICI, DAVID

TROJAHN, MANFRED (born 1949)

5006. Schibli, Siegfried. "Das Eigene im Fremden: Neuere Entwicklungen im Schaffen Manfred Trojahns." NZM 146/5(1985): 26-29.

TULL, FISHER (born 1934)

5007. Tull, Fisher. "*Sketches on a Tudor Psalm*: Analysis by the composer, edited by Dr. James Neilson." JBR 13/1(1977-1978): 20-26.

TURINA, JOAQUIN (1881-1949)

5008. Powell, Linton Elzie, Jr. "The piano music of Joaquin Turina (1882-1949)." PhD dissertation (Musicology): University of North Carolina, 1974. UM 75-15,689. DA XXXVI.1, p.19-A.

UNGER, HERMANN (1886-1958)

5009. Heldt, Gerhard. "Hermann Ungers Klavierlieder: Versuch einer Standortbestimmung des deutschen Liedes nach Max Reger." Fs. Schreiber: 135-158.

URBANNER, ERICH (born 1936)

5010. Urbanner, Erich. "Mein Kontrabasskonzert 1973." ME 31 (1977-1978): 207-212.

USSACHEVSKY, VLADIMIR (born 1911)

5011. Bailey, Donald Lee. "A study of stylistic and compositional elements of *Anthem* (Stravinsky), *Fragments of Archilochos* (Foss), and *Creation Prologue* (Ussachevsky)." DMA dissertation (Performance): University of Northern Colorado, 1976. 218 p. UM 76-23,159. DA XXXVII.4, p.1859-A.

VALEN, FARTEIN (1887-1952)

5012. Windebank, Florence Leah. "The music of Fartein Valen, 1887-1952." PhD dissertation: London, 1973.

VAN DIEREN, BERNARD *see* **DIEREN, BERNARD VAN**

VARÈSE, EDGARD (1883-1965)

Density 21.5
5013. Baron, Carol K. "Varèse's explication of Debussy's *Syrinx* in *Density 21.5* and an analysis of Varese's composition: A secret model revealed." MR 43(1982): 121-134.
5014. Cope: 25-29.
5015. Guck, Marion. "A flow of energy: *Density 21.5*." PNM 23/1 (1984-1985): 334-347.
5016. Gümbel, Martin. "Versuch an Varèse *Density 21.5*." ZM 1/1 (1970): 31-38.
5017. Kresky, Jeffrey. "A path through *Density*." PNM 23/1 (1984-1985): 318-333.
5018. Nattiez, Jean-Jacques. *"Densité 21.5" de Varèse: Essai d'analyse sémiologique.* Montréal: University of Montréal, 1975. 100 p.
5019. ----. "Varèse's *Density 21.5*: A study in semiological analysis." MA 1(1982): 243-340.
5020. Siddons, James. "On the nature of melody in Varèse's *Density 21.5*." PNM 23/1(1984-1985): 298-316.
5021. Varèse, Edgard. *"Density 21.5."* SCORE 19(1957): 15-18.

Hyperprism
5022. Morgan, Robert P. "Notes on Varèse's rhythm." Van Solkema: 9-25.

Intégrales
    5023. Mâche, François-Bernard and Gilles Tremblay. "Analyse d'*Intégrales*." RM 383-384-385(1985): 111-123.
    5024. Morgan, Robert P. "Notes on Varèse's rhythm." Van Solkema: 9-25.
    5025. Post, Nora. "Varèse, Wolpe and the oboe." PNM 20(1981-1982): 135-148.
    5026. Ramsier, Paul. "An analysis and comparison of the motivic structure of *Octandre* and *Intégrales*, two instrumental works by Edgard Varèse." PhD dissertation (Music Education): New York University, 1972. 193 p. UM 72-26,609. DA XXXIII.4, p.1772-A.
    5027. Strawn, John. "The *Intégrales* of Edgard Varèse: Space, mass, element and form." PNM 17/1(1978-1979): 138-160.
    5028. ----. "Raum und Klangmasse in Varèses *Intégrales*." Melos/NZM 1(1975): 446-456.
    5029. Wilkinson, Marc. "Edgard Varèse: Pionier und Prophet." MELOS 28(1961): 68-76.

Ionisation
    5030. Chou, Wen-Chung. "*Ionisation*: The function of timbre in its formal and temporal organization." Van Solkema: 27-74.
    5031. Gruhn, Wilfried. "Edgard Varèse (1883-1965): *Ionisation* (1931)." Zimmerschied: 55-72.

Octandre
    5032. Post, Nora. "Varèse, Wolpe and the oboe." PNM 20(1981-1982): 135-148.
    5033. Ramsier, Paul. "An analysis and comparison of the motivic structure of *Octandre* and *Intégrales*, two instrumental works by Edgard Varèse." PhD dissertation (Music Education): New York University, 1972. 193 p. UM 72-26,609. DA XXXIII.4, p.1772-A.
    5034. Swan, John. "Varèse's *Octandre* as a source piece for the demonstration of three twentieth-century compositional procedures." CAUSM 2/1(1972): 53-74.
    5035. Wilkinson, Marc. "Edgard Varèse: Pionier und Prophet." MELOS 28(1961): 68-76.

Poème electronique
    5036. Cope: 170-174.

Other works
    5037. Bernard, Jonathan W. "Pitch/Register in the music of Edgard Varèse." MTS 3(1981): 1-25.
    5038. ----. "A theory of pitch and register for the music of Edgard Varèse." PhD dissertation (Theory): Yale University, 1977. 2 vols. UM 77-27,059. DA XXXVIII.6, p.3125-A.
    5039. Block, David Reed. "The music of Edgard Varèse." PhD dissertation (Theory): University of Washington, 1973. 246 p. RILM 76/10838dd28. No DA listing.
    5040. Carter, Elliott. "On Edgard Varèse." Van Solkema: 1-7.

5041. Chou, Wen-Chung. "Varèse: A sketch of the man and his music." MQ 52(1966): 151-170.

5042. Cox, David Harold. "The music of Edgard Varèse." PhD dissertation (Music History): Birmingham, 1977.

5043. Parks, Anne Florence. "Freedom, form and process in Varèse: A study of Varèse's musical ideas, their sources, their development, and their use in his works." PhD dissertation (Musicology): Cornell University, 1974. 471 p. UM 74-17,688. RILM 75/1588dd28. No DA listing.

5044. Stempel, Larry. "Not even Varèse can be an orphan." MQ 60 (1974): 46-60.

5045. ----. "Varèses *Awkwardness* und die Symmetrie im *Zwölftonrahmen*." SMZ 119(1979): 69-82.

5046. ----. "Varèse's *Awkwardness* and the symmetry in the *Frame of 12 Tones*: An analytic approach." MQ 65(1979): 148-166.

5047. Stenzl, Jürg. "Varèsiana." HJM 4(1980): 145-162.

5048. Tremblay, Gilles. "Acoustique et forme chez Varèse." RM 383-385 (1985): 29-46.

5049. Wehmeyer, Grete. *Edgard Varèse*. Regensburg: G. Bosse, 1977.

5050. Wilheim, Andras. "The genesis of a specific twelve-tone system in the works of Varèse." SM 19(1977): 203-226.

5051. Wilkinson, Marc. "An introduction to the music of Edgard Varèse." SCORE 19(1957): 5-14.

5052. Yannay, Yehuda. "Toward an open-ended method of analysis of contemporary music: A study of selected works of Edgard Varèse and György Ligeti." DMA dissertation (Composition): University of Illinois, 1974. 131 p. UM 75-11,887. DA XXXV.12, p.7952-3-A.

VAUGHAN WILLIAMS, RALPH (1872-1958)

Operas

5053. Doonan, Michael Robert. *"The Pilgrim's Progress*: An analytical study and case for performance of the opera by Ralph Vaughan Williams." DM dissertation (Music Literature and Pedagogy, Voice): Indiana University, 1980. No DA listing.

5054. Forbes, Anne-Marie H. "Motivic unity in Ralph Vaughan Williams's *Riders to the Sea*." MR 44(1983): 234-245.

5055. Reber, William Francis. "The operas of Ralph Vaughan Williams." DMA dissertation (Performance): University of Texas, 1977. UM 77-28,988. DA XXXVIII.7, p.3796-A.

Symphonies

5056. Clarke, F.R.C. "The structure of Vaughan Williams's *Sea Symphony*." MR 34(1973): 58-61.

5057. Dickinson, A.E.F. "Toward the unknown region (an introduction to Vaughan Williams's Sixth Symphony)." MR 9(1948): 275-290.

5058. ----. "Vaughan Williams's Fifth Symphony." MR 6(1945): 1-12.

5059. Ottaway, Hugh. "Vaughan Williams's Eighth Symphony" ML 38(1957): 213-225.

5060. Schwartz, Elliott Shelling. *The symphonies of Ralph Vaughan Williams: An analysis of their stylistic elements*. Amherst: University of Massachusetts Press, 1964.

Other works

5061. Bergsagel, John Dagfinn. "The national aspects of the music of Ralph Vaughan Williams." PhD dissertation (Musicology): Cornell University, 1957. UM 22,194. DA XVII.9, p.2026.

5062. Curtis.

5063. Dickinson, A.E.F. "The legacy of Ralph Vaughan Williams: A retrospect." MR 19(1958): 290-304.

5064. Hawthorne, Robin. "A note on the music of Vaughan Williams." MR 9(1948): 269-274.

5065. Hesse, Lutz-Werner. *Studien zum Schaffen des Komponisten Ralph Vaughan Williams*. Regensburg: G. Bosse, 1983.

5066. Kimmel, William. "Vaughan Williamss' melodic style." MQ 27 (1941): 491-499.

5067. Payne, Elsie. "Vaughan Williams and folk-song." MR 15(1954): 103-126.

5068. Rubbra, Edmund. "The later Vaughan Williams." ML 18 (1937): 1-8.

VELKE, FRITZ (born 1930)

5069. Velke, Fritz. "Concertino for Band." JBR 2/1(1966): 9-18.

VERDI, GIUSEPPI (1813-1901)

Aida

5070. ASO 4(1976).

5071. Bleiler, Ellen H. *Aida*. Dover Opera Guide and Libretto Series. New York: Dover, 1962.

5072. Gossett, Philip. "Verdi, Ghizlanzoni, and *Aida*: The uses of convention." CI 1/2(1974-1975): 291-334.

5073. John, Nicholas, ed. *Giuseppe Verdi: Aida*. London: J. Calder, 1980.

Un Ballo in maschera

5074. ASO 32(1981).

5075. Levarie, Siegmund. "Key relations in Verdi's *Un Ballo in maschera*." NCM 2(1978-1979): 143-147.

5076. ----. "A pitch cell in Verdi's *Un Ballo in maschera*." JMR 3(1979-1981): 399-409.

5077. Parker, Roger and Matthew Brown. "Motivic and tonal interaction in Verdi's *Un Ballo in maschera*." JAMS 36(1983): 243-265.

5078. Ross, Peter. "Amelias Auftrittsarie im *Maskenball*: Verdis Vertonung in dramaturgisch-textlichem Zusammenhang." AM 40(1983): 126-146.

Il Corsaro

5079. Town, Stephen. "Observations on a cabaletta from Verdi's *Il Corsaro*." CM 32(1981): 59-75.

Don Carlos

5080. Leibowitz, René. *"Don Carlo* ou les fantômes du clair-obscur." Leibowitz/F: 175-204.

5081. Reti, Rudolph. "Die thematische Einheit in Verdis *Don Carlos.*" OMZ 30(1975): 342-350.

I Due Foscari

5082. Biddlecombe, George. "The revision of *No, non morrai, chi i perfidi*: Verdi's compositional process in *I Due Foscari.*" SV 2(1983): 59-77.

Ernani

5083. Kerman, Joseph. "Notes on an early Verdi opera." SN 3(1973): 56-65.

Falstaff

5084. Hepokoski, James A. *Giuseppe Verdi: Falstaff.* Cambridge: Cambridge University Press, 1983.

5085. John, Nicholas, ed. *Verdi: Falstaff.* London: J. Calder, 1982.

5086. Linthicum, David. "Verdi's *Falstaff* and classical sonata form." MR 39(1978): 39-53.

5087. Sabbeth, Daniel. "Dramatic and musical organization in Falstaff." *Atti del IIIo Congreso Internazionale di Studi Verdiani: Il Teatro e la musica di Giuseppe Verdi, 1972.* Mario Medici, ed. Parma: Istituto di Studi Verdiani, 1974: 415-442.

La Forza del destino

5088. John, Nicholas, ed. *Verdi: The Force of Destiny.* London: J. Calder, 1984.

5089. Lawton, David. "Verdi, Cavallini and the clarinet solo in *La Forza del destino.*" V 2/6(1963-1965): English 1723-1748; Italian and German: 2149-2185.

5090. Zecchi, Adone. "The chorus in *La Forza del destino.*" V 2/5 (1962): Italian 793-814; German and English:

Macbeth

5091. Antokoletz, Elliott. "Verdi's dramatic use of harmony and tonality in *Macbeth.*" ITO 4/6(1978): 17-29.

5092. ASO 40(1982).

5093. Christen, Norbert. "Auf dem Weg zum szenischen Musikdrama: Verdis *Macbeth* im Vergleich der beiden Fassungen." NZM 146/7-8(1985): 9-15.

5094. Osthoff, Wolfgang. "Die beiden Fassungen von Verdis *Macbeth.*" AM 29(1972): 17-44.

Otello

5095. Archibald, Bruce. "Tonality in *Otello.*" MR 35(1974): 23-28.

5096. ASO 3(1976).

5097. John, Nicholas, ed. *Verdi: Otello.* London: J. Calder, 1981.

5098. Klein, John W. "Verdi's *Otello* and Rossini's." ML 45(1964): 130-140.

5099. Lawton, David. "On the *Bacio* theme in *Otello*." NCM 1 (1977-1978): 211-220.
5100. Noske, Frits. "*Otello*: Drama through structure." Fs. Fox: 14-47.

Rigoletto

5101. Chusid, Martin. "Rigoletto and Monterone: A study in musical dramaturgy." *Report of the Eleventh Congress of the International Musicological Society, Copenhagen, 1972.* København: 1974, I: 325-336. [Also in V 9(1982): 1544-1588]
5102. John, Nicholas, ed. *Verdi: Rigoletto.* London: J. Calder, 1982.
5103. Lawton, David. "Tonal structure and dramatic action in *Rigoletto*." V 9(1982): 1559-1581.
5104. Leibowitz, René. "The orchestration of *Rigoletto*." V 3/5(1973): Italian 931-949; English and German: 1248-1274
5105. Osthoff, Wolfgang. "The musical characterization of Gilda." V 3/8(1973): German 950-979; English and Italian: 1275-1314.
5106. Zecchi, Adone. "Choruses and coryphaei in *Rigoletto*." V 3/7 (1969): Italian 124-146; English and German: 510-544.

Simon Boccanegra

5107. ASO 19(1979).
5108. Cone, Edward T. "On the road to *Otello*: Tonality and structure in *Simon Boccanegra*." SV 1(1982): 72-98.
5109. Kerman, Joseph. "Lyric form and flexibility in *Simon Boccanegra*." SV 1(1982): 47-62.
5110. Neuls-Bates, Carol. "Verdi's *Les Vêpres siciliennes* (1855) and *Simon Boccanegra* (1857)." PhD dissertation (Music History): Yale University, 1970. UM 70-25,234. DA XXXI.7, p.3578.

La Traviata

5111. ASO 51(1983).
5112. Della Seta, Fabrizio. "Il Tempo della festa: Su due scene della *Traviata* e su altri luoghi Verdiani." SV 2(1983): 108-146.
5113. John, Nicholas, ed. *Verdi: La Traviata.* London: J. Calder, 1981.

Il Trovatore

5114. ASO 60(1984).
5115. Petrobelli, Pierluigi, William Drabkin and Roger Parker. "Verdi's *Il Trovatore*: A symposium." MA 1(1982): 125-168.

Les Vêpres siciliennes

5116. ASO 75(1985).
5117. Conati, Marcello. "Ballabili nei *Vespri*: Con alcune osservazioni su Verdi e la musica populare." SV 1(1982): 21-46.
5118. Neuls-Bates, Carol. "Verdi's *Les Vêpres siciliennes* (1855) and *Simon Boccanegra* (1857)." PhD dissertation (Music History): Yale University, 1970. UM 70-25,234. DA XXXI.7, p.3578.

Other works
5119. Barbera, C. Andre. "Choruses of revolt in Verdi's operas of the 1840's." *Journal of Fine Arts* 1/1(1977): 32-60.
5120. Budden, Julian. *The operas of Verdi*. London: Cassell, 1973-1981. 3 vols.
5121. Gerhartz, Leo Karl. *Auseinandersetzungen des jungen Giuseppe Verdi mit dem literarischen Drama: Ein Beitrag zur szenischen Struktur-bestimmung der Oper*. Berlin: Merseburger, 1968.
5122. Jablonsky, Stephen. "The development of tonal coherence as evidenced in the revised operas of Giuseppe Verdi." PhD dissertation: New York University, 1973. 465 p. No DA listing.
5123. Kerman, Joseph. "Verdi's use of recurring themes." Fs. Strunk: 495-510.
5124. Kimbell, David R.B. *Verdi in the age of Italian romanticism*. Cambridge: Cambridge University Press, 1981.
5125. ----. "The young Verdi and Shakespeare." PRMA 101 (1974-1975): 59-73.
5126. Lawton, David. "Tonality and drama in Verdi's early operas." PhD dissertation (Musicology): University of California, Berkeley, 1973. 2 vols. No DA listing.
5127. Lusk, Franklin Lynn. "An analytical study of the Verdi *Romanze*." PhD dissertation: Indiana University, 1975. No DA listing.
5128. Noske, Frits. "Ritual scenes in Verdi's operas." ML 54(1973): 415-439.
5129. ----. *The signifier and the signified: Studies in the operas of Mozart and Verdi*. s'Gravenhage: M. Nijhoff, 1977.
5130. Osborne, Charles. *The complete operas of Verdi*. London: Gollancz, 1969.
5131. *Quaderni dell'Istituto di Studi Verdiana*. Venice, 1953- Vol.1: *Il Corsaro*; Vol.2: *Gerusalemme*; Vol.3: *Stiffelio*; Vol.4: Genesi dell'*Aida*.
5132. Siegmund-Schultze, Walther. "Some thoughts on the Verdian type of melody." V 2/4(1961): German 255-284; Italian and English: 671-710.
5133. Travis, Francis Irving. *Verdi's orchestration*. Zürich: Juris, 1956.

VERESS, SÁNDOR (born 1907)

5134. Terényi, Ede. "Laudatis musicae: Hommage à Sándor Veress à l'occasion de son 75e anniversaire." SMZ 122(1982): 213-224.
5135. Traub, Andreas. "Melodische Artikulation: Zur *Sonata per violoncello solo* von Sándor Veress." SMZ 120(1980): 15-26.
5136. ----. "Die *Passacaglia concertante* von Sándor Veress: Eine analytische Studie." MF 37(1984): 122-130.
5137. ----. "Zur Geschichte der *Musica concertante*." SMZ 122(1982): 228-237.

VERMEULEN, MATTHIJS (1888-1967)

5138. Ketting Otto. "Prelude as postlude: On Matthijs Vermeulen's Second Symphony, *Prélude à la nouvelle journée*, and the song *Les Filles du Roi d'Espagne*." KN 3(1976): 42-45.
5139. Vermeulen, Matthijs. "Matthijs Vermeulen: Seventh Symphony, *Dithyrambes pour les temps à venir*." SS 29(1966): 24-36.
5140. Wagemans, Peter-Jan. "Matthijs Vermeulen and the dialectic of freedom." KN 21(1985): 3-7.

VIERNE, LOUIS (1870-1937)

5141. Bölting, Ralf. "Die Orgelsinfonien Louis Viernes und ihre Vorgeschichte." MK 48(1978): 112-118.
5142. Kasouf, Edward J. "Louis Vierne and his six organ symphonies." PhD dissertation (Musicology): Catholic University, 1970. UM 70-22,717. DA XXXI.5, p.2422.
5143. Long, Page Carrol. "Transformations of harmony and consistencies of form in the six organ symphonies of Louis Vierne." DMA dissertation: University of Arizona, 1963. UM 63-06,725. DA XXIV.5, p.2071.

VIERU, ANATOL (born 1826)

5144. Grigorovici, Lucian. "Elf Fragen zu Anatol Vieru." MELOS 35 (1968): 236-243.

VILLA-LOBOS, HEITOR (1887-1959)

5145. Farmer, Virginia. "An analytical study of the seventeen string quartets of Heitor Villa-Lobos." PhD dissertation (Performance): University of Illinois, 1973. 135 p. UM 73-17,533. DA XXXIV.1, p.352-A.
5146. Galm, John K. "The use of Brazilian percussion instruments in the music of Villa-Lobos." William Kearns, ed. *Musicology at the University of Colorado*. Regents of the University of Colorado, 1977: 182-199.
5147. Orrego-Salas, Juan A. "Heitor Villa-Lobos: Man, work, style." IAMB 52(1966): 1-36.
5148. Peppercorn, Lisa M. *Heitor Villa-Lobos: Leben und Werk des brasilianischen Komponisten*. Zürich: Atlantis, 1972.

VLIJMEN, JAN VAN (born 1935)

5149. Baaren, Kees van. "Jan van Vlijmen: *Construzione* per due pianoforti." SS 9(1961): 12-17.
5150. Bois, Rob du. "Jan van Vlijmen: *Gruppi* per 20 strumenti e percussione." SS 21(1964): 17-21.
5151. Hartsuiker, Ton. "Jan van Vlijmen: *Omaggio a Gesualdo*." SS 53(1973): 1-11.
5152. ----. "Jan van Vlijmen's *Serenata I*." SS 31(1967): 1-9.
5153. Markus, Wim. "*Axel* or the rejection of life." KN 6(1977): 19-32. [*Axel* by Reinbert de Leeuw and Jan van Vlijmen, co-composer]

5154. ----. *"Quaterni* theses." KN 15(1982): 36-47.

VOGEL, VLADIMIR (born 1896)

5155. Hines: 220-236.
5156. Oesch, Hans. "Wladimir Vogels Werke für Klavier." SMZ 97 (1957): 51-57.
5157. Schuhmacher, Gerhard. "Gesungenes und gesprochenes Wort in Werken Wladimir Vogels." AM 24(1967): 64-80.
5158. Vogel, Wladimir. "Klaviereigene Interpretationsstudie einer variierten Zwölftonfolge (1972)." SMZ 116(1976): 22-24.

VOLKMANN, ROBERT (1815-1883)

5159. Hopkins, William. "The solo piano works of Robert Volkmann (1815-1883)." Fs. Kaufmann,W: 327-338.

VOORMOLEN, ALEXANDER (born 1895)

5160. Bakker, M. Geerink. "Alexander Voormolen: *Chaconne and Fugue.*" SS 24(1965): 12-15.
5161. Reeser, Eduard. "Alexander Voormolen." SS 22(1965): 1-11, 23(1965): 18-25.
5162. Wagemans, Peter-Jan. "Alexander Voormolen: From international *avant garde* to Hague conservatism." KN 15(1982): 14-23.

WAGENAAR, BERNARD (1894-1971)

5163. Fuller, Donald. "Bernard Wagenaar." MM 21(1944): 225-232.

WAGENAAR, DIDERIK (born 1946)

5164. Wagenaar, Diderik. *"Liederen*: An analysis." KN 10(1979): 28-32.

WAGENBRETH, PETER

5165. Oehlschlägel, Reinhard. "Zwischen Handlungensoper und absur-dem Theater: Zu *Itzo-Hux* von Hans-Joachim Hespos und Peter Wagen-broth." MTX 8(1985): 46-48.

WAGNER, RICHARD (1813-1883)

Eine Faustouverture
5166. Macy.
5167. Voss, Egon. *Richard Wagner: Eine Faust-Overture.* München: W. Fink, 1982.

Die Feen
> 5168. Saar, Harold E. "*Die Feen*: Richard Wagner's first opera." PhD dissertation (Musicology): Catholic University, 1964. UM 64-8966. DA XXV.5, p.3021-2.

Der fliegende Holländer
> 5169. ASO 30(1980).
> 5170. John, Nicholas, ed. *Wagner: The Flying Dutchman*. London: J. Calder, 1982.
> 5171. Lefrançois, André Emile. *Le Vaisseu fantôme: Opera romantique de Richard Wagner: Étude thematique et analyse*. Paris: A. Lefrançois, 1983.
> 5172. Prax, Lothar. "Gestalt und Struktur von Wagners *Der fliegende Holländer*." PhD dissertation (Musicology): Köln, 1974.

Götterdämmerung
> 5173. ASO 13-14(1978).
> 5174. Kinderman, William. "Dramatic recapitulation in Wagner's *Götterdämmerung*." NCM 4(1980-1981): 101-112.
> 5175. Lefrançois, André. *"Crépuscule des Dieux" de Richard Wagner: Étude thematique et analyse*. Paris: A. Lefrançois, 1979. 108 p.

Das Liesbesverbot
> 5176. Engel, Hans. "Über Richard Wagners Oper *Das Liebesverbot*." Fs. Blume: 80-91.

Lohengrin
> 5177. Lefrançois, André. *"Lohengrin" de Richard Wagner: Étude thematique et analyse*. Paris: A. Lefrançois, 1980. 83 p.
> 5178. Solyom, György. "*Lohengrin*: Höhepunkt und Zerfall der grossen romantischen Oper." SM 4(1963): 257-287.

Die Meistersinger
> 5179. Finscher, Ludwig. "Über den Kontrapunkt der *Meistersinger*." Dahlhaus: 303-312.
> 5180. Kühn, Hellmut. "Der Niedergang der popularen Oper und Wagners *Meistersinger von Nürnberg*." NZM 134(1973): 272-279.
> 5181. Lefrançois, André. *"Les Maître-chanteurs de Nuremberg" de Richard Wagner: Étude thematique et analyse*. Paris: A. Lefrançois, 1974. 144 p.
> 5182. McDonald, William E. "Words, music, and dramatic development in *Die Meistersinger*." NCM 1(1977-1978): 246-260.
> 5183. Voss, Egon, ed. *Die Meistersinger von Nürnberg*. Reinbeck: Rowohlt, 1981.

Parsifal
> 5184. ASO 38-39(1982).
> 5185. Bauer, Hans-Joachim. *Wagners "Parsifal": Kriterien der Kompostionstechnik*. Berliner Musikwissenschaftliche Arbeiten 15. München: E. Katzbichler, 1977.
> 5186. Beckett, Lucy. *Richard Wagner: Parsifal*. Cambridge:

Cambridge University Press, 1981.

5187. Chailley, Jacques. *"Parsifal" de Richard Wagner: Opéra initiatique*. Paris: Buchet/Chastel, 1979.

5188. Hollander, Hans. "Zum Symbolismus der drei *Parsifal* Vorspiele." NZM 129(1968): 336-338.

5189. Lefrançois, André. *Parsifal: Drame sacre de Richard Wagner: Étude thématique et analyse*. Paris: A. Lefrançois, 1980. 95 p.

5190. Lewin, David. "Amfortas's prayer to Titurel and the role of D in *Parsifal*: The tonal spaces of the drama and the enharmonic C-Flat/B." NCM 7(1983-1984): 336-349.

5191. Ludwig, Ingeborg. "Die Klanggestaltung in Richard Wagners *Parsifal*." PhD dissertation (Musicology): University of Hamburg, 1968.

5192. Neuwirth, Gösta. "Musik um 1900." Fs. Schuh: 89-134.

5193. Seelig, Wolfgang. "Ambivalenz und Erlösung: Wagners *Parsifal*: Zweifel und Glauben." OMZ 37(1982): 307-317.

Das Rheingold

5194. ASO 6-7(1976).

5195. Breig, Werner. "Der 'Rheintöchtergesang' in Wagners *Rheingold*." AM 37(1980): 241-263.

5196. Lefrançois, André. *"L'Or du Rhin" de Richard Wagner: Étude thématique et analyse*. Paris: A. Lefrançois, 1976. 89 p.

Der Ring des Nibelungen [see also individual titles]

5197. Bailey, Robert. "The structure of *The Ring* and its evolution." NCM 1(1977-1978): 48-61.

5198. Breig, Werner. "Das Schicksalskunde-Motiv im *Ring des Nibelungen*: Versuch einer harmonischen Analyse." Dahlhaus: 223-233.

5199. Chapman, Kenneth G. "Siegfried and Brünnhilde and the passage of time in Wagner's *Ring*." CM 32(1981): 43-58.

5200. Dahlhaus, Carl. "Formprinzipien in Wagners *Ring des Nibelungen*." *Beiträge zur Geschichte der Oper*. Heinz Becker, ed. Regensburg: G. Bosse, 1969: 95-129.

5201. ----. "Tonalität und Form in Wagners *Ring des Nibelungen*." AM 40(1983): 165-173.

5202. Darcy, Warren Jay. "Formal and rhythmic problems in Wagner's *Ring* cycle." DMA dissertation (Composition): University of Illinois, 1973. 423 p. UM 74-05,549. DA XXXIV.11, p.7264-A.

5203. Donington, Robert. *Wagner's "Ring" and its symbols: The music and the myth*. London: Faber & Faber, 1963.

5204. Floros, Constantin. "Der 'Beziehungszauber' der Musik im *Ring des Nibelungen* von Richard Wagner." NZM 144/7-8(1983): 8-14.

5205. Gloede, Wilhelm. "Dichterisch-musikalische Periode und Form in Brünnhildes Schlussgesang." OMZ 38(1983): 84-92.

5206. Hutcheson, Ernest. *A musical guide to the Richard Wagner "Ring of the Nibelung."* New York: Simon & Schuster, 1940.

5207. Jacobs, Robert L. "A Freudian view of *The Ring*." MR 26(1965): 201-219.

5208. Jiránek, Jaroslav. "Die philosophischen Grundlagen des *Ring*-dramas." BM 5(1963): 169-182.

5209. Kempter-Lott, Max. *Einführung in Richard Wagners dramatische Dichtung "Der Ring des Nibelungen."* Zürich: Hug, 1941.

5210. Kneif, Tibor. "Zur Deutung der Rheintöchter in Wagners *Ring.*" AM 26(1969): 297-306.

5211. Kolland, Hubert. "Zur Semantik der Leitmotive in Richard Wagners *Ring des Nibelungen.*" IRASM 4(1973): 197-212.

5212. Kroó, György. "Licht-Alberichs Lehrjahre." SM 22(1980): 111-136.

5213. Laing, Alan Henry. "Tonality in Wagner's *Der Ring des Nibelungen.*" PhD dissertation: Edinburgh, 1973.

5214. Mackey-Stein, Christiane. "Les Motifs de la femme et de l'amour dans la tetralogie: Note de recherche." MJ 31(1978): 47-51.

5215. Nitsche, Peter. "Klangfarbe und Form: Das Walhallthema in *Rheingold* und *Walküre.*" Melos/NZM 1(1975): 83-88.

5216. Orlando, Francesco. "Propositions pour une sémantique du leitmotiv dans *L'Anneau des Nibelungen.*" MJ 17(1975): 73-86.

5217. Oskar, Andree. *Richard Wagners "Ring des Nibelungen".* Stuttgart: Mellinger, 1976.

5218. Reynaud, Bérénice. "*L'Anneau de Nibelung* du mythe à l'intention musicale: Pour une analyse structurale." MJ 22(1976): 19-63.

5219. Winkler, Franz Emil. *Richard Wagner: Der Ring des Nibelungen.* Schaffhausen: Novalis, 1981.

Siegfried

5220. ASO 12(1977).

5221. Bailey, Robert. "Wagner's musical sketches for *Siegfrieds Tod.*" Fs. Strunk: 459-494.

5222. Brinkmann, Reinhold. "'Drei der Fragen stell' ich mir frei': Zur Wanderer-Szene im 1. Akt von Wagners *Siegfried.*" JSIM (1972): 120-162.

5223. Coren, Daniel. "Inspiration and calculation in the genesis of Wagner's *Siegfried.*" Fs. Albrecht/S: 266-287.

5224. John, Nicholas, ed. *Wagner: Siegfried.* London: J. Calder, 1984.

5225. Lefrançois, André. *"Siegfried" de Richard Wagner: Étude thématique et analyse.* Paris: A. Lefrançois, 1979. 111 p.

5226. McCreless, Patrick. *Wagner's "Siegfried": Its drama, history and music.* Ann Arbor: UMI Research Press, 1982.

Tannhäuser

5227. ASO 63-64(1984).

5228. Daverio, John. "Narration as drama: Wagner's early revisions of *Tannhäuser* and their relation to the Rome narrative." CMS 24/2(1984): 55-68.

5229. Lefrançois, André. *"Tannhäuser" de Richard Wagner: Étude thématique et analyse.* Paris: A. Lefrançois, 1982.

5230. Strohm, Reinhard. "Dramatic time and operatic form in Wagner's *Tannhäuser.*" PRMA 104(1977-1978): 1-10.

Tristan und Isolde

5231. ASO 34-35(1981).

5232. Bailey, Robert. "The genesis of *Tristan und Isolde* and a study of Wagner's sketches and drafts for the first act." PhD dissertation (Musicology): Princeton University, 1969. UM 70-08,346. DA XXX.11, p.5011.

5233. ----, ed. *Wagner: Prelude and Transfiguration from "Tristan and Isolde"*. Norton Critical Scores. New York: W.W. Norton, 1985.

5234. Barford, Philip. "The way of unity: A study of *Tristan und Isolde*." MR 20(1959): 253-263.

5235. Beeson, Roger. "The *Tristan* chord and others: Harmonic analysis and harmonic explanation." SN 5(1975): 55-72.

5236. Burstein, L. Poundie. "A new view of *Tristan*: Tonal unity in the Prelude and Conclusion to Act I." TP 8/1(1983): 15-42.

5237. Chailley, Jacques. *"Tristan und Isolde" de Richard Wagner*. Au delà des notes 3. Paris: A. Leduc, 1972.

5238. Cone, Edward T. "Yet once more, O ye laurels." PNM 14/2-15/1(1975-1976): 294-306.

5239. Dahlhaus, Carl. *"Tristan*: Harmonik und Tonalität." Melos/NZM 4(1978): 215-219.

5240. Dommel-Diény, Amy. "Encore l'accord de *Tristan*." SMZ 105(1965): 31-37.

5241. Enix, Margery. "Formal expansion through fusion of major and minor: A study of tonal structure in *Tristan und Isolde*, Act I." ITR 1/2(1977-1978): 28-34.

5242. Enix.

5243. Flechsig, Irmtraud. "Beziehungen zwischen textlicher und musikalischer Struktur in Richard Wagners Tristan und Isolde." Dahlhaus: 239-257.

5244. Friedheim, Philip. "The relationship between tonality and musical structure." MR 27(1966): 44-53.

5245. Gauldin, Robert. "Wagner's parody technique: *Träume* and the *Tristan* Love Duet." MTS 1(1979): 35-42.

5246. George, Graham. "Tonality and the narrative in *Tristan*." CAUSM 3/1(1973): 63-70.

5247. ----. "Tonality and the narrative in *Tristan*." CAUSM 4(1974): 21-43. [This is an expansion of the preceding entry]

5248. Gostomsky, Dieter. "Immer noch einmal: Der *Tristan*-Akkord." ZM 6/1(19750: 22-27.

5249. Grunsky, Hans. *"Tristan und Isolde*: Der symphonische Aufbau des dritten Aufzugs." NZM 113(1952): 390-394.

5250. Jackson, Roland. "*Leitmotive* and form in the *Tristan* Prelude." MR 36(1975): 43-53.

5251. John, Nicholas, ed. *Wagner: Tristan and Isolde*. London: J. Calder, 1981.

5252. Kinderman, William. "Das 'Geheimnis der Form' in Wagner's *Tristan und Isolde*." AM 40(1983): 174-188.

5253. Knapp, Raymond. "The tonal structure of *Tristan und Isolde*: A sketch." MR 45(1984): 11-25.

5254. Kropfinger, Klaus. "Wagners *Tristan* und Beethovens Streichquartett Op.130: Funktion und Strukturen des Prinzips der Einleitungswiederholung." Dahlhaus: 259-271.

5255. Lefrançois, André Emile. *"Tristan et Isolde" de Richard Wagner: Étude thématique et analyse.* Paris: A. Lefrançois, 1973. 91 p.

5256. Luschinsky, Eva. "Studien zur Morphologie des *Tristan*: Konzept und Realisierung." PhD dissertation (Theater Studies): Universität Wien, 1977.

5257. Maisel, Arthur. "*Tristan*: A different perspective." TP 8/2 (1983): 53-61.

5258. McKinney, Bruce. "The case against tonal unity in *Tristan*." TP 8/2(1983): 62-67.

5259. Mitchell, William J. "The *Tristan* Prelude: Technique and structure." MFO 1(1967): 162-203.

5260. Poos, Heinrich. "Zur Tristanharmonik." Fs. Pepping: 269-297.

5261. Raymond, Joely. "The *Leitmotiv* and musical-dramatic structure in Tristan's third narrative of delirium." ITR 3/3(1979-1980): 3-17.

5262. Richter, Christoph. "Hermeneutische Grundlagen der didaktischen Interpretation von Musik, dargestellt am *Tristan*-Vorspiel." MB 15/11(1983): 22-26, 15/12(1983): 20-27.

5263. Scharschuch, Horst. *Gesamtanalyse der Harmonik von Richard Wagners Musikdrama "Tristan und Isolde" unter specielle Berücksichtigung der Sequenztechnik des Tristanstiles.* Regensburg: G. Bosse, 1963.

5264. Straus, Joseph N. "*Tristan* and Berg's Suite." ITO 8/3 (1983-1984): 33-41.

5265. Truscott, Harold. "Wagner's *Tristan* and the twentieth century." MR 24(1963): 75-85.

5266. Vogel, Martin. *Der Tristan-Akkord und die Krise der modernen Harmonie-Lehre.* Düsseldorf: Im Verlag der Gesellschaft zur Förderung des Systematischen Musikwissenschaft, 1962.

Die Walküre

5267. ASO 8(1977).

5268. Jenkins, John Edward. "The *Leitmotiv* 'sword' in *Die Walküre*." PhD dissertation: University of Southern Mississippi, 1978. No DA listing.

5269. John, Nicholas, ed. *Wagner: The Valkyrie.* London: J. Calder, 1984.

5270. Kresky, Jeffry. "A study of the end of Act I of Wagner's *Die Walküre*." Kresky: 135-150.

5271. Lefrançois, André. *"La Walkyrie" de Richard Wagner: Étude thématique et analyse.* Paris: A. Lefrançois, 1975.

5272. Serauki, Walter. "Die Todesverkündigungsszene in Richard Wagners *Walküre* also musikalisch-geistige Achse des Werkes." MF 12(1959): 143-151.

Wesendonk Lieder

5273. Gauldin, Robert. "Wagner's parody technique: *Traume* and the *Tristan* Love Duet." MTS 1(1979): 35-42.

Other works

5274. Bertram, Johannes. *Mythos, Symbol, Idee in Richard Wagners Musik-Dramen.* Hamburg: Hamburger Kulturverlag, 1957.

5275. Brinkmann, Reinhold. "Tannhäusers Lied." Dahlhaus: 199-211.

5276. Burbidge, Peter and Richard Sutton, eds. *The Wagner companion.* London: Faber & Faber, 1979.

5277. Dahlhaus, Carl. *Das Drama Richard Wagners als musikalisches Kunstwerk.* Studien zur Musikgeschichte des 19. Jahrhunderts 23. Regensburg: G. Bosse, 1970.

5278. ----. *Richard Wagner: Werk und Wirkung.* Studien zur Musikgeschichte des 19. Jahrhunderts 26. Regensburg: G. Bosse, 1971.

5279. ----. *Richard Wagners Musikdramen.* Velber: Friedrich, 1971. 163 p.

5280. ----. *Richard Wagner's music dramas.* Trans. Mary Whittall. Cambridge: Cambridge University Press, 1979.

5281. ----. "Zur Geschichte der Leitmotivtechnik bei Wagner." Dahlhaus: 17-36.

5282. Dowd, John Andrew. "The Album-Sonate for Matilde Wesendonk: A neglected masterpiece of Richard Wagner." JALS 10(1981): 43-47.

5283. George, Graham. "The structure of dramatic music 1607-1909." MQ 52(1966): 465-482.

5284. Josephson, Nors S. "Tonale Strukturen im musikdramatischen Schaffen Richard Wagners." MF 32(1979): 141-149.

5285. Kirsch, Winfried. "Richard Wagners biblische Szene *Das Liebesmahl der Apostel.*" HJM 8(1985): 157-184.

5286. Knepler, Georg. "Richard Wagners musikalische Gestaltungsprinzipien." BM 5(1963): 33-43.

5287. Laudon, Robert T. "Sources of the Wagnerian synthesis: A study of the Franco-German tradition in nineteenth-century opera." PhD dissertation (Musicology): University of Illinois, 1969. UM 70-13,388. DA XXXI.2, p.787.

5288. Lichtenfeld, Monika. "Zur Technik der Klangflächenkomposition bei Wagner." Dahlhaus: 161-167.

5289. Lorenz, Alfred. *Das Geheimnis der Form bei Richard Wagners.* Tutzing: H. Schneider, 1966.

5290. Newcomb, Anthony. "The birth of music out of the spirit of drama: An essay in Wagnerian formal analysis." NCM 5(1981-1982): 38-66.

5291. Newman, Ernest. *The Wagner operas.* New York: Knopf, 1949.

5292. Noske, Frits. "Das exogene Todesmotiv in den Musikdramen Richard Wagners." MF 31(1978): 285-302.

5293. Osthoff, Wolfgang. "Richard Wagners Buddha-Projekt 'Die Sieger': Seine ideelen und strukturellen Spuren in *Ring* und *Parsifal.*" AM 40(1983): 189-211.

5294. Overhoff, Kurt. *Die Musikdramen Richard Wagners: Eine thematisch-musikalische Interpretation.* Salzburg: Pustet, 1967.

5295. Sommer, Antonius. *Die Komplikationen des musikalischen Rhythmus in den Bühnenwerken Richard Wagners.* Schriften zur Musik 10. Giebing über Prien am Chiemsee: E. Katzbichler, 1971.

5296. Stein, Herbert von. *Dichtung und Musik im Werk Richard Wagners.* Berlin: W. de Gruyter, 1962.

5297. Stephan, Rudolf. "Gibt es ein Geheimnis der Form bei Richard Wagner." Dahlhaus: 9-16.

5298. Treiber, Roland. "Die Todesszene in den Bühnenwerken Richard Wagners." PhD dissertation (Philosophy): University of Heidelberg, 1976.

5299. Voss, Egon. *Studien zur Instrumentation Richard Wagners.* Studien zur Musikgeschichte des 19. Jahrhunderts 24. Regensburg: G. Bosse, 1970.

5300. ----. "Über die Anwendung der Instrumentation auf das Drama bei Wagner." Dahlhaus: 169-175.

5301. Weiner, Marc A. "Richard Wagner's use of E.T.A. Hoffmann's *The Mines of Falun.*" NCM 5(1981-1982): 201-209.

5302. Whittall, Arnold. "Wagner's great transition? From *Lohengrin* to *Das Rheingold.*" MA 2(1983): 269-280.

WALKER, GEORGE (born 1922)

5303. De Lerma, Dominique-René "The choral works of George Walker." ACR 23/1(1981): 1-29.

5304. Ennett, Dorothy Maxine. "An analysis and comparison of selected piano sonatas by three contemporary Black composers: George Walker, Howard Swanson, and Roque Cordero." PhD dissertation (Performance): New York University, 1973. U 73-30,062. DA XXXIV.6, p.3450-A.

5305. Newson, Roosevelt. "A style analysis of the three piano sonatas (1953, 1957, 1976) of George Theophilus Walker." DMA dissertation (Piano): Peabody Conservatory, 1977. UM 78-23,373. DA XXXIX.6, p.3214-A.

WALTON, WILLIAM (1902-1983)

5306. Decker, Jay C. "A comparative textural analysis of selected orchestral works of William Walton and Paul Hindemith." DMA dissertation (Performance): University of Missouri, 1971. UM 72-29,458. DA XXXIII.5, p.2409-A.

5307. Fulton, William Kenneth, Jr. "Selected choral works of William Walton." PhD dissertation (Fine Arts): Texas Tech University, 1981. 223 p. UM 81-21,886. DA XLII.4, p.1363-A.

5308. Howes, Frank Stewart. *The music of William Walton.* London: Oxford University Press, 1965.

5309. Merrick, Frank. "Walton's Concerto for Violin and Orchestra." MR 2(1941): 309-318.

5310. Murrill, Herbert. "Walton's Violin Sonata." ML 31(1950): 208-215.

WARD, ROBERT (born 1917)

5311. Kellner, Hans. "Devils and angels: A study of the demonic in three twentieth-century operas." JMR 2(1976-1978): 255-272. [*The Crucible*]

5312. Larsen, Robert. "A study and comparison of Samuel Barber's *Vanessa*, Robert Ward's *The Crucible*, and Gunther Schuller's *The Visitation.*" DMA dissertation (Conducting): Indiana University, 1971. No DA listing.

WARLOCK, PETER (pseudonym of Philip Heseltine, 1894-1930)

5313. Copley, Ian A. *The music of Peter Warlock: A critical study.* London: Dobson, 1979.
5314. ----. "Peter Warlock's choral music." ML 45(1964): 318-336.
5315. ----. "The published instrumental music of Peter Warlock." MR 25(1964): 209-223.
5316. Yenne, Vernon Lee. "Three twentieth-century English song composers: Peter Warlock, E.J. Morran, and John Ireland." DMA dissertation (Performance): University of Illinois, 1969. No DA listing.

WARTENSEE, SCHNYDER VON

5317. Schneider, Peter Otto. "Zur Militärsinfonie von Schnyder von Wartensee." SMZ 104(1964): 11-21.

WEBER, CARL MARIA VON (1786-1826)

5318. Adams, John P. "A study of the piano sonatas of Carl Maria von Weber." PhD dissertation: Indiana University, 1976. 112 p. No DA listing.
5319. ASO 74(1985). [*Oberon*]
5320. Becker, Peter. "'Freilich ist es wieder Lyrik geworden': Auf der Suche nache dem Exemplarischen bei Weber." MB 15/2(1983): 4-10.
5321. Gras, Alfred H. "A study of *Der Freischütz* by Carl Maria von Weber." PhD dissertation (Music History and Literature): Northwestern University, 1968. DA XXXI.4, p.1832.
5322. Jones, Gaynor G. "Weber's *Secondary Worlds*: The later operas of Carl Maria von Weber." IRASM 7(1976): 219-233.
5323. Kang, Nakcheung Paik. "An analytical study of the piano sonatas of Carl Maria von Weber." PhD dissertation: New York University, 1978. No DA listing.
5324. Leibowitz, René. "Un Opéra maudit: *Euryanthe.*" Leibowitz/F: 145-174.
5325. Marinaro, Stephen. "Carl Maria von Weber: His pianistic style and the four sonatas." JALS 10(1980): 48-55.
5326. ----. "The four piano sonatas of Carl Maria von Weber." DMA dissertation: University of Texas, 1980. No DA listing.
5327. Sandner, Wolfgang. *Die Klarinette bei Carl Maria von Weber.* Neue Musikgeistliche Forschungen 7. Wiesbaden: Breitkopf und Härtel, 1971.
5328. Stephan, Rudolf. "Bemerkungen zur *Freischütz*-Musik." Dahlhaus/S: 491-496.

WEBERN, ANTON (1883-1945)

Opus 1: Passacaglia
5320. Nelson, Robert U. "Webern's path to the serial variation." PNM 7/2(1969): 73-93.

Opus 3: Five Songs from "Der siebente Ring"

5330. Brinkmann, Reinhold. "Die George-Lieder 1908/9 und 1912/23: Ein Kapital Webern-Philologie." BOGM (1972-1973): 40-50.

5331. Budde, Elmar. *Anton Weberns Lieder Op.3: Untersuchungen zur frühen Atonalität bei Webern.* Wiesbaden: Steiner, 1971.

5332. ----. "Metrisch-rhythmische Probleme im Vokalwerk Weberns." BOGM (1972-1973): 52-60.

5333. Hanson, Robert. "Webern's chromatic organization." MA 2(1983): 135-150. [Op.3, No.5]

5334. Ringger, Rolf Urs. "Zur Wort-Ton-Beziehung beim frühen Anton Webern: Analyze von Op.3, Nr.1 aus *5 Lieder* auf Texte von Stefan George." SMZ 103(1963): 330-335.

Opus 4: Five Songs

5335. Brinkmann, Reinhold. "Die George-Lieder 1808/9 und 1912/23: Ein Kapital Webern-Philologie." BOGM (1972-1973): 40-50.

Opus 5: Five Movements for String Quartet

5336. Archibald, Bruce. "Some thoughts on symmetry in early Webern: Op.5, No.2." PNM 10/2(1972): 158-163.

5337. Budde, Elmar. "Anton Weberns Op.5/IV: Versuch einer Analyse." Fs. Doflein: 58-66.

5338. Burkhart, Charles. "The symmetrical source of Webern's Opus 5, No.4." MFO 5(1980): 317-334.

5339. Forte, Allen. "A theory of set-complexes for music." JMT 8 (1964): 136-183.

5340. Lewin, David. "An example of serial technique in early Webern." TP 7/1(1982): 40-43. [Op.5, No.4]

5341. ----. "Transformational technique in atonal and other music theories." PNM 21(1982-1983): 312-371. [Op.5, No.2]

5342. Perle: 16-18.

5343. Persky, Stanley. "A discussion of composition choices in Webern's *Fünf Sätze für Streichquartette*, Op.5, first movement." CM 13(1972): 68-74.

Opus 6: Six Pieces for Large Orchestra

5344. Baker, James M. "Coherence in Webern's Six Pieces for Orchestra, Op.6." MTS 4(1982): 1-27.

5345. Crotty, John E. "A preliminary analysis of Webern's Opus 6, No.3." ITO 5/2(1979-1981): 23-32.

5346. Dahlhaus, Carl. "Rhythmische Strukturen in Weberns Orchesterstücken Opus 6." Webern: 73-80. [Also in BOGM (1972-1973): 73-80]

5347. Elston, Arnold. "The formal structure of Opus 6, No.1." PNM 6/1(1967): 63-66.

5348. Finney, Ross Lee. "Webern's Opus 6, No.1." PNM 6/1(1967): 74.

5349. Hoffmann, Richard. "Webern: Six Pieces, Opus 6(1909)." PNM 6/1(1967): 76-78.

5350. Oliver, Harold. "Structural functions of musical material in Webern's Opus 6, No.1." PNM 6/1(1967): 67-73.

Opus 7: Four Pieces for Violin and Piano

5351. Hanson, Robert. "Webern's chromatic organization." MA 2(1983): 135-150. [Op.7, No.1]

5352. Ligeti, György. "Die Komposition mit Reihen und ihre Konsequenzen bei Anton Webern." OMZ 16(1961): 297-303.

5353. Little.

Opus 9: Six Bagatelles for String Quartet

5354. Bauer, Jürg. "Über Anton Weberns Bagatellen für Streichquartett." Abraham/L: 62-68.

5355. Chrisman, Richard. "Anton Webern's Six Bagatelles for String Quartet, Op.9: The unfolding of intervallic successions." JMT 23(1979): 81-122.

5356. Hansberger, Joachim. "Anton Webern, Die vierte Bagetelle für Streichquartett als Gegenstand einer Übung im Musikhören." M 23(1969): 236-240.

5357. Kaufmann, Harald. "Figur in Weberns erster Bagatelle." Abraham/L: 69-72.

Opus 10: Five Pieces for Orchestra

5358. Deliège, Célestin. "Webern: Op.10, No.4: Un Thème d'analyse et de réflexion." RDM 61(1975): 91-112.

5359. Gruhn, Wilfried. "Anton von Webern (1883-1945): Fünf Stücke für Orchester Op.10 (1911/1913)." Zimmerschied: 13-40.

5360. Hanson, Robert. "Webern's chromatic organization." MA 2(1983): 135-150. [Op.10, No.4]

5361. Johnson, Peter. "Symmetrical sets in Webern's Op.10, No.4." PNM 17/1(1978-1979): 219-229.

5362. Smith, Charles Justice, III. "Patterns and strategies: Four perspectives of musical characterization." PhD dissertation (Theory): University of Michigan, 1980. 130 p. UM 81-06,229. DA XLI.7, p.3776-7-A. [Op.10, No.4]

Opus 11: Three Small Pieces for Cello and Piano

5363. Batstone, Philip. "Musical analysis as phenomenology." PNM 7/2 (1969): 94-110.

5364. Escot, Pozzi. "Towards a theoretical concept: Non-linearity in Webern's Opus 11, No.1." SONUS 3/1(1982): 18-29.

5365. Karkoschka, Erhard. "Weberns Opus 11 unter neuer analytischen Aspekten." Webern: 81-92. [Also in BOGM (1972-1973): 81-92]

5366. Marra, James. "Interrelations between pitch and rhythmic structure in Webern's Opus 11, No.1." ITO 7/2(1983-1984): 3-33.

5367. Perle: 21-23.

5368. Williams, Edgar Warren, Jr. "On mode 12 complementary interval sets." ITO 7/2(1983-1984): 34-43. [Op.11, No.3]

5369. Wintle, Christopher. "An early version of derivation: Webern's Op.11/3." PNM 13/2(1974-1975): 166-177.

Opus 12: Four Songs

5370. Bach, Hans Elmar. "Anton von Webern: *Der Tag ist vergangen*, 1915." Kirchmeyer: 211-218. [Op.12, No.1]

Opus 13: Four Songs for Soprano and Orchestra
    5371. Budde, Elmar. "Metrisch-rhythmische Probleme im Vokalwerk
Weberns." BOGM (1972-1973): 52-60.
    5372. Gerlach, Reinhard. "Anton Webern: *Ein Winterabend*: Op.13,
Nr.4 zum Verhältnis von Musik und Dichtung oder Wahrheit als Struktur."
AM 30(1973): 44-68.
    5373. Williams, Edgar Warren, Jr. "On mode 12 complementary inter-
val sets." ITO 7/2(1983-1984): 34-43. [Op.13, No.1]

Opus 14: Six Songs
    5374. Cholopowa, Valentina. "Chromatische Prinzipien in Anton
Weberns Vokalzyklus *Sechs Lieder nach Gedichten von Georg Trakl*,
Op.14." BM 17(1975): 155-169.

Opus 16: Five Canons
    5375. Ligeti, György. "Die Komposition mit Reihen und ihre Konse-
quenzen bei Anton Webern." OMZ 16(1961): 297-303.

Opus 17: Drei geistliche Volkslieder
    5376. Ligeti, György. "Die Komposition mit Reihen und ihre Konse-
quenzen bei Anton Webern." OMZ 16(1961): 297-303.

Opus 20: Trio
    5377. Leibowitz: 206-209.

Opus 21: Symphony
    5378. Abel, Angelika. "Adornos Kritik der Zwölftontechnik Weberns:
Die Grenzen einer 'Logik des Zerfalls.'" AM 38(1981): 143-178.
    5379. Bailey, Kathryn. "Webern's Opus 21: Creativity in tradition."
JM 2(1983): 184-195.
    5380. Borris, Siegfried. "Structural analysis of Webern's Symphony,
Op.21." Fs. Pisk: 231-242.
    5381. ----. "Strukturanalyse von Weberns Symphonie, Op.21."
Reichert: 253-255.
    5382. ----. "Weberns Symphonie Op.21: Strukturanalyse." MB
5(1973): 324-329.
    5383. Bracanin, Philip K. "The palindrome: Its application in the
music of Anton Webern." MMA 6(1972): 38-47.
    5384. Dagnes, Edward P. "Symmetrical structures in Webern: An
analytical overview of the Symphonie, movement II, variation 3." ITO
1/9(1975): 33-54.
    5385. Goebel, Walter F. "Anton Weberns Sinfonie." MELOS 28(1961):
359-362.
    5386. Goldthwaite, Scott. "Historical awareness in Anton Webern's
Symphony Op.21." Fs. Plamenac: 65-81.
    5387. Gruhn, Wilfried. "Reihenform und Werkgestalt bei Anton
Webern: Die Variationen der Sinfonie Op.21." ZM 2/2(1971): 31-37.
    5388. Hiller, Lejaren and Ramon Fuller. "Structure and information in
Webern's Symphonie, Op.21." JMT 11/1(1967): 60-115.
    5389. Hitchcock, H. Wiley. "A footnote on Webern's variations."
PNM 8/2(1970): 123-142.

5390. Jetter, Elisabeth. "Ordnungsprinzipien im ersten Satz von Anton Weberns Symphonie Op.21." MB 10(1978): 151-158.

5391. Kerr, Elisabeth. "The Variations of Webern's Symphony Op.21: Some observations on rhythmic organization and the use of numerology." ITO 8/2(1984-1985): 5-14.

5392. Leibowitz: 211-218.

5393. Nelson, Robert U. "Webern's path to the serial variation." PNM 7/2(1969): 73-93.

5394. Rahn, John. "Analysis One: Webern's Symphonie Op.21: Thema." Rahn: 4-18.

5395. Raiss, Hans-Peter. "Anton Webern: Symphonie Op.21, 2. Satz (1928)." Vogt: 209-228.

5396. Starr, Mark. "Webern's palindrome." PNM 8/2(1970): 127-142.

5397. Stroh, Wolfgang Martin. *Webern: Symphonie Op.21*. München: W. Fink, 1975. 58 p.

Opus 22: Quartet for clarinet, tenor saxophone, violin, piano

5398. Fennelly, Brian. "Structure and process in Webern's Opus 22." JMT 10/2(1966): 300-328.

5399. Leibowitz: 218-223.

5400. O'Leary, Jane Strong. "Aspects of structure in Webern's Quartet, Op.22." PhD dissertation: Princeton University, 1978. 98 p. No DA listing.

5401. Thomas, Jennifer. "The use of color in three chamber works of the twentieth century." ITR 4/3(1980-1981): 24-40.

Opus 24: Concerto for Nine Instruments

5402. Boykan, Martin. "The Webern Concerto revisited." ASUC 3 (1968): 74-85.

5403. Cohen, David. "Anton Webern and the magic square." PNM 13/1(1974-1975): 213-215.

5404. Gauldin, Robert. "The magic squares of the third movement of Webern's Concerto, Op.24." ITO 2/11-12(1977): 32-42.

5405. ----. "Pitch structure in the second movement of Webern's Concerto Op.24." ITO 2/10(1977): 8-22.

5406. Hasty, Christopher. "Segmentation and process in post-tonal music." MTS 3(1981): 54-73.

5407. Ligeti, György. "Die Komposition mit Reihen und ihre Konsequenzen bei Anton Webern." OMZ 16(1961): 297-303.

5408. Stockhausen: 24-31.

5409. Stockhausen, Karlheinz. "Weberns Konzert für 9 Instrumente Op.24: Analyze des ersten Satzes." MELOS 20(1953): 343-348.

5410. Wintle, Christopher. "Analysis and performance: Webern's Concerto Op.24/II." MA 1(1982): 73-100.

Opus 25: Three Songs

5411. Chittum, Donald. "Some observations on the row technique in Webern's Opus 25." CM 12(1971): 96-101.

5412. Escot, Pozzi. "Webern's Opus 25, No.1: Perception of large-scale patterns." TP 4/1(1979): 28-29.

Opus 27: Variations for Piano

5413. Bach, Hans Elmar. "Anton von Webern: Variationen Op.27, 1. Satz, Takt 1-18, 1936." Kirchmeyer: 219-223.

5414. Bailey, Kathryn. "The evolution of variation form in the music of Webern." CM 16(1973): 55-70.

5415. Bracanin, Philip K. "The palindrome: Its application in the music of Anton Webern." MMA 6(1972): 38-47.

5416. Cholopov, Juri. "Die Spiegelsymmetrie in Anton Weberns Variationen für Klavier Op.27." AM 30(1973): 26-43.

5417. Döhl, Friedhelm. "Weberns Opus 27." MELOS 30(1963): 400-403.

5418. Heimann, Walter. "Autonomie und soziale Bindung." MB 10 (1978): 165-173.

5419. Huber, Nicolaus. "Die Kompositionstechnik Bachs in seinen Sonaten und Partiten für Violine solo und ihre Anwendung in Weberns Op.27/ii." ZM 1/2(1970): 22-31.

5420. Jones, James Rives. "Some aspects of rhythm and meter in Webern's Opus 27." PNM 7/1(1968): 103-109.

5421. Kolneder, Walter. "Klang, Punkt und Linie." *Vergleichende Interpretationskunde.* Berlin: Merseburger, 1963.

5422. Leibowitz: 226-241.

5423. Lewin, David. "A metrical problem in Webern's Op. 27." JMT 6(1962): 125-132.

5424. Lincoln, Harry B., ed. *The Computer and Music.* Ithaca: Cornell University Press, 1970: 115-122.

5425. Nelson, Robert U. "Webern's path to the serial variation." PNM 7/2(1969): 73-93.

5426. Ogdon, Wilbur Lee. "A Webern analysis." JMT 6(1962): 133-138.

5427. Schultz/D. [Second movement]

5428. Stadlen, Peter. "Das pointillistische Missverständnis." OMZ 27 (1972): 152-161.

5429. ----. "Das pointillistische Missverständniss." Webern: 173-184. [This is not the same article as the preceding item despite the title] [Same as BOGM (1972/1973): 173-184]

5430. Travis, Roy. "Directed motion in Schoenberg and Webern." PNM 4/2(1966): 85-89.

5431. Westergaard, Peter. "Some problems in rhythmic theory and analysis." PNM 1/1(1962): 180-191.

5432. ----. "Webern and total organization: An analysis of the second movement of Piano Variations, Op.27." PNM 1/2(1963): 107-120.

Opus 28: String Quartet

5433. Döhl, Friedhelm. "Zum Formbegriff Weberns: Weberns Analyse des Streichquartette Op.28 nebst einigen Bemerkungen zu Weberns Analyse eiegener Werke." OMZ 27(1972): 131-148.

5434. Leibowitz: 241-251.

5435. Pütz.

5436. Rauchhaupt, Ursula van, comp. *Die Streichquartette der Wiener Schule: Schönberg, Berg, Webern: Eines Dokumentation.* München: H. Ellermann, 1971.

Opus 29: First Cantata

5437. Hartwell, Robin. "Duration and mental arithmetic: The first movement of Webern's First Cantata." PNM 23/1(1984-1985): 348-359.

5438. Klemm, Eberhardt. "Symmetrien im Chorsatz von Anton Webern." DJM 11(1966): 107-120.

5439. Kramer, Jonathan. "The row as strucutral background and audible foreground: The first movement of Webern's First Cantata." JMT 15/1-2(1971): 158-181.

5440. Ligeti, György. "Die Komposition mit Reihen und ihre Konsequenzen bei Anton Webern." OMZ 16(1961): 297-303.

5441. ----. "Über die Harmonik in Weberns erster Kantate." DBNM 3(1960): 49-64.

5442. Phipps, Graham H. "Tonality in Webern's Cantata 1." MA 3/2 (1984): 125-158.

5443. Pousseur, Henri. "Webern et le silence." *La Musique et ses problemes contemporains.* Paris: R. Julliard, 1963: 190-202.

5444. Rochberg, George. "Webern's search for harmonic identity." JMT 6(1962): 109-122.

5445. Saturen, David. "Symmetrical relationships in Webern's First Cantata." PNM 6/1(1967): 142-143.

Opus 30: Variations for Orchestra

5446. Bailey, Kathryn. "The evolution of variation form in the music of Webern." CM 16(1973): 55-70.

5447. ----. "Formal and rhythmic procedures in Webern's Opus 30." CAUSM 2/1(1972): 34-52.

5448. ----. "Webern's symmetrical row formations with particular reference to Opus 30." CCM 5(1972): 159-166.

5449. Deppert, Heinrich. "Rhythmische Reihentechnik in Weberns Orchestervariationen Opus 30." Fs. Marx: 84-93.

5450. Nelson, Robert U. "Webern's path to the serial variation." PNM 7/2(1969): 73-93.

5451. Reid, John W. "Properties of the set explored in Webern's Variations, Op.30." PNM 12(1973-1974): 344-350.

Opus 31: Second Cantata

5452. Baumann, Jon Ward. "The Cantata Number Two of Anton Webern." PhD dissertation: University of Illinois, 1972. UM 73-17,111. No DA listing.

5453. Luckman, Phyllis. "The sound of symmetry: A study of the sixth movement of Webern's Second Cantata." MR 36(1975): 187-196.

5454. Spinner, Leopold. "Anton Weberns Kantate Nr.2, Op.31: Die Formprinzipien der kanonischen Darstellung (Analyse des vierten Satzes)." SMZ 101(1961): 303-308.

5455. William, Wolfgang. *Anton Weberns zweite Kantate Op.31: Studien zu Konstruktion und Ausdruck.* München: E. Katzbichler, 1980.

Five Songs after Poems by Richard Dehmel

5456. Gerlach, Reinhard. "Die Handschriften der *Dehmel-Lieder* von Anton Webern: Textkritische Studien." AM 29(1972): 93-113.

5457. ----. "Die *Dehmel-Lieder* von Anton Webern: Musik und Sprache im Übergang zur Atonalität." JSIM (1970): 45-100.

5458. Roman, Zoltan. "From congruence to antithesis: Poetic and musical *Jugendstil* in Webern's songs." MMA 13(1984): 191-202.

5459. Stein, Leonard. "Webern's *Dehmel Lieder* of 1906-1908: Threshold of a new expression." Hans Moldenhauer, ed. *Anton von Webern: Perspectives.* Seattle: University of Washington Press, 1966: 53-61.

Four Pieces for Orchestra (1913)

5460. Barkin, Elaine. "Analysis Symposium: Webern, Orchestra Pieces (1913) Movement 1 (*Bewegt*)." JMT 19(1975): 47-64.

5461. Marvin, Elizabeth West. "The structural role of complementation in Webern's Orchestra Pieces (1913)." MTS 5(1983): 76-88.

5462. Olson, Christin. "Tonal remnants in early Webern: The first movement of Orchestral Pieces (1913)." ITO 5/2(1979-1981): 34-46.

5463. Travis, Roy and Allen Forte. "Analysis Symposium: Webern, Orchestral Pieces (1913) Movement I (*Bewegt*)." JMT 18(1974): 2-43.

Other works

5464. Abel, Angelika. *Die Zwölftontechnik Weberns und Goethes Methodik der Farbenlehre: Zur Kompositionstheorie und Ästhetik der neuen Wiener Schule.* Wiesbaden: Steiner, 1982.

5465. Anthony, Donald B. "Microrhythm in the published works of Anton Webern." PhD dissertation (Musicology): Stanford University, 1968. UM 68-11,265. DA XXIX.3, p.922-A.

5466. Bailey, Kathryn. "A note on Webern's graces." SMUWO 6(1981): 1-6.

5467. Beale, James. "Weberns musikalischen Nachlass." MELOS 31(1964): 297-303.

5468. Beckmann, Dorothea. *Sprache und Musik im Vokalwerk Anton Weberns: Die Konstruktion des Ausdrucks.* Regensburg: G. Bosse, 1970.

5469. Bradshaw, Merrill Kay. "Tonal structure in the early works of Anton Webern." Master's dissertation: University of Illinois, 1962. [Opp. 1-5]

5470. Broekema.

5471. Brown, Robert Barclay. "The early atonal music of Anton Webern: Sound material and structure." PhD dissertation: Brandeis University, 1965. UM 65-14,414. DA XXVII.5, p.1391-A.

5472. Buccheri.

5473. Buchanan, Herbert Herman. "An investigation of mutual influences among Schoenberg, Webern, and Berg (with an emphasis on Schoenberg and Webern, ca. 1904-1908)." PhD dissertation (Musicology): Rutgers University, 1974. UM 74-27,592. DA XXXV.6, p.3789-A.

5474. Budde, Elmar. "Metrisch-rhythmische Probleme in Vokalwerke Weberns." Webern: 52-60.

5475. Busch, Regina. "Über die Musik von Anton Webern." OMZ 36 (1981): 470-482.

5476. Cone, Edward T. "Webern's apprenticeship." MQ 53(1967): 39-52. [Early works]

5477. Craft, Robert. "Anton Webern." SCORE 13(1955): 9-24.

5478. Dahlhaus, Carl. "Analytische Instrumentation." Fs. Blankenburg: 197-206.

5479. Deppert, Heinrich. *Studien zur Kompositionstechnik im instrumentalen Spätwerk Anton Webens.* Darmstadt: Tonos, 1972.

5480. ----. "Über einige Voraussetzungen der musikalischen Analyse." ZM 4/2(1973): 10-16.

5481. ----. "Zu Weberns Klanglich-harmonischen Bewusstsein." Webern: 61-72. [Same as BOGM (1972-1973): 61-72]

5482. Dimond, Chester Arthur. "Fourteen early songs of Anton Webern." DMA dissertation (Performance): University of Oregon, 1971. 213 p. UM 72-14,722. DA XXXIII.7, p.3692-A.

5483. Döhl, Friedhelm. *Webern: Weberns Beitrag zur Stilwende der neuen Musik: Studien über Voraussetzungen, Technik und Ästhetik der "Komposition mit 12 nur aufeinander bezogenen Tönen."* München: E. Katzbichler, 1976. 457 p.

5484. Fiehler, Judith Marie. "Rational structures in the late works of Anton Webern." PhD dissertation (Musicology-Mathematics): Louisiana State University, 1973. 378 p. UM 74-18,335. RILM 74/2745dd28. No DA listing.

5485. Forte, Allen. "Aspects of rhythm in Webern's atonal music." MTS 2(1980): 90-109.

5486. Gerlach, Reinhard. "Kompositionsniederschrift und Werkfassung am Beispiel des Liedes *Am Ufer* (1908) von Webern." Webern: 111-126. [Same as BOGM (1972-1973): 111-126]

5487. ----. "Mystik und Klangmagie in Anton von Weberns hybrider Tonalität: Eine Jugendkrise im Spiegel von Musik und Dichtung der Jahrhundertswende." AM 33(1976): 1-27. [Early works]

5488. Godwin, Paul Milton. "A study of concepts of melody, with particular reference to some music of the twentieth century and examples from the compositions of Schoenberg, Webern, and Berg." PhD dissertation (Theory): Ohio State University, 1972. UM 73-02,003. DA XXXIII.8, p.4453-A.

5489. Goebels, Franzpeter. "Bemerkungen und Materialen zum Studium neuer Klaviermusik." SMZ 113(1973): 265-268, 329-331.

5490. Gruhn, Wilfried. "Bearbeitung als kompositorische Reflexion in neuer Musik." M 28(1974): 522-528. [Transcription of Bach Ricercare]

5491. Hanson, Robert Frederic. "Anton Webern's atonal style." PhD dissertation (Musical Analysis): Southampton University, 1976. 316 p. [Op.10; Four Pieces for Orchestra (1913)]

5492. Johnson, P. "Studies in atonality: Non-thematic structural processes in the early atonal music of Schoenberg and Webern." PhD dissertation (Musicology): Worcester, Oxford, 1978.

5493. Karkoschka, Erhard. "Hat Webern seriell komponiert?" OMZ 30 (1975): 588-594.

5494. ----. *Studien zur Entwicklung der Kompositionstechnik in Frühwerk Anton Weberns.* [n.p.: n.p.] 1959.

5495. Klemm, Eberhard. "Das Augenlicht: Analytische Betrachtung zu einer der späten Kantaten Weberns." MG 33(1983): 696-699.

5496. Kolneder, Walter. *Anton Webern: An introduction to his works.* Westport, CT: Greenwood Press, 1982 (1968).

5497. ----. *Anton Webern: Einführung in Werk und Stil.* Roden-
kirchen/Rhein: P.J. Tonger, 1961.

5498. ----. *Anton Webern: Genesis und Metamorphose eines Stils.*
Wien: Lafite/Österreichische Bundesverlag, 1974.

5499. ----. "Klangtechnik und Motivbildung bei Webern." Fs.
Müller-Blattau/65: 27-50.

5500. Marra, James Richard. "Rhythmic stratification in the 'atonal'
instrumental music of Anton Webern (1913-1914)." DMA dissertation:
Cornell University, 1977 163 p. UM 78-06,309. DA XXXVIII.11,
p.6391-A. [Op.10, No.1; Op.11, No.3; Op.9, No.5]

5501. Mason, Colin. "Webern's later chamber music." ML 38(1957):
232-237.

5502. McKenzie, Wallace Chesseley, Jr. "The music of Anton Webern." PhD dissertation (Musicology): North Texas State University, 1960.
LC Mic 60-2792. DA XXI.3, p.640.

5503. ----. "Webern's posthumous music." BOGM (1972-1973):
185-192.

5504. Murray, Edward Michael. "New approaches to the analysis of
Webern." PhD dissertation (Theory): Yale University, 1979. UM 79-27,644.
DA XL.6, p.2974-A.

5505. Nielsen, Henning. "Zentraltonprinzipien bei Anton Webern."
DAM 5(1966-1967): 119-138.

5506. Ogdon.

5507. Olah, Tiberiu. "Weberns vorserielles Tonsystem." Melos/NZM
1(1975): 10-13.

5508. Overby, Patricia. "Variation techniques in the music of Anton
Webern: An analysis of selected works by Anton Webern, demonstrating
the use of traditional constructive devices in a new stylistic setting." MM
dissertation: University of Iowa, 1969.

5509. Perle, George. "Webern's twelve-tone sketches." MQ 57(1971):
1-25.

5510. Pisk, Paul. "Webern's early orchestral works." Hans Moldenhauer, ed. *Anton von Webern: Perspectives.* Seattle: University of
Washington Press, 1966: 43-52.

5511. Poné, Gundaris. "Webern and Luigi Nono: The genesis of a
new compositional morphology and syntax." PNM 10/2(1972): 111-119.

5512. Ringger, Rolf Urs. *Anton Weberns Klavierlieder.* Zürich:
Juris-Atlantis, 1968.

5513. ----. "Sprachmusikalische Chiffern in Anton Weberns Klavierlieder." SMZ 106(1966): 14-19.

5514. Rubin, Marcel. "Webern und die Folgen." MG 10(1960):
463-469.

5515. Schollum, Robert. "Stilistische Elemente der frühen Webern-
Lieder." BOGM (1972-1973): 127-134.

5516. ----. *Die Wiener Schule: Schönberg-Berg-Webern: Entwicklung
und Ergebnis.* Wien: E. Lafite, 1969.

5517. Schulz, Reinhard. *Über das Verhältnis von Konstruktion und
Ausdruck in den Werken Anton Weberns.* München: W. Fink, 1982.

5518. Snow, Rosemary Allsman. "Cadence or cadential feeling in the instrumental works of Anton von Webern." PhD dissertation (Musicology): Case-Western Reserve University, 1977. UM 77-18,848. DA XXXVIII.3, p.1108-9-A.

5519. Somfai, László. "Rhythmic continuity and articulation in Webern's instrumental works." Webern: 100-110. [Same as BOGM (1972-1973): 100-110]

5520. Spill, Angelike. "Weberns Kompositionstechnik und Goethes Methodik der Farbenlehre." PhD dissertation (Musicology): Marburg, 1980.

5521. Spring, Glenn Ernst, Jr. "Determinants of phrase structure in selected works of Schoenberg, Berg, and Webern." DMA dissertation (Composition): University of Washington, 1972. 61 p. UM 72-28,670. DA XXXIII.5, p.2417-A.

5522. Stadlen, Peter. "Das pointillistische Missverständnis." OMZ 27 (1972): 152-161.

5523. Stephen, Rudolf. "Zu einigen Liedern Anton Weberns." Webern: 135-144. [Same as BOGM (1972-1973): 135-144]

5524. Stroh, Wolfgang Martin. *Anton Webern: Historische Legitimation als kompositorisches Problem.* Göppingen: A. Kummerle, 1973.

5525. Todd, R. Larry. "The genesis of Webern's Opus 32." MQ 66 (1980): 581-591.

5526. Venus, Dankmar. *Vergleichende Untersuchung zur melodischen Struktur der Singstimmen in den Liedern von Arnold Schönberg, Alban Berg, Anton Webern, und Paul Hindemith.* Göttingen, 1965.

5527. Westergaard, Peter. "On the problem of 'reconstruction from a sketch': Webern's *Kunfttag III* and *Leise Düfte*." PNM 11/2(1973): 104-121.

5528. Wilsen, William. "Equitonality as a measure of the evolution toward atonality in the pre-Opus 1 of Anton Webern." PhD dissertation (Theory): Florida State University, 1975. UM 75-15,510. DA XXXVI.1, p.24-A.

5529. Special Issue: OMZ 27(1972).

5530. Special Issue: R 2(1958).

WEILL, KURT (1900-1950)

5531. Collisani, Amalia. "*Der Jasager*: Musica e 'distacco'." RIM 17 (1982): 310-332.

5532. Harden, Susan Clydette. "The music for the stage collaborations of Weill and Brecht." PhD dissertation (Musicology): University of North Carolina, 1972. UM 72-24,795. DA XXXIII.4, p.1767-A.

5533. Kemp, Ian. "Harmony in Weill: Some observations." TEMPO 104(1973): 11-15.

5534. Rienäcker, Gerd. "Thesen zur Opernästhetik Kurt Weills." JP 3(1980): 116-134.

WEINZWEIG, JOHN JACOB (born 1913)

5535. Keillor, Elaine. "John Weinzweig's *Wine of Peace*." SMUWO 9(1984): 79-92.

5536. Webb, Douglas John. "Serial techniques in John Weinzweig's divertimentos and concertos (1945-1968)." PhD dissertation (Theory): University of Rochester, 1977. No DA listing.

WEISGALL, HUGO (born 1912)

5537. Balkin, Alfred. "The operas of Hugo Weisgall." EdD dissertation (Music Education): Columbia University Teachers College, 1968. UM 69-9905. DA XXX.4, p.1583-4-A.

5538. Blumenfeld, Harold. "Hugo Weisgall's 66th birthday and the new *Gardens of Adonis*." PNM 16/2(1977-1978): 156-166.

5539. Brooks, James Anthony, Jr. "Technical aspects of the music in the major operas of Hugo Weisgall." PhD dissertation (Performance): Washington University, 1971. 166 p. UM 71-27,318. DA XXXII.4, p.2114-A.

5540. Saylor, Bruce. "The music of Hugo Weisgall." MQ 59(1973): 239-262.

WEISMANN, WILHELM (born 1900)

5541. Köhler, Siegfried. "Ein neues Vokalwerk von Wilhelm Weismann." MG 10(1960): 330-331. [*Lieder und Balladen aus "Des knaben Wunderhorn"*]

5542. Mainka, Jürgen. "Realität und Phantastik des Volksliedes: Zu Wilhelm Weismanns Liedschaffen." JP 3(1980): 33-53.

WEISS, ADOLPH (1891-1971)

5543. Kopp, Sister Bernadette. "The twelve-tone techniques of Adolph Weiss." PhD dissertation (Music History): Northwestern University, 1981. UM 81-24,931. DA XLII.6, p.1845-A.

WEISS, HARALD (born 1949)

5544. Liesmann-Gümmer, Renate. "Harald Weiss: Grenzgänger unter den jungen deutschen Komponisten." NZM 144/2(1983): 14-19. [*Endstation* and other works]

WELLESZ, EGON (1885-1974)

5545. Redlich, Hans F. "Egon Wellesz." MQ 26(1940): 65-75.

5546. ----. "Egon Wellesz: An Austrian composer in Britain." MR 7 (1946): 69-79.

5547. Scheider, Günter. "Egon Wellesz: Studien zur Theorie und Praxis seiner Musik, dargestellt am Beispiel seiner musikdramatischen Komposition." PhD dissertation (Musicology): Innsbruck, 1981.

5548. Swedish, Stephen John. "The piano works of Egon Wellesz." DMA dissertation (Piano Literature and Performance): Indiana University, 1978. No DA listing. [*Drei Skizzen*, Op.6; *Idyllen*, Op.21; *Fünf Tanzstücke*, Op.42]

5549. Symons, David John. "Egon Wellesz and early twentieth-century tonality." SMU 6(1972): 42-54.
5550. ----. "Tonal organization in the symphonies of Egon Wellesz." PhD dissertation (Musicology): University of Western Australia, 1981.

WENZEL, HANS JÜRGEN (born 1939)

5551. Baethge, Wilhelm. "Die Analyse: Hans Jürgen Wenzels *Händel-Metamorphosen*." MG 28(1978): 273-277.
5552. Belkus, Gerd. "Die Analyse: Hans Jürgen Wenzels Konzert für Violine und Streichorchester." MG 26(1976): 76-80.

WERFEL, ALMA (SCHINDLER) MAHLER (1879-1964)

5553. Schollum, Robert. "Die Lieder von Alma Maria Schindler-Mahler." OMZ 34(1979): 544-551.

WERZLAU, JOACHIM (born 1913)

5554. Kleinschmidt, Klaus. "*Unser Leben im Lied*: Eine Kantate von Joachim Werzlau." MG 9/1(1959): 17-19.

WESLEY, SAMUEL SEBASTIAN (1810-1876)

5555. Hiebert, Arlis J. "The anthems and services of Samuel Sebastian Wesley (1810-1876)." PhD dissertation: Northwestern University, 1965. UM 66-10,701. DA XXVII.5, p.1395-A.

WESTERGAARD, PETER (born 1931)

5556. Crumb, George. "*Variations for Six Players*." PNM 3/2(1965): 152-159.

WHITE, DONALD H. (born 1921)

5557. White, Donald H. "*Miniature Set* for Band in retrospect." JBR 13/2(1977-1978): 41-55.

WHITE, JOHN (born 1936)

5558. Smith, Dave. "The piano sonatas of John White." CT 21(1980): 4-11.

WHITE, MICHAEL

5559. Chittum, Donald. "Current Chronicle." MQ 55(1969): 91-95. [*Metamorphosis*]
5560. ----. "Current Chronicle." MQ 57(1971): 129-131. [*Opposites*]

WIDOR, CHARLES MARIE (1844-1937)

5561. Wilson, John R. "The organ symphonies of Charles Marie Widor." PhD disertation (Theory): Flordia State University, 1966. UM 67-319. DA XXVII.1, p.3899-A.

WIEGOLD, PETER (born 1949)

5562. Barrett, Richard. "Peter Wiegold." CT 27(1983): 28-32.

WILBRANDT, JÜRGEN (born 1922)

5563. Mainka, Jürgen. "*Beppino*: Ein Liederzyklus von Jürgen Wilbrandt." MG 10(1960): 10-14.

WILDBERGER, JACQUES (born 1922)

5564. Wildberger, Jacques. ". . . *die Stimme, die alte, schwacher werdende Stimme* . . .": Ein Triptychon für Solosopran, Solovioloncello, Orchester und Tonband (1973/1974)." SMZ 117(1977): 345-348.

WILDER, ALEC (born 1907)

5565. Roberts, Jean Elizabeth. "The piano music of Alec Wilder." DMA dissertation (Performance): University of Texas, (n.d.)

WILLAN, HEALEY (1880-1968)

5566. Campbell-Yukl, Joylin. "Healey Willan: The independant organ works." DMA dissertation (Performance): University of Missouri, 1976. UM 76-25,156. DA XXXVII.5, p.2476-A.

5567. Marwick, William. "The sacred choral music of Healey Willan." PhD dissertation (Music Education): Michigan State University, 1970. UM 71-11,911. DA XXXI.11, p.6100-A.

5568. Telschow, Frederick H. "The sacred music of Healey Willan." DMA dissertation (Church Music): University of Rochester, 1969. No DA listing.

WILSON, OLLY (born 1937)

5569. Logan, Wendell. "Olly Wilson: *Piece for Four*." PNM 9/1 (1970): 126-134.

WINTER, PETER (1754-1825)

5570. Zeller, Gary L. "The string quartets of Peter Winter (1754-1825)." PhD dissertation (Musicology): Catholic University, 1977. 361 p. UM 77-15,063. DA XXXVIII.1, p.22-A.

WOHLGEMUTH, GERHARD (born 1920)

5571. Fleischhauer, Günter. *"Telemann-Variationen* von Gerhard Wohlgemuth." MG 15(1965): 727-729.

5572. Siegmund-Schultze, Walther. "Gerhard Wohlgemuths Violinkonzert." MG 13(1973): 599-601.

WOLF, HUGO (1860-1903)

Corregidor
5573. Cook, Peter. *Hugo Wolf's "Corregidor": A study of the opera and its origins.* London: P. Cook, 1976.

Goethelieder
5574. Moman, Carl Conway, Jr. "A study of the musical setting by Franz Schubert and Hugo Wolf for Goethe's *Prometheus, Ganymed,* and *Grenzen der Menschheit.*" PhD dissertation: Washington University, 1980. 164 p. UM 81-03,693. DA XLI.9, p.3776-A.

5575. Seelig, Harry E. "Goethe's *Buch Suleikas* and Hugo Wolf: A musical literary study." PhD dissertation (Musicology): University of Kansas, 1969. 306 p. UM 70-11,071. DA XXX.12, p.5458-A.

5576. Tenschert, Roland. "Das Verhältnis von Wort und Ton in Hugo Wolfs Goethe-Liedern." OMZ 8(1953): 53-58.

Italienisches Liederbuch
5577. Levi, Vito. "L'*Italienische Liederbuch* di Hugo Wolf." RIM 1 (1966): 203-217.

5578. Resch, Rita Marie. "The role of the piano in Hugo Wolf's *Italienisches Liederbuch.*" DMA dissertation (Performance): University of Iowa, 1973. No DA listing.

Mörikelieder
5579. Böschenstein, Bernhard. "Zum Verhältnis von Dichtung und Musik in Hugo Wolfs Mörikeliedern." *Wirkendes Wort* 19/3 (May-June 1969): 175-193.

5580. Kinsey, Barbara. "Mörike poems set by Brahms, Schumann, and Wolf." MR 29(1968): 257-267.

5581. Schmalzriedt, Siegfried. "Hugo Wolfs Vertonung von Mörikes Gedicht *Karwoche.*" AM 41(1984): 42-53.

5582. Stein, Jack M. "Poem and music in Hugo Wolf's Mörike songs." MQ 53(1967): 23-28.

5583. Tausche, Anton. *Hugo Wolfs Mörikelieder in Dichtung, Musik und Vortrag.* Wien: Amandus, 1947.

Penthesilea
5584. Metzger, Raphael. "Hugo Wolf's symphonic poem, *Penthesilea*: A history and analysis." DMA dissertation (Orchestral Conducting): Peabody Conservatory, 1980. 214 p. UM 80-21,960. DA XLI.4, p.1274-A.

Songs [see also individual cycles]

5585. Boylan, Paul C. "The Lieder of Hugo Wolf: Zenith of the German art song." PhD dissertation (Musicology): University of Michigan, 1968. UM 69-12,054. DA XXX.3, p.1192-3-A.

5586. Egger, Rita. *Die Deklamationsrhythmik Hugo Wolfs in historischer Sicht.* Tutzing: H. Schneider, 1963.

5587. Gülke, Peter. "*Sterb ich, so hüllt in Blumen meine Glieder . . .*: Zu einem Lied von Hugo Wolf." M 33(1979): 132-140.

5588. Lewis. [*Mignon Lieder*]

5589. Sams, Eric. *The songs of Hugo Wolf.* London: Methuen, 1961.

5590. Stein, Deborah J. *Hugo Wolf's Lieder and extensions of tonality.* Ann Arbor: UMI Research Press, 1985.

5591. Thürmer, Helmut. *Die Melodik in den Liedern von Hugo Wolf.* Schriften zur Musik 2. Giebing über Prien am Chiemsee: E. Katzbichler, 1970.

5592. Youens, Susan Lee. "*Alles endet, was entstehet*: The second of Hugo Wolf's *Michaelangelo-Lieder*." SMU 14(1980): 87-103.

5593. -----. "Charlatans, pedants, and fools: Hugo Wolf's *Cophtisches Lied I*." SMUWO 8(1983): 77-92.

Other works

5594. Eppstein, Hans. "Zum Schaffensprozess bei Hugo Wolf." MF 37 (1984): 4-20.

5595. Hantz, Edwin. "*Exempli gratia*: Le Dernier cri (?): Wolf's harmony revisited." ITO 5/4(1979-1981): 29-32.

5596. Spitzer, Leopold. "Hugo Wolfs *Manuel Venegas*: Ein Beitrag zur Genese." OMZ 32(1977): 68-74.

WOLFF, CHRISTIAN (born 1934)

5597. DeLio, Thomas. "Sound, gesture and symbol: The relation between notation and structure in American experimental music." I 10 (1981): 199-219. [*For 1, 2, or 3 People*]

5598. Lovallo, Lee. "Incipient pan-serialism in Wolff's Duo for Violins." ITO 2/1-2(1976): 35-43.

5599. Natvig, Candace. "*Caribou Tracks*: Eine Einführung in vom Interpreten realisierbare Musik am Beispiel von Christian Wolff's *For 1, 2, or 3 People*." N 1(1980): 156-164.

WOLF-FERRARI, ERMANNO (1876-1948)

5600. Hamann, Peter. "Die frühe Kammermusik Ermanno Wolf-Ferraris." PhD dissertation: Erlangen-Nürnberg, 1975.

WOLPE, STEFAN (1902-1972)

5601. Brody, Martin. "Sensibility defined: Set projection in Stefan Wolpe's *FORM* for Piano." PNM 15/2(1977): 3-22.

5602. Hasty, Christopher. "Segmentation and process in post-tonal music." MTS 3(1981): 54-73. [String Quartet, 1969]

5603. ----. "A theory of segmentation developed from the late works of Stefan Wolpe." PhD dissertation: Yale University, 1978. No DA listing. [String Quartet, 1969; *Piece in Two Parts* for Flute and Piano, 1960; *FORM* for Piano, 1959]

5604. Levy, Edward. "Stefan Wolpe: For his sixtieth birthday." PNM 2/1(1963): 51-65. [Pieces for Two Instrumental Units]

5605. Post, Nora. "Varèse, Wolpe and the oboe." PNM 20(1981-1982): 135-148. [*Suite im Hexachord*]

WORK, JOHN WESLEY III (1901-1967)

5606. Garcia, William Burres. "The life and choral music of John Wesley Work III (1901-1967)." PhD dissertation (Choral Literature): University of Iowa, 1973. UM 73-30,921. DA XXXIV.7, p.4312-A.

WRANITZKY, PAUL (1756-1808)

5607. Abert, Anna Amalie. "*Oberon* in Nord und Süd." Fs. Gudewill: 51-68. [*Oberon, König der Elfen*]

WUORINEN, CHARLES (born 1938)

5608. Hibbard, William. "Charles Wuorinen: The Politics of Harmony." PNM 7/2(1969): 155-166.

WYNNE, DAVID (born 1900)

5609. Jones, Richard Elfyn. *David Wynne.* Cardiff: University of Wales, 1979.

XENAKIS, IANNIS (born 1922)

5610. DeLio, Thomas. "Iannis Xenakis' *Nomos Alpha*: The dialectics of structure and materials." JMT 24(1980): 63-95.

5611. Frisius, Rudolf. "Xenakis und der Rhythmus." NZM 144/4(1983): 13-17. [*Metastasis; Hiketides; Persephassa*]

5612. Naud, Gilles. "Aperçus d'un analyse sémiologique de *Nomos Alpha*." MJ 17(1975): 63-72.

5613. Roberts. [*Pithoprakta*]

5614. Sward, Rosalie La Grow. "An examination of the mathematical systems used in selected compositions of Milton Babbitt and Iannis Xenakis." PhD dissertation: Northwestern University, 1981. No DA listing.

5615. Vriend, Jan. "*Nomos Alpha* for Violoncello Solo (Xenakis 1966): Analysis and comments." I 10(1981): 15-82.

5616. Waugh, Jane. "Xenakis and chance." CT 10(1974-1975): 6-13. [*Duel; Strategie*]

YOUNG, LA MONTE (born 1935)

5617. Mertens: 19-34.

5618. Schulze, Brigitte. "Im Klang sein: La Monte Young und die indische Musik." MTX 9(1985): 40-43.

5619. Smith, Dave. "Following a straight line: La Monte Young." CT 18(1977-1978): 4-9.

YUN, ISANG (born 1917)

5620. Schmidt, Christian Martin. "Etüden für Flöte(n) Solo von Isang Yun." Melos/NZM 2(1976): 16-20.

5621. Schwake, Andreas. "Hören durch Sehen: Der latente Tanz in Kompostionen von Isang Yun." NZM 146/4(1985): 22-26.

5622. Vogt: 421-435. [Sonata für Oboe, Harfe und Viola, 1979]

ZBINDEN, JULIEN-FRANÇOIS (born 1917)

5623. Zbinden, Julien-François. "Concerto pour Orchestre, Op.57 (1977)." SMZ 117(1977): 280-284.

ZECHLIN, RUTH (born 1926)

5624. Röhlig, Eginhard. "Die Analyse: *Situationen* für Orchester von Ruth Zechlin." MG 32(1982): 75-79.

5626. Siegmund-Schultze, Walther. "Die Lidice-Kantate von Ruth Zechlin." MG 9/1(1959): 14-17.

ZEISL, ERIC (1905-1959)

5626. Cole, Malcolm S. "Eric Zeisl's 'American' period." CM 18(1974): 71-78.

ZELTER, CARL FRIEDRICH (1758-1832)

5617. Barr, Raymond. "Carl Friedrich Zelter: A study of the Lied in Berlin during the late eighteenth and early nineteenth centuries." PhD dissertation: University of Wisconsin, 1968. UM 69-00,870. DA XXX.1, p.352.

5627. Forbes, Elliot. "*Nur wer die Sehnsucht kennt*: An example of a Goethe lyric set to music." Fs. Merritt: 59-82.

5628. Grace, Richard M. "Carl Friedrich Zelter's musical settins of Johann Wolfgang Goethe's poems." PhD dissertation (Performance): University of Iowa, 1967. UM 68-933. DA XXVIII.8, p.3209-A.

5629. Havranek, Roger A. "Carl Friedrich Zelter: Fifteen selected Lieder set to Goethe poems." DM dissertation: Indiana University, 1978. No DA listing.

ZEMLINSKY, ALEXANDER (1871-1942)

5631. Fiebig, Paul. "Zu Alexander Zemlinsky's *Lyrischer Sinfonie*." NZM 134(1973): 147-152.

5632. Neuwirth, Gösta. "Musik um 1900." Fs. Schuh: 89-134.

5633. Oncley, Lawrence A. "The published works of Alexander Zemlinsky." PhD dissertation (Musicology): Indiana University, 1975. UM 75-17,061. DA XXXVI.2, p.591-A.

5634. Rooke, Keith J. "Alexander Zemlinskys *Die Saejungfrau.*" SMZ 121(1981): 85-91.

5635. Weber, Horst. "'Figur und Grund': Secessionistic instrumentation of Alexander Zemlinsky." MMA 18(1984): 181-190. [*Der Triumph der Zeit*]

5636. ----. "Stil, Allegorie und Secession: Zu Zemlinskys Ballettmusik nach Hofmannsthals *Der Triumph der Zeit.*" Fs. Schuh: 135-150.

5637. ----. "Zemlinskys Maeterlinck-Gesänge." AM 29(1972): 182-202. [*Sechs Gesänge*, Op.13]

5638. Wildner-Partsch, Angelika. "Die Opern Alexander Zemlinskys: Betrachtungen anhand zweier repräsentativen Werke." SZM 33(1982): 55-126. [*Eine florentinische Tragödie*, Op.16; *Der Kreiderkreis*]

ZENDER, HANS (born 1936)

5639. Vogt: 399-409. [*Canto IV*, 1970)

ZIMMERMANN, BERND ALOIS (1918-1970)

Perspectives
5640. Schubert, Reinhold. "Bernd Alois Zimmermann." R 4(1960): 103-113.

Photoptosis
5641. Müller, Karl-Josef. "Bernd Alois Zimmermann (1918-1970): *Photoptosis*, Prelude für grosses Orchester (1968)." Zimmerschied: 309-329.

Piano works
5642. Imhoff, Andreas von. *Untersuchungen zum Klavierwerk Bernd Alois Zimmermanns (1918-1970).* Regensburg: G. Bosse, 1976. 328 p.

5643. Niehaus, Manfred. "Bernd A. Zimmermann: *Monologue* für zwei Klaviere, 1960/64 (Collage)." Kirchmeyer: 224-227.

Die Soldaten
5644. Funk-Hennigs, Erika. "Zimmermanns Philosophie der Zeit: Dargestellt an Ausschnitten der Oper *Die Soldaten.*" MB 10(1978): 644-652.

5645. Gruhn, Wilfried. "Integrale Komposition: Zu Bernd Alois Zimmermanns Pluralismus-Begriff." AM 40(1983): 287-302.

5646. Herbort, Heinz Josef. "Bernd Alois Zimmermanns Oper *Die Soldaten.*" MB 3(1971): 539-548.

5647. Seipt, Angelus. "Bernd Alois Zimmermann: *Die Soldaten* (1965)." Vogt: 371-381.

Viola Sonata
5648. Hübler, Klaus-K. "Zimmermann the conservative: Anmerkungen zu seiner Viola-Sonate." MB 18(1981): 360-365.

Other works

5649. Imhoff, Andreas von. "Der frühe Bernd Alois Zimmermann." Melos/NZM 1(1975): 359-265.

5650. Karbaum, Michael. "Zur Verfahrensweise im Werk Bernd Alois Zimmermanns." Fs. Schenk: 275-285.

5651. Kühn, Clemens. *Die Orchesterwerke Bernd Alois Zimmermanns.* Hamburg: Wagner, 1978.

5652. Müller, Karl-Josef. "Erleben und Messen: Zu Bernd Alois Zimmermanns Anschauung der Zeit in seinen letzten Werken." MB 9(1977): 550-554.

ZIMMERMANN, HEINZ WERNER (born 1930)

5653. Oehlmann, Werner. "Inmitten der pluralistischen Welt." M 29(1975): 50-52. [*Missa profana*]

5654. Oertel, Heinz-Georg. "Kirchenmusik und Jazz: Heinz Werner Zimmermann (geboren 11.8.1930)." Fs. Mauersberger: 197-213.

5655. Salević, Marion. "Heinz Werner Zimmermanns amerikanische Psalmvertonungen." MK 49(1979): 170-177.

5656. Schütz, Adelbert. "*Missa profana* von Heinz Werner Zimmermann." MK 51(1981): 217-223.

ZIMMERMANN, UDO (born 1943)

5657. Böhm, Hans. "*Sonetti amorosi* von Udo Zimmermann." MG 18(1968): 754-761.

5658. Gerlach, Hannelore. "*L'Homme*: Meditationen für Orchester nach Eugène Guilleric von Udo Zimmermann." MG 23(1973): 455-460.

ZIMMERMANN, WALTER (born 1949)

5659. Fox, Christopher. "Walter Zimmermann's local experiments." CT 27(1983): 4-9.

5660. Leukerl, Bernd. "Das nie verglühende Opfer: Zu Walter Zimmermanns *Spielwerk*." MTX 12(1985): 21-24.

5661. McGuire, John. "In der Luft der eigenen Ätherik auflösen: Walter Zimmermanns *Lokale Musik*." MTX 12(1985): 33-35.

5662. Zimmermann, Walter. "*Lokale Musik*: Eine Projektbeschreibung." N 1(1980): 80-86.

5663. ----. "Vom Alten zum Neuen: Zum Klavier-Stück *Beginner's Mind*." MTX 12(1985): 38-40.

ZUMSTEEG, JOHANN RUDOLF (1760-1802)

5664. Maier, Günter. *Die Lieder Johann Rudolf Zumsteegs und ihr Verhältnis zu Schubert.* Göppingen: A. Kümmerle, 1971.

AUTHOR INDEX

Abbate, Carolyn, 1572

Abel, Angelika, 5378, 5464

Abendroth, Walter, 3410

Abert, Anna Amalie, 1505, 2060, 2637, 4191, 4692, 4784, 5607

Abraham, Gerald, 180, 897, 898, 1479, 1790, 1989, 2030, 3209 3627, 3627, 3628, 4221, 4222, 4344, 4356, 4431, 4500, 4964, 4965

Abraham, Lars Ulrich, 323

Adams, Beverly Decker, 3129

Adams, Frank John, 365

Adams, John P., 2512, 5318

Adams, Stephen, 3726

Adelson, Deborah M., 811

Adensamer, Michael, 1204

Adorno, Theodor W., 712, 3972, 4693

Adrio, Adam, 3351, 3364, 3365

Agawu, V. Kofi, 121, 2897, 2912, 3235, 4143, 4279

Ahrens, Christian, 4357

Ahrens, Joseph, 4

Ahrens, Sieglind, 3130

Albee, David Lyman, 30

Albèra, Philippe, 772. 3834

Albers, Bradley Gene, 3330

Albert, Thomas Russell, 2407

Albrecht, Christoph, 2233

Albrecht, Klaus, 4694

Albrecht, Michael von, 11

Alexander, Metche Franke, 827

Alfred, Everett Maurice, 1651

Allen, Judith Shatin, 1629, 4192

Allihn, Ingeborg, 1815

Allison, Rees Stephen, 3557

Allorto, Riccardo, 1418

Almond, Frank Ward, 3447

Alston, Charlotte LeNora, 2137

Altmann, Peter, 780

Alviani, Doric, 1892

Ameringen, Sylvia van, 59, 123, 3114

Ames, Charles, 14, 2238, 3248

Amman, Douglas D., 1882

Anagnost, Dean Z., 4983

Anderson, Lyle John, 2821

Anderson, Peter James, 2024

Andraschke, Peter, 2053, 2378, 2951, 2959, 3622

Andreae, Hans, 3759

Andrewes, John, 1535

Andrews, Harold L., 2123, 2164

Andrews, Ralph E., 3109

Andriessen, Louis, 4911

Angerer, Manfred, 3236, 4395

Anhalt, Istvan, 29, 314, 770, 773, 2703, 2878, 3727

Anthony, Donald B., 5465

Antokoletz, Elliott, 118, 205, 206, 223, 224, 5091

Antonicek, Theopil, 481

Applebaum, Edward, 2666

Appledorn, Mary Jeanne van, 1573

Archibald, Bruce, 632, 736, 3431, 5095, 5336

Argento, Dominick, 2422

Armstrong, Thomas, 4690

Arnold, Denis, 536, 2165

Arnold, Stephen, 43

Arnold, Willy, 3767

Asafev, Boris Vladimirovich, 4956

Asarnow, Elliot Bruce, 3857

Ashbrook, William, 1744, 1745, 1746, 3511

Ashforth, Alden Banning, 409, 3973, 3974

Ashizawa, Theodore Fumio, 3373

Ashley, Douglas Daniels, 4321

Ashley, Patricia Ruth, 3474

Atkinson, Neville, 4994

Auh, Mijai Youn, 983, 1932, 2768

Austin, William W., 94, 1601, 1852, 2265, 3311, 3432, 3483, 3711

Avron, Dominique, 775

Avshalomov, David, 3818

Ayrey, Craig, 615

Baaren, Kees van, 3732, 5149

Babbitt, Milton, 53, 181, 8913, 3975, 4869

Westergaard, Peter, 48, 5431, 5432, 5527

Westerman, Richard Martyn, 4633

Westphal, Kurt, 480

Westrup, Jack A., 1825

Westwood, Shirley Ann, 2674

Wetschky, Jürgen, 1066

Whalen, J. Robert, 1714

Whaples, Miriam K., 3003, 4124, 4133

Wheeler, Charles Lynn, 890

White, A. Duane, 1801

White, Charles Willis, 2763

White, Donald H., 5557

White, Eric Walter, 4757, 4792, 4861, 4927

White, John D., 1471

White, Maurice L., 1332

White, Pamela C., 3966

Whitesell, L.A., 4368

Whitesitt, Linda, 31

Whitman, Ernestine, 1687

Whittall, Arnold, 203, 316, 1012, 1131, 1154, 1155, 1156, 1279, 1534, 1689, 3056, 3057, 3947, 4063, 4718, 4811, 4999, 5302

Wichtmann, Kurt, 3605

Wickes, Lewis, 3741, 4074

Wieland, Renate, 410

Wieninger, Herbert, 359, 1197, 2202

Wiesel, Henry Meir, 601, 4727

Wiesel, Siegfried, 2115

Wijdeveld, Wolfgang, 1931

Wilcox, James H., 1187, 1188

Wildberger, Jacques, 444, 1484, 4179, 4928, 4465

Wilde, Denis S., 4712

Wildner, Johannes, 3746

Wildner-Partsch, Angelika, 5638

Wiley, Roland John, 4956

Wilheim, Andras, 5050

Wilhelm, Kurt, 4671

Wilke, Rainer, 1016, 3564, 4064

Wilkey, Jay W., 718

Wilkinson, Harry, 4552

Wilkinson, Marc, 5029, 5035, 5051

Will, Roy T., 3247

Willfort, Manfred, 4129

William, Wolfgang, 5455

Williams, B.M., 4841

Williams, Edgar Warren, Jr., 5368, 5373

Williams, Robert, 1731

Williams, Roger B., 4065

Williamson, Clive, 2028

Williamson, John, 2946, 2957

Willms, Franz, 2241

Wilsen, William, 5528

Wilson, Dean C., 3259

Wilson, Eugene N., 1552, 3534

Wilson, John R., 5561

Wilson, Karen Sue, 2744

Wilson, Olly, 2854

Wilson, Paul, 122

Windebank, Florence Leah, 5012

Winfield, George, 1247

Winking, Hans, 515

Winkler, Franz Emil, 5219

Winold, Allen, 3340

Winrow, Barbara, 216

Winter, Ilse, 2040

Winter, Robert S., III, 459, 527

Winterhager, Wolfgang, 4713

Winterhoff, Hans-Jürgen, 3505

Wintle, Christopher, 58, 5369, 5410

Winzer, Dieter, 1688

Wise, Ronald Eugene, 1839, 1881, 2251

Witte, Gerd, 3357

Wittelsbach, Rudolf, 4661, 4682

Witten, Neil David, 1336

Wittlich, Gary, 3794, 4102

Witts, Richard, 315, 902, 3462, 3463

Wöhler, Willi, 3036

Wohlfahrt, Frank, 1189

Wolf, Eugene K., 2162

Wolf, Werner, 91, 1250, 1950, 2570

Wolff, Christoph, 4180, 4190

Wolff, Hellmuth Christian, 141, 222, 302, 303, 1087, 4369

Wolff, Konrad, 2789, 4125

Wolfurt, Kurt von, 2962

Wollenberg, Susan, 2196, 4257

Wolterink, Charles Paul, 4929

Wood, Hugh, 1998

Wood, Jeffrey, 3856

Wood, Vivian Poates, 3456

Woodbury, Arthur, 3323

Woodward, James, 120

Woollen, Russell, 1690

Woolsey, Timothy Dwight, 4390

Worbs, Hans Christoph, 2163

DATE DUE